Tiger Claws

Tiger Claws

JOHN SPEED

St. Martin's Press ❧ New York

This is a work of fiction. All of the characters, organizations, and events portrayed in this novel are either products of the author's imagination or are used fictitiously.

www.stmartins.com

LIBRARY OF CONGRESS CATALOGING-IN-PUBLICATION DATA

Speed, John.
  Tiger claws : a novel of India / John Speed.—1st ed.
    p.   cm.
  ISBN-13: 978-0-312-32551-0
  ISBN-10: 0-312-32551-7
  1. Indian—History—1526–1766—Fiction.   2. Mogul Empire—Fiction.
3. Shivaji, Raja, 1627–1680—Fiction.   4. Aurangzeb, Emperor of
Hindustan, 1618–1707—Fiction.   I. Title.

PS3619.P438T54 2007
813'.6—dc22

                                                    2007020704

First Edition: September 2007

10   9   8   7   6   5   4   3   2   1

AUTHOR'S NOTE

To all avatars, all God's messengers, all perfect masters, all sadgurus, all qutubs, all walis, all friends of God, all saints, all lovers of God, I bow down.

—MEHER BABA

I first heard about Shivaji and Aurangzeb while reading the Australian poet Francis Brabazon's *The Silent Word*, where he discusses those ancient foes with his guru Meher Baba. Maybe, as Meher Baba says, Shivaji was an incarnation of Vishnu, much like Krishna or Rama. Maybe that is why his story filled my dreams.

In 1982, when my obsession began, books about these men and their times were few. At that time, they were not merely minor historical figures, they were practically forgotten. I read through several shelves of books on Indian history at Duke University and the University of North Carolina, and found only about two hundred pages dedicated to them. Finding out-of-print books such as *The Grand Rebel* or *Aurangzeb and Shivaji*, in those days before the Internet, was difficult and expensive.

Sometimes new stimuli transform and overwhelm the individual—all those wonderful, potential addictions like booze, sex, drugs, Haägen-Dazs coffee ice cream, and so on, that finger some button in the brain. I dreamed of those times, daydreamed of them. I became a menace on the road, with my hands on the steering wheel, and my mind in Agra. To the drivers that I ran off the road and scared half to death, I now apologize.

It was years before I scraped up enough money to visit India. Instead, I transformed my world: eating dal and rice, taking darshan at local temples, spinning with local Sufis. At used record stores I found obscure LPs of vina ragas and *qwalis*. My Indian friends tolerated my constant pestering questions, and my naïve lectures to them about their own history, about which, quite truthfully, they knew very little.

By the time of my first pilgimage to the Deccan, I had already written five or six hundred pages of my story. It was pretty shocking to discover that I often had more information about the places I visited than their official guides. In fact, I felt that my visit was a waste of time until I entered Aurangzeb's tomb.

The last great Mogul, perhaps the greatest Mogul, has no great marble and sandstone edifice above, no *charbagh* gardens. You'd probably get lost, as I did, trying to find it in the sleepy town of Khuldabad. There's a small sign over a set of stairs that leads to a narrow gateway into a courtyard. A simple sidewalk surrounds a plot of bare ground: beneath that ground lies Aurangzeb.

No one was there but me, no attendants, no touts, no beggars. The utter simpicity of the place was so unexpected that I went back and reread the tiny sign two or three times just to make sure I was in the right place.

When I sat next to Aurangzeb's grave, a strange moment occurred. I had a rush of sensations. I come from a pretty dysfunctional family: To be at Aurangzeb's grave felt like visiting my parents' house, sitting again at the kitchen table: a sense of great familiarity and deep emotional distress, a sense, for better or worse, of being home.

I don't know quite how to tell what happened there. I've settled for this description—I felt as if a hypodermic of light pierced my brain and injected a package of a thousand memories. In the days that followed, back in the States, the package opened, the memories unfolded, and this book emerged.

I have spent more than twenty years working on this book, and it shows. Originally conceived for only my own pleasure, with no expectation that anyone else would read it, I wrote whatever the hell I pleased. No one was writing the kinds of books I loved most anymore: big, sweeping stories filled with large characters, convoluted plots, operatic conflicts, and minute detail; stories based loosely on history but in the end reflecting more the author's imagination. In my solitude, I chose as models Shakespeare, Tolstoy, Dumas, Scott, Dickens, and Clavell.

I knew a little about writing. I'd written plays, speeches, editorials, essays, and the like. I learned the craft of novel writing on the job. But I was inspired by my subject. Inspired—I use the word in its old sense: to be breathed on, or breathed into.

Basant, originally an extremely minor character, suddenly shoved himself forward and demanded center stage. The eunuch Brotherhood appeared, and the tunnels under Agra fort (only much later did I discover that these tunnels actually exist). The old hero Iron rode into a chapter unbidden, bringing with him the horrific story of taking Torna Fort. And Afzul Khan showed up in my nightmares.

Shivaji, whom I had written as a Standard Matinee Hero, withdrew from sight—his words suddenly unexpected and his motivations obscure—and I could no longer figure out what made him tick. Aurangzeb, my plaster villain, became complicated and contradictory, both charming and horrific.

I spent fifteen years imagining this tale in silence, writing nothing. I visited India perhaps a dozen times, and I spent that time not studying in the usual sense, but absorbing sensations.

After a windfall gave me enough money to do so, I wrote for about eighteen months: seven days a week, sometimes twelve or thirteen hours a day. I wrote more than three thousand pages. For my own pleasure. My book took on a life of its own. I've spent countless hours trying to whip it into some sort of readable shape, and wish, pretty much on the hour, that I'd stuck with my original plan of keeping it private. My obstinate book had other ideas.

Since I started the story, the world has changed. The Hindutva movement in India lifted Shivaji from obscurity to icon. What had been Bombay Airport was now Shivaji Airport. What had been Victoria Terminus was now Shivaji Terminus. Aurangabad, the city named for Aurangzeb, was renamed Sambhaji-nagar, for Shivaji's son. And so on.

And what of Aurangzeb? He had been vilified for years for imposing sharia law on a non-Muslim people. (In fact, he was the first to codify sharia into civil statutes.) But as more Muslims began to demand political expression of their religious beliefs, Aurangzeb was elevated in stature, and they hailed his example. Some began to call him "The Fifth Right-Guided Caliph."

These two figures—ignored only a few years before—had now become polarizing rallying points. To describe them as human, with weaknesses and failings that all humans have, became an inflammatory political-religious insult. For articles I have edited on Wikipedia—in what I believe to be a neutral, scholarly way—I have received hateful e-mails full of threats of violence.

Because of such threats, I have taken a pen name. For if such violence results simply from telling facts about Aurangzeb or Shivaji, how much more insulting will my creative speculation be?

So, to the readers of this book, I apologize. I'm compelled to say: In this work of fiction, any resemblance to actual persons long dead is purely coincidental. If, in attempting to understand history in human terms, I imagined my characters in ways that offend you, forgive me. They deserve a better storyteller than I. Take comfort that my words can do little damage to their shining memory.

I give thanks for many friends who suffered through the creation of this sprawling book. The Wolfwriters novel workshop, led by my writing coach Michael Wolf, gave early drafts a sound drubbing; I am forever in their debt. Jean Naggar, agent extraordinaire, held firm to her faith in this story even when I ran off the rails. I can't thank her enough. Jean led me to Maureen Baron, who managed to cut my "condensed" manuscript to half its length, without, as she had threatened, simply deleting every other word. Daniela Rapp, my editor at St. Martin's, suffered my flailing conversation and missed deadlines with wonderful humor and grace (I'll always treasure how she asked, ever so gently, whether one of my more graphic sex scenes could be "a little less moist"). She treated me like an artist, and worked wonders with my book.

I must also mention with gratitude Tony Thornley and Irwin Jacobs, former president and chairman of Qualcomm. Bought at $10; sold at $1,600; took time off to write the book. Thanks, guys.

Most of all, I offer my inadequate thanks to my one darling, my dear wife, Barbara. She said this story was determined to be told. Her faith inspired me. She is more precious than jewels. Her ways are ways of delight, and all her goings are peace.

I dedicate this book to her: with my full heart, I place this volume, the work of my life, at her feet.

—JOHN SPEED
Cardiff-by-the-Sea
February 25, 2007

MAJOR CHARACTERS
IN ORDER OF APPEARANCE

Note about nicknames: Nicknames are used in situations of familiarity and intimacy. *Shivaji* is often addressed by his nickname *Shahu.* More typically, nicknames are shortened versions of given names. In addition, the respectful, intimate suffix *"ji"* may be added or dropped based on context. So in some conversations, *Hanuman* might be addressed as *Hanu* or *Hanuji.*

BASANT	Eunuch of the first rank, servant to the Mogul princess Roshanara
SHAISTA KHAN	Shah Jahan's former general, ambassador to Bijapur
ROSHANARA	Mogul princess, daughter of Shah Jahan
HING	Shah Jahan's *khaswajara* (eunuch in charge of the household)
DARA	Shah Jahan's heir apparent
AURANGZEB	Shah Jahan's younger son, Viceroy of the Deccan
MIR JUMLA	Aurangzeb's general, a Persian adventurer
ALU	A young eunuch, Jumla's *khaswajara*
JAI SINGH	Dara's general, a Rajput; the king of Amber

SHIVAJI	A Hindu chieftain and highwayman. Also called *Shahu*
TANAJI	Shivaji's mentor and lieutenant
O'NEIL	An Irish trader. Also called *Onil*
MAYA	A devadasi (temple dancer) sold as a slave
JYOTI	Maya's maid
JIJABAI	Shivaji's mother
SAI BAI	Shivaji's wife
DADAJI	Shivaji's regent, founder and administrator of Poona
HANUMAN	One of Tanaji's twin sons
LAKSHMAN	Hanuman's twin brother
BALA	Dadaji's counselor and Shivaji's secretary

Tiger Claws

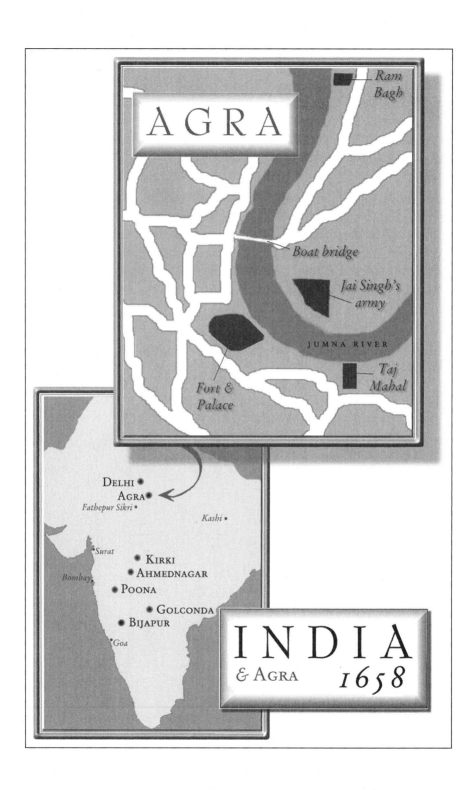

AGRA

Ram
Bagh

Boat bridge

Jai Singh's
army

JUMNA RIVER

Taj
Mahal

Fort &
Palace

DELHI
AGRA
Fathepur Sikri

Kashi

Surat

KIRKI
AHMEDNAGAR
Bombay
POONA

GOLCONDA
BIJAPUR
Goa

INDIA
& AGRA   1658

CHAPTER 1

ᏇᏉᏇᏉ

The brothers say that pleasure cures all fears. But Basant's fears are many, and his pleasures few.

The lights of the butter lamps dance like fireflies across the marble floor, stopping just short of his jewel-encrusted slippers. Time and again he has studied those lights, and the shadows their flickers form. And now Basant shrinks into a corner, praying that the dark will conceal his plump belly from the palace guards.

To cure his fear, he dissembles, though no one sees him. Basant takes pleasure in dissembling. Though he cowers in the shadows he feigns a charming smile and presses a dimpled hand to his heart, just so, as if to say: *Dear me! Did I drift off? I often daydream, here in these shadows; it is nothing special! Anyway, it is my right to be here.* Even so, he shivers, though the night is warm, and a bead of sweat carves any icy path down his neck.

His eyes lift to the crescent moon in the blue-black sky above the river Jumna. Far off he sees the domes of the starlit Taj Mahal, like bubbles floating above the river mist.

The brothers say that pain is but a dream. And Basant is a constant dreamer.

He dreams of a time when he knew his name.

ᏇᏉᏇᏉ

He is a child, an orphan. He is thirsty, for he hasn't been given even a sip of water all day. He sits on the floor of his tent, with his hands tied to a post driven in the ground behind him. And though it is still day, his tent is dark, shut tight and hot, lit by a cheap lamp that hangs from the center pole. He knows he must be a very bad boy indeed to deserve such punishment, but he can't think of what he's done.

The tent flap opens, and the gentle men come in. Their hands are soft as they wrap cords around his torso and thighs. They speak with voices like doves, patting his hair as they tug the bindings tight.

The cords cut into his child's flesh, and he cries out, and the gentle men shush him and call him sweet names. One of them holds a cup to his lips, and with some hesitation he drinks: it is wine, spiced wine maybe, or maybe something else. But it smells all wrong, and its bitter taste numbs his tongue; even so he drains the cup because he is so thirsty.

His mouth grows dry, and his thoughts swirl: his lips feel thick now, and they tingle; and the smells inside the tent—hot canvas and dry wool and dust—converge like harsh music; the guttering flame of the lamp above him flickers with eerie complexity.

Again light pours through the tent flap as the slavemaster enters, and with him a strange-smelling man with pale skin like a pig's, and gray eyes. And he thinks (the way little boys think, with astonished excitement), That must be a *farang*! The boy is sure he will never forget this day.

The flap drops; the tent is again dark as a cave. The cramped air is hot with hot breath. Never have so many people been in my tent, the boy thinks with pride. At a grunt from the slavemaster, the gentle men lift him up and tie him, cords and all, to a wide flat board. The *farang*'s eyes, gray like Satan's, sparkle like a madman's.

From within the folds of his robe, the slavemaster reveals a magic wand: a crescent moon of silver on a stem of jasper. The slavemaster shows it to the *farang*, and both men touch the moon, and whisper in excited voices and drag their thumbs across its edge. And suddenly it is not a wand. It is a knife. The men are testing its silver blade, a blade like the crescent moon.

The gentle men ignore the blade and the whispering, and look only at him, and pat his hands and face, and one of them begins to cry: dark trails glistening on dark cheeks. The boy has never seen a man cry before. The sight begins to scare him. There, there, he says, trying to stop those tears. Smiling for the man, There, there, he says. He doesn't know what else to say. But the tears still come. So he floats out of his body, floats like a bubble, and the tent grows silent, as if no one dared to breathe.

Then the slavemaster takes the knife, and with a quick sweep, whispers the blade through the boy's clothes. The gentle men tuck the tatters away, exposing his smooth skin. He can feel the softness of their cool hands, and the ragged breath of the slavemaster on his bare stomach and bare thighs, and the cords that bite into the flesh of his legs and chest.

He sees his tiny lingam exposed in the flickering lamplight. The slavemaster tickles it until it tingles and begins to stiffen and grow, and the *farang* chuckles, but his breath has grown raspy and his eyes blaze.

The gentle men look away. Their faces are solemn and totally elsewhere. The crying one whispers that he shouldn't worry, that the slavemaster is an expert. It takes the boy a moment to realize that the words are meant for him. I'm fine, he says. The crying one tries to smile.

With hands now careful, the slavemaster's thumb probes slowly along the root of the lingam and also the testicles; these he rubs between his fingers with great care. Then with expert quickness the slavemaster slides the silver moon across his smooth round belly.

The boy feels his lingam come loose, and roll, and then fall. He feels it lodge between his thigh and the board he is tied to. Where his lingam used to be he sees a tiny fountain of blood.

The slavemaster presses a heavy thumb on the fountain: his long fingers curl around the boy's testicles. This seems to happen very slowly.

The moon blade flashes once more. The boy watches it slide in an expert silver arc.

He thinks: Someone in this room is screaming. Like a speck of down, Basant drifts around the tent, looking for the source of the screams. The gentle men are busy, pressing cloths against his bloody groin. He sees the slavemaster's bloody palm, and on it are his testicles in the tiny sack that used to hang between his legs. (He wonders, How will the slavemaster get them back on?) The *farang* leans close, his eyes wide and his face pale.

With the curved point of the silver knife the slavemaster teases the sack, deftly slipping the testicles onto his wide palm.

The screaming stops. He stares at his tiny testicles on the slavemaster's palm: In the lamplight they look like living gems, and he is fascinated by their colors, pinks and grays and blue. They pulse, still alive in the slavemaster's hand.

⊖⊃⊂⊙

The *farang* bending his head to the slavemaster's palm.

The *farang*'s face lifting, eyes aflame. His swallow and his sigh.

That moment.

That pain that is just a dream.

That Basant remembers.

❧

The slavemaster drops the empty sack of flesh on the floor, as one might drop an orange peel.

The gentle men lift the boy, still tied to the wide board, and press his wounds with cloths. He feels his lingam roll from beneath his thigh, and wonders what will become of it. He never sees it again.

They bandage him and place him upright in a hole dug in some sand. They bury him up to his neck. He is so little, the hole is not very deep.

He stays buried three days. He gets a fever. He has never been so thirsty, so that each breath burns.

Sometimes people come to stare and shake their heads; he sees the slavemaster and the *farang* pass by, glancing at him with sidelong looks.

From time to time the gentle men visit him, and feel his forehead and his cheeks (for all but his head is buried in the sand), and they cluck their tongues and shake their heads, and let him sip the bitter wine (but only a sip now, never a drink). Sometimes they wash his face and he licks the drips that slide down his cheek.

On the third day, using only their hands, two of the gentle men dig him out. With soft fingers they brush away the sand. They frown as they unwrap the bandages, and then smile, when they see the wound.

One produces from his turban a thin silver tube, like the quill of a feather. While the other holds him still (for his hands and feet are still tied to the board, and the cords still cut into his flesh), the man pushes the silver quill into the hole where his lingam used to be. It feels cold and enormous, but he does not cry out.

Then he feels it pop into place—somehow he knows it is in place—and he begins to pee. He pees and pees, the stream passing through the silver quill to form a puddle at his feet. Some blood is mixed with the urine. The gentle men examine the stream carefully and nod and smile some more. They release the heavy cords that tie him to the board. He collapses.

One carries him like a baby to the eunuchs' tents.

❧

From that day, he lives among eunuchs, travels in the eunuchs' cart, sleeps in their tent. The gentle men who cared for him are there, and others. He thinks they must be very old. He is the only child in the tent. The slave children he used to play with aren't allowed. Many of the eunuchs have dark, brown skin, but his skin is like cream, golden like a lightly roasted *kachu* nut. He wonders if he will grow dark when he gets old. He makes friends with them. When one of the eunuchs is sold, he misses him.

The eunuchs smile, and pat him and bounce him on their plump laps. They hide him from the slavemaster. They give him a special name— Basant, which means "springtime"—and after a while, he forgets the name he used to have.

Years later, Basant tries to remember his forgotten name. In dreams he hears it, but when he wakes, it's gone.

Basant's wounds heal clean, and the scars look not so bad. He carries the silver quill in his turban. He thinks it is fun to pee through; although he misses his lingam a little, he likes the silver quill nearly as much.

☙☙❧❧

As they travel, rocking on the rough road in the eunuchs' cart, his new friends tell him stories. Mostly they are in verse, and the verses are about lingams. How to rub them, how to lick them, the pleasures they can give. How odd, thinks Basant, now that I haven't got one, to discover how pleasant they might be. The first time he hears a new verse, he laughs and laughs; they seem so silly and so clever.

When they camp at night, they teach him dances and these are easy to learn: shaking his bottom, mostly, back and forth and side to side. They make him sit on a funny seat for hours at a time; it hurts at first, but not as much as the knife, and then it scarcely hurts at all, even when they enlarge each day the nasty part that squeezes into his little bottom.

Sometimes Basant sees the eunuchs speaking with the slavemaster. Basant thinks it odd that the slavemaster should look at him as though he were a sack of gold waiting to be emptied onto the slavemaster's wide palm. He sees the *farang* sometimes, hiding behind a tent, snatching glances.

One night they set up camp in a big town with a big domed mosque. The eunuchs dress him in satins and silks; they rub his *kachu* skin with perfume and stain his eyelids with kohl. They lead him to a special tent, with walls of fine red silk and velvet cushions and butter lamps, and they place him on a soft bed plump with cushions. It is the finest tent he ever has seen. One by one the eunuchs kiss him and duck out through the curtains until he is alone with only the flickering butter lamps for company. Wisps of incense curl through the air, but he can't find where.

He is puzzling about this when the *farang* comes into the tent.

It is not pleasant.

Soon Basant finds he understands the answers to many puzzles. He understands with great suddenness, as one understands a fall down a well, or a fist to one's nose. He understands it all.

Then, after an eternity of night, he falls asleep, and thankfully he has no dreams. The next morning the *farang* is gone, and only then does he weep.

He wipes the trails of his kohl-stained tears, and with some difficulty walks to the eunuchs' tent. He hears them inside, but no one comes out to greet him. He stares at the flap, unable to enter. Instead he goes to the bathing place and washes himself, using bucket after bucket of cold water.

In time the eunuchs come to him and try to make him smile.

Night after night Basant goes to the soft bed of the rich tent. He has many visitors. He still remembers how they smelled.

❧❧❧❧

But as Basant hides in the shadows his memory fades until once more he is himself: clumsy, scheming, fat, rich, and terrified. He gazes at the sky, at the sliver crescent moon, and wills himself to breathe. He has suffered much, but achieved much—now he is here, a person of substance, in the very heart of the empire.

So why then does Basant, Eunuch of the First Rank of the Private Palace of Mogul Emperor, now risk everything? Why risk his status, even his life, on this foolishness? Why?

If you asked him, of course, he would turn aside and say nothing. Such is his way, and the way of all the *mukhunni*. But if you could lift the tent flap of his heart and peer inside, you would understand: he does it for love; for the love of his mistress, for the love of the Princess Roshanara.

Of course he would deny this. He would ask: How might a eunuch love any woman, let alone a princess? He might joke about the speed of his fingers, or the deftness of his tongue, and wink and leer as if to say: When they can't get what they really want, then they want me. For isn't it said the *mukhunni* also have no hearts? So Basant would have you believe.

But Basant has a heart, and he has made of it a shrine to Roshanara, the princess he has served for nineteen months and four days. So he hides, by her command, in the shadows, in the terrifying darkness.

Basant hears each sound that emerges from Roshanara's apartments. And even though tonight at his command the drapes over the windows and breezeways all are lowered, and even though he has ordered drapes of the densest velvet, lined with quilted muslin, winter drapes though it now is spring, despite it all, Basant hears through them every whisper, every grunt. With each noise his terror mounts; his pulse raises like a tabla at the end of a raga. Bad enough that he hears Roshanara, but Basant can also hear her partner: his growls, his filthy words. To explain such sounds would take time, and baksheesh: and he's had no chance to make arrangements; for Roshanara had tossed this rendezvous together with unexpected haste.

Basant wonders desperately whether these sounds are really so loud as they seem to his anxious ears; whether they echo through the palace; whether the emperor who snores in a nautch girl's arms but twenty yards away can hear each groan. He wonders if guards will hear them and burst in, swords whistling.

He can barely keep from running away, particularly when he hears the frantic squealing of the princess in her frenzy, and the groaning of her partner like a bull; that ancient song that Basant can hear but never sing.

Then, as if Allah in his mercy had not yet piled enough worry on his servant, Basant hears a sound more frightening: he recognizes the voice of Muhedin, second captain of the palace guards, the smartest of all the captains and the most suspicious.

Basant curses his fate; that Muhedin should be keeper of the watch this night, of all guards the most attentive! He knows Muhedin's habits, what things might catch his eyes and lead him to investigate. Maybe it will all work out—maybe Basant can keep himself and Roshanara's lover in the shadows and out of sight. Maybe no alarm will be raised. It is not so far to the tunnels. Just act, he orders himself. Now!

But of course he can barely move.

Basant creeps to the edge of the shadows and glances toward the battlements. The only guards nearby are the two Tartar women who stand outside the emperor's bedchamber—strange pink women from a place where it is always cold. And they will not care.

Hesitating in front of the entrance to the princess's apartments, trying not to imagine what he will find within, Basant at last pushes aside the velvet entry drape, heavy with jewels and golden thread.

As the drape falls behind him, pleasure mingles with his fear. To be in her presence, in the heart of her home, amidst the flickering lamps, amidst the incense, amidst the flowers and leaves carved in the walls and burnished with gold! He feels such pleasure as a lover might.

Basant's eyes grow accustomed to the dim light and he makes out the clothing strewn around the room; the bed in attractive disarray with cushions haphazard everywhere; the princess's thick raven hair spread wild across her pillow; the edge of her pretty ear peeping through the tresses; her arm with its silken skin poking from beneath a satin cover.

And he sees the body of her lover: the man's dark limbs sprawled on the bed and his bare ass, sagging in his sleep.

Maybe jealousy clouds Basant's heart. Oh, he knows that he can never possess Roshanara, not as a man might possess her. But he can give her pleasure that a man cannot, for he has been trained to use his tongue and fingertips in ways that only eunuchs know. He can exhaust his sweet princess, thrilling her until she begs for mercy. What man can say that? He eyes her hairy lover with the envy that only eunuchs know.

His eyes fly open as if he can feel Basant's stare, and he rolls from the cushions to crouch by the bed. Facing him with dark malevolent eyes, even naked, even with his fat old lingam hanging down for all to see, the man looks deadly. The flickering lamp traces the bright edges of an ugly knife, one meant for use, not for show. Basant nearly faints.

"I need more light," the man growls. He speaks quietly, clearly used to being obeyed instantly. As Basant lifts a lamp, the man paws through the bedding, looking for his clothes. The musty smell of sex rises from the cushions. Roshanara sleeps through it all like one exhausted.

"Get dressed, uncle," Basant whispers. "We must go quickly." The man scowls at him; he has found his inner turban and he begins to wrap his long hair. Hurry, hurry, you old oaf, Basant thinks, the harem soon will wake. On the man's chest Basant sees a patchwork of livid scars. One runs the length of his body, from his left shoulder to his right hip.

The man puts on his robe; it hangs down nearly to his ankles, Bijapuri-style. He gathers his underwear, turban, and belt and rolls them into a tight ball, then stands and pushes them roughly at Basant. He is used to having others care for him. Basant takes the bundle while the man searches for his cloak.

The princess stirs but doesn't wake—her hair falls back from the fine features of her round face, and she hugs a pillow to her perfect breasts. Basant watches her, fascinated.

Suddenly he yelps at a sharpness in his side. The man has crept up beside him and now prods him with his knife—still sheathed, but to Basant the point of the sheath is as unpleasant as the point of a dagger.

"Let's go." The man pokes him again. "No, wait," he says. He pivots Basant roughly by the arm, turning to face him. He is short, not much taller than Basant, and his black eyes are empty and terrifying, like a tiger's eyes. "Let's get one thing straight. You take me to the Delhi Gate. Understand? No tricks. And no tunnels!"

"No tunnels, uncle? How shall I keep you hidden?"

"I know all about the tunnels. And about the well. You get me? No tricks. No tunnels. No well. Understood?"

"But what well, uncle?" But even Basant can hear that this response is unconvincing.

The man lets out a long hiss. "The Delhi Gate. Now."

Again the point probes Basant's ribs. "But uncle, how shall I take you there safely?"

"I'll tell you how, *hijra*." The cruelty of the term is not lost on Basant. "We'll go to your rooms. You have rooms nearby, don't you? I'll put on clothes like a eunuch and we'll walk right out, our heads held high. Understood? Like men, except . . ." He chuckles at his own wit.

Swiftly Basant considers his options and finds none. With a last glance at his princess, he draws back the drape and walks swiftly to a shadowy corner. The man follows him step for step.

Basant looks for the next shadow, and the next, tracing a zigzag path that leads to the eunuchs' apartments. He becomes almost confident. There are no guards at the doorways; once the emperor has retired, only his Tartar women guard his bedroom; guards above suspicion and beyond attack. Sentries patrol only the perimeter, but they face outward, and are easy to avoid by sticking to the shadows and creeping silently along the walls.

They come to the mezzanine overlooking the enormous water tank at the foot of the stairs. Only the edge of the tank is in shadow; the walkway is lit by the lamps in niches along the walls of the Fish Building.

Basant is disgusted to have to live in a place called the Fish Building; he is sure it has been named that just to insult the eunuchs who live there. It is well known the nautch girls call the eunuchs "fish."

They step swiftly along the edge of the mezzanine. Basant now sees his door and hurries toward it. Too quickly. His foot strikes a night bucket some fool has left at the tank's edge. He stumbles. The bucket clatters as it rolls; it falls, clanging twice with a sound like a broken gong that fills the night. The echo takes forever to fade.

Basant fears he will die, and wants to. Then he feels a rough hand grab his robes; his collar bites his neck, strangling him so he gasps for air. The princess's lover drags him along the edge of the tank. If there are any more buckets here, Basant thinks, this will be a good way to find them. But the man moves furiously, carelessly. "Where? Where?" he whispers through clenched teeth. Basant points miserably toward his door.

The man shuts the door, his teeth clenched so tightly that it's clear he restrains his fury only with enormous effort. "You were drunk and you stepped out to pee. Understand?" They hear the soft knock at the door.

Sharp steel whispers as the dark man draws his blade. Then he presses against the wall: when the door opens, he'll be hidden behind it.

Basant cracks open one side of his double door. "Evening, Basant," says Muhedin, the sentry captain. "Everything all right?"

"Certainly, captain." Basant can scarcely believe his voice works. "I was a little drunk and went to pee, and . . ."

"Mind if I come in and have a look around?"

"Actually, it's not too convenient, uncle. I'm afraid I had a bit of an accident. It happens to us *mukhunni* sometimes: just a splash of urine, but so unpleasant . . ." Basant tries to give a laugh.

"Is anyone there with you, Basant?"

Of course there is, Basant wants to say. Can't you hear him breathing? Can't you smell the garlic? "No, uncle," Basant replies.

"The thing is, someone thinks they saw two persons out there, Basant. Someone thinks they both came in here."

Basant can't breathe. Perhaps, if he played it right, he could manage to have Muhedin kill this awful smelly man. A thief, uncle! Sneaking into the palace, uncle! He made me bring him here! See his ugly dagger! And Basant was good at lying. But as he considers this, he feels a sharp jab beneath his arm; not blunt like before; the tip of that nasty, incessant dagger, now unsheathed and sharp as a needle. Basant wonders how long he has been silent . . . did it seem unnatural? "No, uncle, I'm fine, all by myself, just a fat old eunuch nobody cares for. . . ."

"But we must come in, Basant. Regulations." Basant hears "we," and peers through the crack until he sees a second guard behind Muhedin. Good, he thinks. "Oh, two of you," he says pointedly, glancing at the man as if to say, You are finished now.

He opens one of the doors, the one that will hide the smelly man— Basant doesn't wish to die too soon, after all. Outside, Muhedin is smiling pleasantly; but a skinny guard with a drawn sword stands behind him. Basant bows and steps aside, waving them through.

As Muhedin steps across the threshold, a rough hand thrusts out to push him across the room. He sprawls to the floor.

He looks up to see Muhedin's startled face. Before the captain can even reach his sword, the dark man sweeps his knife. The blade glides through the captain's neck, making a wet slapping noise, like a cleaver cutting cabbage. As Basant watches from the floor, a necklace appears around the front of his neck, like a thin scarlet thread. Then the captain's head flops back-ward, and a deep red river erupts from his exposed neck. The captain's legs buckle, and he falls to his knees: it seems as though he is praying. A shud-der runs through his body and he falls over, convulsing, his heart still pumping dark buckets of blood.

From first step to shuddering death has taken less than a second.

His weapon still raised, the man now lunges through the door and lurches back, the hand of the other guard locked in his grasp.

The man yanks the hand so hard that the guard's head heaves back, chin toward the ceiling. The man thrusts his knife through the soft spot under the guard's chin and drives the point into his brain.

The guard's head snaps forward, and Basant sees his astonished eyes, and his mouth still open, and his tongue pinioned on the blade, squirming on the blade like a pink slug on a skewer.

Then with vicious force the man wrenches the blade back. The body crumbles next to the captain's. Other than the sigh of the knife and the soft thuds of bodies falling, there has been not a sound.

"I am Shaista Khan," says the man, wiping his blade on the robes of the guard. "I must not be found here."

Basant feels liquid warmth at his feet and assumes that he has soiled himself, but then he sees that it is the puddle of Muhedin's blood that seeps through his jeweled slippers. He swallows back bile.

Shaista Khan glances up and down the mezzanine. Satisfied, he closes the door, quietly, carefully, and heaves the bolts. Then Shaista Khan arranges the bodies on the floor, forming a sort of dam to contain the blood and shit seeping from them. With unexpected gentleness he moves Basant aside. He bends down, removing Basant's jeweled slippers with his own hands, and tosses them amidst the bodies and blood. Taking a pillow from the bed, he uses it to mop the floor. Basant's hands dangle at his side like dead things.

"Change of plan," Shaista Khan whispers. "Straight to the Delhi Gate. Dressed as we are. Right now." Quietly he opens the door; quietly he looks for trouble. "Come. Now. The fools came alone."

He steps behind Basant, his hands on Basant's waist. "I need you, eu-nuch. I'm lost here. Which way?" whispers Shaista Khan. Basant turns al-most imperceptibly. Shaista Khan presses him in that direction, and so they go: Shaista Khan half-follows, half-guides him. Like two odd dancing part-ners, clinging to the shadows, at last they reach the Delhi Gate.

CHAPTER 2

ⓒⓈⓒⓈ

Basant wakes, bathed in sweat.

He's in his servant's tent. Tiny streams of light leak through pin-sized holes in the old fabric punctuating the brown darkness. Outside the muezzin sings the call to morning prayer. Haridas, his servant, is already gone.

Fears descend on him like biting insects. Though it seems to him he has not slept, through patches of the tent the sun now shines so bright that the air is filled with light. Basant hears the muffled sounds of life going on outside: the calls and chatter, the clangs and rattles of a typical day.

He creeps to the entry, opens the flap, and blinks at the brightness. He realizes he is barefoot; and in a sudden memory remembers Shaista Khan tossing his blood-soaked slippers on the broken bodies in his rooms. He passes his hand across his brow hoping to drive that image from his mind.

He steps behind the tent and takes the silver quill from his turban. He eases it into the scar in his groin and pees copiously into an open ditch that acts as sewer. But even as he sighs with relief, the dark image of dead men in his room closes over him like sudden night.

Haridas, his servant, walks toward him, his freshly shaved head bare in the morning sunlight, his old face lined, but bright and eager.

"I have brought you clean clothes, son," he says. "Bathe quickly and put them on." He motions Basant to a bathing area near his tent. The alley is alive with people, mostly low-level servants and servants of servants, and they stare at Basant as he passes. What is a eunuch of the first rank doing here? they wonder, glancing over their shoulders at him as they pass by.

"Where did you get these clothes?" Basant asks.

"From your rooms, son," Haridas replies.

"My rooms? You went to my rooms?" Basant licks his lips. "Was any-thing . . . amiss?" he asks, as casually as he can manage.

Basant's reedy voice seems unusually tense; Haridas sees the panic in his eyes. He sits next to Basant, the clothes in a neat pile on his lap, and pats the eunuch's shoulder. "When I woke, I saw you would need new clothing for the audience today. So I went to fetch some clothes for you."

"Didn't the guards try to stop you?" Basant asks.

"I am well known in the Fish House, son. It is my great honor to be known as your servant, and people accord me the respect due the servant of a eunuch of the first rank, and so the guards recognized me."

"But did no one ask your business?" Haridas shakes his head no. "Did no one challenge you?" Again, no. "Guards around my rooms?" Haridas frowns uncertainly. "No bodies? No blood?" Basant blurts out at last.

Haridas sighs, as if suddenly relieved. "You are making a joke with me, son. You will have your fun with your old servant."

Basant holds his head in his hands and begins to laugh. Or perhaps to cry. He can no longer tell the difference. Haridas looks on, confused, his shaved head cocked at a quizzical angle, uncertain about what he should do. At last Basant stands, passes his plump palm over his face, and draws a deep breath. "I need to bathe."

Twenty buckets of cold water later, Basant feels clean and sweet. His fresh clothes gleam in the morning sun, his gems catch fire in its light. The palace shines like a jeweled casket in the bright sun, the walls glisten like wet pearls: the jasper and carnelian embedded in the flesh-white marble flash as he passes; the carvings in the marble sparkle.

Basant's hands tremble as he walks. Behind each column, a guard stands waiting to arrest him. Of that he is sure. He reasons with himself: here in the public palace, no one knows him; he is just another eunuch. See? No one even glances his way. But Basant is certain they mean only to give him false comfort before they pounce like tigers.

The call of muezzin from the Moti Masjid throws Basant into turmoil. Not now! he thinks. I have no time to pray! But even so Basant stops where he is: touching his ears, touching his knees, bowing in the dusty street. He is too frightened to say his prayers, and too frightened not to pretend to.

Then the air erupts with the harsh roar of war horns, the clash of cymbals, the booming of elephant drums, a thunderclap of sound.

It is Dara arriving. The prince spent the night with his armies across the river, and now marches to his father's audience in full pomp.

Basant scurries toward the Diwan-i-Am. Not only will he lose face if he is late for Dara's arrival, but he wants to see!

Sights and sounds assault him with such immense profusion that all his worry evaporates. Musicians by the hundreds spill through the immense Delhi gate, shoving forward in enthusiastic confusion, and the blare of their music echoes and crescendos through the courtyard.

Nobles and bureaucrats and a group of newly honored merchants (who have just received grants of land) crowd into the immense arched courtyard Diwan-i-Am. Though the hall is designed to accommodate thousands, today there is scarcely any space to be found. The crowd pushes forward so that people drop from the edges of the dais in a constant human waterfall.

Finally the musicians blast their instruments mightily as they shove haphazard toward the end of the courtyard. Behind them come row after row of riflemen, with matchlocks gleaming, with turbans piled ridiculously high (it is their regimental pride to wear those sensational turbans); then come five hundred horsemen, their energetic stallions prancing and pawing, crabbing sideways as they look for somewhere to stand.

The courtyard is jammed with commoners and townspeople who have come to see the spectacle; they press forward in a scramble to find a place, and their crush increases the chaos. By contrast, the nobles stand serenely on a platform near the throne clapping at Dara's arrival. In the blare of the trumpets and drums, no one hears them.

Mounted by fierce riders from the mountains and deserts of Rajputana, the war camels now enter in stately ranks through the gates, small cannons gleaming on their humps.

One by one, the elephants enter as the cheers increase and the drums beat louder. Painted and caparisoned, stately and terrifying, heavy brass war spikes fixed to their brilliant tusks, the elephants are daunting, enormous; they lumber slowly, unconcerned by the noise and chaos.

At last Basant glimpses Dara, son of the emperor, the heir to the Peacock Throne, resplendent on a gold and red velvet howdah on the back of a giant Ceylon elephant. Dara's golden turban laced with rubies glitters in the brilliant sun, and his face is no less radiant.

The common folk in the courtyard rush toward his elephant like bees to a flower: they call and wave in a frenzy as the music crescendos even louder. Dara is another Akbar, another Timur!

Dara scatters gold from his howdah, and the people roar and paw through the dust to catch the coins, and call out Lord! and King! But Dara in his splendor seems not to hear. His face is resolute, calm. He motions his mahout to guide the elephant forward.

Basant has been screaming Dara's name with the rest, though he has been unconscious of doing so. As the elephant moves with glacial pomp toward the hall, and bends its knees before the steps of the dais, the music stops and the crowd grows quiet. In the sudden silence, Dara slips gracefully from the howdah's height to land with a bouncy spring, like an athlete. With stately dignity he approaches his golden chair at the foot of his father's throne. The nobles on the dais, a sea of bobbing heads and faces, sweep their hands across the ground and motion toward him, heads bowed.

Dara slides through the crowd. His Rajput bodyguards push along beside him, clearing a path for the prince, but he pretends not to notice and instead walks closer to the crowding nobles, touching a hand, a face. He moves with easy grace through the tumult of faces. When he reaches his golden chair, lifting his hands in acknowledgment of the nobles' presence, he sits gracefully and shuts his eyes, as if in contemplation.

Basant glances back. A number of horses move toward the dais. Basant admires the richness of their jeweled headpieces and bright silver bridles, manes braided with gems. The riders, he supposes, are Dara's generals and advisers; but these were not the ones that Dara typically brings to an audience.

Basant recognizes few of the faces.

Then he sees one he knows.

No, he tells himself. But it's true.

A compact man briskly mounts the dais. Basant recognizes not his face, but his walk: he moves like a coiled spring. His dress is simpler than the others but no less elegant: few jewels but large ones, simple cloth but expensive. From his silk sash hangs a sword in a plain leather scabbard, its handle of ivory, not gold, and the ivory is dark with use.

And there's that dagger, a dagger and a sheath, and Basant knows the feel of both.

The general notices Basant as he passes, and seems about to nod, then shakes his head as if realizing his error. But Basant's blood has frozen at the sight of him: Shaista Khan, the general; Shaista Khan, the seducer; Shaista Khan, the murderer.

☙☙☙☙

Another assault of trumpets and drums blares from the Drum House of Delhi Gate. Basant's head jerks up, startled out of his panic.

Three lone horsemen ride toward the dais. Two are mounted on elaborately liveried stallions. Their silk jama robes flutter in the morning breeze, jeweled headpieces and sword hilts glitter in the sun. They dismount and wait for the third rider to come.

The last man rides in calmly, more slowly than the other two, his eyes lowered as if lost in thought and unaware of the tumult around him. From time to time he strokes his graying beard as if he were in a room somewhere by himself, lost in thought, or in prayer.

At the steps of the dais he dismounts, cavalry style, kicking his leg in front of him, over his horse's neck, one hand on his sword hilt.

His white horse, so fiery that it can scarcely be led away by the attendant, wears no fancy livery. Its rider too dresses simply: white cotton pants, white jama, white turban, plain shoes, a green belt with a simple wooden-handled sword such as any field soldier might carry.

It is Aurangzeb. Dara's brother. The viceroy of the Deccan.

The Deccan is hot, volatile, an area that is always erupting into trouble. The Emperor Shah Jahan could not subdue it, Dara tried and failed; now it is Aurangzeb's problem. And every day, Dara tells his father how Aurangzeb cannot keep the Deccan under control. Always it is up to Dara to bail out Aurangzeb when things go wrong. Or so he tells the emperor.

As Aurangzeb makes his careful way to stand beside his brother (for only Dara, the emperor's favorite son, may sit in the Presence), the emperor emerges through the golden doors of the darshan platform. Musicians raise their silver trumpets. The nobles bow from the waist and sweep their hands across the marble floor, bobbing up and down three times as is customary.

And in the courtyard the commoners raise shrill shouts, and the soldiers and attendants begin to cheer as they catch sight of the King of the Earth, and the mahouts strike their beasts to make the elephants stand on two legs and lift their trunks and trumpet with thunderous joy; the whole courtyard an ocean of noise.

The emperor, leaning on the arm of his ancient *khaswajara*, steps to the edge of the darshan platform and turns his head to sweep the entire scene with his gaze. Lowering himself to his cushioned throne, he arranges the cushions to his satisfaction, spits his wad of pan into a jeweled spittoon held by a eunuch, adjusts his clothes, and whispers to the *khaswajara,* smoke pouring from his lips.

The *khaswajara* is Basant's boss, a dry and shriveled eunuch called Hing. Keeping his face down, he pushes toward the jali screen, in purdah with his mistress the Princess Roshanara, hoping Master Hing won't notice. Like most old eunuchs, Master Hing's eyes are failing, so Basant has little to fear. Past the sour-faced eunuch who guards the jali door, and he's done it. Safe! Here with his princess.

Basant blinks until his eyes adjust to the dark purdah chamber: a wide, shallow space beside the throne room where harem women watch the goings-on at the Diwan-i-Am. Roshanara has dressed simply: a maroon sari of heavy silk, its dark surface dense with gold embroidery. A few dozen ruby-studded bangles clunk heavily when she moves her arm. A gauze veil is fastened around her head with a rope of pearls the size of chickpeas. Her thick, long hair is pulled tight and sleek against her head.

Her veil is so light, since she is hidden from public view by the intricately carved marble jali screen, that through it Basant can discern all of Roshanara's elegant features, her moon-round face, her charming nose, her small, even teeth. She glows to see him, and extends her hand. Even her arm is shapely, thinks Basant, as he gently takes her hand, and allows himself to be pulled to her side, like a favorite pet. He nestles in the cushions and she tugs her skirts toward her, giving him room to sit close.

There are a few other women there; hostage wives mostly, hoping to catch a glimpse of a husband or a son while the audience goes on.

Roshanara leans over. "I can barely walk," she informs him. "As if I rode a stallion all the night." Her eyes flash, only for him. "Bareback," she says with emphasis, her smooth teeth gleaming behind perfect lips. She giggles at him, then turns away and giggles some more. Basant feels his heart grow cold, but he says nothing; he just smiles and smiles. Through the jali he watches the throbbing mass of people jostle beneath velvet canopies.

He spent years pursuing a place amidst this grandeur, years desiring it, years seeking it. Always he thought of it as a dream he might someday gain; but he now sees it, for the first time, as something he might lose.

The thought strikes him like a cold wind, just so.

He sees that even the dear princess will be part of his life for only a little while, and wonders how long that little while will be. He nearly kisses Roshanara's hand, but he masters himself, but strokes her fingers as she grasps his hand. She doesn't notice.

She leans this way and that, trying for a better view. "There! There!" she whispers. "Do you see him? Isn't he beautiful?" Basant assumes that she is speaking of Shaista Khan, but that vile man is nowhere to be seen—perhaps he has slipped behind one of the Dara's other generals.

But Roshanara is nodding toward her brother . . . not to Dara, sitting smugly on the golden chair at his father's feet, but rather at the modest face of Aurangzeb, who stands nearby, as a beggar might stand waiting for the bread thrown at the end of a royal procession.

"He looks well, don't you think, Basant? He looks rested, in spite of his journey. You know he sleeps on the bare ground in the battlefield, like a common soldier! He looks well in spite of it. I think he's lovely."

Aurangzeb seems to Basant extremely plain. "Oh yes, such a fine-looking man," he says, "a lovely man." He's learned to agree promptly.

"Yes lovely, but more than lovely," she whispers, as if suddenly aware she has been speaking out loud. She glances around the room, and leans close to Basant's ear. "Have you heard? He's to be emperor."

She looks at Basant knowingly and nods. "Yes, dearest love. Dara is through." She whispers this, looking at the other women in the room as if daring them to overhear. Then she giggles, and comes so close that her sweet breath tickles his ear, "And soon. Sooner than you think!" She glances hastily around her. "So be ready," she says. "Be ready."

Basant's eyes bounce from the princess, to Dara, to Aurangzeb, then back. He is speechless. Dara—through? Basant is too fearful of treason even to consider what this whispered news might mean. And as his troubled brain sorts through her news, he peers through the jali at Aurangzeb, who looks calmly downward as the tumult bustles all around him.

Then, as if he needed more confusion on this day, a tall man in a gray cloak steps up and frowns at the jali screen, as by squinting hard enough Basant's face would be visible in the purdah shadows.

"Time to go," Roshanara announces. Her mood spins like a tail-less kite. With some effort, Basant hoists himself from the cushions, then extends his hand to help Roshanara. He scoops up her veil and helps her drape it. Once she is covered, they walk from the purdah chamber to the private, inner palace of the emperor.

The palace door swings open, revealing a tall dark eunuch guard, complete with shield and pike, who nods them past. Then up a long staircase: the steep, high stairs of the narrow passage designed for easy defense; the palace, after all, is but a small part of Agra's vast, impregnable fort. The climb is hard for Basant, who loses his breath easily.

Emerging breathless at the top of the staircase, where another dark and heavily armed guard nods them through, Basant notices that there are many guards today, positioned in clusters along the mezzanine of the Fish House: all of them eunuchs.

Again he feels a sense of panic . . . something bad is up. The image of the dead guards flashes past his eyes, and he nearly stumbles.

Across the mezzanine he can see the door of his room. Two eunuch guards stand there. He pretends not to notice.

The princess has been talking to him as they walk, he realizes, although he hasn't heard a word. "I said there was some trouble here last night. Did you hear anything about it?"

Basant tries to think what to say, but before he can answer, Roshanara has stopped in mid-stride and wheeled on him. "Well? Do you know anything about it?" she says again. Behind the dark and heavy outer veil, her eyes are angry and a bit scared.

"I think I must know very little, princess," he replies.

"You must attend to your own welfare," she whispers. Some note in her voice, some look in her eyes, disturbs Basant. His stomach churns as though he were staring into a bottomless well. But Roshanara unexpectedly pats his shoulder, and he wonders if he had simply misunderstood.

"I need you to do a favor for me, Spring Blossom," she coos. "You are the only one I trust in all the world. Will you make me beg?" It seems to Basant that he can actually hear her pouting.

"You know you have only to ask," he answers, his voice husky.

"I have a letter for my brother. For Aurangzeb. You must deliver it. Please, my darling, say you will," she says. Her hand presses his plump fingers as they walk. "But not here, darling. Not where anyone can see."

"Where, then?"

"Cross the river. Take it to his camp, in the Rambagh." Her eyes stare out from the veil, pleading with him. Basant, of course, agrees.

"When you see him, Basant, dear, tell him everything. Leave out nothing." She nods meaningfully to the guards around the Fish House, toward his heavily guarded rooms. "He can help you, or no one can."

"I'm not sure that I need help, princess." But the lie falls from his lips and lands at his feet with a clang. "Besides, Little Rose, I can't see how Aurangzeb can help me."

But now they are nearing the Diwan-i-Khas, the hall of private audience, and already many of Shah Jahan's closest advisers are gathering. It was here, not in the public audience downstairs, that the real issues would be discussed and real decisions would be made. "It looks quite a crowd gathering, Basant," Roshanara remarks, casually. "Can you imagine why?"

"No, princess," he answers, honestly mystified. He fears that somehow the answer has something to do with him, with the bloody deaths of the guards, with Shaista Khan, but they pass the Diwan-i-Khas and no one, not even the captain of the eunuch guards, seems to glance his way.

"Why are all these *hijra* here?" Roshanara wonders. Basant winces at the word: "*hijra*" was a commoner's word for eunuch, for eunuchs who dressed as women and did many unclean things, and it hurt Basant to hear the brothers called this name, especially by his princess.

Like most of the brothers he preferred the gentler, politer, name, *mukhunni.* For the Prophet knew of eunuchs, and accepted them (not like the Hindis who drove them from their homes and forced them to live on the streets like dogs). So Basant worships at the mosque, Basant says his prayers (when he manages to remember) with full confidence; he is one of Allah's *mukhunni,* one of Allah's own. The brothers like the word because it means "short-tusked"; they like being compared to elephants.

Yet what *were* all these eunuchs doing here? The eunuch guard had many formal functions, mostly to protect the harem in the imperial caravans. Rarely were eunuch guards seen in the palace, and never in such numbers.

He sees far off that same tall, gray-cloaked man he had seen at the jali screen, now talking to the two eunuchs guarding his rooms. "Look," he whispers to Roshana. "Do you know that man?"

But before she can answer, a small, dark eunuch boy in sumptuous clothing comes running up. "Uncle, uncle," he pipes, tugging at Basant. "Please come quick. Master *Khaswajara* wants you right away. Come, come, uncle!" the boy insists.

"Go, my dear," Roshanara says sweetly. "Your duty calls. I am nearly at my room. But don't forget your promise, darling," she adds, nodding meaningfully. "Come and see me soon."

Basant allows himself to be dragged by the eunuch boy. "I will see you at the private audience if I can break away," he calls to her.

"If!" she replies and giggles.

◈◈◈◈

The boy takes Basant's pudgy hand in his tiny, nervous fingers, fingers awash in jewels, baubles lent by Master Hing. Who has more jewels to lend than Hing? The emperor is lavish in his gifts to the *khaswajara.* And why not? When Hing dies, he leaves no heirs; all those gifts fall back in the emperor's lap, just so. But the *khaswajara* appears not to care: he is generous with his borrowed wealth, and lends it freely to his favorites.

The boy leads Basant across the chowk, a vast courtyard filled with sunlight that dances in the jets of a hundred laughing fountains. At last they come to a set of tall, stately doors and remove their jeweled slippers.

Together they enter the apartments of the *khaswajara*, the most trusted of the emperor's deputies—the master of the emperor's private life: his home, his harem, his meals, his leisure. Nowhere is the emperor more vulnerable; and knowing this, the emperor places his trust in one most fiercely incorruptible. For Shah Jahan, that one is Hing, the fading, wrinkled eunuch.

Basant frames a calm face for himself, though his mind churns. The boy holds his hand as they step into Hing's apartments.

In a makeshift circle on the floor of the main room, surrounded by cushions and pillows of rich velvet and much gold, a dozen eunuchs sit quietly surrounding their master.

Hing looks up. He wears heavy spectacles tied with satin ribbons around his head; these make his eyes seem to float beyond the plane of his wrinkled face, aged and scaled as an old lizard; his withered, wrinkled lips sneer around yellow teeth, worn and stained. He is old for a eunuch, for the brothers tend to die young. The odor of decay clings to his breath.

"How good of you to join us, Basant," he whispers, his voice like a rasp. "Please take your place."

Basant approaches slowly, deferentially. He is prepared to grovel, but has not yet felt the need to so. The eighth and tenth eunuchs of the first rank scuttle sideways, clearing room for him, and he sits between them.

"And these are extraordinary times, brothers," Hing says. His eyes, spectacled like fishbowls, sweep around the circle. "Last night two members of the palace guard went to the rooms of one of the brothers, but they never returned." Basant shifts uncomfortably. No one looks at him.

"Basant!" Hing calls, lifting his wet, spectacled eyes. Basant bows as near to the floor as he can. "What do you know of what happened last night? Of the disturbances that alarmed the guards? Of their fate?"

Basant's left eyelid starts to twitch. His groin is clammy with cold sweat. He opens his mouth, but nothing emerges except a tight squeak. He's ready to confess everything when Hing speaks for him:

"Nothing." Hing looks around the circle significantly. "Our brother knows nothing. For he was with the princess. Giving her an energetic ride, no doubt, on the tongue camel."

Hing pauses to allow the snickers from the brothers to fade. "Then, for some reason—and by the knife, I don't want to know—he spent what little was left of the evening in his servant's tent."

Hing glares at the circle as if inviting them all to share his cynical incredulity, and then his eyes rest calmly on Basant, staring deeply at him, as if directly into Basant's fearful heart. "Perhaps he needed his servant's help to massage his exhausted tongue. If so, we must all be grateful for his present silence. There are other ways to become a eunuch of the first rank," he says coldly, "than with the fingers, or with the tongue."

"For example, with the ass," whispers one of the eunuchs, and though Hing scowls at them, it is clear he has no idea who has uttered this mockery.

"I mean, with the mind!" Hing glares at the brothers, but his eyes are too weak to see the hidden sneers: for what unites this brotherhood most, Basant knows, is its careful mocking of its master.

"So the eunuch guard is here, Rampfel," Hing continues, as if in answer to a question, "until I feel confident in the palace guards again. There's an investigation under way. Until then, the palace guards are relieved."

Rampfel, the fifth eunuch, bows his head. Then, realizing how futile such a gesture may be to half-blind Hing, he says quietly: "Yes, sir."

"Good," says Hing. "Anything suspicious—anything even slightly out of place—is to be reported to me at once. Or to Ali Khalil Khan, a man most trusted by me—he is a cousin of the emperor." Clutching the dark eunuch boy's hand, Hing struggles to his feet. "You may go."

Rampfel taps Basant's shoulder. "What do you think got into him?" he whispers. Basant shrugs, unable to think of anything except escaping from this uncomfortable place. Before he reaches the door, however, he hears the sound he has been dreading: "Basant! Come here!"

❧❧❧❧

Basant turns back to Hing, who stands unsteadily, leaning heavily on the eunuch boy. Rampfel hesitates for a moment, then catches up and joins Basant. "I didn't ask for you, brother," Hing says to Rampfel coldly. "Never mind. You can stay." Hing turns his spectacled eyes to Basant and stares at him for a long time.

"You have such friends, my dear," the old eunuch says. "Such friends to care for you. Do you think you are fortunate in your friends? With such friends caring for you, you should take even more care, my dear."

Basant stares back, uncertain how to respond. "Ah, yes," Hing continues, "you don't know what I mean. That's a good plan, not to know what I mean. I'm old and will be dead soon anyway." Hing shakes his head wearily and whispers to Rampfel, "Here's a brother you should cultivate, my dear. He has so many friends."

Then Hing turns to Basant, and asks, as if offhand, "Tell me, Spring Blossom. Have you been to the tunnels lately?" The question surprises Basant. Hing bares his yellow teeth. "Well? Have you?"

"No, sir." His answer sounds hollow. "I nearly went last night, but . . ." He breaks off, uncertain. "But . . . I didn't. I didn't need to."

"No, of course . . . no need. Still you felt the need to kick a night bucket down the corridor. Hopeless fool! Did you think no one saw?"

Basant stares at Hing helplessly. "I wouldn't know . . . " he stammers.

"Rampfel, you see that you learn from this brother," Hing coos. "What does it take to succeed in the palace these days? Just quick fingers, I suppose, and an agile tongue."

Hing draws so close that Basant sees each flaw in his lined and spotted face. "There's a body in the well." Hing's old eyeballs are magnified to the size of duck eggs by his thick spectacles. "Yes, a body! A new body. Ask him," Hing nods at Rampfel. "He found it. Found it this morning." Hing's breath wheezes, the only sound in the room. "Well? Rampfel didn't put it there. Know anything about it? Ring any bells for you?"

Basant shakes his head.

"Well, what about your precious princess? Think she knows anything? Think she even speculates? In between her climaxes, I mean?"

Basant knows better than to answer.

"Never mind," says Hing. "It's no one's fault. It's a clerical error—a number entered in the wrong column that spoiled all the sums. I don't suppose we'll ever know who he is." He gives a long sigh; it smells musty, like air from a cave. "But who knows about the well, eh? No secret is more secret. You two, myself, and perhaps one or two others. So how can there be a body in that secret well if none of us knows how it got there?"

Basant shakes his head, but of course he notices the exquisite dark eunuch boy who holds Hing's hand. How much has he heard? How many other boys have stood in that same place, their turbans dripping with Hing's borrowed jewels? How many others have heard Hing's secrets, long after Hing has forgotten them? Until this moment, Basant has hated Master Hing, but trusted him. Suddenly he realizes that Hing is dangerous in many, many ways. He finds himself thinking of Hing's cryptic remarks, and wonders who his real friends are.

Hing shakes his head. "Go now. Surely you have better things to do than to listen to a pathetic old eunuch." He turns away, holding the eunuch boy. "All my friends will not desert me." Leaning on the eunuch boy, he walks away with slow and painful steps.

"What was that about?" whispers Rampfel when Hing is out of earshot. "Such nonsense! Did you understand a single thing he said?"

Basant shrugs. "I must join the princess at the audience," he says.

Rampfel chatters on, hardly noticing that Basant has moved away. "I doubt that we will join you. The Princess Jahanara goes less and less. I think it saddens her to see what her father is becoming. Odd that Roshanara doesn't mind, eh? They are sisters, yet so different."

But by now Basant has slipped through the doorway to the chowk, leaving Rampfel by himself.

⊘⊙⊘⊙

"Basant, what luck. May I walk with you, sir?"

Basant, somewhat blinded by the sunlight, takes a moment to find the owner of that honey-smooth voice.

A tall man, exquisitely groomed, steps beside him. Basant sees the deep dark eyes, the trimmed beard, the silver turban. He sees the sweeping dark gray cloak that swirls majestically as the man matches Basant's padding footsteps with his smooth and flowing tread. "My name is Ali Khalil and I have the honor of being a distant relative of the Lord of Light himself, may he live forever. Perhaps you have heard of me?"

Basant nods silently. His voice has suddenly fled.

Ali Khan's smooth lips pull back to reveal pearl-white, even teeth. "As chance would have it, I attended the rising of the lord my cousin this morning. At that time I was asked to look into certain discrepancies that have caused our dear lord some concern. It seems that two guards disappeared last night while on duty, and no one knows where they have got to. Our lord is worried some treachery may be afoot. Unworthy as I am to receive the honor, it is my task to know what may be known."

"Whatever help I can give is yours, uncle. You need only ask." Basant bows calmly, but his heart races. So this is the face of my death, he thinks. I'll be arrested, carted off, and executed. To his own surprise, Basant finds that he is calm. Perhaps he is too tired to care. All he feels is hunger. All he hopes is that he'll get a last meal before the end.

"I knew I could count on you, Basant," the man replies, all courtesy. With a beautifully manicured fingertip, he smoothes one of his mustaches. "Perhaps you know that there was a disturbance last night in the Machi

Bahwan?" Basant is amused to hear the Fish Building called by its proper name. "The guards thought it might have come from near your rooms."

Basant tries his best to look noncommittal. "What then?" he asks.

"What then, indeed?" Ali Khalil now stops completely, facing Basant. "There's a disturbance. The captain and another guard investigate. Then the captain and the guard disappear."

Ali Khalil's dark eyes stare calmly into Basant's round face. This is a contest, Basant thinks, and the first to speak will be the loser. He wills himself to hold his tongue, that tongue which is the source of all his troubles and his triumphs. He stares back, silent.

In the end, it is Ali Khalil who speaks. "But then what could you know? You were with the Princess Roshanara for much of the night. And, if your servant is to be believed, you joined him at his tent near dawn." Basant says nothing: silence, so far, has been his friend. "I thought that part odd," Khalil says. "To sleep in an old tent instead of the palace."

Basant says nothing. "It is as I thought," Khalil continues, satisfying himself with his own answers. "You had some business, but you are discreet. A eunuch of the first rank, I told myself, will keep his own counsel." Khalil inclines his head, inviting Basant to agree with this compliment.

"I can have no secrets from such a one as you, Ali Khalil."

"You flatter me," Khalil says, bowing. "By the way, Basant, do you know anything about tunnels?"

Basant's heart stops, but he tries as best he can to keep his face serene. "Tunnels, uncle? For what purpose, sir?"

"I can't imagine. The guards tell me that the eunuchs use secret tunnels to bring visitors—men—to the harem without being seen. Sounds like a lonely soldier's fantasy to me." Khalil laughs and with an inclination of his head invites Basant to laugh with him. Of course Basant joins in.

Still chuckling, Khalil bows deeply to Basant, more deeply, strictly speaking, than Basant deserves, and swirls away majestically, his dark gray cloak sweeping behind him, leaving Basant squinting in the sunlight.

After watching him go, Basant hurries to the Diwan-i-Khas, staggering like a deer dazed by a hunter's near miss: not wounded, but confused. Basant hopes to see no more people today; he has had enough of people. His heart yearns for the safety and the quiet of the purdah chamber, for the gentle voice and hands of Roshanara. He hurries on.

The Diwan-i-Khas is like a jeweled miniature of the public audience hall. Only the greatest noblemen, those most dear to the emperor, may enter this pavilion, and see the King of the World seated on his Peacock

Throne. The golden peacock's tail that spreads over the emperor's head is so studded with jewels and gems that it seems about to collapse from its own weight. Within a silver railing stand those who have permission to speak; inside a golden railing those closest to Shah Jahan, his sons: Dara (who sits) and Aurangzeb (who stands), also his ministers and secretaries, and kneeling at the foot of the throne, his vizier, Assaf Khan, who truly controls the empire in Shah Jahan's name.

ᘒᘒᘒᘒ

At this very moment a battle is raging in front of the Peacock Throne that will shape the nature of the empire for the next fifty years. Basant, however, walks past without a second glance; he hasn't even noticed.

Perhaps if the warriors wielded swords, Basant would better see the battle in its fury. But these two warriors use only words as weapons—Prince Dara, and Aurangzeb's general, Mir Jumla.

The heart of the matter is this: Each of Shah Jahan's four sons controls a quarter of the kingdom. That at least is the theory. In practice, Dara owns the lion's share, and now has Aurangzeb's quarter, the Deccan, firmly in his sights. Aurangzeb knows this, and now joins the battle here.

Aurangzeb's commander Mir Jumla has the floor. Ten years ago, he explains, the Deccan belonged to Dara. Within five years, Dara had all but lost it. The local kings first reduced their tribute, then stopped paying altogether, then openly rebelled. Dara retreated, Jumla explains with flowery words, and became viceroy of Bengal instead—a docile and agreeable place that gives little distress.

Aurangzeb was then made viceroy of the Deccan. For five years he has set about winning back the lands that Dara lost. One by one the rebel kings have fallen, one by one, their tributes have returned. "The wealth of the Deccan," Jumla continues, "has been underestimated. The wealth of some of those small kingdoms rivals all the rest of the empire combined."

Shah Jahan, hearing this, lifts an eyebrow skeptically.

It is time for Jumla to make his point. He calls for his servant to bring a box covered in black velvet. He takes the box, and with a sweeping bow, places it in Shah Jahan's quivering, outstretched hand. "From Aurangzeb and all your faithful servants," Jumla intones.

Shah Jahan fiddles with the small box, unfastening its clasps, and finally lifting the lid. His eyes grow wide. "It's not real," Shah Jahan whispers. He is too fascinated by the contents to notice Jumla's assurances that it is, indeed, real. At last, Shah Jahan lifts from its velvet casket a stone clear as glass, a diamond bigger than an egg, faceted and brilliant. Except for the startled gasps of some of the courtiers, the hall is silent, as they marvel at the stone's size, its clarity, its fire.

"This jewel beyond price," Jumla says, "this diamond beyond compare, was captured by your son, Aurangzeb from the Golcondan king. And this gem is but a fraction of their treasure, a mere hint of the wealth of that kingdom." Shah Jahan seems lost in fascination (for he has already taken much opium that morning), but Assaf Khan is listening hard, as is Dara.

"Aurangzeb is now breaking down the very door of Golconda. Our armies have laid siege for months. Wealth such as you see is within inches of your fingertips."

Now Dara speaks, again pretending that the audience is Shah Jahan, but stealing glances at Assaf Khan all the while. "But general, our dear friend the king of Golconda has written us. He begs to know why our brother Aurangzeb storms his gates. He has promised tribute and sued for peace. And what, we would know, should we tell that poor man? We are at a loss why our brother should attack a man so ready to yield. Unless my brother's purpose is at odds with our dear father's?"

Aurangzeb stands silent on the other side of Shah Jahan, his head bowed slightly, his eyes half-closed, as if praying. Mir Jumla responds, "The Golcondan king thinks that he can get a better deal from you than from Aurangzeb." His eyes narrow. "I think he's right."

The courtiers nearby are shocked by this exchange, and expect that Shah Jahan will intervene, but the emperor seems too intrigued by the brilliance of his new plaything.

"It is our father's will that all his dominions be at peace. Lift the siege at once," Dara replies, recovering.

"When I hear it from your father's lips."

"I have spoken. That is enough."

Maybe Jumla expects the court to be shocked at this statement, but as he looks around the assembled nobles, he discovers that Dara's assertion is not news.

Jumla glances at Aurangzeb for guidance. Perhaps he finds it in Aurangzeb's impassive face. He wheels on Dara angrily. "This is your will, Dara, not your father's. You are fearful of Aurangzeb and wish to spoil his victory. You fear that his radiance will outshine yours."

Dara looks at Jumla, pleasantly, but slightly irritated, like a man tiring of the games of a favorite nephew. "General, you have been in the company of one who cares little for ceremony, and, in truth one who cares little for our father. He has proven this a hundred ways. But here in Agra, sir, you would be wise to think before you speak."

At that moment, all the hall again grows quiet, anticipating some great outburst, some outpouring of emotion. Even Shah Jahan grows still; placing the diamond in his lap, he looks up, as if dazed.

Jumla is about to reply, but when Aurangzeb raises his hand, he stops. The courtiers shift their glances, from brother to brother, taking each man's measure. They look at Dara in his silks and jewels, the eldest, the favorite, and at Aurangzeb in his simple robe, the plainest of men.

"I am but a beggar on this earth," Aurangzeb says quietly. "In this as in all things I will obey my father's will. But is it truly my father's will that you have spoken, brother?"

"It is," Dara replies, looking directly at him.

"I would hear my father say so." Aurangzeb looks to his father. The emperor faces his younger son with some confusion, then turns helplessly to Dara—who says nothing—and then to Assaf Khan.

"It is your father's will that the siege of Golconda be raised," Assaf Khan says, hardly glancing at the emperor. Shah Jahan's eyes have drifted away. "As his vizier, I say this. Hear and obey."

Aurangzeb peers at the faces of the courtiers who watch him with anxious fascination, scarcely breathing. He then bows to his father, tapping the floor with his hands three times, and walks slowly from the hall without a word or even glance to Dara. Jumla follows, neither bowing or nodding.

And as they leave, Basant enters the dark shelter of the purdah chamber of the private palace. In the dim light he approaches Roshanara, kneeling on her cushions "What's going on?" he asks.

They stare through the jali at the scene in the audience hall. The nobles have begun to breathe again, and now are whispering with one another. Assaf Khan is speaking anxiously with Shah Jahan. Only Dara seems unaffected, sitting on his golden stool, alone; it seems odd to Basant that no one is talking to him. "What did I miss?" Basant asks again.

Roshanara turns to him, tears streaming from her eyes. To Basant's surprise, she throws herself on his shoulder and weeps. Embarrassed, he puts his plump arms around her. "There, there," he whispers. "There, there." He doesn't know what else to do.

❦ ❦ ❦ ❦

Basant knows the touch of women on the boil, churning with the heat of passion. He knows the smell and taste of their desire. He knows the thrashing and squealing, as they clench his head between their thighs and melt into moaning, throbbing delight.

But he never feels their softness, their yielding. Such gifts, thinks Basant, they save for men, not for those like me. For what has he, deformed and maimed, to offer a woman? Cut off a man's leg, and even though it is gone he can feel it itch. What happens if you cut off his lingam?

Can it be that Basant feels something like desire? Is this why, when he holds Roshanara just so, he begins to dream of serving girls and pillows, and *sharbats*, and swings?

Here is a secret he would never tell: Sometimes he dreams of being Roshanara's husband, of being cradled in her arms (sometimes she is naked in these dreams; and sometimes so is he); and she feeds him sweet milk full of sugar from an ivory cup.

Now his dream is close, now as he holds her. Thoughts of pleasure fill his head; he floats as on a cloud of some unnamable desire.

Only he is not with some daydream, but with the real Roshanara—and Roshanara shares no one's dreams. She twists from his embrace and pushes him away. "The hand is dealt. I must not fear my role. It is now: not soon, but now." She blots her eyes with her palms, as a child might, and she snaps at him: "Come, fool. We have work to do."

The familiar twisting dread returns.

She flips back the veil that covers her face, and peers into a miniature mirror that she wears as a ring on her right thumb. Patting a wayward lock of hair, she scowls at her reflection. Angrily she strides out. The marble walls echo as the heels of her slippers clap against the tiles.

❧❧❧❧

Basant, forlorn, forgotten, watches her shadow disappear through the door. He blinks and follows. A taste like acid burns the back of his throat, making his eyes water. A fool might say that I've been crying, he thinks.

They step into the light-drenched hallways of the harem. After the shadows of the purdah room, the bright sunlight of the seraglio bruises his weary eyes. The warming air is already heavy with damp smells of beauty—of hot bathwater, of attar of roses and *chandan* oil, of patchouli and musk. Breezes from the river carry a breath of orange blossoms, and fetch the laughter of water splashing in the scented courtyard fountains.

The harem is buzzing—maidservants, serving girls, eunuchs of the lower ranks, all walking quickly here and there; ill-mannered children dash between them, giggling. The wives complain to the eunuchs, who turn and scold the maids, who then bark at the serving girls, who chase off on some errand near tears.

But Basant feels only the burning stares of the eunuch guards. Since these guards are suddenly important, brought in to cope with unknown danger, they are especially watchful. And because they are eunuchs, laughed at by the regular guard, they are more watchful still.

And the guards are everywhere, halting people, asking questions—acting in the same intrusive way that drove Shah Jahan to command their removal from the harem in the first place. The eunuch guards scrutinize even the Tartar women, Shah Jahan's most trusted guardians. It is clear from their pink, angry faces that the women despise the eunuch guards.

In fact it seems to Basant, as he watches the comings and goings, that everyone and everything in the harem seems upset, off balance. He has never seen the harem like this. It would be hard for him to say exactly what strikes him as wrong. Perhaps it is only his own anxiety that he projects around him—yet it seems that every eye he sees darts fretfully away, every face turns furtively aside. Anxiety perfumes the air; it pervades each breath that Basant takes. Something terrible is about to happen.

Roshanara, walking purposefully, veiled—although here in the privacy of the zenena, veiling is unusual—moves quickly toward the wing of concubines of the first rank. Basant follows at her heels as she thrusts open a great ebony door. Whose room is this? Basant wonders. He doesn't recognize it. He steps tentatively inside.

Here the world moves at a different speed. Sunbeams float above them, lazily catching the incense smoke spiraling from braziers hanging from the ceiling. Two young and beautiful women are bathing, assisted by attentive serving girls and eunuchs who at this moment are pouring salvers of steaming water over their heads and backs.

The sunlight glistens on their smooth bodies and dances in wisps of steam rising from their hair and shoulders. It sparkles on the surface of the bathwater in the twin, swan-shaped tubs, on the girls who look impossibly beautiful. Basant feels like a dervish glimpsing paradise.

Though he has never entered these particular rooms before, Basant of course recognizes the two women who are bathing. They are Shah Jahan's favorite nautch girls; twin sisters, barely fifteen, so similar in looks and temperament as to be indistinguishable.

I'd forgotten they'd been moved in here, Basant thinks.

Their nautch names are Sun and Moon. The wags in the court call them Breakfast and Lunch. From all indications they are insatiable.

What a shame they are so stupid.

Around them Shah Jahan has no self-control. Master Hing loves to recount how the emperor actually commanded that they both be brought to his bed at the same time. Hing, of course, was horrified, and although he expected to die for it, he refused to obey. Later—as Hing recounts at every opportunity—the emperor apologized to him for this sinful lapse and sent to Hing a robe of honor for his steadfastness, and, no doubt, to buy his silence.

Hing subsequently had given vehement and explicit orders to assure such a scandalous act never occurred. Such a sinful act could destroy the emperor's authority to govern.

Basant winces at the rude and disdainful greeting Roshanara gives the twins. The twins raise their sleepy beautiful faces to her—round, wet, and innocent of any disturbing thoughts, or of any thoughts at all. Though the servants bow low to Roshanara, and stay prostrate excessively long (and one even says "highness" very loudly, as if to give the sisters a hint), the two girls gape at her with their dark, blank eyes.

Without raising her voice, Roshanara commands all the servants from the room; they scramble to their feet and dash for the door before she finishes speaking. Then she turns and orders Basant to bring Tambula the apothecary to her immediately.

Basant is stunned, not only by the command, but by its unexpected tone—stately and demeaning. But he gathers his wits, and moves to obey. As he leaves, he looks back hopefully. Maybe she will call him back, say that she was only teasing her dear Spring Blossom—but as she turns with a scowl to the twins, Basant thinks she looks angry indeed.

◌◌◌◌

He hurries down the long hall to the red sandstone archway that separates the harem from the palace. Guards patrol this gateway: on Basant's side of the gate stand eunuch guards who nod at him as he passes, on the other side stand a few of the now disfavored palace guard. Once he steps beneath the arch, a palace guard calls out "Hey! Hey you! Stop!" and drops his tasseled lance across Basant's path.

Basant toys with the idea of running. For a moment he remembers being five years old, with all his parts intact, and he wishes he had run then when he could run. Cursing silently, he halts.

"Aren't you Basant? Basant the eunuch?" the guard demands.

"I have the honor to be a servant of the emperor, a eunuch of the first rank, and personal attendant to Princess Roshanara Begum, second daughter of the emperor. By her am I called Basant, and by my friends."

"That's enough," the guard sneers, unimpressed. "Wait here, *hijra*." The words thud in Basant's ears, like rocks heaved into a shallow pool.

Across the sunlit courtyard Basant sees a door open, and the guard who stopped him leads a familiar-looking man toward him: It is that same man, Ali Khalil—the friend of Hing, the cousin of the emperor, the pain in the ass. He looks just the same as earlier, and Basant hates him for it, hates that he should be smiling and friendly and impeccably groomed when Basant sweats in cold panic.

"Good day, Basant," Khalil says, stepping toward him.

"He don't like that name," says the palace guard, pretending, as soldiers do everywhere, to be stupider than he really is. "That name be only for his friends, he says." The guard sneers at Basant with smug amusement.

Khalil thinks this over, and fixes the guard with his charming smile. "But you see, I am his friend." And he beams at Basant. "Am I not your friend, Basant?"

Basant beams back, thankful to have something to do besides perspire.

Basant notices that the other palace guards have moved closer. They are watching Khalil—waiting for his subtlest sign before stepping into action.

"Ali Khalil," Basant says, giving the appearance, he hopes, of bored annoyance, "I come on an errand at the order of my mistress, the princess. Already she will be asking for me—I dare not delay."

"Do me a service, Basant?" Though he phrases it as a question, Khalil speaks it like an order. He draws the eunuch away from the arch. Khalil's hand feels hot, like the hand of a man hot with desire. Surely that's impossible! Basant thinks.

Khalil puts his face close to Basant's ear. Basant can feel his smiling breath. "What a lot of trouble you have made for me," Khalil whispers, the words blowing warm and soft in his ear, like a caress. "And for yourself, Basant," Khalil whispers. The sound curls in Basant's ear like a snake.

Basant wants to flee, but where can he go? "Could you look at something with me?" Khalil says, peering into Basant's face with his plaster smile. "It may be something that concerns you." Basant's knees are shaking so much that he can feel his silken pant legs quivering.

"This way, Basant," Khalil says gently, and he motions to his palace guards. They step forward, almost offhandedly forming themselves together into a tight unit. This subtle action nearly undoes Basant; he thinks he must collapse. Instead he walks beside Ali Khalil to a small storeroom. Khalil stands by the door while one of the guards pushes it open.

A moist smell of damp wool emerges, then the sour smell of old dust. The room is dark. "Show him," Khalil says, gesturing with his chin to something in the shadows. With a heave, two of the guards push the end of a big wet carpet through the door and into the sunlight. It lands in a tented heap in front of Basant's feet. A dark puddle forms beneath the carpet, spreading toward Basant's jeweled slippers.

"Seen this before?" Khalil asks.

It is the carpet from Basant's own room—a deep blue Persian carpet of Sarouk design. "Never," Basant replies.

"We fished it out of the moat this morning. Someone thought it might be yours," Khalil looks at him levelly.

"Someone is mistaken."

Khalil looks at him carefully, the way a man might watch a bubble, waiting for it to pop. Basant looks back, forcing his eyes to be soft, half-asleep. Whoever speaks next loses, Basant thinks.

"Well, that's what we told him. We looked in your room—the carpet's still there." Khalil seems embarrassed by the admission. "Then he said the one in your room was a new one." Basant sniffs, disdaining even to answer. Who is saying these things, he wonders, though he keeps his face blank. "Any idea where this came from? How it ended up in the moat?" Khalil asks, almost pitifully. Basant shrugs. "Put it back," Khalil says to the guards.

Khalil shakes his head. "Intruders in the harem. A guards captain missing . . . and his lieutenant missing. A carpet in the moat . . ." His voice trails off. "The emperor so terrified of treachery that he removes his own guard in favor of the eunuch guards! Well, I can't expect you to help me. Sorry to trouble you." His smile is unchanged as ever, but there is a wan, defeated quality in his eyes. "I was sorry to hear about the death of your servant," Khalil adds, his plaster smile unchanged. "He died over there. Fell down those stairs. They say he broke his neck."

"Haridas? When?" Basant croaks.

"A few hours ago. His family collected the body."

"He had no family."

Khalil seems not to hear. He bows deeply to Basant, swirls his sumptuous gray cloak around him with a flourish, and glides away.

The guards look Basant up and down and then follow Khalil down the hallway of the palace. Leaving Basant behind, gasping for breath.

ᏚᏬᏪᏬ

In the neat herb gardens Basant sees Tambula's long, thin form bent over a row of tall plants.

Basant allows himself to breathe. It seems he has hardly breathed all day. The garden air smells full of tangy, pungent scents.

In the far corner Tambula picks carefully through a row of plants held up by stakes and strings. Now and then he plucks a leaf and places it gently in one of the sacks he has slung over his shoulder, dropping others less than perfect disdainfully to the ground.

Basant and Tambula have been friends since childhood, since they were made brothers by the same slavemaster. Tambula had a keen mind and an infallible memory—unlike Basant, whose main talents are a pleasant demeanor and an artless willingness to do whatever he is asked. Tambula, young though he was, became harem apothecary. Now of all the brothers in the harem, Tambula has the position of greatest trust. Only the Mir-Bakawal, the royal taster, has a post of greater trust, and he is not a brother and has never seen the inside of the harem.

Tambula straightens and lifts his chin in greeting. One of his two front teeth is much longer than the other, and gives him a sweet and slightly dopey appearance, which, Basant knows, is entirely misleading but very appealing. Basant waves back. They exchange a few pleasantries, and almost immediately Basant tells him why he has come.

"But do you know what she wants, brother?" Tambula asks. "Is she ill? Fearful? Too sad or too happy? Are her menses uncomfortable?"

To each question Basant merely shakes his head and shrugs, unable to bear any delay. "Just come quickly, brother."

But Tambula moves slowly, carefully lifting each sack over his head and handing it gently to his apprentice, who sets it tenderly on the marble walkway that surrounds the garden. Tambula then removes and folds his apron; he hands this to his apprentice as well.

Basant can barely contain himself. "Hurry, hurry," he says, glancing at the archway to the harem.

Tambula brushes the dust from his trousers and kicks the dry soil from his sandals. He opens a fine old, wooden box: plain, about the size of a harmonium. Tambula throws back the lid and studies his portable apothecary kit—full of vials and potions arranged in neat rows of corked glass bottles. Running a jeweled finger across the display, he quickly tallies what he has and what he lacks.

"I have no rue," he says.

"Never mind, just come," Basant says. "We must hurry."

"It's for painful menses."

"It doesn't matter. Just hurry."

"But what if the princess has painful menses?" Tambula slips the em-broidered strap over his head, and stands so the heavy apothecary box rests on his left hip.

Together they hurry back toward the concubines' quarters. Tam-bula's long legs easily outpace Basant, who has to waddle extra fast to catch up.

"Sorry about your servant. I know how you loved him," Tambula mentions as they walk. "But I was there, you know. I held his hand and of-fered prayers, but he was already dead."

Basant can barely speak. "Did he suffer?"

"No, dear. And the fall didn't kill him, you know. Somebody broke his neck for him and then shoved him down the stairs. You could see his neck had been wrung like a washcloth."

Basant stops walking. His world seems to go black. When he comes to himself, he has to run to catch up. When he reaches Tambula's side once more, Basant is puffing hard.

"I could give you something to make you skinnier," Tambula offers.

"Perhaps some other time," Basant replies.

Never has Basant seen so many eunuch guards. All of them seem to be peering at him with accusing eyes. When they pass one, Basant positions Tambula between the guard and himself, altering his pace carefully to keep himself hidden. But he knows it is impossible to hide his quivering bulk behind the rail-thin Tambula. Tambula looks at Basant quizzically.

They reach the door of Breakfast and Lunch. The scene is much as Bas-ant left it: Roshanara is still standing near the two nautch girls, but they have left their baths and stand wrapped in muslin sheets.

The faces of Breakfast and Lunch, those empty-eyed faces so beautiful and serene a few moments ago now appear agitated and fearful. The twins cower together as Roshanara strides nearby, dark and powerful. Basant wonders what Roshanara could have said to frighten them so. As she mo-tions impatiently for Tambula to enter, she says brusquely to Basant, "Fetch their other servants."

Basant bows. Tambula hurries to Roshanara's side. She is already whis-pering to him fiercely when Basant goes out the door.

When he returns, he sees Roshanara watching imperiously as Breakfast and Lunch swallow potions handed to them by Tambula. They make wry, wrinkled faces and reach for cups of wine. With that Roshanara turns straight for Basant. "Now pay attention. This time nothing must go wrong. When these two . . . women are dressed, take them to the Diwan-i-Khas. Yes, the purdah room, of course. When they are done there, come to my room. I'll have a letter for Aurangzeb. Is that quite clear?"

It isn't until after Roshanara strides from the room, scowling, that Basant realizes he doesn't know what he's supposed to do with two nautch girls in the purdah room. He feels his cheeks growing hot and tears welling up in his eyes, but he refuses to let her see him cry.

He closes the door behind the princess, and turns back into the room. Tambula has come to his side. The apothecary's face is pale and his eyes are wide—Basant can see that Tambula too is shaken.

"I had no idea, brother," Tambula whispers hoarsely. "No idea at all. You are fortunate in your friends. Indeed, I hope you will remember our friendship in days to come." He seems to Basant almost to bow. "Even so, my dear, promise me that you will never say a word of this to Hing!"

"What can you mean, brother?"

"What if he finds out that I have had a part in this—the act that he has so explicitly forbidden?" His face is ashen. "The princess stakes everything on one throw of the dice." He gives a resigned shrug. "Anyway, I suppose my secret's safe enough with you. If things go wrong, I mean—why, you'd be the first one Hing would kill."

Tambula turns to watch the servants dress the twins, leaving Basant to sort this out as best he can. "I've given them each dravanas," Tambula explains. "Double doses. I don't know what the princess said to them, but whatever it was, I've never seen them so upset."

"What did she say to you?" Basant asks.

"You can imagine," Tambula answers, appearing disturbed just by the memory. "In any case, she was quite explicit about what I was to do with these two. They'll be as horny as lepers in a few minutes. Then you can take them to the purdah room." Tambula bites his lip. "I'm concerned they might have convulsions. I can't help them much if they do. I've never given anyone such big doses before. They're young, so they'll probably be all right. I'll just watch them for a while, I think."

Convulsions! He is about reply when he notices that Tambula's hands have dark swellings, like thick pustules.

"Oh those," Tambula says, as if answering the question Basant is too embarrassed to ask.

While they watch the twins being dressed and prepared by their serving girls, Tambula quietly tells Basant the story of those odd swellings. He speaks quietly and discreetly, slipping into Bengali, which all the brothers speak when secrecy is helpful.

❦❦❦❦

It happened, Tambula says, after 'taj Mahal died—giving birth to her fourteenth child: what does that say about Shah Jahan's vigor? After a period of mourning, Shah Jahan called Tambula's predecessor, a eunuch called Kela, for a consultation. At that time Tambula was Kela's apprentice.

Every man, of course, experiments with *vardhanas* at some point—every man wants to add an inch or two to the length of his lingam. But in this endeavor as in others Shah Jahan was determined to surpass all other men. He let Kela know he was prepared to tolerate any manner of agony to achieve his goal—to have the grandest lingam the world had ever known.

Kela's method required enormous effort—Shah Jahan ended up lying facedown in a hammock for more than a month. His lingam poked through a hole with small weights suspended from its tip. The shaft Kela wrapped in wool soaked in mustard oil, into which he and Tambula had ground up the stingers of a thousand *jalshuks*. Since a man might swell up and die from a single jalshuk sting, Kela had paid dearly for them: a full rupee apiece for each of the brilliant green bugs.

Though they wrapped their hands in rags before they applied this ointment to Shah Jahan's lingam, no precaution was adequate. Touch even a few drops of the oil and hands and fingers would blister and swell to enormous size; and though they soaked their hands in *dahi* for hours, even that could not cool them. But Shah Jahan bore the treatment day after day, never sleeping for the pain, never uttering a sound.

At last, though more blistering oil was applied, the skin had become so thick and blackened that no more growth could be achieved.

For some weeks, the emperor used to show the results to anyone who asked, and also to those who did not ask. Tambula says that the court called it the *Jahan-minar*—the tower of the world—just to please him.

Since Basant never saw it, Tambula describes it to him: The emperor's lingam is enormous—long, thick, but hideously misshapen; twisted, distorted, bulging, and in some places black.

Nevertheless, the emperor seemed delighted with the results. He only sees its size, says Tambula, not its deformity. Apparently he could make it function well enough, and that was the main thing.

He gave Kela jama robes of honor and a casket of jewels. And of course at that point Kela made his tearful goodbyes, and gave Tambula his apothecary box. Two days later he was dead. Shah Jahan could not bear that Kela might help another man achieve such a masterwork.

Shah Jahan's wives and concubines quickly learned to bite back their horror at the emperor's monstrosity: rather they learned to admire the results if they knew what was good for them.

As he listens to Tambula describe this lunacy, Basant wonders what Shah Jahan was like when Taj Mahal was alive. He has only seen him as he appears now: old, sneering, overwhelmed by wine, opium, and endless *vajikaranas*. The brothers shake their heads when they speak of Shah Jahan.

Basant asks Tambula about it. Tambula confirms the stories. Yes, Shah Jahan had congress twenty-two times in one night. Three or four times an hour! Think of it! Recently he collapsed on his eleventh partner and couldn't be roused, even with her screaming in his ear and the brothers rubbing ice on his hands and feet.

"Why do you think I am so honored by the emperor? He knows that no one can match my skill in *vajikarana*," Tambula says ruefully. "Without my help, he'd have a stalk like a limp radish."

Tambula speculates that all these drugs must be having an effect: He thinks that Shah Jahan's strength is being squeezed from his limbs and out through his lingam, leaving his organs shriveled and dry like dates. He and his apprentice like to guess about which woman will squeeze the last drop from Shah Jahan and toss his brittle husk aside.

And yet, Shah Jahan still rules the empire. Though he may be dying slowly, he rules, and wisely, and well, Basant thinks. The empire thrives, its people are happy. The beauty of Agra, of Lahore, of Shahjahanabad; these reflect a sensibility and intelligence rarely seen in a king. Taxes are fair, he has been told, and collected with only minimal violence; justice is meted out with reason and charity—with only enough tortures and executions each week to make consequences apparent and memorable.

Basant likes to show a sophisticated interest in politics. But before he can consider matters further, as often happens, reality intrudes. The girls are dressed and ready, and showing no ill effects. Tambula places his long fingers first on the neck of one, then of the other, and pulls down their lower eyelids without a word. Appearing much relieved, he settles the vials in his apothecary case and slings it over his shoulder. "I've done enough damage here," he says. "Get them to a man fast or they'll attack each other. And pray to God he can stay hard for a month."

Turning to Basant as he leaves, he says, "You were right, brother—it wasn't her menses. I wonder if she even is a woman. Don't say I said so—though I imagine she'd take it as a compliment. Be careful, brother."

❧❧❧

Basant soon finds himself walking the corridors of the harem with Breakfast and Lunch.

At last they enter the purdah room. The girls' eyes are unfocused, glazed, but burning with fierce, purposeful desire. They glide across the room arm in arm, heads close, whispering secrets to each other.

In the dim light that filters through the jali their heavy pearl necklaces slide across their perfect, perfumed breasts perfectly visible through blouses of silk mesh. A heat rises from them; they glow like hot coals; eyes dark and wild that both mock and invite; lips red and full, licked by nimble tongues; nipples painted with kumkum and opium; silk skirts whispering across sleek thighs. The girls seem to float to cushions at the edge of the jali screen, attracted by the light. Basant takes a seat in a darker corner, and nearly trips over the legs of someone already seated in the shadows.

It is Hing.

Basant mixes an apology and a greeting into an embarrassed confusion. "Well, well," Hing rasps, his red, rheumy eyes looking up at him through globelike spectacles. "Spring Blossom, as I live and breathe. The very brother I wanted to see. And accompanied by two such upstanding young women. Why are you with them, I wonder? Taking a step down, are we?" He casts a disdainful glance around the room. "Or maybe a step up."

"Let's see," Hing continues, "I gave three strict orders to protect our beloved emperor from his own outsized desires, to wit. One: No daytime visits from Breakfast and Lunch. Two: Absolutely those two strumpets will be kept from the purdah room. Three: Never feed those animals aphrodisiacs before evening. But what have we here?" Hing looks around the room, as if surprised to find the twin nautch girls nearby. "Really, how amusing you are, Spring Blossom. Why one might think you didn't care a fig for my orders."

Hing enjoys Basant's discomfort. "I am old, Basant. I enjoy so few things anymore." He stares at Basant with those wet, sick eyes. "You won't believe me, but it amuses me to see you gaping there. Makes me feel like a child again.

"So, darling, enjoy yourself. Disobey whenever you wish! Pay no mind to me." Hing's breath wheezes. "You see, that's the way of things these days. You can do almost anything if you amuse the right people."

Hing waves a shriveled, jewel-laden hand, and his eunuch boy suddenly appears from the shadows. He steps to Master Hing's side, and the feeble old eunuch begins the long process of standing. "I know better, Basant, than to be your enemy. You have so many friends now. I too shall be your friend. But, dear Spring Blossom, let me give you some advice: You would do better to have me as an enemy than as a friend."

Basant scarcely knows what to say. "But I would want you as my friend, master, unworthy though I am."

"So you disregard my advice?" Hing sighs. "No matter, Spring Blossom. Oh, dear, look at this . . ." Hing grimaces, gesturing toward the activity in the Diwan-i-Khas.

Through the screen, they see the nobles standing at the silver rail, and an attractive slim-hipped youth in a fine, sky-blue jama steps forward.

The youth calls on Dara to recite. Dara agrees, glowing at the request, and the youth turns aside, blushing. Without any preamble Dara starts to recite his latest work: a translation of the Hindu Upanishads into Persian. He lifts his head and closes his eyes, intoning his majestic words with artful solemnity. Those in attendance nod appreciatively, extending their hands at particularly poignant passages. Only about half of them understand Persian.

"Look at Dara, look!" Hing says. "Head over heels for a little boy who scarcely has a beard. Disgusting." Hing snorts. "In my day, a prince would be happy with his wife, or he'd take a concubine. Worse come to worse, he'd find a eunuch. What was wrong with that?" He scowls at Dara, shaking his head. "This modern custom of bringing your fancy boys to the palace—it makes me ill. And think of what he has given him—a *mandsab* of five thousand horses. For what, I ask you? For having long hands and a soft ass." He fixes Basant with a glare. "Remind you of anyone?"

Outside the jali, Dara lilts along in perfect Persian. Inside, Hing is struggling to stand. Basant puts a hand under his elbow, and Hing twists away. Then he relents. "I forgot you wanted me for a friend," he wheezes, offering his elbow. With Basant's help the old eunuch gets to his feet.

Hing is nearly to the door when he stops and looks down at Basant's feet. "Ever think about those shoes of yours, Spring Blossom? I think about my shoes, sometimes. Once I wore satin slippers. Now see! They are covered with jewels. Same as yours, my boy. I wear them wherever I want. I am the *khaswajara* now, at least for a little while. The only place I remove my slippers is in the emperor's own bedroom." He looks wryly at Basant. "And what about you? Where do you remove your slippers, Basant? At the emperor's quarters, and at my door. And nowhere else! Think of that, Basant. What other people in this palace—slave, free, princess or prince, can say as much? We are so very fortunate, Basant. I thank Allah each day for my good luck."

He pauses, and Basant wonders if Hing might be dying. "How hard it is to be patient, Basant. Yet I would advise you to be patient. Though I am old, I still I have my teeth. Do you see?" He looks to Basant as if he wants pity. "I used to be young like you, my darling. Like this one, too," he adds, gazing at the sweet face of his bejeweled eunuch boy. Hing shuffles to the door. "Don't follow those girls when they leave the purdah room, not if you know what's good for you."

Before can Basant can answer, Hing is gone.

ಲಿಲಿಲಿ

At the jali screen, leaning against the pierced marble, the sisters snuggle. Heads touching, their hands caress each other through transparent silk.

And they are moaning.

Through the jali, Basant sees Shah Jahan's attention waver. He has heard the moans, of course; they were intended for his ears. Breakfast slips her long, pink tongue through a space in the jali screen and wiggles it. Basant is amazed to see that it is long enough to pass clear through the cutouts of the white marble. The girls now can barely hold back their laughter. Their eyes glitter with the dreamy, manic light of opium and *dravana*.

Maybe Shah Jahan sees the moist red tip of that extraordinary tongue through the jali screen, or maybe his ears are tuned to the music of the moans and giggles of his favorites, or perhaps he senses their dark heat, which seems to spill through the jali and spread across the room like smoke.

Basant thinks, They'd never try it if Aurangzeb were around.

Even Dara notices. He pauses in his endless recitation and reluctantly glances over to the jali screen; he looks away, clearly disturbed. Now all pretense of order in the hall has ceased; all eyes are fixed on that screen. And the men around Dara stare at the jali with disgust, envy, fascination, trying to make out the shadows of Shah Jahan's women.

Without any explanation or fanfare, Shah Jahan stands. His pants tent out obviously, forcing everyone around to glance away. The emperor appears unconcerned. He leaves the velvet cushions of his throne and slips quickly through the door to his private apartments. He is gone with such suddenness, the pretty young eunuch boy who holds the peacock feather umbrella over his head must hurry to catch up.

A few alert courtiers manage to bow before Shah Jahan has entirely left the room, those less alert bow toward the door that closes behind him.

Everyone in the room, however, shares a sense of gratitude that they no longer must observe the emperor's embarrassing behavior.

In the purdah room, behind the jali, the two sisters watch the emperor head for his chambers. They nuzzle against each other, and then, unable to contain themselves, they kiss each other full on the lips, lingering long, tongues and teeth darting, gazing into each other's eyes. Then they leave the purdah room to join the emperor. Basant watches with disgust and fascination. How much of what occurred was part of Roshanara's plan?

He heeds Hing's advice, and lets the girls go without following them.

☙◖◗❧

When Basant enters her rooms, Roshanara is staring at the river, her back to him. Her hands play idly with something in her lap; Basant sees only a flash of gold and white—a miniature portrait. Of whom, he wonders.

Without looking up, she dismisses her other servants, and asks him for a full report.

Basant sketches out the events. He speaks softly, barely loud enough for his voice to reach the princess's ears—someone might be listening.

As he speaks, he realizes that his feeling of dread and doom is growing. He finds it increasingly hard to speak. By the time he tells the story of the nautch girls and Dara's spoiled recitation, his throat is so tight his voice is husky and barely above a whisper. He just manages to tell the story of her father's exit before his voice seems to altogether fail him.

"My father. My father." She spits out the words, like a cobra spitting venom. And then Roshanara begins to shake with laughter. Or so it seems at first. But the shaking continues too long and Basant realizes that sobbing racks her slender body.

The sight of her tears overwhelms Basant; for a while he merely stares at her. His own troubles and uncertainties seem so ominous and large, but he realizes that something is working on Roshanara as well. He places a tentative hand on her shoulder. She turns to him, her face wet with tears.

"Basant," she says, her voice full of desperation, "do you love me?"

Basant blinks and his mouth drops. "Do you love me, dear?" she demands. She clutches his pudgy hand.

"My princess, yes, of course!" He bends close to her. His voice is so husky, he wonders if she can hear him.

"Tell me. Tell me you do!"

"Of course, of course. How could you not know? I love you!" He strokes her dark hair. "I love you, Little Rose."

"Darling, darling," she whispers and kisses his hand. She has never done that before. Her eyes, dark as wet jasper, stare into his. "Would you still love me if I were bad, darling?" Basant uses his thumb to dry her tears on her cheek and shakes his head: the question is too ridiculous to answer. "I can be very bad, you know. I think I shall live in hell, I am so very bad." She grasps his fingers. Both their hands are wet with her tears. "Promise you will never stop loving me, no matter how bad I have to be."

Basant stares solemnly at Roshanara's anxious face. "I promise, Little Rose, oh my dear little rose! always, always, always!"

"Darling, you must write a letter for me," she says when she has at last recovered her voice. Basant nods. He moves a small writing table near her and kneels before it. Taking a piece of paper, he chooses a quill pen and dips its tip in the ink and waits.

Then she begins to dictate a letter. Basant transcribes her whispered words, which seem on their surface entirely benign—but of course he can guess for each a dozen deeper meanings.

When she is done, he again dips his pen, but she interrupts him. "Don't sign it!" she hisses. He nods, confused, and flips the paper over. "And don't, for heaven's, sake, seal it! Hide it. Give it to my brother only. Destroy it rather than let another read it!"

Basant places the letter in the folds of his shirt.

"Go quickly to my brother in the Rambagh. Take my palanquin." She crosses to him and pats his heart, where the letter lies hidden. "Go with God," she whispers. "Go with God." Basant is so touched he can barely respond.

"Remember your promise!" she calls as he leaves her. "Keep your promise to your Little Rose!" For a moment he can't place the promise she refers to, but then he understands: to love her always, even if she is bad. Well, that shouldn't be too hard, he thinks. He lowers his head, walking backward from the room. He finds her maid outside the door, and tells her to have Roshanara's bearers bring the palanquin.

Basant looks up to see Roshanara slink through her door, head down. Keeping her eyes to the floor, she shuffles toward her father's chamber, like a condemned man going to the gallows.

The eunuch guards at the chamber door eye her uncertainly—she shouldn't be here, but she is the princess; what are they to do? Before they have time to act, she bursts forward and throws open the bedchamber door. Basant catches a glimpse of the emperor, naked with the two nautch girls. Before he can blink, Roshanara slams the door behind her.

CHAPTER 3

Carried on the shoulders of sweating men, Basant floats above the fragrant streets of Agra. His palanquin bearers must brave the open sewers. They squeeze through the market crowds, and tiptoe past the garbage.

Through curtains of silk gauze Basant watches as hawkers cry out for customers, housemaids bargain at the top of their lungs, beggar children whine for coins, dogs bark. The road is jammed: the palanquin is outpaced even by the skinny cows that amble through the twisting streets.

Basant adores Agra.

Unlike the palace, no one planned Agra; no one owns it, or controls it. The city streets dance to a wild, secret music unheard inside the palace walls. Just as the smack by a heavy wave renews an ocean swimmer, so the tumult of Agra restores Basant. Agra, bursting with life, gives Basant hope.

The brothers say that hope clouds the will and muddles the judgment. Hope is a cruel joke.

But right now, inspired by the unfettered bustle of the city, Basant dares to do his sums: Fourteen hours have passed since the guards were murdered in his rooms, yet no one has arrested him. That fool Ali Khalil found his bloody carpet in the moat and let him go. Somehow, by the grace of the Lord All-Merciful, he has managed to squeak through.

Here in the streets of Agra, carried on the shoulders of sweating men, Basant floats on a cloud of hope. He ignores the dangers on every side: the eunuch guards, the strange actions of the princess, Hing and all his riddles, the murder of his servant. He would rather die in hope than live in fear.

Across the Jumna, a few miles from the palace, lies a perfect garden, built by Babur, the first Mogul emperor. Babur never loved the land he conquered. Compared to Samarkand, his home, Agra seemed wild and misbegotten. So he built a garden like paradise, with fountains and orchards, with peacocks and deer.

His garden, the Rambagh—so simple, so pure—fell into disfavor as his grandchildren built ever grander gardens of their own. But Aurangzeb has loved that old garden since he was child—its simplicity and calm. It is there that Aurangzeb has set up his tents, using its sandstone pavilion for his temporary headquarters. It is there Basant will meet him.

The palanquin approaches the Rambagh. The road grows wider, and the way more sunny. Set in the clearing are a dozen large tents. War tents, not the majestic harem tents with gilded tent poles that Basant is used to: these are no-nonsense affairs, quick to set up and quick to strike; soldiers' tents, arranged in a circle, surrounded by bedrolls and makeshift cots. Near one tent a green banner flies; the flag of the viceroy of the Deccan.

After they set him down, Basant pads along the sandstone walkway that leads through the gardens. The sun is bright, but in this expanse of green, its light feels gentle. Water chatters beside the walkway in sandstone channels cut through the lawn. Tall trees shade the walk; fountains send sprites of water dancing. The air is damp and fresh.

Soon Basant reaches the marble platform that marks the center of the garden. As Babur would have wanted, Basant takes a moment here to enjoy the layout of the garden; a large enclosed lawn cut by four causeways, like the four rivers of paradise meeting at the throne of God. Then he follows the walkway to Aurangzeb's pavilion.

It's an informal building surrounded by columns of red sandstone. Basant notices the peacocks and elephants carved into the tops of each of the columns, for it was built by a man who considered charm more important than majesty. Silk drapes of gold and green hang from chains run through large iron rings embedded in the walls.

A slender young man in elegant clothing the color of old ivory walks toward him. As he approaches, Basant sees that he is a brother, but one he has not yet met. The slender eunuch bows. "You must be Basant. Prince Aurangzeb told me to expect you. I am your younger brother, Alu."

"Your master is Aurangzeb?" Basant asks as he lifts his head.

Alu leads Basant to the anteroom. "I have the honor to be of occasional service to his highness. But my master is General Jumla, the Persian. I am his *khaswajara*." Basant blinks with surprise. This sweet-spoken eunuch seems too young to be *khaswajara* to one so grand as Jumla. It makes Basant feel old and backward that he is only Roshanara's *mukhunni*. He examines the brother with a bit of envy. Alu is striking: tall, thinner than most of the brothers, who tend to get padded with fat . He speaks with a charming, husky voice. His eyes are dark, sensuous, set far apart, and one of them trails off to the side, giving him a mysterious, crafty air.

"The prince is with my master. There's quite a storm brewing, of course." Alu looks at Basant as though he were fragile. "You *are* ready aren't you? When the storm breaks, we'll all need friends. Do you know who your friends are?"

Alu's words confuse Basant. They remind him of Master Hing's mysterious comments—like he is being given a password, but doesn't know the countersign. "I think many people like me," he replies uncertainly.

"I forget with whom I speak." Alu lowers his husky voice to a whisper. "Who of all the brothers is more fortunate than you?" Alu inclines his head in a respectful bow that confuses Basant even more. Alu for a moment manages to fix both of his dark eyes on Basant before his right eye starts to wander. "You will remember me, won't you, brother?"

Before Basant has a chance to puzzle through what this might mean, they hear angry words from the behind the wall. Suddenly General Jumla wheels angrily into the courtyard, shouting over his shoulder. "I'll give you one day!" he bellows. "If you can't deliver on your promises, you've seen the last of me!" The general stomps off.

"Aren't you going to him?" Basant asks Alu.

Alu shakes his head. "What could I do for my master in such a state?" he asks. "Besides," he says confidingly, "my master learned the value of bluster when he was a merchant—how do you think he got so rich? His anger means little. My duty now is to attend the prince. After sundown, he refuses any service. Did you know Aurangzeb eats with the regular soldiers? He even sleeps on a mat, under the stars, with his saddle for a pillow." Basant of course has heard all this before. "He asked to see you when the general left. Do you wish to go in?" Not waiting for an answer, Alu claps his hands twice; the sound *pings* against sandstone walls.

A huge shape lurches around the corner into the courtyard—a man so large Basant gasps. The peak of his turban brushes against the doorway as he bows his head to enter. His face looks craggy, like thick skin stretched across a grotesque skull: a heavy brow and protruding cheekbones; an uneven, shaggy beard covers his thick, misshapen jaw. The giant bows, but Basant is too overwhelmed to move.

"This is Karm, the prince's bodyguard," Alu explains. "He needs to search you. The prince will have no weapons in his presence. Please don't take any insult, brother. Even Jai Singh was searched."

"Jai Singh?" Basant asks. "Is he here?"

"Of course. He came for his chess game."

Odd that Dara's own commander would be visiting Aurangzeb, Basant thinks, but then the thought is driven from his mind as Karm's fingers (the size of cucumbers) delicately press and probe his person.

Karm finds the silver tube tucked into Basant's turban and lifts it questioningly. The dark palm of Karm's hand, big as a platter, dwarfs the slender silver quill that rests on it. "It's nothing, Karm," Alu assures him. "Just the same as my gold one."

Gold? thinks Basant.

The giant gently returns the quill, and then his fingers, massive and delicate, probe along Basant's arms to his neck and shoulders, where he finds the necklace; a chain and pendant.

Drawing it out, he holds it up and frowns. The giant lifts his huge eyes to Basant, staring at him from deep beneath his shaggy eyebrows. "It's just a keepsake," Basant explains. His lips are dry and his voice is hoarse; he hadn't come prepared for a giant. "A gift from long ago."

Karm tilts his head inquiringly. Alu moves to get a better view.

"Well, I think it's from my mother, if you must know," Basant blurts out. "I've had it as long as I remember." He takes the pendant—a coin from an unknown country, the writing indecipherable, sawed in half on a rough, jagged line—and thrusts it back under his shirt.

The giant's enormous face peers at Basant. His breathing sounds labored and phlegmy, like an old camel. He finds nothing else. Basant's skin tingles as though he has been massaged. "Thank you, Karm," Alu says.

The giant grunts and moves back to the prince's room. "He can hear, but he can't speak," Alu says softly to Basant. "They pulled his tongue out by the roots when he was a child. He can barely swallow." Alu *namskars*. "Go in, brother. Talk to me afterwards if you have the chance."

Basant slips into the receiving room, where Karm stands by the entranceway. Basant looks up into his huge eyes and he sees in them deep wells of sadness, loneliness, and pain. They share a bond, Basant thinks, that only a maimed child can know. But he forces himself to look away from the giant's dark eyes, steeling himself for his talk with Aurangzeb.

❧❧❧❧

A huge Persian carpet covers the entire floor. Cushions of various sizes, covered in velvets and brocades, are scattered haphazardly around the room, as if many people are expected. But other than Karm and Basant, and a tired-looking manservant who stands patiently by the back wall, only two men are in the room, seated near a low ivory chess table, at the far end where they can catch the river breeze.

Basant recognizes Aurangzeb right away. He wears his simple white jamas. Even his cushion is simple, covered in cheap muslin. The other man, of course, dressed in elegant silks, is Jai Singh, Dara's general. The silver scabbard on his belt is encrusted with gems to resemble the scales of a fantastic fish (one of the many gifts Jai Singh received from Shah Jahan in gratitude for donating the land where he built 'taj Mahal's tomb)—but it holds no sword. *The prince will have no weapons in his presence,* Alu had said. *Even Jai Singh was searched . . .*

Of course, Jai Singh ties his jama on the left side to show he is a Hindu, but the robe is cleverly tailored so that at first glance, the fastenings appear to be on the right, the Muslim side.

Like Aurangzeb, Jai Singh wears a neat white turban—but Jai Singh's is pinned at the front with an elegant peacock feather made of diamonds and emeralds. His beard is manicured, rust-colored from henna. Aurangzeb just lets his gray whiskers show.

Basant waits for someone to acknowledge him. Finally he falls back on protocol, which never fails, and he forces a long bow. He knows he will grunt with the effort, and that will surely draw attention his way.

In response, Aurangzeb waves his hand without looking up from the game board. "No ceremony here, Basant. Save fawning for others. Come. Sit. Jai Singh is teaching me a lesson."

Jai Singh shrugs as if the compliment were undeserved. It seems to Basant a very simple gesture for a man so great. He motions for Basant to sit on a dark velvet cushion near his side.

Jai Singh plays the white pieces, Aurangzeb the black. Both men have lost their viziers; Jai Singh has his king, two horses and an elephant; Aurangzeb has the king, a camel, a horse, and an elephant—so they are fairly matched. Jai Singh, however, has four *pyadas*; while Aurangzeb has only two.

Basant can play chess, but not well. Still he appreciates the contest. He speculates about how important those extra pieces will be. After all, these men are both generals—on a real battlefield would an extra foot soldier or two make any difference to the outcome of a battle? So why should it on the chessboard?

"What will you do about Jumla, lord?" Jai Singh asks quietly. He seems unconcerned that Basant will hear.

Aurangzeb strokes his beard thoughtfully but doesn't look up. "I will do what I can. I don't wish to lose Jumla, not any more than I wish to lose Golconda, or the Deccan for that matter."

"Yes, he is the key to the Deccan," Jai Singh agrees. "You know that I suggested you attack Bijapur, not Golconda. Those forts guarding the trade routes could have been ours, you know. We could have allied with that rebel, Shahji, but we moved too slowly. Now what do we face? Danger."

He says this in an offhand way, but Basant notices how Aurangzeb's breath grows still. "Then why not attack Bijapur?" Aurangzeb asks.

"Sadly, Prince Dara does not agree."

Aurangzeb moves his elephant to the last file of the chessboard, a few spaces from Jai Singh's king. "Excuse me, uncle," he says softly, "but my brother does not yet rule the land. Our future rests not on him, but on the emperor my father. Danger!"

Basant is surprised by Aurangzeb's last word. Then he realizes that Aurangzeb refers to the chessboard, saying that Jai Singh's king is in danger.

Jai Singh now stares relentlessly at the chessboard, and Aurangzeb lifts his head for the first time "Do you play chess?" he asks Basant.

"Very badly, lord."

Jai Singh moves his camel between his king and Aurangzeb's elephant. "Death in three moves, I think, sir," he says.

Aurangzeb considers the board for so long, his eyelids droop sleepily over his dark eyes, "Shall we make a wager?" he says at last.

Jai Singh's clear eyes flash. "What shall we bet?"

"Wager that service we discussed, general," says Aurangzeb softly.

Jai Singh stares steadily into Aurangzeb's sleepy eyes. "Such a wager is not trivial, sir."

"No," Aurangzeb answers, eyes hooded, staring at the chessboard. "No, I did not mean for it to be."

Unconsciously, Jai Singh begins to rub his hands together. "You ask not only for my help, sir, you ask for my honor."

"Forgive me if I see it otherwise, general," Aurangzeb says. "Am I not a son of the emperor, beggar though I be? To ask that you help me . . . does this go against honor?"

"It may," Jai Singh replies, "if your enemy is Prince Dara."

"How can my brother also be my enemy?" Aurangzeb asks.

Jai Singh turns away. "And what will you wager on your side, sir?"

"Ask for what you want, uncle."

Jai Singh's neat fingers brush his trim, pointed beard. "A promise."

"What promise?" Aurangzeb asks, surprised.

"Never to come against me. Or my family. Or my heirs."

Basant can sense the tension in the room. Both men stare fiercely at each other, as though the fate of nations would rise or fall on the outcome. Aurangzeb almost lazily closes his eyes and then, slowly, inclines his head, giving a nearly imperceptible nod. Jai Singh sits ramrod straight.

The wager is made.

Without hesitation, Aurangzeb slides his camel next to Jai Singh's king. "Danger," he says.

Jai Singh's eyebrows rise and his eyes widen. His face looks suddenly very old indeed. He stares at the chessboard, eyes darting from piece to piece. Basant notices that Jai Singh's hand is small and delicate, like a child's hand, and though the general is clearly agitated by the game and the wager, his hand is steady. His moves are careful, not indecisive.

"My tutors were fools," Aurangzeb says while Jai Singh considers. "My tutors taught me Arabic and rhetoric. I wish someone had taught me about my life—about the life of a Mogul prince." He waves to his manservant and silently motions for him to bring refreshments. Basant realizes the manservant is deaf. "I am the son of an emperor. What fate for me but an early death?"

"You exaggerate," Jai Singh says, still staring at the board.

"I have but two choices: death—or the throne. I swear I do not seek the throne. But whoever takes it next will kill me." Aurangzeb shakes his head. "Though I renounce the throne, how is the next emperor to trust me? I am but a beggar, after all. Who trusts the word of a beggar?"

"Yes, I agree. Your fate is certain," says Jai Singh with no trace of irony. "If the history of your family teaches anything, it is that siblings of the new emperor don't live long."

Aurangzeb looks hard at Jai Singh. "If I don't wish to die by my brothers' hands, what choice is left me? Shall I say it aloud, uncle? My only recourse is to depose my father and seize the throne myself." He squeezes his eyes shut as if his head hurts. "Allah pushes us like *pyadas* on a chessboard. Kill my brothers or be killed myself? Why has Allah, the all compassionate, placed this choice before me?"

Jai Singh stares at Aurangzeb. "But I do not think you can avoid this choice." He slides his camel across the board. "Danger."

Instead of looking at Jai Singh's move, Aurangzeb looks directly at Basant. "Did I not tell my father that I abjure the Peacock Throne? Did I not leave this world behind to prove my vow? For twelve years I wandered homeless, with only the clothes on my back. I dwelt with dervishes and walis. I slept in the shadow of *dargahs*. I lost myself in ghazals and *qwalis*."

He shakes his head. "Then my father called me back—against my will—to be viceroy of the Deccan. The very post I had left twelve years before! Of course I obeyed. It was not my portion to renounce this world. I resumed my duties as a prince. I married. I had sons. Such was Allah's will."

He lifts his hands, appealing to Basant, to Jai Singh, to Allah. "Am I to die for this act of loyalty? Where else but in Agra is filial devotion a death sentence?"

Basant is struck by Aurangzeb's passion. Yet to some part of his mind the words sound rehearsed. The prince, Basant thinks, speaks with an underlying apathy that belies his words. But Basant thrusts this thought away, for he is determined to be convinced of Aurangzeb's sincerity.

Aurangzeb fixes Jai Singh with a hawklike stare. "Do you believe me when I say that I abjure the Peacock Throne?" Jai Singh does not move. Aurangzeb turns to Basant, as if in despair. "Do you believe me?"

"Of course, lord," Basant says immediately. How can Roshanara even imagine that this humble prince would ever struggle for the throne?

Aurangzeb looks at the chessboard. "My life is a chess game that I am bound to lose."

"Then take the needle, if you mean this," Jai Singh replies.

Aurangzeb looks back at Jai Singh, clearly unprepared for this suggestion. "Blind myself, you mean?"

"Even if you do not seek the throne, the winner must eradicate you as a threat." Jai Singh looks at Aurangzeb sorrowfully. "Will the winner choose to kill you, or only to blind you? The best you can hope for is blinding. History bears this out. Why not avoid the worst? Remove the threat. Take the needle to your eyes. No one wants a blind king."

Aurangzeb peers into Jai Singh's eyes. "Are these Dara's thoughts or yours, uncle? On whose behalf do you speak?"

"You know my feelings, sir," Jai Singh says.

"Yes, uncle, I do. To understand a man, you need only look to what he wagers." Aurangzeb nods at the chessboard. "Danger."

Aurangzeb turns fully to Basant, unexpectedly casual. "The general said 'Death in three moves,' did he not?"

"Yes, lord, that is what I heard him say."

"And how many moves has it been since then?"

"Two moves. lord, I think." Basant wishes he had paid closer attention.

Jai Singh looks. "Perhaps I spoke too soon," he admits. "But while I may mistake the timing, I do not mistake the outcome."

"Allah's will, and not our own, determines all things, uncle. That is why we must trust in him." He turns, looking significantly at Basant. "And we must trust our friends as well. How is my sister?"

"She is well, lord."

"You had an easy journey over the river?"

"Easy enough, lord," Basant replies, surprised at the simple friendliness of these questions.

"What did you think of Jai Singh's army?" Aurangzeb asks.

"I scarcely know, lord. I'm sure I didn't notice it."

Jai Singh looks up. "You didn't notice two hundred thousand men? Ten thousand tents? You didn't notice?"

"I'm sorry, lord. I had many things on my mind," Basant manages to mumble at last. He doesn't want to say that he fell asleep as he crossed the boat bridge across the Jumna.

Jai Singh huffs. He reaches out his neat hand to the chessboard and takes Aurangzeb's camel with his elephant. "Your move," he says. He glances at Basant and huffs again.

Aurangzeb moves his *pyada.* Jai Singh looks at him. "You see that your elephant is in danger?" he asks. "Take back your move, if you wish."

Aurangzeb looks at the board and raises his hands resignedly. Jai Singh takes the elephant as if it is a sad duty, but he cannot hide his pleasure.

Aurangzeb moves his camel one square.

Jai Singh is again about to move when Aurangzeb says, as though the thought suddenly struck him, "Danger."

Jai Singh's stares at the board. He looks up, mystified. "How can this be?" he asks. "It's impossible!" He turns to Basant. "Do you see?"

"What, lord?"

Jai Singh now plays both his pieces and Aurangzeb's, calling out each move. "I move my king. His elephant takes my horse. Danger. Again I move my king, and so his *pyada* here—this miserable little piece—reaches the final rank and becomes a vizier." He replaces the pyada with the elegant ivory vizier. "And now my king is dead. So." Jai Singh tips the king over, gently laying the piece on its side.

"I have won." Aurangzeb says, bowing his head.

"Take pleasure in your victory, sir." Jai Singh returns his bow.

"I take pleasure in our wager, uncle," Aurangzeb answers. "With Allah's mercy, your service will never be required—we can hope so, at least. But to know that it is now mine eases my beggar's heart. Those *pyadas* made all the difference, eh, Basant? It is so important to remember the little pieces, is it not?" Aurangzeb sighs. "We must always pay attention to the little pieces."

The manservant discreetly comes near, offering juices from a silver tray. Basant chooses melon mixed with mango, and a candy wrapped in silver foil. Aurangzeb takes only water, a fakir in the midst of splendor.

ତ୨ତ୨

Basant knows how Aurangzeb decries extravagance, but his little drink seems sad without a bit of ice to clink against his cup.

In the harem, ice is so common that Basant has forgotten that it is worth its weight in silver. Basant has seen the icewallahs floating rafts of ice down the Jumna while children swim nearby hoping to chip away a piece when no one sees; ice rafts that started in the Himalayas as chunks of glacier a thousand times heavier. Master Hing has told him that ice is the harem's single greatest expense, more than clothing, food, or gems.

Basant looks through the arches to the river, at the children swimming amidst a herd of sleek black water buffalo in the slow-moving current. Their laughter, he realizes, is mingling with shouts from the garden behind them. The shouts increase, and soon at the entrance a whole crowd of men appears; Aurangzeb's soldiers. "My lord, I couldn't stop them," Alu cries. "Look, this dispatch has just come from the palace." The men crowd into a tight circle, all eyes on Aurangzeb as he takes the parchment.

General Jumla pushes through the crowd. "Has it come?" he asks.

"As we hoped, general," Aurangzeb replies. "Please, open it and read it aloud." Jumla and Jai Singh both seem surprised that Aurangzeb would hand Jumla the scroll without first reading it himself. It is a firman—an imperial order, heavy with sealing wax and ribbon—signed by Shah Jahan himself. Jumla reads aloud and as he reads, his eyes widen with surprise.

Shah Jahan has completely reversed the morning's decisions. He now orders the army to attack Golconda and Bijapur without quarter. But the language is so flowery that even Basant has trouble understanding it. At last Aurangzeb translates it into plain soldier-talk: "We attack! The Deccan is ours!" he shouts, and the men cheer.

The firman goes on, however. As if Shah Jahan's reversal of the morning orders were not surprising enough, he now makes Jumla a *mandsabar* of fifty thousand men and ten thousand horses. In effect, he gives him half the army of the Deccan. Further, the emperor orders that Jumla should lead not only his own troops, but Aurangzeb's also.

The firman makes Jumla the supreme commander of the Deccan army, a hundred thousand strong. Jumla stops reading and looks up slightly embarrassed. The soldiers look confused, puzzling over what the fancy talk all means. Again Aurangzeb interprets: "Jumla's in charge, men," he says. "He's the general of us all, now."

The men cheer at first and then their shouts fade. It seems wrong to cheer Jumla while Aurangzeb stands nearby. Aurangzeb, however, congratulates Jumla. His words are plain, though his demeanor is formal. The soldiers cheer uncertainly again.

"That's all," Alu says at last. "Let's leave these men alone—I'm sure they have things to discuss." Encouraged by Alu, who is backed by Karm's silent presence, the soldiers slowly turn and walk off.

"Congratulations, general," Jai Singh says to Jumla. "This recognition must be very satisfying."

Jumla nods, but seems embarrassed. "Is this what you expected?" he asks Aurangzeb uncertainly. "Is this what you wanted?"

Aurangzeb looks at him coolly. "I am only a beggar, general. I tell you this but I fear you don't believe me. I am resigned to Allah's will. I extend my congratulations." Basant can't decide if Aurangzeb is the calmest man he has ever known, or the angriest.

"Sketch out the campaign, general," Aurangzeb says when Jumla bows in reply. "If I may request it humbly, please make haste."

"For tonight's meeting, you mean," Jumla says, then suddenly clasps a hand over his mouth. "Forgive me, lord!" he gasps.

Aurangzeb's smile never wavers. "I'm meeting with my staff tonight," Aurangzeb says casually to Jai Singh. "There is nothing to forgive, general." Jumla, clearly embarrassed, backs out of the room. Basant wonders why such a meeting would cause Jumla to be embarrassed.

"This firman brings unexpected news, lord," Jai Singh says.

"Do you find it so, uncle?" Aurangzeb replies. He turns to Basant. "You heard the firman, Basant. Would you care to share your reflections?"

"Shall I speak frankly, lord? Many people think that Shah Jahan is the puppet of Prince Dara. But this firman reveals that the emperor still rules."

"The eunuch is right. Your father has openly taken your side," Jai Singh agrees. "Golconda is clearly a threat. Dara is a fool to accept the assurances of the Golcondan King. Shah Jahan knows this. Also, Shah Jahan knows he's bleeding the treasury—too many monuments and mosques, too many mistresses. But Golconda is so rich, its fall will fix all that."

"And about Jumla—" Aurangzeb asks.

"I may say something that offends you, lord," says Jai Singh. "The decision to give Jumla command means only one thing. Your father fears you. If he weakens you, he assures the succession will be Dara's." Unconsciously, Jai Singh pats his forehead with the cuff of his silk shirt. "It is an ill wind that blows no good. Despite his preference for Dara, your father has done you a service by removing you from command. Without an army, you reduce Dara's need to kill you. Consider that."

Aurangzeb looks at him squarely. Jai Singh continues: "And think of this: Why has he given an order like this only to you? Why not strip your other brothers as well? Here's what I say: Murad is no threat; he cannot lead. Shuja is no threat; he is a wastrel. Dara can subdue them easily. I'll speak frankly: it would be no great loss for those two to die."

Basant finds himself interrupting Jai Singh in his eagerness. "He's right, lord. You alone are a threat to Dara; only you confuse the succession. Shah Jahan realizes this. He wishes to neutralize you, for Dara's good and also for your own good. I think he loves you, lord, though I think you are a mystery to him. You do not love the things your father loves."

Basant halts suddenly, realizing he has said too much.

"I am not like Dara, you mean," Aurangzeb says, shaking his head. "I, unfortunately, have a conscience."

"You see it clearly, sir," Jai Singh agrees. "Your integrity is unassailable."

The room is silent for a long time. Only the sounds of the river in the afternoon sun can be heard. At last, Jai Singh asks leave to return.

"But remember our wager," the prince says as he walks the general to the door. "You have promised me a service, uncle."

"A wager is sacred debt, a debt of honor, sir," the general answers. Basant wonders what service Aurangzeb could want that would be so difficult for the general to provide. "Let us hope that the need for that service will never arise. It seems to me that Shah Jahan, with this order, may have made the fulfillment of my promise unnecessary."

"Let us pray it will be so," Aurangzeb agrees, bowing thoughtfully. "A safe journey, uncle. I will return to the Deccan with tomorrow's sunrise. Let us hope that we play chess together soon."

"Next time I'll be more careful of my wagers!" Jai Singh answers, and they both laugh politely.

☙☙☙☙

When Jai Singh has gone, Aurangzeb seats himself by the arch that frames the river. Basant takes out Roshanara's letter.

Aurangzeb glances at it. "You wrote this," he says.

"Yes, lord."

"My sister's script is indecipherable." He smiles, Basant notices, with only one side of his mouth. "Your script is quite attractive."

"Thank you, lord." Aurangzeb stares into space, and motions with his hand. Basant supposes he wants the letter read aloud.

There is the usual puffery at the start—what a wonderful person Aurangzeb is, how he shines brighter than the sun and so on. Basant, who wrote this flattery now feels embarrassed. Spoken before a man dressed in cotton, not silk, who wears no jewels, who drinks warm river water from a plain cup, the courtly prose seems silly and extreme. Basant hurries to the core of the letter—Roshanara's concern for Aurangzeb, and her plans.

First, Roshanara introduces Basant—she calls him "that best of servants, the *mukhunni* we discussed." Basant, she says, is her closest confidant, instructed to be open and truthful. Privately she emphasized—Tell him anything! Everything! Hold back nothing!

Then she affirms her love for Aurangzeb. She uses words that Basant finds embarrassing between a brother and a sister—yet when he suggested alternatives, she pinched him and ordered him to write as he was told.

Next she tells Aurangzeb not to be concerned about their father's decision—soon she will set things right, she says; the Deccan will be Aurangzeb's. There are ways, she says, that she is not afraid to use.

"She risks too much," Aurangzeb mutters. "Some treasures are so cursed that only fools will dig them up." He nods at Basant significantly, as though Basant understands his cryptic remarks. Basant closes his eyes to give the impression that he thinks the same dark thoughts himself.

Basant continues: " 'The tiger is on the leash, ready for riding. . . .' "

Again Aurangzeb stops Basant. "What do you think of that, Basant?

There's an old saying—The problem with riding a tiger is when you try to get off." The prince stands abruptly. "Let us walk along the river."

Here it comes: this is the test, Basant thinks, but he can't guess what is to be tested. Grunting, he lumbers to his feet, brushing his silks. Aurangzeb has already moved a few paces ahead of him, and he chuffs along trying to catch up. Finally Aurangzeb stops to gaze across the river. Basant falls in beside him, peering up at his hawklike profile.

Basant always thinks of Aurangzeb in profile, perhaps because it is rare for him to see the prince's face full on. Aurangzeb never looks squarely at him; Aurangzeb never seems to look squarely at anything.

After a few more paces, Aurangzeb gestures, and they move down the steps of the pavilion, past a garden full of fragrant roses, blood red. Basant is too nervous even to look at them; if Aurangzeb has noticed, he gives no sign. His mind seems fixed beyond the gardens. "Tell me, Basant: what do you think of my sister? Is she to be trusted, do you think?"

Basant remembers watching the court artists in their workshop; how before they paint a bird, they trap it under a heavy glass jar. Sometimes they fill the jar with water to see the drowned bird magnified. Now he knows how those birds feel. "My lord, do you trust her?" Basant replies at last.

At this the prince snorts. "Do you love my sister?" he asks.

"I am a eunuch, lord."

"Surely, Basant, eunuchs can love." Aurangzeb steps in front of him, and looks him full in the face. "Would you do me a service, Basant?" the prince whispers. His deep-set dark eyes, shaded by black eyebrows peppered with gray, glow like banked embers.

Basant is struck by their power. "Any service you require, lord."

"Don't agree so quickly, Basant," Aurangzeb cautions, his forefinger raised, reminding Basant of a mullah or a dervish making a point. "Suppose this service were of great moment—not just for me, but for the kingdom. Would you do it? Even though it broke your heart, would you do it? For in truth it breaks my heart to ask you."

Again Basant finds himself blurting out, "Of course, lord, of course!"

Aurangzeb lifts his head and glances around the garden, with an expert furtiveness that surprises Basant. The prince leans close to Basant's ear.

"Would you kill Roshanara for me?" he whispers.

ᕤᕦᕤᕦᕤ

My life is over, thinks Basant.

He weeps inside the curtained palanquin, wailing, not caring who might hear. Back in his room, the last red rays of the setting sun bathe the white marble walls with a light that glows like the fires of hell.

Why, oh why had he answered Aurangzeb so?

He had said no. Then yes. Then no again. But before he could change his mind once more, Aurangzeb had drawn back, and wearily, sadly, waved him away.

☙☙☙☙

Yesterday his was a child's life: everything was provided for him; he lived with women and had little to do with nasty, hairy men. The world was simple and he would always be happy.

Today he is a child no longer. But what does that mean for Basant, who can never be a man?

Finally he understands Master Hing: he had always thought of him as twisted, shriveled, vile, soured by the bile of his anger. Finally he sees that people slowly become what they are, never conscious of the steps that brought them there. Maybe Hing too was happy once, gentle once, and had watched his life collapse around him.

☙☙☙☙

On the sleeping cushions that lie strewn across his carpet (his new, red carpet), is the package that Alu gave him as he left the Rambagh.

How much does that damned *hijra* know?

As Basant walked dazed from his talk with Aurangzeb, Alu had caught up with him, still all sweetness and flowers. "This token is from the prince," he told Basant, handing him a small parcel. "He says to tell you that he has the other, too."

Of course it would have been bad manners to untie the colored string right then, so Basant waits until he is in the palanquin. While his bearers lurch down the bank that leads to the river, cursing Basant's weight with each struggling step, Basant unfolds the heavy white paper that wraps his gift. Basant yelps, and clasps both pudgy hands over his mouth. It is a jeweled slipper, the delicate slipper he had worn only yesterday, now brown with dried blood.

Basant remembers the hard hand of Shaista Khan lifting his feet, and the slap of each wet slipper landing on the bodies and the blood. He was so glad that the bodies had disappeared that he gave no thought to how, or who. He simply gloried in his escape from disaster, and reveled in Ali

Khalil's confusion. When those bodies had disappeared like the morning mists, he convinced himself he had been dreaming.

Muhedin dead, Muhedin who had been his friend, and with him some poor man he had never met. And Haridas dead, his own servant, his neck snapped like a bird's. And in his lap, a token: more will die.

Basant, would you kill Roshanara for me?

If he would kill his own sister, what will he not do to me?

Basant thinks of the goat, staked as bait, a noose around its neck, slashed along its flanks to lure the tiger with the scent of blood. Did it matter to the goat if it was eaten or merely bled to death?

He has heard too much. His life is worthless. And what about Roshanara? Can I save myself? Can I save my Little Rose? Must we suffer? Must we die? Then he knows what he must do, and as quick as that knows also how to do it.

Across the room he has a lacquered chest with many drawers. It belonged to his predecessor: a gift, Haridas had told him with some pride, from the empress herself.

Then twisting one of the drawer pulls, and sliding a false bottom aside, the servant showed Basant the secret drawer.

With eyes moist with tears, Haridas looked at the contents of that compartment. Without showing them to Basant, he quickly stowed each item in his pocket. Only when it was empty did Haridas step aside and let him see.

Though Basant lives with rich clothing, jewels, paintings, carpets, he is not rich; they are but on loan, not his. He has no family, no heirs: they'll go back to the emperor when he dies.

What was his, really? Things hidden in the bottom of this secret drawer; precious, worthless things: A rose, now fragile as tissue, that Roshanara had touched to her lips the day they met; the small plain quill he used the day he had been made; the paper that wrapped the broken coin he now wore on a chain around his neck (and tucked inside, a thin braid of long black hair); his bill of sale, written in extravagant calligraphy (for after all, he had cost a small fortune), which he had stolen from Master Hing; and last of all, a gift from Tambula, precious indeed—a small vial of delicate greenish glass that holds a thick, greasy-looking syrup.

The dark liquid clings to the glass vial as Basant examines it, turning it in the red light of the setting sun.

He sets the vial on the low table near his bed. His hand drifts to his hidden necklace, grasping the coin through the filmy cotton of his shirt.

He can feel the saw marks of its ragged edge. For a moment he thinks about putting it into the drawer as well. Of all his treasures, it is his most precious. But when he shuts the drawer, the coin still hangs around his neck.

◎◎◎◎

He picks up the vial, its smooth glass cool and pleasing to his fingers. Who will know about that secret drawer when I am gone? he thinks. Now that Haridas is gone, who will tell my successor about that secret drawer? Who will collect my things into his pockets?

As the shadows creep into his room, he quickly takes fresh silks from a nearby chest: jama, pants, brocaded girdle, skirt of gauze and silken cloak the color of midnight. He puts on slippers, soft and quiet as a cat's paws. He then pockets the vial and steps into the corridors of the harem.

While the serving eunuchs bustle past with *sharbats* and fruit drinks in gold salvers, pitchers of wine and chilled candies, while the nautch girls ready themselves on the dancing platform that rises from the fountains of the Khas Mahal, while the youngest concubines splash their feet in the rose-water pool before the emperor's door, Basant heads for the apartments of Roshanara. Tonight, no joy for him.

As he approaches Roshanara's door, he hears far-off singing: a ghazal full of yearning and despair, the cry of a lover spurned by her beloved. His heart aches at the sound of it, almost he begins to weep. He despairs at what he is about to do.

The door opens, as he expects, even as he approaches, but it is not Roshanara who emerges, but her maid Shaheen. "Our mistress will not need you tonight, Basant," she says, and begins to shut the door.

But Basant is not to be put off. "She must see me, Shaheen."

"'Must'?" Shaheen repeats, her lips pursing. "I think not." She again begins to shut the door.

"I beg you to let me in. It is . . ." He's about to say "a matter of life or death," but realizes that it sounds too foolish, even if it is true for once.

Shaheen seems to sense his anxiety. "Let me see what I can do," she says, closing the door. Finally Shaheen reappears, but from her face alone Basant knows she has bad news. "She doesn't wish to see you, Basant. I'm sorry. I don't know what you've done. She says . . ."

Basant waits for her to go on. "Please," he says quietly, "please tell me."

Shaheen bites her lip. "She says she has a new eunuch."

It seems to Basant that the ground has slipped suddenly from beneath his feet. "Who?" he gasps.

"She says never mind who."

"Did she say that? A new eunuch, never mind who? She said that?"

Shaheen looks away, shamefaced. "I have to go." Then she whispers, careful that the princess won't hear, "Come back tomorrow, Basant. You know how she loves you. I'm sure things will be different."

Shaheen begins to shut the door. "Wait! Tell her . . . tell her . . . " he starts to say, but the words simply will not come. His hand clutches the green glass vial as he walks slowly away.

Now he is more resolved than ever.

CHAPTER 4

For what seems like hours Basant watches Roshanara's quarters. Her door opens at last, and Shaheen slips gently away; Basant now moves unnoticed from shadow to shadow. His hand has nearly reached the handle of Roshanara's door when he hears a noise and steps back. Her door opens.

Roshanara's new eunuch slips quickly from her room.

Like Basant, he wears a cloak whose hood obscures his face, and he too hugs the shadows. Basant decides to follow him. The new eunuch is slender, and moves quickly. Basant thinks for a moment that he might be Alu, that eunuch from the Rambagh. But it's too dark to be sure.

Soon Basant is sweating and puffing, struggling to quiet his breath as he follows: the other eunuch walks quickly. Near the Diwan-i-Khas, he takes a butter lamp from its niche and then slips around a corner.

Basant snorts; the eunuch has just entered a dead end. He expects him to reappear any second and so waits a few yards away, catching his breath.

But the eunuch does not reappear.

What's he doing? Basant wonders. There's nothing there but a court-yard, not even a fountain, nothing. At last he figures it out.

The tunnels.

Where else could he have gone? He goes back to the corner to fetch a butter lamp, puzzling how this unknown eunuch would know about the tunnels, a secret known to few.

At the edge of the outer wall, he stretches on tiptoe to press a marble dado with his fingertips. When he feels it click, three sandstone blocks in the wall beside him pivot to create a narrow door.

ᘒᘒᘒᘒ

Basant hates this entry: it is *so* narrow. Thrusting the butter lamp through the passageway, he squeezes in; the rough sandstones scraping his shirt. Only as an afterthought does Basant worry about the safety of his green glass vial. He feels through the cloth: the vial is in his pocket.

The tunnel passage is so inky dark that he wonders whether the eunuch even entered there at all.

When he pushes against the stones to close the secret door, he nearly drops the butter lamp. He doesn't relish the idea of being in the tunnels without a light. This opening was designed to be only an entrance, not an exit. He would need to trace his way through the tunnels for several hundred yards to find a way out. Without a light such a journey would be difficult, for the tunnels were filled with traps both intentional and unintentional, traps hard enough to see holding a lamp in one's hand.

How much his safety depends on that one little lamp. The tunnels are a maze of passages beneath the foundations of the fort, built long before Babur, the first Mogul emperor, acquired Agra as his capital. They are centuries old: even the air trapped inside the tunnels must be hundreds of years old, dank and unhealthy, the rough walls slimy with ages-old mildew.

Basant steps down a steep, rough-hewn staircase, now steadying himself with his free hand so his lamp wavers unprotected in the stale air. The risers of the steps are so deep that Basant can scarcely reach the step below without pitching forward. He crab-walks down, clinging to the sandstone walls as tightly as his sausage fingers allow, puffing hard.

At last he reaches the main tunnel, a wide passage that runs the length of the fort. Hiding the light of his lamp, peering into the shadows, listening hard: He hears nothing but the echoes of water dripping from the ceiling and striking the stone floors with a soft slap. His eyes, adjusting to the dark, seem to see dark shapes swimming through the shadows, but when he blinks, they disappear. He hopes they are tricks of the light, not ghosts.

The main tunnel runs from beneath the courtyard of the Diwan-i-Am to the moat. He seems to sense more than see a faint lightness to his right, toward the moat. *How much the day has changed me!* Basant thinks. A little light is enough for me to follow now: to follow I know not where!

ေ ⁇ ⁇ ⁇

The glass vial bounces rhythmically in his pocket as he pads down the passage, ducking every so often when he passes beneath the beams that reinforce the ceiling. He knows this part of the tunnels so very well that he scarcely needs his lamp; even so he shields the flame.

The tunnels' echoes magnify every footfall, every breath. Shielding the precious flame of his butter lamp, Basant hurries through the stale air, deep into the bowels of the palace. The path is marked, but the marks are secret and subtle. The tunnel is meant to be confusing. The tunnel winds and twists, and every crossing leads to traps and wells and death in many forms.

Basant knows the way well enough to walk quickly. He's confident that the new eunuch, even if he knows how to find the secret marks, will be more timid. Basant should be able to catch up with him soon.

Suddenly Basant hears a *bang,* and involuntarily stops and presses against the wall as if expecting to be shot. It's only some noise from farther down the tunnel. He guesses it is the sound of the river exit swinging shut; that means the other eunuch is now only a few yards ahead.

In a few minutes, he too reaches the river exit. At his feet he finds not one, but two butter lamps, their wicks still smoking; a tiny ember still glowing on the end of the wick of one of them. Two lamps, thinks Basant. He was certain the eunuch had only taken the one.

Basant places his own lamp beside them and steps out into the star-filled Agra night. The exit is hidden by a tall thicket of briar roses. He pushes the stone door back into place and steps carefully down the narrow path. The other eunuch is nowhere to be seen.

At last Basant emerges from the bushes. He stands on a narrow embankment at the foot of the enormous walls of the fort; the embankment descends quickly to the moat, its waters stocked liberally with crocodiles. In times of war, sentries patrol this embankment, but tonight all is quiet. Basant hears laughter and soft music from high above, the sounds of the harem at play. Beyond he sees the lights of fishing huts along the river's edge.

A small pier pokes into the moat a few yards ahead. Tonight, unexpectedly, a narrow rowboat, the kind used by fishermen, is tied to the pier. Beyond the pier Basant can just make out the shadows of another boat already gliding across the river. He inches along the embankment, wanting a better look. He pulls the hood of his cloak over his head and depends on the darkness and shadows to protect him from being seen.

So he is surprised to hear a voice in his ear saying, "You're late." From under his cloak Basant sees a peasant: a dark face stubbled with gray beneath his ill-kempt turban. His breath reeks of onions.

"Hey," the peasant says suspiciously, "how many damned eunuchs are we supposed to take tonight? Two isn't enough, now there's supposed to be three eunuchs? Nobody told us that. Nobody told me the third fare would be another eunuch." He looks Basant over, frowning at what he sees. "Not that I care whether you have balls or not. But a fellow likes to be told things."

"Why do you think I'm here, uncle?" Basant replies politely.

But instead of answering his question, the peasant simply snorts and walks to the boat. After a few steps he turns. "You coming or not?"

CSCSC

The slow, steady current of the Jumna pushes them forward. In the dim light of the stars, curls of mist rise ghostlike from the river. Basant can just make out the outline of the Taj Mahal against the black sky, its white marble surfaces so polished it catches the least hints of starlight.

As they slip closer to the Taj, Basant makes out a number of boats in the river. It is unusual for even one fishing boat to be out at this hour. "Hey, we've almost caught up with your buddies," the boatman says.

"How many did you say there were?" Basant asks.

"How many do you think? Just those two."

Basant hopes with his silence to encourage the boatman to say more, but he seems focused only on rowing. So Basant is left to wonder who else may be in that boat. They are beginning to push toward the south bank, toward the river wall of the Taj. Approaching, Basant feels a change. From afar the tomb appeared delicate as bubbles on soft grass; coming closer, its vaulting domes loom overhead: rich, powerful, ominous.

The boatman guides his craft toward a pier Basant had not even seen. Soon Basant is directly adjacent to one of the wooden ladders built into the pier. "This is where you get off," whispers the boatman. "And hurry, will you! I don't want to be near this place. There are ghosts here."

Basant manages to appear calm, though he's rattled somewhat by the daunting prospect of leaving the boat by ladder. But he manages the climb, stands straight, feeling as if he has accomplished something just by reaching the top.

The place is empty. For a moment he considers calling to the boatman, begging him to take him back. Instead he walks to the end of the pier and mounts a sandstone step. This leads to an arched doorway in the river wall, which opens to the rear of the tomb. There a staircase has been built into the *rauza*'s marble plinth.

The Taj looms over him.

☙☙☙☙

He climbs the stairs as quietly as he can, and looks around. At least no one is standing there with a sword, as he imagined, ready to slice off his head. He hears the sounds of conversations somewhere nearby, and sees the gentle glow of lamps. It reminds him of a nighttime picnic.

Who would have the audacity to violate this sacred space with a picnic? Forget the ghosts, he thinks, who would risk the emperor's wrath?

He crouches at the railing that overlooks the mosque. Beside the marble plinth of the mausoleum stretches a wide courtyard; in the midst of this courtyard, a broad, shallow *hauz*: a pool of water where the faithful might wash before prayer. At its edge, Basant sees a group of people gathered in a circle on a large carpet, talking in hushed, intense tones.

They could see him if they looked his way. Though he kneels on the marble floor, behind the low, intricately carved railing that sweeps around the plinth, Basant is in plain sight. Only the shadows hide him, and also that the attention of the circle seems to be focused only on each other.

Basant recognizes most of them even though their faces are lit only by the dim glow of lanterns. At the head of the circle is Aurangzeb. To his right is General Jumla, looking very relaxed now, much different than he looked this afternoon. Beside Jumla sits Shaista Khan, tough as an old wolf.

Yes, thinks Basant as he sees him, you were the start of it all, the start of my ruin. If only I had led you through the tunnels as I planned—if only I had pushed you into the well.

Next to Shaista Khan are two other men that Basant has never seen before. Basant makes out in the shadows the form of Aurangzeb's deaf manservant hovering behind the lanterns. At last, a slender eunuch steps into the circle and sits in the empty place.

So, thinks Basant, it was Alu the whole time. He curses the sweet-faced eunuch, curses Roshanara, curses himself, curses silently but in the midst of his cursing fails to hear what Alu is saying.

The circle shifts, making space, and two new figures join. It is Master Hing, and with him is a different eunuch—Roshanara's new eunuch.

Two butter lamps at the exit, Basant thinks stupidly. Despite the new eunuch's hooded face, Basant sees now that he is shorter than Alu—even his shape is different.

Hing sits down, hunching away from Aurangzeb, making room for the other eunuch, who sits abruptly—almost playfully—next to Aurangzeb.

Then the eunuch tosses back the hood that hides his face. But his face is still veiled from the eyes down.

Her face.

Of course, Basant realizes, her face. Roshanara's face.

ⓒⓄⓒⓄ

What a fool, what a fool I am, Basant thinks, tapping his head with the heels of his hands, and nearly crying for joy. Of course she still loves me.

While Basant thinks his giddy thoughts, even as it dawns on him that there is something odd here, the circle is quickly changing its nature. Instead of soft chatter, the group grows quiet, and seats are shifted so that everyone is leaning toward Aurangzeb.

"Where is Ali Khalil?" Aurangzeb asks Master Hing, looking at some place on the carpet rather than directly at any of the people there.

The old eunuch shrugs. "He knew the plan, your highness. He should have come. The boatman was waiting for him when we left."

"What does it mean that he has not come?" Jumla asks. "He is a danger."

"I will see to it," Hing replies in his scratchy, piping voice.

"I regret it, but it must be so," Aurangzeb says, not lifting his eyes.

"And what of Jai Singh? What of him?" It is Shaista Khan who speaks. Basant notices that he seems to feel free to be aggressive with the prince, and that Alu and Jumla look at him with the same disapproving expression.

Aurangzeb sits impassively, staring at the carpet. "He will not come."

"Then I will manage it," Shaista Khan says.

"No," Aurangzeb says quietly, and for the first time raises his head. "I did not ask him to come, nor did I tell him of our plans." He nods to Alu. "You were there."

"Yes, lord," the eunuch answers, his voice a husky whisper. "You achieved your goal with him but never revealed your purpose. It was masterful."

Alu describes the chess game, the end game where Aurangzeb turned the tables on Jai Singh, emerging victorious. "In your wisdom, lord," Alu continues, "you wagered against him on this game: If you won, he must lend support for your cause. Your victory was deftly done, lord."

"Then where is he? Why isn't he here?" Shaista Khan demands. Jumla bristles, but at a motion from Aurangzeb's hand he settles back.

"He is not here because there is no need for him to be here," Aurangzeb says. "He lost the wager; he gave his word; all is settled."

"His word? You expect a Hindu to keep his word?" Shaista Khan blurts out angrily.

For the first time, Aurangzeb turns to face him. "He is a gentleman."

"Not like the rest of you," Roshanara says, and she laughs, and the others, except Shaista Khan, laugh with her.

Even Aurangzeb chuckles. Then his face straightens, and he says quietly, "It isn't necessary for him to know our plans, provided—"

"Provided that he is in your pocket, brother," Roshanara says. Basant has noticed how much Roshanara likes to burst in to others' conversations.

"As you say, sister," Aurangzeb says, giving the impression of someone who has learned patience through much practice. "Tomorrow, at the order of my father, we return to the siege of Golconda; I and General Jumla." He nods to the eunuch across the circle. "Alu, of course, will be with us."

Aurangzeb looks from face to face. "This may be our last chance to speak together, friends. Sadly we must speak the unspeakable. We must lay our plans now, plans that by Allah's grace will never be used."

Hing stirs uncomfortably in his seat, like someone rousing himself from sleep. "So you say, highness, but forgive me, I must disagree. I am old now and soon I shall die. So forgive this old *hijra* if I speak those words you say are unspeakable." He waits silently until they turn his way.

"Suppose there were a ruler who was no longer fit to rule," Hing says at last. "Suppose he once nurtured his empire, once built grand monuments across the land ..." Hing waves his hand vaguely toward the looming domes of the Taj. "Suppose that he once was loved by all. Now suppose that man had changed, thinking now only of women, opium, and wine.

"Suppose that man were now so vile, so besotted, as to have congress with two women at once, in ways most sickening and contemptible.

"Suppose that man, that weak and foolish man, were now so mired in his debauchery that his own daughter could use his vile predilections against him. If his gentle daughter could extort him thus, to rescind his own military orders, I ask you—what might some other do?"

Jumla shifts in his seat. "Is that how the order of command was changed?" Aurangzeb says nothing, but Roshanara now turns to face the Persian general. "Changed by blackmail?"

"What does it matter how?" Roshanara spits back. "It only matters that the order was changed. Or would you prefer it changed back? Is Alu the *hijra,* or you?"

"I must know why I was named commander instead of Aurangzeb," Jumla demands. "Was that your idea or your father's?"

"Neither mine nor my father's," she answers.

"Whose then?"

"His." She tilts her head toward Aurangzeb.

All faces turn to the prince. He does not look up.

"I thought Shah Jahan had chosen me." Jumla turns away.

"I changed his mind for him, with my sister's help—is that not enough? Golconda is yours; the army is yours? What more could you want?"

"Respect," Jumla whispers.

Hing glares at Jumla. "What sort of man are you, general? Would you seek the approval of a profligate?"

"Look upon my brother," Roshanara says. "Isn't his merest nod worth more than a dozen robes of honor from my father?"

☙☙☙☙

"My lords, you see how it is?" Alu speaks now. "You are angry. Confused. You bark and growl at one another like ill-bred dogs. For your master has lost his way. Which is more foolhardy? To be ruled by an unworthy king, or to rise up against the might of his throne, uncertain of the outcome?"

"Look at our house," Roshanara says, "look at our history. Time and again, it has only been through rebellion that our empire has been saved. Why, this is the very way my father came to power!"

"That doesn't make it right," a soft voice says. The speaker is Aurangzeb. "There is a great chasm between discussing this act and doing it, and I am not yet sure that the time is right to leap across it."

"Then why the hell are we here?" Shaista Khan sputters. "If we are not here to act, then I was misled."

"Then leave," Jumla answers. His hand rests on the hilt of his sword.

"Leave with your life, Shaista Khan," Aurangzeb adds gently. "No harm will come to you."

"I meant no offense," Shaista Khan says. "But my question remains. Why are we here, if not for action?"

"Why you are here, I cannot say," Aurangzeb replies, with a hint of sadness. "I am here to consider a dreadful undertaking, to learn the counsel of wiser men than I. For when the moment comes, Shaista Khan, you will have your wish—there will be no time for thought, but only for action."

Aurangzeb looks around the circle, as if to read each man's heart. "Who will utter those terrible words, the words that I cannot say?"

But no one answers.

Finally, Jumla lifts his head. "Take it, lord. Take the throne. We're behind you. Others will join us. Take it. Save the empire." He looks firmly at Aurangzeb. "You know that this is Allah's will."

"No," says Master Hing, his voice like ice water. "You cannot simply take the throne, highness. There must be a reason. Without a reason, your father and your brothers will come against you, and anyone with a conscience will join them. There must be a reason."

"What reason can I have, Master Hing?" Aurangzeb asks.

"Well . . . there's always God," Hing replies.

"That is the perfect reason!" Shaista Khan says. "Let's be rid of the Hindus! Your father coddles them, and worse. Make them the enemy! Who will stand against you if God is on your side?"

Aurangzeb turns to Alu. "What do you think?"

"It's dicey, lord," Alu answers. "What would you do to the Hindus? Kill them? We depend on them too much."

"Force them to convert," Shaista Khan bursts in. "Make them bow before Allah the All-Merciful."

"And how would you do that?" Alu responds.

"Tax them," suggests Jumla. "Tax them until they bleed. Restore the *jizya*. All who do not bow to Allah must pay the *jizya*, so it is written."

"But Shah Jahan has been trying to collect the *jizya* for years," Hing puts in. "He's had no success."

"Then it must be done with emphasis," Jumla asserts. "At the point of the sword. At the head of an army, tearing down temples as we go."

"Dara won't stand for it," Shaista Khan says. "He's too close to Jai Singh. He won't levy the *jizya* tax on Rajputana. Dara depends on the Rajputs for his very life. He trusts them more than Muslims."

"You mean only that Dara trusts Jai Singh more than you, general," Roshanara says. "With good reason, apparently."

Shaista Khan bristles. "Why shouldn't I be trusted?" he shoots back. Bits of saliva spray as he talks. "Do you think Jai Singh can be trusted? Do you think Dara doesn't have meetings like this himself?" Aurangzeb looks up, and Shaista Khan realizes that he has stepped into a trap.

"Well, general," Aurangzeb says. "Tell us of Dara's meetings."

"He's had one or two," Shaista Khan allows; each word painful.

"So Dara plots as well," Hing interrupts. "Is anyone surprised to hear it? Knowing this about him, what shall we do?"

Unexpectedly Aurangzeb answers. "I will move when Dara moves. Not before." He looks steadily around the circle. "But when Dara moves, I will not attack the throne myself. I will support Murad, my brother."

☙◗◑◖❧

Those in the circle lean back as if shocked at these words—but the faces of the eunuchs brighten. "Excellent, lord," Hing tells Aurangzeb.

"But Murad can't lead!" Shaista Khan bursts out. "I won't stand for him being king!"

"Of course not, general," Hing says, his voice croaking cheerfully. "And neither will anyone else. That is the beauty of this plan. With Aurangzeb as an ally, Murad can crush Dara. Dara will be isolated."

Shaista Khan laughs. "And no noble will bet his family's ass on a potential loser. But I must protest—Murad is more fool than your father. He is not worthy."

"That's the beauty of this thought," Alu explains. "Once Dara is clearly doomed, the nobility will beg Aurangzeb to lead."

"And nothing is more honorable than agreeing reluctantly to a heartfelt plea," Hing says, with a cackling chuckle. "But what of Jai Singh?"

"When the time comes, Jai Singh will turn. If you cannot trust Jai Singh, then trust me. If Jai Singh comes against us, I myself will present this neck to you. Take my head and feed my eyes to the crows. Or take it to Murad, or to Dara, and use it to buy your peace." His face hardens—the first time Basant has seen him angry.

"I don't like this," Roshanara says. "Waiting for Dara to move? That could take forever. He's undependable, damn it. You can't even depend on his treachery!"

Aurangzeb and the others chuckle. "I think I know how it might be accomplished, lord," Hing says softly. "If I might suggest a plan. . . ."

☙◗◑◖❧

So much has happened to Basant since the moon rose last night that he might be forgiven for ignoring the obvious. As he sits leaning against the railing of the Taj's marble plinth, peering out from the shadows and listening to treason, it doesn't cross his mind to wonder why *he* has not been invited. Why isn't he sitting in that circle, instead of watching uninvited from afar?

But Basant ignores such thoughts: he has begun to dream again as he watches that cluster of treachery plot and plan. He will tell of this conspiracy and make his fortune.

For years he has drifted rudderless on the waves of Fate, enduring the tragedy and insult, as all slaves must, and never had the power to respond.

Until now.

Fate has favored him, for a change. She has placed under his hand so many great ones. He has only to lift his finger and all of them will die. For just a word, Shah Jahan would give him anything he can dream of. Dara would give him even more.

Every fault, every slight, every outrage will be requited. Justice will be done: on earth, not in heaven; and by him, not by Allah; and before his eyes.

He will make them all pay. For the castration, the molestations, the indignities, the servitude, the deaths—all will be repaid. No more will Basant walk in fear, but all shall fear him.

☙☙☙☙

In the pride of his thought, Basant has failed to account for a missing piece. He can feel it—something nagging, something important. It is the feeling he gets when he plays cards: He looks at his cards and thinks, I have won! These cards can't be beaten! Only to find out too late that he missed a trump, a little card held by someone else, and watches his victory bleed away.

What is it, what is it, what is it? he asks himself. But he cannot answer, he cannot name it, any more than he can remember to count the trump cards in his hand. It is not his nature to notice the obvious.

Instead, he makes plans.

The first thing, he decides, is to get back to the palace. With studied care he starts to tiptoe back to the stairs that lead to the river.

And then it happens: the glass vial must have shifted in his pocket. When he stands up, it falls out. He sees it drop, tracing an arc to the white marble tiles. He nearly screams.

But the vial does not shatter into a million noisy pieces after all. It bounces. Then it rolls, making the clinking, singing sound of blown glass rolling over marble. Dumbstruck, Basant watches. Suddenly his right arm stabs with pain. His chest is crushed. He doubles over as if pushed down by an enormous weight. He feels an enormous hand squeezing his shoulder so mightily that his arm grows numb, and he must gasp for breath.

This is the thing he has forgotten. That he is mortal. That he can be broken. Most of all he has forgotten the one who can break him. He is lifted off his feet. He opens his eyes and sees: The giant is what he has forgotten. Karm. Aurangzeb, the eunuch, Alu, and the deaf-mute manservant were there. Basant should have realized that the giant would also be around. Since he was not in the circle, he should have guessed that the giant would be patrolling, watching for spies.

Spies like Basant.

ᘓᘔᘓᘔ

The giant Karm hauls Basant along the plinth for several steps and then stops. Without letting go of the eunuch, he bends down and scoops up the vial that has rolled along the tiles. He drops it into the pocket of his tunic and then lugs Basant like a sack to the circle of conspirators.

They are all standing now, all except Master Hing, who is still struggling to his feet. Every eye watches as Karm lugs him into their midst and sets him down a few feet from Alu.

Basant's eyes flick from face to face: the dubious, uncertain faces of the generals who have never seen him before; Shaista Khan, who stands with sword drawn, wishing he had killed Basant last night; Alu, disappointed but curious; and Hing, who gives up his struggle to stand, and sits like an old, old man, shaking his head. Basant then looks at Aurangzeb, and finally, hesitantly, to Roshanara. "Oh, Basant," he hears her say.

The words strike his heart, filling Basant with a righteous courage. Now that he is hopeless and helpless he sees his path clearly. I may be dead, he thinks, but not yet in the grave. "He asked me to kill you," Basant tells Roshanara. "Your saintly brother." He turns to the circle. "This prince you all think should be king? He's a murderer." It seems to him that his little boy's voice is at that moment commanding and strong.

"And what did you answer when I asked you this favor, Basant?" Aurangzeb asks quietly, looking beyond Basant, at the crescent moon.

"I refused!" Basant cries out. "I refused," he whispers.

Master Hing raises his hands to his ears to shut out the sound of Basant's words. He lifts his head and Basant sees the watery, fishlike glistening of Hing's eyes in the moonlight. "You fool, you young fool," Master Hing mutters. "I am sorry, highness, so sorry."

Aurangzeb nods at Karm. The giant moves to Basant, but the eunuch shies away. "I can walk," he says. Karm points toward the orchard gardens, and Basant, taking one last look into Roshanara's exquisite eyes, goes where he is told.

With Karm following, Basant walks blindly into the shadows, stepping off the sandstone pathways and onto the orchard grass now damp with dew. He barks his shins against low bushes hidden in the darkness. Why don't you lead, you big oaf, Basant thinks. On he wanders deeper into the gardens, until sick of it all, he simply stops. He faces the giant, who stands away from him, a vague shape in the shadows, lit only by the bitter light of moonrise. The silver tip of the crescent moon trace the round fullness of the white dome of the Taj, and Basant thinks, Whatever is going to be done to me will be done soon.

Basant's eyes return to the giant, still standing a little way off. Karm doesn't carry a sword or even a knife. His weapons, Basant supposes, are those enormous hands.

Basant can imagine the crushing power of one of those fists. And worse, much worse. As he imagines horror after horror, Basant falls to his knees. "Whatever did I do to deserve this?" he wails. "I beg you, let me go!"

As Basant faces him, crying with his woman's voice, Karm's great eyebrows work up and down, he opens his mouth, but only strangled grunts emerge. At last he crouches and rests a heavy arm across Basant's fleshy shoulders, his big eyes filled with concern.

"Are you going to hurt me?" Basant whispers. The big dark eyes of the giant stare steadily at the eunuch. "You will hurt me, won't you? You will if they make you. That's why they keep you around. You're here only to crush and kill, just like I'm here only to flatter and lick. Oh, we are pitiful, you and I!"

Karm's fingers gently squeeze Basant's shoulder, and Basant, starting again to sob, places his own soft hand over the giant's. "We're not so different, you and I," Basant sniffs, lifting his face to Karm's. "They maimed us—they made us slaves. We're like cattle to them—they just snip off the bits they don't like. What choice did we have? No one ever asked me if I wanted this life." He looks desperately at Karm. "I dreamed of vengeance. I dreamed of making them pay! But it's no good! Listen to me! Forget vengeance! Be happy! There's still time—do what you must to be happy!"

Alu approaches but looks only at Karm. "He's to die. Drown him. Make it look accidental." The words thud in Basant's heart. Suddenly it occurs to Basant that his turban must look dreadful; he reaches up to fix it. It's stupid, he knows, but he can't stop himself.

"Don't do that!" Alu hisses. "You're going to die, you fool! What does your turban matter now? You were to be special, Basant. Aurangzeb's *khaswajara*. It was yours for the taking. Only a fool would throw it away. You deserve this fate. You make us all look like fools."

"Brother," Basant whispers, not knowing what he else to say, but Alu glares at him, unconsciously swiping at his eyes. He's crying.

"Master Hing sends this message," Alu spits out. "You are no brother of his. He has forgotten your name." Alu sobs, but controls himself. "And I too have forgotten you."

But Basant barely hears him. He turns his eyes toward the magnificent onion dome, now silver in the moonlight, more brilliant than ever. He sees the play of shadows as the moonlight falls on the spires and domes, on the finials and minarets; he sees the vast yearning emptiness of the arches; he sees finally that the tomb of this dead queen is a poem written in marble: so glorious it seems now, so pathetic, so full of hope and of despair.

At that moment, Basant thinks, Ah, I understand.

He faces Karm. His heart is at ease, beyond good or evil. "I'm ready," he says. He squares his shoulders, trying to look brave. They walk toward the river stairs. When he sees the place where Karm caught him, Basant looks at the giant as if they share a good joke. Then he walks toward the railing, with Karm beside him, like a huge and silent shadow.

She is still down there, Roshanara. He looks at her, and his chest heaves. She doesn't see him, so he waves, but the shadows still hide him.

"Little Rose!" he calls. And again. She looks up, as do Alu, who stands beside her, and Hing, who is talking to Aurangzeb.

"I loved you!" he calls. "I would never hurt you!" Basant reaches into Karm's pocket—the giant stares at him in surprise but does nothing—and takes out the glass vial. "Look!" Basant shouts, his piping voice echoing against the vast facade of the tomb. "I brought this! I was going to poison myself after I told you . . . After I told you about your brother. He's evil, you know! He's a very bad man!"

He starts to cry. He clutches the vial and shakes it at the princess, although in the darkness, it isn't very likely that she can see it. "I was ready to die for you! Who else loved you so, Little Rose!" As his sobs overwhelm him, he sees Roshanara turn aside, and Alu leading her away

"Come on," whispers Basant through his tears. "Lets get this over with."

They come to the dark opening that yawns into the plinth, the stairs that lead down to the river. The way ahead is black, impenetrable except for a haze of silver at the bottom of the stairs: the door to the shore.

He almost tumbles on a broken step. He turns and starts to tell Karm to be careful, but then he thinks, Why should I warn him? Instead Basant goes outside, and hears with some satisfaction the surprised grunt of the giant as he comes down the last stairs.

Karm must lower his head carefully as he comes through the door, and Basant nearly laughs.

This is it, Basant thinks. This is it!

When Karm sees him, his heavy eyebrows shoot up. Suddenly Basant realizes that Karm is surprised that he did not run away. But where would he go, on his pudgy legs? Karm could catch him easily. Still the thought occurs to him that this play has not yet ended; maybe there is yet hope.

"I'm ready," he tells the giant. "I'm ready to die. I'm not afraid."

Instead of walking along the pier, Karm leads Basant to the edge of the bank, to the shore, to the dhobi stones where the women wash their clothes in the river. Basant's pace slows. At last he wades in—another step, and another. The water is cold, colder than he thought water could be; as it laps around his ankles, he trembles. Karm's hand still holds him fast.

"No!" Basant says, trying to pull away. "Not this way!" His feet slip on the slick round stones of the river bottom and he pitches into the water, landing on his hands and knees.

Karm pulls him out, standing him on his feet. How odd, thinks Basant, he could just have pushed me down. So he stands, cold and dripping; the water comes up to his groin, and chills the opening where his lingam used to be; his cloak, now heavy with water, clings to him. His turban falls off, and he watches it uncoil and tumble over the surface of the river like a dark snake.

"I don't want to die this way," he tells the giant through chattering teeth. "Please don't make me die this way. I can't stand it! I'm so cold."

Karm of course says nothing, the expression on his face a mystery.

"You're not a bad man," Basant says, shivering. "Let me take this." With a trembling hand, he holds up the vial of poison for Karm to see. "It was always my plan to use this. Don't drown me."

Karm shakes his head, but Basant pays no attention. He struggles to break the wax and pull the stopper, but his hands are numb and trembling. No good. He starts to place the glass between his teeth. Why not chew it open, he thinks, swallow it all, even the glass—what difference does it make?

Karm howls and grabs at his hand.

The vial flies off into the river.

Gone.

Basant's mouth opens, lips quivering, teeth chattering, but no words come out this time, only a strangled groan. He falls to his knees in the water, half laughing, half sobbing. Then suddenly, vehemently, Basant thrusts his head beneath the water and tries to inhale.

Instead of holding him down, Basant feels Karm's enormous hand pull him from the water. "Why?" Basant cries. "Why?"

Karm places his great hands on Basant's shoulders, and lowers his heavy shaggy head as though he were about to kiss him. Basant feels his body being tilted backward into the water.

Basant thinks: This is my last breath!

The eunuch's eyes dart in every direction: he sees the cold stars, the thumbnail moon, the firelight flickering through the trees, the haze of dawn along the river's edge. He glances one last time at the dome of the tomb. On the plinth a shadow stares toward him. Somehow he knows it is Aurangzeb, come to watch him die. Watch then, he thinks, watch and be damned.

As Karm leans him backward into the water, Basant's consciousness floats from his body, from the space behind his eyes to some great height where there is no cold.

I can see everything from here!

He sees the endless, sacred river flowing gently to the sea far away.

Life is wonderful!

He sees Aurangzeb staring from the plinth and traces each pathetic feature of the prince's face—the weakness of his eyes, the fear that plays along his lips.

You are pitiful!

He watches a giant gently lower a trembling eunuch into the cold river.

How funny!

He sees one final time the brilliant horns of the crescent moon as it rises above the silvering sky.

I always loved you!

And suddenly he is back, trapped inside his horrible, choking body, gasping as his head is thrust into the water.

He sputters and churns and refuses to drown.

Through the water that laps over his eyes he sees the giant's anguished, determined face. He feels the water bubble into his ears and the cold, stinging burn as it fills his lungs. Finally he feels the giant's thumbs upon his windpipe like weights, and hears a crunching crack.

And then all is light.

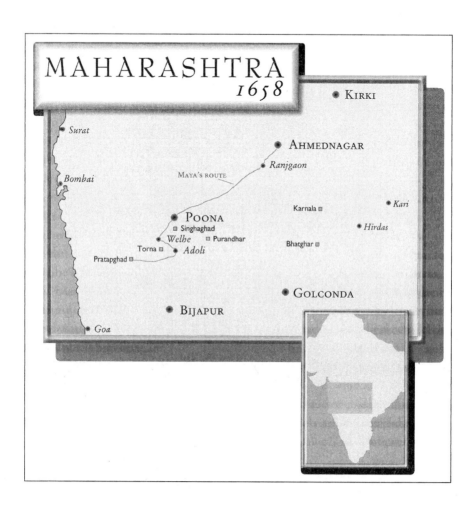

MAHARASHTRA
1658

• KIRKI

• Surat

• AHMEDNAGAR

Bombai

MAYA'S ROUTE   • *Ranjgaon*

• Kari

Karnala ▣

• *Hirdas*

• POONA
▣ Singhaghad

Welhe   ▣ Purandhar   Bhatghar ▣

Torna ▣   • *Adoli*

Pratapghad ▣

• GOLCONDA

• BIJAPUR

• *Goa*

CHAPTER 5

Tanaji sleeps in the manger.

Or rather he does not sleep. He barely fits: one rail digs into his thick shoulder, and his sandals hang in the air. But at least the manger is clean—uncomfortable, but not dirty like the fouled straw of the stable floor. A man my age needs a bed, Tanaji thinks; a man of my position should not sleep in dung.

This, thinks Tanaji, is what comes from keeping promises.

At first it was fun, watching young Shahu use his charm to beguile information from a merchant's wife. Later Tanaji and Shahu would lie in wait by a roadside, knowing exactly when the caravan would pass, how much gold the merchant carried in his purse. But now—now Shahu must have more; he must sleep in the merchant's bed, cuckold the husband and steal the wife's jewels, while Tanaji, old uncle Tanaji, keeps watch in the stables.

Well, he thinks, maybe old uncle Tanaji has had enough.

He hunches some straw to form a pillow. Even through his turban, the straw scratches. Slowly his breathing attunes to the snores of the horses and his limbs grow heavy in the breath-warmed air.

Then Tanaji sits up with a start, his hand on the hilt of his *katar*. What woke him, he wonders. Then he realizes—the *clip* of horses' hooves on the cobbled courtyard.

No, no, no! Tomorrow! he thinks. You're not to come home until tomorrow!

In the pale light of the crescent moon he sees two riders: the merchant-husband followed by his servant. Except it isn't the merchant after all: from the glitter of his jewels under the silver moon, Tanaji sees that it's a nobleman, a Bijapuri from the look of him, man big as a mountain.

Gods help us, thinks Tanaji, it can't be. Not him!

As the men dismount, Tanaji gathers his wits. Through the shadows, huddling in a crouch, he races to the nearby guesthouse. As the riders fuss with their horses, he silently opens the narrow door and steals inside.

Somewhere, somewhere in this house Shahu is staying, and Tanaji must find him, and fast. Then get out, fast. For Khirki is a Muslim town, and if he finds them, a Muslim will be within his rights to kill Shahu, and the cheating wife. And Tanaji for good measure. But if the rider is Afzul Khan, as Tanaji fears, quick death would be the best of outcomes. By the thin light of the moon through a window, Tanaji sees Shahu's form sprawled across the bed, naked, legs and arms intertwined with a woman's. He kicks the bed. "Shahu! Wake up! He's back!"

The pretty wife, not Shahu, blinks awake. Her arms are pinned under Shahu's muscled shoulders and her face registers increasing panic until, with some effort, she tugs free. As she slides from the bed Tanaji catches a glimpse of warm skin, of firm breasts and a shapely belly. She hears the noise outside.

Shahu yawns and stretches. The woman scowls as she rushes to her own room, pretending to cover her creamy nakedness by hugging herself. "Get up!" Tanaji barks, no longer caring if anyone hears. Shahu looks up dazed. His clothes are scattered in a trail to the bed. Tanaji throws Shahu his pants. As he pulls them on, Tanaji scoops up everything he can find; they'll sort things out later. Meanwhile Shahu unbolts the window shutter. Alert now, he grabs the clothes from Tanaji and tosses them outside.

"I'll never make it," Tanaji mutters, and Shahu laughs. Scowling, Tanaji slides out, scraping his belly, squeezing his shoulders. He feels with his toes, but he can't find the ground, so he simply hopes for the best and drops. The fall is only a couple of feet. Through the window he can hear the angry cries of the husband. "Hurry, Shahu!" Tanaji whispers.

There's a loud bang, and suddenly Shahu pitches headfirst through the bedroom window, somersaulting as he lands on the ground. "Come on!" he shouts, running barefoot into the night. Tanaji frowns and scoops up the clothes. He curses his short legs, and the pile of clothes he clutches to his chest; he's slow enough without them. He turns to see the Bijapuri squeezing through the same window, his legs kicking in frustration.

Shahu reaches the courtyard wall. "Where?" he calls to Tanaji.

"Horses! Other side of the wall. There!" Tanaji is running so hard that the effort of shouting winds him. Shahu shuffles backward, waving for Tanaji to hurry, while looking for a place to crawl over the wall.

When he catches up, Shahu jerks the clothes from Tanaji's arms and paws through them. Rising triumphantly, he waves a small cloth sack under Tanaji's nose. "Great!" he grins, and then tosses the clothing over the wall.

He cups his hands together to give Tanaji a leg up. Tanaji is about to object—he should be helping Shahu, he thinks, but Shahu is the stronger man now. Shahu nearly tosses him over the wall. Tanaji reaches back to Shahu. He sees the Bijapuri charging at them.

Shahu scrambles over the wall; Tanaji barely has time to pull his hand back as the nobleman hacks at it with his sword. "Do you know who that is?" Tanaji shouts. Shahu laughs. Again he shakes the sack, letting Tanaji hear the heavy clunk of the gold coins.

The horses are around the back, where Tanaji hid them as a precaution against just this sort of escapade. Shahu hears the whinny of his Bedouin mare. He laughs again, and snatching shoes from the clothes scattered at his feet, runs toward the sound, hopping madly as he slips on his sandals.

Tanaji follows. In a moment he reaches his sturdy Marathi pony and heaves himself on the saddle. Shahu, already mounted on his tall Bedouin mare, grins at Tanaji, and spurs away. Tanaji gallops after him.

They dash through Khirki, twisting through a narrow maze of alleys and walkways. At last they see the West Gate; beyond lies Poona, and in Poona they will be safe. The elephant door of Khirki's West Gate is bolted shut; only the smaller horse door is open, but a guard sits beside it. Tanaji reins in his horse, thinking Shahu will do the same, but Shahu lowers his head and spurs forward with a great shout, galloping through the horse door like thread through a needle. The guard leaps to his feet.

Tanaji sizes up his options. Spurring his pony so fiercely it rears, he races to the gate. He is shorter than Shahu, but wider, so the cloth of his pant legs clips the sides of the door. The guard spins around just in time to see the pony about to run him down; he scrambles away as the pony's hoofs splinter his spear into the dust.

The Bedouin's long strides easily outpace Tanaji's pony with its stubby legs. With each mile, Shahu's mare moves farther into the distance, and with each mile, Tanaji's irritation grows.

◕◔◑◓

Seven miles beyond Khirki he finds Shahu waiting for him by a tall tree near a crossroad. The soft light of dawn filters through the mists, and warms the damp air, painting the horizon with a gleaming silver glow. They have seen no pursuit: no sound of hooves, no clouds of dust. And once they pass these crossroads, any pursuers can't know which way they went.

Tanaji rides up, scowling. "What were you thinking, Shahu! We could have been killed! What the hell were you doing? That was Afzul Khan!"

"What if it was, uncle? He's only a man, and he has things to steal."

"You don't trifle with men like Afzul Khan! What would your father say?"

"How would I know?" Shahu answers. "My father made his choices. Now I make mine."

Tanaji says no more. They turn their horses down the southern road, toward Poona, toward home. The safety of this road, the gentle pace of his pony's stubby legs, the soft light of morning and the scent of flowers and smoke on the breeze combine to calm Tanaji, and to clear his mind.

Promise or no promise, Tanaji again decides that he has finally had it with Shahu. It galls him that Shahu has not only changed his clothes, but has even wound his turban in the tight, complex folds that he prefers. How did he manage that? Tanaji wonders.

Shahu looks fresh, as if their escape had been some fine adventure.

Tanaji looks like he slept in a stable.

What the hell am I doing? he wonders.

CISCIS

By the time they reach the fords of the Godavari, the sun has reached its zenith. Tanaji spurs his pony into the shallows. He looks back to see Shahu's tall Bedouin mare crabbing skittishly along the bank. Shahu reins the mare skillfully, but she won't be calmed. Shahu shortens up her reins, pressing her flanks hard as the mare snorts and whistles.

In the midst of this commotion, Tanaji sees one of Shahu's saddlebags splash into the water, where the current catches it and tumbles it downstream. Alarmed, Tanaji clumsily fishes the bag from the river.

It's the cloth sack Tanaji retrieved from the bedroom, the sack that Shahu waved, laughing with triumph. Tanaji slogs back to Shahu. "Isn't this your money?" he shouts. "Didn't you even notice when it fell?" He shakes the dripping bag under Shahu's nose.

Shahu, trying to calm his horse, answers in a soft voice. "Hold it for me, please, uncle. You're right—I must be more careful."

"You'll never grow up so long as I'm around!" Tanaji slumps back to his pony and ties the wet cloth saddlebag to the horn of his wooden saddle. As he spurs his pony up the steps of the temple ghats on the far bank, he makes up his mind. He is tired of adventures, tired of escapes. Tired of his promise. Enough, he decides, is enough.

He's just about to speak his mind when he turns and looks back. Shahu, dressed in white silk, framed against the misty shadows of the mango trees on the far bank, sits handsome and proud on his elegant mare. The river light glints and sparkles like jewels. Then a flock of river cranes bursts from the water; they soar past like white-winged *asparas*.

Tanaji is not a man with words to tell his feelings. Seeing this he remembers Shahu's stories, the ancient tales where gods are born as men and live among us. And like river cranes rising effortlessly into a cloudless sky, Tanaji's resolution begins to dissolve. This is what always happens: He loves Shahu so much that he can't bear to be parted from him, even if it seems right that he should go.

Once they get to the far bank, they find a quiet grove near a deserted temple. Hobbling their horses and letting them graze, Shahu and Tanaji open their packs and eat, and before long both fall asleep.

Later as they ride west into the glaring sun. Tanaji considers how the gods mock men's intentions. Look at him, he thinks, eyeing Shahu on his prancing mare. I promised his father I'd raise him in the ways of peace. But he was his father's son: once Shahu tasted danger, he craved more, as a drunkard craves wine though it kills him. He is reckless and rash, thinks Tanaji. He's a thief and a fool, and despite Tanaji's efforts, he's going to end up hanging from a tree, his hands cut off and strung around his neck as a warning to others. My promise ruined him, Tanaji thinks.

He spurs his pony to catch up. "We've got to hurry if we want to make Ahmednagar by sundown."

"We're not going to Ahmednagar," Shahu answers. "We're going to that old dharmsala in Pimpalgaon."

"That old place? What for?"

"The Bijapuris are sending some sort of treasure to Surat. The caravan will stay there tonight."

"Is that what the woman told you?" Tanaji takes Shahu's silence for a yes. "Did she say what the treasure was?" This time he takes the silence for a no. "It's not worth it, Shahu. What if it's a trap?" Shahu rides on in silence. "So, what's your plan?"

"Scout things out at the dharmsala. If anything looks promising, catch up with them on the road tomorrow."

Tanaji sighs. "Let's go into town, Shahu. Get a bed and a hot meal."

Shahu turns. "She's probably dead, uncle. Do you think she's dead?"

"Probably. If it was Afzul Khan we saw, probably. He's a killer."

"Then it's the least we can do, uncle."

"That makes no sense!" Tanaji exclaims. But by that time Shahu has spurred his horse to an angry gallop, and is too far away to hear.

۞۞۞۞

As the sun drops in the western sky, they see the green gates of the old dharmsala, and beyond, a glimpse of its quiet courtyard planted with roses, and grapes, and flowering trees. After riding all day, the dust has dried in Tanaji's nostrils; his lips are chapped; his clothing sticks to his skin. The soft breeze, cool and perfumed with the smell of blossoms and water, re-freshes him. He and Shahu coax their tired horses to a trot.

To their left they pass goats and sheep grazing in meadows of dry grass; to their right, green shoots of *bakri*, bright green against the dark earth. The farmers have blocked off their fields into small squares bounded by low walls of soil, lined by trenches for routing water from a wide pond. Outside their low mud huts, the farmers' wives cook chapatis for the evening meal on iron griddles heated by small dung fires. Children, nearly naked, toss rocks and sticks into the branches of the tamarind trees, hoping to knock down the tasty seedpods.

Tanaji and Shahu ride into the dharmsala's serene courtyard, refreshed by the fragrance of flowers and moist, shaded earth. The sun that blazed on their heads all day now drifts, huge and red, behind the cone-shaped hill.

Shahu stretches as he swings from his saddle; his muscled form bends like a young tree. His turban is still tightly wound despite a day's riding. Though dusty, he still looks well groomed: his eyebrows trimmed and neat; his beard shaped and oiled; his cheeks carefully shaved where they peep over the edge of his beard. His tunic and jama robes of ivory-colored damask are simple in design but precise in detail, embroidered with thread of that same fine ivory color; his sandals shine. Even his hands are fine: long-boned fingers and well shaped nails, trimmed precisely. He has that cultivated look that men of action detest, and women notice.

Tanaji grunts as the blood returns to his butt. Making a big show of ignoring Shahu, he loops the reins of each horse over his elbow, and leads them to a watering trough. Tanaji's legs are bowed. His wife can't stop him from dressing like a bachelor. His simple clothes and rolling walk give him an informal, affable air. As the horses drink, Tanaji dips his kerchief in the water and wipes it on his dusty neck.

When the horses have had their fill, he leads them to the dharmsala stables. Tanaji doesn't like dharmsalas—he tries to avoid anything run by the government. But even though most are plain, even uncomfortable, merchants traveling with goods prefer dharmsalas to private inns because they provide safe lodging, guaranteed by the shah.

This dharmsala is one of Ahmednagar's oldest. Once the new road was built, it became a quiet place, frequented only by merchants who appreciated its privacy and beauty. Though more comfortable than most dharmsalas, it still falls to its guests to provide for themselves.

When Tanaji enters the stables he finds a groom caring for some tired horses. The two men nod at each other, wary but polite. After a while they fall into the easy conversation of servants at work away from their masters. Tanaji notices three small dots in a line along the crease of the man's elbow. Probably a caste mark, he thinks, but he doesn't recognize the symbol.

ᘛᘚᘛᘚ

Just as Tanaji is finishing up, Shahu appears in the courtyard, accompanied by the dharmsala's caretaker: a small dark man in cotton jamas that probably were once white. He walks with an exaggerated limp from a short left leg. He talks as he bobs along, trying to keep pace with Shahu's effortless strides. In front of the guesthouse sits a palanquin, and a bored guard rests against a nearby wall, a bare sword across his knees.

Tanaji meets them in the middle of the courtyard, the packs slung across his back and under his arms. Shahu makes no move to help. "You'll be Master Bhisma's servant," the caretaker says. Tanaji blinks at the name but notices Shahu's fierce look and says nothing.

As they walk together, the caretaker chatters on about his miserable life: "Always there are too many guests or none at all, sir. And now here comes this *farang* big shot, and all his guards, I tell you. *Farangs!* You never know with those devils, sir." The caretaker's head bobs between them as they pass the foreigner's guard sitting by the guesthouse door. "Look, sir. An armed guard sitting there just like that, sir! I am appalled to see such a thing in my dharmsala! Who will hurt him at my place, I ask you?"

The caretaker leads them across the courtyard to another building opposite the guest quarters. "The guesthouse is already full," he explains, "and these quarters are reserved for the arrival of government officials."

The special quarters look similar to the guesthouse, but there's no covered verandah, just a slate patio in front. As in the guesthouse, each room has a narrow double door. These doors can be locked on the outside or on the inside, by a bolt that slides from one door to a fastener on the other

The caretaker slides his hip up to the lock so his long key can reach without having to remove the key ring from his belt. The bolt sticks, squeaking noisily, and finally opens with a *bang* that echoes in the empty room. Inside, the rooms are dark and cool. Thick whitewashed walls reach up to a soaring thatched roof with a high window for ventilation; the furnishings: a low wooden bed, and a bedside table with a single oil lamp.

"These rooms, of course, are just the same as the guest quarters across the way," the caretaker says. He ignores Tanaji. "But it is a special building, actually, sir, designed for privacy. Very quiet, sir, away from all the snoring, and only opened for dignitaries so that they can sleep in peace, and also for newlyweds so everyone else can sleep in peace."

"Why didn't you give it to that *farang* big shot, then?" Shahu asks. Don't egg him on, thinks Tanaji.

"I tell you, that fellow is a prick, sir! *Farangs* are not gentlemen, I tell you. They demanded that room on the end. Do I run this dharmsala or not, I ask you, sir? Am I the shah's servant or theirs?"

"Well, I hope they give you something for all your trouble. You may be certain I appreciate your courtesy," Shahu says, handing the man a few coins. "I would be grateful if you could give my servant a room."

"I suppose he might be allowed to sleep in the next room," the caretaker replies, scowling at Tanaji.

After many more compliments and bows, the caretaker at last bobs out of the room. He doesn't look at the coins immediately, but Tanaji can see his fingers in his pocket, testing their heft.

Tanaji sets the saddlebags on the floor. "Who's Master Bhisma?" he asks.

"It's how they know me here," Shahu replies casually. He stretches on the low bed. Its mattress is a thick cotton pad resting on a net of stout ropes. The pad has a musty smell, as though the room had been shut up for too long. "What did you find out?" he asks.

"The groom says they've come from Nagpur. One of the *farangs* rides in that covered palki. He wears a big veil that hangs on his hat. None of the guards have ever seen his face. The other *farangs* never go near the palki. When he takes a shit, the whole caravan must turn its back. The *farangs* keep their pistols out in case anyone wants to take a look."

"Who needs a guard to take a shit?"

Tanaji nods. "Also the guards have too much money—they're over-paid. You're sure this is the right caravan?"

"Yes. And the caretaker told me they'd paid with gold. Did you hear anything about the cargo?"

"Sure, I heard. The groom said they're carrying prayer rugs to Surat. A groom, four guards, a captain, and three *farangs,* all for prayer rugs."

"They must be impressive rugs," Shahu says. "What do you think?"

"Jewels, probably. There's no indication they've got anything heavy."

Shahu looks pleased. "Fine. Easy for us to steal. We'll get a good sleep, leave early, and waylay them on the other side of town tomorrow morning." Tanaji nods. "Did you learn anything else, uncle?"

"I've learned your bags are too damned heavy. I'm sick of carrying them. Maybe I should be the master again." As Tanaji complains, Shahu takes his bedroll and flips it onto the bed. The roll opens to reveal a fierce-looking sword that Shahu quickly hides beneath the bedclothes. "Don't wear your weapons here. Keep them hidden tonight," he says quietly to Tanaji. Shahu looks at Tanaji's expression and adds, "I mean it."

"Why?" asks Tanaji, annoyed. Shahu looks at him but says nothing. For Tanaji, these unexplained orders are one of the more unpleasant aspects of his recent life with Shahu. He remembers the old days, when he gave the orders. "Then if you have nothing further for me, sir, I'll go to my own room now, sir, if you don't mind, sir."

"Keep your mace under your blanket," Shahu insists.

"All right, all right," Tanaji replies. "Don't forget: that mace has saved your life more than once." He drags his bags outside, to the room next door.

Shahu closes the door. By the dim light of the high windows, Shahu examines his sword. The blade of dark steel has been sharpened until the razor edge glistens like a bright silver thread.

There are many kinds of sword blade, each suited to a particular style of fighting, a particular temperament: blades narrow, long and flexible, with a needle-sharp point for stabbing from a distance; heavy, moon-shaped blades with a sweeping edge, designed for a rider to hack from above; blades thick and deep, like an elongated ax head.

The blade that whispers beneath Shahu's thumbnail, however, is narrow, light, sharpened to glide smoothly through flesh and sinew. Every blade has drawbacks; this blade will snap if caught in live bone; the steel, designed for sharpness, is brittle. But for close-quarter fighting, for speed and quiet action, no blade could compare.

Hearing a knock, Shahu sheathes the sword and secretes it beneath his bedroll, then swings back the inner bolt to open the door. It's the caretaker bringing pitchers of fresh water. As he places the pitcher on the bed table, Shahu asks casually about the guarded room. "I think that *farang* bastard may be sick," the caretaker says. "I think maybe leprosy."

Shahu straightens up, looking shocked. The caretaker's face is shocked as well. Having said the words aloud, they no longer seem unreasonable to him; suddenly the caretaker thinks he may be right. "No one has seen him. He came in a closed palanquin. He ducked straight into his room. He was covered from top to toe—you couldn't see his face, his hands, nothing. He wore one of those big hats—you know the kind *farangs* wear, sir, like a tray on the head? A veil on the brim—it looked like a big black sack over his head."

They agree that it's all very strange, and not like the old days. The caretaker limps to Tanaji's room with the other pitcher.

Shahu takes up a towel and goes to the nearby well for a wash. Tanaji is already there bathing. "I don't like it if he's a leper," Tanaji mutters as Shahu shares the news. "You can never go wrong keeping a big distance from a leper, that's my view."

"Fine," Shahu says gently. "Then keep an eye on his guards and see what they're up to. If he's a leper, they'll know."

"You don't believe it?"

"Look at those guards—do they seem worried?" Shahu dries his face. "We'll stick to my plan, leper or no."

The first bell of evening begins to ring and they head for the common area near the courtyard verandah. Shahu takes long, easy strides, and Tanaji must bustle on his stumpy legs just to keep up.

Among the blossoming bowers of roses, cloths and cushions have been set on the ground, where the guests of the dharmsala are gathering for supper. As they approach the courtyard, Tanaji and Shahu see two *farangs* in their bizarre costumes seated there.

Tanaji and Shahu find seats, trying not to stare at the foreigners, who sit on wooden chairs and talk among themselves. *Farangs* are still so few, so unusual, that they have a compelling novelty; it is all too easy to stare.

The guards, some of whom are playing cards, nod casually at the two new arrivals. From their belts hang swords, knives, and punch daggers. The *farangs* carry long straight swords and pistols tucked into their belts.

One of the *farangs* notices Tanaji eyeing his pistols. "Ever fired a *pistola*, captain?" he asks in heavily accented Marathi. Tanaji is too shocked to be addressed by a *farang* even to reply. The *farang* laughs, and then leans back, poking the other *farang* in the arm, and they laugh together. Something about their laughter perturbs Tanaji.

"I am a Portuguese," the *farang* says proudly. "My *farang* name is"—here he says some blather of syllables—"but my Hindi friends call me Deoga." He nods to Shahu. "You must be Master Bhisma."

Shahu *namskars* politely, folding his hands and bowing his head. Deoga *namskars* in reply. Then he pushes his hand forward as if reaching for Shahu. "This is how we greet each other as *farangs,*" he explains, grasping Shahu's hand and swinging it up and down. "There now, we've met properly." The guards are clearly amused.

"My friend is an English," Deoga continues, pointing to the other *farang*. "His name is Onil. You want to greet Onil?" Shahu finally understands, and with some trepidation, pushes his hand forward.

"Other hand, captain," Deoga whispers.

With a pleasant smile, Onil takes Shahu's hand in his and squeezes it while moving it up and down. It is not so unpleasant when Onil does it.

Tanaji examines the *farangs*. They're about the same age, and bigger than most Hindis, more dense and fleshy. Both wear loose white shirts, dark sleeveless tunics fastened by small silver disks, dark trousers that cling tightly to their legs, fastened along the outside edge with disks of bone, and heavy boots that come up to their knees. Tanaji imagines they would be very difficult to walk in. Deoga's hair is dark brown, but Onil's is that odd coppery-golden color that some *farangs* have, and he has the ghostly blue eyes that go with it. Both have beards and pale, pasty skin, and Onil's skin is blotchy with small orange patches and lumps.

But Tanaji senses something else in these men, an agitated air that clings to them like an odor. Deoga impresses Tanaji as a typical *farang*: open, loutish, overbearing, pushy. He acts as if he doesn't realize how loud he talks, or doesn't care. Onil, on the other hand, seems careful, reserved. He hangs back at every moment, watching, waiting, considering his next move. Tanaji doesn't trust him.

Shahu returns to his seat near Tanaji, looking relieved to put some space between himself and the *farangs*. The guards chuckle; it's clear they think the *farangs* are a fine joke.

At that moment the caravan captain walks up, looking very ill humored. "All right boys," he says, "eat up. Then draw lots for watch. First watch starts in an hour. Questions? None? Good."

Tanaji approves of his style: quick and direct, the captain acts like a professional. Like all good captains, he strides off confidently the moment he stops speaking, his orders still ringing in the air, hoping to give his men the impression that the orders came from God's own voice, and those with questions or doubts are fools.

The caretaker, meanwhile, limps to the gate of the dharmsala. Two bars of iron hang from a tree near the gate; he vigorously strikes one against the other, setting up a terrific *clang*.

As the ringing fades, his thin voice shouts the official formula, "In the name of Allah the Munificent and his excellence the Nizam Shah of Ahmednagar, may he live forever, the gates of this dharmsala are about to close." With these words, he swings shut the iron gates with a *boom*. Then he resumes shouting, "Let all who remain sleep in peace! Look to your possessions!" With that the caretaker locks the gate with a long iron lock. This ritual over, life in the courtyard returns to normal.

While they argue over their watch assignments, the guards are cooking vegetables in big iron pots. The hot oil and smoky spices fill the air with fragrance. The *farangs* are talking, sounding to Tanaji like bleating goats.

As he stretches his arm, Tanaji notices three black dots in the crease of his elbow.

One of the guards is laying out banana leaves. Soon warm and fragrant food has been piled on each of the leaves. As if at a silent signal, the guards move to seat themselves; Shahu and the *farangs* come when Tanaji calls them to eat.

As he takes his place, Shahu glances over to the guarded door of the missing *farang*. Tanaji leans over to Shahu. "He has to come out sometime. Even if he doesn't eat, he's got to pee."

"I wonder." He glances at the *farangs,* who have left their wooden chairs to sit politely on the seating cloths set on the ground. Their stiff knees jut up into the air. Deoga uses his knife to probe at the vegetables he has been given; Onil uses his right hand like a civilized person, but is as clumsy as a child. Bits of food fall on his shirt just as his fingers reach his lips. The guards snigger.

The captain dispatches a guard to bring food to the missing *farang*. "Have you boys got your schedule all set?" he asks brusquely, eating with quick motions. "All right. First watch in five minutes. No complaints!"

The skies now are nearly dark: the last rosy glow of the setting sun has faded, and the crescent moon won't rise until it's nearly dawn.

"You expect trouble, captain?" Deoga asks. He has lifted the banana leaf and shovels the food into his mouth.

"Maybe," he replies. "There are many robbers in these hills."

The caretaker limps up. "Robbers indeed," he sputters. "This dharmsala has never been robbed!"

"A first time for everything," the captain replies. "You've got about ten bands of robbers in a thirty-mile radius of here. But most of them won't bother us. We only need to worry about three: Kalidas, Shivaji, and Chandbibi. The rest are lazy scum. But those three show some initiative, and initiative is what you don't want in your robbers."

"No thief would dare enter this dharmsala!" the caretaker says.

"Better too careful, than not careful enough," the dark *farang* says. "What concerns you about those three?"

The captain seems pleased by the *farang*'s question. "First, Kalidas. He is crazy. The crescent moon tonight is sacred to his goddess Kali. He has been quiet lately. I'd bet his men are getting restless.

"Next, Shivaji. Mostly he works the roads west of here. Attacking a dharmsala isn't Shivaji's style. He prefers the open road, but he likes surprise. So maybe he'll surprise us. But he's a coward—so if the guards stay awake, he'll never come near. Still, men get weary, you know? Sometimes they're paid to fall asleep.

"Last, Chandbibi. She could charm her way in here and never spill a drop of blood. Our guards have been away from their women too long. Let Chandbibi show a bit of thigh, and so much for discipline." His eyes sparkle. "She has excellent thighs," he adds, as if remembering.

"Most caravans are robbed by their own guards," Shahu says. The captain responds with an icy stare. "So if there's anyone to fear, captain, I'd say it's your men. Or you." The captain's hand moves slowly toward his sword. Shahu, unarmed, stares back, stone still. The fire crackles.

Finally Deoga laughs. "God, you Hindis would murder each other over a penny!" He leans forward. "By God, captain, let's not fight!" But no one speaks, and Shahu and the captain do not break their stare.

Then the caretaker pipes up loudly, "Sri Bhisma is a storyteller! Maybe you can tell us a story, sir?"

The *farang* forces another booming laugh, but his eyes are stern. "Yes, captain, tell us a story! Only go slow or my friend won't know what you are saying." He nods to Onil, who smiles politely, uncertain of the joke.

"All right," Shahu says. "What shall I tell?"

"Tell us the story of Shivaji," the captain says coldly. "You're from his part of the country, I think."

"Suppose instead I tell you the story of Shivaji's grandfather," Shahu replies. "That story is more interesting. It so happened that a poor farmer called Maloji lived in a village called Khed."

"Maloji had been plowing one day when a glittering green snake coiled at his feet, looked up at him with golden eyes, and then slithered down into a nearby hole, like a rope of emeralds. The next day, from that same hole, Maloji saw a woman's hand emerge, green as a shoot of *bakri,* long and graceful as a snake, the hand of a goddess living in the the soil, beckoning, beckoning.

"He dug where the goddess showed him: deeper, deeper, deep as a well, a well so deep he could not see the sky, but found nothing. Exhausted, miserable, about to give up, he suddenly found, wrapped in a snake-green cloth, a treasure: a trove of weapons and gold.

"Maloji took these blessings, put on armor and bought a horse. Risking all, he rode fully armed to the court of the Nizam Shah of Ahmednagar. The Nizam Shah, impressed by his audacity, made him a *mandsabdar* of a thousand men and a hundred horses.

"Maloji used his wealth to build an army: the bravest men and the strongest horses the shah had ever seen. He rode at the vanguard of the shah's battles, gaining glory.

"Maloji then sought a wife for his only son, Shahji: One day he rode into the midst of the *swayamvara* of a princess, and in the face of all her suitors hauled her on his horse, and rode away.

"When the kidnapped princess saw Shahji, her intended groom, she fell in love at once and married him and they lived in joy. The Nizam Shah gave the newlyweds a glorious kingdom, if Maloji could conquer it. So Maloji led his army, and took those lands. With those battles the Sultan of Bijapur became Maloji's enemy forever, and his son Shahji's enemy as well."

"Wait, no more!" interrupts the captain. "Bijapur was Shahji's savior, not his enemy!" He grows agitated. "When Shahji couldn't beat old Wagnak, he ran to Bijapur to hide. On his knees, like a woman! Shahji begged for Bijapur to save him."

The captain frowns at Shahu. "That farmer Maloji was tough—a real man. Took what he wanted. Chewed up his enemies and spat out the bones. Not like his son. The blood was weak in Shahji. Wagnak pushed him and he collapsed. So the Bijapuris made him a deal: just give us everything. Shahji so feared Wagnak that he surrendered all his lands, the coward."

"Who is Wagnak?" asks the dark *farang.*

"The name means 'tiger claws'. It's the Marathi name for Aurangzeb," the captain answers.

"You mean Viceroy Aurangzeb? The emperor's son? Why call him that?"

The captain spits. "Aurangzeb—Wagnak—what's the difference? He was the best general I've ever seen. I mean the worst. His attacks were like the mouth of hell." The captain stares at the fire, as if ghosts surround him. "Not long ago, these lands were stained red. The coward Shahji couldn't face Wagnak. He lost and lost, and then he ran and ran, the shit."

"That's not true," Tanaji breaks in. "Shahji was a hero. He fought well—he had the Moguls on the run."

"Shahji just sat in his fort and let his armies bleed," the captain fires back. "And I should know. I was one who bled.

"A real man would have died fighting. All those forts! The trade routes to the sea! They all were Shahji's. A real man would have attacked. But Shahji ran, throwing everything away, his forts, his lands. His men, abandoned in battle, dying and bleeding. But maybe you already know this." The captain turns to the *farang*, nodding toward Tanaji, "I think maybe this man is a Malve. Malves thought Shahji's shit didn't stink." He fixes his eyes on Tanaji. "A Malve would suck Shahji's prick like a eunuch."

Tanaji's black eyes blaze. But Shahu reaches out a hand to Tanaji's shoulder.

The captain turns away, and now faces the *farang*. "Shahji got a sweet deal, all right. He got rich, got a place at the Bijapuri court, and a nice new wife, soft, young and tight as a glove. All this for running away. So he gives up his army! So what? And his forts! So what? And also his wife. So what? She was God's own bitch! And to top it off, his own child, his little rat-boy son"—the captain pretends he's still talking to the *farang*—"he gave up his only son so he could live like a *padshah* in Bijapur. The wife gets shit and the brat gets shit. So what? It's only his wife! It's only his son! Why, any damned Malve would sell his wife and son for a couple of annas!"

"But this sounds like too much, captain!" the Deoga protests. "Why do they offer him so much?"

"Don't you see? Those forts . . . Shahji's forts . . . They were like gold to Bijapur! Add Shahji's forts to Bijapur's and they form an unbroken line: they cover every mountain pass to the coast. What made Bijapur so rich? It's because every ounce of ocean trade must cross through Bijapur. Think of the taxes! Even a haji on his way to Mecca must pay his toll to Bijapur! So Bijapur threw the coward a bone, and Shahji, the dog, licked their hands."

"You're telling lies!" Tanaji blurts out. "Shahji was no coward. He saw he couldn't beat the Moguls. He'd sacrificed too many men already. So he allied with Bijapur . . . That's leadership, not cowardice! And he's a commander for Bijapur now—their best general!"

The captain smirks. "He left his wife and son in a garbage dump, where nothing prowled but wolves. That's your man, sir. I spit on a man with no honor. No wonder his son Shivaji is a thief: What else should become of that dog's pup, stuck in a hole like Poona with no one but his mother for comfort, and her a queen bitch?"

The captain bows to Shahu. "I apologize, storyteller. You touched a nerve. I never knew Maloji, but I knew Shahji, the shit. Sorry if I disturbed your story." He strides off.

A long quiet moment follows. Finally the caretaker speaks: "It was here, you know. In this dharmsala Shahji signed his treaty with Bijapur. He stood right there." The caretaker nods to a spot a few yards away. "Wali Khan stood there beside him," the caretaker whispers. "Many other nobles, too. And that monster, Afzul Khan. Do you know him, sir?"

"We ran into him last night," Tanaji mutters. "Sri Bhisma stole his gold."

The caretaker grins. "Your servant likes jokes, I see. Anyway, I thought it was a good story, sir," he says. "I always like your stories, sir."

"You can't please everyone; a storyteller learns that early on." The caretaker lights a couple of tapers, and Shahu and Tanaji head for their rooms.

"Why did you tell that story?" Tanaji grumbles. "Anyway, you know it's a lie."

"It just occurred to me to tell it. And it is half-true."

"Which half?" Tanaji replies.

Around them, night birds are calling; bat wings glint in the firelight. Shahu looks around the courtyard of the dharmsala warily. "You know that mark? The three dots? The captain's got that mark," he whispers.

"You're sure? The one cooking the vegetables had dots, too." Tanaji strokes his mustache. "What do you think is going on?"

"I don't know. But I'm not sleeping tonight. Something's up."

Tanaji considers this. "Wake me at midnight. We'll split the watch."

CHAPTER 6

❧❧❧❧

From his travel roll Tanaji takes his battle mace—a weapon of steel, roughly the size and shape of a sword, and with a hilt and a handle like a sword: a weighted, clublike bludgeon welded to its end, forged with knife-like edges. Tanaji's mace is brutally simple: It swings with the speed of a sword, splintering bone and flesh; if extra damage is needed, a quick twist of the bludgeon mangles the wound into a bloody crater. This weapon suits Tanaji's style; he hurtles into battle, screaming his war cry.

Tanaji places his mace at the bottom of the bed, settles himself on the bed fully dressed, and slips into a soldier's easy sleep.

After what seems like only a moment, he bolts up, blinking in the guttering light of the oil lamp. His room echoes with a huge *bang*. It takes him a moment to realize what the sound means.

His door has been bolted—from the outside.

He hears Shahu yelling through the thick walls. "I'm locked in!" He hears cries outside, and the ring of steel on steel. That sound awakens him fully. He seizes his mace and lurches from the bed. He shakes the door, but it holds fast. "Hang on, Shahu! I'm coming!" he yells through the walls.

Tanaji kicks the door. Nothing. Through the wall he hears Shahu trying the same thing. He slams his mace against one of the door panels. It shivers encouragingly. Again he pounds it, and again. Splinters fly.

With a few more blows he has banged a hole big enough for his arm and shoulder to push through. He stretches, fumbling for the outside bolt, feeling with his fingers. The door is only bolted shut, not padlocked. His fingers claw at the bolt. He manages to slide it, and the door pops open—but now he can't free his arm from the hole he has made.

One of the caravan guards races straight toward him, brandishing a sword. His arm still trapped in the door, Tanaji swings his mace wildly and deflects the blade, which drives into the door just inches from Tanaji's head. The force of the blow swings the door outward and Tanaji—still stuck—with it.

Now they struggle: Tanaji trying to release his arm even as the guard tries to tug his sword free. The door jerks back and forth with their efforts. Tanaji swings his mace wildly: the guard lurches away so violenty he stumbles to the ground, his sword still stuck in the door.

Ignoring the pain, Tanaji jerks his arm from the splintered door. The guard scrambles to his feet, a punch dagger in his hand. Tanaji swings, but the bludgeon misses, heaving past an inch short of the guard's nose.

The guard's face displays that strange expression of terror and delight seen only in battle, the astonishment of a man who has seen death miss by inches. He stares at Tanaji, too shocked to move.

Calmly, Tanaji swings the mace backward with both hands.

The guard's face explodes as the bludgeon tears off his jaw.

A gurgling scream rises from what used to be a mouth. The guard clutches his head, choking as blood pours into his throat. He's drowning: with his jaw gone, the blood pours from his broken face, down his throat, over his naked tongue, through his clutching fingers, soaking his sleeves.

Tanaji turns away as if the guard no longer existed. The evening campfire is roaring, about twenty feet away: someone has poured oil on it so its flames leap shoulder high. The dark *farang* circles the firepit holding two men at bay: the captain and another guard. Stabbing over the flames, the *farang* has his hands full. Across the courtyard, Tanaji can make out the other *farang*, swinging his sword against an opponent that Tanaji can't see.

Tanaji reaches Shahu's door, and slides the outer bolt.

Shahu bursts out, sword in hand, eyes full of fire. "What's going on?"

"That man," he says, pointing to the guard who now is writhing incoherently a few feet away, "attacked me."

"It's a double cross," Shahu concludes. "The guards locked us in. They're ambushing the *farangs*, and they wanted us out of the way."

"So, whose side are we on?" Tanaji asks.

"The *farangs*," Shahu replies.

"Damn," Tanaji snorts. "In that case we've got our work cut out. I'll take the fire; you take the guesthouse," Figuring the captain for the toughest of the lot, Tanaji hopes to give Shahu the easier part.

Shahu sprints toward the guesthouse. As he moves to the fire, Tanaji does the arithmetic. There's the captain, also four guards. On their side, two *farangs* (three if the leper is strong enough to fight), and now him and Shahu. He's knocked off one guard. So now it's a fair fight, he thinks—two against two at the fire; two against two at the guesthouse.

But Tanaji has miscalculated. He hears a thin voice screeching to his right, and sees the caretaker carrying a spear so large he can barely lift it. Rising and falling as he runs with his one short leg, the spear bounces every which way. Tanaji crouches, gauging his situation. He doesn't want to kill an old lame man. Instead, as the caretaker comes in range, Tanaji deflects the spear with his mace. But it all goes wrong: the caretaker stumbles and buries the point of the spear into the ground; the shaft slams against his body in mid-stride. He lurches forward, past Tanaji, past the *farang*, and with a thin scream, stumbles into the flames.

The old man struggles to his feet, reaching out with a flaming arm. Oil has soaked his clothes: His pants are burning, his shirt. The caretaker's screams grow shrill as the stink of his burning hair and flesh fills the air.

A movement to his side makes Tanaji realize that he has miscounted again: He has forgotten the groom who is now running straight for the *farang*, silent except for the padding of his bare feet, his sword raised. Only Tanaji sees him coming—the others have stopped their fight to stare at the caretaker—but the groom, apparently expecting Tanaji to be locked harmlessly in his room, doesn't notice him.

The groom's sword is a few inches from the *farang*'s head when Tanaji's bludgeon catches him in the spine. The force is so great the groom is lifted from his feet, his sword flying into the air like a child's toy. He collapses at the *farang*'s feet, his torso twisted around his broken back.

Tanaji sees the sword glinting in the firelight, flipping end over end; then it falls, whirling through the air. By the time he figures out what's about to happen, Tanaji can't even speak. He watches open-mouthed and helpless as the sword, glittering like one of Indra's lightning bolts, hits the *farang*'s right shoulder, and slices through his arm. The *farang* screams and drops to his knees, grabbing at his shoulder as if he might somehow reattach his arm, while dark blood stains his white shirt.

But now the captain and the guard have seen Tanaji. They ignore the *farang* whimpering by the fire, the caretaker collapsing in flames: their eyes narrowed like wolves', they shuffle toward Tanaji, swords waving in lazy circles. Now they are only a few feet away, close enough to strike.

Unequal odds frighten Tanaji. He knows that it is his nature only to think of one thing at a time; two opponents place him at a disadvantage. So he attacks. Taking his punch dagger in his left hand, he knocks at the point of one sword, then the other, *clang, clang,* just so. The men step back, but keep close together. Tanaji lunges at the captain with his dagger. The captain leaps away. Then Tanaji drives the mace toward the guard; he moves just enough to dodge the blow. But now, at least, they are apart.

Then Tanaji senses the captain behind him and he turns to see his death descending—the captain's sword swinging in a long, horrible arc.

Tanaji pays no attention to the sword. Instead he looks into the face of his death: the captain's face, with eyes as black and hot as a jackal's.

Tanaji now sees every whisker, every pore. He cannot move, not even when he hears the blade whistle toward his head like a black wind. He wonders how his head will feel when the cap of his skull spirals into the darkness, when the cold night air whispers over the wet surface of his exposed brain. He hopes it will not take too long to die. And all the while he thinks these thoughts, he stares at the solemn beauty of these last sights: the languid dance of a string of spittle slipping from the captain's lips; the yellow teeth licked by his coated tongue.

Then some magic begins: Tanaji watches enchanted as a small dot appears on the captain's forehead, just over the right eye. From this dot a rose begins to blossom.

The captain seems puzzled to discover that a flower would burst from his head. His head snaps sideways in surprise, and twists on his neck, like a broken puppet's. As Tanaji watches fascinated, the captain's sword whispers harmless past his ear, falling from the captain's hand. He watches the captain drop like a cut tree, his body landing heavily on the ground.

The captain spasms and shivers, and then stops forever. Tanaji pushes himself to his feet. Behind him he sees what has saved him: the *farang* struggling for breath; in his left hand, a smoking *pistola.*

I'll think about that later, Tanaji decides, and turns his mace on the guard. He doesn't have time to aim, but with a mace that doesn't matter. The bludgeon clips the guard on the hip and before the guard has finished spinning, Tanaji has swung again and splintered his skull.

Without a look behind him, Tanaji now walks toward the guesthouse, panting from the exertion of his killing. When he reaches the verandah, he can hear shouting and the *clang* of steel but can't find where it comes from.

"Inside," whispers a voice from below him. It is the other *farang*, the spotty one, collapsed beneath the body of a guard, barely alive. The *farang* nods weakly toward the door of the leper.

Despite his fear of disease, Tanaji kicks open the door and bursts in, ready to kill or die. Within he finds Shahu and the last living guard stepping in cautious circles, facing each other in the tight space between the bed and the wall. On the low bed Tanaji sees the *farang* leper still wearing the wide-brimmed hat and dark veil that the caretaker described. The *farang* is squeezed against the wall with fright, head buried between his drawn-up knees.

The guard tries a feint and then a lunge, but the space is too small; his blows glance against the wall and Shahu steps calmly away. Tanaji assumes that the guard is more of a chopper than a swordsman. In this small space he's at a disadvantage. But Shahu is a fencer; it's a pleasure to watch him feint and dodge.

The guard looks up to see Tanaji, and his face falls. What does it mean that he stands alone against two men—men thought to be harmless, to be locked safely in their rooms? Where are his friends? Why doesn't anyone come to help him? The more he considers, the more his face tightens. "Put down your weapon and live," says Shahu quietly.

"Look, your friends are all dead," Tanaji tells the guard, as if trying to be helpful. "There's no need to join them."

The guard looks from Shahu to Tanaji. Suddenly resolution appears in his eyes, and he leaps up onto the low table by the bed. The oil lamp clatters down, and spilled oil slides across the floor. Soon a ribbon of black smoke rises from the flame that dances along its surface.

The guard brings his sword-edge at the neck of the *farang*. "Let me go or I kill him," he says.

"Go ahead and kill him," answers Tanaji. "What the hell do I care? Put the damned leper out of his misery."

The guard's eyes flick from Tanaji to Shahu; the point of his sword traces small erratic circles near the *farang*'s ear. Flames ripple on the surface of the lamp's spilled oil. The *farang* seems too terrified to move.

Suddenly Shahu thrusts. His blade whips the air, but the guard is just out of reach. With sudden agility the guard swivels away from the point of Shahu's sword.

Shahu had planned for his sword to hit solid flesh, but instead it sails through thin air, pulling him off balance. He pitches forward and the sword point digs into the wall; his full weight falls onto it, and the blade snaps. The point clatters to the floor beside the bed.

Shahu holds the rest shattered in his hand.

Tanaji realizes he needs to help, but the room is too small for him to swing his mace. He considers his punch dagger, but Shahu stands between him and the guard, and there's no way to squeeze through.

The flames from the oil lamp lick the far wall; the room fills with damp smoke.

Time in the room stands still. Here is the guard, on the table, wild with terror, sword in hand, flames inches from his feet. Here is Shahu with a pitiful, broken sword, as if guarding the *farang*. There is Tanaji, uncertain of how to proceed. Nothing can be done, so nothing is done.

Then Shahu takes a fearsome lunge. Perhaps he slips on the spilled oil: his feet slide out from beneath him and he crashes to the floor.

The movement triggers the guard and he leaps over Shahu with a shout, swinging his sword at Tanaji, who blocks the door. Tanaji raises his punch dagger in front of his face to ward off the guard's sword blow. The guard collides into him, and they collapse to the floor. Tanaji lies under the guard, his right arm pinned beneath him, his fingers pinched on the grip of his now useless mace. The guard lifts himself, pressing his forearm across Tanaji's windpipe. He looks around while Tanaji squirms beneath him gasping for breath.

Then the guard's head snaps back. Blood bubbles from his mouth. His sword drops harmlessly beside him. Blood pours into Tanaji's face and eyes, blinding him. He feels the body of the guard roll away, and he wipes his eyes with the back of his hand. Shahu stands over him, offering him a hand up. Beside him is the guard, the hilt of Shahu's broken sword thrust into the back of his neck, right below the skull.

Tanaji gets up with Shahu's help. The walls are burning. They dash through the door when Shahu looks behind him and curses. Then he runs back into the room.

"He's a leper!" shouts Tanaji. "Leave him!"

His foot bumps into the confused pile of bodies outside the door. There is the *farang* he took for dead, still pinned beneath the body of one of the guards. As Shahu and the veiled *farang* emerge coughing from the burning room, Tanaji heaves the body from the *farang*.

Onil, the light-haired *farang*, smiles wanly. A deep gash bleeds across his chest. "Where other man?" the *farang* whispers. He raises his eyes to see the veiled *farang* next to Shahu; then his head pitches forward.

The veiled *farang* starts to cough, a high, sick-sounding hacking that won't stop. Shahu watches the *farang* for a moment, and gives up, turning instead to Onil who is at least capable of speech. "Listen to me," Shahu shouts. He pulls Onil's head back roughly and pull his face up close. "Listen! Your treasure! Where is it?" Onil shakes his head. "Damn you, listen!" Shahu insists. "Where is the treasure? The building is burning and we don't have much time!"

"No treasure, no treasure . . . ," Onil says, listlessly.

"Of course there's treasure. Everyone is dead, do you hear? Your treasure is still here!"

Onil points to the veiled *farang*. "She has treasure," he whispers. Then he shakes his head. "No! No! I say wrong!"

Shahu points to the veiled *farang*. "Do you mean, he has the treasure?"

"No," says Onil, struggling for the words. "Mean, she is treasure." He smiles as if satisfied and then his head flops forward.

Shahu feels and finds a pulse. "What does that mean?" Tanaji asks him.

The other *farang*, who has at last stopped coughing, throws back the veil that has covered his face. Only, of course, it isn't his face, it is her face. And she is no *farang*; her face is beautiful and fierce, with kohl-stained eyes and dark lips. And now they both realize what they knew all the time. Of course it was a woman. Now it all makes sense.

Shahu stares at her for a only a moment, then returns to his question as if unaffected by her beauty. "What about the treasure?"

Her voice is soft but powerful. "I am the treasure. I am a nautch girl sent by the court of Bijapur to Viceroy Murad of the Moguls. My worth is more than gold, or so they say. Such is the price of desire." The thick dark hair hidden beneath the hat has spilled to her waist, framing a face that is golden in the flames. With dark eyes blazing, she faces Shahu. "My nautch name is Maya. And you, who stole me from these flames where I had hoped to die, what is your name?"

He stands before he addresses her. "My name," he answers, "is Shivaji."

CHAPTER 7

☙☙☙☙

Tanaji recovers his wits. The fire is spreading—flames leap from the thick, low-hanging smoke and lick the outer walls, a fire too large to be put out by the two of them. In a few minutes the dharmsala will be engulfed. The *farang* Onil is unconscious, breathing steadily and deeply. The woman Maya looks calm, but it won't be long before she realizes that she's standing in a pile of corpses. Shivaji is standing, but breathing hard.

Tanaji's clothes are wet with the blood of dead men. The smell sickens him and he hurries to a trough near the stable. In the flickering firelight, the blood that washes off looks dark and oily. He wipes his face with his kerchief and then drops it, disgusted. Meanwhile Shivaji brings their horses from the stables: they toss their heads and try to pull away from the fire. Tanaji goes to lend a hand and make a plan. Shivaji ties Tanaji's pony next to his own Bedouin mare. "We've got to get out of here," says Shivaji.

"Right. That fire is going to attract some attention. There's a lot of dead men around. We better move quickly." Tanaji nods to the girl. "She comes with us. Anyone who isn't dead comes with us."

Shivaji nods. "How many horses do we need?"

"You, me, the girl. Three. What about the *farang*?" Tanaji gestures with his chin to Onil. "Will he live?"

"Maybe. What about the others?" he asks. "What about the guards?"

Tanaji shakes his head. "So. Four horses. You get them saddled. Set the rest free before they burn. I'll scavenge what I can." Taking up his mace, he strides back to the courtyard. The ghostly light of the flames gives the scene a nightmarish air. He hurries to his room, past the splintered door, trying to avoid puddles of oozing blood. He shoves his few belongings into his bag. Next door he does the same with Shivaji's.

But he can't bring himself to do the neccessary.

Come on—you've seen worse, he tells himself as he heads back to the courtyard. It's hard work, though, even for a hard man. Ignoring the twisted bodies, the burning flesh, the blood and brains splashed on the dust, he pats the pockets of the dead men, slipping what he finds into his pack.

As he walks past the ashes of the caretaker's burned body, he remembers something. He pats the body, feeling the charred skin crackle beneath his palm. Nothing. Then he draws his hands through the dust nearby: at last he finds the iron ring of keys.

"Captain, captain," one of the corpses moans. Tanaji leaps to his feet, mace ready. It's the *farang* Deoga; pale and dying. "I'm thirsty."

Tanaji forces himself to come closer. "You're dying," he tells the *farang*. "Water will only make it worse."

The captain closes his eyes and nods. "Listen, captain," he gasps. "I'm sorry for all the very bad things I have done ever."

Tanaji scowls at him. "Die like a man." He smells the rusty odor of warm blood dripping into the dust and aches to get away.

"Take my purse, captain. Give my money to the poor. Do a favor, captain. You owe me."

Tied around the *farang*'s neck, Tanaji finds the purse, soft yellow leather. Hanging from the same cord is a *farang murti*: a small dark sculpture of a man in a lungi, his arms and legs tacked to a thin cross. Tanaji cuts the cord with the edge of his dagger. He lays the *murti* gently on the *farang*'s gurgling chest; the purse he places in one of his pockets.

Without looking back, he leaves the *farang* to die.

By the time Tanaji returns, the whole guesthouse is in flames. Oily smoke spreads like fog around his feet. He hurries over to Onil, for the fire is moving toward him, and pulls him away from the fire.

"Wait," Onil gasps, choking in the smoky haze around him. "Help up, please." With Tanaji's help, Onil struggles to the horses. Tanaji can hear Shivaji in the stables. The woman is nowhere to be seen.

"Let's have a look," Tanaji says, trying to appear unconcerned. He peels back Onil's shirt: the damage is less horrible than it might be—a heavy, ragged cut across the chest down to the belly, bleeding but already scabbing over in places. Onil too has a silver pendant dangling from a string around his neck: the image of a goddess, maybe.

Tanaji goes to the watchfire and takes two handfuls of cold ashes from the edge. He comes back and rubs the ashes hard along the wound, forcing them into the cut. Onil grimaces, but makes no sound.

"That will only make it worse." Maya has come up behind him.

"Is that stuff yours?" Tanaji replies.

"I'm a slave," she answers. "I own nothing."

"It's hers," interrupts Shivaji, coming from the stables with two more saddled horses. Maya glares at him defiantly.

Tanaji reaches into his bag. He twists one of his shirts into a long roll that he presses against the cut. "Hold this," he tells Onil, Then he ties their bags to the horses Shivaji has saddled. He strokes each horse after he has done, and they calm beneath his soothing hand. The other horses, released by Shivaji, trot around the courtyard nervously whinnying.

"Mount up," he tells the woman.

"Ride that horse—by myself?" She laughs. She has a cold laugh that cuts through Tanaji like a poison. Taking her by the waist, he heaves her on the back of one of the Bedouins.

She is feather light—far too light for all the force he used. He didn't need to be so harsh—but, after all, in those *farang* man's clothes, who could tell she was so delicate? She must be very young, he realizes. His empty hands still feel her waist; it felt vibrant when he lifted her. He chides himself: bad manners, lifting her like that. But she doesn't curse him as he deserves; she just sits fiercely silent atop that big horse.

"Time you learned to ride by yourself," Tanaji snaps. He shortens the stirrups and puts her feet in them. She wears women's slippers; inside them, her feet are round, smooth, like a child's feet.

Tanaji scolds himself for getting distracted. This woman, he realizes, is provocative. They are going to have their hands full. Oh yes.

Tanaji wraps Maya's fingers around the reins. "Pull like this for left, like this for right. Pull like this to stop."

She snatches the reins from his hands. "But how do I make it go?"

"Squeeze your legs and rub his flanks with your heels," he answers, more gruffly than necessary. He can still feel where she placed her fingers on his rough hands. Shivaji, meanwhile, struggles with Onil. Whenever he sits him upright in the saddle, the *farang* just faints and falls off. In the end he lashes Onil to the horse: he slumps over, but stays in the saddle.

"Let's get out of here," Shivaji says.

Tanaji takes the caretaker's keys and unlocks the gate. As the dharmsala fire begins to roar, Shivaji trots past, leading Onil. Maya spurs her horse as it swings open. "I thought you never rode before," he calls.

"I haven't," she replies, but rubs her heels against the horse's flanks like an expert, and the horse breaks into a brisk trot.

Shit, thinks Tanaji, struggling to mount before she gets too far away. He spurs his pony. In spite of the smoke, he can still smell her perfume.

ᘜᘝᘜᘝ

A mile from the dharmsala, Tanaji glances at the *farang*. "How's he doing, Shahu?" he asks.

"I think he'll live," Shivaji replies. "Are we always going to be in trouble, uncle?" Tanaji shakes his head. Trouble is like a clever beggar; it can always find them.

Maya is no longer riding easily. Suddenly her beginner's luck has run out. She kicks the horse violently, but now when he begins to trot, his gait jostles her and she pulls back on the reins to keep from falling. The poor horse can't figure out what she wants him to do.

"Hold his reins steady and he'll keep moving," Tanaji tells Maya. "You don't need to keep kicking him." She glares back, and continues riding exactly as before: push-pull, start-stop.

A nautch girl and a man who's mostly dead, thinks Tanaji. Which is slower? He trots back to Shivaji. "Let's leave them," he suggests. "Neither of them can ride worth a damn. Let's get to Poona fast. This fellow is all but dead. And the girl? Hell, she can take care of herself." Then thinking of Shivaji's soft heart, Tanaji adds, "We'll just involve them in our troubles. For our good and for theirs, we need to leave them and get going."

"They are too valuable to leave behind," Shivaji answers.

"It was just an idea," Tanaji mumbles. "Let's at least get off the road. That's a shepherd's path—let's try it."

Tanaji trots forward, and without a word, grabs Maya's bridle. Despite her protests, he leads them down the narrow path. Tree roots and sharp stones punctuate the rough surface. Tanaji's sturdy pony has no trouble negotiating the uneven ground, but the Bedouin's hooves slide dangerously. And the girl grunts whenever she bounces in her saddle. When Tanaji shushes her, she glares back. "I'm being as quiet as I can. You should be glad I'm not screaming." Behind them Tanaji sees Shivaji struggling with the slumping form of Onil.

After a few hundred yards the track levels off as it leads along the edge of the cone-shaped hill. Despite the darkness, Tanaji can make out an over-hang of rock. It will provide some protection, like the roof of a house.

When he reaches it, he slips off his pony and then halts Maya's horse as well. She whines for help getting down but he ignores her—he's happy to have her stay put until he gets his bearings.

Soon Shivaji and the *farang* join them. Shivaji dismounts and he helps Maya down. Instead of thanking him, she simply chides Tanaji for his bad manners. But Shahu ignores her, and this irritates her even more.

They see the orange glow of the dharmsala's flames edging the horizon behind them. "Let's split up," Shivaji says to Tanaji. "The moon's bright enough to follow this trail. I'll take the *farang*. You bring the woman when the sun comes up. Meet at that toddy shop on the Daund road."

Tanaji knows better than to argue with Shivaji, though it seems to him that they should all just wait for daylight.

"Take my pony," Tanaji insists. "It's got better footing, and you're not going to be able to see where you're going, not in this light."

Shivaji agrees. They untie the *farang*, and sling him onto the pony. In a moment Shivaji and the *farang* are gone, and it's just Tanaji and Maya, alone under the lonesome overhang of that secluded hill.

❧❧❧❧

Their rest is short. As soon as the first hint of dawn pinks the horizon, Tanaji orders them forward. But their mood has improved. With Tanaji riding beside her, Maya even seems able to keep her horse moving.

"Do you know that you haven't said your name?" she says.

Tanaji blinks in embarrassment. She's right. So he tells her. He feels so embarrassed, he tells her the name of his wife, and his twin sons, and his pet lizard. With her smiling encouragement, Tanaji talks freely. He doesn't realize how often she bends the conversation toward Shivaji. In a few minutes he has told her about Shivaji's wife and son, his interfering mother, Jijabai, and the father who abandoned them. He tells her how he took Shivaji into the hills to hide from the Bijapuris, of years spent living in caves, riding with bandits.

Behind them, the sun rises: a fierce yellow disk in a hazy sky. Far to their right they see Ahmednagar, the city a shadowy mist in the dawn light. The sun begins to warm their backs. Tanaji now begins to ask Maya questions, and with each answer, his wonder grows.

She tells him that her temple sold her for a slave to some *farangs* who took her to Goa, and from there to Bijapur where she was to be given to the grand vizier. But there'd been some trouble—she wouldn't go into it—and next she knew, the Bijapuris had decided to send her to Murad, the Mogul Viceroy of the West Provinces. "They said I was a peace offering," she says in a soft, detached voice. "The seal on some alliance they arranged."

"What alliance?" Tanaji asks, suddenly alert. But she has no answer. "So why were you with *farangs*? Why not Bijapuri guards?"

It had been a secret caravan, she answers. "The stakes were so high, they feared their own people would betray them."

"Why?" asks Tanaji. "How much are you worth?"

"Seven lakh hun, I think," she answers without looking up. The figure is so staggering, Tanaji pulls up his mount and sits blinking. She's lying. She's mistaken. But he has heard of nautch girls sold for more than whole towns are worth. Could she be one of those? Who decides these things? And all the while, hoping she won't notice, he steals curious glances.

The path opens onto a narrow lane, and that lane joins a well trampled road, with big trees planted along each side. Soon they come to a green canopy set up in the middle of the road: the tomb of a Muslim saint. At the side of the white marble tombstone, a man is praying, burying his face in the green tomb cloth. He looks up at their approach. It's Shivaji.

"This way," he motions, leading them to a nearby grove of trees. Somewhere Shivaji has found farmer's clothing to wear—a simple white shirt and a faded lungi—and has replaced his tight turban with the pile of loosely wrapped cotton favored by farmers in the area. His feet are bare.

The horses, half-hidden by the trees, chew calmly on the yellow grass. On the ground in the shade, Shivaji has propped Onil against the saddles, and covered him with saddle blankets. Onil is pale but breathing easily in his sleep. Nearby is a small fire. Shivaji has set out for them a few small thick-peeled bananas, and several *bakri* chapatis.

"The perfect host," Tanaji says, smiling.

Tanaji slides off his saddle. Before he can help her, Maya slides from her saddle and smiles triumphantly. She still wears her *farang* clothes, and now she sits on the ground, tailor-fashion, as any man might do. She reties her hair, which has loosened considerably with the riding, and stares comfortably at Shivaji. "Those clothes suit you," she teases.

"They should," Shivaji replies, more seriously than she expects. He pokes a stick through one of the chapatis, and wafts it over the small flames of his fire. "You know my family were farmers." When the chapati is warmed, he passes it to her at the end of the stick.

She takes it and flips the flat round bread from hand to hand until it cools. "You were dressed like a merchant when I first saw you, or like a prince," she says quietly, glancing away. After a moment, she looks again.

It's her first chance to examine him in the light. She sees right away that he is attractive: tall, lean, quick and precise in his movements, sleekly muscled, beautifully proportioned. His face is strong and his eyes are large. A brightness burns inside him; she thinks stupidly of a moth being drawn to a flame. But maybe the moth finds that a pleasant way to die.

Shivaji hands her a banana. Of course she scowls at him: A banana and *bakri* chapati are scarcely the foods that she should be offered. As she takes it she notices the scars that cross the palms of his hands, like thick white threads embedded beneath the skin. But before she can ask about them, he has walked away.

The food is tastier than she expects, and she is famished.

Tanaji scowls when Shivaji hands him a chapati. "You know, I made a vow never to eat *bakri* again," he complains. "Eating this makes me look capricious." He grins, clearly pleased to be using a fancy word.

"Knowing your vow, I thought there would be more for me!" Shivaji replies. "I spoke to the cook," he relates, more seriously. "He already knew about the fire." At this, Tanaji stops chewing. "The fire was so big that no one survived. Everyone burned—beyond recognition. Everyone dead."

"They don't know about us!" Tanaji says. "The fire covered our tracks!" Maya thinks he looks ready to dance in his happiness. He eats a chapati, and a banana, and another and another. Humming to himself, he walks around the grove of trees. Shivaji glances at Maya, who is sharing his amusement at Tanaji's happiness. She can see that he likes Tanaji immensely.

"There is one other thing though, uncle," Shivaji says. "The cook said that two Bijapuri guards had ridden through yesterday. From Khirki. They were looking for two travelers. Offered a reward. Three rupees."

Tanaji whistles. "Three rupees? These travelers they seek—they didn't sound like . . . us, by any chance?"

Shivaji nods. Tanaji considers this. "And I was thinking . . ."

Tanaji looks up. It's never good when Shivaji starts to think.

"Well, there's her," Shivaji says, nodding to Maya. Maya instantly takes offense at being referred to as though she weren't able to hear. "Somebody is going to wonder what happened to her."

"No. She died in the fire, remember? We all died in the fire. Easy."

"Easy? Maybe. If she disappears and no one ever sees her again, maybe. Even so, somebody is going to wonder why all those bodies in the fire were men. Somebody will wonder why there isn't a woman's body."

Tanaji considers this and frowns. "There's something you need to hear, Shahu." He turns to Maya. "Tell him about yourself."

Maya, a little frightened, repeats the story she told Tanaji earlier. When he hears the figure of seven lakh hun, Shivaji whistles.

"If it's true," Tanaji says, "then we've gone and stepped in it. Maybe we should let her go."

Shivaji's eyes harden. "Well, what about the *farang*? What happens when he wakes up? Where does he go . . . Back to the Bijapuris? Won't he lead them straight to us? And those thieves, those guards—three dots . . . That's a clan sign, uncle. What if the rest of the clan comes after us? They might even start a *wagnak*." Shivaji looks hard at Tanaji.

"Seven lakh hun will buy a lot of enemies, Shahu," Tanaji says. "We've got to do something. She's got to disappear."

Maya doesn't like being discussed as if she's a problem to be solved. Men trying to be rid of her? That she has never experienced before. She wonders if they are capable of murdering her.

Tanaji's face grows hard. "We're in trouble, Shahu. We're too obvious. Her and the *farang*, they make us obvious." He looks around and each item he sees upsets him more. "Look—these horses. And the saddle. Anyone with half a brain could recognize them. Shit, we're tethered goats!"

Maya can't take any more. "Can't you see? You are just weaving your own troubles!"

Maya's outburst surprises them as much as if a rock spoke. Tanaji and Shivaji are not used to women who speak without being addressed. They know that nautch girls are supposed to be frank and straightforward in bed—that's their appeal, after all—but neither had any idea that this behavior extended past the bedroom door. They scarcely know how to react. So they ignore her, and this irritates her even more.

"So what shall we do? Sell her?" Tanaji suggests.

Maya bristles. "Sell me? You don't own me!"

"Speak when you're spoken to," Tanaji answers. "Don't tempt me with the obvious solution." His hand moves toward the hilt of his mace.

"You wouldn't . . . ," she whispers.

"Don't put it to the test," Tanaji answers, looking into her eyes with a cold, lifeless stare. Maya backs away and sits on the ground near Onil.

"Hold her," Shivaji proposes, "for ransom."

"Ransom from who, Shahu?"

"The Bijapuris were sending her to the viceroy in Surat. The *farangs* were supposed to be delivering her. So take your pick—the Bijapuris, the Moguls, or the *farangs*!"

"Maybe all three?" Tanaji laughs. "But what about now? We need a place to hide."

All is silent except the sound of a dog barking far away. Then Shivaji's eyes light up. "Have you ever been to Ranjangaon temple?"

☙☙☙☙

So Tanaji waits with the girl while Shivaji and the *farang* leave separately for the temple. The plan is that Shivaji will return with a horse cart.

Hidden from the road by the dense bushes, Tanaji sits with his back to a tree, staring into space and digging into the dust at his feet with his mace, never looking up, especially never looking at Maya.

Of course he wants to look at her. But the nightmare memories of last night are closing in. He can't bear to look at her while he is thinking his dark thoughts.

☙☙☙☙

Run away! Maya thinks.

But she does not run.

She has her own dark thoughts: her vulnerability in a land of farmers—why, they might do anything to her, a woman, alone, and dressed in men's clothing. She might take one of the horses, and ride for safety—maybe a horse would protect her from bumpkins on the road—but where would she ride? Into Ahmednagar?

If she were found in Ahmednagar, who knows what might happen to her?

Someone might simply capture her and sell her for a slave. And what then? Why risk the road, risk death or rape, merely to end up a slave once more? And not just any slave, she thinks: a new slave; a new whore begging for scraps in some rich man's house.

After years living in poverty at the temple, as a nautch girl she found wealth beyond imagining. Was it odd that she hesitated to run?

She had learned whom to gratify, whom to mock, whom to frustrate, whom to join in congress—and in what manner, for there were many, and men were so silly about asking. She had been taught well and learned much. Now she was at the peak of her desirability, prized not just for her beauty, but for her knowledge, not just her sex, but for her skills. And more: desired for the price paid to buy her. She had achieved honor by her value, clear to great and powerful men.

But to be sold again, without a patron, without history, without a story: she could end up flat on her back for every cook and groom and fly-swatter in some second-rate nabob's court.

Better to chance the plans of her current captors; they would ransom her back into a world where she was known and valued . . . valued even more, she reasons perhaps, by someone who had paid to ransom her.

And perhaps there is another reason why she stays.

ᘉᘓᘉᘓ

Shivaji returns.

Instead of riding on Tanaji's pony, he walks beside a bullock cart. He looks every inch a farmer. He plods toward the grove slightly bowlegged, the hem of his dusty lungi dragging in the dust. That's a nice touch, thinks Tanaji.

The cart is old, its two great solid wooden wheels broken and patched many times, and Tanaji starts to laugh. "Where did you get that piece of junk?"

"Get in the wagon," Shivaji says to Maya.

"I won't ride in that," she answers. She tries to hide behind one of the Bedouins.

Tanaji picks up a short, thin branch. "Act like a whore and be beaten like a whore."

"Stop!" Shivaji orders.

Tanaji turns to him. "We can't have this, Shahu," he explains as if to a child. "She must learn who's boss. What if she calls out, or runs away! We'll take her, and bind her and gag her—for her protection as much as ours."

"No," Shivaji answers with finality. "She'll ride hidden in the cart and she won't make a sound. And she'll do it willingly."

"Why?" asks Maya, suddenly intrigued. "Why will I do that?"

"Because we will ask you to. Politely." He bows his head and says clearly and slowly, "Please, Maya, hide yourself in the cart."

It is the first time he has said her name.

"Make him say it, too."

"I ask you to get in the cart," Tanaji says.

She waits.

"Please," he croaks out, finally.

As though she were dressed in heavy silks instead of *farang* pantaloons, Maya walks elegantly to the cart. To Shivaji's surprise, she reaches out a hand as if waiting for him to help her.

When he takes her hand, neither of them says a word, but Maya looks into Shivaji's dark eyes with such intensity that Tanaji is taken aback. She's just trouble, he thinks to himself.

ᴄᴊᴊᴄᴊ

A half hour later, Maya sticks her head from under the sacks where she hides. "It's getting hot," she complains.

"Well, so long as no one is coming, you can keep your head out," Tanaji says.

"Anyway we're practically there," says Shivaji. They have reached the top of a long rise at last, and now Shivaji motions toward a sweeping valley They can see the high, conical dome of a large temple, and the smaller domes of the lesser temples that surround it.

"What's that place?" asks Maya.

"That's Ranjangaon," Shivaji answers. "A temple to Lord Ganesha."

"I've never heard of it," Maya says. Suddenly she scrambles out of the sacks to kneel at the railing of the bullock cart. "What's that?" she points, eyes gleaming. To the side of the main temple, they can just make out a raised platform.

"That's the dance temple," Shivaji replies, and her eyes grow bright. He smiles at her pleasure.

CHAPTER 8

The temple gate leads to a cool arched stone corridor and into the court-yard. It is almost like entering a fort, Tanaji thinks.

Against his bare feet, the bricks of the walk feel smooth and cool. The edges of the walk have been decorated with tangled designs drawn in lines of rice flour and kumkum—triangles, mangoes, swastikas, all melded together with vines traced in elaborate profusion and brilliant colors.

On a raised platform at the end of the walk stands a tall lampstand of sculpted brass: from its branches hang a dozen or more butter lamps with flames burning steadily in the still morning air. A brazier of frankincense and sandalwood fills the courtyard with a heady tang. A mandala fashioned of fresh flower petals covers much of platform.

Beyond, Tanaji sees several temples, constructed of the dark volcanic stone common to this part of the county. The temples share a common lay-out: four colonnaded wings, and above each, a dome, the shape of an elon-gated beehive, meant to resemble Vishnu's celestial home, Mount Mehru. Most are small. The larger temples have been decorated with free-standing sculptures and with bas-reliefs: gods, animals, devas, asuras, heroes, vil-lains, chakras, chariots—each temple a sculpted library of stories.

The most lavish is a temple to Ganesha: its sculptures are not mere life-less stone; all have been painted in bright, shocking colors: they vibrate with life, but only hint at the effulgent glory of the gods, at the forms that might be seen only by their grace.

Tanaji gapes at the temple. The god that lives there must be very rich. "You haven't been here before?" Shivaji asks.

"No," says Tanaji. In the distance, he sees the dance temple, with the raised platform that Maya pointed out from the top of the hill. He blinks, and takes another look. "Is that her? Is that Maya up there?"

"Yes, uncle. She made straight for the dance temple," Shivaji answers.

"What was her hurry?" Tanaji asks.

"She's a nautch girl . . . a devadasi, uncle," Shivaji says, turning to look at him. "Where did you think she'd go, first chance she got?"

"I thought she was just another whore," Tanaji answers. High class, maybe, a rich man's toy, maybe, but a whore is a whore.

"Real nautch girls are temple dancers. Devadasis. At least that's what they used to be—what they're supposed to be. The best ones still are—brought up from two or three to be dancers for the gods."

Tanaji shrugs. "How do they turn into whores? Because that's what they are. You can't deny it."

"Not all of them. Not here. There are temples where the brahmins make a trade in them. They raise them for sex, not for dance, and then sell them as soon as they ripen. But not here."

They soon reach a long row of rooms, much like those at the dharmsala: pilgrims' quarters. The walls are painted with pictures of gods and goddesses. In one, Onil lies comfortably on a mat, face washed, eyes open. Nearby sits a young girl, fanning him. She is too young to mask her fascination at seeing a *farang* this close; she stares at Onil's red hair, at his strange pink, freckled skin. She startles when Shivaji and Tanaji enter, and turns away even when Tanaji tries to give her a reassuring grin.

"You come back," Onil says. "I think you leave me here. Think I am dead man." His wan smile only emphasizes his damp hair and clammy, white skin. "Little girl won't say her name. What your name, little girl?"

"Tell us your name, child," Shivaji says gently.

The girl looks up at him, her large, kohl-stained eyes luminous in the light from the tiny window. "Upala."

"Ah, see! For you she say!" Onil shakes his head. You good girl. Good girl, Upala." She gives Onil a quick smile. And even this small gesture makes Onil happy; he beams at her as if she were his own daughter.

"You're looking better, *farang*," Tanaji lies. His skin shouldn't be so gray, Tanaji thinks. He's dying.

"Sure, good, good," Onil replies. "Doctor comes. Gives me some mud to drink, taste like puke. Now feel very good. Also on chest puts some smell bad stuff, maybe cow shit. I don't care. Smell bad, feel good."

He bows his head. "I now much grateful both of you. I grateful for my living. I dead man many times last night. Now maybe not dead, so now I grateful." Tanaji thinks maybe he is thanking them too soon.

"Go find the others, Upala," Shivaji says, ignoring Onil for the moment. "They're all down by the river, I expect."

"Sure, good. Come back soon," Onil puts in. The little girl walks off with that solemnity only little children and royalty can muster. The bells of her ankle bracelet jingle pleasantly.

"Nautch girl," Shivaji whispers to Tanaji, nodding at Upala.

Tanaji doesn't quite know what to make of that. He hasn't ever thought of all those whores as little girls before.

"What do we do with you?" Shivaji says, kneeling near Onil's bedside.

Onil looks at him with gratitude: this is what he has wanted to ask, but there was no polite way to do so. "I go wonder this same thing."

Tanaji becomes aware of the smell in the room. The doctor probably did use cow dung on Onil's wound, he thinks. Even with all the herbs and powders they mix into it, they can't hide the smell. He has come to associate that dark tangy smell with sorrow; the smell takes him back to battle.

"The doctor says you are too weak to travel. You can stay here for a few days. Then I invite you to come to Poona and stay with me. Stay as long as you wish. You understand?" Shivaji says.

"Sure, good. I know you," Onil says. "I much grateful for your kind to me, I now owing you. How can I pay that . . . that owing?"

"Keep your mouth shut about the dharmsala," Tanaji tells him gruffly. "You were never there. You never saw us. It never happened. You understand? Even here, say nothing about the dharmsala. You understand?"

"Sure, I know not talk." Onil pauses and licks his lips. "What about girl? What about treasure girl?"

Shivaji glances at Tanaji. "She comes with us."

"You are boss now. She stay with you. Sure, good." To Tanaji he seems troubled, as though he had been thinking up his own plans. "She yours if you want her. Very good for congress. I give her to you."

"She is not yours to give," Shivaji replies. It is as though Onil has stepped across a hidden boundary. They look hard at each other and a chill fills the air.

At last Onil shrugs. "Sure. She just a girl. Anybody's girl. Your girl, maybe. Maybe nobody's girl. Just a girl." It's clear to Tanaji that this is not the response Shivaji wants, but it will have to do.

ᏣᎧᏣᎧ

A commotion has been growing outside. Tanaji goes to the door to see a large procession moving through the courtyard. Brahmins in lungis lead the way back from the nearby river, banging drums and gongs and blowing conches that bellow like great horns. Behind them come a host of young men carrying shoulder poles: at each end hang large silver pots full of water; following them a great crowd of local pilgrims.

Among this crowd Tanaji sees the nautch girls—a dozen devadasis at least, maybe two—young ones and old, wearing yellow and orange saris, their long hair plaited with flowers and ribbons, with ankle bells jingling brightly as they spin and leap. The procession chants: Jai! Jai! Ganapati! Jai! Jai! Ganesha! To its infectious tune, the dancers clap and whirl their way to the main temple. It is time for Ganesha's bath.

"I'm going to watch," Tanaji calls to Shivaji. He catches up with the procession just as it gets to the temple steps. The clatter of the drums and gongs and the deep blasts of the conch shells mix with the singing. He sees Upala, pretty as a flower, twirling with her eyes closed, hands in the air.

Jostling, bumping, Tanaji pushes forward. Everyone is squeezing forward, trying to get into the sacred center of the temple. And by the time he and the others have mounted the steps, Tanaji has changed. He breathes as one with the others, moves as one with them, chants as one.

The brahmins place frankincense on big braziers of charcoal, and the heavy smoke pours across the room, into their lungs, and out once more, so that they become part of the smoke that rises to the deity and up into heaven.

He sees Maya now. She stands ahead of him, dressed now in a yellow sari like the other nautch girls, swaying, spinning with the others. Tanaji feels no surprise at her transformation. His arms are waving over his head, his voice is ringing: *Jai! Jai!* Ganapati! *Jai! Jai!* Ganesha! The pounding of the drums crescendos; the stone room has itself become a drum.

The brahmins move ahead to the pounding heart of the temple, to the red velvet drapes that veil the inner room, the very home of the god himself. A *shastri* slowly draws the drapes aside.

The form of the god can be seen in his holy place—hazily, of course, for a curtain of silk gauze still hangs across the door. But even this first glimpse of the deity is enough to stir the crowd, to push their emotions to the brink. The drumming grows yet louder. The chant is shouted now, not sung. The nautch girls leap so high they seem to fly.

The brahmins raise butter lamps and sandalwood on silver trays. They wave the trays in long circles, and chant their praises of the god. In the crowd, bodies now vibrate with the echoes of those huge drums, of those clanging gongs and roaring horns, like the walls and the floors, the people themselves now throb with the universe's own unending hymns of praise.

The priests now beg the deity to wake and bless them with his darshan, their chants mingling with the smoke and light and sound. And at that moment the sun bursts through a window in the dome and strikes the face of the deity. The temple explodes in sound as the brahmins bow and lower their *arti* trays and pull the last gauze curtain aside.

Silence. Silece that roars as loud as an ocean. The echoes fade, like the last quiet hum of a great gong. It is he: Ganesha.

What a delightful sight he is, always curious, always refreshing, like clear air that has never before been breathed. Ganesha, the child of Shiva, the delight of all the gods.

Ganesha was only a child when he defied his father Shiva on his mother's orders. In his anger, Shiva, who had never met his child, sliced off his head with the light of his third eye. How Shiva grieved when he found that he had killed his own son! So Shiva killed a passing elephant, attached the elephant's head to the tiny corpse, and resurrected the boy with his tears.

This is the *murti* that Tanaji sees: Ganesha with his chubby body and elephant head now pink and perfect like a child's; Ganesha with his four hands displaying his munificence—one hand open as a sign of comfort, the others holding signs of power and affection: a lily, a discus, and a bowl of candy for his lovers. At his feet is a rat, for of all the animals, the rat goes anywhere and none can keep him out—so, too Ganesha removes all obstacles and none can restrain him. He sits on a silver throne with his consorts—Buddhi seated near one knee, Siddhi at the other, sweet, slim-hipped goddesses with naked breasts as round as custard apples.

The body of the *murti* glows rosy pink in the sun, the palms of his hands and feet bright red. His painted eyes—divinely, exquisitely human—are long-lashed and languid and serene. Those who look into those eyes and have his darshan are blessed: their sins, their obstacles removed.

With soft prayers, the priests now bathe the god using the water carried from the river, pouring pot after silver pot over his head until the *murti* gleams like a great pink jewel. They dry him with soft cloths, then dress him: in rich silks shot with gold, and heavy brocades and velvets. They offer him sweets—*pedas,* his favorite, little cakes of boiled milk and sugar. Once he has eaten his fill, the priests take the bounty that remains to offer to the crowd as Ganesha's *prasad.*

And now the crowd begins to disassemble, to step out of its ecstasy, to fall from the height of heaven back to earth. Instead of one people, they become many persons; they form into lines and approach the railing that separates them from the deity.

One by one they come to take Ganesha's holy gifts. They waft fingers through the flames of his sacred butter lamps, and touch the fire to eyes and lips. They receive a spoonful of the water that bathed the god's body: from their palms they swallow a drop, and sprinke the rest on their heads. Finally they take from the brahmin's hand a *peda,* Ganesha's sweet *prasad,* food that comes from the mouth of god.

Each one steps away from that railing silent, blessed, filled, once more an individual, with all the frailties and worries and tiny joys of the day to face, but now with hope.

Tanaji edges to the railing, his eyes fixed on the Lord Ganesha's eyes— they are beautiful; he is reminded of Maya's eyes. Suddenly he is inspired to perform *palikarsha:* Crossing his arms in front of him, he grabs his earlobes and bobs up and down three times—the silly gesture that the deity enjoys, for he is still a child at heart. The gesture makes Tanaji forget the horrors of the previous night; it makes him too, feel like a child. He waves his hands through the flame offered by the priest, and sprinkles water on his hair, and takes a *peda,* and then two more.

He walks backward so as not to turn his back on the deity, and heads back to the pilgrims' quarters, munching on the *peda* as he goes. There Tanaji finds Onil. "For you," he tells the *farang,* handing him the *prasad.*

"What is it?"

Tanaji thinks about how best to tell Onil about the darshan he has received, about the blessings and generosity of the elephant-headed god, about the holy *prasad* that has fallen from Ganesha's very lips, from the god who removes all obstacles, this blessing that now rests in Onil's hands.

"Candy," he explains. "Eat it."

Onil eats the small ivory-colored cake. "Sure, good," he says. "Shivaji go talk some woman."

"Maya?" Tanaji asks.

"No—old woman, very old woman," Onil replies. "He very happy. Maybe she is his mother, I think."

Tanaji snorts. "If he was happy to see her, it wasn't his mother."

At that moment he turns to see a dark, slender girl of about sixteen who raises her folded hands to her forehead. "I have come for my mistress's things," she announces. "Which bags are hers?"

Tanaji sputters for a second—he never reacts well to sudden pronouncements, particularly from women. "Who the hell are you?"

"I am Jyoti. I live here. Premabai, my old mistress, has just made me the servant of Mayabai, and I have come to take her things to her quarters in the dancers' school."

"Mayabai?" Tanaji asks. "You mean the nautch girl?"

"She is no nautch girl, sir! She is a daughter of the goddess," Jyoti replies, offended. "You might as well call her a whore!"

He might indeed. And then he might also beat this girl for insolence. But he is a stranger here. He mumbles an apology. "Her stuff is there." He nods casually to a couple of cloth bags pushed up against the wall near the door. Jyoti doesn't move. "Well?" he asks.

She glares at him. "You can't expect me to carry her bags?"

Tanaji picks up Maya's things, swearing under his breath. Jyoti leads him across the courtyard to a small complex of buildings behind the new dance temple.

The buildings face a small courtyard. Jyoti lifts her hand to indicate a door. Nearby Maya paints henna on the hands of Upala, the little girl who tended Onil. "Just put them there," Maya says, without looking up.

"Oh yes, madam." Tanaji snarls.

If she is bothered by his tone, Maya makes no sign; she focuses on the intricate design she traces with the cone of dye on the little girl's pudgy hands. "Oh, and pay her please," Maya adds, not looking up.

"Pay who?"

"Jyoti," Maya answers, as if this were the most obvious thing in the world. "Well, I don't have any money, do I?"

Jyoti serenely holds out her hand while Tanaji splutters. At last he claws out his purse and spills some coins into his palm. He can barely speak for anger. "How much?"

"Ten annas," Maya says.

"Ten? For the month? That's a lot for a serving girl."

"For the week. And she isn't a serving girl. She's my maid. It's what they're paid in civilized countries. Perhaps you wouldn't know that." Maya continues to decorate Upala's hand.

"I'm giving her seven," Tanaji replies at last.

Maya glares at him, but she sees the anger in his face. So she lowers her eyes and says with a practiced quaver, "You are kind to me, uncle." Her voice is sweet like cool water. Tanaji is mystified by his response. All his anger vanishes.

"That will be all," Jyoti tells him. Before he knows what has happened, he finds himself staring at the door that Jyoti has closed in his face. He struggles to make sense of his situation. Life is strange, he decides.

He finds Shivaji in the portico of the dance temple, talking with a gray-haired woman. Shivaji motions for Tanaji to join them. "Who is the deity of this dance temple?" Tanaji asks as he sits next to Shivaji.

The gray-haired woman seems pleased by his question. "This temple houses the goddess, who has many forms, but only one essence," she says. From her yellowed teeth, Tanaji realizes that she is much older than she first appears, for her face is bright and hardly wrinkled and her eyes are clear. "Here the goddess is pleased to share with us her form as Bhavani. Do you know this aspect of the goddess?"

"Sure," Tanaji replies. "You worship Bhavani, don't you, Shahu?"

"Yes, my little Shahu knows her well. Don't you, sweet?" Shivaji turns away with a bashfulness that Tanaji has not seen before. "You don't know me, do you?" the old woman says to Tanaji. "But I know you. Your father brought you here when you were just a baby. Your father was Balaram, a great favorite of Maloji. And your mother was a beauty, but I forget her name. I'm old, you see."

"You knew my parents?" Tanaji asks. "They died when I was young."

"Your father was a great warrior," the woman tells him, raising her hand to his, pulling him down beside her. "Without him, Maloji was nothing. Balaram and Maloji—they were fearless! Princes, but born as farmers by some whim of the goddess. And such adventures! To become princes in their own time! Yes, I knew your father. He was a friend of mine, child."

"I scarcely remember my father, and my mother not at all. Maloji raised me with his own son, Shahji. Maloji never said that my father was important."

"Important!" the old woman exclaims. "Essential! Without your father, Maloji would not have been a prince, and without Maloji, this temple would never have survived." She squeezes Tanaji's hand surprisingly hard.

"Her name is Premabai," Shivaji tells him. "She has been a temple dancer here since before this temple was built. She was a great favorite of my grandfather. He visited her often." It takes a moment for Tanaji to realize that Shivaji is saying that Premabai was his grandfather's mistress.

Premabai's knotted fingers still squeeze Tanaji's hand. "I am so glad you brought my sister here," she whispers. "Mayabai, I mean."

"That nautch girl? Maya?"

Premabai's expression is one of such grief that Tanaji wishes he could cut out his tongue. She looks at him with that tolerant forgiveness reserved for the very old. "That's not such a nice word, you know. She and I are devadasis, and daughters of the same mother. What you say of her, you also say of me. You think like others, that all nautch girls are whores."

Tanaji hangs his head.

"We devadasis have only one mother, our dear guru—she becomes our mother, our father, our family. Mayabai and I both were chelas of the same teacher, Gungama of Bengal. You've heard of her?" Tanaji lifts his hands uncertainly. "Never mind," Premabai says sadly. "It is not her portion to be famous in this lifetime."

She shifts so she can look straight into Tanaji's eyes. He is surprised by the force of her look. "You must do me a kindness, little one. I am too old for you to refuse." Again she takes his hand, pressing it urgently. "Promise me to keep her safe. Do you understand?"

"Maya, you mean? Mayabai?" he asks, and she nods her head.

"Promise me, little one, that you'll care for my sister when I cannot," she begs.

"Yes, mother, yes," he answers.

"It was for this reason that you have returned here. I have seen this," she tells him, as if revealing a great secret. She peers into his face, and he feels a joyous peace flowing from her eyes into his.

"We must let you go, Premabai," Shivaji rises and *namskars*.

"Can I help you up, mother?" Tanaji asks, offering his hand.

"I shall stay here." As the two men walk off, she draws the end of her sari over her head and begins to chant, rocking gently with the words.

ⒸⓈⒸⓈ

Lunch. On a rush-roofed verandah the temple residents sit shoulder to shoulder on a flagstone floor, banana-leaf plates in front of them. Servers inch between the rows, ladling food from pots they carry wrapped in thick towels—rice, dal, *dahi*. Tanaji turns to Shivaji. "We're in danger here. We stick out. Someone here will inform on us. Those Khirki men will find us and there's no way out. We'll die here, most likely."

"I agree. We'll leave tomorrow. By oxcart. Dawn."

"You mean to take the girl?" Tanaji asks.

Shivaji doesn't even need to answer.

"Maybe she should stay here," Tanaji suggests, thinking of Premabai.

"No."

Tanaji looks into Shivaji's face. There's no room for argument. "And the *farang*?" Tanaji asks.

"Forget the *farang*," Shivaji replies. "He's dying. I'll give the *shastri* some money to bury him. That's their custom, I think. Buried in the ground like Muslims."

Tanaji notices a man looking at him: dark, dirty, his hair and beard matted with dust; wearing rags so tattered they hide very little, so grimed by dust and sweat that they look almost like part of the earth itself. People keep their distance from him. Even when Tanaji looks away, he can feel the rag man's eyes burning into him. Then, unexpectedly, the rag man's face breaks into a toothy, extravagant grin.

As if he needed any new element to strain his reason, the strange smile of this strange man completely unnerves him. Suddenly Tanaji's mind starts overheating. "We shouldn't be seen together," Tanaji says with sudden urgency. "We're being watched. We should sit apart."

"Uncle," Shivaji says, frowning with concern, "don't tell me you're worried. That is only Ram Das. You know Ram Das. He's that crazy holy man. He wanders from town to town—you've seen him before. Ram Das is harmless! You're tired, uncle. Finish your food. Get some sleep."

At the very word "sleep," Tanaji feels so weary he can scarcely keep his eyes open. Suddenly a question pops into his mind. "Why do they call you Master Bhisma, Shahu? What's that all about?"

"You know the story of Bhisma, uncle. From the Mahabharata."

"Sure. The prince who made the terrible vow. The gods showered him with celestial flowers."

"That's the one," Shivaji says. Tanaji looks back with uncomprehending eyes. "You know of the vow we took—your sons and me?"

"That was all some child's game, Shahu."

Shivaji looks up, as if pained by Tanaji's words. "We made our vow here, uncle, at this temple. That's why they call me Bhisma." Shaking his head as if lost in memories, Shivaji walks off.

"But I don't understand!" Tanaji calls after him. "What was so terrible? The gods didn't shower you with flowers, did they, Shahu?"

Shivaji waves, without turning his head.

ଔଓଔଓ

The bells wake him. For a moment O'Neil is back in Dublin, listening to the bells of Saint Finian's—asleep in his big wooden bed, his wife still alive, his daughter still alive. For a moment the constant ache of his heart disappears. But how, he wonders, has Dublin got so hot? When did it start to smell of jasmine and dung? And the bells don't sound right—usually they peal forth like angels, not clanging and banging to wake the dead.

And then he knows. He is in Hindustan, far from home and alone. Absently rubbing his eyes with the back of his hands, he refuses to acknowledge, even to himself, that they are wet with tears.

His clothing is soaked: sweat mixed with blood and dung and herbs. An ugly stain crosses the once white cotton of his shirt. I need a drink, he thinks, wishing for whiskey. A pitcher stands near his bed, and he picks it up. Empty. He can't remember drinking it, but he must have done.

Where's that girl? He stands, and darkness swims before his eyes.

He tries to ignore the smell rising from his chest, the smell that seeps through even the heavy odor of cow dung and herbs. He knows that smell too well: the sick rotten sweetness of a festering wound. Once it gets in your nose, it takes hours before it goes away. Now, sweet Mary, that smell rises from him.

He struggles to walk to the door. He needs water, some food, the girl, something. He is exhausted just by the effort of getting this far. But he won't turn back and he won't lie down again: he has the soldier's fear that if he doesn't move, he will fade into a slow, still death.

With each step his lips move soundlessly—*Ave Maria, gratia plena.* Silently he begs the Virgin to forgive his clumsy prayer, to forgive that he hasn't tasted the Host in months, and with tears in his heart, he begs Her to look after his sweethearts, to lift them from the muck of purgatory to join with Her in Blessed Paradise. He prays a lot these days.

Some man comes up to him, half-naked, wearing nothing but a skirt tied around his waist, and across his chest that bloody string they all wear. "Something something," the man says, trying not to stare at O'Neil. "Other man something."

"Pardon me but I do not speak your language very well. Please talk to me slowly, and use small simple words," O'Neil answers, the formula he has memorized. His wound is starting to throb now: his chest is on fire.

The man nods and now talks as though O'Neil were deaf. "Taaannnnaaaaji. Slleeeeping." He points to the door of the next room, and mimes someone napping.

"My friend, I very thirsty. You having water nearby?" O'Neil croaks.

The man frowns, looking confused for a moment, and then nods enthusiastically. He points toward some building, a small temple maybe. Odd to put water in a temple, O'Neil thinks.

Suddenly he feels a wave of clammy cold. His stomach twists. Taking a deep breath, he clasps his arms across his chest, struggling not to fall. He stumbles toward the temple, eager to find water. He shivers and sweats. Oh Blessed Mary, he thinks, I should never have done this. But there's no well, no water. Looking back to where the pointing man had stood he now sees no one. Bloody hell, he says to himself, setting his teeth and lurching forward. All he can think about is water. Maybe there's some inside.

My boots, he thinks with a sinking heart when he reaches the doorway, and sees the row of *chappals* and shoes. He leans against a wall and tugs them off, grunting mightily. The effort triggers another bout of ague. This time he can barely control the tremors in his hands. As he drops them, his boots clump noisily to the floor. Strange that there would be water at a temple. He's too exhausted to worry about it. Cold sweat bathes his limbs.

The smooth black tiles feel cool on his bare soles as he weaves forward through the hall, dimly lit by butter lamps. He stumbles toward the brightly lit *griha,* the inner room that houses the image of the god.

Surrounded by a chanting, swaying multitude, sweating, maybe dying, he stares at the brightly lit idol. He thinks it's a female god, but of course it's hard to tell—these Hindi sculptors carve their male idols with curves every bloody which way, so they look like women. But this one is wearing a big round gold nose ring. She's been carved out of dark-colored rock, and her face is deep green. But O'Neil is bothered by her eyes.

He's seen this sort of thing before: The carvers paste bright crescents of white shell where the eyes ought to be. In the center of the white they paint a dark black iris. The contrast is startling, fixing the face in a fierce stare that to O'Neil seems almost evil.

Those bright shell eyes now bore into him as a paroxysm of ague consumes him. He falls, first to his knees, then forward on his hands. Blackness clouds his eyes. Holy Mother, he thinks, Holy Mother, this is death.

He manages to crawl to a nearby wall, gasping for breath. His ears begin to close down: the din of bells and drums now seems to come from far away. He can't wrest his eyes from the unblinking white stare of the goddess. The sweet, dead smell of his wound curls up from underneath his shirt and fills his nostrils. Holy Mary, he thinks, Holy Mary.

From the corner of his eye he notices a bundle of rags on the floor beside him, dirty rags the color of old leaves rotting. Who would leave a pile of rags lying about in a busy temple? Then as he watches, the bundle begins to breathe, to change its form: lengthening and narrowing, until it takes on a shape like a shaggy, dark peapod.

This is what happens when you die, O'Neil thinks. Your eyes go, and your mind goes, and a pile of rags begins to breathe. He wants to get away, but he can no longer move. And he can't take his eyes off those damned rags. Holy Mary, pray for us sinners.

Suddenly, the peapod of rags splits down its length, like a cocoon opening. The sides fold back. O'Neil wants to shut his eyes, but can't. And so he sees it: an old withered body lying in the rags, a body with gray flesh and gray hair, thin and contorted with age, covered in grime.

Yet a sweetness fills the air. The gray body itself splits down the middle, just like the rag cocoon did a moment before, like a dry husk. Tilting up from the husk a form emerges: lean, smoothly muscled, the flesh glowing like burnished mahogany; radiant, perfected.

The glowing form floats to O'Neil. "Brother of one mother," the form says, lifting his graceful glowing hands to his forehead. "Be not afraid. I am Ram Das. She has sent me. I will bring you drink."

The glowing rag man walks or floats or dances toward the *griha*. No one seems to notice him. I'm delirious, O'Neil thinks. The thought comforts him; at least he's not going crazy.

From the feet of the idol, the rag man takes a brass water pitcher left by the brahmins. His feet scarcely touch the ground as he returns. He holds the lip of the pot to O'Neil's lips. "She says, Drink what you want."

O'Neil smells the stale river water in the pitcher, and nearly vomits. Never mind, he would drink no matter how it smelled.

But the flavor when he swallows is that of an icy stream that ran by his home when he was a child.

"Yes, you like that," the rag man's eyes gleam. "Drink what you want, she says. She is very happy with you."

The rag man pours more liquid between O'Neil's parched lips, and this time: My God! It is whiskey, real whiskey, the best he has ever drunk. He gulps it down: sweet smoky warmth pouring over his throat, into his heart. He drinks and drinks.

"She hears your prayers," the rag man says. "She sends you blessings." The rag man is speaking Persian, which O'Neil learned years before.

"She says, Don't worry about your wife and daughter. They are with her in perfect bliss. They send you blessings. They are safe in the arms of the blessed mother." The rag man nods toward the idol in the *griha*.

"But she's not the one I meant," O'Neil splutters. He wonders if he's speaking Persian or English, or if he's even speaking out loud at all. "I meant the Virgin, not some bloody idol."

The rag man purses his lips in amused rebuke. "She is that same one!" he laughs. "She has so many forms! She loves to tease, that one!" He grows more serious. "Maybe you did not know to whom you prayed. But why would she care? She accepts all prayers, even yours! Even mine! She takes our prayers of lead and spins them to bright gold that they may be worthy of her. Who can understand her ways? She is all compassion, that one." He places the pitcher once more to O'Neil's dry lips. This time the water tastes delicate, like sunlight and honey, or mother's milk.

"Your women are with her, dear one," the rag man tells him. "With her they bloom like roses, watered by your prayers. And someday, they will fall like petals back to the earth. And she says, you will see them again, and again, for never does love die."

O'Neil begins to sob. Putting the empty pitcher on the floor, the rag man places his hands gently on O'Neil's shoulders. The touch is soft and warm. The rag man looks toward O'Neil; not at him, but through him.

The rag man draws his right hand across the *farang*'s chest, tracing the length of his wound with his index finger. The sensation is deep and exquisite; O'Neil groans; whether with pleasure or pain he could not say. It feels as though the rag man is reaching through the flesh itself.

When again he opens his eyes O'Neil sits alone. A few yards away, an old man so dirty he seems covered in chalk sits on a pile of rags. Despite the dust that clings to him, the rag man smells sweet. O'Neil sees that his hands are knotted with age, the fingernails yellowed and long.

The noise of the temple begins to reemerge. "Good, good," says the rag man, no longer speaking Persian. "You good now, *farang*, stay good!" He gestures with his chin toward the *griha*, toward the image of the dark goddess on her silver throne. "Something, her! Always something, her!" The rag man lies back in his cocoon of rags, and merges into them, drawing into himself like a ball, until the bundle looks just as it did when O'Neil entered, a forgotten pile of rags.

ᘓᘓᘓᘓ

O'Neil gets to his feet. His fever has broken, his thirst is gone, his wound feels cool. At the temple steps, he picks up his boots, and finds that he can pull them on without pain. It's like waking from a dream.

As he walks toward the pilgrims' quarters he feels buoyant, cheerful, as if he were being pulled by invisible strings of light.

"Hey, hey, Onil!" O'Neil sees Tanaji ambling toward him. "Hey, Onil, why are you smiling so much?" Tanaji calls. "Hey, Onil, are you drunk?" O'Neil has never seen Tanaji at ease before. "Look at you," Tanaji says, slapping his shoulder. "I thought you were going to die!"

"Not dead. Feel better. No more sick. Hungry now."

"And you smell bad. Come on. You need a bath."

"Bath good," O'Neil says gratefully. Tanaji leads him to a well where he draws several buckets of water. "Off," he tells O'Neil, nodding at the *farang*'s clothes. O'Neil peels off the shirt, then his boots, stockings, pants, and with some hesitation, his underwear. It's hard enough for him to get used to bathing. He remembers Deoga telling him that all the Hindis bathed, and if he were going to survive, he'd better do so, too.

So O'Neil bathes, he even strips down like a Hindi with his Master Tom flopping in the breeze and his bare ass shining for all to see.

Tanaji starts dousing him and soon he is thoroughly soaked. O'Neil finger combs his long coppery hair and beard, glad to have the dust rinsed from it, and hand scrubs his face. The poultice of cow shit and herbs melts off, forming a greenish oozy puddle around his feet.

Tanaji comes closer to him, frowning. "Look. That shit worked good." O'Neil looks. The wound, festering before, is now closed, and the skin is a livid pink, like a scab has been picked away. There is no sign of bleeding or infection. "You're going to have something," Tanaji says—a scar, O'Neil thinks, noting the word, "but you won't die. Not today, *farang*." Tanaji laughs and O'Neil, with great relief, laughs, too.

O'Neil begins to shiver. "You need some clothes," Tanaji says. "Not those, they smell like shit," he says. Before he leaves, Tanaji finds a horse blanket. It is heavy and scratchy, but O'Neil throws it across his cool shoulders gratefully. Tanaji strides off.

He looks up to see a young farmer leading two dusty ponies into the courtyard. The ponies walk oddly as though they were lame or diseased. But as the ponies draw closer he realizes that the farmer is Shivaji. Seeing him, Shivaji gives a look of pleased surprise. Just then Tanaji rounds the corner, carrying fresh clothing, "Look at our *farang*," he calls out.

"Give me clothes," O'Neil says to Tanaji.

Tanaji hands him the clothing. "Most of your stuff was dirty," he tells O'Neil. "I brought you some of my stuff."

"Thanks," O'Neil says in English, for while there really is no Marathi word for "thank you," he still doesn't feel comfortable taking a kindness without saying something in reply. Tanaji shrugs.

Shivaji and Tanaji talk, quietly and quickly. O'Neil can understand only a few words. He's busy anyway, trying to dress in the clothes Tanaji has bought. The clothes are Hindi clothes, of course. O'Neil pulls on a light brown shirt, a pair of baggy cotton pants and a gauzelike roll of cloth about two yards long, to wrap around his privates.

Tanaji and Shivaji keep stealing glances at O'Neil as he dresses; they are particularly amused as he struggles to wrap his privates. Bloody hell, O'Neil thinks—he has seen men do this, but never tried it himself. Bloody in front of the whole bloody world, he thinks. He puts on the long shirt first, hoping that this will improve his privacy. But the bloody shirt seems to make things worse: he ends up wrapping both shirt and undercloth into his privates.

Naturally, his struggle delights Tanaji and Shivaji even more. At one point they try unsuccessfully to pantomime instructions to the *farang*, but instead, what with waving their hands and wiggling their asses trying to mime how the undercloth is worn, they end up laughing even harder.

At last he's dressed. He tugs on his heavy leather boots, since of course Tanaji owns no stockings and his *chappals* would never fit a *farang*'s wide feet. Feeling a perfect fool, O'Neil steps over to the two men with a valiant smile. "Now look like Hindi," O'Neil announces.

"Now look like fool," Tanaji laughs. "I am telling how you now are not sick. Very good." O'Neil feels embarrassed to be addressed by Tanaji in what clearly is simplified language, but since he can't keep up otherwise, he is grateful.

"Good now, very good, all good," O'Neil agrees. He lifts up his shirt to show Shivaji the wound. "All good now."

Shivaji bends forward to look critically at the long line of bulging pink skin that marks where the slash had been just an hour before; after examining it for a moment, he looks at O'Neil with a puzzled expression. "Very good now, yes. But how? Should be very bad."

O'Neil doesn't have the words to describe his experience in the temple. "Man fix good," he tells Shivaji.

"Yes, doctor very good," Shivaji replies.

"Not doctor. Other man. In . . ." But he can't remember the word for "temple."

Shivaji isn't paying attention; rather he holds O'Neil's scapular gently in his hand, peering at it with unexpected fascination. "Something?" he asks, looking into O'Neil's face.

O'Neil, not sure what he means, follows his glance. "Name is Mary," he says. "God Woman. Mother of God."

"She is Bhavani? Bhavani, yes?" Shivaji asks as if he hadn't heard. He points to the temple where O'Neil met the rag man, the temple with the dark green statue of some goddess.

Bloody hell, no, O'Neil wants to say, she's not some bloody cow idol, it's the Virgin bloody Mary. But Shivaji is waving for Tanaji to come look.

Tanaji stares at it. Then he folds the medal in his hands and brings it to his forehead. *"Har, har, mahadev,"* he whispers.

This reaction confuses O'Neil. He gently takes his medal from Tanaji. Somehow the Virgin's face has changed: dark now, dark green, except for the eyes; there the untarnished silver shines bright. Even O'Neil is reminded of the dark green idol in the temple. He stares at the dark face of Mary for a long time. It's just some bloody kind of tarnish, he thinks.

"It's a sign," Tanaji whispers. Shivaji closes his eyes and nods.

It's no bloody sign, O'Neil thinks. But at the same time he looks up at the two men. The golden glow of sunset touches their faces, highlighting their features. They seem to him noble, like kings of ancient times. It seems that he has known them all his life, maybe many lifetimes.

Bloody hell, I'm thinking like a bloody Hindi myself. He looks at the scapular and it changes before his eyes: now the Blessed Virgin, now the idol goddess. She is that same one, the rag man said.

O'Neil shakes his head. If he were home, if he were with his friends, he'd know how to deal with this nonsense. But home is half a world away. Now Hindustan is his home. Now these must be his friends.

Who can understand her ways? the rag man said.

He folds the medal between his hands, and raises it to his forehead as he saw Shivaji and Tanaji do. The last red rays of the setting sun bathe them in light like fire. *"Har, har, mahadev,"* he says, deciding.

ೞೞೞೞ

They had left Ranjangaon temple in the dim light of dawn: Maya and her
maid Jyoti hidden under blankets in the old oxcart; Shivaji and Tanaji
dressed like farmers, walking beside. Now the sun lifts higher; the air warms
and the shadows lessen. It's breakfast time, and Tanaji is hungry. They stop
at a small food hut near the road.

Tanaji loves places like this: good country people cooking good country food. No seats, no tables, just a fireplace and a packed-dirt verandah:
beneath a rush roof, the floor freshly polished to a dark, translucent green
with the cow dung slurry.

The men wash in a nearby basin. Soon Jyoti and Maya join them. They
sit together on the green floor. Tanaji orders chapatis for everyone. Wheat
chapatis.

Looking at his farmer's clothes, the woman raises an eyebrow. *Bakri*
chapatis, she suggests. Wheat, Tanaji insists. And *dahi*.

He has to put some coins in front of him before she is convinced.

"Are you going to take that from her, uncle?" Jyoti demands. "She has
insulted you!"

"What do you want to me to do?" Tanaji replies. "We'll all get along
better if you deal with your business and leave me to deal with mine."

"You are her business," Maya puts in. Her voice reminds Tanaji of
tamarind, that tastes at once both sour and sweet. "She is my maid, and you
are my keepers."

Tanaji takes a long look at Maya. It's only been a day, but she looks so
different now. She wears a sari the color of yellow roses, traced with vines
of green. Her eyes are brighter, lighter, clear amber flecked with gold. Her
dark hair catches the morning sunlight.

"Please think of us as your hosts," Shivaji says.

"If its soothes you, I will say so. But I now rely on you, don't I? So your
actions—are they not her business? If you wander off drunk, or get yourself
killed, or even if you let any pissy old serving woman insult you, is that not
her business?" Maya says all this calmly, holding Jyoti's hand.

Tanaji squares his shoulders and fixes Maya with a cold eye. "Listen to
me. I don't know what sort of life you've been used to, but the new rules
are these: You'll do what you're told and take what you're given. And
you," he says to Jyoti, "will keep your thoughts to yourself."

At that moment the chapatis arrive. The woman sets them down in a stack on a rough clay plate, still steaming, and puts near them a bowl of fresh buffalo milk *dahi,* the curds firm and creamy white.

"Best if you think of yourselves as our guests," Shivaji says.

"Guests then," Maya replies. "So may your guests inquire what plans you have for them?"

"We're going to my home in Poona. There's a guesthouse in our compound, and you'll be welcome there. You'll stay—as guests—until you can be returned to your proper home. We don't mean to keep you at all."

Maya considers this. What is she to think? She looks away again, a little frightened.

☙☙☙☙

Jyoti can't remember having been this far from home, from the temple where she has lived since she was a baby, where she worked for so many years beside her mother, where her mother's ashes now lie scattered. She felt brave when she offered her services to Maya; but now outside the temple walls, seeing the new world she is entering, her heart beats like a bird's.

She clutches Maya's hand, and thinks of the story of the kidnapped bride Subhadra, gripping the silver railing of Prince Arjuna's war chariot in ancient times, feeling the wind in her face as the prince raced from the pursuing armies of Krishna.

Jyoti talks when she is afraid. She asks if Maya likes stories, and without waiting, she starts to tell story after story: of love forbidden, of love requited. Maya sits against the rocking rickety rails of the oxcart, deep in thought. She cares nothing for love stories. She may seem young to have a heart so hard, but there it is. Love, she thinks, is the fool's name for desire.

She knows about desire: not the desire of Jyoti's stories, a gentle longing of heart for heart. Maya knows the essence of desire; knows it well: the fierce ragged beast that explodes through the quiet skin, yearning to possess, to hold, to own—the brutal hunger of the hands to grasp, of the tongue to lick, of the empty aching yoni to be filled.

Soon they reach a shallow ford where the Poona road crosses the river. Maya's eyes dart along the heavy woods across the river. Jyoti is reciting the story of a queen exiled to the forest. Is that her fate as well? Oh gods, she thinks, How will it be, how will it be? Maybe I should run.

☉☉☉☉

At least the forests had been cool. The trees growing in tangled profusion had muted their steps, their words. The gentle rocking of the oxcart had lulled the women to nap. But now there is no shade. The sun glares down, its light assaulting them. Their faces shine with sweat. The road weaves up and down over increasingly steep hills.

"Tell me where we are, uncle," Maya calls to Tanaji.

"Close. Once we reach the top of this hill, we might even be able to see Poona."

"Whose lands are these, uncle?"

"No one's, now. Maybe his. Maybe he owns them, if anybody does," he says, nodding to Shivaji, who has now fallen far behind them.

"Him, uncle . . . Shivaji?"

"Shahji, his father, conquered this territory. But he gave everything over to Bijapur when he made peace. Anyway, the Bijapuris wanted Shahji's forts, but they didn't give a shit about these old hills." Tanaji hums to himself as if remembering. "This is where I brought Shivaji and my boys when he was on the run from the sultan. There's lots of caves around here."

"He gave them to Bijapur? To the sultana?" Maya asks.

"No, to her husband, the sultan who died. This was years ago, when Shivaji was a child. Hell, Shivaji probably killed him, spitting in his eye the way he did." Tanaji laughs and answers Maya's next question before she asks it. "No, he didn't really spit. He just refused to bow to the sultan—then he turned his back on him when he left the *darbar*. Ten years old, and turning his back! Of course that put his father Shahji into a very unpleasant position. So he tried to make Shivaji apologize to the sultan."

"And did he?" Maya asks, glancing behind her, where Shivaji walks through the dancing shadows of the trees.

"Him? Apologize? Of course not. He stole his father's horse, instead. That's right: He stole Shahji's horse and rode it into the marketplace, and for good measure knocked down the butchers' stands. Meat, you understand. Couldn't bear the sight. He was so full of his mother's notions then, you know—Hindus must not bow down to Muslims; Hindus don't eat meat, like that. He was just a kid. But what a mess." Tanaji glances back at Shivaji, and Maya realizes that he is looking not at a man, but at that boy. "So it fell to me to get him out of sight while Shahji and Dadaji tried to square it with the sultan. In the meantime, there was a price on Shahu's head. So this is where we hid," Tanaji waves his arms to the horizon, "here in these old hills."

At the crest, the road twists to the right, and suddenly the land drops off below them into a wide plain that stretches west as far as they can see. "It looks smooth, doesn't it, like a big table," Tanaji says.

"Like a dancing platform, uncle," Maya replies, enjoying the vista.

"The Deccan plateau," Tanaji explains. "Over there is Poona, where we're going. And where you're going—to Shahu's palace. The Rang Mahal—the Painted Palace."

Jyoti's eyes grow wide to hear this. "A palace?"

"It's just a house," Shivaji says, suddenly drawing near them. "You'll see it soon enough. I'm sure Maya has seen better."

Tanaji nods to some distant mountains to the south. "We're in Shivaji's fief now. From here to . . . well, can you see the forts high on those hills over there? And there," he adds pointing north. "From here, to there, to there—all this land is his."

"This land is ours," Shivaji says quietly, correcting him.

"But I thought Bijapur owns . . ." Maya's voice trails off before she finishes the question.

Shivaji looks away. Tanaji answers for him, "Shahji made a deal with Bijapur, but they haven't held up their end. So by rights . . ." Tanaji shrugs. "It's complicated."

Again Maya sees in Shivaji's eyes the same fierce fire, but now burning even hotter, as though with his fief stretched out before him he is nearing the heart of his desire.

"It's not complicated." Shivaji turns to Tanaji, teeth clenched. "Bijapur has taken everything."

"But, Shahu, we . . ." Then Tanaji stops, and hangs his head. An uncomfortable quiet falls as they stare at the bright lands that lie around them. Shivaji moves to the head of the procession, and Tanaji takes his cue and steps to the rear, and no one speaks a word.

❧❧❧❧

The sun bakes the road. Shivaji, his shirt stained with sweat, reaches for the water jug, pouring a long draft into his mouth from above, and then splashing some over his face.

"Me, too," Jyoti says, flirting. Shivaji lifts the jug over her head. She drinks and then moves suddenly so the water pours onto her breasts, soaking them.

Cow, thinks Maya. Is that what I shall have to do now? she wonders.

They start down the road again, but now Shivaji and Tanaji walk close together, far ahead, talking softly. Maya can't hear what they're saying.

"I wonder what they're up to . . . ," she says to herself.

"Men are a mystery, mistress," Jyoti says. And Maya notes that Jyoti is watching Shivaji as she says this. "He's married," she says, as if Jyoti doesn't know this.

"But he's a man, isn't he?" She leans toward Maya.

"They say that he is very adept. They say that he is the master of a hundred different kinds of congress, and that he has seduced the wives of two hundred Muslim merchants."

"Muslims?" Maya says aloud. "Surely not."

"They say that. The women have not complained, they say, though their husbands beat them after. Many merchants want him dead." She gives a mischevious look. "A wanted man. Wanted by the husbands, wanted by the wives. They say he paid for our temple with their love gifts. So do you think it matters that he's married?"

"I forbid you to flirt with him, Jyoti," Maya whispers. "It's not right."

Jyoti shrugs, and Maya bristles. It's clear that Jyoti thinks she's trying to keep Shivaji to herself. That isn't true, Maya tells herself. But some part of her knows that Jyoti is right.

Despite herself, Maya finds her eyes again drifting toward Shivaji. Even when he is walking slowly so Tanaji and the bullock can keep up, an intense energy seems to pour from him, as though he might suddenly gallop off.

He's a panther, Maya thinks: dark, graceful, full of coiled power. A panther in a cage. And if the cage should open . . .

"Dangerous," Jyoti whispers. She gazes at Shivaji, neither cautiously or circumspectly. It's embarrassing. Oh, gods, thinks Maya, am I as obvious as her?

ভাঃভা

The road snakes toward Poona. Now they see more signs of life: children driving water buffalo, cooking fires, mud farmers' huts. The land is broken into neat squares, marked with stone fences.

Tanaji hasn't forgotten the riders from Kirkhi—but despite this he feels easy. Khirki's looking for two bandits fleeing on horseback, not for a couple of sweaty farmers with women in an oxcart.

"They're hard to see with this haze, but there are caves in most of those hills," he says to the women. "That's why bandits love this area."

"Did you see bandits when you were hiding here, uncle?" Maya asks.

"We were bandits." His voice trails off. Suddenly, he seems old.

"And what will we do in Poona, uncle?" Jyoti asks.

"You two will stay at the palace, I suppose. There's room. Sai Bai will insist, I expect."

"What's she like, uncle?"

Tanaji takes a moment, considering his words. "She grew up well. Shahji arranged the marriage before he went to Bijapur. It took some doing after Shivaji's insults, but Dadaji and Shahji worked out the deal. That's how we stopped living in caves. A couple of years after we got there, Shivaji got married. Shahji never showed up. But Sai Bai was so pretty. Prettiest little girl I think I've ever seen. Every time I see her I still see that bright-eyed little girl. She makes me laugh, Sai Bai. She's a sweetheart."

Jyoti continues on: "And do they have children, uncle?"

"There's a boy, about eight or nine. Nine, I think. Sambhuji." He looks around cautiously. "And Shahu's mother. Jijabai."

"Is she a sweetheart too, uncle?"

"Nice enough, I suppose." He licks his lips. "Like any mother, I suppose." Now he rubs his nose. "She's fine. She's a good woman. Look, you'll meet her soon enough. You can draw your own conclusions."

CHAPTER 9

Standing at the Rang Mahal's great doors, Jijabai sees her son approach, dressed as a farmer. A farmer! She can see that even from here. What is one more disappointment for Jijabai? It is her karma to be humiliated, time and again.

But she does not surrender. She defies her fate.

To punish her for some ancient sin, the gods had given her Shahji for a husband. But she did not decline. So they gave her Shivaji for a son. Still she would not crumble. They exiled her to this backwater, to Poona, and set the halfwit Dadaji for her protector. Even then, she would not bow.

They would not break her, no, not without a fight. She was a queen, and the daughter of a queen. She would not yield.

So now the gods had taken merely to insulting her.

As she gazes at her pathetic son, she feels the thorn again thrust deep into her heart. That she should live to see this day: to see her son, her son who should be king, wearing the filthy lungi of a farmer.

But she does not bend, nor weep nor wail. No, she stands tall: noble but wronged, watching her useless son approach. By the gods, she watches him! no matter how her heart should break.

And that fat fool beside him, Tanaji. This must have been his idea: Oh Shahu, let's dress up like bumpkins! What fun! The fool! Without Tanaji's interference, my son might have seized his destiny.

But are the gods content with these heartaches merely? No, they mock her once more: Jijabai sees the women in the bullock cart. She recognizes what they are at once, and despite herself, she catches her breath. She grasps the doorjamb so she will not faint. Oh you gods, she wails silently. Do what you will, you shall not triumph!

But her heart feels the piercing of another thorn, this one sharper and longer. Now he brings home his whores! Isn't his useless wife trouble enough? Must I now suffer nautch girls in my house?

I am doomed forever to play out this pitiful life. How will Shahu ever be a king? He might as well leave that lungi on, and take a mattock, and go into the fields and dig. I might as well go with him.

But Jijabai buries her anguish where no one can see, for she is a queen despite the gods, and queens have above all their dignity.

She sees her little grandson, as always playing in the dirt. Now all her hopes rest in that dirty, round-faced boy. Now the grandson is her only hope. She will raise Sambhuji to be a king despite his father. "Sam," she calls. "Fetch your good-for-nothing mother. Tell her that her husband has come. As if she cares. Hurry."

"Yes, grandmother," says the boy. He at least has learned to obey without question. He scurries off. "Mama, mama, daddy's home!"

His nose needs blowing, scowls Jijabai.

◌◌◌◌

Shivaji greets Jijabai. How small she is. She is getting old, he realizes, but her face is still vibrant: tiny eyes see everything, high cheekbones worthy of a queen, and a mouth that never smiles. She still wears her marriage necklace, though she hasn't seen Shahji for over fifteen years.

"I greet you, mother," Shivaji says, kneeling to place his forehead to her feet. This is proper respect, and it somewhat placates her. But it makes her feel her age. He used to be so small! But as she looks down at the man kneeling before her, she thinks: even so, he's so beautiful. She is, after all, his mother.

She sniffs. "Where did you find those rags? Have you no dignity? Is this how I raised you! If you care nothing for your own reputation, think what you do to me, your own mother!"

"I beg your forgiveness, mother, though I am unworthy." By now he is adept at such apologies.

"And what, pray tell," Jijabai asks, raising her chin ever so slightly to indicate Maya and Jyoti, "is that?"

"A guest, mother, and her servant."

"Is that what they're called these days? Very pretty."

"Maya, please come here," Shivaji calls. Exchanging timid glances, the women come slowly, eyes lowered, sari ends pulled up to hide their hair.

At that moment, however, Sambhuji comes bursting around his grandmother's skirts. "Daddy," he shouts, leaping to throw his chubby arms around his father's neck. Through the doorway, Shivaji sees his wife, Sai Bai. Her green sari that blends with the shadows. She has tossed its end across her head like a veil, and keeps her face turned down. There is stillness in her movements, like the slow ripples on a deep tank of water.

She starts to kneel at Shivaji's feet, but he pulls her up. "Please let me greet you, lord," she says.

"The sight of you is greeting enough, Sai Bai."

"You flatter me, husband." There he stands, dressed in rags, wearing that look of despair he gets whenever his mother disapproves, which is always. Her dark eyes sweep the scene. Whores. No wonder Jijabai scowls. It is never easy to be his wife.

But she recovers. "We must see to your guests," she says.

"This is Maya," Shivaji says, "and her servant Jyoti." The women raise their folded hands in greeting. "Maya is a devadasi."

Jijabai closes her eyes and sighs. "A nautch girl."

Maya says nothing, but lifts her head and stares into Jijabai's gray eyes until Jijabai flinches and steps back. But Sai Bai moves between Jijabai and her son, and raises her delicate hands to her forehead. "Our house is blessed by your presence."

"Sai Bai," hisses Jijabai, "don't you know what she is?"

"Yes, mother," she replies. "She is my husband's guest, and now mine." She lifts her head. In a heartbeat Sai Bai sees in Maya's eyes a story unfold, a story vast and tragic, hearts shattered and tears shed.

Then, in Maya's eyes, she sees her death.

She straightens, becoming for a moment as stiff and formal as Jijabai. "I am Sai Bai, wife of Shivaji, most noble of men. We must be sisters."

"Let it be as you say," Maya replies, and adds, tentatively, "Sister."

"Disgusting," says Jijabai.

☙☙☙☙

Tanaji lives in a wooden house on the north side of the palace compound. It's empty: Nirmala is probably in the marketplace, shopping and gossiping as usual, the twins are gone hunting, and the servants, of course, are nowhere to be seen. So he yawns and throws himself on the bedmat, and in a moment is snoring loudly.

He wakes to find Nirmala sitting by him. Her round face, as always, seems to be both laughing and scolding. She has gotten thicker as the years pass, and a little less nimble, but to Tanaji she still looks like the bride he married as a boy. He still enjoys a tumble with her now as much as when they were youngsters, his voice cracking and his lingam a sprout that seemed never to get soft. Many things have changed, but she will always be the little girl he married.

"Well, it's a mess over there," she says as soon as his eyes open. "What possessed him to bring a nautch girl here is beyond me. And that sweet wife of his, ready to do anything he wants, anything. And him always leaving her alone for days, and having congress with anything that wears a skirt, and Muslim women, too. She deserves better." She smiles at Tanaji. "But then, everyone can't have the best husband in the world."

"No," Tanaji agrees. "You are very fortunate."

They talk about a hundred things; about nothing; a husband and wife who know each other well.

Nirmala sighs and shakes her head. "Jijabai won't talk to her." It takes Tanaji a moment to realize that she has turned her thoughts once more to the big house. "She sent them to the servants' quarters, but Sai Bai wouldn't hear of it. She almost raised her voice to Jijabai, she was that upset. Sai Bai gave up her own room for them."

"What did Shahu say?"

"He's gone to talk with Dadaji. Trust a man to avoid a conflict."

"He'll settle things when he gets back."

"I think not. I think we know who rules that house."

ᏣᎤᏣᎤ

Shivaji watches Dadaji add up another line of figures.

A white-bearded man with a long sad face, Dadaji sits cross-legged on a low wooden platform, near a short-legged writing table. Everywhere papers surround him, in baskets, in boxes—he even holds papers between his long, wrinkled toes. The room is small—not really big enough for two grown men, Shivaji thinks. Yet when Shivaji appeared at the door, Dadaji had shooed away four or five assistants—his secretary, his accountant, and some others. Shivaji can't imagine how they found room.

Dadaji takes a paper from between his toes, shakes his head, and with a scratching flourish of his feather pen, scribbles a total. Even the slightest interruption makes him lose his concentration, forcing him to start from the beginning. "You see how it is, Shahu." Dadaji holds out the paper with his bare right arm. "We're practically out of money. What will happen when this little bit is gone?"

Now why Dadaji's arm is bare is this: Years ago he had planted an orchard of mango trees in the eastern part of the compound, and forbade anyone to touch the fruit, or lose his arm. One hot day he was strolling through the orchard, and without thinking, he plucked a ripe mango. When he realized what he had done, he cried out for his servant to bring a sword.

The servant fetched Shivaji instead of the sword. At last the boy convinced his uncle not to do the horrible deed. Dadaji agreed, but as penance ripped the sleeve from his shirt, and never covered that arm again.

Shivaji glances at the number. "This is not so bad, uncle," he replies. "We can do well for six months easily with this much in our treasury—even more if we are frugal."

Dadaji snorts. "When did you learn to be frugal? I'm telling you our situation is desperate. That wall costs a lot of money. Do you intend to leave it incomplete? I am telling you, we must raise taxes."

"No." The finality of Shivaji's word allows no argument.

"Always no. So what is your plan then, Shahu? How will you maintain this city? Our taxes are a quarter of what the Bijapuris took. We could double them and still be heroes. Maybe you think bankruptcy is better?"

"I have a plan." Quickly, Shivaji tells Dadaji about Maya, about her value as a slave and the ransom she can bring.

"There are far too many ifs in your plan to satisfy me," Dadaji replies, but already he is counting the ransom and calculating its effect. "How long will this take, do you think?"

"Four or five weeks, no more," Shivaji responds. "Send for Balaji to write up a ransom demand."

"It must be worded carefully," Dadaji responds, "or you will invite reprisals. You might be thought a thief yourself," he adds. "And to whom shall the letter be addressed?" Dadaji asks. "Viceroy Murad? The king of Bijapur? The Portuguese?"

"Why not write three letters?" Shivaji asks. "We'll sell her to the highest bidder."

It pleases Dadaji that his little Shahu has become such a man. He tests and probes Shivaji's plan many ways, and finds it well constructed, if risky. He's like his father, thinks Dadaji—he thrives on tossing the dice. Poona is a city founded on risk; Shivaji is its ideal leader, Dadaji thinks.

"Shahu," he says, "that fool from Singhaghad fort came here again. What's his name . . . Ali Danyal. He now wants only one lakh hun."

"Only one lakh? Only a hundred thousand hun—and for that he will betray Bijapur? That's a bargain," Shivaji says, looking very amused.

"In six months his price has come down from two lakh hun," Dadaji chuckles. "At this rate he'll be paying us to take the fort off his hands in two months." They both laugh.

"Still, uncle, one lakh hun . . . if we had Singhaghad . . ."

"It might as well be one crore hun, Shahu—where would we get that kind of money? What good is one fort, and that bribed away from the Bijapuris? It would poke a finger in the sultana's eye. I only mentioned it because the fool is so insistent." Dadaji frowns. "Shahu, promise me that you won't take this seriously."

After Shivaji leaves, Dadaji continues to work. At lunchtime his servant tells him about Sai Bai and Maya and Shivaji. Dadaji shakes his head. What kind of man must Shivaji be? What kind of man brings a nautch girl as a guest into his home? Yet who sells off a guest to the highest bidder?

He longs for the old days, for General Shahji who did things right. I'm sorry, commander, he tells Shahji mentally, I've done a piss-poor job of raising your son. Selling a guest to the highest bidder! Sighing, Dadaji turns back to his work.

ભ

"Now Shahu!"

"Soon, mother."

"It has been nearly a month!"

"Maybe it has only been two weeks, mother."

"She has to go!"

"She will go."

"Now!" Jijabai looks as though she has bit into a chili.

"Very soon, mother. I promise."

Jijaibai reaches for the door of Shivaji's bedroom. "She destroys my peace! Everyday comes some new insult, some new crisis!" She whirls around. "Who will rid me of that rakshashi!"

"Soon, soon, I promise, mother."

"You have been saying so, but that demoness remains!" She sees Sambhuji dashing through the hallway. "Sam!" she calls. "Stop that running."

Sambhuji shuffles to his father's door with his head down.

"You know better than to run. You are prince of the blood, Sambhuji. What will the servants think?"

"I'm sorry, grandmother. I'm on an errand for Auntie Maya."

Jijabai pulls Sambhuji into the room to face his father. "Do you hear this? Your own son calls her 'auntie'!"

Sambhuji peers up at his father. "I was just on my way to find Jyotibai. Auntie Maya needs her. She knew I could find her, quick as fire. She says I'm really fast. But I should have fetched Jyoti by now!"

"We do not fetch, young man. Dogs fetch. That is why the gods made servants." Jijabai turns to Shivaji. "You see her influence! It spreads from her like a disease. First your wife, and now your son."

"Where she belongs."

"Please, grandmother. I have to get Jyoti. Auntie Maya wants her bath."

"Her bath!" Jijabai sputters. "She would have a bath every day. Every day! And hot water, too!"

"But I bathe every day. Father makes me," Sambhuji puts in.

"We bathe by the well, son," his father says, trying to smooth things over. "So our baths are not so difficult for your grandmother."

"You must forbid this! She should bathe like a regular person or not all! A hot bath every day! Is she some sort of queen? Even I . . ." Shivaji's large eyes bore into her. She stops, for she has come to the heart of the matter. Well of course she is jealous! Who wouldn't be jealous? Some whore treated like a queen! While Jijabai herself, truly a queen, must watch and suffer? "I blame your wife," Jijabai whispers, and strides from the room.

"Did I do wrong, father?" Sambhuji asks.

"You did fine, son." Shivaji tousles his son's hair with his strong fingers. "Now, don't you have an errand?" With that, Sambhuji dashes from the room.

ৱ৩৫৩

On the stairs, Shivaji meets Jyoti hurrying to Maya, with Sambhuji tagging behind. Now that she has been away from the temple, her face seems longer, more sophisticated. But she still walks with an energetic bounce, as if any minute she might begin to skip.

"Well, you have been summoned, I see," Shivaji says, winking at his son. "And it is not morning any longer; the noon bell rang some time ago. Time for your mistress to be up, I think, or there may be trouble."

Jyoti laughs. "My mistress can make trouble without leaving her bed, master. Come on, Sam."

As they slip past Shivaji on the narrow staircase, he pulls Jyoti aside. "I don't think Sambhuji should be there when your mistress bathes," he says, careful that his son not hear. "I know that in a harem boys are allowed . . ."

"My mistress bathes in privacy," Jyoti replies. "Frankly, your son is the least of my worries. It's those others . . ." Jyoti stops suddenly.

"What others?"

"No one. It's nothing." But finally, glancing anxiously at Maya's door, Jyoti allows that she has seen men trying to peek into the bathhouse.

Shivaji's face grows cold. "Who?" he says, his voice harsh.

"I don't know, sir," Jyoti responds, suddenly timid. "I'd say if I could, sir. When I go to chase them away, they are gone."

"Maybe it's just children."

"Maybe," Jyoti replies.

"I will take care of it," he says finally. "Go to your mistress. Tell her she won't be bothered by this insult again." He looks angry, Jyoti thinks, as he clatters down the narrow staircase.

☙☙☙☙

The shutters of the house have been sealed since dawn, trapping the morning air. Outside, the heat is already fierce. Before he gets to Tanaji's house Shivaji is damp with sweat.

He glances at the wooden bathing house behind the Rang Mahal: an older, simpler building. Some of its wooden sideboards have cracked with age. Anyone could peer in and get an eyeful.

He finds Tanaji sitting on his verandah, using a flat stone to sharpen the blades of his mace. "Morning, Shahu. Dadaji's coming for breakfast. Maybe you'll join—"

"Who has been spying on Maya in the bathhouse?" Shivaji asks.

Tanaji looks up, his eyebrows hunched and his lips pursed. "How would I know?" Shivaji says nothing. Tanaji stares at Shivaji, and slowly an unpleasant idea strikes him. He sets the mace between his crossed legs. "Hey, boys!" he calls. "Boys! Come out here."

In a moment the twins come out. Shivaji knows them well: they have been playmates, have hunted and gambled together. But now instead of greeting them, Shivaji stares at them as if he is sizing them up for a fight.

Tanaji frowns. His sons are a few years younger than Shivaji. Both sport wide, flowing mustaches, and like Shivaji, they look trim, strong, and proud. Hanuman and Lakshman are almost indistinguishable, although a close friend can see that Hanuman's face is slightly heavier, more apt to smile, and that Lakshman's eyes often flash with anger.

"You boys seen anybody prowling around the bathing house?" Tanaji asks.

They glance at one another. "What's going on, Shahu?" Hanuman asks.

"He's accusing us, brother," says Lakshman softly, eyeing Shivaji.

Shivaji stares back. "Not both of you."

"Speak up if you know something," Tanaji says.

Hanuman lifts his hands in confusion, but Lakshman speaks. "I've seen nothing others haven't seen."

Shivaji glares at him. "She is my guest."

"She's a whore."

"Lakshman!" Tanaji barks. But Lakshman is used to speaking freely.

"Say, Shahu," says Hanuman, "take it easy. So he watched her. So? She's used to it, right? Anyway, isn't the plan to sell her off? So he got a look at the goods . . . what difference does it make? No harm done, Shahu!"

But Shivaji and Lakshman are locked in an edgy staring contest. Tanaji feels compelled to add his voice, "Shahu, where's the harm? She's just a nautch girl!"

Shivaji bristles. "You call her 'daughter.' She calls you 'father.' But now she's just a nautch girl?"

"I call my mare 'sweetie,' but she's still just a horse. And I keep her in the stable, not in the house!"

There's wildness in the air, a fight on its way, ripping through the hot air like a thunderstorm about to burst. Tanaji waves Lakshman to stand behind him. Lakshman doesn't move, except for his right hand, which fumbles in his pocket. Shivaji, for his part, is standing easy, eyelids half-closed so it's hard to see where exactly he is looking.

If it were just another fight his brother had brought on himself, Hanuman would know what to do, but he's got his father to deal with, and Shahu as well. "Let's take a breath, all right? Why are we all getting so excited?" He looks up to see a barrel-shaped brahmin passing, his head shaved but for a small topknot, his chest bare except for the sacred thread. It is Trelochan, a young priest. Hanuman calls to him.

Trelochan ambles over, and then senses the tension. "What's going on?" he whispers to Hanuman.

"That girl . . . ," Hanuman replies.

Trelochan shakes his head. "You see how it is, Shahu? All Hanuman needs to say is 'that girl' and immediately I know! What does that tell you? Let us sit down and discuss this like men," he says, lowering himself to the floor. "Shahu, please, come sit. Tanaji, please."

So they all sit with exaggerated casualness, careful not to touch.

"Show me your hand," Trelochan says to Lakshman.

Slowly, Lakshman lifts his bare hand—bare, that is, but for three black rings on his fingers. Suddenly he makes a fist and thrusts it a thumbs-breadth from Trelochan's nose.

Jutting out from between his fingers are three dark dagger blades, each sharp, double-edged, about two inches long.

Lakshman gives Trelochan his sneering grin.

"Very nice," says Trelochan. "Tiger claws. Let me keep those for now."

Lakshman first stretches his hand flat—the blades hide neatly between his fingers; the weapon disappears. Then he pulls the weapon's rings from his fingers, and lays the tiger claws on the brahmin's open palm.

Just as Trelochan thinks he's settled matters, a door opens in the rear of the big house, and Sambhuji comes out, and Jyoti, and last of all that girl herself, the source of all the trouble, wrapped in a robe of sheer silk that clings to her limbs. Her round hips sway. No one speaks until they have followed Maya's silken walk across the courtyard. Finally the door of the bathing house closes.

"Really, Shahu," Trelochan says. "Something must be done. This arrangement is no good. Maybe you could move the bathing place closer to the house. It would be less distracting."

"Just tell Maya she needs to learn to enjoy being dirty like the rest of us." Tanaji grins. They all laugh, but Shivaji least of all. As for Lakshman, Trelochan notes that he keeps glancing toward the bathing house, and sometimes to the black tiger claws resting on Trelochan's lap.

Trelochan turns back to the men around him. "Look . . . Dadaji is coming. It is a good omen."

When Dadaji sees the gathering on the verandah he frowns. He is bare-foot, and he carries his beautiful bright red shoes tied on his belt, another indication of his well-known frugality.

Coming with him is a tall, nervous young man: his apprentice, Bala. Bala, as always, is grinning happily, as if the simple act of walking is his greatest pleasure—with such big ears and wide lips, his toothy smile is infectious. His dark head gleams in the sunlight, for Bala is gloriously bald. No hair on his head, his face, his body: no eyebrows, no lashes, no mustache, no beard, no pubes. As with every part of his life, this oddity seems to delight him.

Dadaji looks around, then seats himself with a formal dignity, as though recognizing that there is an official quality to this gathering. "Well?"

"It's about the girl," the priest replies.

"Ahcha." Dadaji slumps back. He's been expecting this. "Well?"

Lakshman starts to tell his story: He may have glanced at Maya in her bath. By accident.

Dadaji turns to Tanaji, not Lakshman. "You see how it is? Your sons need wives, Tana," he declares. "It is not good for them to be alone. You must find them wives."

"What harm has been done?" Tanaji asks. "A man sees a naked whore—what's the harm?"

Dadaji looks at Lakshman. "I am embarrassed that your son feels no shame." Then he notices the tiger claws resting in Trelochan's lap. He picks them up between finger and thumb, as though lifting a dry dog turd.

"*Wagnak*," he whispers, using the old Marathi word for the weapon. "Whose?" The priest nods toward Lakshman. Dadaji sighs.

"How long will this girl remain, Shahu? You see the trouble she brings." He turns to Bala. "When did you send those ransom letters?"

Bala's smile is frozen and painful to see. "Master, maybe they did not go right away."

Dadaji bristles. "When did you send them?"

"To be perfectly accurate, master, I might say that those particular letters still await actual sending."

"What?" Dadaji shouts. He slaps at Bala, but Shivaji catches his hand.

"It's not his fault. I told him not to send the letters." Shivaji hesitates. "It did not now seem right to me. As I considered it, it seemed to me that this was no more than selling her for a slave."

Dadaji stares at him. "You might have told me. Supposedly I'm still in charge. Anyway, she *is* a slave! You must not interfere with her karma!" Dadaji turns to Trelochan for support. "Am I not right?"

The priest shrugs. "Maybe, sir, but . . . it has occurred to me that . . . well, since Shahu took the girl by force, by kshatriya law, they are already married."

Another vein pops pulsing into the skin of Dadaji's forehead. "Married?" He lifts his hands to the gods. "Has everyone gone mad?"

"That is the law of the kshatriya caste, sir. Marriage by force is the most honorable form of marriage for a warrior."

"Enough nonsense!" Dadaji shouts. "Shivaji is not a kshatriya!"

Trelochan speaks without thinking, excited now. "Oh but he is sir! He is a kshatriya prince! My preliminary research . . ."

"I say, enough!" Dadaji stands, an old man filled with righteous anger. "The day of the kshatriyas has passed. That caste is dead. Those ancient laws do not apply. Kshatriya law was written for kshatriyas, not for us. We don't gamble and whore and hunt and kill for pleasure. We don't have a dozen wives. And we don't marry by kidnapping!" Dadaji glares. "We need no kshatriyas! We need men! Real men! Men of honor!" He looks directly at Shivaji. "Men who keep their word!" Slowly he lowers himself down. "I'm old. Perhaps the time has come for me to leave."

The men around the circle know the coming speech by heart.

"I shall wander the roads, a naked sadhu. I shall die in the Ganges," he says, raising his eyes to the heavens.

"No, uncle, please stay, I beg you." Shivaji presses his forehead to the floor, and Dadaji closes his eyes, mollified.

"Still, why not let her stay?" asks Hanuman. "I think it's wrong to sell her."

"You answer," Dadaji says to Shivaji.

"Very well, uncle: You would have me say that she is dangerous because she is valuable. She has been stolen from powerful men. Next you would have me say that she is dangerous because of her nature. She is beautiful and desirable. A wise man hides such a treasure. Besides, our city is poor and the money she would fetch could help much."

Dadaji looks at him proudly. "Now you answer as a man worthy of being a prince."

"Even so, uncle," Shivaji says, "I will not sell her. I mean no disrespect. I must be a man before I am a prince. No man could bear to see her sold. I regret I suggested it." Dadaji's answering glance is withering.

Trelochan speaks. "But Shahu, look at what she's done to your friends, to your house. Even to you! If you won't sell her, at least send her away."

"What about taking her back to Ranjangaon temple?" Tanaji suggests. "She's a devadasi. She belongs dancing in a temple."

"Dangerous," says Shivaji. "Too close to Khirki and that dharmsala. Too busy, too. Someone might recognize her."

"What about Adoli temple?" Bala says. "It's just a few miles from Welhe. That's Iron's place. Remember Iron? He was a great friend of Shahji."

"It's a little village," Hanuman says. "Same sort of trouble will get stirred up there as here, don't you think?"

"She'll be in the temple, not the village. A Bhavani temple. There's a dancing school. Maya could help."

"They'll find her," Hanuman says. "She's worth a lot, a girl like that. Just because Shivaji has some honor . . ."

"Iron will protect her. He is a real man," Dadaji says firmly. "A devadasi he will keep safe."

"But the road to Welhe will be dangerous," Hanuman insists.

"Do it carefully, then," Tanaji says. He lifts his chin, pointing to the sky. "In a week or two monsoons will start. You won't find anybody traveling those roads then, not even bandits. Wait until it rains.

"Can't use a cart though, not on those roads, not in the rain," Tanaji realizes. "They'll have to learn to ride."

"I'll see to it," Hanuman says, unable to disguise his pleasure.

This final plan meets mumbled approval. The mood at last is pleasant.

Except for Dadaji. Dadaji considers Shivaji. Measuring him, the way a man measures the beam he lays on a foundation, wondering if it will serve.

And except for Lakshman. Unnoticed, he has moved into the shadows on the other side of the courtyard. He waits there as Maya comes out of the bathing house, like a flower blossoming in the morning still wet with dew.

Watching.

As the monsoons approach, the days grow darker. The sky changes. For a while, the sun peeks through the haze. Then the haze becomes thick, and there is only a glow where once the bright sun shone.

It will only be days, perhaps hours before the rains come to Poona. The air grows dense with moisture; sweat hangs on the skin, clothing will not dry, mold grows on sandals and mildew stains walls.

Jijabai finds Shivaji sitting on the verandah, looking at a stack of papers. For a moment, she remembers herself as young woman, scarcely more than a girl, carrying him in her belly in all that heat, holding him to her nipple as he suckled, carrying him on her hip through these forests as they first came to Poona. What hopes she had.

Now she is hopeless. Looking down she doubts that he will ever achieve anything. He is truly his father's son, she thinks. So she stands over him rather than sit beside him.

Jijabai scowls. "The girl," she says at last.

"You wanted her gone. She's going. We'll leave when the rains start; in a day or two. Isn't that what you wanted?"

"What about the ransom?" she says, choking out the words.

Shivaji bobs his head noncommittally. "No ransom, mother."

"Why should you throw away the fortune that the gods have placed in your hands?" Jijabai stamps her foot. "Dadaji has told me. The treasury is nearly empty yet you will give away your prize! Have you gone mad?"

"There is plenty. In fact I will take a thousand rupees to the temple as *bhiksha* . . ."

"A thousand!"

"There's plenty in the treasury, mother. Dadaji—"

"How dare you ignore your uncle and adviser!"

Shivaji doesn't look up. "It is wrong to ransom her."

"That's not what you said before! This is her doing. You've been manipulated. She's leading you around by your lingam. You and all your men—like dogs smelling a bitch!"

"Mother," Shivaji whispers.

But Jijabai doesn't care if her voice carries up the stairs. Let her hear! "She is no fragile flower, Shahu. Her yoni is no unopened bud. I'm sure you've found that out. Under your own roof, with your son not twenty feet away!" She bites her lip, determined not to weep. "Oh, Shahu," she moans. "What will become of us? I won't die poor. I won't!"

"Mother, such talk! Who says you will be poor?"

"The treasury is nearly empty. How will we live?"

"There's plenty left, mother. Plenty for many months."

"Not enough if the Bijapuris demand a larger allotment." She watches with satisfaction as Shivaji considers this. Now, maybe, he understands the reason she is so upset. "You must raise the tax. If only to appease the Bijapuris." She ignores Shivaji's puzzled look. "Of all the jagirs in their realm Poona has the lowest taxes. Why do you think so many farmers are moving here? Don't you think it attracts their notice? How long can you expect them to ignore us? Soon they will come in anger!"

"But they made a treaty with my father," Shivaji protests.

"Oh, you are a child," she sighs.

☙❦☙❦

In a small fenced ring, Jyoti and Maya trot their ponies in an easy circle. In the center of the ring stands Hanuman, from time to time flicking the the ponies with a long willow branch.

Hanuman smiles to himself. If they go in the rain as Tanaji plans, when will they even find a place to trot? When will they do anything but slog through a river of mud? Still it is enjoyable to teach them.

Sometimes Jyoti's pony will suddenly break into a canter and when this happens, she laughs. Hanuman notices the way Jyoti responds, enjoying the sudden roughness and surprise. He finds himself thinking thoughts that have nothing to do with horses.

Maya on the other hand is quiet as she rides. But she is a much better rider: calm where Jyoti is excited, still where Jyoti bounces. Already the horse and Maya move as one.

"You're both doing very well today!" Hanuman calls out. "You're ready for the trip, I think." He looks at the sky, squinting, sniffing the air. "Rain tonight. So we'll leave tomorrow or the day after. You'll do fine."

"You are too kind, dear sir," Jyoti says with too much formality. "That makes us feel much better than yesterday."

Hanuman frowns. "What about yesterday?"

Jyoti laughs. "Yesterday you were not so pleased. Yesterday you shouted at us both, and insisted on giving Maya private instructions."

Hanuman frowns. "I gave you no lesson yesterday."

Maya's face changes: first laughter, then shock, then horror.

Jyoti just laughs, not noticing her mistress. "Of course you gave us lessons. I have the stripe on my backside where you missed the horse!"

"No," says Maya quietly, studying his face. "No. It wasn't him."

ଓଠଓଠ

Tanaji has decided to take twenty-five men along to Welhe. He has two worries: the girl and the gold.

Everyone in Poona knows about the thousand pieces of gold they carry. And Poona buzzes with the tale of Maya's price of seven lakh hun. If Poona knows, everyone knows. And someone might try something. And the girl is like some witch's charm that lures men to lust. He has felt that charm; he has seen it at work on Shahu, and on his sons. It seems the whole town has become bewitched. If he takes along enough men, he reasons, the effect might be diluted. They can't all be smitten at once.

Besides the girl, there is the gold: Shivaji, as Tanaji expected, wants to take a casketful of gold to the temple. There is nothing like giving gold to the *shastri* to improve your welcome. But gold, Tanaji knows, has a voice; it calls out as it travels, and villains hear its call.

Outside, he hears nervous, prancing hoofbeats, and a grating voice with a horrible accent.

It's O'Neil.

There at the gate of the compound, arguing with the gatekeeper, riding Shivaji's fine black Bedouin, with the other Bedouin tethered behind him.

"I never thought we'd see you again!" Tanaji calls.

"See, don't I tell you I good friend Shivaji?" O'Neil calls back. "Look: I am bringing here your Bedouins see? Like promise, I do."

"Very good, Onil," Tanaji says. "I never thought we'd see you again, to tell the truth."

"Where Shivaji? Must talk Shivaji. Where that girl?" O'Neil asks, looking around the courtyard.

Tanaji looks from the *farang* to the lowering sky. "Don't unpack," Tanaji says.

ೕಀೕಀ

In a cave on the edge of Poona is a temple, carved from the living rock. Thick black columns form its wide colonnade. In the heart of the cave a temple to Shiva has been carved from the basalt, and in the center of that small temple is a shivalingam.

Sai Bai steps into the darkness of the inner temple. She rings the dark bronze bell that hangs from the ceiling. It peals deeply, and a rich, low hum reverberates in the heavy air. She likes this dark place, its coolness and its silence, the ancient temple and the more ancient cave. She comes here when her heart is troubled.

There are no priests here, only the lingam and a tiny butter lamp: it is quiet, cool, and dank. She walks once around the lingam and stands before it, adoring it, quieting her heart. Then she whispers her prayer.

The lingam itself is only about a foot tall. And maybe by design or by the ravages of time, it is not smooth; it seems almost to have veins carved into the black stone. It glistens in the darkness. At its base are flower petals, bits of incense, and a few coins.

She says her prayer, then she waits for a sign that the gods have heard.

In a moment a drop of water forms on the dark ceiling and falls onto the lingam with a plop.

ೕಀೕಀ

Leaving the temple, she sees him in the shadows, meditating cross-legged on a wide platform of rock, in a part of the cave where the carving was never completed. His head nearly touches the low-hanging ceiling. His eyes are closed and his hands are on his knees.

When she was a child, her auntie told her the story of Karna, the foundling child of a charioteer, really the son of the sun god. When she met Shivaji she thought of that son of the sun: his skin always golden, his face radiant, his eyes like jewels.

She wishes she were enough for him.

Shivaji's face brightens when he sees Sai Bai. "Did the gods answer?"

"Husband, do you have some trouble on your mind?"

"Maybe some money trouble. Taxes and allotments. Mother thinks Bijapur may raise our allotment, even attack us."

"What will you do?" He tells her so little about his life outside the palace. But Sai Bai picks up pieces and assembles them in her heart.

"I trust that the path of dharma will be clear. I'll do what I must."

She can no longer hold back. Here in the silence of this cave, as the storm gathers round them, she cannot be silent. "I see your heart. I see the madness that you plan."

Shivaji stares at her. "This is not like you."

"You must not do it, husband. I see on every side around you blood and death and grief. You must not do this thing."

"Why not?" he shouts, and his words echo in the cave.

"Because it is the path of darkness. And you . . ." She cannot finish. "Give up, husband," she says abruptly. "I have prayed for the courage to say this, so, please, dearest, don't interrupt me." Sai Bai takes a deep breath, staring into her husband's eyes. "Let me care for Sam and Jijabai. Go away from here. She is so beautiful and her heart is pure and she loves you, dearest. She doesn't know this, yet, but she does. Trelochan says you are already married. So leave these troubles. Give up your mad plan. Take her to some sweet valley in the forest and live lives of pleasure."

Shivaji lowers his head. "I do not think that is my path."

"Then make it your path. I know your heart. You have the strength to make it so. Like Kunti and Pandu, be happy in the forest. Be happy, husband, as I will be happy for you." The faint light highlights tears in the corners of Sai Bai's eyes.

Shivaji says nothing for a long time. "What about Madri? She was Pandu's other wife. She went to the forest, too. They were happy together, the three of them, were they not?"

Sai Bai scarcely dares to breathe. "Yes, lord," she says. "Yes, Madri was happy, too."

"But it cannot be so with us, Sai Bai," Shivaji says.

Sai Bai closes her eyes, feeling as though the knife has fallen through her heart. "No," she says weakly. They are so close, she can hear his heart beating while her own heart breaks.

"I have but one wife, dearest. Why would I seek another? I have but one home. If you think you know my heart, then you must know this."

"But I thought . . . and she's so . . . perfect . . ." Sai Bai's throat is tight and she has trouble speaking.

"But she is not my wife, no matter what a priest may say. You were chosen for me, and for that I thank the gods."

Sai Bai throws herself against him, her tears now flowing onto his shirt.

"Marry her, husband. I wouldn't mind. Trelochan says a kshatriya must have many wives."

"I have you. What man could ask for more?"

"But those women . . . all those Muslim wives . . ." Sai Bai says the words before she can stop herself.

Shivaji looks into her eyes. "They are not women."

"Not women! What are you saying? I don't understand."

"Don't try to understand. Just love me."

So she clings to him. When they leave the temple, on the open road where anyone may see, she pulls away. But still she feels his weight against her. A wind gusts suddenly in the midst of the dark, humid air. The trees rustle, branches sway in the wind. Then a fat raindrop plops onto her forehead, and one on her arm, and soon the dusty ground begins to jump as big globs of rain splash on the dry earth.

The monsoon has come.

CHAPTER 10

As a fish leaps from the water, eager to catch the baited hook, Ali Khalil saw his chance and leaped.

The life of a lesser nephew of the emperor, simple and obscure, filled with petty handouts and dubious favors—such a life might satisfy some men, but not Ali Khalil. He cadged an invitation to live at the palace; once there he had won his uncle's trust. But his uncle, Shah Jahan, emperor of Hindustan, would not be emperor long, he soon realized. Ali Khalil was no fool.

So he turned his thoughts to winning the confidence of the next emperor. Of course he assumed that the successor would be his cousin, Dara. Everyone assumed this. But after spending time in Dara's company, Ali Khalil saw that the empire would not long tolerate such a self-important fool. And the other princes—Murad, Shuja—he had seen and dismissed: they were ciphers; ineffectual, even laughable, unsuitable as emperor.

But then Aurangzeb arrived at court—quiet, introspective, adamant, modest Aurangzeb. Ali Khalil saw that the sun would soon rise on Aurangzeb even as it set on Shah Jahan. Aurangzeb too was no fool. So Ali Khalil had made himself available; he charmed, he flirted.

At last his moment had come, when he received that secret note from the old *khaswajara*, Hing. Ali Khalil leaped.

Following Hing's instructions, he had found the old path that led to the moat. But when he got there, there had been no boat.

No boat.

He had stood there like a fool, pressed against the red sandstone walls, staring at the slow-moving river. With each step back to his rooms he faced a flood of doubt and dread.

They had duped him. They had forced him to show his hand. His anger at his folly was matched only by his terror; the penalty for betrayal was death: swift, certain, secret, painful death. Curled up on his bed, he awaited the crack of the door bursting its hinges, the rush of guards, the pitiful end to his pitiful life.

But a day had passed, then another. When he tiptoes from his room, he is ignored. No one greets him. No one, it seems, even looks at him. A week passes. He must sneak into the servant cantonment to buy food, or he would starve.

They know. They all know, he realizes. He locks his door, and pulls the drapes, and determines to fast until he dies. But Ali Khalil, nephew to the emperor, will not be defeated easily. Ali Khalil makes a plan.

For he realizes that betrayal is two-edged sword. What is *his* betrayal? Nothing! Especially compared with the betrayal of the *khaswajara*, that pathetic eunuch Hing. Ali Khalil has done no more than to receive a note! What about the traitor who *wrote* that note? What about Hing?

He will bring the old *khaswajara* to justice, he decides, that shriveled eunuch who betrayed him. The wheel of justice will turn full circle!

Seeing now that it is Hing, not he, who has the most to lose, Ali Khalil begins to wonder—on whose behalf did Hing deceive him: on Shah Jahan's? Or Dara's?

If only he were wiser; if only he had been raised at court instead of in his mother's country house, maybe he would not be in such danger—danger exacerbated by his ill-formed plan.

Ali Khalil writes a hasty note to the captain of the palace guard, signs it, and seals it with wax. He opens his door, fearful of being seen delivering it. But then, the Prophet be praised, luck shines on him: A boy comes his way, a carefree African boy, dark as shadows, his teeth gleaming white against his black lips. In a moment Khalil has sent the boy scurrying.

While he waits, he himself sponges his elegant gray cloak—for he is poorer than he would like to appear, and it is the only one he owns. He hears a timid knocking at his door. The boy has brought an answering note. The captain suggests a time when they can meet in secret; when the inner palace will be deserted.

It never occurs to Khalil to wonder why the note is unsealed.

⊖⊙⊖⊙

As the note instructed, he waits in a colonnade near the Diwan-i-Am. Behind him he hears a heavy groan. Beneath the shadowed archway of the colonnade, the palace wall begins to bulge, and a secret door appears, formed from the wall of heavy sandstone blocks.

From the shadows of that dark doorway, a hand signals him. Khalil glances around, assures himself that no one is looking, and then heads into the shadows of that open door, a man chasing blindly to his death.

The door groans shut, closing with a deep *thoom* that seems to echo for miles, and the world is plunged into shadows. Stepping from the white brilliance of the morning into the inky dark, Ali Khalil can sense but not see the cramped and narrow passageway.

He smells dust and damp stone. Then the small flame of a butter lamp floats in front of him. Slowly his eyes adjust: he sees then the long fingers and narrow hand that holds the lamp; the arm and slender waist and finally the body and face of the man who holds it.

The eunuch who holds it.

One of the eunuch's dark eyes drifts outward: it's hard to tell which eye is really looking at him. "Who are you?" Khalil asks.

"Didn't you want to see the captain of the guard?" The voice is throaty, but commanding. "In secret?"

"Yes . . . but who are you?"

"I serve the one who answered your note. Is that not enough for you to know?"

"Perhaps," Khalil says.

"What do you wish with the captain of the guard?"

"That I will say to him alone."

The eunuch seems about to answer but shakes his head. "You might have saved yourself some trouble if you had spoken first to me, Ali Khalil. But never mind; that is not your fate." With that he starts off, casting Khalil into shadows as the lamp proceeds into the darkness.

At this point, Khalil is in turmoil. A eunuch! Since when was the captain of the guard attended by a eunuch? "Wait," he cries. His voice swirls into a mush of echoes. Ali Khalil hurries toward the flame like an unsuspecting moth.

He catches glimpses of the dark stones that line the narrow hall—great stones, roughly cut, jammed in place with lots of mortar and no finesse. The floor is uneven, and he often stumbles as he struggles to keep up with the slender eunuch and his quick, swaying step. Khalil slides his left hand along the stone wall as he walks in the near darkness. Unconsciously he begins to lean against that hand, steadying himself when he starts to trip on the uneven floor. But suddenly the wall disappears from beneath his hand. He cries out and stumbles.

"Are you all right?" the eunuch asks.

In this light, his eyes look like an animal's, Khalil thinks. "I'm fine," he answers. "Where's the captain?"

"Try to keep up. It won't be long. Do be careful, Ali Khalil. From here on we start to go down."

Why didn't he answer me properly? thinks Ali Khalil.

ⓈⓄⓈⓄ

"Stop!" Ali Khalil calls out after what seems like hours of walking. "I will go no further! Let the captain of the guard come here!" He is nearly screaming, he realizes, and his voice echoes and echoes and echoes.

The eunuch comes near, putting out a hand. Ali Khalil flinches. "Calm yourself. You must be calm. If you don't keep your head these old paths can be treacherous."

"Treacherous, indeed," says a voice behind him. Khalil swings around. The flickering light reflects on thick spectacles, the rheumy eyes behind them wet and cloudy, like the eyes of a fish that is starting to rot.

"You surprise me, Ali Khalil," Hing says to him. "And I've grown so tired of surprises. Maybe you should try Alu instead. He likes surprises. He likes so many things."

The old eunuch looks to the other. "Well, Alu? Would you like Khalil to surprise you? I understand that he's your type." Hing starts a chuckle that dissolves into wet coughing. "Alu likes the company of rugged men. You're rugged, aren't you Khalil? Alu, do you find him attractive?"

Maybe Alu responds—Khalil pays no attention. His stomach is churning now, his mind reeling. He's walked into a trap! How long did Hing hide there? "What do you want, *khaswajara*?" Khalil says. His voice sounds surprisingly confident. Already the first threads of a plan are weaving in his mind.

"I want so little, Khalil." Khalil sees the spectacles bobbing as Hing walks. "I'd like to eat food again, something with more substance than rice. I'd like a friend. Not the sycophants I'm plagued with; toadies like you. I'd like to have Nur Jahan for empress again. Now there was a real queen." Hing pauses. "Am I boring you?"

"No," Khalil lies.

"And I'd like . . . let's see . . . I'd like to have my balls back, please. And my dick. Is that too much to ask? They've had them for so long; you'd think they'd be done with them by now." Now Hing moves closer, and Khalil can see that he steadies himself by placing his hand on the shoulder of a beautiful African boy, a boy as dark as shadows.

Khalil curses Fate. He is right to do so, for it was Fate that brought Hing's little eunuch to his door, Fate that put Kahlil's note into his black hands, Fate that he carried the note straight to Hing, his teeth gleaming white against his black lips all the while.

Hing sighs. "But you didn't truly mean to ask what I want, did you? You wanted to know what's going to happen to *you*." Khalil draws back from the yellow, decaying smell that seems to ooze from his body. "You're going to die, my boy. You're dead already, in fact. You've been dead for hours. You're just too stupid to lie down."

Khalil sees a shadow of movement in the flame of the butter lamp, and sees that the slender eunuch now has a long knife in his hand. Instinctively, he reaches for his belt. But of course, he brought no weapons. He was meeting the captain of the palace guard, after all.

"You see how it is Khalil? Alu likes surprises. Don't you, Alu?"

Alu's thumb twitches on the edge of his knife's narrow blade.

"You should have come with us, Khalil. You have no idea what a world of trouble your absence caused."

"I tried, but there was no boat!"

"Pity you weren't there on time. It seems someone else took your boat instead. A nice enough fellow—out of his depth of course. A pity. He drowned. But you knew him! Basant—the eunuch who killed those guards!"

"Basant killed the guards? How? He hadn't the strength . . ." Despite his situation, Khalil is intrigued.

"Yes," Hing says, suddenly congenial. "Little Basant. Harmless Basant. Would you like to see how he did it? We're not far from where they died."

"They died here? In these tunnels? Can you show me?" Khalil feigns curiosity, interest, respect. He'll buy time, he thinks. Khalil bows his head. And it works. With a vague smile, Hing leads the way. Amazing that Hing could be manipulated so easily. All Khalil had to do was show a little interest and Hing was ready to take him on a tour instead of killing him.

He must know these tunnels blindfolded, Khalil thinks.

Khalil shapes a plan. Hing he can kill with his bare hands: that dry old neck will snap like a twig. The boy—he'll be a nuisance, but Khalil will manage. It is Alu, the young slender eunuch, that is the key. He holds a knife, he's young; strong enough to fight back. Khalil might surprise him; even overpower him.

But Alu also holds the lamp. What if he were to drop it in a struggle? Then Khalil would be trapped in this maze of darkness. Hing might know his way in the darkness, but not Khalil. Could he leave Hing alive long enough to lead him out through the dark? Wouldn't Hing realize he'd be the next to die?

It's like a puzzle where the final piece won't fit.

What Khalil doesn't realize, of course, is that there is no escape. He already draws his last breaths. Instead, Khalil's eyes dart like his thoughts, from Hing to Alu, from Alu to Hing. Which to attack? Which to kill?

All the while, his own death is only a few steps away.

Khalil sees Hing's shadow hobbling into some kind of passageway ahead, one not yet lit by Alu's wavering light. Khalil reaches out like a blind man. Here water trickles down the stone walls, water that smells harsh, almost acidic. He pulls his hand back at its touch, then calms himself—it's only water, after all—and once more feels along the damp wall until he finds the doorway, where the wall disappears into emptiness.

With his hands, with his toes, he probes the utter darkness, for Alu's lamp doesn't yet shine into this passage. But Khalil moves forward, he wants to appear confident.

Hing, however, knows Khalil's true state of mind. He has brought many men to this place, men whole and brave. He knows how the heart quails and the mind begins to squirm, walking through the damp shadows. He knows that by now Khalil has stopped planning, that his mind instead has begun to churn with nightmare images of shadowed fangs and great pale eyes.

With each tentative step Khalil takes into the noiseless black, into shadows so dark they seem to have weight, with each anxious breath of that stale dank air, his senses struggle and his panic rises.

When Hing reaches out, and touches him, touches him softly, just so, Khalil screams, and his own scream frightens him so much, he screams again. But after he screams, Alu appears in the passage carrying the light. Khalil is so grateful that he presses his hands against Alu's arm. "Here is where it happened," Hing says quietly. "Here is where they died."

His voice doesn't echo, exactly. It seems to drop away, as if the words were heavy, as if they fell spinning from his lips to an unfathomable depth. And as he speaks, Khalil is aware of a strange odor, or a mix of odors: water,

160

definitely—but nasty water, stale, and old and rotten. It brings to Khalil's mind an image of oozing flesh dripping from wet bones. And it seems to him he hears moaning, and sees in his mind's eye the faces of dead men with lidless eyes, like severed heads scattered on a battlefield.

"What is this place?" Khalil cries out, now truly frightened. For though his mind has not yet comprehended it, his body knows: he has come to the Door of Hell.

"Why, Ali Khalil, it is the place those guards died—you wanted to come here, remember?" Hing takes his hand; Khalil is too stupid with fear to resist. "Bring the lamp this way," Hing says.

Khalil now sees that they stand on the edge of a deep, deep well. There's no protecting wall: just a vast circle of emptiness about fifteen yards across. The lamplight flickers, casting shadows down into its endless depths.

The little African boy tosses something; a coin maybe.

They wait.

Hing turns to Khalil with a quizzical expression on his face. They wait. Khalil wonders if he only imagined the coin being thrown. They listen. They wait, now scarcely breathing.

Plink.

The sound is so soft that Khalil's first thought is to doubt his ears. No well can be that deep. "Show him," Hing whispers.

Alu steps to the very edge, the toes of his satin shoes actually reaching out into the emptiness. He balances there like an acrobat, extending the lamp outward. "Look," says Hing, nudging Khalil forward.

Khalil follows Alu's example. He tries to appear calm, but his eyes are wide and his lips quiver. He shuffles to the edge, inch by inch, his hand unconsciously tightening on Hing's as he moves.

He looks down, down into inky, endless black. It takes a long time for his eyes to adjust as the flame flickers into the deep shadows. At last he sees the bottom of the well, the dank circle of water glimmering in the pale light. Then he sees—can it be?—poking out of the black water, human forms. He squints: an arm, a leg, the top of someone's head perhaps, and a dim, watery oval that might once have been a face. He trembles.

Then he sees one more sight and cries out.

"What's wrong?" Hing asks quietly, still holding Khalil's hand.

"There's something down there!" Khalil cries. His words swirl eerily, echoing against the stones.

"Yes," says Hing.

"No, something's moving! Something's alive!"

Hing sighs. "You know, we wonder about that sometimes. Does the fall kill them? Do they drown? But those guards: they've been there for three days now, so in my opinion, they must be dead. Or nearly." Hing moves closer to Khalil, still holding his hand. "Still—there might something down there. Perhaps a turtle."

Khalil pulls back from the edge with a sudden violence. "A turtle! There can't be a turtle in a well that deep!" He shouts, much more vehemently than he should. Some part of him has realized that he has peered into his own future.

Hing shrugs. "A turtle is the most logical explanation. Don't you agree, Alu?"

"As you say, master." Alu eyes Khalil strangely. "It is an amusing idea. More pleasant than the alternatives." He steps back from the edge and inches closer to Khalil. Khalil sees that Alu has thrown his sleeve over his long blade, as one hides the knife from an old bullock whose time has come.

"And so, Ali Khalil, you have seen them, those guards of Basant's. Now you know the answer to your questions. Now there remains but one question more for you to answer."

"And what question is that?" Khalil asks. But now everyone is silent: Khalil, Hing, Alu, even Hing's African boy, his teeth gleaming even in this shallow lamplight, gleaming white against his black lips all the while.

Alu stands with his left hand extended, holding the butter lamp far from Khalil, his right hand low with the knife blade pointing to Khalil's ribs.

Khalil considers the effect of that long knife thrusting into his heart. Would he feel the tearing and the bursting? Or would he die before he felt the pain?

Or there's the other way, he thinks. A step and a moment of fright, and then darkness.

He leans slightly out, over the dark pool far, far below him. The well seems to pull his head forward, for just one more look into its depths. He can hardly resist, so fierce his the desire. Even standing unmoving, the image fills his brain; that dark pool, those gray limbs, the ripples in the black water.

Peaceful, he thinks. Even the trip to reach the bottom . . . not so bad, maybe. And then to join those peaceful, endless depths.

Maybe he wouldn't die, though.

Maybe he wouldn't die, but linger in that deep pool, gasping, drowning, a broken mass of dying pain.

Or face that knife. And have Alu's crooked smile be the final image that he sees.

He's deciding, thinks Hing. Always they decide. The thought fills Hing with perplexity. Here, with death inevitable, he might easily throw me in the well, or Alu, or both of us. We stand here helpless, inches from death—yet we are forgotten.

That was the secret of this well, Hing's master had told him years ago. When they peer down it, when they see the very bottom, somehow the well traps their eyes. Their eyes can't rest until they see its depths again. And then the whispering begins. For the well whispers to its victims, it draws them. It calls to them to see once more its peaceful depths, its cold shadows, its endless night.

Hing's master had been right. Khalil is listening; he hears its whispers; he thinks its soft enticements are his own wise thoughts. He believes he's deciding—but all he's doing is listening to the whisper of the well.

In a moment, just as Hing expects, a gleam appears in Khalil's eyes. Decision resolves itself upon his face. He looks like a man victorious in battle. He glances to Alu's face, and then to Hing's, and snorts with contempt.

It seems for a moment that he will say something, some final word of triumph, some farewell.

Instead he simply steps: over the edge of the well, confidently, as one walks through a doorway; head held high, as though his foot will soon land on something solid instead of dropping through the dead forgotten air.

Poor Khalil begins to tumble as he drops.

He hadn't counted on that.

Toward the last, he screams.

The echo ends with a wet, hollow smack that rings against the damp stones and fades into silence.

After some time, Alu speaks. "Is it always so, master?"

"Have I not said so? It is the power of the well. Once you see its depths, it calls you." Hing's wet eyes search Alu's. "Do you not feel it calling you, even now?"

Alu snorts—as though he were a child to be frightened by such tales. The old eunuch stands statue still, staring back, saying nothing.

Alu's mocking smile lasts for a moment, then begins to fade. Soon he is not smiling at all. His eyes grow wide and doubt appears. His face grows grave, as though he hears a strange, unnerving sound, like the drone of a tamboura buzzing its endless chord, and he steps toward Hing with knife raised.

"Yes," says Hing, "this is why I brought you here, to hear the music of the well. Here we are equals, brother. So, as equals, it's time we had a talk. You and I must come to an understanding. Otherwise I fear one of us must die."

Alu looks at Hing with uncertain eyes: his knife raised almost helplessly; his grip now appears so weak that even Hing might break it.

"You've made your way quite satisfactorily. Good looks and a good brain. Unusual for a brother to have either, and you, dear one, have both. You will achieve much. If you don't die young."

Some part of Alu struggles to regain his will, while some other part of him feels compelled to peer again down into the fathomless inviting darkness of that deep well.

"Here we stand, you and I. You have your knife at my ribs and your foot on the edge of emptiness. So what we say here has the force of death behind it, do you see?"

Alu nods. Hing says: "Be my heir. I have no one left! I'll confess, for all his stupidity, I liked Basant. It was my weakness. I thought he might grow wise in time. Alas he was far more stupid than I thought. But not you, Alu. I don't like you very much, but my heart has proven a poor guide. You're pretty and you're smart. You'll do, and do better than most.

"Be my heir. I have no goods to leave you—rings and trinkets and what not? You'll get enough of those on your own. No, Alu, I mean: be my heir for power. Succeed me—lead the brothers when I die. Do you know who rules Hindustan today? It is I, the *khaswajara*, no one else. I have only to say the word, and Shah Jahan will do as I tell him. Can Assaf Khan say as much? Or anyone?"

A pale light comes into Alu's eyes. Hing's words seem to be entering his brain, driving out the relentless droning of the well. "What must I do, master?"

"Do? Why, whatever you please!" Hing shrugs. "Well, perhaps from time to time I may ask some small favor. A token. Nothing much. Nothing difficult. Besides, you like killing. I can tell." Hing steps close to the young eunuch, staring into his dark wayward eyes, so close his dank breath swirls in Alu's nostrils. "Be the next *khaswajara*. Work with me; follow my footsteps. Don't just call me master, acknowledge my mastery! Or kill me. Or die.

"Whichever you choose. I no longer care, you see. My days are dwindling. Soon I will be gone. Someone will be *khaswajara* in my stead. Why not you, brother? Why not you?"

In Alu's mind Hing's words are like a slender, brilliant rope thrown to a drowning man. "Let it be as you say, master."

"Then put your knife away, and let us go together, you and I."

Alu slips the knife into his scabbard. Hing lifts his gnarled hand and Alu grasps it with his smooth long fingers.

"Brother," says Hing.

"Master," says Alu.

They embrace. Alu's hands can feel Hing's body through his clothing like the bones of a naked skeleton.

"And there's this, brother," Hing says gently to Alu. "Aurangzeb must not be emperor. That would destroy us, brother, destroy our only legacy, the legacy of our power."

Alu frowns. "But not Dara, master . . . ," he begins to protest.

Hing holds up his hand. "Shah Jahan—Dara. The power of the Brotherhood depends on that succession. We will play Aurangzeb for the fool he is, but Dara will be our champion. So long as I live, I swear it: Aurangzeb will not sit on the Peacock Throne."

Alu bows his head. "So be it, master."

In a few minutes, as they walk together in slow silence up the rough floor of the tunnel, the howling begins.

Alu shivers as the howl winds through the still air of the tunnels. A howl that chokes off in a splutter, and then starts up again. Its echo slides along Alu's spine like wet ice.

Hing seems not to hear. Perhaps he is deaf, or deaf to some sounds.

"Master?" Alu says at last, his husky voice choked in his throat.

Hing stops and turns to Alu, his enormous eyes glimmering. "It happens sometimes. Sometimes the fall isn't enough. Sometimes it takes a while."

Another howl shivers through the dark.

"How long?"

"A few hours perhaps. Maybe more . . . a day maybe . . . if he decides to eat."

CHAPTER 11

☙☙☙☙

The bright green parrots squawk as they swarm around the lake, terrified by the racket of the beaters.

Though the tiger hunt is nearly a mile away, the birds feel the noise with their fragile bodies; the slap of the clapping sticks, the bang of the squibs, the shouts of the beaters and the roar of the elephants, the crack of breaking trees. The parrots fly in frenzied clusters, pivoting in midair like schools of fish, and each time they light, the clamor blares anew, and off they fly, shrieking.

At the edge of the lake stand three hundred silk tents. The largest and grandest stand twenty feet tall, as wide around as a stable, brightly colored, with pennants and banners snapping in the breeze.

Returning from his inspection, General Jai Singh rides to the second grandest tent. A great dark blue banner flutters on a silver flagpole, on its upper corner is the sacred swastika; for Jai Singh, Dara's first general and a Rajput king, is a Hindu. His banner waves bravely in a forest of pennants bearing the crescents and swords and stars of Islam.

On the fifth hour of every fourth day Jai Singh inspects his troops. Even a royal tiger hunt is no reason to change his routine. So Jai Singh had sent regrets in response to Dara—anyone else would have dropped everything, viewing the invitation to the tiger hunt as a royal command. Still he promised to join Dara as soon as his inspection was over.

With Dara and the others gone to the hunt, Jai Singh enjoys a few moments of privacy. His heart is troubled by the letter he has just received from Shanti, his dear wife and queen. At this moment he misses her exquisitely. He wishes he were beside her, standing in the gardens of their palace in Amber fort, watching mountain eagles soar across the lake far below.

He unrolls the letter and studies it again:

My dear husband,

Bad news, they say, is never gentle, and I fear my tale will break your tender heart. Dear husband, know first that your dear son Man Singh and I are safe and happy, except that both of us long to see you soon.

The sadness is about your friend, Behram Singh. He was the most trusted of your men, the captain of the royal bodyguard. Yes, sweet husband, I say "was," for alas, Behram Singh is no more. And I do not doubt that you will find the circumstances of his death as troubling as do I.

Two days ago I received your last letter. How I enjoyed hearing about your chess game with Aurangzeb! Of course I told Behram Singh of your good wishes as you asked. He seemed happy to hear them, husband—how extraordinary in light of what soon followed!

Last night I was awakened in my bed. Standing over me was Mohmoud Das, captain of the Mogul imperial honor guard. In his hand was a bloody sword, at his feet was Behram Singh, stabbed through the heart.

Captain Mohmoud explained that he had seen Behram Singh enter the seraglio, and followed him to my apartments. Behram Singh had come to kill me, but Captain Mohmoud saved my life.

Captain Mohmoud says that if Behram Singh could turn traitor, the entire bodyguard was suspect. He has therefore sequestered the royal bodyguard and placed himself in charge. So now, the whole palace is carefully guarded by his troop of Mogul guards.

I long for you so to return to set things right.

I am with deepest adoration, your own,
Shanti

I have forgot to say this word of comfort, my husband: You will be glad to know that Behram Singh did not suffer. Though his clothes were soaked, there was scarcely any blood on the floor around his body. It was almost as if he had been killed elsewhere. Captain Mohmoud assures me that this is the sign of a quick and painless death.

His hands tremble as he sets the letter down. Her hints seem obvious. The captain of his bodyguard is dead, and his wife is a Mogul hostage. This is Dara's work, Jai Singh thinks.

What must I do?

Although his blood is hot, he refuses to let emotions rule him. He sets the problem to the side, knowing it will take time to solve and in that time new elements will come to light. He wants to find out what Dara knows about the events at Amber. He wants to see Dara's eyes when he asks him.

ଈଓଈଓ

About a half mile from the edge of camp, near the simple cloth tepees of the camp whores, where the *dhobiwallahs* spread wet laundry on the tall grass, Jai Singh approaches the hunt. The noise of the beaters grows wilder as they hem their prey in an ever-shrinking circle. Birds burst into the air from the dense trees, flapping in terrified confusion. Jai Singh can't see them yet, but he knows the drill: a slowly tightening noose of men and elephants pushes through the forest, driving any animals toward the killing field, a clearing bounded by an array of mounted hunters.

Jai Singh has often said that a hunt is like a battle: when the tiger appears, order and reason fly, and the true measure of a man appears. Now Jai Singh wants to sample the measure of the man he obeys, the heir presumptive, Dara.

This is a small hunt, quickly gathered. No more than thirty elephants are crashing through the forest. Drummers thump the huge drums slung on the elephant's backs. Between the elephants walk men with bamboo beating sticks; behind them, noisewallahs blow trumpets or bang field drums or light firecrackers.

Just as in a battle, the men on foot have the worst of it. As the forest animals run, some grow agitated and frantic until, frenzied by the noise, they try to break through the marching line of beaters.

On horses and elephants around the killing field are Dara's friends and courtiers. In front of them stand soldiers with bright spears pointed toward the clearing; the first line of defense. The richest courtiers sit in jeweled howdahs strapped to the backs of elephants. Those wishing to be thought brave push to the front; wily men and cowards hold back. Their elephants wait nervously, sighing loudly and rocking from foot to foot.

The grandest elephant is Prince Dara's, a yard taller than any other. Beneath the green velvet canopy of the royal howdah ride Dara and his companion, a doe-eyed young man with a sky-blue turban.

The sun is bright, the air humid and still. The smell of smoldering beeswax fills the heavy air: the burning fuses of the hundred matchlock rifles. The warm wax smell mingles with the sting of smoke from the firecrackers, with the tang of forest dust, with the leafy smell of the vegetation cut to clear the killing field. The air is nearly too thick to breathe.

With the circle of beaters closing, animals begin to dash from the forest. First come the monkeys: angry, not frightened. They leap into the clearing, sharp white teeth bared in their black faces, screaming as the spearmen let them pass. Next come the mice and squirrels. Tensed for big game, however, the spearmen startle at the skittering of tiny paws across sandaled feet and the mahouts struggle to calm their elephants. Now the larger animals race from the woods: mongooses and possums and weasels, spinning and skidding into the unexpected clearing.

The real action is about to start.

A big-antlered buck and two does run from the forest. A chorus of matchlocks crack in quick succession, filling the air with smoke. One doe is shredded as a half-dozen rounds crisscross through her, while the other flips backward, like an acrobat somersaulting head over heels. The buck staggers forward, antlers down for an attack, blood spurting from its belly and neck; after a few steps, it kneels on its forelegs and topples over.

The black smoke begins to swirl off. Even the smoke from these few shots makes horses cough, and men wipe their tearing eyes. The beaters are now only yards from the clearing. Their elephants thrust trees aside. The trunks snap, the trumpets blare, the drums boom, the beaters shout and clack their sticks. The noise reverberates through the clearing.

Jai Singh sees shadowy forms prowling at the clearing's edge. Two cats. Maybe three. One tiger dashes into the clearing; Jai Singh sees its bright coat and dark stripes, sees it whirl and disappear back into the shadows. But there is no safety left. Suddenly two tigers slide raging into the clearing. A third follows. Then, unexpectedly, a frightened-looking bear.

At last the beaters reach the clearing and their thunder stops. The air seems flooded by the sudden silence. Everyone's ears are ringing. Jai Singh can barely hear the hunters' shouts of orders and encouragement. The men on the howdah beside him begin to sing a drunken song. Idiots, he thinks.

From his jeweled howdah high above the others, Prince Dara calls out, "Hold! Hold!" This is Dara's party; it is his right to take the first shot.

The tigers wheel madly, testing the line, hoping to find some place of weakness. But the men drive their spears into their path.

For a moment, the tigers seem to give up. They start a slow, prowling walk, snarling, roaring. Jai Singh stares; they are so powerful, so grand. The bear sits in the midst of the clearing, scratching its chest, looking calm, even stupid, except for his wild, flashing eyes.

The sun beats down on the ring of men and animals. For a moment all is quiet, even peaceful. But, just as in a battle, the silence is misleading. The breeze turns, and now the smell overwhelms the circle: the smell of big cats, of urine and blood and meat eaten raw. The elephants stamp and moan, rocking the passengers in the howdahs.

What is Dara waiting for? wonders Jai Singh. Take your shot, and let's go home. These tigers could turn at any moment.

He squints to see Dara's arm draped over his companion's shoulder, his face close to the young man's cheek, instructing him on the aiming of the matchlock. Dara's fancy boy is trying to follow the prowling of the tigers, and as time passes, the cats move faster and the shot grows harder.

Think of those men facing the tigers with nothing but spears, Jai Singh wants to shout, and take the damned shot!

Then it happens.

The biggest of the cats, a gangly, hungry-looking male, unexpectedly whirls and attacks. But the line holds firm; the men whip their spears to stop him. The tiger skids and reverses course, his feet splaying. He drives headlong toward the beaters on the other side of the circle.

Dara sees the danger, and shouts for his friend to fire. His companion's doe eyes seem about to pop. The long rifle booms, belching a cloud of smoke. The round misses its mark, tearing past the tiger, drilling into the flank of an elephant on the other side of the circle. Mad with pain, the elephant rears, blood spurting from the wound. Its mahout falls and scrambles away.

The tiger coils and leaps in an astonishing arc, grabbing the hurt beast's trunk. Throwing its head to shake off the cat, the bellowing elephant flails around the circle, straight into the line of beaters. Some are lucky; the elephant crushes them at once. From beneath the clinging tiger's claws, blood pours in rivulets down the elephant's trunk.

Now the bear ambles over to paw through the wounded men, tearing off chunks of flesh which he swallows with a toss of his head. Oh, he's hungry, thinks Jai Singh stupidly. The other elephants lurch away; in their howdahs the marksmen and matchlocks heave from side to side. Some drop their rifles; unintended shots get fired as sparks fall from the fuses into the firing pans. Black smoke pours into the clearing.

The other two tigers see the break in the line and make a dash. A hundred matchlocks now blast away. The air is filled with the shouts of the hunters and the groans of the injured, with elephant's bellow and tiger's roar.

Jai Singh has to wheel his Bedouin away from the elephant beside him; for the big beast is crabbing sideways. In the howdah its drunken passengers spill first to one side and then the other. A matchlock falls from the howdah, striking Jai Singh's shoulder and nearly knocking him from his horse. The fuse keeps burning despite the fall. Gods, thinks Jai Singh, it's loaded! I might have been killed! He sets the stock on his knee, pointing the barrel upright. He considers snuffing out the fuse, but seeing the confusion all around him, decides it might be better to be armed.

Just as in a battle, order has dissolved into men concerned first with saving their own hides and only second with doing their duty. The uninjured beaters try to save their fallen comrades. More get trampled, adding to the screams. Shots blast out, aimed at who knows what. Stinging smoke drifts across the clearing.

Then through the smoke Jai Singh sees an amazing sight: In the center of the madness, armed with only a spear, is Prince Dara.

The wounded elephant, the tiger clinging still to its trunk, drags its bloody head to the ground in hopes of scraping off the cat. The huge copper drums on its sides clatter and boom as it turns. Dara moves toward the tiger clinging to its bleeding trunk. Oh gods, thinks Jai Singh, he wants to be a hero. Dara slides his feet like a fencer, eyes on the tiger, spear held firm.

The elephant shakes its head in a violent spasm, throwing off one of the tiger's paws. The striped arm is bright red with blood. In a last gasp, the elephant runs blindly, straight for Dara. The tiger paws the air with his bloodred arm. Which is, miraculously, exactly what Dara might have wished.

As the elephant pitches toward him, Dara is perfectly placed: facing the tiger's dripping jaws, staring into its fright-crazed eyes. He holds his spear in form—hands opposing, elbows in, shoulders down. With unerring accuracy, he drives the long spear into the neck of the astonished tiger.

In awe, Jai Singh watches through the fog of smoke. Dara moves as in a dance, smooth and fluid, and with unearthly speed.

As the bright metal bites through his throat, the tiger's roar turns into an unearthly squeal, like a burning child. Blood and bile pour over its black lips. Its heavy, muscled body writhes and twists on the spear that runs through its neck like a pin.

Dara jams the shaft of the spear into the ground, and the elephant's forward motion impales the tiger on its point.

Before Jai Singh has a chance to respond, his smarting eyes notice a darkness swirling in the clouds of dust and smoke. Like a bad dream, the black bear steps suddenly forward.

The bear. He had forgotten.

Blood streams from its snout, for the bear's nose has been shot off. It staggers forward on its hind legs, arms spread, mouth open, eyes rimmed with white, mad with pain. In one paw it clutches a partially eaten hand, a ring still on the thumb.

The bear is heading right for Dara.

Dara doesn't see his danger. The mad bear approaches from behind like a rakshasa in fury. "Shoot, shoot!" Jai Singh shrieks.

It can't be up to me, he thinks, hoisting the fallen matchlock. Jai Singh's bad marksmanship is legendary. The matchlock's barrel is cold, and so heavy that the sight sinks slowly downward as he starts to aim.

The bear is nearly on Dara.

As the fuse clip flips to the strike pan, it occurs to Jai Singh that the barrel might be obstructed from its fall. I'm going to die, he thinks.

There is a terrific boom and a belch of smoke.

The bear collapses as though a carpet had been pulled from under its feet. Dara looks up from the struggling tiger to see the bear behind him, flailing and bellowing on the ground. In an instant his sword flashes and the bear's head rolls from its body in a spray of dark blood. Dara stares at Jai Singh lowering his matchlock. Then he turns around and pierces the squirming tiger through the eye. That way, he knows, makes the best trophy.

From a half dozen voices around the circle, Dara hears a feeble cheer. No one else has seen what happened. "Bring the *hakims*!" Dara shouts. "Men are hurt here!"

Jai Singh slips off his horse and begins to move among the bloody men. Some are struggling to their feet; Jai Singh urges them back to the camp, and focuses instead on the bodies lying on the cleared ground. He turns the dead on their faces and the injured on their backs for easy identification. Some of the men marked as dead thrash desperately, trying to turn themselves on to their backs.

Dara is doing the same task. All too many men are being turned facedown. What a waste, thinks Jai Singh. Dara approaches him, his handsome face blood-spattered and beaming. "What a hunt!" he says. Jai Singh can't find the heart to answer. "General, I owe you my life."

"Anyone might have done the same, lord," Jai Singh replies.

Dara face is flushed. "Did you see that kill?" he asks, nodding toward the tiger. "Do you think Aurangzeb could have done such a thing?"

"I doubt he would ever have done so," Jai Singh answers truthfully.

There he is, thinks Jai Singh, the next emperor: a man who will leap into the path of a tiger, who will risk his life and others' for a kill. Reckless and brave and foolhardy. So unlike Aurangzeb. So much more exciting.

Around him, the *hakims* have come to tend to the wounded. There are calls for water and stretchers. Dara waves for his servants to help.

"And we must mount this bear, general!" Dara calls.

"Yes, lord," Jai Singh calls back.

"We'll have paintings made; you shooting that bear while I spear my tiger. We'll have a poem written."

"Thank you, lord," Jai Singh replies. Then he looks away, for in the midst of so much death, he suddenly remembers Shanti and his son.

Dara senses his distraction. "You're concerned about your wife, general."

Jai Singh is surprised by Dara's insight. "Yes, lord."

"I received Captain Mohmoud's dispatch. Terrible thing, treachery."

Jai Singh recognizes at once the two-edged thrust of an ambiguous remark. "It is indeed a terrible thing when a friend is revealed as an enemy, lord."

The prince has not yet wiped the tiger's blood from his face. He lifts his hands toward Jai Singh. "General, you have lost a friend. Let me replace him. Let me be a better friend to you than that traitor."

"Then you would be a friend indeed, lord."

"When your own bodyguard betrays you, who can you trust, general?" Dara looks him square in the eye as he says this. Suddenly it seems to Jai Singh that much of Dara's foppery could be an act, a ruse to appear weaker than he really is. Dara's look now, in fact, reminds him of Aurangzeb, but with a worldliness that Aurangzeb will never have.

"I tell you, lord, I know no longer whom to trust," Jai Singh says.

"Except Shanti. Your dear wife Shanti. And your son."

Is that a threat, Jai Singh wonders. With Dara, it's so difficult to tell.

"Be glad my guard is there. I myself will guarantee your family's safety. Take this from this," Dara says dramatically, pointing to his head and neck, "if there be any dishonorable act."

"Lord . . . ," Jai Singh protests, but Dara *tut-tuts* and stops him. In any case, Jai Singh knows that cutting off Dara's head would be only the first of his reprisals in the case of treachery.

But now is not the time for suspicion, for there is Jai Singh, facing Dara, his cousin and the heir presumptive; and there is Prince Dara offering Jai Singh his friendship. "What must I do, lord?" Jai Singh asks.

"Why, cousin, I beg you, do nothing at all. Trouble yourself not at all. It is I who must do for you. Return to Amber. If I may offer some advice, take my men for your bodyguard. Send your Rajputs to the main army. Let them prove themselves in battle, and only then offer them reinstatement. For there will be battles soon enough, cousin."

"I like this advice," Jai Singh replies.

"But cousin, come back quickly. I shall have need of you soon."

But before Jai Singh leaves, he turns. "So you know this Captain Mohmoud? You trust him?"

"Trust him? Yes, cousin, yes! Even though I have never met the man. Is he not Aurangzeb's old playmate? My brother recommended him for that post. And whatever you may think of my dear brother, you must admit, he is a great judge of the character of men."

Again Jai Singh bows, now anxious to be home. Instead of calm, his heart is more turbulent than ever.

Aurangzeb!

ꙮ

That evening, after celebrating the hunt at a grand banquet, Shaista Khan— lover of a princess, killer of guards, favorite of Dara, secret ally of Aurangzeb—stands with a few of his fellow courtiers, watching the fading sunlight from a sandstone balcony of the lake pavillion. A half dozen cranes, white as ashes, sweep across the somber sky, ruffling the heavy air with the rush of wings. Fishermen in long rowboats bob gently on the barely flowing surface of the water, singing as they wind their lines and prepare to scull to shore. The men watch in silence.

"It has been more than a month," he says at last.

"A month, Ibrahim?" the man in black beside him asks.

While Ibrahim stares across the river, the other two men glance at the garden behind them. Their aides have been stationed at the stairways. There may be listeners hidden in the shadows, but at least the balcony is free of spies. Even so, they keep their voices hushed.

"A month since that night. You know when I mean, Khurram. The night that eunuch drowned."

Odd, thinks Shaista Khan, that Ibrahim recalls it as the night the eunuch drowned. So much happened on that night Shaista Khan had nearly forgotten about that part. "A month, then, Ibrahim," he says politely.

General Ibrahim seems reluctant. "I've heard nothing. Have you?"

"Nothing, Ibrahim," Khurram says.

"Nor I," Shaista Khan says flatly.

"How am I to believe you? Either of you?" Ibrahim asks.

"What you believe is your look-to, general. If my word is not enough then the hell with you." Shaista Khan turns on his heel.

If he leaves, Khurram thinks, then he is lying. His fingers slip unconsciously to the jeweled dagger hanging from the belt of his black jama.

But Shaista Khan turns back to the railing. Khurram's fingers relax. "Do you think it's off?" Khurram asks.

"It's not like Aurangzeb to make a plan and not execute it," Ibrahim says.

"How would you know?" Shaista Khan snaps. "How many coups have you plotted with him before this?"

"Calm yourself, general," Ibrahim says. "Let's just say that I would have expected some communication from Aurangzeb."

"For that matter, general," Khurram says, "why did Aurangzeb not take you with him when he went to Golconda?"

"Because, general, I'm supposed to be Dara's man," Shaista Khan replies. "You know that."

"Maybe he left you here to spy on us, general?" Ibrahim suggests.

Shaista Khan glares back. "You two are priceless," he growls. "You focus on me like I'm your enemy, you focus on Aurangzeb the same way. Haven't you noticed that we've got some real problems?" He struggles to keep his voice low. "So, we haven't heard from Aurangzeb. Is that so difficult to understand? I think not. But what about those others, eh? The *khaswajara*, for example, that damned *hijra*, Hing. You can find him sucking Dara's farts, two or three times a week. What's that about, if he is supposed to be Aurangzeb's man?"

"Maybe he's trying to lull Dara . . ."

"I say never trust a *hijra*. Hing's like every goddamned *hijra*, Khurram—they can none of them decide which hole they prefer. What if he's using both of them?" Shaista Khan spits over the balcony. "Second point," he continues. "Where's damned Jai Singh?"

"Shaista Khan, really, you must be calm. Jai Singh went to Amber. An assassination attempt—" Khurram looks annoyed at having to explain.

But Shaista Khan interrupts. "Doesn't that story seem a little . . . how shall I say it . . . contrived?"

"But he told me that that captain of his bodyguard had attacked his wife!" Ibrahim protests.

"And you believed him?"

"Why should I doubt him? I've known him twenty years! Longer than I've known you, general." Ibrahim straightens. "If not for the captain of the imperial honor guard, Jai Singh's family might be dead."

"Oh, yes," Shaista Khan drawls. "Captain Mohmoud. Isn't it fortunate that the imperial guard was there just when it was needed?"

"Mohmoud is Aurangzeb's man," Ibrahim says.

"That's not what I've heard," Shaista Khan replies. "Dara sent that company to Amber, and Dara gave Captain Mohmoud command."

"I'm just a simple soldier, general," Khurram says to Shaista Khan. "Perhaps you'd better explain this to me."

"I'm just pointing out the obvious, gentlemen. Don't worry about Aurangzeb. That's a distraction. What you should ask is: What's Jai Singh's game?" A boom of thunder throbs through the humid air. "This empire depends upon the Rajputs! Think about it—the great Akbar couldn't beat them. That's why he married a Rajput bitch. Since then every Mogul emperor has had a Rajput wife. Shah Jahan himself is three-quarters Rajput. Three quarters! And still he calls himself a Muslim and a Mogul. Ever wonder why the Moguls bow and scrape to the Rajputs so? Why they have so many Rajput brides?" Shaista Khan asks. "Can it be that Rajput women have such nimble yonis?"

"Nimble my ass. They just lie there and make you do all the work," Ibrahim says.

But Shaista Khan's eyes glint. "I'll tell you why they love those Rajput wives: Rajput soldiers. But face it: they're Rajputs first, soldiers second. They'd follow a Rajput general into the jaws of hell—but what about a Mogul? Would they obey one of us, for example? Depends on what they had for breakfast." Shaista Khan looks at them. "Not clear enough yet? Try this: To control the empire you must control the Rajputs. And who controls them? Not a Muslim. Not a Mogul. So who?"

"Jai Singh," Khurram whispers.

"Right. And who controls Jai Singh?"

Khurram glances uncertainly at Ibrahim then back to Shaista Khan. "Well, Dara says that he does. But we know . . ." His voice trails off.

"Aurangzeb?" Ibrahim says, somewhat doubtfully.

"And why do you say that, general?" Shaista Khan says carefully.

"Well, didn't he tell us . . . ," Ibrahim replies, his face clouding with uncertainty at what had seemed to him a fact just a moment ago.

"Yes, he told us. He sat there big as life with his sincere frown and told us." Shaista Khan chews his lip. "So? Doesn't Dara say the same?"

"Then whose side are you on, Shaista Khan?" Ibrahim whispers.

"I tell you, friends, I'm a fool. I lie, I pander, I conceal. Is it not so with you as well, my friends? Do you both dissemble as do I?" The other two hang their heads but do not answer. "This is how Jai Singh behaves as well," Shaista Khan continues. "Now all we have is the word of Dara and the word of Aurangzeb. Of the two, I trust Aurangzeb—I'm sure he believes he has Jai Singh's support. But what does Jai Singh really mean to do?"

Khurram shrugs. "Are you saying he is Dara's man?"

"My friend, I've heard both those bastards claiming Jai Singh for an ally. Yet I haven't heard a single word from Jai Singh. Have you?"

"So you think this assassination attempt—" Ibrahim begins to say.

"It could be Dara's plot—just to let Jai Singh know who's boss. That'd be like Dara. Maybe it's Aurangzeb's . . . Maybe Aurangzeb wants to cast suspicion on Dara; that'd be like Aurangzeb. Hell, maybe Jai Singh did it himself, just to get home for a few days."

Khurram frowns. "You fear your own shadow, general."

Shaista Khan's eyes glitter. "We've pledged to support Dara and Aurangzeb—both of them, mind you—and join with them in taking down our living emperor. We are a fine bunch of loyal generals, are we not?"

Shaista Khan lets out a mirthless chuckle. "Let me speak for myself: When the smoke clears, I want to be sitting on the winning side. Which side will that be? Whichever side has Jai Singh!"

"What are you suggesting, Shaista Khan?" whispers Ibrahim.

"I'm watching Jai Singh. My eyes are on him. Where he goes, I go. I suggest you do the same." Shaista Khan looks at them severely, as though he truly believes what he has just said and now dares anyone to challenge him. Lightning snaps across the sky, and soon thunder shakes the still night air. The men look up; they've become so engrossed that they haven't noticed the figures strolling toward them, dressed in silks pale as moonlight.

"Hush," whispers Khurram as the figures mount the steps. The men straighten and try to strike casual poses.

☙☙☙☙

It is Prince Dara walking toward them. Beside him, holding his arm, is a woman. The generals cannot help staring. For the woman wears no veil. Her face is naked for all to see. "Your mouth," Shaista Khan whispers, for Ibrahim's jaw has nearly reached his chest.

The prince, resplendent in silks and lace, his turban decked with emerald peacock feathers, nods to the woman. She glances at the men for

a moment, then looks away. "Gentlemen," Dara says with his sophisticated smile, "I think you know my wife, the princess Ranadil."

One by one, the generals manage to steal their eyes from Ranadil's
pale, exquisite face, and bow, Ibrahim the deepest and longest of all. Shaista
Khan sees that her fingers are curled so tight around Prince Dara's arm that
her nails are white. Dara nods, pats his wife's anxious hand, and the two of
them begin a slow stroll along the balcony.

"By the Almighty, she is lovely. I had no idea!" Khurram whispers.

"I can't believe what I have seen," Ibrahim gasps. "Do they have no
shame?"

"Women—" Khurram starts to say, but Ibrahim interrupts.

"It wasn't her idea! You could see that. He forced her! He put her on
display! Naked! I have made up my mind, friends. I can't bear the shame of
having that depravity sitting on the Peacock Throne. Whatever may come,
I will support Aurangzeb."

"I hope for your sake Jai Singh feels the same," Shaista Khan replies.

Ibrahim nods. "I agree, Shaista Khan. Jai Singh is key. But that makes
me think: Why not Jai Singh for emperor? He at least has honor. He has
dignity. And despite his religion, he is a moral man. His wives at least are
covered. He understands such things. He has military power. And most
important: as a politician he is a mere child. We would install him as a fig-
urehead. The real power"—here Ibrahim glances to either side—"would be
elsewhere."

"I don't like the idea of a Hindu emperor," Khurram replies.

"What do you think Dara would be?" Shaista Khan snaps. "That
whelp is more Hindu than Jai Singh." He looks into Ibrahim's dark face.
"It's time we generals did some thinking on our own."

"Yes, I agree," Khurram says. "Jai Singh then . . . Or maybe . . . one of
us?"

"Not I," Ibrahim says quickly.

"Nor I," agrees Shaista Khan.

"I did not mean myself, my friends," Khurram adds hurriedly, hoping
that their memories are short.

CHAPTER 12

On ponies they ride across the mountains, drenched by the elephant rains, twenty-five riders in a broken line: Jyoti and Maya in the middle; Hanuman behind them; Lakshman, Tanaji with others in front. Jyoti turns in her saddle to see Shivaji far to the rear. Beside her rides the *farang* from the temple, the one with the copper hair and those strange, catlike eyes.

Now as they reach the final pass, the rain subsides. The ponies, glad for the sudden break from the monsoon, shake their heads. Water droplets flip from their manes. The riders have packages wrapped in wax cloth tied to their saddles: flat, narrow, sharp at the ends. Bows, Jyoti realizes. Bows and arrows.

Just then Hanuman rides up. "That's Poona back there," he says. "You can just see the place the river bends—not much else . . . In front of us, that's Welhe: that's where we're going. Well, not you two, I suppose."

Jyoti notices that he is dripping from head to foot, and that there are tiny spots of mud on his nose, and she finds herself wondering how she must look to him. Frightful, she thinks. Her eyes linger on his face and she turns aside, embarrassed. Why hasn't he married? she wonders, and finds herself looking at his profile instead of at the fort he is pointing to.

"That's Torna." He points to a ragged piece of stone on the knifelike edge of a mountain nearby. "A little fort, very pretty inside. A good place for picnics. But I wouldn't want to be there in the rains."

"Is it Shivaji's fort?" Maya asks.

"Shivaji's fort?" Hanuman frowns. "Sort of . . . it was Shahji's; his father's I mean. And Shivaji is Shahji's heir, so . . . it's complicated. . . ."

Maya asks, "How can everything about Shivaji be so complicated? Is it his fort? It's a simple question."

"Well, it's supposed to be. That's the treaty: Shivaji is to get back the forts when he comes of age. But what's Shivaji supposed to do? Walk up to Torna gate and knock? Hello, may I now have my fort back, please?"

"What about Shahji? Can't he do anything?"

"He lives in Bijapur and he's married to the sultana's niece. He's a big general now—ten thousand horse, I hear. What's he going to do? Shahji made his deal. Now he just wants a nice life." All too soon the rain returns. Raindrops large as marbles, pounding them like hammers. Jyoti pulls a waxcloth cape around her, but it does no good.

Suddenly the road dives into the dense foliage of the mountain forest. The smell of wet ground and wet leaves hangs dense around them. Water pours down as if from buckets, collected into thick streams by the canopy of leaves above them. They ride in single file, and water sheets down the path so fast it looks like the rapids of a small river. Mud and pebbles mingle in the stream and rattle against the hooves of the ponies.

❧❧❧❧

God, I'd give anything for a map, thinks O'Neil. What had Da Gama told him? There's not a map to be found in Hindustan unless a *farang* draws it. And never has O'Neil wanted a map more than today.

O'Neil remembers him often these days: Da Gama, his mentor, now dead, that the Hindis called Deoga. Hindustan is paradise and Hindustan is hell, Da Gama had told him. O'Neil is still waiting to find paradise. He had always imagined hell as a place of fire and heat, but perhaps hell is a mudslick mountainside beaten with rain, where you ride a feeble pony that seems ready to somersault down the side.

Through the rain, O'Neil sees Bala riding just ahead. What a treasure Bala is, he thinks. To have found a man such as Bala in Maharashtra: one with connections, intelligence, humor, and best of all, a man who speaks Persian.

If what Bala had told O'Neil were true, there is a very different situation in Hindustan than the picture painted by the Moguls.

At the dharmsala—the night Da Gama died, he reminds himself, the night his life changed utterly—O'Neil had begun to puzzle over Shivaji's story. Da Gama had scoffed at him: "For Hindi there's no difference between the truth and a lie. Never believe anything they say."

But he had heard something momentous. A Hindu general. Hindu tribes arming themselves and rebelling. Taking forts and raising armies.

In the pictures drawn by the Persian-speaking Mogul tradewallahs, no such conflicts were revealed. Oh, there were hints of difficulties between the Moguls and Bijapur and Golconda, but the tradewallahs acted as though such conflicts were the minor adjustments required when great nations danced in exquisite unison.

But with Bala's help, O'Neil was learning that the tradewallahs from these different groups were colluding: presenting a unified front to the *farangs,* setting high prices and miserable terms.

What O'Neil has learned may make him rich.

He understands much better the importance of those forts around him. He must have seen half a dozen in the fifty miles between Ahmednagar and Poona. Bala says that there are a dozen more in these hills as well.

Control those forts and you control the trade routes to the sea.

That was why Bijapur was so ready to negotiate with an upstart Hindu chieftain: By taking just a few forts, Shahji had a stranglehold on Bijapur.

Also Bala told him that although Bijapur has manned those forts, their garrisons are dwindling and complacent.

O'Neil looks at the riders around him. He has seen the vast armies of Bijapur: the war elephants, the camels and the horses, the hordes of Abyssinian mercenaries. Hard to believe that Shahji had taken riders like these up against such forces, harder still to believe that they had won.

What stops from Shivaji from doing the same? What does he need—money? Guns? The factors in Surat can provide these things and more. Confidence? Perhaps O'Neil can provide that, too.

For there is treasure to be had here. Treasure that the tradewallahs don't even realize they own, like those vast forests of teak on the road to Poona.

Though the factors had asked about teak—the best wood for building boats and worth a fortune—the tradewallahs said they had none; not even the Bijapuris had mentioned those forests. Thanks to Bala, O'Neil now begins to understand: these teak forests officially still belong to Shahji. Or perhaps Shivaji. In any case, no one now has outright title.

Perhaps it's time for Shivaji to stake his claim.

He peers through the misty shadow to the tall form of Shivaji riding at the rear. He might do it, O'Neil thinks. With my help, he might.

God, I'd give anything for a map!

By the time they reach the temple gates there is hardly light enough to see. The temple wall, covered by dense, big-leafed vines, looks to Jyoti like a shaggy shadow. Beyond it, she can see the dark suggestions of temple domes rising into the air.

A man in a dark cloak, comes up to Jyoti, takes the pony's bridle, and leads her up to the temple. Another man from the temple is guiding Maya the same way. While the riders dismount, their guides lead Maya and Jyoti toward some nearby buildings. Four tall temples stand there, with a stone platform connecting them; raised above the platform is a makeshift canopy made from long bolts of waxcloth. The cloth slaps in the wet breeze, but most of the platform is dry.

While Jyoti and Maya dismount, a big, burly man with a wide nose and a gray-flecked mustache, stands up from the small dung fire. He *namskars* long and low, as though they are royalty, and looks out at them with eyes serious and sad. "We heard you two were coming. Well, now you're here. We'll find the *shastri* and get you settled. Was the ride hard?"

Jyoti and Maya look at each other in some confusion. The man is strong, tough, his turban messy. Something about him reminds Jyoti of Tanaji. "It was very wet, sir. Two days ride in constant rain, sir," Jyoti replies.

"Two days, eh? Then you made good time, across those hills in this weather." With this observation the man has apparently run out of things to say. His face begins to sag with the strain of being polite. It strikes Jyoti why this man reminds her of Tanaji: He's a warrior, she thinks.

Then Jyoti becomes aware of a familiar sound coming from one of the temples: drumbeats, and the shaking of dozens of tiny bells.

"Do you hear it?" Maya asks Jyoti. Jyoti nods.

The man waves toward one of the temples behind them. "Oh, that racket goes on all day. It should stop soon, gods be praised."

"Dancing?" Maya asks softly.

"Yes, yes. Bloody dancing. Damned girls racing everywhere." Maya is about to speak when the man looks up and begins to curse. "Who let you in here!" he shouts. "This means your death, you bastard!"

"My death! Shit! It's I who have come to finish you off, captain!"

Jyoti huddles against Maya as the men square off.

"Iron!" says Tanaji, grasping his shoulders and laughing. "You've gotten old and flabby. Maybe I should start to call you Rust now, instead of Iron."

"I can still take you, any time, captain. Just try me." Laughing, Iron looks at the others. "Who is this? It can't be Shahu?"

"Yes, uncle. It is good to see you once more."

Iron shakes his head. "You were this big. How's your father?"

"I don't see him, uncle," Shivaji replies without a hint of emotion.

Iron blinks, then shrugs. "No, no, of course not. He was a great man."

Iron studies Shivaji's face as if he is looking for something, some mark, some sign. It's not clear whether he sees it. "That new dancing guru keeps making a fuss about your coming. Says you're a marked man, Shahu. Said I could see it for myself." He frowns. "I don't see anything."

While Iron greets Hanuman and Lakshman, and is just telling Tanaji how big those sons of his have grown, a shout goes up from one of the temples—a chorus of high-pitched children's voices. "Oh, gods," Iron groans. "Lesson's over. Here they come." From behind the farthest temple a stream of girls in bright dresses comes running. Iron shakes his head resignedly.

"Is that the dancing school, then?" Tanaji asks.

Maya follows the girls with her eyes until every one of them has ducked into a doorway. Then she sees one last form emerge—but as Maya watches through the veils of rain, she sees that this one wears a sari instead of a dress, and moves with labored steps, and her long hair is white. Maya's eyes grow wide, and she lifts her hand to her mouth as though she fears to speak.

A gray-haired woman appears, wearing a dark wax cloth cloak. "The guru has sent me to fetch the women," she says.

The woman nods impatiently for them to follow and leads them toward a low house full of lights. Jyoti looks back. Hanuman smiles at her as if to say goodbye.

"Tell me, sister," Maya whispers to their guide. "What is the guru's name?"

"You don't know?" the woman sneers. "Her name is Gungama."

"Mother!" Maya gasps.

☙❧☙❧

"Where is everyone, Iron?" Tanaji asks. "The place seems deserted. Where are the *shastri* and the brahmins? Isn't there some sort of dancing school? All I see around here are your people."

"Ah, the dancing school. Those girls will be the death of me! All day long, it's all you can hear, the *clack* of their drums, and that damned guru yelling. Then when they stop it's worse! Little girls, running around, running and shouting and never a moment's peace!"

"You never married, did you, Iron?" Tanaji asks, his eyes sparkling.

"Eh? What about it?" He glares at Tanaji. "It's a festival, that's where they all are. The festival of the mother, so naturally those girls will make a big deal about it, here at a Bhavani temple. Running around, doing heaven knows what. They'll be in the main temple soon, I suppose. It's *purnima*, the full moon, so they'll be singing *kirtan* all night."

"The crow's baby is a big deal to the crow," Tanaji agrees.

"I don't mean to make it sound so bad," Iron says, looking embarrassed. "It's nice, if you don't mind a little noise. People like dancing, right?" He says this as though such a thought would never cross a soldier's mind. "Even so, it hurts me to bring you to this place, but under the circumstances it seemed best. I didn't know where else to put you."

The flames of the dung fire glint golden on the dark faces of the tired men. "I thought I'd bring you to my place in Welhe," Iron continues. "It's just a run-down shack compared to yours, Shahu." This raises a few chuckles; Iron's compound is elegant. "The rains started a week ago. After the rains had fallen for five days and nights without stopping, I heard a pounding on my gates, a big ruckus. When I got to the door, what did I see?

"There in my courtyard was Hamzadin, the captain of the garrison at Torna fort, and around him maybe thirty men, the bunch of them looking like drowned rats. He was polite, but his eyes were crazy.

"He wanted me to put them up! Him and his men! So much rain up there on the mountain they couldn't stand it anymore! He had a near mutiny, so Hamzadin decided to bring everyone to town where there maybe was a dry blanket and a dry floor."

Tanaji slaps his thigh. "They ran away from rain? You must be joking."

"Well a few days ago, it was really coming down. But you're right—what kind of captain runs from a little drizzle?"

The men shake their heads. O'Neil, who has followed a little of this talk, however, thinks of the surging floods that have fallen on him nonstop for two days, and wonders what it would be like if, as Iron says, it was "really coming down."

"So the whole garrison is at your house, Iron?" Bala asks.

"He rotates three or four men from the house back to the fort every day. There's maybe half a dozen up there." Lakshman sneers, as if to say that he would know how many men were left at that fort. Iron ignores him.

"So even if I still had the room to put you up, which I don't," Iron continues, "I asked myself if it was a good idea. Bijapuris and Poonis in the same place? I thought that it would be more peaceful to bring you here.

"The Bijapuris are living well on my food and drink. My drink especially; they do love their wine." Iron shakes his head. "But I had this canopy set up for you, and food sent for you and the animals, and I've made arrangements with some villagers to look after you."

Iron nudges Tanaji. "Of course the *shastri* ordered that there's to be no toddy here. So don't tell him that I gave you this." He hands Tanaji a flask. Tanaji drinks and passes the flask around the circle. O'Neil splutters after a sip; only Shivaji passes it without drinking. Soon that flask is empty, and another, and the men's faces glow as they speak. Iron's people work like magic: bedmats roll out on the floor, dishes of hot dal appear in their hands.

"I owe this fool my life," Iron says to Shivaji, nodding toward Tanaji, "and I owe your father for my good fortune. I don't forget this. He was a great man, Shahu, a great man."

Shivaji stands up. "I'm going to check on the horses." He finds his cloak and steps out into the downpour.

☙☙☙☙

Iron has provided well: Shivaji's men have blankets enough, and food and drink in plenty, and the ponies are dry and comfortable.

Shivaji then picks his way across flooded walkways to the stone stairs of the main temple. The night air, full of rain, is getting cold. At the sides of the temple steps are two tall stone columns, shaped like huge combs with wide stone teeth. On each tooth sits a flaming oil lamp. The flames sputter as the rains splash into the oil, but still they burn. But just as he's about to climb the steps, a small gray-haired woman appears, beckoning him to follow. She moves quickly, glancing behind her to be sure that Shivaji is keeping up.

She leads him past the windows of the low house that he assumes is the students' quarters, empty now. Around the corner they come to a dark door at the end of the building.

Maya answers his knock, her eyes red from weeping.

"What's wrong?" Shivaji asks.

"It's my guru. She's here." Her tears brim up. "I thought she was dead. "Come," she says, wiping her cheeks with her fingertips, "she wants to see you."

☙☙☙☙

An old voice calls him, a voice so old that it's hard to tell whether it's a man or a woman. "Come here, darling one."

On a tiger-skin rug that has been spread on the dirt floor sits the tiniest woman that Shivaji has ever seen; maybe the oldest woman he has ever seen; maybe the happiest woman he has ever seen.

She is smaller than Sambhuji, so that makes her smaller than a nine-year-old. Her hair is long and completely white, the thin skin of her face crosshatched with fine lines, her eyes penetrating and bright.

As he enters, she struggles to stand, taking Maya's quickly offered hand to steady herself. Then she shuffles to Shivaji's side like a child peering up at a giant.

"You brought my daughter back to me." Though her teeth are stained and ground with age almost to stumps, her smile is bright. She must lean her head back just to see into Shivaji's eyes. "Did you hear me calling you, my darling? I've been calling and calling. I've so wanted to see you. Sometimes I thought I would never live this long, to see this day, to see you both together, in my own room." She looks over to Maya. "Now I can die."

Though Maya's eyes are full of tears they beam at the old woman. "This is Gungama. My guru. Did you know she would be here? I thought she had died long ago."

"Sit right here, darling," Gungama says, taking Shivaji's hand and leading him to her tiger-skin rug.

"Not here, mother," he protests. "A skin such as this is a guru's place. I should sit elsewhere."

She shushes him. "It is a king's place, my darling." She guides him onto the tiger skin, and then tugs at him until he sits.

"That's better." Gungama beams at Shivaji. She fusses with his turban, which he accepts with a mixture of tolerance and amusement. When she is satisfied, she steps back and sinks to her knees, looking into his eyes with clear delight. "I have sat you on tiger-skin. I have brought you incense and butter lamps burning bright. But I am too weak to wave these things before you as I should. So this will have to do."

"Mother, I deserve none of this."

"That, dear, is not for you to say. Not yet" She leans forward, and stretching out her back in a long and graceful curve that seems impossible for one so old, places her forehead on his feet.

"No, mother, no," Shivaji protests. Maya watches in confusion, still sniffing her tears.

Then Gungama begins to moan. She begins to lean first to one side, then the other, and the moan continues longer and longer, until Maya realizes that Gungama is *singing*. The words are strange, a language she has never heard before, and the tune is scarcely more than tiny variations in her guru's croaking voice. The effect is fascinating, comforting, disturbing, beautiful.

Maya catches her breath, for the swaying song of Gungama is like the song of the heart of the earth, a song that seeps skyward from the dark oceans deep beneath the ground, a song that grates against the bones of the world to emerge in wisps through the soil, an ancient melody gathered by this tiny woman, placed before Shivaji's feet like a flower.

At last Gungama opens her eyes. "One more thing to do before I die," she says. She leans forward, balancing on her knees, and catching Shivaji's head in her hands, presses her thumbs into the spot between his eyebrows. His face widens in shock, and he tries to pull away from those gnarled, tiny hands, but he cannot. She squeezes his face so hard his flesh pokes out between her fingers, she presses her yellowed thumbnails into his forehead so hard that a drop of blood oozes from beneath them.

Tears begin to well up in her old eyes when she sees that drop of blood, and she stops, leaning back on her heels. "Well, darling, that wasn't too bad, I hope. It had to be done, you know, but it's over now."

"So," she says, patting the floor, "Maya." Maya hurries to her guru's side. "What took you so long, darling?" she asks, turning to Shivaji, who is still rubbing his forehead. "I've been calling for you over these many weeks."

"Mother, how would we hear your words? We're so far away."

She looks shocked. "Your ears must be made of stone. I called and called. I called even louder when my daughter here begged me for my help."

"Whenever did I do that, mother?" Maya asks in surprise.

"About a month ago, I think." The old woman's beams, but seems puzzled that the incident isn't obvious. "Shall I describe the scene? You, dear child, sitting on a low bed in the dark, wearing some nonsense that covered all your pretty face. And pressed against your sweet throat, child, a sword. And then a fire—flames everywhere. Oh yes, child, you were calling your poor old mother. You called her very hard.

"And so, what did I do, eh? I called him! Didn't I, darling?" She nods to Shivaji. He nods his head noncommittally. "I called for you to help her—and you did! Things looked so difficult. Yes, darling, yes: you even broke your sword trying to help her! But everything," she says brightly, "has worked out in the end. Just as it is supposed to. And now, look at us: we three. And in my room. What a sweet world we live in."

Her bright eyes flash from face to face. "And neither of you believes a single thing I've said." She chuckles. "But what do I care? Now I can die.

"Let's see: first, there's the problem of your sword, the broken sword. That at least is easily remedied. Daughter, please give him yours. He broke his own in your service, I think it is the least you might do in return."

Maya looks shocked. "I have no sword, mother," she answers.

"Don't be obtuse, daughter, of course you do. Haven't you known all along that this moment would come?"

"But, mother, it's . . ."

"It's been waiting for him, child. Go and get it."

Maya goes to her bedmat and brings her long bag. She opens it, and takes from it a shallow box of cheap wood nearly as long as the bag itself, tied with a wide ribbon of faded silk. She places it in front of Gungama, bowing her head to the floor. "I am your slave entirely, mother."

"Sit up, child. You are very formal today. Show him what you've got in there." Her eyes crinkle at Shivaji. "Now, I don't pretend to know about such matters. So you just tell me exactly what you think, darling."

Maya pulls on the faded bow until the knot gives way. She sets the ribbon aside as though it were very precious, and then tugs on the box's lid. It resists as though it has been shut a long time. Maya lifts from it a long shape, wrapped in silk as though wearing a fine robe. "I've had this all my life," she explains. "I think it was my father's. I like to think that it was."

Shivaji takes it and pushes aside the wrapper to reveal a rapier blade that glistens in the lamplight: not a whole sword, but the blade of a sword. Instead of a hilt there's only a raw-looking tang, scratched and ugly compared to the limpid beauty of the blade.

"This is a *farang* blade," he says, moving it easily, catching the light on its gleaming edge. "It's exquisite. Your father's, you say?"

"Child, have you not told him your tale?" Gungama asks.

"It is of no consequence, Mother," Maya answers.

"This is a fine blade," Shivaji says. He tests its lightness, its balance; runs his finger along its edges, flexes the point. Whorls and swirls of gray shine in the bright steel. "Can this really be steel?" he asks. "It's so flexible. There's no sign of rust."

"So, it's good?" Gungama asks.

"Very good," Shivaji replies.

"And, child, don't you think it should be his?"

Maya lowers her head to Shivaji. "Please take it, sir. You saved my life. Take this sword as a token of my gratitude."

"And . . . ," Gungama says.

Maya looks up, surprised. She looks into her guru's eyes, and lowers her head, suddenly embarassed. "And of . . . my affection," she whispers.

Gungama's gaze lingers on Maya and she smiles, as if remembering or imagining. Then she turns back to Shivaji. "So it can be repaired, dear? Good as new?"

"Yes, Mother," Shivaji says. "All that's missing is the hilts."

Gungama claps her hands as though this is delightful news. "So what will you do with your new sword?" She pauses, but Shivaji doesn't answer. "That blade is a token, darling. A sign. Now you must act."

"But what am I to do, Mother?" Shivaji asks.

"Stop pretending you're so thick-headed. Can't you see that you are missing something obvious?"

"What? What am I missing?" But Gungama only looks at him as though he is teasing her. An expression of pity crosses her face. "You have forgotten why you are here, darling," she says at last. She nods to Maya. From her bag Maya slips out a smaller one and lifts it for Shivaji to see: a net of gems; two or three dozen gold-set stones—diamonds the size of chickpeas, a hundred pearls of equal size—woven into a glittering mesh by threads of gold. She slips it over his hands, the stones glittering.

When he takes it, his hands dip involuntarily—it is that much heavier than he expects. "What is it?" he says at last. Whenever he moves his hands the gems glitter unexpectedly, catching the golden light.

"It is a wedding headdress. My mother had it."

Shivaji lifts an eyebrow. "It's exquisite." He holds the headdress out, and she takes it with care.

For a moment their fingers touch.

Maya lifts a final treasure. It is a small golden coin. Or rather half a coin, for it has been sawn roughly down the center with a jagged, uneven cut. Its markings are in some strange language.

"What is this?" he asks. But Maya looks away and will not answer.

Gungama laughs. "You have more questions, darling?" Gungama waves her hand toward the sword in Shivaji's lap, then over the headdress and coin. "You must wake up, darling boy. The world puts the answers at your feet."

Shivaji suddenly reaches for his forehead; the thumbnail mark between his eyebrows has begun to throb. "What have you done to me?" he demands.

"It's always so hard to wake up, darling." She looks into his eyes levelly. "Tell me, what story do you read here? Sharp sword, jeweled headdress, broken coin. What do these signs tell you?"

Shivaji rubs his forehead. "I don't understand."

"That's because you're a hard case, darling."

Shivaji rises, holding on to the wall to steady himself. Perspiration beads up on his forehead. Maya gets up to help him, but he brushes her away. "Take some air," Gungama says. She stands with the careful effort of an old woman, yet she seems at this point steadier and stronger than Shivaji. The old woman motions toward the sword. "Bring it just like that," she says to Maya as she pushes Shivaji to the door.

Bring it? Where? wonders Maya. But she wraps the sword in its silk cloth, and follows.

ᏬᏬᏬᏬ

The temple is crowded. Drones and flutes mix with the splash of finger cymbals and tambourines, with the deep thump of tablas and clay drums. The stone walls ring with song. No one pays attention to Shivaji, though he lurches through the crowd like a drunkard, supported by Gungama and Maya.

In the temple chamber, Shivaji seems to rouse himself. Before them is the ancient *murti* of the goddess Bhavani: as Bala had said, little more than a rock with eyes.

This rock, this idol, is a self-incarnating *murti,* an image formed by the goddess herself, found by a lucky farmer in his field in the old times and worshipped for generations since.

The rock, naturally dark green, has been carefully stained to show more clearly the image of the goddess that inhabits it. Brilliant eyes of white shell have been placed on the goddess's face, on which dark black pupils have been painted. The stone goddess has been dressed in heavy silks, garlanded with golden necklaces, and crowned with gems. Above her spreads a silver umbrella held aloft by sculpted peacocks.

Gungama lets go of Shivaji's hand, pushing him forward. "Give it to him, hurry," she whispers. Maya places the cloth-wrapped sword in Shivaji's hands. Though he grips it tight, his gaze is fixed on the bright eyes of the goddess. He lurches to the very foot of the rock idol and falls heavily to his knees. The chanting seems, impossibly, to grow louder; the temple walls echo like thunder.

Shivaji shuffles forward on his knees, the sword outstretched. Finally he tumbles forward at the base of the idol, letting the sword fall at the goddess's feet.

"Now. Now!" says Gungama, tugging at Maya's arm. "Dance!"

ᏂᏂᏂᏂ

When he opens his eyes, Shivaji sees not the black basalt stones of the temple, but bright light, glinting golden on the green face of the goddess.

How did the temple come to be so full of light, he wonders? The *murti* has changed: it has begun to breathe. The rock grows soft, and from it emerges the goddess, no longer rough and obscure, but smooth, distinct, throbbing with life. The goddess is glorious: her flesh is green and dark, and her eyes are brilliant white, but the heart of them is black as the night sky. Her eyes are full of stars.

Next to the goddess swirls a whirlwind: a million strings of light; each string a different brilliant color, each vibrating at a different pitch, making music unlike any he has heard before, the sound of light.

The whirling spirals of light move toward him as a storm and soon engulf him. He swirls inside the maelstrom until he himself dissolves.

He flows like water over the face of the goddess. Galaxies swirl in her dark eyes. She opens her green lips and swallows him whole. He is everywhere and also beyond everywhere. Now he soars through her, inside her. He sees that her mouth contains the whole earth. The rolling plain is but the surface of her tongue; the mountains are her teeth.

ᏂᏂᏂᏂ

The next thing Shivaji sees is a tiger chewing on a corpse.

The tiger lifts its head. Flesh trails from its black lips; blood reddens its long yellow teeth. Shivaji sees that the tiger's eyes are filmed; that its teeth are worn away; that its fur is graying and moth-eaten.

The tiger is dying, but it is not yet dead. No, it is alive and looking straight at him. Those horrid teeth loom toward him. Swelling to enormous size, towering over him, the tiger opens its jaws to swallow him.

Shivaji runs. He sees hills, and runs to them for shelter. But they are not hills, but heaps of rotting, burning corpses: of children, of horses and elephants, of women and men.

The dying tiger too prowls there. Sour smoke swirls around his heaving sides. He may be dying, but his claws are sharp as razors. The tiger kills each thing it touches, eats each thing it kills.

Then beneath his paws, from beneath the smoking corpses, the earth begins to twitch. The soil churns; it becomes a sea of rats. The rats skitter up to the beast's huge legs. The tiger slaps out, claws flashing, but they are too fast, too many, skittering away only to circle back again.

A rat nips at the tiger's tail and runs. A drop of blood flows from its bite along the yellow fur. Another rat runs up to snap at the tiger's tender belly. Then by twos and threes, the rats dash forth and back, nipping, biting, gnawing. The tiger gets to its feet, enraged, anxious now to stop these nasty, painful bites. It roars, it stamps, it bats the ground. But still they come: biting, biting, biting. Blood pours in rivulets from the tiger's paws. The smell of blood maddens the roiling sea of rats.

A fat black rat gnaws through the tiger's belly, and dives inside his gut with a dozen of its brothers.

The tiger roars and crashes to the ground, but it does no good. As the tiger screams, the blood-soaked head of the fat black rat emerges from his chest. And now a hundred hungry rats are leaping on the tiger, a hundred tiny gnawing mouths are feasting on its dying flesh. Soon the tiger's roars are merely groans.

The tiger dies a wretched living death, his hide a living blanket made of gnawing rats. And then the fat black rat, the one who first dove into the tiger's belly, runs up and sits upon his haunches at Shivaji's feet.

In the eyes and nose and bloodstained mouth of that fat rat, Shivaji seems to find a face he knows. He leans his head closer, closer, eye to tiny eye. It seems to him that the rat has many arms, and many human hands.

The rat bows its head and touches Shivaji's feet.

"Why do you bow to me?" Shivaji asks.

"I bow to the king of rats, lord," it replies.

❧❧❧❧

While Shivaji lies unmoving at the *murti*'s feet, Maya dances. When she sits down exhausted, even when the *kirtan* stops, Shivaji does not move. Gungama sends for the *shastri*; he feels Shivaji's pulse but cannot wake him. At last they carry him from the temple to the *shastri*'s home, as motionless as when he first collapsed before the *murti* of the goddess.

❧❧❧❧

For three days and nights Maya stays by Shivaji's bedside. It is her guru's wish, and so she stays. Amba, the *shastri*'s wife, brings food: samosas, *dahi*, *bhel*. Sometimes Maya takes water, but the food remains untouched.

The *shastri* doesn't know what's wrong with him. The doctor shakes his head. Only Gungama smiles when she comes to see Shivaji. "Good, good, good," she repeats each time; just that and nothing else.

Sometimes Jyoti comes, and only then will Maya allow herself to take a little nap, resting her head against Jyoti's shoulder.

On the third evening, Amba calls Maya into the main room of their tiny house. There, seated on the floor around a butter lamp are the *shastri* and Gungama.

The brahmin is much older than his wife, the stubble of his shaved head glinting silver in the flickering lamplight. After a few pleasantries, Gungama takes Maya's hand firmly with her tiny, wrinkled fingers. "Daughter," she says in her hoarse croak, "tonight I leave you. I've spoken to the *shastri*. You'll be in charge of the dancing school now. You are the new guru. I know you will not disappoint me."

"No!" Maya says despite herself. "It's wrong, *ma*, it's wrong!" She sobs. "I know so little!"

"What you don't yet know about temple dance, you shall discover on your own. I will help you. I will pray for you. But I must leave you now."

"But I'm not ready," Maya protests. "And Shivaji . . ."

"Why should you worry? Whether he lives or dies, is it not God's will?"

Maya blanches. "Is he going to die?"

Gungama looks at her with loving eyes and shakes her head. "No, daughter, he will not die. Tonight he'll wake up. Or perhaps tomorrow. He'll be fine. Fine . . . but different."

"Different how?" Maya asks

"In ways I cannot see," Gungama replies. "I brought him here to wake him up, daughter. That was all my job, and now it's done. I do not know the consequence." Gungama stands with an effort, using Maya's hand for support. Then she lays her old hands on the young woman's forehead. "Take my blessing."

The *shastri namskars* as Gungama shuffles past him to the door. Amba hands the old woman a package of food, and helps her into a wax cloth cloak.

"No!" Maya shouts. "I may never see you again, mother."

Now Gungama laughs. "Child, don't be foolish. You've danced so many stories—the Mahabharata, the Ramayana, the tales of Janaki and Shakuntla. In all those stories, doesn't the guru wander into the forest? And always, daughter, doesn't the guru return?

"Even so, child, the Author of my story won't let me leave so easily, I fear. Much as I would like to climb the ladder into heaven, the Author, I expect, has other ideas. And you have much to do before this story is complete." Now Gungama stands on tiptoe and places her arms around Maya's neck, kissing her once on each cheek. "Take care of my girls. Take care of those sweet lambs. Remember me." Maya nods. The *shastri* opens the wooden door, and Gungama steps into the pouring rain.

҈҉҈҉

She goes back to Shivaji's bedside, her heart charged with doubt and wonder. Because of Gungama's assurance, she expects Shivaji to wake. Instead he lies there, as quiet as ever.

Amba looks in to see if there is any change, but of course there is none. She shakes her head and says goodnight. Soon Maya hears them climbing into bed; soon she hears them snore. And still she sits near Shivaji's sleeping form, waiting against hope. Sometimes she brushes back his long, dark hair. And still he does not stir.

And sitting there, in the dark that is broken only by the guttering butter lamp in the room next door, sitting by his bed in the never-ending rain that seems to grow ever louder, her sleep-starved mind begins to twist with unnamed fears. She starts to feel her skin crawl, as though some evil rakshasa had slipped into the room. Knowing she is foolish, against her will, her face turns toward the window.

There standing in a cloak is Hanuman.

No. Lakshman. Watching.

She shivers. Never has he done anything but look at her, but, still, those burning eyes! And she is helpless. She turns to Shivaji. "Wake up," she whispers.

But Shivaji does not move. At last, she falls with her face upon his chest, and weeps until she has no more tears to cry. With her cheek pressed against his damp shirt, she rests there, until lulled at last by the slow and steady beating of his heart she falls asleep.

҈҉҈҉

Maya wakes to see blue sky through the window. The rain has ceased to beat upon the rush roof. She realizes that Shivaji's bed is empty.

Shivaji sits across the room, leaning his back against the wall.

"You looked so beautiful, I couldn't bear to wake you."

"Are you all right?"

"I was hungry," he says. He lifts the tray *shastri*'s wife had brought her; all that's left are crumbs. "How long was I asleep?"

"Three days. Are you sure you're all right?"

"Were you here the whole time, Maya?"

It pleases her to hear him say her name. The sound of his voice saying it seems to pour across the ragged surface of her heart like warm oil. "Oh, yes," she answers. For a long time, they look at one another.

It must be early morning, Maya thinks, staring into his dark eyes. She can hear the snoring of the *shastri* and his wife; they will not wake for hours. She could latch the door and no one would come in.

Still their eyes linger. Want what I want, she thinks. But he turns away. "I had a funny dream, you know," he tells her, as if trying to sound casual.

The moment, she can feel, is gone. If he loved her, he would have acted. I am a fool. "Tell me about your funny dream."

"I dreamed I was the king of all the rats."

"Then it was a good dream," she says, pleased for him. "It means that you will overcome all obstacles to reach your goal. Ganesha himself has given you this vision. Only Ganesha crowns the king of rats. Ganesha loves rats, for they ignore obstacles." She seems almost to plead with him. "Nothing can stop you! Ganesha's blessings rest upon you! Take what you want!" She can't stop looking at him.

Then she sees the mark that rests on his forehead, on the place that Gungama drew blood. On his forehead there she sees a purplish "V," like the *tilik* of a priest. The sight disturbs her. She reaches out her hand, tracing the "V" upon his brow with her finger. Her face grows taut. The mark seems to rest below the surface of his skin. Its color shifts from dark purple to a reddish brown, like a thing alive.

She pulls back her hand and then she laughs, but her laugh is cold. She has seen the veil pulled back at last. She laughs again, a sad, mirthless laugh, and turns away. Her mind is racing, filled with memories of Gungama and the words she spoke. "Look what she has done to you! And me! Yesterday I was a slave. Today I'm the guru. She has pulled me from one prison and cast me in another. She always finds the way to demolish me."

"You talk as though your guru is your enemy," Shivaji says.

"What do you know of it?" Maya flares. "She taught me to dance and then deserted me! I was young, alone, driven into slavery, turned into a . . ." Again the word is hard for her to say. ". . . a whore; a rich man's whore. She could have saved me. She had the means." Shivaji moves to comfort her, but she shrugs him off.

"But look how much she has given you—"

"She doesn't give; she takes! She smiles and smiles, and steals away everything I love. I hate her!"

"But what has she stolen? I don't understand."

"She's stolen you!" Maya cries out. "She took away hope . . . my hope of you." Again she laughs, cold and bitter. "You don't know what she's done to you, do you?"

"What has she done?"

"I don't know, not all of it. But I know enough . . . I know she's cut off from you that part that once belonged to me."

"I never—"

Again she lifts her hand, stopping his words. "I know what I know." How different she feels now when she looks at him. She starts to cry again, to mourn the loss of what she never had.

"Did she tell you she was doing something to me?"

Maya turns away, disgusted. "She said you would awaken."

"Anything more than that?"

"You heard her! She said you should remember why you're here."

He seems to consider this; his eyes are veiled and thoughtful. "Why do you think I'm here?" he asks at last.

She sighs. "You wanted to get me away from your house. And you couldn't go to Welhe; all those soldiers from the fort got there first. You're . . ." But she stops as she sees a strange expression cross his face.

"Yes," he says, his dark eyes gleaming. He tosses back his flowing hair. "Yes, that's it. That's why I'm here!" Already he's heading for the door.

Wait," she calls. Shivaji turns and looks at her. Such a beautiful smile, she thinks. And then he's gone.

◑◐◑◐

Tanaji feels someone shaking him. He opens his eyes and sees sunshine. Sunshine, after more than a week. He sits up, ready to be glad.

"Hello, uncle," Shivaji says cheerfully.

"You're up!" Tanaji says. But no one seems to listen.

There are others standing around the bed. Hanuman, Lakshman crouching near his shoulder. Beside him sits Iron, looking thoughtful.

"What is this, a war council?" Tanaji says, making a joke. He glances at Iron, who merely nods his head noncommittally. Tanaji looks from face to face. "Wait, what's going on?" he says.

"Father, Shahu has a plan," says Hanuman.

"I can't think when I first wake up. This is well known, Shahu. I need to piddle. I need some breakfast. Then I can think."

They continue to sit in silence as Tanaji takes a third *idli*. Though he knows something's up, Tanaji won't ask, and the others know it's impolite to interrupt. But the quiet doesn't last.

"We're taking the fort," Hanuman blurts out.

Tanaji gawks at Hanuman, the cup of *sambhar* and half-finished *idli* motionless in his hand.

"Maybe you'd better let me put these things down," he says, "before I hear this bright idea."

Hanuman and Lakshman unveil the plan. There are only six or eight men guarding Torna fort. It's a rotation; four men get sent back every day; four from the fort come down. They'll waylay the rotation, and go in place of the four-man guard sent up today. Once inside, they'll overpower the current guards, and take the fort. Simple.

As he listens, Tanaji's frown gets deeper. He squints from time to time to Iron, but Iron simply grunts and looks away.

With Hanuman interrupting, Lakshman takes charred stick and draws on the courtyard tiles: roads, gates, walls, cannons; black lines on the gray tiles. Tanaji looks on, weighing what he sees. "Can this be done?" he asks Iron when the twins have finished speaking.

"Yes," Iron says after a few moments. "Maybe." He looks at Shivaji, then the sooty drawing, then back to Tanaji. "With the right men."

"Your men?" Tanaji asks.

Iron seems to think this over. "Maybe," he answers, hoping Tanaji will understand, one grown and wiser man to another.

"Say you take Torna," Tanaji says, turning to Shivaji. "Then what?"

"Then it's ours, father," Hanuman exclaims.

Tanaji's dark eyebrows knit tight. "I'm asking him." He turns back to Shivaji. In the window the sun has moved behind Shivaji, and the sunbeams dance amidst the stray hairs of his head, sparkling so it seems he has a golden halo. It's a lucky thing I'm not a superstitious man, Tanaji thinks. "I asked you a question, Shahu. What happens if you take it?"

"Take it back, you mean, uncle."

"After all," Iron puts in, "it's his fort, isn't it? Wasn't that why Shahji fought, Tana? For his son? Isn't that why we fought beside him? For a kingdom? A succession? Wasn't that the point?"

"But are you prepared to die for it, Iron? Are the rest of you?" As Tanaji asks this, he sees the grim darkness of Iron's tiny eyes, the clinched muscles of his broad face. And his sons, their faces beaming. And Shivaji, glowing like a god.

You're grown now, Shahu, Tanaji thinks. Today I set aside my promise to your father. I can't keep you from pursuing what you want. And my sons are in love with the thought of conquest. You don't know what you're asking. But you, he thinks, looking at Iron, you know my heart too well. If only Dadaji were here, I'd know better what to do!

"Let's find out what Bala has to say," suggests Tanaji.

ⓈⓈⓈⓈ

They're still discussing the plan when O'Neil comes up to see Shivaji. Shivaji comes away from the circle. O'Neil lifts his hands politely. "Hey, Lord Shivaji, I hear you going fight soon."

"Lord?" Shivaji replies. "Where did you hear that, Onil?"

"About fight is everywhere. All say fight come very soon."

"It's not certain yet. Not sure, you understand? It must be legal." O'Neil strains to understand that word, and Shivaji tries to explain its meaning to him.

"Lord, you must be joking. Legal? It must be the strong man that takes that fort. Strong man takes what he wants. Legal . . . No legal."

"Maybe," Shivaji replies, amused.

"Sure, sure, maybe. But I think maybe yes, lord. So why I come. I wish to ask you a par-tic-u-lar favor." He sounds out the syllables carefully.

Shivaji's eyebrow shoots up. "A favor, Onil? A *particular* favor?"

O'Neil grins. "You like that? I learn Balaji. He good teacher. He speaks very good Persian. Smart man, Bala. Good man."

Shivaji agrees, nodding. "What is your particular favor?" He tries not to enjoy the word too much.

"Lord, at the edge of your jagir is a forest of teak. I say right?" O'Neil says. "This teak is a particular favorite of our ship makers. *Farang* men make big boat, you see? Ship men liking this wood, very good. This forest of teak would be most valuable to the *farangs,* particularly the Portuguese and Dutch. You understand, Portuguese and Dutch? Means *farangs,* yes?"

Shivaji's amusement and curiosity show. "You've been practicing this, haven't you, Onil?"

O'Neil's spotty face glows red. "Bala help me get good words. You like my good words, lord? These particular words?" O'Neil laughs. "Listen, lord, that tree place very good, very good trees. Long, you understand?

Very long, means very good. Much gold for long trees. I get this gold for you. You give me trees, I give gold."

"Wait, Onil: those trees aren't mine."

O'Neil listens carefully and seems to think over what Shivaji has said. "Sure, I understand. But Bala say, sure, trees belong you. You are the true and rightful owner of that land, that Bala say. I say this right?"

Shivaji looks behind him, to Bala who at this moment is arguing with Tanaji, then back to O'Neil. "Maybe," he says.

"You want gold? You want gold for trees?" O'Neil asks, his pale eyes glowing.

"No," Shivaji replies. O'Neil's face falls. A peal of thunder comes from far away, shattering the morning calm. Shivaji looks steadily at O'Neil. "No, you misunderstand. I'll give you trees, but not for gold.

"Bring me guns," he whispers.

☙☙☙☙

Jyoti finds Maya in Gungama's old room, her arms curled around a pillow. Thunder is rolling down the mountain, booming and cracking wildly.

"Mistress," Jyoti whispers. Maya's eyes open so quickly the maid realizes that she wasn't really asleep. "Your girls are waiting, mistress. Your *chelas*, mistress. They're in the dance pavilion, waiting for their guru. For you, mistress." Maya sighs, as if her doom is sealed. "You should be happy, mistress. You will be a great guru."

"Do you like this temple, Jyoti? This room? I hope you do. This is our home, I guess, until we die."

Jyoti clucks her tongue. "You make it sound bad. I know what you would rather have, but no one gets every wish."

"What would I rather have?" says Maya, suddenly facing her maid.

Jyoti avoids Maya's eyes. "They'll be leaving soon, you know. Hanuman came to tell us goodbye just a moment ago. They're saddling the horses even now," she says to Maya.

"No!" Maya cries, standing up. Her hair cascades around her shoulders like a shawl. She runs to the door. A blast of thunder crashes through the tiny house as though the sky were breaking overhead. There in the courtyard Maya sees the men from Poona mounting their ponies. From beneath their cloaks she sees the gleam of sword and mace, bows and arrows with bright feathers.

"Maya."

She turns. There he is, Shivaji, motioning for her.

"Are you going away?" she asks. No matter how she tries, her voice is filled with anguish.

"Not for long," he answers. "I'll see you very soon."

"But when?" She doesn't care that people watch. The storm wind has started blowing now—it whips across the temple walls and gusts across the courtyard, shaking the trees, sending her sari fluttering. The wind is heavy with the scent of rain.

"Soon. Very soon."

"Don't lie to me," she whispers.

"A day or two, no more," he laughs. Then he throws back his hood and points to his forehead. "I'll never lie to you. I swear by this mark."

She's surprised to see that he's wearing a saffron-colored turban, the color that holy men and renunciants wear. "Oh, gods," she breathes. The first great drops of rain begin to splatter from the sky.

"Go now in peace." His voice is far too fatherly to suit her. "Go."

"No!" she answers, standing by his pony, looking up into his face. A fat drop of rain smacks her cheek as she stares up at him.

"Let's ride," shouts Tanaji, waving his hand.

The rain now beats down heavier than ever.

If she had looked behind her Maya might have seen her maid standing in the portico, following another horseman with longing eyes, with tears spilling down her round cheeks. As it is, Maya waits in the rain, her empty arms outstretched long after all the riders have gone, long after the temple gates are shut, until at last Jyoti comes and leads her silently inside.

CHAPTER 13

"It ain't fair!" one of the Bijapuris whines. "I was just up there two days ago. Shouldn't be my turn until tomorrow." With the rain crashing down upon them, the cloaked soldiers ride with hoods pulled over their faces, two in front, two in back. Their horses pick their way along the mud-slick road that leads to the foot of Torna mountain.

"Quit bellyaching," comes a voice from beneath another wax cloth hood. "The cook up at the fort is sick. He needs to come down. It's just the way the dice fell."

"Well, I'm sick, too," the first man replies, kicking his horse's flanks. "I'm sick of this shit. I miss my wife."

"Close your mouths, the both of you," a third man says, lifting his hood just enough to show a pair of angry eyes. "Shut up and be like him," the sergeant says. "He keeps his mouth shut and just rides."

"Maybe he's dead," the first man says.

"Maybe he's drowned," says the second man. "Who'd know?"

But before they can laugh at this wit, the trees on either side of the road begin to rustle. The sergeant pulls up, but before he can say a word, he sees a pony's head emerge from the brush, and a bow and arrow pointed at his heart. In a moment a dozen bowmen on ponies encircle them.

There was no sign, the sergeant protests silently, cursing Allah. They just appeared out of nowhere, he thinks, already preparing his excuses. It wasn't my fault!

Then it strikes the sergeant that a bigger problem requires his immediate attention. "Don't shoot," he says, raising his hands. Cold rain pours down his chest and arms, cascading over the edges of the wax cloth cloak. One of the ponies steps forward. The sergeant sees a nasty-looking mace hanging from the rider's saddle.

The man with the mace lifts his hooded head, and rain pours down the ends of his mustache. "How'd you boys like a little relief?"

"Sounds great," the first rider says.

"Shut up," growls the sergeant.

◎◎◎◎

"Put them over there," Iron says, nodding to an empty stall.

The four Bijapuri horsemen are led inside a dark stable, heads down and cloaks dripping. The sergeant sees that the stable is full of his men. Captain Hamzadin sits miserably against the wall, bound hand and foot. "What happened, captain?" the sergeant says. "Have they captured everybody?"

Hamzadin growls, "We put up a fight. Did you?"

"At least I won't be the one explaining this to Bijapur," the sergeant says. Hamzadin curls his lip and spits.

◎◎◎◎

"But I want to go," Iron says. "It's my right to go."

"A four-man job, uncle," Shivaji answers. "Besides, you need to give a younger man a chance."

"No," Iron rumbles. "This is my chance. You are my chance. I served your father. That fort belongs to you, Shahu. I want to get it back for you. It is my right to go, and my pleasure. You cannot deny me this, Shahu."

"He's right, Shahu," Tanaji says, coming up to join them. "He should go."

"Their routine is to rotate four guards—just four," Shivaji replies. "So just the four will go. A fifth would be suspicious."

"But they know Iron, Shahu," Tanaji says. "I was thinking about this. Who will talk to the guards up there? They're not going to let us in like that, not when they've never seen us before. They know him, Shahu. They like him. Everybody likes Iron, right?"

Shivaji simply closes his eyes.

"Come on, you," Tanaji says to Iron. "Let's see if you remember how to fight."

❦❧❦❧

There had been grousing when Tanaji selected the twins to make up the rest of the party. But the two of them are the best bowmen in Poona, and who can blame Tanaji if he wants family for a job like this? Still, what kind of father sends his children to face death?

Iron lends his favorite old sword to Shivaji before they leave the compound. It's a little heavier than Shivaji likes, but it will serve. Near the hilt the blade has twenty-nine notches.

"I'm like your dad," Iron says to the twins as they begin to ride. "I like a mace. Gives you a feeling of protection, a mace." He pats the heavy weapon that hangs from his horse's saddle. Iron's mace has a hammerhead bludgeon instead of the knife-edged one Tanaji prefers. The twins wince at these old men who place such store in bashing their enemies' heads. They'd rather slice a throat with a shiny arrow from a hundred yards away.

❦❧❦❧

Water cascades off the face of the mountain, spilling across the pathway.

"Have they got guns?" Tanaji shouts to Iron as they slog up the narrow, winding path to the fort. The wind whips the rain right in their faces.

"Sure, they've got guns," Iron shouts back. "But what good are guns in this weather?"

Even nearly empty, even poorly defended, a fort is a force unto itself. Tanaji twists his head, peering into the rain sheeting from the gray sky, peering up at the fierce rock walls of Torna.

Torna mountain is tall and narrow, thrusting like a knife blade from the plains. And even if the rain were less, it would be hard to tell exactly where the mountain ended and the fort walls began. The walls rise up in a smooth face that curves around the edge of the mountain's knifelike peak.

The road to the fort is a narrow switchback path, its surface left intentionally uneven, full of half-formed steps and potholes. It would be hazardous in sunshine, but rain-slick and blasted by the mountain winds, it's terrifying. From hidden drains in the walls above them, cold rivers of rain arc through the air and crash to the winding road. They're getting soaked.

❦❧❦❧

The first gate on the road—about three quarters of the way up the mountain—is open. The Bijapuris have no enemies on this side of Hindustan, and no one expects a move upon this small and insignificant fort. Why else would the captain feel comfortable leaving it all but deserted? "Eight men only up there, maybe ten at most," Hamzadin had told them. He'd said the same even after they twisted his arms till he screamed.

But as he waits for the others to gather beside him in the shelter of the gatehouse, Tanaji begins having second thoughts. Eight or ten men in this fortress, tiny as it is, could harry an attacking army. If the eight men were determined, if they could use guns. Their plan depends on surprise. He hopes surprise will be enough.

Beneath an overhanging rock, Tanaji halts and makes them rehash the plan once more. Then he tells them all to pee.

"Spoken like a true soldier," Iron laughs.

"I don't need to," Hanuman says.

"Better to try anyway," Iron tells him. "It's embarrassing to pee your pants in a fight."

"Iron speaks from experience," Tanaji says.

They pass through the second gatehouse: the gate is open here as well, but passing beneath the high stone arches seems to disquiet Hanuman. It's not the first time he has been to a fort, but it's the first time he has gone to capture one. As he moves beneath the gateway arch, he looks up into the machicolations, where defenders, if they wanted, could simply wait above the gateway to pour down boiling water, or a rain of arrows. Suddenly Hanuman regrets he didn't say goodbye to Jyoti.

Hanuman doesn't realize that such a feeling of dread is just what his ancestors intended—this fort designed by cruel and clever men fascinated by violence and death. The thick dark walls jut outward to rise menacingly over them; the narrow viewing slots peer down like empty terrifying eyes; the shifting, shadowed crenellations along the tops of the walls jut up like the spines of some ancient lizard made of stone; the vast wooden gate, made of whole tree trunks clenched by iron, black with age, bristle with black, barbed spikes. Every aspect of this structure was meant to unsettle and unnerve. It does its work on Hanuman, and on the rest of them as well.

Only Iron seems not to mind: He rides casually, hands easy on the reins. When he nears the great black gate, he tosses back his hood, rain be damned, and shouts, "Hey! Hey boys!" his big voice just audible above the blustering wind. "Hey boys, wake up! It's Captain Hamzadin come on an inspection! Wake up, boys!" Rain pours from his turban and streams down his mustaches. He stares at the silent gate, eyes glittering.

They wait a long time. There's nobody here, Hanuman thinks. We've come all this way for nothing. They've all got sick and died. Then Tanaji points his nose almost imperceptibly toward the wall; Hanuman follows his nod to one of the viewing slots. He wonders if he just imagines a darker shadow moving behind it. He notices for the first time that there is a banner on the flagpole; the green flag of Bijapur hanging limply, streaming with rainwater, like someone's forgotten wash hung out to dry.

Iron just sits there, face out and open, friendly as a snake. The other four huddle behind him, seated on the captured horses, huddled in their prisoners' dark cloaks, wondering if they will pass for the relief party. There are no hiding places here, and a forced retreat on that rough road would lead only to a spilling, tumbling dive to certain death.

This is a bad plan, Hanuman thinks. Five against ten. What fools we are. They're trapped by their plan. Now there is no way but forward. He's about to yell out: Turn! Run! But at that moment, the shadow moves away from the viewing slot and a hooded figure appears above the gate. "Hey, Iron! You're a fucking liar! That ain't the fucking captain!"

Still keeping his place behind Iron, by feel alone Hanuman notches an arrow on his bowstring beneath his cloak. He becomes aware of Lakshman stirring beside him, and knows that he has done the same.

"Do you think I'm fucking stupid?" the sentry shouts.

"I think you're fucking sober," Iron shouts back. "But I can fix that." He pats the bundle on the saddle behind him where he has hidden his battle-hammer mace. "Toddy, my boy. Toddy for his loyal guards, compliments of your shit-faced captain," Iron yells. "Iron's best brew, guaranteed to burn your guts out. Pure Hindu poison. Your captain's already gone blind. He can't remember his name. Your buddies here can hardly ride." He waves an arm at the four men behind him. "Stinking drunk, the bunch of them, puking on themselves. Disgusting, aren't they?"

"What's wrong with the sergeant?" the sentry asks. "He don't look right. Hey, sarge!"

"He's passed out," Iron shouts back. Behind him he motions subtly with his hand for the others to stay calm. "Lucky he got up here at all. If you call getting up to this pisshole luck. Hey, sentry, let's just stand out here. I love getting soaked. Makes me feel like a man when my pecker's freezing off."

The sentry disappears from the wall. Hanuman wonders if he is the only one whose stomach is twisting. "When the time comes, don't hesitate," Tanaji had told them all. "You'll have to move fast, faster than you want to. You strike, then think about it later. It's the nature of a surprise attack that somebody's going to die who doesn't need to die. Let's make sure it's none of us."

All right, thinks Hanuman. Let's go. I don't care anymore. I'm ready. Let's go. He thinks of Jyoti suddenly, wondering what she'll say when he comes back. What if he comes back dead? Don't be a fool, he tells himself. You strike, then think about it later. So stop thinking about it now. In the lower part of the huge wooden gate, a smaller door opens, big enough for a horse. Hanuman slips his bow and arrow in front of him. A movement to his right suggests that Lakshman is doing the same. But Tanaji waves a hidden hand behind him: Calm, calm, wait for it.

Iron leads his horse to the open doorway. Hanuman can see him talking to the sentry but the rain and wind obscure the words. The sentry moves in the shadows and Hanuman sees him lift his hand. There's something in it. What's he doing?

Beside him, Hanuman hears Lakshman's bow: *thwoop, thwoop*—two arrows slice through the rain. At that same moment, the sentry bangs a triangle alarm with a metal rod.

Almost instantly the sentry spins and falls when an arrow pierces his neck. Iron turns to Lakshman, his face a mask of rage, and then runs inside the gate, black battle hammer twirling in his hand.

Tanaji leaps off his horse and Lakshman follows. Together they race for the gate. Shivaji runs up to Hanuman. "Your brother's a fool," he shouts.

Hanuman feels his arrows rattling as he runs. How many did I bring? he thinks suddenly. Not enough. He steps through the horse gate and sees the sentry rolling in the mud, clutching his throat. Dark blood swirls in the rainwater. Hanuman turns and vomits. He looks up to see Iron swing his battle hammer. After the sentry's skull cracks open, his body flops in spasms on the ground for a moment, then lies still.

"Who gave the order to shoot, dammit? He was supposed to be a hostage!" Iron whispers at Lakshman, his face contorted with anger.

"You should have taken him, then. Your inaction killed him, not me," Lakshman replies.

"Shut up and apologize!" Tanaji yells.

"Shut up or apologize? Which do you want?" Lakshman shouts. Hanuman looks up, stunned by his lack of respect.

"Hurry, " Shivaji says. "He was signaling when we shot him."

"When that fool shot him," Iron says, and spits.

Lakshman picks up the iron bar from the dead sentry's hand and walks toward the triangle. "Let's try the doorbell," he says.

Iron's eyes grow wide.

"Go ahead and hit it," Shivaji says.

"What's the plan?" asks Hanuman.

"There is no plan," Tanaji mutters.

"Just kill everything in sight," Iron says.

Lakshman wails on the triangle like a delighted child.

"So much for surprise," Tanaji says.

❧❧❧❧

Lakshman returns to huddle with the rest behind a cannon. "Shit. I left my other quiver on my horse," he whispers. Iron glares at him.

Shit, thinks Hanuman. I did the same.

The rain pounds harder then ever, spattering with soft cymbal sounds as the drops hit the cannon's bronze. They wait, holding their breaths, weapons ready, water dripping from their hands.

Nothing happens.

Then they hear the *clink* of keys, the snap of a lock being opened, the rattle of short chains. Shivaji signs: Get ready.

From within the giant gate, the smallest door begins to creak, the one designed to admit a man on foot. Lakshman's bow *twangs* as he lets an arrow fly. The point gets buried in the opening door.

"Move!" shouts Shivaji. "Move!" His cloak thrown back, his sword bare, he runs toward the gate, with Tanaji and Iron following close behind. Iron's feet slide on the wet cobbles; he falls right next to Hanuman, but when Hanuman reaches to help, Iron shakes him off and thrusts forward on all fours. Lakshman chases after him, looking smug.

"Get through, get through!" Tanaji screams. "If they go up the wall we're dead! Get through." Now that they realize they're under attack, the Bijapuris pull the small door closed. Shivaji, reaching the door just in time, drives his sword through the opening. He thrusts it violently, recklessly, wrenching it in the closing gap, hoping to keep the Bijapuris away from the latch and lock, twisting so hard he slips to his knees in the swirling mud. In a moment, Tanaji appears at his side, driving the blades of his mace's bludgeon into the narrow opening, sending splinters flying.

Iron steps back, giving them room. Lakshman and Hanuman run up, but Iron keeps them from the door, pointing to the high walls above them. The twins twist nervously, swinging their bows to aim at every shadow.

"This is fun," Lakshman says.

Shivaji leans away as Tanaji slams the mace against the door, making a hole just large enough to squeeze the bludgeon through. He rams the bludgeon against the frame and, using the heavy handle of his mace, levers the door open.

He screams as an arrow pierces his left bicep and pins him to the gate.

Tanaji starts to follow but Iron stops him. "Come on, boys!" he yells, waving the twins through the door instead. "Bowmen on the other side," Iron shouts. "Go! Go!" The open door waits like the mouth of death. Bowstring drawn and arrow cocked, Hanuman runs through.

Beyond the gate is another narrow passage. Hanuman can't see anything to shoot. He swings in arcs, hunting for a target. Rain pours into his face, spilling down his arms, down his pants. He could pee now and no one could tell. He hears Lakshman clambering through the door behind him.

An arrow whistles past his ear. "Shit." He can't tell if he says this out loud. Then he sees Shivaji, half-crouched behind a bench, his left arm, pulled unnaturally away from his body, pinned by an arrow to the black gate itself.

Shivaji raises his sword to a point above them. Behind one of the stones, Hanuman catches a glimpse of glinting metal. He looses two arrows and hears the thud of one striking home. A body tumbles from the wall.

Another arrow sings past his head, this from another direction. Shivaji points to a different wall, a different shadow, and again Hanuman shoots. He hears a thrashing, then a gurgle, then silence. Notching another arrow, he catches a glimpse of someone running away.

"You're good," a voice says behind him. He turns to see Iron standing next to him; Hanuman had no idea he was so nearby. "Done this before?"

"Not in a fort, uncle," Hanuman answers.

Tanaji comes through the door, and moves quickly to Shivaji, looking over the arrow and the arm. "This isn't bad, Shahu," he says. Shivaji grunts.

At the end of the passage is a narrow, winding stair. "There'll be swordsmen on those stairs, or I miss my guess," says Iron.

"I agree," Tanaji says. "Lakshman, give me your knife."

"What's wrong with yours?" Lakshman asks. But when his father blazes at him, he shrugs and takes his serpent blade from its sheath. "Careful," he whispers as he passes it. One edge of the long wavy blade is toothed like a saw, the other edge as sharp as a razor.

"This might hurt," Tanaji says as he saws with the toothed edge through the arrow shaft in Shivaji's arm. Hanuman sees the shaft jumping and vibrating as Tanaji cuts; he watches Shivaji grimace. In a moment, though, the black-feathered shaft clatters to the wet stones. Carefully

Tanaji lifts and slides Shivaji's arm off what's left of the arrow. Shivaji groans, and his eyes roll back. Tanaji lowers him to the ground.

"Watch the stairs," Iron says to the twins. "I mean you, too," he snarls at Lakshman. Then Iron and Tanaji stretch Shivaji out along the ground. Using Lakshman's knife, Tanaji cuts Shivaji's sleeve, and ties it in a thick knot around the wounded bicep.

"I've seen worse," Iron says. But Shivaji doesn't answer. Maybe he's fainted. Iron slaps him. "Hey, Shahu, do you hear me? I've seen worse. I've seen plenty worse."

"Shut up," Shivaji mumbles.

Iron slaps him again. "No sleeping now, Shahu. Work to be done, boy." Iron lifts Shivaji to a sitting position. "Time to get going."

"Why don't we just leave him," Lakshman says.

"He might be captured, or even die. We need to get him moving."

"We all need to get moving or we all will die," Hanuman says. "Lakshman, watch the stairs!" For he sees shadows slide along the stairway's edge.

"This is man's work, boys," Iron says. "Step aside and let us grown-ups show you how it's done." He looks up at Hanuman. "You. Come here and get him up. Get him to his feet, whatever it takes." Then Iron stands, twirling his battle hammer in his hands so the black hammerhead spins like a top, and steps next to Tanaji. Iron whispers in Tanaji's ear. Tanaji shakes his head, but as Iron keeps up his whispered talk, he slowly nods. The two come back, eyes trained on Shivaji.

"Us two, then you two. Then him."

"I don't think he . . . ," Hanuman begins.

"I can do it," Shivaji says, but his voice is weak. "I can fight."

"But look at him . . ."

"He looks good. I've seen worse. Haven't you?"

"Sure," Tanaji agrees.

"Right. That captain told us that there's eight or ten up here. We got three—if you killed that last one, Hanu—so five to seven left. Good odds," Tanaji says.

"One of them is sick. I heard the relief party talking about it; the cook is sick," Hanuman says hopefully.

"Right," Iron says, "even better. One of them is sick."

"Well, one of us is sick, too. He's not doing so good," Lakshman says.

"I'm all right," Shivaji replies, but his eyes have trouble focusing.

"He's just shook up," Iron suggests. "He'll be fine in a moment."

"And while we're standing here, they could be getting ready to attack," Lakshman complains.

"They won't attack. They've seen you two shoot. They're waiting for us," Iron replies.

"Maybe we turn back now," says Lakshman, glancing at his father.

"They'll come after us," Iron says. "If not these boys, then an attack party from Bijapur. We discussed this."

"There's only one path, son," agrees Tanaji, nodding.

"Two, if you count dying," Iron chuckles. No one laughs.

"You ready, Shahu?" Iron asks. Shivaji nods. "Let's go, then."

"Just five or six," Hanuman says. "Just five or six." He looks at Shivaji. *"Har, har, mahadev,"* he says.

Hanuman watches Iron and Tanaji run straight to the stairs. A moment ago, his father had been wrestling with his fear, but now he's eager to face those shadows on the stairs. "Let's go," Hanuman says, turning to Lakshman. Lakshman smirks as though it were all a big game.

But as they start to run, Shivaji lumbers between them and races past.

"Hey," Hanuman shouts, splashing across the courtyard, trying to catch up. "We're supposed to be next. Wait!"

"Dammit," Lakshman storms after him.

Through the rain they hear the *clang* of steel, the groan of men fighting, the kiss of metal meeting flesh.

As they reach the passage opening, a heavy body tumbles down, bumping down the stairs headfirst. The face is smashed and gone. For a moment, Hanuman thinks it is Iron, or that it's his father, but then he sees that it's only one of the Bijapuris. Just four or five to go, he thinks.

He and Lakshman mount the stairs together, the way twins can move in perfect unison, bows leveled, arrows ready. What's left of the dim daylight disappears. It is madness. Five men going up ten feet of dark and narrow stairs. Weapons are nearly useless here: as likely to bang and glance against the wet stone walls as to hit their targets.

But there is a *thung* as Lakshman looses an arrow, and a grunt as it pierces a Bijapuri's heart. His body somersaults backward down the stairs like rag toy; Hanuman must jump aside to keep from tumbling down the stairs beside it. He sees Iron, hammer in hand, gaping at the empty place where his opponent stood; Iron's thigh is cut and bleeding.

The air whistles before him. Hanuman sees a sword slicing through a Bijapuri's body, like a knife through a roast; a sword held by Shivaji, face pale, mouth open, fighting for breath. The body sinks to its knees with a burbling cry, blood and shit pouring into the rainwater rushing down the stone stairs. As Shivaji tugs out his blade, foulness fills the air.

Shivaji drops, his hands on his knees, gasping. Blood and water drip from his left arm. Lakshman kicks the body down the stairs.

Hanuman's eyes are drawn to the darkness higher up. A fight is raging: it must be Tanaji. They hear the muffled sounds of punches.

Hanuman pushes Iron aside, and runs past Shivaji, up the stairs. The steps grow narrow as he ascends; there is no room for weapons here.

He can just make out his father's eyes bulging wide, the hands that grip his father's neck. Using his elbow, Hanuman whacks his father's foe across the head.

Hanuman punches the man, blindly, calling Lakshman for help. The attacker seems impervious to his blows. Tanaji has stopped even gasping.

Hanuman reaches into his quiver and takes out his few arrows. Holding them in a bundle, with all his strength he drives them into the man's side, pulls them out and then drives them in again.

The man lets go his father's neck. Tanaji clatters to his knees. The man, arrows still embedded in his side, lurches forward, falling against Hanuman, a burbling in his throat. Hanuman looks with horror into the man's dying eyes and shoves him away. "Father?" he calls.

"Here," Tanaji croaks, collapsing into his son's arms. "You saved my life."

Iron comes up. Hanuman glances at Iron's thigh, the wound tied with a strip of cloth. "It's not so bad," Iron says. "I've seen worse."

"We're not done yet," croaks Tanaji. "Eight or ten men. We've killed six or seven. Still two or three more to go."

"Where the hell are they, father?" Lakshman asks.

"They could hole up here for days," Iron replies. "But this is the last line of easy defense, these stairs here. Once we're through that door up there, we're set." He nods to a narrow exit hole above them, where the stairs mount onto the floor above.

All five men look up at the square opening at the top of the stairs. "It's one of those places, isn't it?" Lakshman says, figuring it out. "They stand up there with swords and wait for you to come up."

Dread falls on them like the cold rain. Water pours through the opening as the rain beats down. The afternoon light has faded, but the open square is bright compared to the darkness of the stairway passage.

"You need to look at the bright sky first," Iron says. For the first time,

Hanuman realizes that Iron is afraid. "Look at the bright sky first so you don't shoot blind."

"I'm out of arrows," Hanuman says. The words cast a pall over the five men. The odds are looking worse all the time.

"I have six," Lakshman says, offering three to Hanuman.

"You won't need more than that," Iron says grimly.

"Six arrows for three men?" Lakshman sneers. "You must think we're great shots."

"I mean you'll have one chance to kill the swordsman up there before he kills whoever goes first." Iron moves close to Lakshman, his face now only inches from Lakshman's nose. "Do you understand, boy? Here's your chance to be rid of me. I'm going up there, I'll be first. Just shoot a half a second late, that's all, and you're done with me for good."

"Not my way, old man," Lakshman replies. "Don't want you to die by accident, do I?"

Iron bristles, but turns again to the opening above them. "How do we work this?" he asks.

The narrow stairs are crowded, slippery with rain. Their clothes are soaked, heavy with water. The smell of wet cloth mixes with sweat and fear.

"Let's throw them a corpse," Lakshman suggests.

Everyone glances around, trying to see who will object to this disgusting suggestion. "Come on," whispers Lakshman, reaching down to grab the body at their feet.

Iron swings his weight behind Lakshman's, then they all join to hoist the corpse toward the opening. The body is cumbersome, heavier than it looks, slippery with rainwater and blood. Somehow they manage to boost it nearly to the top of the stairs. Then they grunt and hoist the corpse up through the stairway opening.

In a flash they hear a clang of swords above them, and the corpse's head topples from its body and bounces past them down the stair. They drop the headless body and it bumps down after it.

"Well, now we know," says Iron. "Two of them. One left, one right.'

"Get ready. I'm going to be the bait. Get ready," Shivaji whispers.

"You've never done this before, Shahu," says Iron, stepping forward. "I have. Time for you to watch and learn." He steps to the top of the stairs, and nudges Tanaji and Shivaji, until they move reluctantly down. Then he shows Lakshman and Hanuman where to stand. Lakshman is hunched in a corner, Hanuman is lying nearly prostrate on the stairs. "Can you shoot in this position, boys?" Iron asks. The boys nod. "Then get your arrows ready. You'll get one shot each." As they each notch an arrow, Iron hands his battle hammer to Shivaji. "Give me the sword, Shahu. This is sword work here." He takes Shivaji's sword, checking its heft.

He's delaying, trying to muster his courage, Hanuman realizes. Iron expects to be killed.

"Will you please get the hell on with it," Lakshman bursts out.

"Give a man a chance, boy," Iron hisses back. He stoops to look at Tanaji and Shivaji, one last look, maybe. Then he sighs and stands, gripping his sword and shouts, "One! Two! Three!"

He jumps up into the opening. There's a *clang* of steel almost at once, and the twang of bows.

But Iron's body crashes down the wet stone stairs. Then his sword clatters down, sliding stair by stair behind him. Tanaji and Shivaji watch Iron's body slump to a stop. They turn to the twins, and from the twins to the opening.

"I got my man," says Lakshman. "Got him through the neck. What about you?"

"Maybe," Hanuman says.

"Shit," says Lakshman.

"I'm going up," says Tanaji.

"I'll do it," Shivaji says.

"They're my boys," Tanaji replies and he moves to the top of the stairs before Shivaji can stop him.

"Arrows ready?" he asks. The boys hardly have a chance to nod before he too shouts, "One, two, three," and dashes up the stairs.

The twins don't move; there's no one there to shoot at. Shivaji follows up the stairs behind Tanaji, now holding Iron's battle hammer in his hand.

They step out onto an open stone roof, the rain blustering in sheets around their feet. Tanaji, a few steps away from the stairway opening, sees Shivaji, points to a spot not far from where Shivaji stands, and continues a low sweeping prowl across the roof.

They're in the heart of the fort now; there are no more tricky defenses. Past this point it will be hand to hand. Shivaji looks where Tanaji indicated. There's a dead man splayed on the stones, an arrow through his eye.

Lakshman steps up the stairs now, arrow drawn. He looks at the corpse that Shivaji shows him. "I thought I hit him in the neck," he whispers, as rain pours down his face. "That leaves one more; the one that Hanuman missed. Maybe two."

"Yes, the cook; the sick cook," Shivaji says. "Where's Hanuman?"

"Went to look at Iron. Poor bastard."

Tanaji has found another staircase on the other end of the roof. He signals to Shivaji, then, mace held high before him, he crab-steps down the stairs to the central courtyard of the fort.

Shivaji is about to follow when Lakshman taps his shoulder. In the fading afternoon light, they can just make out a patch of red slowly dissolving into the rain; a few steps beyond it is another patch, and then another; these small and dense, fresher. Lakshman and Shivaji take slow, careful steps, following the bloodstains to a rush-roofed storage hut.

A few steps farther on, they find an arced scimitar lying on the stones beside a pool of blood, the wide blade bent and deeply notched, as though it failed to cut through something hard. Holding Iron's battle hammer, Shivaji moves toward the hut, Lakshman at his heels, arrow notched and ready. The hut is windowless, its door but a stoop hole. Shivaji creeps up and stands beside the low opening, Lakshman now at his side. The light is so dim that the inside of the hut seems night black. The two of them listen but all they hear is the pounding rain and whistling wind.

Shivaji flashes an unexpected grin at Lakshman, then ducks through the hut's low door.

There won't be room enough to swing a mace in there, Lakshman thinks.

But in a moment, Shivaji creeps back. "There's a body in there."

"Dead?" asks Lakshman.

Shivaji glares at him. "Yes, dead."

"That's it then," Lakshman glances at Shivaji's troubled face. "What's wrong, Shahu? We wiped them out."

"He didn't have any wounds. So where did these bloodstains come from?"

Lakshman stifles a groan. "You can always find something wrong, can't you? Why can't you ever just be happy? We've won!"

At that moment, Tanaji comes toward them, mace gripped tight.

"You can relax," Lakshman says. "They're all dead."

"That's it, then, I guess," he whispers hoarsely. "The lower fort is deserted. I guess we got them all."

"I thank the goddess for this victory," Shivaji says, raising Iron's mace above his bowed head.

Lakshman laughs. "Hey, Shahu, your turban's running in the rain. There's orange all over your shirt."

Tanaji curses, disturbed that Lakshman has spoiled this moment. "You too, should be grateful, boy. You alone escaped unhurt." He looks sadly at Shahu. "I can't believe they killed Iron. After all these years, to see him go."

"His karma finally caught up with him," Lakshman laughs. "Why do you think I'm uninjured?"

"Don't tempt the gods," Tanaji warns. Sometimes he can't believe that Lakshman is his son. Then Tanaji sees Hanuman running up the stairway.

"Iron!" pants Hanuman. "He had a helmet wrapped beneath his turban. The metal's sliced clean through, and part of his scalp is gone. I thought he was dead, but he started breathing again. He's still unconscious. Maybe he broke something, falling down the stairs."

"What's it take to kill that son of a bitch?" Lakshman says. He leans against the hut, away from the others, shaking his head.

"Shut up, Lakshman," Hanuman snaps. "He saved our lives."

"He saved shit—" Lakshman starts to say, but a hand grabs him from behind and pulls him off his feet. Lakshman shouts as he falls; his bow skitters across the roof.

Now Lakshman is staring at a familiar-looking knife. The point of his own black serpent blade hovers over Lakshman's left eye, held by an unknown hand, set to plunge into his brain. The other men stand like statues.

"Put down the knife," Shivaji says to Lakshman's captor, advancing inch by inch. "Put down the knife and live."

"Throw down your weapons or he dies," the man replies. Lakshman smells the sour, sick odor of the man's breath as he speaks.

"We can make a deal," Hanuman says.

"Nice words after you kill my friends." The man half-drags Lakshman toward the stairway opening. The Bijapuri's eyes are wild; full of crazy energy. He sits behind Lakshman, his back near the stairway opening, and raises the black serpent blade just inches from his captive's face. Rainwater fountains along the edge of the knife, streaming onto Lakshman's chest.

"We don't want to hurt you," Tanaji says.

"Well, I don't want to hurt him," the man replies. "But I will. I might be a cook, but I still know how to kill." He flicks the knife like lightning at Lakshman's eyebrow, sending blood streaking down Lakshman's wet face. "Sharp knife," he says. "Cooks say a sharp knife will never cut you." He flicks the knife point again, making a tiny bleeding "X." "Another lie."

The cook leans back, though he still holds the knife to Lakshman's eye. "Say, come here, you," the cook says to Hanuman. Hanuman moves with slow steps. "Closer." Hanuman understands, and brings his face close to that of his twin. He can feel Lakshman's, anxious breath on his wet skin.

"You look the same," the Bijapuri says, faintly amused, glancing from face to face. "Almost."

"He's my brother," Hanuman says. "Let him go, and . . ."

"Brothers? Twins?" the cook says. "Not quite the same, though." With unimagined quickness the cook swings the serpent blade. Hanuman screams, pushing himself away, his hands over his eye.

"Now you look the same," the cook says. Hanuman lurches back and Tanaji pulls his son's blood-drenched hand away from his eye to check the damage. The rain spills across his eyebrow, over a fiercely bleeding "X," just like the one carved on Lakshman. "That's just to let you know that I can do whatever I want," the cook says. Lakshman whimpers.

"Tell us what you need," Shivaji says. "To go free? Done. Release him. There are horses outside the gate. Take one and go."

"Don't know what I want," the cook replies, suddenly thoughtful. He licks his lips as though savoring the taste of the rain on his tongue. "Might want something more. Don't know. Might want a lot more. Might want something from his brother, too." The man leers, his eyes glittering and rolling back in his head so they see the bloodshot whites.

He slides the knifepoint down over Lakshman's face, gently dragging it along the skin, hard enough that it leaves a stark white track on the cheek and neck, but not deep enough to cut. He slides the serpent blade along the chin, the jaw, bringing it at last to the bottom of Lakshman's ear.

The Bijapuri looks to the three men that watch him, as if inviting them to pay attention. Suddenly the long serpent blade swings in his hand. Tanaji grimaces, sure the cook means to plunge the point into his poor son's throat. Instead the cook stops with sudden precision, and flicks the razor-smooth blade outward with a snap of his wrist.

Lakshman's earlobe flies through the air to land at Hanuman's feet.

"Stop!" Tanaji yells. "Take me instead! Do what you want to me!"

"You the daddy?" the man asks, his glittering eyes suddenly full of understanding. "You the daddy of these sweet boys?" Pulling Lakshman's head upward, he takes the knife and now presses its point under Lakshman's chin until a tiny drop of blood wells up. "Your sweet boy's peeing his pants, daddy. I can feel it. It's warm."

"Let him go or die," Shivaji says, glancing up behind the cook.

"You can't fool me like that, friend," the cook replies, his gap-toothed grin widening. "I know there's nothing there behind me."

"You're wrong, boy," says Iron's voice. He staggers up the stairway opening. His turban gone, blood drips along his forehead from underneath the headpiece of the torn helmet he still wears. The cook doesn't look around, so he can't see Iron weaving on his feet. "Drop the knife."

"Or what?" the cook replies. "Or what?" he says, sliding the blade up over Lakshman's face again.

Hanuman sees the world around him moving in awful slowness. He sees Iron's sword whirling in an axlike arc, whistling through the air as Iron slams it home. As Iron swings his sword, the cook slides the point of the serpent blade in a ragged trail along his brother's quivering face.

Hanuman sees the cook's head burst beneath Iron's heavy sword. The skull splits like a block of wood. The halves cave away, flopping to his shoulders like a melon split in two.

The serpent knife flies from the cook's senseless hand and slides across the puddles and the stones, but its awful work is done. Lakshman lifts his head. As Hanuman stares, the razor cut across his face begins to ooze red. He watches horrified as the sliced skin slides apart. Lakshman's eye spills out like jelly, gushing down the gash of the deep and perfect cut the blade has made. Blood and rain bubble from his wound.

Hanuman is clutching his brother's face, frantically trying to scoop the streaming jelly back into Lakshman's socket. The screams he hears are Lakshman's and his own.

Iron is swaying over Lakshman and the man he killed, looking down at them in anguish. "Lakshman! Lakshman!" he moans, his face held up into the pelting rain. "This is my fault! What have I done?"

Tanaji's face grows pale and his eyes dart from son to son. His battle mace clatters from his hands and he sinks to his knees.

He looks up to Shivaji and the rain pours down his face. "Is this is my reward, Shahu? So your have your fort—is it worth the price? Tell me, is it worth the price?"

Around their feet the blood-red puddles swirl.

CHAPTER 14

More rain! So much rain! thinks Bala. Nowhere does so much rain fall as in these Purandhar hills. How do people stand to live here in all this rain?

Looking up from his morning prayers, Bala's gaze turns to the dark hills where Torna fort lies hidden by low clouds. I wonder what it's like for them up there, he thinks. The plan is to send a company up the mountain today. If all has gone well, the raiding party should be in charge to welcome them, and the Poonis can occupy the fort. If not, well, they'll find that out soon enough. Either way, Bala will have work to do today.

For it will fall to him to explain to Bijapur what they have done, either way. Yesterday, with very little ceremony, Shivaji appointed him ambassador. In truth, all Shivaji actually said was, "I'm sending you to Bijapur." But Bala understood. And by the light in his eyes he knew that Shivaji understood as well. Torna fort was going to be just the beginning. What's happening up there, he wonders, as he squints at the hidden mountain.

As Bala walks he sees the *farang* O'Neil, saddling a Bedouin, a traveling bag at his feet. "Good morrow, Onil. Thou'rt preparing for a journey?" Bala asks in Persian, the tongue they both speak fluently.

O'Neil bows. His red hair is tied into a bushy queue. "I must away for Surat. My lord Shivaji has given me leave to barter for his teak."

Bala's eyebrows lift—actually his bald forehead where his eyebrows would be, if he had any hair. "This is good news, Onil. Dost know about Torna?"

"A little, maybe. Wouldst tell me more?"

Bala explains how the raiding party left yesterday afternoon to recapture Torna, how Shivaji is legally the rightful master of the fort.

"Bijapur will be angry, Balaji," O'Neil says.

"Less, maybe, than thou thinkest. Bijapur cares little for forts. They want only the taxes. Just give them their allotment, which they believe to be their proper due—and thou mightst then keep any fort."

"And if he does not pay, Balaji?"

"Then I think an army of elephants will thunder through these hills, with guns and cannons blazing."

"So he must pay, Balaji!"

"I do not think he likes to pay. In any case I will go to Bijapur, Onil. Maybe I can soothe them with my words. Wouldst come with me?"

"I go to Surat first, master. I must tell the Portuguese of the death of their man, Da Gama. And I must seek out the Dutch and speak to them of teak." O'Neil mounts the wooden saddle. Bala walks beside him.

As they reach the gate, the wind shifts, now from the north, cool and dry, blowing the haze from the sky. O'Neil points to the peak of Torna mountain, to the gray walls of the fort. Floating high above the walls, a saffron-colored banner, long, thin, billows on the breeze.

"A saffron flag!" whispers Bala. Bala forgets about O'Neil and runs back into the temple. "They've done it!" he shouts. "They've taken Torna fort!"

ෙඛෙ

Soon everyone from the temple is heading to Welhe, dancing, laughing, eager to congratulate the triumphant raiding party. When they reach the village, they gather in the courtyard of Iron's house. Bala finds himself talking to his friend Govindas. "I'll tell you what I think, Balaji," Govindas says. "This is the start of something, make no mistake. This is Shivaji's sign. He's telling the world that he's taking back what's his."

"Maybe," Bala answers.

"I see them!" someone shouts, pointing to a hill just visible over the village's stone walls.

ෙඛෙ

When he hears the cheering, Iron straightens, a man aware of the importance of appearances, lifting his head, though it weighs a hundred pounds. "We're all right!" Iron shouts, his face determined that it should be so. But even Bala's smile fades when he sees Lakshman clutching his bandaged eye, the blood oozing over his fingertips. "Get a doctor," Tanaji growls. But his voice is so hoarse, Bala can hardly hear him.

"We have no doctor," Iron says. "Get the *shastri*."

"The *shastri* is here, uncle," Bala responds, jogging along beside Lakshman. "Hold on, brother, help is here. Hold on." Bala runs back to the gates.

"I'm all right," Lakshman says, not realizing that Bala is already gone.

Tanaji reins in his horse and waits for Shivaji to catch up. "Now I quit, Shahu. I'm done with you." When he sees the look on Shivaji's face, Tanaji nearly repents. But he's been thinking and now his mind is made up. He speaks quickly before he changes it again. "I promised your dad I'd help you grow to manhood. Well, I'm done. If you can take a fort, you're a man—that's how it seems to me."

"Uncle, don't say this. Not now," Shivaji says, and his eyes are so plaintive that Tanaji nearly reconsiders. But a look at Lakshman is all it takes to steel him.

"Look at my son. Haven't I sacrificed enough, Shahu?" Tanaji's voice chokes. "Time you take the consequences of your actions."

"You are my general, my minister, my friend. I will have no other one but you, uncle. I cannot replace you. I won't even try. I need you, uncle."

"No more, Shahu. Look at my sons, broken and bleeding. Enough."

Shivaji lifts his head, in a way that reminds Tanaji of General Shahji. "The day of reckoning comes, Tana. The die is cast, there is no bringing it back."

"Not with me, Shahu. I'm done." When Shivaji reaches out to him, Tanaji spurs his horse, to ride next to Lakshman.

"Forget it, Shahu," Hanuman says, turning in his saddle. "He's just upset. It's hard on him seeing Lakshman hurt. Give him a day or two, and everything will be back to normal."

"I don't think that's going to happen," Shivaji replies. "I think he's right. Don't you?" And without waiting for an answer, Shivaji reins his horse briskly to the head of the line.

Hanuman looks after him, wondering: Has Father really broken their friendship with those few short words? What does that mean for me?

೧ ಅ ೧ ಅ

By the time the riders reach the crowd, the cheers have faded. Shivaji goes to the front of the line, close to Iron. "Here is your hero!" Shivaji calls. Iron struggles to smile, though it's clear he is hurting; he raises his hand. A few voices cry out "Iron! Iron!" but mostly people simply crowd around his horse, trying to touch him, as though to offer comfort.

Some of the men from Poona, on the other hand, rush toward Lakshman. With them is Jyoti, who along with Maya has made her way from the temple. Gathering up her skirts, she runs right through the puddles, calling: "Hanuman! Hanuman!"

By the time she reaches his side, her face is wet with tears. All she sees is that he is whole. She stands near his horse, just staring. For of course, what else may she do? She is a servant, and he is a soldier. It's not as if they are married or betrothed. She can't even touch his hand.

So she gazes up at him. And he lifts his hand ever so slightly, moving his fingers so she might see.

◖◗◖◗

They won't let Iron walk from his horse to his house and they carry Lakshman in as well. The servants make up a bed in Iron's small bedroom where Lakshman can be tended. Iron's old manservant chases everyone away but the *shastri* and his wife. Tanaji, Hanuman, and Shivaji he allows to sit in the next room; the rest must wait outside.

Maya peers through the crowd, her arm around Jyoti. She nods as Jyoti describes Lakshman's terrible injuries and Hanuman's apparent good fortune, but listens all the while for word of Shivaji. She caught only a glimpse of him, riding tall on his great Bedouin, his hair flying in the morning breeze.

The sky grows dark. Thunder rumbles. Some of the people from the temple eye the sky and talk of heading back. Others wait. They want to know what happened. Maya thinks: Who can blame them? She wonders why Shivaji doesn't come out to tell them.

The door to Iron's house groans open. It is Amba, the *shastri*'s wife. "Maya!" she calls, waving her hand. Maya picks her way toward the door, aware that many eyes are looking at her. Jyoti clings to her elbow. Amba pulls her inside the house. "We know your skill in healing. Can you help?"

"Maybe," Maya answers. "I will do what I can, auntie." She steps into the bedroom and forgets everything else.

What takes Maya's breath away is Lakshman, lying flat on a bedmat on the floor before her. His bandages removed, she sees his ghastly wound, and she has to turn away. Jyoti holds her arm, as if to give her strength.

The *shastri* sits near Lakshman's head, dabbing slowly and gently at the twists of skin that hang from his face. His flesh, purple and swollen, has fallen away to expose a bleeding mass of muscles, veins and fat. The eyelid dents downward over the empty socket where his eye should be, the eye-lashes glued shut by dark, dried blood. A trail of orange oozes from its corner. The *shastri* lifts his sorrowful face to Maya.

"Can't you help, dear?" Amba whispers in her ear. Maya takes a soft cloth and a bowl of warm water from the *shastri*. Steeling herself, she stares directly at the injury. She begins to drench the wound, and as she does so, Lakshman lurches on the bed. His good eye opens wide, and his hand snakes around her wrist. "Kiss it and make it better?" he whispers.

"Let her go, Lakshman," the *shastri* says. "You don't know what you're doing."

"Trust me: I know." His breath comes in harsh, angry rasps.

"Get bhang," the priest says to his wife. Instantly she vanishes from the room. Jyoti stares, uncertain of what she ought to do. At least I can keep my mistress company, she thinks. She smooths her hand along Maya's arm. Then she slowly pries Lakshman's fingers from Maya's wrist.

Through it all, Maya simply stares at the floor, as though she were in pain; pain worse than Lakshman's.

ଏ୨ଓ୧ଚ

Soon Amba returns, a cup in her hands. Lakshman makes a terrible face when he drinks the warm brown cup of bhang. It smells like old leaves and earth.

With each swallow Lakshman grows a little easier. In a few minutes he closes his eyes and begins to hum; after a while, his humming stops.

"I saw something like this fixed once," Maya explains to the *shastri*. She drenches the wound again and again, until no blood colors the water. Then she lifts the torn skin, gently spreading its curled edges, pushing the flaps over the tissues they used to cover, stretching the skin with gentle fingers. She probes and presses until the edges match up fairly well. Lakshman stirs beneath her touch when she does this, but he does not wake.

The *shastri* chants an endless Sanskrit prayer while Maya presses on the wound. Outside the sky darkens, and thunder tumbles through the stone walls of the house. Sweat drenches Maya's sari, though she hardly moves. Beneath her touch the angry flesh, once dead, seems to glow.

When she's done, she leans back, exhausted. The ragged edges of his skin are pink now; they nearly join in places. Amba hands Maya a hair-fine needle threaded with a single strand of silk. She passes the needle's point through Lakshman's wounded flesh. Then she ties an exquisite, tiny knot.

She makes a score of tiny knots along Lakshman's ravaged face. Amba brings a bowl of neem leaves ground with myrrh. Maya paints the greenish paste across the ragged seam of Lakshman's wound, presses his broken face with a clean cotton cloth, and ties a bandage over his cheek.

Lastly she sighs as if steeling herself for one final, difficult encounter. She places her hands on Lakshman's head, closes her eyes, and breathes deep, as though breathing through her hands and arms into Lakshman's face. Her breath comes deep and strong.

When Maya lifts her hands, the *shastri* thinks he sees them joined by threads of light, all red and golden. "She's a wonder," he whispers to his wife, as Maya shuffles out with Jyoti by her side. "I thought she was a just nautch girl. I didn't understand why Gungama chose her."

"And do you now know, husband?" the *shastri*'s wife asks.

"I'll never look at her the same way again," he says with awe.

"That will be a relief," his wife replies coolly.

☙☙☙☙

Hanuman gets to his feet and goes to Iron's bedroom. The *shastri* and his wife are picking up their things with a formal finality. A terrible fear overcomes Hanuman. He glances at his brother, and sees his face so peaceful it seems to him he must be dead. Hanuman lets out a stifled cry.

"Do you think we'd let him die?" Amba exclaims.

"That nautch girl . . . ," the *shastri* says, then corrects himself, "that devadasi, it was she who fixed your brother. I can't imagine where she learned to do all those things she did."

"He's going to be well?" Hanuman asks, hardly daring to believe. The *shastri* nods. "And Iron?" Hanuman whispers.

"It would take more than a sword to kill that old log," Amba snorts.

☙☙☙☙

Shivaji stands when Hanuman returns, his long hair still loose over a clean white shirt. He places his hand softly on Hanuman's shoulder. It is an unexpected gesture, formal yet intimate, the gesture of a kindly general toward an untried lieutenant. Hanuman looks into Shivaji's dark, intense eyes.

"I need a right-hand man to help me in my work, Hanu," Shivaji whispers.

"I'm always here to serve you, Shahu." That last word bothers Hanuman. "Lord, I mean."

"Have we stopped being friends, Hanu?"

"No, lord," Hanuman answers. "But things are different."

"And more changes are coming, Hanuman. More than you can guess." Shivaji nods toward Lakshman on the bedmat. "You and your brother are more dear to me than life itself. Do you know that? Your brother's task is hard, far harder than I had any notion of. The pain that he must face . . ." Shivaji winces as though thinking about some unnamed horror. "I feel unworthy of the honor he does me. You won't fail me, either," Shivaji sighs, as if he's heard Hanuman voice some binding oath. "You have the easier path to tread, Hanu, if that's any comfort. Or at least the shorter one."

"What path, Shahu?" Hanuman whispers, but Shivaji does not answer.

"Come," he says, nodding toward the verandah door and holding out his hand to Hanuman, "I must talk to these people." As Hanuman stands beside him, Shivaji stares at him once more. "Say you'll do whatever I ask."

"Why, Shahu?" Hanuman asks.

"I want to hear you say it."

"I'll do whatever you ask," Hanuman replies simply.

Shivaji lifts his hand to Hanuman's face. For a moment, Hanuman thinks Shivaji might slap him, but instead he pats his face with his broad, soft palm, once, twice, three times. "Good man," he says.

As they walk to the verandah door, a thought strikes Hanuman. "Is this about that vow we made, Shahu? Years ago, at the temple?"

Shivaji grins, the old familiar grin that Hanuman remembers. "You guessed." He nods. "Yes, Hanu. Yes." His eyes crinkle as though with pure delight. "Don't you think it's time we did something about that vow?"

Hanuman grins back. "It's way past time, Shahu."

☙☙☙☙

When Shivaji and Hanuman step outside, the waiting crowd barrages them with questions. Shivaji stands motionless as if he is listening to some far away sound. One by one people fall silent. Hanuman motions for them to sit, then he takes a seat before Shivaji. There is some shushing and hushing as people wait for Shivaji to speak.

Shivaji has told so many stories in his life that even when he simply wants to give some news, he tells it like a story. He spins the tale for them, and the crowd responds with wide eyes. He weaves the scene: the fight at the gate, the battle of arrows, Tanaji's and Hanuman's struggles, Iron's courage on the stairs, Lakshman's torture, Iron's valor. Every one of them a hero, except Shivaji himself. When he is finished speaking, some of the men brush tears from their eyes; women weep.

Near the verandah door is an open window. Suddenly the curtain is pulled aside, and Tanaji thrusts his head out. "Very nice," he croaks. "It wasn't really nice, though, was it, Shahu? Why did we kill those men, men no different from ourselves? Why did we bleed? For what, Shahu?"

Shivaji gazes at the floor. "Ask him," he says, nodding to Hanuman.

Hanuman looks shocked. "It just seemed right," Hanuman begins, speaking directly to Shivaji, but Shivaji nods for him to face the crowd. "Why shouldn't that fort be ours?" he continues, his voice gaining volume as he starts to speak. "Why should Iron's village be held captive to some far-off king?"

"Queen," Bala says.

"Queen, then," Hanuman says. "That fort was built by Hindu hands, by the sweat of our grandfathers' grandfathers. And up until a hundred years ago, we were ruled by Hindu kings! Kings we knew!" As Hanuman speaks, a man near him pats his knee. "Maybe our fathers lost some war. That was years ago! What about today? What about us? Must we live beneath the heel of a far-off king because our grandfathers were weak?"

"Queen," Bala says again, and this time everyone laughs.

"It's your father's fault, Shahu!" Tanaji says from the window when the laughter falls away. "It wasn't our fathers that lost that fort. It was your father! It is Shahji that's the villain!"

"Shahji was no villain," one of the Poona riders says. Some people nod and agree, others seem to wonder. Shivaji says nothing.

"Let me tell you about Shahji," Bala says. People are surprised to see that Bala is not smiling now. "My father fought with Shahji. Lots of our fathers did." Bala looks at Shivaji. "Of all of us here, who got the worst deal when Shahji surrendered? Shivaji did. Shivaji might have been a king today. Do you blame him, Shahu? Do you call him villain?"

Shivaji says nothing.

"No," says Bala. "And why should you condemn him? After all, Shahji tried, didn't he? He took back the land . . . the forts our grandfathers built, this home we called our own for countless generations! He failed. But at least he tried!" Bala looks around him: few of the people here have heard him speak this way. "That fort up there, where the saffron flag now flies, that fort is ours! And so it should be! That was Shahji's bargain: the forts to be returned when Shivaji came of age."

Anger begins to show on people's faces, the bruises of old insults.

"I knew I might get hurt," Hanuman says above the murmurs of the crowd. "I knew I might die. I'm sick of being some queen's hostage, paying some queen's taxes. Sure we got hurt, but look up there!" The saffron flag flutters on the hill far above them. "Shivaji went up, same as us. He was the first to bleed! Show them your arm, Shahu! Shot through the arm! Pinned to the wall!"

"He didn't bleed as much as Lakshman," Tanaji growls.

"You were ready to die, father, and for us to die beside you," Hanuman replies. "You chose us to go. You hate your choice now? Fine. I stand by my decision. Lakshman, I do not doubt, will stand by his as well."

"Tell us what's next, Shahu," Balaji speaks up, sensing that the crowd now is ready to listen to a leader.

"Tell us, Shahu," Hanuman whispers. "Tell us," many voices ask.

"We're going to take back what's ours," Shivaji says quietly.

Eyes dart from side to side, faces turn frowning, waiting for him to speak again. But Shivaji holds his silence. Then, one by one the people seem to reconsider what he said. "Take back what is ours!" a voice shouts. "Take back what's ours!" others call. Then cheers erupt, and clapping, and thumping as hands strike the wooden floor, as the crowd at last realizes that a line of battle has indeed been drawn, and Shivaji has drawn it.

Then as the shouts subside, eyes turn to Shivaji, eyes bright now, full of fire. "Who's with me?" Shivaji says.

Across the verandah, people cheer again, getting to their feet. "Shivaji *ki jai*!" Bala's voice rings out.

"Shivaji *ki jai*!" Victory to Shivaji, everyone shouts. "Shivaji *ki jai*!"

Soon the crowd is chanting, bouncing on their feet, dancing in place. Shivaji walks among them as they shout, pressing each man's hand, looking deep into each face. "*Har, har mahadev!*" Even the *shastri* and his wife are shouting, holding on to one another's hands, dancing. Then Shivaji takes Jyoti's hand, and presses it, and then Maya's, who looks at him with tearful eyes.

"It's over now," she says.

"It's just beginning," he replies above the din. Even when he shuts the door, the chant goes on and on: *Har, har mahadev!*

❧❧❧❧

"You'll be in charge," Shivaji says to Hanuman. "Take twenty men and occupy the fort. Pick five men to march the Bijapuri prisoners back to Bijapur. Put Govindas in charge of the escort. No injuries are to befall them."

"Yes, lord," Hanuman replies. It seems right to say this, now.

"Prepare an inventory. Guns, gold, anything of value. Send it to me as soon as possible."

"Yes, lord. The horses?"

"Keep them here for now. Send the prisoners back on foot.

"Bala," Shivaji continues, "prepare a letter for my signature. To the sultana of Bijapur: Tell her that her Captain Hamzadin was derelict in his duty, and I have relieved him of command."

"Just that, lord?" Bala replies. "You need to press your case . . ."

"What do you suggest, Balaji?"

"Tell her that the fort remains in the keeping of its rightful owners," Bala says. "But about the allotment, lord?"

"Suggest that nothing's changed, but say that cagily as well."

"Of course, lord. So I understand . . . you don't plan to pay?"

Shivaji looks up and smiles, as though surprised Bala needs even to ask. "Ride for Bijapur as fast as you can. I want the letter to arrive before any rumors reach them. I want *you* to tell them of the capture of the fort."

"And what about you, Shahu? What will you do?" Hanuman asks.

"In a day or two, I ride for Poona. I'll send money and replacements."

"What about me, Shahu?" says a hoarse voice. Tanaji sits with his back against a wall, looking miserable.

"You're tired, uncle, and hurt. What sort of man would I be to take offense at words spoken in sorrow? You didn't raise me to be a man like that."

"No," Tanaji replies, but his face is still pinched. "But I should maybe not have said . . ."

"Speak to me later, uncle, when we both have had more time to think," Shivaji replies and turns as though Tanaji were not even there.

☙☙❧☙

Thunder rumbles through the mountains, but the rain still holds back. In the courtyard, Hanuman has assembled a dozen men and ponies. They are checking their livery, pulling cinches, tying bags across their saddles. Shivaji comes from the house and says goodbye to each.

"Keep everything you find at the fort safe. Prepare an inventory. There's a mosque there, I think . . . don't let the men harm it. Treat it like a temple. Do you want me to tell them?"

"No," Hanuman replies. "That's my job."

Shivaji seems delighted by his answer. "If you find their holy book, wrap it in white cloth, and bring it with you when you come. That's important, Hanuman."

"I won't forget, lord."

"You'll be in my prayers, cousin," Shivaji says, *namskar*ing.

Hanuman nods and waves the company forward. Shivaji watches as they walk out the village gates, and looks up to the fort where the saffron flag billows lazily against the dark sky.

He turns to see Maya coming from Iron's house. "I must also say goodbye," Maya says to him, after a long silence. They stand awkwardly, facing each other from a few feet away.

"For a little while, goodbye. We will never be apart for long, I think. And always I will hold you in my heart."

"Keep me always in your mind as well," she whispers. Suddenly she steps forward, quick as a doe, and taking him by the shoulders, raises her face to his. She brushes her lips across his, feeling for a moment their softness, tasting for a moment their sweetness. When she steps away, her face is full of longing.

But if he sees, he makes no sign. His indifference makes her catch her breath. A sound escapes her, like a laugh maybe, or a single sob. She pulls the end of her sari over her head, and she walks backward, eyes on his.

After Maya leaves, Jyoti comes to Shivaji. She's been waiting, giving her mistress time alone. "Is Hanuman still here?"

"I've sent him away," Shivaji answers.

Jyoti's face falls. "I never told him goodbye."

"He hasn't gone far enough to bother with goodbyes," Shivaji answers. "He's up at the fort. I'm sure he'll want to come down to the temple as often as he can . . . I know how much he loves to see the goddess there."

It takes a moment before Jyoti understands and answers with a smile.

CHAPTER 15

As he clears the top of a gentle rise on his borrowed Bedouin mare, Bala sees the dome of the Gol Gumbaz peeking over the walls of Bijapur.

After riding through two days of endless rain, Bala enjoys the hard gleam of the morning sun. Through the sparkling air, light spills across the brown fields. Tiny green pennants of wheat sprouting in dark soil dot the wide plateau that approaches the city gates. Although dark clouds clump in the eastern sky, it seems to Bala that the monsoon rains have begun to wane. The morning air is so crisp that he can see each detail of the far-off city.

Only once before has Bala come to Bijapur: with his father, Manji, the famous carpet trader—before his father joined with Shahji and was killed. He had been only a boy. He remembers the winding streets and tall build-ings, not much more.

First a bath, and then the queen, he thinks. His horse's hooves begin to *click*, for from this point, the city road is paved in stones. The dome he's seen for miles looms large. He can see the city gates, tall as ten men. Bronze cannon bristle atop the city walls.

His horse prances nervously along the main avenue. Merchants push flat wood carts, farmers lead flocks of sheep and naked children drive water buffalo. Soldiers carry bright spears. Yellow dogs scurry past.

Directly before him towers a huge, menacing cannon, placed at the en-trance of the city: Malik-i-Maidan, the Monarch of the Plain. Longer than a tree trunk, wider than a house, its barrel large enough to hold a sitting man. The cannon is fashioned like a lion, its barrel the lion's mouth. Jeweled earrings glitter in the lion's ears. The gun is covered by a great green cloth. Bala has heard that the gun has never been fired in war; only in executions. They found parts of one man's body three miles from the city.

ೕಲೀ

Every wall in Bijapur bears in stone or metal an image of the crescent moon. For the Bijapuri sultans came from Turkistan, and the crescent moon recalls their ancient lineage. Bala rides beneath the towering dome of the Gol Gumbaz, the largest in the world, they say. Its walls are covered in turquoise-colored tiles, inlaid with lapis and jasper. Bala smells the stink of a nearby butcher shop, but bites back his disgust.

Passing through the busy bazaar, he turns toward the city palace. Here, at least, the way is quieter, for army guards patrol the streets and let no merchants pass. He sees the walls of the palace. Between its minarets hang long chains of stone: delicately carved from a single piece of white marble, the links so light that they flutter in the breeze, clinking softly.

Just in front of the palace stands the Mosque of the Relic, that holds, they say, a crystal vial with two of Muhammad's hairs. A few hundred yards from the palace, he finds what he wants: a public bath.

ೕಲೀ

He wears his best robes and finest slippers, which he brought with him from Poona to Welhe. You never know when your best clothes might be needed. You never know when Shivaji might suddenly decide to name you ambassador to Bijapur, and send you to the sultana with an urgent message.

But here in sophisticated Bijapur even his very best clothing looks plain. So Bala focuses his thoughts on Bhavani, and begs the goddess for guidance.

She provides help immediately as she always does:

It doesn't matter.

The words ring in his heart. It doesn't matter, he tells himself as he hands the frayed reins of his borrowed Bedouin to a palace groom. It doesn't matter, he tells himself as he climbs the marble stairs to the doorway of the palace, because I come with urgent news, and can't be expected to waste time primping. It doesn't matter, he tells himself again as he knocks on the vizier's door, because I am a Marathi, and they expect rustic clothing on folk like me.

All that matters—he tells himself as the vizier's secretary considers his request—is my mission. My letter—he thinks, as the secretary looks him over, curls his lip, and then lowers his head in welcome, leading him gravely to the throne room—gives me power. And since Shivaji's father is the Bijapuri commander—he thinks, as a eunuch whispers his name to the sultana's major domo—attention must be paid, however I may look.

But I'm frightened, ma, he tells the goddess.

Be frightened later, Bhavani replies.

And so despite his clothes Bala's name is called out at the entrance of the Diwan-i-Khas, and the low chatter of the throne room grows silent as he approaches the sultana, the queen of Bijapur.

☾☽☾☽

She perches on the edge of the wide and shining silver throne like a bird of prey. Her tiny figure is covered top to toe in black silks shot with gold. The fabric seems to have a structure of its own; like a tent she sits inside, rather than a dress she wears. Only her flickering eyes emerge from behind her veil, eyes like those of an aging hawk. Cabochon rubies on chains of gold droop from her headdress so her head tilts forward from their weight, and when she lifts her hidden hand to straighten her long, dark skirt, heavy diamond bracelets *clunk* dully against each other.

A little brat about Sambhuji's age sits at her feet, playing with a set of tiny silver soldiers. Everyone else in the room is standing. Bala glances from face to face, trying to guess which courtier is which. That, he thinks, must be Whisper, the queen's *khaswajara*—no other eunuch comes so near her side. And that, he guesses, looking at the fat and oily fellow standing on the stairs of the dais at her feet, must be the grand vizier, Wali Khan. Others are there, but none he recognizes. He smiles at everyone anyway.

Then Bala notices a huge, broad man who steps out from behind a marble column. To Bala he seems to have the menacing presence of a mast elephant: a dark and shadowed face that emerges from a vast, bloated body. Bala has heard the tales about him and his voracious appetite: Afzul Khan, the sultana's nephew, and Shahji's chief rival at the Bijapuri court.

If Afzul Khan is here, Bala thinks, then General Shahji must be, too. Bala expected that he'd remember him, even after all these years. But his eyes pass over Shahji twice before he recognizes him.

He's shorter than Bala remembers, shorter than Shivaji. And his face has grown softer, the big eyes Bala remembers now peering over fattened cheeks. But the general's bearing remains, though he has put on weight, and he holds his head as he always did, squinting quizzically down his long, beaklike nose. Bala nods to him, but the general merely stares back.

As he approaches the silver throne Bala becomes aware of a deep ticking echo from the walls: *thock, thock, thock.* At the foot of the dais is the royal timekeeper, a bored-looking fellow who stares languidly as sand spills through a wide hourglass. Next to him is something Bala has heard of but never seen: a thick, platter-sized machine, ticking regularly, so loudly that the noise echoes through the room. With each tick a single, arrow-shaped pointer jumps a notch on its intricately carved face. A Persian clock. Bala stares. Why would anyone want a contraption like that when a beautiful, quiet hourglass serves the purpose?

Aware of the stares that follow him, Bala steps to the edge of the dais. Now he can see close-up the Abyssinian Christian guards; the deep black crosses they have burned into their faces, ear to ear and forehead to chin. Does their god make them do that? If O'Neil worships that god, why has he not burned his own face just so?

☙❧☙❧

Bala can smell the tension in the air. After all, Shivaji's refusal to bow to the old sultan was the insult that forced his exile to Poona; the courtiers want to see what Shivaji's emissary will now do.

Bala stretches full length on the heavy Persian carpet, burying his head beneath his arms. When he stands, Bala feels the court's approval; having been forced to grovel so often themselves, they appreciate seeing Bala do what his master would not. Only Shahji scowls; when Bala rises he turns away. Even the sultana's wary eyes are crinkled with amusement over the edge of her golden veil.

"Oh, your highness," Bala says loudly, bowing his head, "forgive this fool. He would not dare to enter your presence on his own accord. He only hazards this task at the bidding of his master, your faithful servant, Shivaji of Poona." At these words the sultana arches an eyebrow toward Shahji, who stands listening impassively across the room. "This lowly fool is but a messenger from one great person to another."

There is much consternation, for his speech is full of subtle contradictions: his bow, his greeting, describing Shivaji as the sultana's servant—all these of course are pleasant and surprising. But those last words, "one great person to another," cause many eyes to open wide, including the sultana's. For a moment, the eunuchs who fan the throne with gold-handled whisks stop swaying, as if they expect lightning to crash down.

"What kind of riddle is this, you who call yourself a fool?" the sultana asks. Her voice is muffled by her veils. Though her words are sharp, her demeanor is calm, and as she speaks she runs her fingers idly through her son's thick black hair. "We understood only you brought us news. Now you claim to be the emissary of some great person. If that is so, what presents do you bring?"

Bala smiles; he prepared for this. "The fool before you is a poor servant, madam, dispatched in haste. I have no presents but this letter. My master Shivaji, that great person, bade me place it at your feet, a token of his humility before your greatness." With that, ignoring the eunuch boy that the *khaswajara* sends to intercept him, he steps briskly up the dais stairs to the very foot of the sultana's throne. There he kneels and places the leather message tube beside her jeweled slippers. As Bala tiptoes backward to his place, the boy sultan puts down his silver charioteer and hands the letter casually to his mother. She glares at him, for now she's forced to take it.

It is as much as Balaji might hope for. "Your highness is too kind to this poor fool," he says, bowing deeply.

"We agree," says the sultana, her dark eyes glaring over the veil. She hands the tube to Whisper, her *khaswajara,* who passes it to the vizier, who in turn passes it to a secretary.

" 'Most effulgent of the lights of Allah, most fragrant rose of the master's garden, more graceful than any bird in heaven . . . ,' " the secretary reads out, translating Bala's Persian.

"Yes, yes, get on with it," the sultana says. "I don't need every word." She fluffs her robes, for it is hot already in the throne room.

The secretary clears his throat. "The writer goes on to say that your Captain Hamzadin was derelict, madam. He left Torna fort unattended. He and all his men fled the fort, lord, or so this letter says."

"Fled? Were they under attack? Has war come to Torna? Why was I not informed?" Wali Khan asks, looking levelly at Balaji. But Balaji simply shrugs.

"It seems the captain grew weary of the monsoon rains, lord," the secretary says, trying to hide his amusement.

"Hamzadin is your man, isn't he, general?" Wali Khan says to Shahji, a vacant look on his round face.

"As well you know, lord," Shahji replies, "he is not my man." Shahji bows both to Wali Khan and the sultana.

"Then whose man is he, general?" the sultana asks after a suitably indifferent pause.

"May I suggest you ask your nephew, madam?"

Her veiled face turns to the imposing form of Afzul Khan, who stands on the other side of the room. "This letter, madam," says Afzul Khan, "is Marathi lies." His voice trumpets across the throne room.

From the corners of the Diwan-i-Khas, courtiers begin to stir, suddenly conscious of a conflict, anxious for some gossip to share later with their mistresses and wives. They begin to converge, like so many carrion birds at the first smell of blood. Among them is a short, tough-looking man with dark intense eyes and a graying beard. It is Shaista Khan, the Mogul ambassador, just returned to Bijapur from Agra. His sharp eyes dart between Afzul Khan and Shahji, sizing things up, looking for opportunities.

"Well, fool?" asks the sultana, peering over her veil at Balaji.

"It is easy to say that a letter lies, madam," Bala replies. "For how will a letter, which is nothing but a dead thing, defend its honor?" He bows to Afzul Khan. "So now I speak for Shivaji." Bala looks directly at Afzul Khan. "Call me a liar, if you will. I say that Hamzadin was derelict. I say that they fled the fort like cowards, afraid of a little shower of rain. Do you hear me? Come and say I lie. For I am no dumb letter, sir. I may be a humble fool, but even a fool might defend his honor."

"It seems this fool can talk, nephew," says the sultana, settling back upon the ornate silver throne.

"By his own admission he is a common servant, madam," Afzul Khan replies, his face flushed. "There is no honor in answering a fool."

"Read on," the sultana commands.

"Here the letter states that Shivaji has acted on your behalf, madam. Mindful that even your benevolence would not tolerate cowardice, Shivaji arrested Hamzadin. Then your affectionate servant garrisoned the fort with his own men, and at his own expense."

"Affectionate? Does it really say that—affectionate?" the sultana asks, her eyes crinkling. "Well, General Shahji, what do you say to that?" the Sultana says, her voice full of amusement. "Your own son says he is our affectionate servant. Affectionate, mind you—just think of that! Are you also affectionate? Are you mindful of our benevolence?"

General Shahji has been fighting battles in the throne room for many years. "My affection, madam, is to the crown of Bijapur."

Though the movement is scarcely visible beneath the voluminous pyramid of fabric; the sultana prods her son's foot with her toe. The boy straightens up and attempts to look more royal.

"As always, you have made a clever answer, general," says the sultana. "Do not think we are so blind or so stupid that we would miss your point. But answer this, general, if you will: Whose words do you think seem to us more pleasing? Yours or your son's?"

Shahji makes a low bow, keeping his eyes fixed on the sultana even as he drops his head. All around the throne room can be heard the quiet murmurs of the courtiers, speculating on the meanings of the words they hear.

"Is there more?" the sultana asks.

"Only this, madam," says the vizier. "Shivaji says that he holds the fort in trust, keeping it for its rightful owner. And he sends Hamzadin and his men back to Bijapur with an escort."

"They should be here in two or three days, madam," Balaji puts in.

"Well, gentlemen," she says at last. "What shall our answer be? Shall we thank him, this grand person, this affectionate servant? Shall we leave him there to hold that fort for its rightful owner? Or shall we send an army to retake that fort and punish him for his insolence?"

"An army, madam!" Afzul Khan calls out. "My army stands ready, awaiting only your command." He lifts his head and glares around the throne room. "The word of a Marathi may not be trusted."

"We are certain you were not thinking of our friend General Shahji when you spoke, nephew," the sultana says, but her eyes reveal nothing. "Wasn't it your army that we sent before? Hamzadin was your man, was he not, nephew? Wasn't the garrison yours, too?" The sultana then looks to Shahji. "But we would hear your opinion, general. He's your son, after all."

Shahji spreads his arms, as if he is about to make a great speech. But then he drops his hands. "No," he says quietly. "He's not my son."

Bala's eyes go wide. There is a buzz throughout the throne room; no one expected this. "What are you saying, general?" cries Wali Khan.

"I say ignore those flowery words, madam. A man writes that he's taken your fort! If anyone else wrote those words to you, how would you respond? That the writer was once my son should not enter into it."

"But the letter says, general," Wali Khan argues, "that he holds the fort for its rightful owner."

"Lord," Shahji replies, "Who does Shivaji think is the rightful owner?"

"Bijapur is the rightful owner of Torna fort—of all the forts you ceded to us, general," Wali Khan replies. "Until Shivaji comes of age and swears an oath of fealty. Have you yet seen him here, bowing to our queen?"

"I say this letter is a feint, designed to breed confusion," Shahji continues. "Shivaji pretends no harm, but he means to keep that fort!"

"I must say that I'm surprised to hear such thoughts from your lips, general," the sultana says.

And Bala too is shocked. He stares at the general, not even smiling for a change, surprised that Shahji has seen so clearly what the others appear to miss, and that he speaks against his own son.

"The point," says a raspy, treble voice, "is only this: will Shivaji send the allotment?" The throne room quiets; people shush each other, trying to hear Whisper, the *khaswajara*. "That's all that counts, madam."

"You are right to say so, Whisper," the sultana replies. "When is the next allotment due?"

"In six weeks, madam," Whisper replies instantly.

"Then in six weeks, we shall see, Whisper. Shall we not?"

Afzul Khan takes a bounding step forward. "You can't be serious, madam. You plan to wait?"

"And what if we are serious, nephew?"

"What about the treasury?" Afzul Khan chokes out.

Bala's bald eyebrows snap up. Treasury? The sultana glances toward Wali Khan, lifting an eyebrow.

"There is that, madam," the grand vizier replies.

"Tell us."

Wali Khan glances to his secretary, who is already busily stooping over a pile of cloth-bound books. At last he grunts and lifts a large folio. Briskly turning page after page, he reads: "Nine hundred and eighteen rupees. That was last quarter's accounting." Bala tries to hide his excitement: Why that fort holds nearly as much gold as Poona's whole treasury!

"Not worth wasting lives over such a triviality," the vizier says thoughtfully.

"But add to that the guns, madam! Who knows how many weapons are up there!" Afzul Khan calls out.

"Eight fixed cannon, four small wheeled cannon, fifty matchlocks, and miscellaneous small arms." Shahji enumerates from memory.

"Thank you, general. As you see, that also is not so much, madam," Wali Khan suggests.

"Not so much?" Afzul Khan sputters. "He takes our money and our guns. It is an insult at the very least!" He wheels toward Shahji, graceful despite his bulk. "What do you think he'll do—that son of yours?"

Shahji stares up calmly at Afzul Khan, whose face burns with scarcely concealed anger. "Tell me what you would do, General Khan, if you had all that money and all those guns?"

"I'd figure out how to use them, general. And I wouldn't think too long before I put them into action."

"So would I, general. That's just what I would do."

You would imagine, Bala thinks to himself, that with these words of agreement Afzul Khan and Shahji would make a momentary truce. Instead, they glare at one another more fiercely than ever. Does this go on every day? Bala wonders. The courtiers look on: eyes darting from one man to the other as if they will be called upon at any moment to place a wager.

The sultana's muffled voice tries to ease the tension. "General Shahji, using stolen guns from a conquered fort is exactly what you did to us, if we recall correctly."

Shahji bows. "Madam, I must protest. My victories were on the battlefield. I didn't simply move into an empty fort."

"Are you unhappy with your son's tactics, general?" The sultana's voice seems to Bala genuinely interested.

"Not what I would have recommended, madam."

"Still why shouldn't he have done so, general?" Wali Khan suggests. "For as soon as he swears his fealty that fort and many others will be his."

"Then let him do it, lord! Let him swear, as I did!" Shahji answers, his voice harsh. "Let him do it first, though, before he starts occupying forts; let him prostrate himself before the throne, the benevolent throne! Let him bow his head like a man!" In the vast hall all that can be heard now is the sound of Shahji's breathing, and the *thock, thock, thock* of the Persian clock.

In the midst of this discussion, Bala, the cause of it all, stands forgotten. Perhaps he could now just slip away unnoticed. But of course that is not his mission.

"At times like these we miss our husband," the sultana says, her muffled voice so soft that Bala has to strain to make out her words. "What do you think that we should do, general?" she says, turning to Shahji.

"Send a letter, madam. Tell Shivaji to prostrate himself before the throne. Then when he refuses, attack with unassailable strength."

"You think he will refuse, general?"

"He may have changed. It's been years since I last saw him."

"But the leopard, general, as they say . . . ," the sultana says.

"Yes, madam, the leopard," Shahji replies.

For a long time, the sultana merely sits with eyes closed. Bala wonders if she is well, when she last ate.

"We have decided . . . ," she begins.

Just then her son throws a dozen of his toy soldiers in the air. They land on the marble steps of the dais and spray along the stairs, clanking as they spin to a stop. "They all died," he explains. "They got blown up by a *farang* bomb." Only Afzul Khan laughs. It's the first time Bala has seen him smile.

"We have decided to follow a different course," the sultana says at last. "We will write to Shivaji and demand the return of the treasury. We will regard that return as an indication of his fealty. We will command him to send it, along with the allotment, within six weeks."

"And when he doesn't pay? For he won't, you know!" shouts Afzul Khan.

"He'll pay, nephew," the sultana says, eyes gleaming not at Afzul Khan, but at Bala. "His father's fortune is at stake. He'll pay." Bala stares right back at the bright black eyes that peer above the veil. He glances for a moment at Shahji, who stands, rigid but pale.

"Fool, inform that great person Shivaji of our decision," the sultana continues. "Tell him that he is now the master of his father's fate, and of his own. Let him show loyalty in actions as well as in words—then he will be honored as his father has been. Or let him prove false, and he will suffer, as his father will. Let him decide."

Bala stands silently, eyes fixed on the sultana's. "You're done, sir," says the vizier's secretary at last.

Bala bows deeply. Only as he steps away does he begin to tremble, as the fear he set aside so long falls on him. He steps into the courtyard and his stomach heaves so hard he has to lean against a column.

From the throne room a grim-faced man approaches, dressed in rich silks, but carrying a simple, ivory-handled dagger. "Good day, sir," he says to Bala. "I'm Shaista Khan, ambassador of the *padshah*, the Great Mogul, Shah Jahan." He looks at Bala's clammy skin, and his hard eyes soften. "You did well in there. No shame in being frightened now."

"I am honored that you would speak with me, lord," says Bala, struggling to bow. "I only did my best, lord."

"Others have done worse. But don't call me lord. We're peers," Shaista Khan replies, ignoring the obvious. "Both of us ambassadors in a far-off land, doing our best to serve our masters."

"You are too kind, lord," Bala replies.

"Enough formality, lad," Shaista Khan answers. "Have you established an embassy here in Bijapur yet?" The idea is so ludicrous, Bala can barely keep from laughing, no matter how ill he feels.

"Stay with me," Shaista Khan says, with a look that might seem friendly, if it were on a different face, from a different pair of eyes. "I have plenty of room. And I can even lend you some clothes."

Bala licks his lips. His mouth tastes sour and he longs for sleep. "But why, if I may ask without offending?"

"We need to stick together, lad, strangers in this evil court. Evil everywhere you turn. Good men need friends. They must be strong together. Besides," he adds, "we might have been allies. We nearly were." Shaista Khan smiles at Bala's confusion. "Yes. Shivaji's father had the chance. He might have made a peace with the Moguls. Instead he chose the Bijapuris. You see what a mess that has made of things."

"Do you not say *'Ishvara Allah'*? What God wills . . . ," Bala answers.

"Good men can change God's will," Shaista Khan replies. "The fathers failed to make the peace—Shahji, I mean, and Shah Jahan. But the sons might fix that. Shivaji and Aurangzeb should be allies." Again Shaista Khan's wolf grin peeks out from the graying beard. "Your master's in trouble, lad. Maybe he doesn't know how much. Aurangzeb is the man he needs."

Silently, Bala prays to Bhavani. Whatever does Shivaji have that the Moguls want? He looks into Shaista Khan's unblinking eyes, and thinks of a cobra hypnotizing its prey.

ʘϽϾʘ

"Well, Iron, what will you do now?" asks Tukoji. "Now you've taken, Torna, what now?"

Iron's friend and cousin Tukoji, the *deshmukh* of Kari, arrived in Welhe yesterday with his son Jedhe and his nephew Bandal. When they heard the news they galloped there immediately.

Iron lifts his hands helplessly. "What can I do, Tukoji? The cards are dealt . . . I'll play them."

"That's horseshit, Iron."

If any other man had said this, Iron might have bristled; instead he grins. "Yes, it's horseshit," Iron chuckles. "But Shahu has sent a letter to Bijapur. He marched the fort commander back to Bijapur. He's garrisoned the fort with the men he brought from Poona."

"How many men from Poona?" Tukoji asks, lifting his heavy eyes to Iron as if all this information wearies him.

"Maybe twenty."

"Hmm. Not many. Not enough."

"Twenty men could hold Torna for a year," Iron replies. "Twenty men with the will."

"Ah, but do they have the will, Iron?" Tukoji asks, lifting a dark eyebrow. He leans back, sighing. "What do you think about General Shahji these days, Iron?"

Iron's face grows still and his eyes narrow. He glances carefully around him, then leans forward to whisper "You know what I think. I've sworn *wagnak*. I'll kill the son of a bitch like a dog if I ever get the chance."

Tukoji takes a long look at Iron. "Shall I tell you a secret? I checked your hands before I embraced you. After all, I too made peace with Bijapur, as Shahji did. Don't you mean to kill me as well?"

Iron holds up his hands, spreading his fingers. "No tiger claws for you, old friend."

"But why not, Iron? Am I not a traitor, just like Shahji?"

Iron dislikes thinking. He notes the signs of Tukoji's prosperity: the stiff folds of his crisply pressed clothing, the heaviness of his turban, the breadth of his belly, the soft refinement of his hands. Iron feels ashamed to be sitting in his cotton jamas. "You made the best of the bad deal, as did I," Iron says at last. "Once Shahji left us with our dicks flapping in the breeze, it was every man for himself. You made a deal—I made a deal. But that bastard Shahji left us both high and dry."

"But what about the son? Kill the son and you'll punish the father right enough."

Iron shrugs. "Thought about it. Didn't seem right somehow. The boy's not so bad."

"I heard he was a shit."

"Maybe . . . I guess we're all shits when you come down to it. Still, he's been respectful to me, and loyal. Besides, this action at the fort will make pain for the traitor Shahji."

Tukoji pretends to share Iron's amusement. "But back to the point, Iron. What will you do now, eh? Think your situation through, Iron. This is your chance to make a new deal with Bijapur. A favorable deal."

"Why would Bijapur cut a new deal with me?"

"Iron, listen: so far as Bijapur is concerned, everything is Shivaji's doing—the attack, the takeover of the fort, the arrest of the Bijapuri garrison . . ."

"Wait, wait," Iron protests, "Bijapur is bound to hear something about my part. It's not like I wasn't there . . ."

"Sure. But maybe you only went there to help, eh? Maybe you tried to keep things from getting out of hand. Who's to say? Iron, listen: Bijapur will think whatever you tell them to think."

"You're confusing me."

Tukoji's heavy lips curl into a dark smile. "There's still time, Iron. You might send men today to take back the fort from Shivaji's garrison. You might send a letter yourself to Bijapur, repudiating Shivaji's actions. Small steps, really, but you might end up in a much better position."

"I don't know. It's not my nature . . ."

Tukoji presses on. "You'll get invited to Bijapur in honor. You'd get close enough to Shahji to use those tiger claws. And what would that be worth, eh? How much would the sultana pay to be rid of the son of a bitch? If not her, then Afzul Khan, or for that matter the Brotherhood."

Iron looks at Tukoji with the cold eyes of an old gambler. What does Tukoji gain from all this . . . why is he so insistent? "I don't know," Iron grunts. "Going against Shivaji . . . I was just starting to like him."

"Enough to face a war? When the Bijapuri elephants stomp this little town of yours to splinters, will you still like Shivaji so much?" Iron says nothing. "Does he even know about your *wagnak* oath, Iron?" Tukoji asks.

"Speak quietly. He's right over there." Iron glares. "Anyway, how could I take back that fort, with Shivaji's garrison up there and all?"

This is what Tukoji has been waiting for. He leans forward to whisper to Iron.

௧௨௧௨

Seated on the verandah on the other side of the courtyard, Shivaji is preparing pan with his newly met cousins, Jedhe and Bandal. It's Jedhe's pan set, and like all of Jedhe's things, it is expensive. He watches Jedhe set out his pan *dan*; a matching set of small round gold-enameled boxes for the supari nuts, the betel leaves, the cardamom and clove, and a special box with a small spoon that holds the astringent chunam powder.

Iron had explained the family tree when he introduced them: how Iron and Jedhe's father had ridden with Shahji, how the two of them had played together as babies, and so on. An old man's introduction, full of an old man's memories. Jedhe had caught Shivaji's eye with a quick, mocking look at Iron before formally lifting his hands to his head to greet Shivaji.

Iron continued: "This other fellow is Bandal. He just became *deshmukh* of Hirdas—a month ago, wasn't it?"

"It has been ten weeks now, uncle. You came to my father's funeral." Bandal bows.

"Anyway you youngsters are all cousins, you know. Why, you are practically brothers!"

Soon after Iron leaves, the "youngsters" are enjoying the familiarity even this thin thread of blood tie affords. As family, they forgo the need to find common bonds of friendship. They launch immediately into talk of family members known and unknown, scandals and annoyances. Soon they are laughing.

Even now Shivaji is chuckling at one of Jedhe's jokes. He seems to have an endless supply. Jedhe wears a whisper-thin mustache, and his eyes are clear and hard: they dart quickly as he talks, like the eyes of a hunting bird.

Bandal, a head taller than Jedhe, watches silently, his face so dark it seems smudged with charcoal, his eyes plaintive, never looking directly at either.

As his hands deftly prepare the pan, Jedhe describes a wedding he attended, focusing especially on the expression of the eleven-year-old bridegroom seeing his twelve-year-old bride. He mimes the boy's wide-eyed expression: the fear and desire. But there's more: hidden by his cloak, Jedhe has stuck his hand down his pants; now he pokes out his thumb to mime the boy's stiffening lingam. He shows the boy: now frantically trying to push it down, now squeezing it between his legs, finally showing it off to his young bride. Shivaji laughs until tears dampen his eyes.

"Uncle Iron told us you have a *farang* sword, Shahu," Bandal says, changing the subject. "Might we see it?"

"When I get it back . . . It's at the smith's," Shivaji replies. "I'm having it fitted out as a *pata.*"

"A gauntlet sword . . . excellent. The hand can be a swordsman's most vulnerable spot," Bandal says.

"How did you come to get a *farang* sword?" Bandal asks.

"It was a gift," Shivaji answers. The others wait but nothing further comes.

"Ahcha . . ." Bandal says at last, as if Shivaji's silence has imparted a secret.

Soon they are describing their *watans.* "How many horse do you have now, Bandal?" Jedhe asks, referring to the stipend Bandal gets from Bijapur.

"I am a two thousand horse, cousin," Bandal replies.

"My father is a four thousand," Jedhe tells him. "What about you, Shahu?"

"I'm not a *mandsab,*" he says quietly but firmly.

The cousins glance at each other. "But your father . . . ," says Bandal, pressing him. "Isn't he the Bijapuri commander?" Shivaji shrugs. The others stare in uncomfortable silence. "I heard you kept an army," Bandal asks—for of course their "horses" are simply terms of ceremony.

"I personally maintain a force of seven hundred," Shivaji says.

"That's a lot of mouths to feed," Bandal says. "How many forts do you control?"

"Including Torna?" Shivaji asks. "One."

The two others look at each other as if they're not sure how to take this statement. "So many men, and just this one fort, cousin?" Bandal says, threading his way carefully.

Jedhe looks at Bandal and begins to laugh. "I'll tell you what, Shahu. I'll give you a fort. Then you'll have two." He moves behind Shivaji, putting his head near Shivaji's ear, and points to the mountain next to Torna. "Do you see that peak, Shahu? That's Bhatghar. You can have that. There. Now it's yours. Now you have two forts."

"Pay no attention to him, Shahu. He thinks he's funny."

"No, no!" Jedhe insists, returning to his seat. "It's a fort."

"Maybe it used to be a fort. Years and years ago, maybe. Now it's nothing but a clod of earth."

"The foundations are still there. I've seen them. You'd have to fortify it, Shahu. Build a few walls. You could do that, couldn't you? Easier than fighting a battle, eh? Anyway, nobody else has claimed it; it might as well be yours. Now you have two forts." Jedhe laughs at his joke.

Shivaji laughs along. "All right, I have two forts. Is that better?"

Bandal shakes his head. "It's still a lot of men, Shahu."

Shivaji looks as if knows what he says next will be even more shocking. "We also support a lot of widows. Maybe a thousand, I suppose, whose husbands were killed in Shahji's battles."

"Why, Shahu?" Jedhe asks. "How the hell can you afford it?"

"I steal," whispers Shivaji.

Jedhe looks as though he's about to laugh, but he considers Shivaji's serious face and holds back. "I've heard this," Bandal says. "I always thought . . . well, people exaggerate."

"I steal from women mostly, from merchants' wives mostly, Bijapuri and Moguls, mostly." Hearing this, Jedhe looks away, studying the wood planking of the verandah, but Bandal stares at Shivaji. "I rob caravans as well. Usually small ones. Usually it's just Tanaji and me, but sometimes Hanuman or Lakshman comes along." Shivaji looks at them in silence. Jedhe and Bandal stare at him doubtfully. Why would anyone be so frank?

They sit in silence until finally Jedhe nods to the bustling activity in the courtyard. "Iron really knows how to throw a party," he says, anxious to change the subject. "What's this all for, anyway?"

"Well, for me, partly," Shivaji says. "To celebrate taking the fort."

"Well, well," Jedhe says, looking to the bustle: women and men hanging lanterns and flags, thick garlands of marigolds and roses being draped over doors and windows. The workers have laid out a patchwork of wax cloth to cover the courtyard: bright blankets, sheets, bolts of cloth of all descriptions. Tables have been carried to the edge of the verandah, and women hurry out with steaming trays of chapatis and puris. But Shivaji looks like a man at a funeral.

"Cousin, what's wrong?" Bandal asks him.

"Just what I've said, cousin," Shivaji replies. "What man likes to tell the truth about himself?"

"Why, then, Shahu? Why did you tell us this?"

"Well, I'm going to need allies, aren't I?" Shivaji says, standing up. "You should know what you're getting yourselves into; that's how I see it."

As Shivaji walks away, they look at each other too surprised to speak. "Allies?" Jedhe says at last. For a moment it seems that he'll make another joke, but some light in Bandal's eyes stops him cold.

At the temple in Adoli, the *shastri* paces by the bullock cart in front of his small house, waiting as always with exceptional forbearance for the women. Young girls climb in the back of the cart, dressed in bright colors, garlands of tuberoses and marigolds woven in their hair. The *shastri* scowls at them when they start to giggle, then scowls across the temple courtyard at Maya's door. "Come! We're late. Soon it will rain!" he calls out.

In Maya's room, Jyoti jumps up and heads for the door, but just as she reaches it, she turns and steps back inside. "I'm not going."

"Don't be foolish," Maya exclaims. "You have to go!"

"Well, you're not going!"

Maya crosses her arms over her chest and stands, looking like an impatient mother, though she's scarcely older than Jyoti. "What has that to do with anything? You said you'd look after the girls who are going. You promised the *shastri*. Now go."

"No, I don't want to now," Jyoti says, though anyone can see that she both longs to go and is frightened to death that no one will stop her.

"Oh, silly," Maya laughs, "you'll have a wonderful time!"

"If it's going to be so wonderful, why won't you come along?"

Maya's gold-flecked eyes narrow, growing sad and distant.

"You'll have to see him sooner or later," Jyoti says to Maya's silence. "Come with me. Please, Maya. I can't go alone."

"You don't need me, dear. I'd only be in the way."

Again they hear the *shastri* calling, this time threatening to leave without them. "If I see him, do you want me to give him a message?" Jyoti asks.

"Tell him I hate him," Maya says.

"You don't!" Jyoti cries.

Maya lowers her eyes. "Maybe not, but say so anyway. Now go, before the party's over!"

Jyoti lets herself be bustled through the door.

"I'm not going to tell him anything then," Jyoti declares. "I'll just walk right past him like he's not there!"

"Just what I'd do myself." Maya gives her a swift hug.

☙☙☙☙

Shivaji walks back from the smith, smiling, swaggering even; a warrior who has just taken possession of a beautiful weapon. Hanging from his belt is a scabbard, long, narrow, of red velvet. In the scabbard, the *farang* sword, Maya's gift, outfitted now with a gauntlet hilt.

When Iron proposed that his village smith modify the *farang* sword, Shivaji's face had fallen, and Iron had laughed. Now Shivaji understood. Whatever was a smith of such skill, such artistry doing in this tiny village?

The bright damascened blade had been sharpened and polished: the smith himself had admired it—Moorish steel, he called it. Despite his complaints to Iron when pressed to finish the job in just two days, the gauntlet hilt he had added was a work of art.

Shivaji rests his hand gently on his sword's new hilt. The steel is cool and smooth, polished so it shines, inlaid here and there with silver and gold. The gauntlet is fashioned as a ram's head; the sword seems to emerge from its angry mouth, the wide curling horns of the head of the ram provide the space for Shivaji's hand to hold the crossbar hand grip inside. The ram gauntlet covers the whole of his forearm.

Townspeople seeing Shivaji strut down the street lift their hands. When he walks by, they remark to each other how like a kshatriya he looks, how regal, how courageous. Then they shake their heads—for of course, the kings of old are dead and gone, all the kshatriyas are gone (for no one believes the lying Rajput rulers and their claims). They feel happy to see Shivaji so full of life. Of course the Bijapuris will destroy him, but let him have his fun now while he can.

He walks past boys playing near a well, fighting with long stalks of sharp sword grass: "I get to be Shivaji!" "No! You were Shivaji last time! I'm Shivaji! You be Iron!" Near the gates of Iron's compound, Shivaji sees Tanaji trying to catch his eye.

"We've got trouble," Tanaji says, leading him to the stable. After making sure no one's watching, Tanaji pulls Shivaji by the arm to a dark corner, where Hanuman is standing near an old bullock cart from the fort.

"Look at this," he says, pulling aside the gunny on the cart to reveal a pile of canvas bags. "This is bad."

Shivaji opens one of the bags. It's surprisingly heavy. Inside he sees a jumble of long, uneven cylinders wrapped in silk, each tied with blue string and sealed with lumps of wax. He lifts one of the cylinders and tears the silk away, revealing a stack of gold coins.

"Huns, Shahu," Hanuman says, his eyes gleaming. "Mogul huns. I can't believe the captain just left it all there. Gold huns, Shahu, still wrapped and sealed."

"How much?" Shivaji asks in a hoarse whisper.

"Two lakhs," Tanaji answers.

"Two lakhs, nineteen thousand seven hundred," Hanuman corrects him.

"This changes everything," Tanaji whispers.

"For the better." Hanuman grins.

Tanaji glares at his son, as though he blamed Hanuman for the gold's existence. "That commander was an idiot! Who would abandon a fort with two lakh hun in the strong room! I tell you Shahu, we're deep in shit now."

"Calm down, father," Hanuman says, which only increases Tanaji's agitation. "What's wrong with money?"

"I'm ashamed to be the father of a man who can't see what this means. Two lakh hun! Where did it come from? Do you think the bitch queen of Bijapur will sit quietly while we take two lakh hun from her pockets?"

Hanuman snorts and rolls his eyes. "Oh, hell. Forget the money, father—they're already going to kill us for taking the fort! And even Bijapuris can't kill you twice."

"You'd be surprised what they can do." Then Tanaji glares at Shivaji. "This won't be good for your father."

Shivaji's face grows cold. Until now he'd been enjoying the argument between Tanaji and Hanuman, and the weight of the gold in his hands. "What about my father?"

"They'll use him to get this back." Tanaji stares levelly into Shivaji's eyes. "You know they will."

"I don't care," Shivaji replies. "How will they use him?" he asks as if as an afterthought.

"Maybe they send your father with an army. Would you fight against him, Shahu? Or worse, maybe they begin to send the little boxes: a finger in one, an eye in another." Tanaji waits for Shivaji to consider his words.

"I don't get it," Hanuman bursts in. "So we found some gold. So what? If we have to, we give it back. All's well. Right?" Hanuman glances from his father to his cousin, waiting. "Right?" he insists.

"Except we don't give it back, do we?" Tanaji says quietly.

Shivaji looks up, places the silk-sheathed cylinder in the canvas bag with its many brothers. "No," he says. "We don't give it back."

There's silence for a moment. "This is going to change everything," Tanaji whispers, and stomps off.

They watch as Tanaji walks away. "What's wrong with him?" Hanuman murmurs. "Why is he so angry?"

"He's scared."

"Scared of what? He's been in battles before."

"Scared for you, maybe. After what happened to your brother . . ."

"Scared to tell our mother, that's what he's scared of."

Shivaji looks carefully at Hanuman. "You could have kept this, cousin. You could have lived like a *padshah*."

"Now you sound like my father. He said the same thing. Got very pissed when I told him I was giving it to you. Anyway, I was not meant to be a rich man, Shahu," Hanuman says.

"He's right," Shivaji replies at last. "This will change everything."

☙◌◑◌☙

"No, it's not going to rain," Iron shouts over the drummers. In the cool dark evening air the cloud of Iron's breath bursts forth warm and damp and sweet with toddy. "I paid a fortune to the blasted *shastri* to say the right mantras. Clear skies guaranteed!" Firelight brightens the faces of the men on the dais; golden, like the faces of gods. Iron's soldiers celebrate by doing yet another dance before the dais, beating wildly on double ended clay drums, making a great racket while they turn and jump and dip and kneel, never missing a beat.

Lakshman, his eye bandaged, sits alone at the edge of the dais. Perhaps everyone has someone else to talk to. No one would admit wanting to avoid him. Even so he sits apart. He holds his head still, as if his wound might burst apart if he moved too quickly. Lakshman's good eye plays across the faces in the crowd like he's searching for someone. In spite of his obvious discomfort, he's smiling. He has always been proud of his charming smile, and still is proud of what remains of it.

The entire village has filled the courtyard to overflowing, an unexpectedly orderly jumble of villagers seated in long rows that stretch from wall to wall of the compound, from the far gate almost to the dais's edge. Boys run through the gathering, blowing on terra-cotta whistles.

Iron knows how to celebrate. Everyone is drunk; gloriously, wildly drunk. Shivaji has only had a cup or two of toddy, but he is in the minority; others are soaked in the stuff. Every few minutes, a drunken villager stumbles up to the dais and bows before Shivaji, usually offering fruits or flowers. So many garlands now hang around his neck Shivaji seems to be wearing a robe of marigolds and tuberoses. Beside him, Iron sways in his seat, the happiest of hosts, calling constantly for more toddy; making sure that the food never stops, nor the music.

Other than his friends on the dais, Shivaji sees few people he knows: most of his men are on duty up at the fort or marching to Bijapur; Hanuman himself guards the bullock cart and its hidden gold—Shivaji will relieve him later.

Shivaji had eagerly scanned the faces in the crowd when a few of the young dancing students from the temple got up to perform. He caught a glimpse of Jyoti, but that was all. Now a group of village women gets up to dance: old maids and widows and a young girl or two, walking in a slow circle. Shivaji notices that many of the women give Iron bright glances fueled by too much toddy, and Iron responds with upraised eyebrows and a knowing nod. "Having fun, Shahu?" Iron says to Shivaji. He leans over to hear Shivaji's answer and almost starts to topple.

"It's late and I'm tired, uncle," Shivaji laughs, pushing him upright. "Looks like you're tired, too!"

"I'm too drunk to be tired!" he shouts.

Shivaji looks around the dais. Jedhe and Bandal have gone. "Uncle, I'm going! I have to leave early tomorrow! I am grateful for this honor, uncle."

"Well, if you're not drunk enough to stay up all night, what the hell good are you?" Iron winks at him, and Shivaji realizes that Iron thinks he's leaving to be with a woman.

But as Shivaji stands, a scream tears through the laughter, turning into a choking gurgling rattle.

Shivaji sees a farmer stagger to his feet, clutching his side. For a moment a half dozen bloody snakes squirm between the farmer's fingers. Then Shivaji realizes that what he took for snakes are really the ragged end of the farmer's entrails.

The farmer lurches forward, one hand locked on his gushing wound, the other pawing the air. Then his eyes grow wide and cold, and roll up showing only the whites in the torchlight, and he falls. His head lands on a plate of food, and blood gushes from his lips. A woman screams, and another, and soon the air is filled with anguish.

Nearby another man stands and holds up his bloody hand: his sleeve is stained scarlet and his eyes are afire. "*Wagnak!*" he screams in a mad dance. "*Wagnak! Wagnak!*"

There, shining wet in the firelight, he reveals the hidden knives of death: black tiger claws between his clenched and bloody fingers. "*Wagnak!*" he screams in triumph.

Iron is at the scene almost before the farmer has fallen. He slaps the killer across the face with a heavy hand, and the man collapses in a heap at his feet. Iron grabs the man's arm and tears off the tiger claws, practically ripping off his fingers along with the rings. Some guards move forward, but they are superfluous: Iron's knee drives the man's neck to the ground as Iron spits on his face. "Fool!" he shouts. Then to the guards: "Take him to the caste elders; let them decide his fate."

Tanaji grabs Shivaji's arm and tugs him away from the scene. "There! Do you see! There's your enemy, Shahu! Not the Bijapuris—your own people! General Shahji couldn't control them and look what became of him! How will you succeed where he failed?"

Iron stands and waves the bloody *wagnak* angrily at the assembled villagers. "I'll not have it! Do you hear! I won't have blood feuds in my *watan*!" He shakes his fist at the farmer. "Whatever the elders decide, I add this: You are banished! Banished forever from my *watan*!" Iron strides back to the dais. "Play!" he shouts to the musicians as he takes his seat again. "Toddy!" he yells, and a frightened woman brings the brass pitcher to him quickly.

Tukoji leans over to Iron. "If only that had been General Shahji, eh, cousin? What he deserves, eh?" Iron looks at him for a moment and then turns away, draining his cup and thrusting it forward again.

ⓒⓘⓒⓘ

"You look like hell, you know. Must be quite a party!" Hanuman laughs as Shivaji approaches. But when Shivaji tells him what has happened, Hanuman shakes his head. "You never know, do you? I mean, that's the whole point of *wagnak*—you have to get close . . . You have to win the trust of the man that you despise. Even when he sees the rings on your fingers, he has to say, no, not him; it can't be, not him, not my friend. He has let you sit beside him, let you put your arm around him, until you sink the blades deep into his guts. That's the point, isn't it?"

"What's the point?" Shivaji spits back. "That we must never trust our friends? That we're in danger always, even when we think we're safe?"

"Especially when we think we're safe, Shahu." Hanuman looks at Shivaji. "To swear *wagnak* is to become the hand of Yama, the lord of death. Death comes to us all, Shahu."

"Must *wagnak* come to us all as well?" Shivaji throws himself on the straw near the wheel of the bullock cart, beside the sacks of hidden gold.

"So, Shahu . . . ," Hanuman asks after a silence. "Did Maya come?"

"What concern is it of yours?"

Hanuman holds up his hands. "Easy, Shahu. No concern. But if Maya didn't come, then Jyoti . . ."

"So you'll find someone else. Plenty of women there. Just stand near Iron, he seems to attract them. Go."

"It's not like that, Shahu." Hanuman frowns. "You're just upset. Do you want me to stay?"

"I'll be all right. Go. And I did see Jyoti. She's here. So enjoy yourself."

Hanuman leaves and Shivaji sits staring at a butter lamp, wondering how long it will burn before it leaves him in darkness.

Fog has crept down from the mountain. The air glows in a silver mist when Hanuman leaves the stable. He's about to head toward the courtyard when he senses something—a shadow in the misty darkness. His hand moves silently to the *katar* hanging from his belt. "Who's there?" Hanuman calls.

"I missed you," Jyoti replies, gliding toward him.

"Jyoti," Hanuman whispers as her graceful form emerges from the fog. "You're drunk," he laughs as she comes closer.

"Not so drunk," she answers.

She places her hand against him, tracing a soft trail down his chest. His skin seems to vibrate along her finger's path. Then she turns away, stepping slowly into the silver fog. She walks as though she knows just where she wants to go; he can sense her hips shifting with each step.

Amidst the roses and night-blooming jasmine grows an enormous mango tree, its fog-wet foliage spreading over the garden like a canopy. Jyoti steps onto a wide board swing, its long ropes tied to a high branch. She flexes like a reed, pushing the swing into a slow arc.

"Swing me," she says to Hanuman.

In the dark he finds the pulling line attached to the seat, and he tugs. She begins to giggle. He pulls harder, and she starts to moan, and now as she sweeps past him in a breathless arc, she shrieks out his name with terror and delight, begging him to stop. He has her flying now; soaring up till her face nearly presses against the sky, weightless, suspended; then a sudden backward dive, swinging until she stops in midair, staring straight down into emptiness; then plummeting forward again.

"You like it!" he says as she swings past him.

"Yes!" she laughs, abandoning herself. That word explodes in Hanuman's ears. He leaps up on the swing himself, standing with her face-to-face, pressed against her.

She laughs, and then with unexpected boldness lifts her face to quickly brush his lips with hers. Before he can react, she leans back and begins to pump the swing. "Don't just stand there," she teases. His hands press against hers on the soft ropes. The swing is soaring. Above them the great branch groans against the ropes. Water shakes from the rain-soaked leaves, sprinkling them and the ground below. "Stop," Jyoti cries at last, her face just inches from his.

Before they stop, she has wrapped one of her legs around him, and he has pressed one hand against her breast. She grazes his chest and neck and ears with her soft lips. Her breath stirs against his skin. The swing twists slowly underneath them.

As she feels him press against her, as she feels his urgent breath against her ear, as she shivers when he pulls aside her blouse and traces the soft flesh of her shoulders with his tongue, as she holds him close and whispers to him "yes," she thinks she sees—amidst all this, she thinks she sees—a shadow in the fog.

Like a black wolf, she thinks, or a wild dog.

A strange dog. A dog with one eye only; one eye gleaming in the dark; one eye shining in the mist; one eye hidden in the shadows.

But maybe it is nothing, she thinks. Soon she is too absorbed to care.

❦

Shivaji wakes with a start, his heart pounding. Something's near him, close. In the darkness he can hear breathing, not the warm long breath of the animals; softer, shallower. Closer. He reaches for his *katar*. It's gone! And his belt, gone! "Who's there? Speak!" he croaks out.

An old man, naked but for a gunny rag hanging from his shoulder, peers from the shadows. "Ram Das?" Shivaji asks.

"You remembered! How auspicious!" the old man says.

"Am I dreaming?"

"The exact question you should ask! Are you dreaming? Exactly!" This strikes Ram Das as hilarious. He cackles, until he begins to cough. "They're celebrating your victory, lord." Ram Das continues, "I've come to add my congratulations. I have a present for you." Ram Das leans close to Shivaji, and taking one of his hands in his dry, knotted fingers, presses something into his palm.

"What is it? Tiger claws?"

Ram Das cackles again. "No, not tiger claws; not *wagnak*, lord, not yet. Not yet. Not yet, but soon. Not tiger claws just yet. What do you think it is? Humor your child! Guess again!"

Shivaji tries to think what's in his hand. "It's something hard."

"Sometimes hope is hard, lord. Yes, that's my gift: hope. Hope in the palm of your hand." Ram Das folds Shivaji's fist tight with his dry old fingers. "Don't look until tomorrow. Promise me that."

"Why?"

"Maybe the gift will disappear if you disobey. Maybe it's the silly request of an old man. Maybe it's your duty to humor your servant. Maybe it's the way of the gods."

"Maybe I'm dreaming."

"Maybe," Ram Das says. "But soon those dreams will end."

The light gutters out suddenly, and just as suddenly Shivaji feels only emptiness where Ram Das was standing.

❦

The party is in tatters after the murder, and cannot be resurrected. Despite all of Iron's shouted commands people leave. Trelochan, the *shastri* from Poona, finds himself walking to his room in the company of Jedhe, Bandal, and Tukoji. They had met at the party and discovered many mutual friends.

"You've known him a long time, Trelochan," Jedhe says. "What do you think Shivaji will do, now he has a fort of his very own?"

"Well, he's bound by his oath, isn't he?" Trelochan replies.

"What oath?" Jedhe asks.

Trelochan realizes he has said too much. "Perhaps you should ask him yourself."

But Tukoji stands stock still. "I would hear of this oath, brahmin." The fog presses against them, damp and cool.

"It was a night much like this." Gathering momentum as he speaks, Trelochan spins the tale: he was one of five: along with Shahu, Lakshman, Balaji, and Hanuman. One night seven years before Shivaji had led them to the edge of the campfires of a Mogul caravan. At midnight, beneath a crescent moon, a greenish fog appeared. Soon the whole camp fell into a death-like sleep. The boys filled sack after sack with Mogul gold. Through it all the sleepers never moved. The green fog swirled around them.

At last they rode eastward in the dim light of the misty moon. At dawn they reached the Ganesha temple at Ranjangaon. Shivaji led them to the *murti* of the goddess. "Here is our benefactress," he said at last. One by one they took Bhavani's darshan, and placed their treasure at her feet. Then they lay prostrate before the *murti*.

"Maybe I was tired, uncle," Trelochan says, "maybe I had started to dream. He stood at the goddess's right hand, and I thought I saw a crown of fire on Shahu's head. I thought his hair was burning."

Trelochan's eyes are far away. "He held his naked sword. The morning sun poured down upon him. He bade us each stand up and grasp that sword with him. I thought the blade would cut me."

Tukoji lifts his chin. "Is there a point to this story?"

Trelochan ignores him, lost in memory. "When we held the sword, Shahu called out an oath. It was glorious: to free our homeland from the Muslim kings, to live once more as free men in the land of our fathers." Trelochan's face fills with light. "One by one we took that oath, and kissed the hem of Bhavani's garment. She wore green that day, light green, light as air, the color of the fog we'd seen by moonlight."

Trelochan speaks softly. "Shahu's sword was sharp. His hands were bleeding—you can still see the scars on his palms—white, like the scars that Indra gets from throwing lightning bolts. They still call Shahu 'Master Bhisma' at that temple, lord. After the great prince Bhisma, the one who took that terrible oath in ancient times. Remember him? The gods rained flowers on his head."

"That oath, if I recall correctly," Tukoji replies dryly, "was an oath of celibacy. Was it not? The name of Bhisma hardly suits Shivaji." Tukoji frowns. "Why, Shivaji has done no more than swear revenge for his father's failure. He's wrapped his schemes in the skirts of the goddess. Hardly the sort of act the gods applauded by dropping flowers from heaven."

"If you say so, lord," Trelochan replies quietly.

ᘒᘒᘒ

Shivaji wakes again, but this time the stable is lit by the light of dawn. Hanuman leans against the wheel of the bullock cart, his head bare and his dark hair hanging around his shoulders. "Did you get a nice sleep, Shahu?" Hanuman asks.

"Yes, fine," Shivaji answers. "I notice you got very little sleep."

Hanuman turns away, embarrassed but pleased. "Go get some break-fast, Shahu. I'll stand guard." As he rises, Hanuman notices that Shivaji's fingers are folded tight against his palm. "What's in your hand, Shahu?"

"I don't know," Shivaji answers, extending his hand toward Hanuman. On his palm rest four small jagged rocks.

Hanuman shrugs. "Three rocks, cousin. This one is a just a clod of dried earth. You must have been sleepwalking. Where did you pick them up?" Hanuman nods to the stable around them. "There are no rocks around here like these. These are basalt, Shahu; like they use to build forts."

"Are they?" Shivaji examines them. Three rocks and a clod of earth. His face looks resolute, as if he's come to a great decision. "I'm going to Poona. Today. I have much work to do."

"Today? Taking the gold, Shahu?"

"Oh, yes, Hanuman. And much more than the gold." He stares fasci-nated at the stones in his hand. "This is a sign, cousin," he whispers, as he clenches his hand so tightly his fist begins to shake. "I'm taking hope."

CHAPTER 16

Something was happening.

Something powerful hovered over the Rang Mahal, over the compound, over all the city of Poona. She could feel it, and long ago she had learned to trust her feelings.

Sai Bai had felt it ever since Shivaji had returned, driving into the compound seated on an old bullock cart, Trelochan in the back with Lakshman—poor Lakshman!—and Tanaji riding his pony behind them all, looking more anxious than she had ever seen.

Well, of course he would look anxious, wouldn't he? Seeing his son's face destroyed must have been hard enough—but now he would have to face Nirmala. How to tell his wife that her son had been hurt?

Nirmala, of course, had found out, and in the hardest of ways: she had run outside to greet them both and seen her son's face covered by bandages. Then the wailing had started, and the weeping. Soon Nirmala's cries had awakened the whole compound.

Sai Bai herself had raced across the courtyard barefoot. She had kissed his face right there in front of everyone. Let them talk. Let Jijabai scowl. I'm his wife! I'll kiss him if I please. He had kissed her right back—how long had it been since that happened? She could feel his lips on her cheek. It had been worth it! The hell with them all!

That night he had come to her room—how long had it been since that had happened? Oh my, they had hardly slept. Wonderful, wonderful, she thought. Later, while he snored, she wondered: What happened in Welhe? Maya had been there. Friend or no friend, she was a nautch girl. He was a man. And Sai Bai knows Shivaji's nature all too well.

The next morning she first noticed that strange uneasy feeling. Like the breeze that comes hours before a storm: Shivaji's talks with Dadaji that grew into arguments; Tanaji bursting from Shahu's room, swearing as he stormed down the stairs. Others felt it, too. No one said hello anymore, or stopped to chat. Servants clutched their saris tight around them as they hurried past.

Messengers galloped off each day, secrets stuffed into their saddlebags. Where were they going? Then soldiers started to appear. Some she had seen before; when they had been dressed like farmers or goatherds and their smiles had been easy. But now they rode in looking grim, carrying weapons—swords and maces, spears and bows. Tanaji would greet them.

Just as suddenly as the soldiers began to arrive, the masons departed. The wall was done, the servants had told her, for now of course she scarcely saw her husband. All those months and now the wall was finished! Dadaji, grumbling all the while, had paid extra for early completion. Dozens of new masons had arrived from Rajastan to help complete the job.

Then she heard that the masons had come not simply to finish the wall, but for a different job entirely: on a mountain near Welhe, Shahu was re-building Bhatghar, an old fort, given by his cousin. Bhatghar and Torna. The servants said it had been in ruins, scarcely more than a clod of earth, but soon it would be grand again.

Torna. Bhatghar. Two forts, she thought. Her heart broke when she heard it. Two would only be a taste. He'd want more.

She came upon Jijabai one night, on the verandah, staring out at the moon. "You feel it, daughter, don't you?" Jijabai had asked her. Calling her "daughter"—how long had it been since that had happened?

"I don't know what I'm feeling, mother."

Jijabai turned to her, and Sai Bai grew frightened to see the coldness in her eyes. "You feel war, Sai Bai, the coming of war. Just as you hear the drone of locusts before they hatch, you hear now the drone of coming sorrow. Death gathers in the sky like clouds. The scent of blood hangs in the air. Soon we shall be sad. Our hands will be red with the blood of our men." The old woman stared at her for a while, until Sai Bai felt that Jijabai was staring through her, seeing the flames of war fires and bodies broken on the field, the air thick with smoke and the heavy stink of blood.

Back in her room Sai Bai, filled with dark thoughts, rocked on her bed until Shahu came. She forgot all her anguish in his arms. I must be fickle, Sai Bai thought, to be so easily distracted.

He had started coming to her every night. What had got into him?

When the dawn came, even though he was gone, she felt restored. But she hated seeing Jijabai. Instead of her tantrums, which Sai Bai had learned to bear, Jijabai bore those haunted, widow's eyes.

The evil eye, a maid had told her. She gave Sai Bai an amulet and a mantra to whisper whenever Jijabai came by.

The city grew busier each day, drawing activity to its heart the way a carcass draws flies. Horses arrived and horsemen—Tanaji built hasty pens and stables near the palace—and with them came soldiers on foot, training loudly all day outside the compound walls.

And soon came cooks, and tailors, and tent-makers, and whores. And weapon makers too: smiths of all sorts, caravans of smiths. Hammers clanged all day and half the night, and the air stunk with the smoke from the forges. And farriers arrived, and fletchers, and armorers and saddle-makers and all the rest.

War.

War crept from the ground like locusts. Soon Sai Bai felt its terror continually—it only paused when Shivaji's arms were wrapped around her. But even then she feared for his life, and for the life of her son; sometimes she feared even for her own.

And when he wore that sword—which now meant constantly—that gauntlet sword the nautch girl gave him, she wondered again about Welhe, what might have happened between them. She forced herself to imagine him and Maya twined in congress—then she would find a hidden place and weep.

Then one day he left. Gone on an errand so secret he could not tell even her. "But you told Tanaji," she said, as tears spilled from her eyes. "You told Dadaji. You won't tell me, your own wife? I may never see you again!"

"I will always return for you."

"Someday you won't return," she cried. Later she regretted that those had been the last words she said as he rode away.

◎◎◎◎

Later, Trelochan had come to see her. He told her that Shivaji had received a message from the gods. But he started talking about rocks and a clod of earth, and Sai Bai stopped listening.

CRCR

Three days later, Shivaji rides into the courtyard. Sai Bai runs out, her sandals splashing in puddles. She doesn't care. He's back.

While she serves him breakfast, he tells her how the monsoon rains still pour in the western ghats; how the birds flop on the wet ground of the forests with wings too wet to fly; how clouds billow and fall down the mountainsides obscuring everything.

As he says all this, she nods as if she's happy to hear more, but she longs for him to cease. His words trouble her, and there are better uses for his lips. She takes a deep breath and makes up her mind to tell him this, when Dadaji steps in. "Ah, Shahu, you've come back! What news?"

Too late. He's gone now. And all day long she'll only have her yearning for the night to come.

CRCR

Tanaji looks around the circle of men seated in Dadaji's room. He can't believe that things have come to this.

Tanaji scowls as once again the young *shastri* Trelochan gazes moon-eyed at Shivaji. Since Shivaji's return from Welhe, with his story of the holy man and his gift of pebbles, Trelochan has gone mad. Trelochan thinks the story proves Shivaji's destiny. And now even Shivaji appears to believe it.

Shivaji has brought them here to listen to his latest fantasy. Something about bribing a Bijapuri commander to hand over Singhaghad fort. He wants to use the Bijapuri gold to buy the fort. Of course Trelochan laps it up. It all adds up to a pile of horseshit. "You can't trust a Bijapuri, Shahu! Especially not a Bijapuri traitor!"

"You can when the price is right, Tanaji," Dadaji says. "This commander has been offering us Singhaghad fort for many months. He's serious. For one lakh hun, I think he may be trusted." Tanaji scowls, but before he can speak, Dadaji dives back in: "I've never known a Bijapuri to walk away from a deal when actual gold was involved."

"But the transfer! The transfer is dangerous! What's to stop him from taking the money and then refusing to hand over the fort?" asks Tanaji.

Shivaji shrugs. "I don't think he's smart enough to be dangerous."

"Hell, I'm not smart, but I'm dangerous. If that commander's not smart, that's all the more reason for concern—ask yourself: How did a stupid man come to be commander of Singhaghad?"

"Tanaji is right. The transfer is the moment of danger. The method must be foolproof," Dadaji says. "But what about the price? Is it worth one lakh hun to get Singhaghad?"

"Without a drop of blood, yes!" Trelochan pipes up. Tanaji rolls his eyes. Now brahmins have military opinions.

"We don't need another fort!" Tanaji bursts out. "Why do you suddenly need forts, Shahu?"

"You heard Shahu's story, uncle," Trelochan says, practically bubbling. "Four stones, four forts—"

"I know, I know, I know," Tanaji interrupts. "And one of them needs repair, and one of the stones was a clod of earth, and on and on and on." He pulls on his mustache for fear he'll start to scream. "I can't believe we're basing policy on some stones Shahu found in his hand!"

But Trelochan can't contain himself. "Four stones, uncle! Each stone represents a fort. The clod of earth is for Bhatghar, which Shivaji is fortifying even now. It is a sacred sign! When the gods speak . . ."

"Four forts?" Tanaji glares from face to face, making sure he gets each man's attention. "So where's fort number four, eh, *shastri*? We're about to pay a fortune for a fort, and now you're practically guaranteeing that we'll attack yet another fort, just to make the prophecy come true!" Tanaji lifts his hands, appealing to Dadaji. "Is this how we make policy these days, Dada? Some crazy man shits in my hand, and therefore I need to attack Agra?"

"It's Shahu's gold, Tanaji. He must decide how to use it, not I," Dadaji replies.

Tanaji bristles. "Let's talk about whose gold it is. Who found it, eh? Who bled for it?"

"Shahu bled as much as anybody, uncle," Trelochan answers, for Shivaji again is looking down, his hands open, palms in his lap.

"Lost an eye, did he? Nearly get himself strangled, did he?"

"Shahu was shot, wasn't he? Doesn't that count for something, uncle?"

"If you want the money, Tanaji, take it," Shivaji says softly.

"Fine!" Tanaji replies angrily. "Fine! I will take it!"

Dadaji clucks his tongue. "There, there, Tanaji; control yourself. Shivaji, this does not become you."

"It's not your money, Shahu!" Trelochan insists. "It's a gift from the gods! You are only its caretaker!"

"Those huns came from Bijapur, not from the gods," Tanaji scowls.

"How can you be so blind, old fool," Trelochan shouts back. "The gods are here among us—they are shaping our destinies!" He is too caught up in his fervor to see the frowns of the others. "Why did Shahu succeed at Torna? The goddess sent him a sign, a dream! Five men, taking Torna? Don't you see that was divine intervention? With no deaths . . . with only a little blood . . ."

"More than a little," Tanaji growls.

"And then the gold, appearing out of nowhere!" Tanaji gasps, but Trelochan rattles on. "The gold, coming with the sign of the stones! It can only mean one thing! The gold must be dedicated to fulfilling the sign!"

"The sign, the sign! I've heard enough!" Tanaji stands. "Shahu, don't tell me you really believe this horseshit."

After a long pause, Shivaji looks up. "Tanaji is right. I've been a fool."

"No!" Trelochan cries.

"Don't stop him, now that he's starting to make sense," Tanaji says.

"Shahu, don't be foolish!" Trelochan begs.

"It seems I'm a fool no matter what I say," Shivaji replies.

Dadaji gives Shivaji's shoulder a shove. "Stop feeling sorry for yourself, Shahu. Didn't you know this day would come? I am ashamed to hear you talking about signs and stones. What difference do they make to a man? Don't turn your back on your destiny."

"You don't believe in the stones, Dadaji?" Trelochan asks.

"Those stones are horseshit, *shastri*. That far I agree with Tanaji. But if they inspire Shivaji to fulfill his birthright, who cares if they're horseshit?"

He takes Shivaji's hand. It is an unexpectedly emotional gesture, for Dadaji is the most formal of men. "Shahu, look around you. The walls of the city are complete. You've taken back Torna, and you're fortifying Bhatghar. Singhaghad is in your grasp. It is your destiny to succeed where your father failed. I've known that, Jijabai has known that." Dadaji then looks into Shivaji's eyes. "Those men outside our gates—the army that's massing here. Do you think a single man there believes that crappy sign? Do you think they came to fight because of four black stones?"

"No," Shivaji says. "But they might have come for gold."

"For gold, or for glory, or to get away from their nagging wives . . . Men make excuses, Shahu. They do what they want, and then they make up a reason. That's not why they came, Shahu. Not for gold, not for stones. They came for you."

"What am I to do, uncle?" Shivaji asks.

Dadaji lets go Shivaji's hand, his eyes looking far away. "How would I know, eh? My work is over now, and yours has begun. I can depart in peace. I shall be a *sanyasi.*"

"Like hell, Dada!" Tanaji roars. "We're in a big mess. You're not renouncing anything, not now!"

"Please, Dadaji, stay a with us a little longer," Shivaji says.

"A little longer, yes. But the big mess is yours, Shahu, not mine." Dadaji laughs, even Tanaji laughs.

"I will consider what to do," Shivaji says. "Maybe the gods will make my path clear."

"Listen, Shahu," Dadaji says. "The path of dharma always looks hard. So if your way isn't clear, choose the hard road instead of the easy."

"And about the money, Shahu?" Tanaji asks.

"Maybe the gods will make that clear as well."

After a moment, Dadaji speaks again. "There's another matter. This came from Balaji." The mood of the room changes quickly. "He says that he has put your case to the sultana, Shahu. The arrival of the Torna guard caused a real scene, he says. A letter is being drafted demanding the return of the Torna treasury. I should think we'll have a delegation from Bijapur arriving any day."

Trelochan gasps and Tanaji grimaces. "That ties it, Shahu," Tanaji says. "You want the gods to make things clear? There! Bijapuris at your door! Will you go to war over two lakh hun?"

"Will you hold your tongue? Bala's letter's not done," Dadaji says. "By Bijapur's accounting—are you listening to me?—Torna's treasury held nine hundred rupees."

Tanaji looks up, his lips moving, doing the math. "That's about—what—a hundred hun? That's all?"

Trelochan gasps. "But the gold—it's two thousand times that much!"

"I don't understand," Shivaji says.

"I do," replies Trelochan. "This *is* the sign you were looking for, Shahu. The gods have multiplied the treasure so you can do their will."

"There may be other explanations, Shahu," Dadaji says dryly.

ଔଓଔଓ

The next evening, Shivaji receives a message from Dadaji and hurries to the old man's room. "Come in and see," Dadaji tells him, opening the door. Two or three butter lamps cast a dim glow. On the floor in a cluster sit three men Shivaji has never seen before. They look up and instantly touch their foreheads to the floor.

"Stop that!" Dadaji exclaims. "They keep doing that," he complains softly. "This is Shivaji, master of Poona," Dadaji continues. At once the three men start to bow again. "Enough, enough!" Dadaji says.

From the way they tie their turbans, it is clear that the men are Muslims. "What's this about, Dada?" Shivaji asks. He turns to the men. "Have you come about the fort?" His voice is harsh, and the men cringe when they hear it. "Have you come from Bijapur? Is this about Torna?"

Dadaji gives a small, calming wave. "Listen," he tells Shivaji. "Tell," he commands the men.

The one closest to Dadaji begins to speak. "I am Ahmed, and these are my brothers, Kurshid and Munna," he says. "We have come here, lords, over this." Reaching into a leather satchel, Ahmed removes a long tube wrapped in black silk embroidered with golden crescents. The other brothers watch with fierce and anxious eyes as Ahmed extracts a sheet of rolled up parchment. Extravagant Persian calligraphy dances across the ivory page. The bottom of the paper sags beneath a half dozen heavy seals of embossed wax from which hang multicolored ribbons.

"This is a firman from the sultan of Bijapur."

"I can't read it," Dadaji says.

"No one can, lord. It's supposed to be in Persian, but the writing is so fancy, no one can read it. We all know what it says, though, lord, because it comes with this." Here, Ahmed again reaches into the bag, and brings out a great key of iron; on its badge, the key-maker has carved a bas-relief portrait of a mountain fort.

"This is why we have come. Our father is . . . was, I mean . . . the commander of Purandhar fort, lord. This firman and this key confirmed the appointment." Ahmed continues, "He fell and broke his back. It took him a long time to die. We buried him at the fort, lord."

"But what has this to do with me?" Shivaji demands.

Ahmed speaks uncertainly: "By rights the succession of Purandhar fort should fall to us, lord. But, lord, we cannot tell how this should be!" Ahmed starts to bow, but catches himself in time. "So we come to you, lord, that you should in your wisdom settle the matter for us."

"They want us to decide who will get Purandhar fort, Shahu." Dadaji lifts an eyebrow to underline the significance of his words.

Shivaji nods, as if this sort of occurrence were commonplace. "But surely the eldest would inherit?"

"Our father was clear that we must share the fort," Ahmed explains. "The most deserving of us to take the largest share. But forgive us, lord?

We can't choose who is most deserving. Nor do we know how a fort is to be divided into three."

Shivaji waves that problem off, still concentrating on the brothers' motives. "Why not send to Bijapur for a judgment?"

Again the three men shift uncomfortably. "Your first thought was right, lord," Munna says, glaring his brother Ahmed into silence. "By law of the Koran, the eldest would inherit, unless there is a will."

"Didn't you say that there was a will?" Dadaji asks.

"Not a written will, lord. This disposition was my father's dying wish . . . we all three heard it!" Munna says. He looks to the others. "Our father's dying wish, lord! If we go to our Muslim judges, they'll just give the fort to the eldest. Besides, they'd want a bite."

"A bite? Who?" asks Dadaji.

"The mullahs or whoever," Khurshid, the middle man, puts in.

Dadaji laughs. "But not us, eh? Not us Hindus?"

Khurshid, reveals his few remaining teeth. "Maybe your bite won't be so bad. Anyway, you're a businessman, lord," he says to Dadaji. "Maybe we can work things out. See here, lord. The monsoons were bad for us, you know? Our roofs are broken. They need thatching, eh? Suppose you delivered us some thatch for our roofs?"

"I'm sure we could arrange that," answers Shivaji.

"Let's say we pay you twenty rupees a bale."

"For twenty rupees a bale you could thatch your roofs with gold!"

"We'll need a hundred bales, I reckon," Kurshid continues, and the other brothers grimly nod in agreement.

Shivaji glances at Dadaji and shakes his head. "I think it's better if we don't . . . ," he starts to say, but his eyes drift to the firman, to the key of dull iron.

"Please, lord, we beg you!" Khurshid presses his forehead to the floor. The other brothers join him.

Shivaji glares. "Then stop this horseshit! Two thousand rupees? Tell me the real story and maybe I'll help you."

The brothers lift their heads and glance at each other.

"Please, lord," Munna says. "None of us has slept in days!"

"The story," Shivaji demands.

"It's as we told you, lord. Except that we've been . . . well . . . frightened," Ahmed says.

"Frightened? Of what?"

"Of each other, lord," Munna mumbles. Finally he blurts out: "Ahmed threatened to kill Khurshid, lord." His brothers glare at him, and then at each other. "Then Khurshid swore to kill Ahmed first."

"And then our dear baby brother here took an oath to kill whichever one survived!" Khurshid spits out.

"Do you think we like this, lord?" Ahmed whimpers. "Why do you think we've come to you?"

"Enough," cries Dadaji. "Send to Bijapur. Let the sultana judge."

The brothers share a glance. "That's not possible, lord," Ahmed says at last. "There may have been some . . . irregularities . . . some minor irregularities . . . regarding the allotment. A more precise accounting might prove embarrassing. In fact, faced with certain alternatives, being killed by one's brothers doesn't look so bad."

Shivaji laughs, and Ahmed joins him, and soon Dadaji and all of them are laughing as well. "That's why you're offering to pay us for bringing thatch," Shivaji suggests.

Khurshid nods. "So that there should be no question of a bribe, lord, in the event our request becomes known. Should any questions ever arise, we'll be able to say honestly that we came to you merely to purchase thatch to repair our fort."

"At a fair price?" Dadaji chuckles.

"Let it be Allah's will that others will pay you equally well, lord," Munna says.

"We will do what you ask, gentlemen," Shivaji says instantly, startling Dadaji. "We will pick the most deserving, and decide the method of division. On condition you agree to accept our judgment regardless of who or how we choose."

"Then we all agree," Khurshid says, and the others nod.

"I will begin sending thatch tomorrow," Shivaji continues. "I'll want a written order for this. I'll even have my men help repair the roofs. It seems the least I can do. In the meantime, while we speak with you to determine who is most deserving, you will stay here as our guests."

Once again the three men press their foreheads to the floor. "And we will keep these," Shivaji reaches casually for the firman and the key. For a moment the brothers stiffen, eyeing him as he rolls the firman into its brocaded tube, and then slips the heavy key into his pocket. But it's too late to say anything; they've come too far to go back now.

"What's your plan?" Dadaji whispers to Shivaji as he walks him to the door. "I know you have some mischief in mind."

"Keep them here—don't let them go back to their fort. Lots of interviews. Lots of questions. Who's most deserving, eh? Plenty to discuss for a couple of days. And get that written order for the thatch in my hand by dawn." Dadaji nods, knowing when he's been given a command. "I need two days, Dadaji. They've given me the key."

"The key to Purandhar, yes."

"This is the key to Singhaghad."

Dadaji looks at Shivaji uncertainly. "First Torna, then the gold, then Singhaghad, now this. Bhavani has thrown a treasure into your lap."

"Now you believe in the sign, uncle?"

Dadaji sighs. "Maybe she has given you this chance only to tempt you."

"This is the gift of Bhavani, uncle, not the villainy of Kali."

"They are both that same one, Shahu," says Dadaji.

Sai Bai feels a coldness in the room, like the shadow of a passing ghost, and turns to find Jijabai staring at her. "Whatever are you doing?" the older woman scolds. "Have we no servants?"

Sai Bai struggles to keep her face serene, knowing how that bothers Jijabai. "I prefer to look after Shahu's clothes myself, mother." She smooths an ironed turban cloth, and places it beside an embroidered jacket. "Especially when he faces trouble."

"What do you know of trouble?"

"Your son hopes to take a fort, mother, without an army," Sai Bai shoots back. "Do you think that easy?"

For a moment, for just a moment, Jijabai looks at Sai Bai as though she might reach out, weeping. But she sets her mouth and steels her spine. "This is servant's work! I never laid out my husband's clothes."

"Perhaps you should have, mother."

Shivaji and Tanaji and a line of twenty soldiers ride on Bedouin stallions outfitted in all their finery: tassles and bell bridles, velvet saddle blankets and silver ornaments. It takes only a few hours to ride to Singhaghad. The sun has burst through the clouds by the time they reach the mountain's foot. "The rains stopped early this year, Shahu," Tanaji remarks. He sounds grim. Drought and famine follow a short monsoon.

"It's Bhavani's work, uncle," Shivaji replies. "She is setting all things in motion." Tanaji says nothing. Around them the rolling fields are covered in golden greens as young plants sprout from the tilled ground. Breezes blow down the mountain. Everywhere birds chirp and caw.

They might be going on a picnic—except for the maces and swords, and spears and arrows, and sharp helmet tips peeking through the tops of turbans, and the glint of mail shirts beneath cotton robes.

Tanaji points to the mountaintop, to the battlements of Singhaghad, the Lion Fort, the most impregnable fortress in India, some say. Built on a mountain, three tall, sheer sides drop off into stomach-twisting emptiness. The fort's only access is a broken, one-horse trail that twists and switches like a coiling snake. Only two armies have been foolish enough to attack Singhaghad, and both were beaten back with ease.

Too tall for cannon fire, no access for tunneling. The road is so twisted that elephants—even if they managed to reach the gates—would never get the momentum for ramming. The fort scarcely needs its many guns. The defenders can sit behind the fort's locked gate as comfortable as a merchant in his strong room. No one comes in uninvited.

Of course, getting invited is the key to Shivaji's plan.

❦❦❦❦

Meanwhile, about twenty miles away, Lakshman trudges up the hill to Purandhar fort. Over the bleak road of unforgiving stones, he leads a line of a hundred bare-chested peasants. Each man balances on his head a great pile of thatch. It's hot, hard work.

When challenged at the fort gate, Lakshman pulls from his pocket the order written by the three brothers. It's damp with sweat. The sentry hurries off to find someone who can read, leaving Lakshman and his men standing in a long line that extends a hundred yards down the road. At length Lakshman pitches his bale to the ground and leans against it with a look of irritation. The other peasants do the same. They are too tired to talk.

"It looks all right," a cynical sergeant says, returning with the paper. Lakshman stuffs it in his pocket. The sentries laboriously set about opening the elephant gate, working the big keys in the great locks. It takes two men to unhitch the chain—each link weighs twenty pounds.

Swinging the heavy bundles of thatch back up to their heads, the men pass into the fort, meek and weary. The sergeant shakes his head, as if the procession is yet more proof that all officers are idiots.

With the commander dead, and his sons away in Poona, discipline in Purandhar has gone to hell. Lakshman sees only three or four lookouts on the battlements. Some men play at cards, some at dice, some nap. There are women around as well, looking well paid and available, but it's early and they're not yet getting too much attention. One of the women glances at Lakshman; she winces when she sees his broken face and turns away.

"Who's in charge?" Lakshman grunts.

"Sarge, I guess. Or nobody, more like. Why?"

"We're supposed to repair the roofs. Orders."

The sergeant ambles over. "How long is all this going to take?"

"Not long. A couple of days, maybe."

"You'll be staying down the mountain, at the village?" asks the sergeant.

"We'll be staying up here, at Purandhar fort!" Lakshman bristles. "You're supposed to provide us shelter. Didn't you read the order?"

The sergeant fingers a gold medallion hanging from his neck by a thick black string. "I wanted to know if you had read it."

"Do I look like I can read?" Lakshman sneers.

"All right. We'll find someplace to put you. I suppose you'll want food, too."

"When's dinner?" Lakshman says.

The sergeant glowers at him. "Do some work first." He walks away, unconsciously fingering his gold medallion.

Lakshman watches him leave with a sneering grin. The men round up four or five rickety bamboo ladders and start to hump the heavy bales to the roofs of the buildings. The smell of meat cooking begins to rise from one of the buildings. Dinner soon, Lakshman thinks. It won't be long now.

ଏଓଏଓ

As they approach the towering gates of Singhaghad, Tanaji finds himself remembering the horrors of Torna. I'm getting old, he thinks. It's not like Torna—we have Shivaji's plan, a perfect plan. Nothing can go wrong.

But the memory of Lakshman burns in his heart; he winces every time he thinks of that knife slicing his son's fair face. He should never have had Lakshman volunteer to go to Purandhar; he should have stopped him. Oh gods, he prays, keep Lakshman well.

Despite his doubts, Tanaji presses on. Soon he sees Shivaji nod toward the high gate of Singhaghad, flashing that brilliant, confident smile. Tanaji halts the men with a wave of his hand, lifts his head and calls to the sentries high above: "I bring a firman from the sultana of Bijapur!"

"Who the hell are you?" the sentry barks.

"I'm the one who brings the firman!" Tanaji replies.

"Who the hell are the others?"

"They are with me."

Again a long silence. Tanaji lifts the long tube covered in black silk that Shivaji took from the feuding brothers of Purandhar. He waves it at the sentries. "This firman from the sultana is why we've come. Bring us to the commander, sentry. This concerns him, not you."

In a moment, the small inner door of the great gate opens, and a soldier comes out—just as Shivaji had said would happen. The soldier walks slowly up to Tanaji, his left hand steadying his sword. He's about Tanaji's age; his leathery face is puckered and his mustache gray.

"Give me the firman," the soldier says.

Before he answers, Tanaji looks at Shivaji. Even this look is part of the plan. "No," Tanaji answers. "This firman is for the commander, for Ali Danyal—not a common sentry."

The soldier looks up into Shivaji's bright eyes, considers, then turns. "Let them pass!" They hear the *clank* of iron, the thud of bolts moving, and at last the gates of Singhaghad groan slowly open.

It's like a card game. Either hand can win, Shivaji had explained. It comes down to how we play. The first step is getting inside the fort. Now that he's managed it, Tanaji thinks that first step was the easy part.

The inner gates are every bit as formidable as the outer ones, even more so. But once inside, the path is smooth and the horses walk easily. The inner gates lead to a long, roofed corridor; dark and lit by torches whose flickering flames catch the firing slots in the walls, the holes in the arched ceiling from which hot death can be poured.

As the line of soldiers rides into the courtyard of the Lion Fort, Tanaji holds high the black firman tube. "Ali Danyal, come forward!" Tanaji shouts. "I bear a firman from Bijapur. Come forward, Ali Danyal!"

Around the courtyard, soldiers look up. The riders form a wide half circle around Tanaji and Shivaji. "Come forth, Ali Danyal. Receive the sultana's command!" Tanaji shouts again.

"You!" Shivaji says, picking out one of the Bijapuris. "Fetch the commander at once." The soldier glances around. Who is this fellow to order him about? "Well?" Shivaji says softly.

The soldier considers, then walks to a nearby building.

Quiet. Beneath the relentless sun, men watch each other, fingering their weapons. Tanaji can feel the perspiration sliding down his back.

In a moment, the guards at the door snap to attention and Ali Danyal emerges. He strides forward. He is younger than Tanaji expected: a stocky man with a square, pockmarked face. "I am Ali Danyal, commander of this fort," he says as if he'd never seen Shivaji. "State your business."

Tanaji withdraws the firman from the tube and with a flourish unrolls it, careful that its seals and ribbons can be seen by all. "Ali Danyal!" he shouts. "I bear greetings from Bijapur—this firman from Wali Khan, grand vizier of the sultana!" Tanaji lifts the parchment high and turns in a wide arc on his saddle, displaying it for all to see. "I will translate, sir: 'To our trusty servant Mohamed Sharif Ali Danyal, greetings!'" Tanaji continues, pretending to read. "'Know by this firman that we herewith return the custody of Singhaghad fort, its contents and environs, to its rightful master our trusty friend, Shivaji, *mandsab* of Poona, the son and heir of our General Commander Shahji. In token whereof we bestow on him this key of authority. Make haste to deliver up to him control as quickly as may be.'"

Now Shivaji lifts the ceremonial iron fort key high in his hand. If from this distance anyone can tell that the fort engraved upon its badge is not Singhaghad but Purandhar, his eyes are good indeed.

"Long live the sultana of Bijapur!" Tanaji shouts at the top of his lungs. "*Jai, jai* Bijapur!"

Shivaji's men lift their bows high above their heads and cheer behind him: "*Jai, jai* Bijapur!" Soon, as Shivaji hoped, the soldiers in the courtyard cheer as well. Ali Danyal's eyes are fixed on Shivaji.

After a few more cheers, Ali Danyal lifts his hand, and the soldiers stumble back to silence. "Come with me," he says. Shivaji dismounts, followed by Tanaji.

"No weapons," Ali Danyal says. He waits while they leave their swords outside the door. Before he heaves it shut, he orders his guards to stand away. "What is this shit, sir?" Ali Danyal says quietly, taking the firman. His lips are tight against his teeth.

For a moment, Tanaji is about to answer. But it's Shivaji's turn now, he thinks. He wants it—let him have it. He'll either end up a fool or a king. It's out of my hands.

Ali Danyal waves the firman at Shivaji. "What's this supposed to mean?"

"Read it and tell me."

"It's a fake! A forgery!" Shivaji says nothing. "Suppose I send to Bijapur for confirmation, eh?" Again Shivaji says nothing. So Ali Danyal tries another tack. "I thought we had a deal! One lakh hun! Are you going back on your word?"

"I stand by the deal, Ali Danyal."

"Do you? Haven't you forgotten a small detail? The gold?"

Shivaji turns coolly away, and starts a slow circuit of the commander's room. As Ali Danyal follows Shivaji's movement, Tanaji quietly takes a pair of blackened tiger claws from his pocket and threads the thin black blades between his fingers. When he drops his hand, only the black rings show—the blades of the *wagnak* are hidden by his fingers.

Shivaji stops at Danyal's desk. "I have not come empty-handed, Ali Danyal. On my horse and Tanaji's are twelve bags of gold: the lakh of hun. Take the gold, sir. Take the horses too if you wish."

This is the moment, Tanaji thinks. The gold is in the fort, ready for the taking. Does Ali Danyal shout for his guards—or does he take the gold and flee? His hand grips the *wagnak* tightly.

Ali Danyal walks toward Shivaji, no longer pretending to be civil. "What if I order you killed?" he asks.

"Do you think your soldiers would obey? We are emissaries of the sultana—you heard the cheers. Do you think they'd kill us now?"

Ali Danyal considers his situation. "Suppose I just kill you myself, and keep both the money and the fort?" His hand moves toward his dagger. Before his fingers even touch it Tanaji has slipped across the room. He places his left hand heavily on Ali Danyal's shoulder, and his right hand clenched, so the black *wagnak* blades protrude. Ali Danyal turns to see the points emerging like claws. He licks his lips.

"Ever seen these, commander?" Tanaji asks softly. "Very messy way to die. Nasty. Blood and shit everywhere. One of those ugly, painful deaths; a dirty wound that festers and leaks and smells. You don't want to die that way, commander. Trust me."

"Go ahead!" Ali Danyal spits out, defiantly. "You think you'd leave alive? My men would have their vengeance! Go ahead—test their loyalty."

"A lakh of hun will buy a lot of loyalty, commander," Tanaji answers, giving Ali Danyal's side a little jab.

"Death or gold, sir," Shivaji says softly. "Which shall it be?"

⊙⊙⊙⊙

Back in Purandhar, a boy steps to the mess hall door and clangs the dinner bell. From the rooftops, from the courtyards, the peasants from Poona stop working and stare hungrily as the Bijapuri soldiers amble toward the mess hall. Some of the peasants move hopefully toward their ladders.

"Back to work, you lot!" the sergeant calls out. The peasants stop. "You heard me . . . back to work!"

Some turn to Lakshman, uncertain. Lakshman swings down the ladder and looks the sergeant in the face. "We're hungry," Lakshman says. "A few vegetables, some chapatis . . . is that too much to ask?"

The sergeant looks almost pleased by Lakshman's discomfort. "Your hunger is not my concern," he declares. "Maybe later, after we're through. If anything is left." The glare of Lakshman's good eye, however, unnerves him. "There's usually something left," he mumbles as he turns away.

☙◍❧

"How long is this going to take?" Munna asks as he sits in Dadaji's room.

"Not long," Dadaji replies, opening a notebook and dipping a reed pen in a bottle of ink. "Your brothers have been most helpful."

"How will you make your choice, uncle?" the young man asks. "How will you know who is most deserving?"

"Shivaji will decide who most deserves the fort."

Munna eyes Dadaji suspiciously. Something in the old man's tone rings false. "I want to see my brothers. Take me to them!"

"Not until we're done." Dadaji's eyes have narrowed. "Or shall I tell my master that you no longer accept his judgment?"

A minute passes, maybe more, as Munna weighs his options. "Let's be fast, then, uncle," Munna says at last.

Dadaji nods and sets the pen to the paper. "Your full name?" Munna starts to talk, trying to ignore his unnamed fears, but as Dadaji writes and questions him, his agitation grows.

☙◍❧

Facing the mounted men of Poona, the soldiers of Singhaghad now stand in the courtyard in a long, straight line. With Ali Danyal at his side, Shivaji walks along the line of Bijapuris, giving some a nod, others a smile, here and there asking a question. Ali Danyal has a look of agitated impatience, as though he needs very much to take a shit.

Shivaji's doing what he's seen his father do a hundred times—grabbing the loyalty of a group of soldiers through the simple act of walking past them. When he reaches the line's end, Shivaji gives Ali Danyal a boost onto his saddle. "Go ahead and look," he tells him.

His fingers feel as thick as sausages as Ali Danyal fumbles with the ties of the saddlebag. He throws back the flap and sees inside six canvas sacks. Choosing one at random he tears at the opening, exposing a jumble of silk-wrapped cylinders. Thrusting his hand into the sack he feels for one—not the top one, that would be too easy, he reasons. He scrapes the silk wrapper. The afternoon sunlight just touches it; he sees the glint of gold.

Ali Danyal looks up almost in tears. "You're a rich man now, Ali Danyal." Shivaji turns to the line of soldiers. "Your commander goes in honor to Bijapur to receive the thanks of a grateful queen! Tomorrow, once the handover of the Lion Fort is completed, you shall go there, too. You'll find a special reward awaits you!" The soldiers of Singhaghad who have until now seemed tentative, once more start to cheer.

"*Jai, jai* Ali Danyal!" shouts Tanaji. "*Jai, jai* Ali Danyal!" the soldiers yell.

Ali Danyal turns his horse toward the gate, held open now by two of Shivaji's men. "I expect you'll shoot me as I leave," he whispers.

"When have I done a single thing that you expect?" Shivaji replies.

๑ิๆ๏ะ

All through dinner, the sergeant remembered that look on Lakshman's face, that single eye so full of rage. He finds himself fingering his medallion, something he does when he senses danger. Maybe he should just tell the cook to make a meal for the peasants. How hard would that be? Again he finds his hand toying with his gold medallion. What's wrong with me? Maybe I'll just see how things are going, he thinks. But when he steps through the door of the mess hall, the sergeant finds the two sentries trussed like captured wolves, whimpering through cloths stuffed into their mouths.

Above them stands Lakshman, an arrow notched in a short bow. All the peasants are there. All of them with bows drawn. They wear belts now, and from the belts hang swords and quivers full of arrows.

They hid the weapons in those bales of thatch, the sergeant realizes. As usual, too late.

Hopelessly, he stares into Lakshman's burning eye. Slowly he kneels. The arrow aimed at his heart quivers with the force of Lakshman's hand upon the bowstring. As the sergeant stretches prostrate, his gold medallion drops against the floor. Face in the dirt, hands curled upward inches from Lakshman's sandaled feet. "Mercy," the sergeant says. He lifts head to look into that horrid, pitiless eye. "Mercy. Mercy. Mercy."

Lakshman reaches for his knife.

☙☙☙☙

The three brothers cross the courtyard. Above them the moon glints behind a silver cloud. They've been awakened in the middle of the night, summoned urgently to Dadaji's room. "Something is wrong," Munna whispers.

"Show some courage!" says Ahmed. "Our fate is in the hands of Allah."

As they approach they see a figure striding from Dadaji's door; a fierce-looking peasant who glares at them with one relentless eye. He frightens them even more than the sight of Dadaji, wearing a formal robe and large white turban pinned with a jewel. In the middle of the night, what can be happening? Two guards slip behind them. Dadaji sits gravely before them, like a judge. "I deliver now Shivaji's judgment. He finds that none of you are worthy. The fort, therefore, is forfeit."

The brothers look at each other. "I don't understand!" Kurshid says.

Munna shouts, "I told you! I said we couldn't trust them!"

"Quiet!" Ahmed shouts. He has seen the guards touch their swords.

Dadaji lifts his chin for silence. "My master says he finds the lot of you despicable. Brother ready to murder brother . . . and for what? A clod of earth; a chip of rock. In his beneficence, my master offers you a choice. Stay and face the punishment your treachery deserves, or go back to Bijapur, to your own people, to be judged by them as they see fit." Dadaji's eyes move slowly from face to face. "Well? Which do you choose?"

"We choose neither," Ahmed says, sneering. "We shall return to Purandhar."

Dadaji shakes his head wearily. "Even now our men have captured it."

Ahmed begins to laugh. "The hell with you, uncle."

Dadaji turns and lifts something from a nearby table. He dangles it before Ahmed's eyes; a gold medallion spinning on a thick black thread still moist with blood. "Your men are dead, sir. You may join them if you wish. You have five minutes." Dadaji stands, but this time does not bow. "After that, I'll set the guards upon you."

Dadaji moves quietly to the door, ignoring the brothers' protests. His hand slips into the pocket where he carries the treasure Shivaji gave him. Four dark stones, one of them a clod of earth.

CHAPTER 17

ଶ୍ରୀ

"Why was I kept ignorant about the treasure at that fort?"

Whisper the *khaswajara* stands facing a muslin sheet hung from a cord, which hides the sultana of Bijapur. "If I might but see you, madam."

"When will you cease to vex me, *khaswajara*? No man shall see me," comes the sultana's voice from behind the curtain. "Answer my question."

How did she find out so fast? Whisper wonders. What goes on behind that curtain? Despite his bribes, despite his threats, none of her maids would say. Even the brat would tell him nothing. "You've heard, madam?"

"You think I am without resources? I am the sultan's mother and the sultan's widow. That was eunuch gold."

The words sting. Does she know, or only guess? "The Brotherhood may have had an interest, madam. We would be grateful to recover it."

"And why did you keep this secret from me?"

"I keep many secrets, madam. Many are secrets of yours, madam. Your son, the heir—"

"Enough!" Whisper hears the anger in the sultana's voice, and knows his hint has met the mark. "Tell me what you want me to do."

Leaning close to the muslin curtain, the *khaswajara* whispers his plan.

ଶ୍ରୀ

Has it only been three weeks since he arrived in Bijapur?

What a nice man Shaista Khan is, Bala thinks. He should have been lost in the labyrinth of the Bijapuri court without Shaista Khan's friendship.

And more: clothes, money; introductions; advice, intelligent and subtle, all given with offhand nonchalance, more like an uncle than a Mogul general.

Shaista Khan is welcomed everywhere. Odd, thinks Bala, for Bijapur seems terrified of the Moguls. The court flutters with news of Aurangzeb's campaign against Golconda. Rumors fly that when Golconda falls, Bijapur is next. And no one doubts that Golconda will fall. Maybe that's why Shaista Khan is received so well. He brings with him a hope of peace. He hints that Bijapur is safe; he suggests—through a tilt of his head, through a shrug—that he has secret assurances.

When Bala galloped into Bijapur, he had a purpose. He spoke well and defended his friends. After twenty days, however, no one seems to care about Shivaji. All the talk of attacking Torna appears to be forgotten. People seem to wonder why Bala is still around. Bala too has begun to wonder. He hasn't heard from Shivaji for days.

Suddenly his door bangs open. Shaista Khan strides in. "Get dressed," he commands. "I've just had word. Shivaji has been busy."

Shaista Khan leans on some cushions while Bala dresses. "It turns out that Torna had two lakh hun in its strong room." At the figure, Bala's wide mouth drops open. "The eunuchs were working some mischief, a big bribe probably. Who's on the take, how deep it goes, no one knows. It's a huge scandal. Afzul Khan executed the Torna captain last night, and that's just the start. No one knows where it's all going to end. Also, Shivaji has fortified an old stronghold at Bhatghar, the mountain next to Torna. Also, an entire Bijapuri garrison is on its way here from Singhaghad. Seems the commander took a bribe and handed the fort over to Shivaji. My guess is he's got a few of those missing huns. Also, Shivaji's men captured Purandhar fort yesterday. They may have massacred the entire garrison."

"I don't know what to say, sir," Bala says.

Shaista Khan eyes him, like a trainer looking over a colt at an auction. "No. It's clear you know nothing. All the more reason for you to leave." He turns and shakes his head. "I knew there was something about that Shivaji. Son of a bitch, he's good. Tell him that from me, do you hear?"

"Yes, sir. Thank you, sir."

"There's a horse for you outside. Ride for Poona and slam the gate behind you. I'll hold things together here for as long as I can."

Bala chews his lip. "I'm Shivaji's ambassador. I should plead his case."

"Ambassador? Shit." He softens. "Listen, Bala—at best you're a pawn. They'll hold you hostage. I don't know if that would make a difference to

Shivaji. In any case they'll torture you in their spare time. The Bijapuris are devils. Get out while you can."

"What do you think will happen next, sir?"

"Without you around to kill? They'll go after Shahji. But Shahji's tough, and smart—he'll figure something out. Then they'll come after Shiva-ji. He only has a little while to get ready."

The color drains from Bala's face. "A little while?"

"Maybe a fortnight, maybe a month. Depends on how much fight Shahji's got left. My guess is he'll ask to lead the attack on Shivaji."

Bala's mouth drops. "Attack his own son?"

"Right now his own son is single-handedly destroying Shahji's com-fortable position here at court. Now listen—as soon as you get to Poona send messages to the sultana. Eternal loyalty, it was all a big mistake, Shivaji loves Bijapur—you get the idea. Buy as much time as you can. Send copies to me. I'll do what I can to slow things down. They're still terrified of Aurangzeb—I can use that. Get going, Bala. You have no time to lose."

❧❧❧❧

Two days later, Bala sits in Shivaji's bedroom. "Massacred!" Shivaji whis-pers, incredulous. "Massacred a garrison? What a hideous thought!" Bala shrugs. "Do you think he was just making this up, Bala? Maybe he wanted you out of the way for some reason?"

"I don't think so, Shahu. He seemed convinced."

"That will all be cleared up soon enough," Dadaji says. "The Purand-har garrison should be in Bijapur in a few days."

"But what damage will be done in those few days, uncle," Bala says. "Shaista Khan says we have only two weeks."

Dadaji's eyebrows move against one another as though they are wrestling against the thoughts in his head. "Maybe it was me, Shahu."

Shahu seems stunned. "You would never . . ."

"Something slipped out when I spoke to those brothers. They might have misinterpreted . . . they were terrified. Perhaps they thought . . ."

Bala listens, incredulous. He wonders if Dadaji truly understands the damage he has done.

"There's something else I need to tell you, Shahu," Dadaji says, look-ing very ashamed. "There's been a mix-up in the strong room. We double-counted some of the money. Look for yourself!" he says, brandishing the account books.

"Let me see them, sir," says Balaji. His eyes widen as his finger runs down the page. "Dadaji, this isn't like you! You've carried the wrong balance here, and here, and here."

Dadaji lowers his head. "I resign. I'm making foolish errors, Shahu. Maybe I'm tired. Maybe I'm old. My mind's growing dim. Time I handed over my key, my books." He unties an iron key hanging on his neck, and hands it to Shivaji. "You're not without support, you know. Bala can take care of things. Don't get up. I'll say goodbye before I leave."

"Maybe I should go after him," says Balaji.

"Not this time." Shivaji seems serious, almost angry.

"It's a mistake anyone might make, Shahu."

Shivaji picks up the account book, which has fallen unnoticed from Balaji's lap, and hands it back to him. "How much do we have?"

"It may take me a while to figure it out exactly . . ."

"But you found three mistakes. What do those add up to?"

"Maybe sixty thousand rupees less than we thought."

"That means nothing to me, Bala. Not how many rupees . . . how much time?"

Balaji nods and leafs through the book. He stares at the invisible slate some more, frowns, looks in the book, frowns more. "Three weeks, Shahu. At current rates. There's a big payment due the Rajput masons in two weeks. If we can delay that payment, we have four weeks."

Shivaji sighs. "Three or four weeks? Is that all? I thought . . ." For a moment, Balaji thinks Shivaji is looking at him, but realizes that he's staring at a small altar on a nearby table. There's a small bronze image of Bhavani, another of Ganesha. "What shall we do, Bala? It's like we're burning money."

"What you're doing costs a lot. Bribes. Building. Salaries. Weapons."

"Yes. Weapons. We need cannon, Bala."

"There must be cannon at your forts, Shahu."

"Fixed cannon. Good for defense only."

"Maybe you can put wheels on them, Shahu."

Shivaji shakes his head. "Also we'll need to place cannon at Bhatghar once the fortifications are complete. We can cannibalize the other forts for a start, but it won't be enough if it comes to a war. Without cannon we're nothing, Bala. What is a wasp without a sting, eh?"

"Maybe there's another way, Shahu? Are cannon really that important?"

Shivaji winces. "Leave me, Bala. I need to think."

❦❦❦❦

In her small room near the temple, Maya rolls a lump of wet *mendhi* onto a stiff cloth. She folds the cloth tight around the *mendhi* to a form a flat package, and with a scissors snips off the corner.

Watching from the bed is Jyoti. She holds out her feet unnaturally, letting them dry. Already Maya has traced them, top and sole, intricate twisting lines. Where bits of the *mendhi* have dried and fallen from her foot, Jyoti's skin is stained dark orange. "You do this so beautifully," she says to Maya. "These Ori designs are so much prettier than Marathi designs."

"Now for your hands," Maya says. She presses the cloth envelope and squeezes from the cut-off corner a thin string of *mendhi* onto Jyoti's palm. Carefully she begins to draw another line, concentrating hard.

"Do you really think this is a good idea?" Jyoti says.

"Shivaji likes you, and Hanuman is his friend. He will not disappoint you."

"The *mendhi*, I mean."

Maya looks up. "It's too late now! Besides, you saw it in a dream. It must be right!" She sets back to work.

Jyoti looks at her pretty hands, worrying over them. "But this is what brides do . . ."

"And the friends of brides, and their families. Don't you want to be Hanuman's bride?" Maya looks into Jyoti's face. How bright she looks, Maya thinks, how frightened. "If it is to be, it is to be. So why worry?"

"Do you really think there is a husband meant for me?" Jyoti asks.

"Hanuman, you mean?" Maya laughs. "You know he loves you."

"What has marriage to do with love? I have no parents, no dowry . . ."

Maya stops. Careful not to disturb the *mendhi* on Jyoti's hands, Maya puts a slender arm around her shoulder.

"I suppose it makes no difference. It will be or not be." Jyoti leans her head against Maya's. "Do you ever dream of a husband, Maya?"

"I've had enough of men."

"A husband would be different though! A home together! Suppers. Children. Bed." Jyoti's voice trails off. "Maybe Shivaji . . ."

"Let's speak of something else," Maya says quietly.

❦❦❦❦

On the peaceful verandah of his house in Kari, Jedhe sits amidst a symphony of tiny gold objects, his implements and containers for making pan.

He moves slowly, every gesture careful and meticulous. For what else does Jedhe have to occupy his time? Today at least, Bandal is here. He arrived at Kari in a breathless gallop. Bandal had brought news of Shivaji. Their cousin now has taken three forts from Bijapur. Three forts!

Jedhe shakes his head. He had never guessed his cousin would be so daring. It pleases him to think of what Shivaji has done. Jedhe imagines that he too might be capable of daring acts, if only his father would allow him!

"Are you thinking about joining him, cousin?" Jedhe later asks Bandal. "Despite my father's advice, I mean."

Bandal shrugs. He and Jedhe are close in age, but he seems so much older ... quiet, cynical. "Your father's a wise man, Jedhe. He has advised me well. While my father was dying, he told me to seek your father's counsel."

"You didn't really need to come all this way. His advice never changes: Do nothing. Hold tight. Be sensible. Think twice." Bandal laughs, for Jedhe has captured even Tukoji's frown as he intones his clichés.

"You're not giving your father enough credit, Jedhe. This is big—big enough to cause a war."

"Yes, war, or worse." It is Tukoji himself, come to join them. As he sits beside Bandal, Jedhe hands him a bright green packet of pan. "But maybe war can be avoided. Maybe even some good can come from this misfortune."

"I don't see that it's a misfortune, father," Jedhe starts to say.

"Sometimes the path of dharma is hard, Bandal," Tukoji says, ignoring his son. "I think maybe now is such a time. Our hard path is clear. We must ride against our cousin Shivaji."

"Is there no other way?" asks Bandal.

"He's only a cousin, my dear boy. Why, you scarcely know him ... it's not such a terrible thing, is it? Assign your men to my command. I will lead them down to Poona. I don't think we'll find too much resistance."

"I've heard that Shivaji is assembling his army."

"If that's true, all the more reason to move quickly."

But Bandal's eyebrows knit together. "It's not just Shivaji. We'll have to go against Iron as well, won't we?" Bandal lowers his head. "I like Iron."

"Everyone likes Iron, lad. But when he sees us marching on Poona, he'll do his sums and join us."

"We should be joining Shahu, not moving against him!" interrupts Jedhe. "Why should we be whores for Bijapur? What has Bijapur ever done for us?"

"They've made us rich," Tukoji says with dark finality. "Where do you think your wealth comes from?"

"Then let's be poor. Poor and free. What's wrong with that?"

Tukoji rises to his feet and towers over Jedhe. "I'm glad your mother isn't alive to hear. You don't know what it was like before the truce, before the traitor Shahji surrendered. War everywhere. Famine, drought. Babies dying, widows wailing. Join Shivaji and you'll bring it all back. You want the blood of children on your hands?"

"Better to die fighting, father," Jedhe answers quietly. "What are we to Bijapur? They take almost half of everything we produce."

"They give back, fool. You've done quite well on what they give back!" Tukoji turns to Bandal, waving a finger. "And if we work together, much more will be given back. If the traitor Shahji proved anything, it's that Bijapur pays for loyalty—they pay bloody well." With that he storms off.

"Well," says Jedhe after a while, "that was pleasant."

"Do you have a different idea?" Bandal asks after a long silence. "Maybe you'll find me ready to listen."

☙ ☙ ☙ ☙

"But isn't he coming back, father?" Sambhuji tugs at Shivaji's hand, trying to get his attention, for Shivaji's eyes are focused in the distance. "Father!"

"Probably not," Sai Bai answers, seeing Shivaji's empty stare. "Trust Dadaji to pick the least convenient moment."

Despite the noonday sun and the cloudless sky—for the rains have finished very early this year—the air is cool in the courtyard. At last, his door creaks open, and Dadaji emerges one last time from his room. He clutches his bare chest as the breeze chills him, and shuffles in his bare feet toward the gates where Shivaji and the others wait. His soft belly hangs over the small lungi wrapped around his loins. The rest of his body is thin, almost emaciated, and the skin droops like old parchment from his slender frame. He has shaved his head. Now walking awkwardly in bare feet on the rough ground, he looks like an ungainly naked bird.

Sambhuji runs to him laughing, and Dadaji seems flustered until at last he laughs too, and takes Sambhuji's hand. "Well, isn't this a good joke, Sam," Dadaji says, as Sambhuji leads him toward his parents. There Dadaji lowers his head. "An old man's last foolishness. Wish me well, my dear boy."

Shivaji wraps his long arms around the old man, and he holds him there a long time, his face pressed into Dadaji's neck.

"You know, I had a thought as I was getting ready, Shahu . . ." Tears pool up in Dadaji's eyes. "I couldn't bear to see what's coming next. I couldn't bear to see you war against your father."

"The gods grant it does not come to that, uncle."

"But it will, won't it, Shahu? How can you avoid it? It is the nature of war: father against son, brother against brother. But I don't need to see it. I've already seen too much." He presses a hand to Shivaji's cheek. "But Shahu, think, think, think when you do it. Think of Sambhuji here. Think what it would be like for him to draw his sword against you, or you against him. You've hardly seen him, still Shahji is your father. Remember that!"

At this Jijabai sniffs impatiently. Dadaji turns to her. "What good is a life built on scorn?"

"You dare ask me this?" she replies, lifting her head imperiously.

"And why not? What difference does it make to either of us now? Your life is empty, Jijabai, more than mine. You should follow my example."

She shakes her head. "I don't walk away so easily. I keep my promises."

Dadaji seems about to answer, then shrugs. He shuffles over to Balaji, who falls to his knees and presses his head to the old man's bare feet. "I have no heir, Bala. I leave everything to you."

"You do me too much honor, Dadaji," Bala says.

"It isn't much," Dadaji laughs. "I've left you some notes." He pats Bala's round bald head, and then his own, now newly shaved. "Two bald men, eh? Take care of Shahu, Bala. Don't let him get into too much trouble."

"Where will you go, uncle? Will you head straight for Kashi?" Shivaji asks, raising himself to his knees.

"Not Kashi right away, not the city of the dead right away. Later, Shahu. Please don't rush me. First Nasik, I think. Yes, Nasik first." Dadaji steps to the gateway and raises his hands above his head. *"Namaste!"* he calls and *"Namaste!"* everyone replies. Then he lowers himself awkwardly to the moist, cold ground, and begins: for he intends to be a rolling pilgrim, to make his way by rolling from his back to his stomach, from his stomach to his back.

By the time he reaches the gates, his old body is already thick with dust.

☙ ☙ ❧ ❧

Lakshman rides into the jungle, following the sound of singing.

He follows a stranger who has not told his name. The man had appeared in Poona that morning as if from nowhere.

The stranger knew Lakshman, though. He'd come on an errand, he said: his master had an offer for Shivaji—a plan to give Shivaji "total victory." But his master would negotiate only with Lakshman, and only at his own place.

Lakshman might have walked away. He might have picked a fight. But something about the stranger, the way his eyes sparkled, a hint of mystery in his voice, tempted Lakshman's soul. Two hours later, the sounds of the jungle crowd around him, the shrieks of unknown beasts and the rustle of the great trees. And the stranger's singing, which caresses Lakshman's heart.

Even though the stranger sings of Kali, the black destroyer.

Kali, of course, had terrified Lakshman as a child: a gaunt, dark horror, her eyes huge and burning, a bloodstained tongue hanging like a pennant from her gaping mouth. Weapons she held in each of her eight flailing arms: no sign of peace, no boons did she offer. She wore a necklace of human skulls, and a skirt of human arms.

But the stranger sings of Kali's beauty: the kindness of those gaping eyes, the sweetness of that dangling tongue. In his song, the stranger calls her "Mommy." And even though he can't reconcile the horror of his childhood nightmares with the gentle goddess mommy of the rider's song, Lakshman finds tears flowing down his cheek.

By that song, Lakshman can guess their destination. His guide, he guessed from the start, was a brigand. His song to Kali leaves no doubt.

Kalidas. The singer's master is the worst of thieves: violent, senseless, terrifying. Everyone fears his name. Torture, rape, death—for Kalidas, no act is too depraved. What can Kalidas want with him, or with Shivaji?

ଓଓଓଓ

At last they come to a clearing full of strange huts. Forest creepers thread through their walls and roofs, so the huts look like plants that have somehow grown into houses. There's a big fire where a goat is being cooked upon a spit.

Lakshman sees eight or nine men sitting around idly, and maybe a dozen women or more, all of them young and strikingly beautiful, preparing food, hanging laundry, cleaning pots and dishes, all of them smiling, some of them singing. The men look content, almost smug, eyeing the women as they pass, sometimes reaching out to grab a bottom or a breast. The women giggle and scold them, eyes flashing. Everyone, men and women alike, dresses in extravagant finery: rich silks, necklaces and rings, bright jungle flowers. It's like a dream, thinks Lakshman.

"Do you want some toddy?" one of them asks, and before Lakshman can answer, a jeweled cup is thrust into his hand. He takes a long drink: the liquid is sweet and fiery and he chokes and coughs as the men around him laugh.

Suddenly, though, they stop laughing and step away. A man walks toward Lakshman, dressed all in black—no flowers, no jewels, with bushy hair and a black beard, and large dark eyes that seem hot as fire.

"I am Kalidas," the man says. He looks calmly, almost affectionately, at Lakshman. Since his eye was injured, a straight look is a rarity. Neither he nor Lakshman bows. "Welcome to my humble place."

"I came not for my sake, but Shivaji's," Lakshman answers.

"He can wait. Are you hungry? Thirsty? Fancy a woman?"

Lakshman tries to shrug nonchalantly, but the great black eyes of Kalidas burn through his skin. "No," he manages to say.

"Fresh clothing," Kalidas orders. Two women drop their chores, bringing robes and sandals, jewelry and flowers. Kneeling at Lakshman's feet. The women gently peel away his cotton garments, taking even his lungi.

The women hum as they work. They wrap him in silk. He feels the smoothness of their hands against him, the flutter of their breath against his skin. The rich cloth rests heavily against him, rustling when he moves.

"This suits you," says Kalidas when the job is done. "I have some business. Rest for a while. Then we shall talk." Kalidas then walks into the jungle; his men and women following silently behind, leaving Lakshman alone. The sky grows pale as the sun sets. Lakshman waits in his strange new garments. Loneliness begins to eat at him. He's faced with a dilemma: stay here alone, or follow the others into the deep forbidding darkness.

He hopes the light will last long enough for him to follow the path. As he walks into the trees, his nostrils are filled with jungle smell; green and wet, a rotting lingering sweetness that grows stronger with each breath. Far off, he hears chanting. And another sound, now growing stronger and more clear, a buzzing, a great and endless drone. With every step that drone grows stronger, punctuated by deep drumbeats like the beating of the jungle's heart. He doesn't need to see his way, he can follow his ears.

The path bends and he sees them, huddled in a semicircle before a huge fat man who stands in an enormous swirling cloud of smoke. They chant and wave a tray of lights and incense. The droning and booming grow louder.

But the firelight surges and he sees that he is wrong. It isn't a cloud of smoke at all. It's flies. Millions of flies. That's the drone: Flies so thick that he can hardly see the man standing in their midst. How can he stand so still, in all those buzzing flies? Of course, it's not a man; it's a statue.

Kali.

A huge painted *murti* of a black-skinned, wild-eyed goddess, a long red tongue hanging from her mouth.

She wears around her neck, not skulls, but real heads: human heads, strung together through the ears, dripping and festering with rot. Around her waist, a skirt of arms, real arms: different sizes, different shapes—the thick arms of workmen, the slender arms of young wives—and some of them, Lakshman realizes, the tiny arms of babies.

As Lakshman gapes in horror, the idol's eyes begin to move, turning slowly in their sockets.

It can't be, he thinks, you're just a statue.

At last she finds him where he tries to hide, and then Kali looks at him, and around her dangling tongue her stone face smiles.

ℭ☺ℭ☺

"It's no good, Jedhe," Bandal says. "Your father will not budge."

"I told you he would not, cousin. My father may be a fool, but I guarantee he is a stubborn fool."

"Can you blame him for his stubbornness? He struggled hard to achieve his current status. He's a Bijapuri *mandsab* of four thousand horse! You think he's ready to give it up on your whim?"

"It's not a whim!" Jedhe's usual look of calm amusement is gone, replaced by a fierceness that Bandal has never seen before. "It's what's right."

"You're a fool," Bandal mutters. Jedhe shrugs, his eyes burning. "Well," Bandal says at last, a small smile on the corners of his lips, "we'll be fools together."

ℭ☺ℭ☺

Stars are beginning to glimmer in the skies over Poona. Sai Bai carries a tiny lantern against the coming night, more for comfort than light. In any case she knows the way.

At the entrance of the Shiva cave, she can see within the dim flame burning in the lamp above the tiny shivalingam. If he's anywhere, she thinks, he'll be here. But it saddens her that she might find him here, for she knows this is the place he comes in times of greatest tribulation. He's doing his best, she scolds the gods, so why is everything so hard for him! She sees Shivaji from behind, sitting in the dark, his turban gone and his long hair falling softly on his shoulders. As she moves in front of him, however, she gapes. Shivaji has ripped his shirtfront from neck to navel. He holds in his hand a shining knife, the tip pointing to his heart.

"No!"

He sees her but he does not move. At last his eyes flicker—from the blade to his wife's pale face. Finally he sets down the knife and lifts his eyes to Sai Bai. "At least we first shall say goodbye. I was sad that I did not say goodbye to you, my wife. That was the part I most regretted."

At last she finds her tongue. "What are you thinking? Do you really mean to die here?"

"We all must die, my darling," he says. "It will be best for everyone."

"No!" Sai Bai answers, twisting away. "The god of death alone knows when to pluck your soul. It is Yama's choice to make, not yours."

"I will not be his slave, but my own master," Shivaji replies. "I need no permission. It is a warrior's privilege. Tell me goodbye and leave me."

A silence passes agonizingly between them. "Tell me why, husband, and I will leave. Otherwise I'll do everything I can to stop you. Is it something I have done?"

"No!" Shivaji shouts and the sound echoes from the walls. He has to look away from her before he can speak. "I've made a mess of things. I can feel the hands of the gods about to crush us. I've angered them by my pride."

"But those stones!" Sai Bai protests.

Shivaji lifts his hands to silence her. "Four stones placed in my hand by a madman and look what I do! In a few days, Bijapur will fall upon us like a thunderbolt!" He counts the problems on his fingers: "No cannon. No army—a few farmers, maybe, men whose fathers went to war, but no army! No money—that's right, the money's all but gone! What am I to do, Sai Bai, what am I to do?" Now she cannot stop from throwing her arms around his shoulders, from pressing her face against his cheek.

"Is this the man I love, the husband I married, the father of my children? If you have a warrior's privilege, then you have a warrior's duty, husband! Why are you afraid?"

He lifts his head, each word an agony. "I can't send men to die."

"Is that all?"

"It's enough," he answers. A light seems to flash between them, like a flash of lightning. She squeezes her eyes tight, but sees an echo of that flash behind her eyelids. In it, she sees faces: men that she has never seen. Dozens, then hundreds, then thousands, each face a shrieking mask of agony and pain. "Make it stop!" she cries at last, grabbing Shivaji's hands. "What have you done to me? Make it stop!"

Shivaji whispers: "You see now what I see—every moment. Does this course now seem so bad?" He lifts his knife.

"It's not your choice, husband. Everyone must die. So what if some may choose to die for you! Let them choose! Let them act as warriors, too. Let them follow you, to death if they choose!"

Taking his face between her small hands, she looks into his eyes. "And who are you to say that they will die? Why in a month, a week, a day, all may be changed! Maybe a devi will shower us with gold." Shivaji snorts. "Oh, you laugh at me," Sai Bai pouts. "I'm just a foolish woman! But look, you: Who would have said that today you would hold four forts? Who could guess an army would be at your gates, awaiting your command? Who? Things change, husband. Do not take this coward's blade! If you claim the warrior's privilege, take the duty, too! Stand firm! Be brave!"

He stares into her trusting, gentle face, her face that has no doubt of him at all. "You called me the father of your *children*," he says softly.

"Did I?" She looks away, brushing back a hair that has fallen out of place. The lamplight flickers around them like dancing stars. "Silly of me." He waits for her to speak. "Maybe . . .", she says, and she sees at last that smile of his, the one she longs to see.

"Don't you know?"

"It's early, but . . . Well, I'm woozy every morning, and you have been . . . vigorous." Her voice falters, but her face tells him everything. He lifts her hands to his lips. When they walk back, Shivaji presses her close, his long arm tight around her shoulder.

⊖⊖⊖⊖

"She liked you." Kalidas, chewing on the haunch of a roast goat, lifts a heavy black eyebrow to Lakshman.

"Who?" Maybe from the wine, maybe from the vision of Kali, Lakshman's brain floats in a kind of dream. The thief's hut is furnished like a palace—Persian carpets scattered everywhere, pillows of brocade.

"She has taught me everything," Kalidas says, his voice rich but raw. "I made myself her slave—her child—fifteen years ago. And I had been a good Muslim up till then—said my prayers each day, right up until the day Mommy looked at me." His face grows serious. "She said she'd give me anything I desired. And she has."

He's mad, thinks Lakshman. But he's fascinated by the heavy, dark energy that hovers around Kalidas. "You live well, sir," Lakshman says, nodding at the beautiful furnishings.

Kalidas turns on him. "What you see here is shit. Anyone may get such trash. One has only to reach into the privy. I'm talking about one's true desires, sir. The thoughts a weak man dare not even name."

Lakshman feels clammy. There's a ringing in his ears. Suddenly his mind leaps back in time: He's back at Torna, the cold edge of the serpent knife slicing across his eye, the rain pouring across the bleeding socket. He looks up to see Kalidas. "Yes," the dark voice says. "Yes, thoughts like that."

Lakshman shivers. "That's not a desire!"

"Isn't it?" The question lingers in the air like smoke. Kalidas frowns, and then as if struck by inspiration he claps, and a young servant girl enters, twirling gracefully through the door. "This is Amba," Kalidas says to Lakshman. Then he nods, indicating Lakshman. Instantly Amba falls to her knees before Lakshman, and tugs the drawstring of Lakshman's pants. "Amba is a *houri*," Kalidas whispers, as though explaining to a child. "She's an angel made in paradise for the pleasure of the blessed. You didn't truly think that she was real? She is but Mommy's shadow."

Lakshman finds himself growing stiff, and he tries to hide it. His eyes are glued to Amba's. Suddenly his pants are around his ankles, and he feels her lips upon him, her sliding, wriggling tongue, the moist darkness of her mouth. A deep droning burns in Lakshman's ears; his heart is pounding like a beating drum. "What are you doing to me?" he cries out.

Amba sucks at his lingam as though it were the source of all desire. She fondles her heavy breasts as she works, her face glowing, and always her wild eyes on Lakshman. Kalidas chuckles. "To Mommy it is nothing. To have a woman do whatever you bid, no matter how depraved. To her it is a trifle." But Lakshman now is past the point of speech. "Ahhh," Kalidas sighs as he looks at Lakshman's face. "Yes, Lakshman. Mommy says yes: it can be any woman you desire." As Kalidas says this, Amba's face begins to change. Even as she rubs her wet cheek against his length, Amba's eyes grow lighter, flecked with gold, and her nose grows small and straight; her brown lips shine like bloodred rubies; her breasts grow smaller and more shapely; the hands that fondle them grow delicate and small.

"Maya . . .", Lakshman gasps, his voice constricted.

"Even her," Kalidas whispers. Maya clutches the shaft with both fine hands to her bare breasts, glorying in it, moaning. And all the while Maya's gold-flecked eyes still bore into Lakshman's face.

"Leave us," Kalidas says casually. Maya stands—but, no, now she's turned back into Amba as she was before. Amba stands, pulling her sari clumsily around her as she leaves, still smiling over her shoulder at Lakshman.

"Don't be upset you didn't finish," Kalidas chuckles. "You can have that nautch girl anytime, brother."

"Why are you doing this to me!" Lakshman cries as he struggles back into his pants.

"Have you not yet understood? We have a pact, Mommy and I. She gives me anything I desire . . . I give her anything she asks for."

"What has she asked for now?" says Lakshman. He feels like his whole world is spinning out of control.

"You."

Lakshman closes his eyes when he hears the word; he feels himself sliding into blackness. "And if I say no?"

"Hell, say whatever you like. What you say to her is your look-to, not mine. Mommy just likes you, that's all. She wants you to be her little boy. But I have brought you here for a different reason."

"What reason was that?"

"A secret." He runs his hands through his thick hair, looking very serious. "I talked with Mommy—I told her I was tired of running, tired of robbing and killing. I told her my desire was peace." Kalidas laughs, his voice rich and harsh. "I have a secret. Tell Shivaji. I have a secret that can bring him victory. If Shivaji will guarantee me peace, I'll tell it to him."

☙☙☙☙

Crickets and night birds. And the sound of footsteps. "Who's there?" the young sentry whispers into the darkness.

"Just me." Jedhe moves into the dim light. "Why aren't you asleep?"

"I'm to watch all night, sir. I can't go to sleep."

"Can't you? Thought it was part of the job! You're the first sentry who has stayed up this late."

"Oh, you're joking again sir," the sentry laughs. But his head jerks up. "Who's that with you, sir?" he asks, grasping his lance tightly again.

"It's just my cousin Bandal. We've come to see my father."

"He gave strict orders, sir, not to be disturbed . . ."

Jedhe pats him on the shoulder. "Family business, you understand. Be a good lad and stand away from the door."

Bandal takes the sentry's arm and whispers. "We've got some bad news. He'd be embarrassed if one of his soldiers were to hear him cry. A favorite uncle. Very old. It's been expected, but . . ."

"I understand, sir. I'll stand here where I won't hear a thing."

"That's the boy." Bandal steps back to Jedhe, near the door. "Keep an eye on the horses."

With Bandal beside him, Jedhe pushes the door open gently, and the two of them duck inside. Tukoji huddles in the covers, his snores filling the room. "I'm scared," Bandal whispers into Jedhe's ear.

"It's not dangerous," Jedhe whispers back.

"Maybe. But it's sinful."

"Shall I do this alone?"

Silence for a moment. "No, I'm with you," Bandal whispers.

Jedhe kneels by his father's head. With a start, Tukoji bursts upright, his hooded eyes opening so wide the whites glisten in the lamplight. "What! Who's there?"

"Only us, father," Jedhe whispers. One hand slips into his pocket while the other grasps his father's shoulder.

"Jedhe," sighs Tukoji. "Why are you here? It's the middle of the night!"

"We think you need a change of scene, father. Some fresh mountain air will do you good."

Tukoji is fully awake now. "Why would I be going anywhere?"

Jedhe lifts his hand from his pocket. Tukoji sees the iron rings; he doesn't need to see the blades. "Bandal is placing his fort under Shivaji's control. And we're joining him. We're giving Shivaji our fort—Kari fort, I mean."

Tukoji's face goes blank. He looks to Bandal, who shrugs. "It was Jedhe's idea, uncle," Bandal says weakly.

"The idea is worthless." Tukoji struggles to collect his wits. He looks at his son. "Kari isn't yours to give." Jedhe shrugs and glances at his hand, flexing the fingers just a little, just enough to expose the short, harsh blades between them. Tukoji pulls back. "You can't. I'm your father, damn it!"

Now Jedhe closes his fingers tight, and the bright edges of the *wagnak* glisten in the lamplight. "Being your son has very little to recommend it, father. I suppose some boy somewhere might have enjoyed all your insults. I've grown weary of them, frankly." The hand holding the *wagnak* moves slowly, until its points press against Tukoji's side. Around his shoulder, Jedhe's arm pulls Tukoji toward him. "It's ending, father: now, tonight. I don't much care how. Come with us, or stay here and bleed your guts out. It's all one to me."

"I don't know you," Tukoji whispers, his eyes wide with horror.

"Yes, you do, father. I'm your son. Remember me?"

Bandal hands Tukoji his cloak and a pair of sandals. Watching Jedhe all the while, Tukoji puts them on. "We'll take you to Hirdas, sir. It's not such a bad place," Bandal whispers to him while he dresses. "My father built a summer house there for my mother."

"You see, father? Nice and cool." Jedhe hikes his father to his feet. "Perfect for you." Bandal wraps Tukoji's wrists behind him with a leather thong. Together then the three of them walk through the door. Jedhe keeps one arm on Tukoji's shoulder as though holding him up. Horses are saddled nearby.

The young sentry steps forward, his pale face shining in the darkness. "Do you need some help?" The sentry can see Tukoji trying to catch his attention. The young man glances from face to face, and shakes his head. "I know it's hard, sir, but there's nothing to be done. In time it won't be so bad."

"He knows?" Tukoji asks, incredulous. Bandal shrugs. "Worthless scum!" Tukoji spits out. "Traitor!"

"He's upset," Jedhe whispers to the sentry as they guide Tukoji toward his horse. "Pay no attention. See me when I return . . . I'll show my gratitude for your loyalty."

"Yes, sir," he replies. He watches as they struggle to help Tukoji onto the saddle . . . the old man's grief seems so severe, he can hardly use his hands.

CHAPTER 18

Imbeciles! Fools!

Shaista Khan watches the chaos as the Bijapuri court explodes once again into shouts of recrimination. It's been like this for more than an hour, ever since Wali Khan, the grand vizier, finally acknowledged—after two days of rumors—that Shivaji had captured Singhaghad and Purandhar.

It's just the same as Agra, Shaista Khan thinks bitterly. Just as puffed up, just as useless. But Agra, at least, is quieter. No one shouts in Agra.

Shaista Khan knows why he's been sent to Bijapur. At home, in Agra, he's dangerous. Emperor Shah Jahan needs to put him somewhere safe: away from Agra; away from Aurangzeb—for the two of them together are like gunpowder and fire. Away from Roshanara—for in Agra gossip is like money; and a hint of their affair would be pure gold.

So where to send dangerous old Shaista Khan? Where else but Bijapur?

Odd, reflects Shaista Khan, that the man I most admire in Bijapur is one I've never spoken to. He looks across the churning mob. Only one other man merely watches from the side. General Shahji, he thinks, what an ally you might have been. If only you had chosen us instead of Bijapur.

Shahji had accomplished much, Shaista Khan thinks. He'd taken a couple of dozen forts. He might have made himself a little kingdom—if his army hadn't fallen to pieces, feuding with itself; if the sultan of Bijapur himself hadn't made Shahji an astonishing offer: riches, a new wife, a place at court, command of all the Bijapuri armies. This even while Shahji's own troops were pointing their lances at each other.

I don't blame him for that decision, Shaista Khan thinks. Any man would have done the same. Honor only gets you so far.

Maybe I should speak with him, Shaista Khan thinks. Maybe I should tell Shahji of my admiration. And my admiration for his son. Maybe I could make Shahji our ally. Even Aurangzeb hadn't managed that.

ᕦᕤᕦᕤ

"Please, hurry, madam. It's getting very unpleasant out there."

Yet again, Whisper faces the white, unwrinkled sheet that hangs like a curtain at the sultana's door. How long has he stood there this time? Many maids sweep past him, looking at him—mocking him, he thinks—as they slip behind the white sheet into the place where he may not go. Not even he, the *khaswajara*!

"Madam, I beg you, hurry!"

"I will eat," comes her voice, as if from far away.

But this is no time for eating! Whisper thinks. Sure enough, now come the serving girls: first some with salvers of water for cleansing the mouth and hands; then others carrying dishes from the kitchen wrapped in red cloth and white, all bearing the seal of the royal taster. The girls cover their noses with kerchiefs lest they even breathe upon her food. Behind the curtain, Whisper has no doubt, some other trusted servant tastes it one more time before the sultana eats. If only he could find out who!

"They will not wait much longer, madam!"

"You fret too much, *khaswajara*. They can do nothing without me. You only worry that you'll miss the fun."

At last comes the serving girl bearing *besan* flour. The meal must be over, Whisper thinks, it must be over now! She'll rub her hands in flour to clean them, she'll dip her hands in water, and then at last we'll go.

"I'm dressing now, *khaswajara*," the voice says. He knows she says it only to frustrate him.

"But we must hurry, madam. It is a crisis!"

"It is always a crisis." Another line of maids parades past. These carry silver trays, each with some new adornment: a blouse and slip of lightest gauze, a skirt and overblouse of ivory silk shot through with gold. An overskirt embroidered with a thousand tiny roses. Then jewels: jewels for the ears and nose, jewels for the hair, jewels for the wrist and fingers, jewels for the ankles and toes. A miniature jeweled dagger in a diamond sheath. Jeweled slippers, tiny as a doll's. A mirror ring to slip upon her thumb. Clothes no one will ever see.

Then, carried by two maids, a tray heaped high with velvet cloth, a poison green.

Why even bother with the rest, thinks Whisper. "You must hurry, madam!" But she does not answer. His scarecrow foot taps the marble floor.

At last she comes, like a tent of green silk. She lifts her covered hand to him. He must extend his arm to reach it—her velvet skirts keep him far away. The cloth tugs the floor as she sweeps across the courtyard. He can feel her fingers, small as a child's, but the cloth drapes her hand so he cannot see. Whisper glances at her eyes, buried in the shadows of her veils. Are they angry? Worried? Whisper cannot tell.

The sun streams through the harem courtyard setting the fountains glittering. Laughter echoes from the marble walls: children playing before harem school begins. She does not turn.

He steals another look—does she enjoy their laughter? Resent it? Her hidden eyes give him no clue, and she lets no other part be seen. In silence they sweep past. Former wives and nautch girls bow. He nods in reply; the sultana makes no sign. "How fragile is this paradise, madam," Whisper breathes. "We are only beggars on this earth."

As she struggles up the steps of the main palace, she truly grips his hand. How heavy those robes must be!

They pass through the harem gateway, into the world of men. A dozen guards appear to march on either side of her. Across the palace courtyard stands a massive, guarded door. Even closed they can hear the shouts within. Footmen swing the door at their approach, and the tumult floods out.

The herald strides from the door to the center of the hall. Gongs and drums and trumpets clamor in a deafening blare. With the fading of their echo, the hall grows silent.

Whisper enters first, for she is so formidable in her elaborate costume that she must come through the door alone. But he feels her fingers tighten around his hand, and looks back.

For an instant he sees them, her eyes: anxious, frightened, terrified. For just a moment he sees the court through her eyes: a hundred angry, greedy men; each twice her size; not one of them her ally. For a moment, he understands.

Even so, he leads her to the dais, to the silver throne. He leads her there, and then he walks away.

She has her fate, Whisper thinks, as do we all.

⊖⊙⊖⊙

With Afzul Khan in the lead, the angry nobles of Bijapur stride to the silver-railed dais of the sultana. Bolstered by the men around him, trying to appear as if he comes reluctantly, Afzul Khan steps forward to face the veiled queen of Bijapur. The attendants with their horsehair whisks have withdrawn to the shadows; only Wali Khan, the vizier, and Whisper, her *khaswajara* have the courage to stand by her.

"It is time to face facts, your highness," Afzul Khan shouts. "How can you allow your armies to be led by a traitor?" His followers begins to shout and shake their fists. Wali Khan glances helplessly to General Shahji, as if imploring him to speak on his own behalf, but the general only stares away.

Whisper looks into Afzul Khan's brutal, bloated face. "What are you suggesting, lord?" The eunuch's voice is barely audible. A few of the mob now wave their hands for silence.

Afzul Khan approaches, towering over him. "Of course it's obvious, *khaswajara*. But it's not up to me to say." He fixes his fierce eyes on Whisper, but the eunuch stares back unperturbed. In time Afzul Khan snorts and turns away.

But the mob notices; for they want to end up on the winning side, and Afzul Khan, for all his bluster, still stands outside of the silver rail. Whisper, on the other hand, has stood inside that railing longer even than the sultana. "You're right, lord," Whisper agrees. "It isn't up to you. Do you suggest that Shahji be accountable for the actions of his son?"

With the uncertain look of a bear being led toward a trap, Afzul Khan frowns.

"Don't try to confuse him, Whisper. It's too easy." The voice is muffled, coming from behind the dark veil of the sultana. Whisper bows and moves back to the sultana's side.

"General Shahji!" the sultana's muffled voice calls. "I ask you: If I order you to attack Shivaji and retake the forts that he has stolen, will you do it?"

"Yes, madam," Shahji answers firmly. "I'll do my duty, and if it is the will of the gods, I shall return victorious. But madam, I am your military adviser as well, and I therefore recommend against this course."

To this the nobility responds with sounds of exasperation, some pleading directly to the sultana to be allowed to speak. Wali Khan bangs his baton on the floor, demanding order. "I would suggest, madam, that a battle between the forces of a father and son must invariably be a source of ruin.

Both armies will become dispirited and desperate, the action horrible, the resolution without honor."

"So you recommend what, general? That we abandon all these forts to your son?"

"No, madam. I recommend that you replace me as your commander."

At first unprepared, the nobles realize what Shahji has said. They begin to applaud, then to cheer. "Afzul! Afzul!" someone yells, and soon everyone is shouting.

"Silence!" Wali Khan pounds the floor with his staff until they stop.

"If not you, General Shahji, whom would you recommend as the queen's commander? Who can save us from the threat of Shivaji?" Wali Khan asks.

"Shivaji is a small threat. Bijapur's greater threat comes from the east. Compared to the eastern threat, Shivaji is a nuisance, nothing more. If steps had been taken earlier, as I suggested, things might be different. As it is, we must now defend both borders, east and west."

"Surely you don't think, general," says Shaista Khan, stepping forward with a sweep of his cloak, "that the Mogul is your enemy?" Wali Khan nods gravely to Shaista Khan, and raises a questioning eyebrow to Shahji. One might think that he was smiling.

"I never said so, Lord Ambassador," Shahji replies. "But let me ask you, as one soldier to another . . . where is Bijapur more vulnerable? From the single road that leads across the mountains of our western border—or from the Golcondan plain that is our border to the east?"

"But the forces of the Moguls now protect your eastern border from Golconda."

"And what protects us from the Moguls?" replies Shahji. "As you are a man of honor, tell the queen!"

Shaista Khan feels Shahji's dark eyes burning into him. "In all honesty, majesty, your eastern flank is more vulnerable. Vulnerable from Golconda, I mean, of course. That is one reason why we Moguls march against them, to assure your peace."

Shahji laughs. "The Moguls will come against us, madam, if Golconda falls. As the ambassador well knows."

"You're not going to insist again that we send armies to support Golconda, are you, general?" The queen's voice from behind her veil sounds thin. "Say that you are not. I find the matter tedious, and wish to hear no more."

"Then let me answer for him, madam," Shaista Khan calls out. "A

Mogul victory against Golconda is inevitable. But if, for some reason, Aurangzeb should fail, then beware. Golconda will remember that you left them hanging, and they will attack you. I agree with Shahji: You should send troops east—but to be allied with the Moguls, not with Golconda."

"What is this?" Afzul Khan roars. "Are we now to have all our strategies designed by foreigners?" He strides threateningly close to Shaista Khan. "What business is it of yours, jackal?" Afzul Khan's thick fingers move slowly for the jeweled handle of his *katar,* but Shaista Khan merely stares up at him, as if measuring the man's fat chest to find the perfect spot to thrust a knife.

Afzul Khan spins on his heel. "Remember my words—if these two say look east, I say look west! Can't we see through their lies? The west is where the danger rests!"

"I am certain the ambassador was concerned for our safety, Afzul Khan," says the vizier. "For the second time I ask, General Shahji—if not yourself, who should be commander?"

"I would divide our forces into two armies, lord vizier, an eastern and western part. Many captains have the skill required to lead them. I'd suggest Razoul Khan and Ali Sharif, though others on my staff are just as capable."

"But to command those two, general, to be the commander-in-chief? Who for that post, eh?"

"For that post I would recommend you, lord vizier." Shahji stares levelly at Wali Khan. From the crowd of nobles comes a hubbub of whispers. Afzul Khan looks stunned. A youngish noble pats his broad back sadly. Shaista Khan hears Shahji's answer with surprise.

"I asked my question seriously, general. Pray don't trifle with me," Wali Khan replies.

"I have answered you honestly, lord," Shahji says, looking genuinely hurt.

"Some might wonder, general," Whisper says, and at his soft voice the room becomes quiet, "some might wonder why you failed to name another. Would you tell us why you did not name our Lord Afzul Khan? I'm sure her majesty would wish to know as well."

Before the queen can even nod, however, Afzul Khan strides forward, his face aglow with rage. "I insist," he says in a voice as soft as Whisper's, but full of violence.

Shahji looks back at him easily, more comfortable with open anger than with the covert agendas of the court. "As you wish. I did not name you, sir, because you seek glory. A commander must not desire battle, but find ways to avoid it. He must seek the harder path that leads to peace. Much as he might want a battle," Shahji adds, turning to face Afzul Khan, "the queen's commander must not say so. He must protect the queen. No battle is without cost, sir, and no country, not even Bijapur, is rich enough to bear the cost of endless victories. Bijapur must choose her battles wisely, and win the battles that she chooses."

Afzul Khan seems almost ready to explode. "Coward!" he bellows. The nobles shout and wave their fists at Shahji, and struggle to keep Afzul Khan from attacking him.

"Bloated fool," Shaista Khan whispers, unheard by anyone.

"Silence! Silence!" Wali Khan commands. As the crowd of nobles settles down, Whisper leans close to the sultana and murmurs in her ear.

"Hear my words and obey," says the sultana quietly. One by one the nobles lower their heads. "I will do as General Shahji suggests: divide our forces into two parts. I place Afzul Khan in charge of the western army. The combined forces will remain under the command of Shahji. General, name anyone you will to lead the eastern army; except our trusty servant Wali Khan; we need his full attention as vizier."

Afzul Khan seems uncertain whether to regard this decision as a vindication or an insult, but the nobles around him, eager for his approval, bow and whisper their congratulations.

"Madam," Shahji answers, "I beg you to reconsider."

"You have heard our wishes. I need men of wisdom near me, general."

"But I am not wise, madam."

"We disagree." Beneath the mountainous veil, her head turns almost imperceptibly. "Afzul, prepare with General Shahji a plan to send a force to Poona. It is my hope that Shivaji is indeed, as he claims, the most loyal of my subjects. Should things turn out different, let Bijapur be ready. And General Shahji," she adds, turning like a dark boulder, "do not neglect the safety of our eastern border. Despite the protests of our dear ambassador," she nods to Shaista Khan, "I fear for our safety."

Uninvited, Shaista Khan speaks out once more. "You made wise choices, madam," he says. He hides his pleasure as the nobles glance at him doubtfully, trying to guess the hidden meaning of a Mogul compliment.

The sultana merely nods, and though she may be trembling underneath her enormous veil, she gives no indication of her feelings. Then she stands to leave.

The nobles chatter together when she leaves, none of them satisfied, exactly as the sultana might have hoped.

CHAPTER 19

"Shahu tells me you've managed to get yourself pregnant."

Jijabai glares at Sai Bai, who's stirring a pot of boiling dal. Her tone suggests that her son had nothing to do with it. Sai Bai takes a moment to prepare herself before she looks up. She tries to shape her face into the form of a dutiful daughter-in-law, one who never feels tired, or put upon, or worked to death; one whose life is full of ease and pleasure; one whose mother-in-law is as sweet as buffalo milk, not as shrewish as . . . well, as Jijabai.

"I'm waiting," Jijabai says.

"Mother, I hope so, but who knows? I'm only a few days late. . . ."

"You're pregnant," Jijabai says with finality, as though Sai Bai's uncertainty is all the proof she needs. "Let's hope it's a son." Jijabai glares at Sai Bai. "A daughter's useless now."

"What can I do about it now, mother?"

"You can pray. Go to the temple every day. Trelochan knows the mantras. Make offerings. Be generous."

"Where will I get the money, mother?"

"Just tell Dadaji. He'll . . ." Jijabai's voice trails off, and she curses herself for remembering too late. "I mean Balaji." Jijabai spits out the name. She hates losing face.

"He won't give me money unless Shahu says so, mother."

Jijabai purses her lips. "You'll have to ask Shahu then, won't you?"

"He won't do it, mother. He doesn't care if it's a boy or a girl."

"Fool! Of course he cares. Have you no sense at all?"

"He is my husband, mother. Would you have me contradict him?"

It's always like this, Jijabai thinks. I can't tell if she really is as stupid as she appears, or whether it's just an act designed to irritate me. Why can't she simply obey me? "Listen to me for once. You think I am your enemy. But I'm your friend. You and I are like this; like root and branch. What do we women have except each other? Who else can we trust? I am the mother of your husband, and you are the mother of my grandchild . . . my grandchildren. We must be friends. I need you, Sai Bai, and you need me. Believe me—you have no one else."

Until she says this last statement, Sai Bai had been touched, seeing Jijabai as a real woman, not just a witch sent to plague her. But at those words, Sai Bai rounds on her. "How can you say this to me? I have your son. What more should I need but him?"

A tear rolls slowly down the older woman's cheek. "Don't look at me!" Jijabai's order comes out like a plea. "This is not for you to see!"

"Mother," Sai Bai whispers, and suddenly Jijabai is in her arms, broken with sobbing. "What's wrong, mother dear?"

"Men are like monkeys!" Jijabai sobs. "They hop from tree to tree, not caring. They pick up some shiny thing; they hold it for a little while. Then they grow bored and cast it aside."

"That's what Shahji did to you, mother." Sai Bai pats Jijabai's back, so full of bones.

"You think the son is different from the father?"

Sai Bai straightens. "You say this to me? About your son?"

"*His* son." The words hang in the air between them.

"You're wrong about him."

"Am I? You say this only because he has once more brought you to his bed. Have you forgotten how long he abandoned you? Don't be a fool! Once you get big, believe me, he'll be gone. What happened last time, eh? How long did you spend in your lonely bed, clutching a pillow for comfort?"

"He's changed."

"How long before he grows tired of you? How long until he finds his way to that nautch girl? And how will you stop him, eh? You had no luck last time."

Jijabai's eyes are dark with pain, wrinkles forming where the skin once was smooth. I won't end up like her! Sai Bai vows. And yet how will it be different? She knows Jijabai is right.

Damn her. Damn Shivaji. Now the two of them are sobbing. "He . . . he . . . he was going to kill himself." She hadn't meant to tell this.

Sai Bai begins to weep, and Jijabai weeps with her. "He's tried it before. My poor son! My poor son!"

"What should I do, mother?"

It is the question that Jijabai has longed for, the one she doubted she would ever hear. "You must trust me daughter. Trust me. Trust me." And now it is Jijabai who comforts Sai Bai with her thin, tired arms.

ↀↀↀↀ

Shivaji's strong room is small and damp, a room dug out of the ground, reached by earth-cut stairs, guarded by an iron-bound door. In the lamplight, jewels glisten. "This?" Bala asks, holding up a gem-encrusted pin.

"All right," Shivaji replies.

They are looking for gifts to send to the sultana. Bala lifts a jade spoon, its handle trimmed with tiny diamonds. Shivaji nods, and Bala places it in the velvet bag where he stowed the pin.

Shivaji shows Bala a small dagger, its golden handle enameled with jewel-like glass. Bala shrugs. "Not really something for a queen, is it?"

Shivaji considers. "How about for her boy?"

"Maybe." Bala drops the dagger in the bag as well. His eyes fasten on something. "What about this?" he asks, holding up a necklace.

Shivaji shrugs. "I don't think so. I think . . . I think we stole it from her."

As they walk up the stairway from the strong room, Bala tries out an idea. "Suppose we sent this via Shaista Khan?"

"Why would we want to do that?"

"If we let Shaista Khan act as our representative, let him present our note and gifts, it will give Bijapur something to think about."

"Everyone knows the Moguls seek to annex Bijapur."

"Yes, everyone knows, but no one says so. It's different in Bijapur."

Shivaji frowns, looking at the sun glinting through the immense mango trees that surround the palace walls. "Why don't I just go to the sultana and plead for mercy? What's the worst that could happen?"

"I don't like to imagine the worst, lord. I couldn't imagine anything horrible enough. I heard such stories. That man Afzul Khan . . ."

"But we're nearly out of money. No guns. Our army unready. Bijapur, from all accounts, about to attack us."

"I trust Shaista Khan. He says delay, so let's delay. A note and a few gifts can't hurt, can it? Besides, things change, Shahu. They change like that."

"It's only delaying the inevitable."

Bala looks at Shivaji seriously. "Listen, Shahu, I'll tell you what's inevitable. We have the goddess herself on our side. How shall we fail? We swore to rid this land of Muslim rule. She heard our vow. You are leaving the goddess out of your equations, Shahu. You must not forget her."

"Yet you would have me use a Muslim, a Mogul too, the worst sort . . ."

"I don't hate Muslims, Shahu. I am just tired of living under their thumbs. I say use whatever means we must."

Shivaji eyes are fixed on the ground, his mind working. "If we must ask Shaista Khan to represent us, won't they laugh?"

"No one laughs at Shaista Khan, Shahu."

"All right, Bala. Ask Shaista Khan to present our note and our gifts. But I tell you, Bala, I don't like it. He's still a Mogul for all his pretended friendship. He's got a scheme." Shivaji thinks this over. "Well, what harm can it do? Send the note and gifts to Bijapur by a swift rider. Then see if you can find Trelochan and Tanaji. We need a plan, if only for appearance's sake."

୧୨୧୨

Just before lunch Bandal and Jedhe ride into the courtyard. They are welcomed and hurried into the palace. All through their lunch, they seem about to say more than mere pleasantries, but Shivaji tells them to save business for later, when the others will be there.

So now in Shivaji's upstairs room, Shivaji sits between Balaji and Trelochan; Tanaji, Hanuman, Jedhe, and Bandal surround him, and across from Shivaji sits Iron. Lakshman, as always, sits in a corner.

Iron grins. "It's a regular war party, Shahu. Like when we made plans with your father." Nodding to Jedhe, he adds, "Too bad Tukoji couldn't come. Your father was General Shahji's best lieutenant." Jedhe shrugs.

There's news to tell. First Tanaji describes the army outside Poona. There's two thousand men. The armorers are working day and night. There are plenty of ponies, too. But only a few flintlocks, and no cannon.

"Never mind," laughs Iron. "With you leading them, Tana, they won't need cannon!"

"I won't lead them." Tanaji's words are deep and bitter. "I've told Shahu this. Now I tell you. I'll train them, yes—I'll fight, yes. But I'm through leading men into battle—it will be someone else."

"Then why the hell are you here, Tana?" Iron growls.

"He's here at my invitation, uncle, as are you," Shivaji says softly.

Then Tanaji speaks of how they took Singhaghad and Purandhar. Everyone has heard bits and pieces but now they hear the whole story. Tanaji tells it simply, fact by fact, but everyone is smiling when he's done.

"It was a brilliant move, cousin," Jedhe says, eyes bright.

"That remains to be seen," Shivaji says.

Balaji goes next. "Bala has taken Dadaji's place," Shivaji announces, "I've put him in charge of our business affairs."

"No one can take Dadaji's place, Shahu," Balaji says, lowering his round bald head. Bala then tells of the completion of the Poona wall, and of the progress of the fortification of Bhatghar.

"Iron and I stopped to see that, Shahu," interrupts Hanuman. "It's very good, very strong."

Bala tells of his visit to Bijapur and his meeting with the sultana. Iron's eyes sparkle over his big mustache. "I've still got a friend or two at Bijapur. Seems there was quite a stir when you took those forts. Afzul Khan's in charge of the Bijapuri armies now. Your father's out."

"That's a relief," says Trelochan. "It is not right for a son to go against his father."

Bandal raises his head. "There's a man in my village . . . well, hardly a man any more, not after Afzul Khan got through. He left him his ears and his tongue. No lips though—he can't talk, just drools. No eyes. No teeth. No hands or arms or legs. No dick of course. His wife's a saint. She won't let him die. I'm sure he wants to."

"Lots of them were like that, son," Iron says. "Make you shit your pants, some of them. But Afzul Khan was the worst. He'd drive his men— like something evil. Afzul Khan's a rakshasa."

"Afzul Khan is not our greatest problem," Shivaji says. "Tell them, Bala." Bala describes the strong room, and the treasury, or what's left of it. The gold is nearly gone.

Jedhe turns to Shivaji, ashen-faced. "This is bad, cousin."

"As you say," Shivaji replies. "I will understand if anyone now chooses to leave this council."

Eyes glance from face to face, but only Bandal and Jedhe seem truly disturbed.

"Hell, Shahu, it's always been hopeless," Iron says with a shrug.

"It's not hopeless at all," Bala insists. "We need to dig deep, that's all. Raise taxes a little. We'll be fine."

Iron clears his throat and glances around the circle. "You're speaking like a child, Bala. It's all very well what you say, but . . . we've just collected the allotment for fucking Bijapur. There's nothing left!"

"There's always something left," Bala says coldly. "You just have to want it bad enough to take it."

"Yes, well, then come on try, youngster," Iron answers, barely keeping his temper. "If you want to finance a rebellion, you don't suck your people dry. You need their support as well as their money. More."

"I agree," Shivaji says.

Iron shakes his head. "If Tukoji were here, I can imagine what he'd say. Where is your father, Jedhe?"

Jedhe glances at Bandal, then sits up and looks into Iron's eyes. "I've put him under house arrest, uncle."

"Explain yourself!" Iron yells.

Jedhe instead turns to Shivaji. "He planned to move against you, Shahu. He planned to come against you in force . . . to bring you to Bijapur in a cage."

"Even so, Jedhe," Trelochan whispers in horror, "he is your father. The Vedas say . . ."

But Jedhe sneers. "The Vedas mean nothing to me."

"Silence." At Shivaji's word the men sit back; slowly they regain their composure. "What was your plan, Jedhe?"

Taking a deep breath, Jedhe speaks: "You think you can do this by yourself, Shahu? You've taken over forts, sure, but not by fighting. Sleight of hand. Tricks. Stealth."

"If it works . . . ," Tanaji says quietly.

"It works only for a while, uncle. The time comes when armies must attack, when blood must spill."

"True enough," Iron mumbles. He seems to be mulling something over.

"To gain all, dare all. That's the proverb, eh? Look at you, Iron, and you, Tanaji, and you, Hanuman, and you too, Shahu. You dared all, and so against all odds, you took Torna. See what you've started? I want to be a part of it."

"Me, too," says Bandal. "We're in this together. Tukoji's a fool. I'd rather be dead than a Bijapuri slave!"

"We've come to you, Shahu, to offer our allegiance," Jedhe says proudly.

But Bandal bites his lip. "We . . . we thought you had money."

Tanaji shakes his head. "Shit! I can't believe what I'm hearing!" He rounds on Jedhe, shouting so angrily that spit flies from his lips. "Have you no honor? Money? You arrested your own father for fucking money?"

"No!" Jedhe shouts angrily.

"Yes," says Bandal. His soft, unexpected answer captures the attention of everyone. "Yes, of course, uncle. For money." He continues, his eyes cold and serious, "Yes, fucking money! I'll admit it. What about my people? Every year, the Bijapur allotment grows heavier. Do you think that's right, uncle? Is it right that they should pay out three hun for every four? It's only fucking money? Should I just ignore this burden?"

Tanaji's answering shrug infuriates Bandal. "We've become fucking tax collectors! Fleecing our own people, sending the tax to Bijapur with a fucking smile."

When Bandal stops, though, no one says a word; no one breathes. Finally Lakshman laughs. "Listen, money's no problem. Not anymore. Shahu, listen—I've just come from Kalidas."

"Kalidas the bandit?" Trelochan exclaims.

"He's a day's ride north of here. He's got an offer, Shahu. We can fix our money problems for good. You'll have to grant him protection, Shahu. He wants to be done with banditry, but he wants no reprisals against him or his men. I promised I wouldn't say anything until I heard you say the words. Anyway, then I can tell you." Lakshman grins, but when Shivaji says nothing and the silence grows longer, his smile begins to fade. "Is this a problem? Believe me, Shahu, it's worth it, whatever he's done."

"Kalidas is evil, boy. Just tell us," Iron says. "Then Shahu can decide."

"I promised not to, uncle. First Shahu makes the promise, then I tell the secret—that's what I promised Kalidas."

"If the secret's worth so much, why is he giving it to Shivaji?" Bala says gently.

Shivaji looks from face to face. Finally he speaks. "I will give Kalidas what he requests."

Iron pulls back. "You can't be serious! I can't agree with this, Shahu!"

"Then leave." Iron's eyes grow wide. Shivaji glances around the circle. "Anyone who wants to, leave! Otherwise, stay and obey my will. I asked for your advice. I listened. Now I have spoken." No one has heard Shivaji speak this way before. The sun from the high window falls on his face. "Well?" Shivaji whispers, looking at Iron.

"I'll stay," Iron grunts back.

"I'm glad, uncle. I need you. I'll need all of you.

"You've heard my decision, Lakshman. Tell this to Kalidas. Within my power I will protect him—but only for what he has already done—not what evil he may yet do. Let him stray an inch and he will feel my wrath."

Lakshman bows. "This is what he told me you would say, Shahu." Then Lakshman starts to weave the tale:

Every year the Maharashtran allotment is collected by special guards. Usually each *watan*'s share is carried straight to Bijapur, but this year is different. The master of the treasury has gone to Kalyan for his health, a large city to the west on the Kankonen plain.

The master of the treasury, Lakshman continues, has not gone to Bijapur. To be cooped up in the stuffy treasure rooms of Bijapur—it will do his health no good. So he has gathered the allotment to Kalyan. Once it's counted, he'll send it by caravan to Bijapur.

Tanaji's eyes light up. "All the gold's in Kalyan? How are they guarding it?"

A thousand cavalry, Kalidas had said. Around the circle, eyes grow bright. Though Iron seems almost to be salivating, he warns: "But this information, coming from a villain . . ."

There's more, Lakshman explains. The master of the treasury is a scoundrel. Now the circle grows very still indeed. Many scoundrels sit there, hanging on Lakshman's words.

The master of the treasury is not really sick, of course. All these arrangements have been made with one purpose only . . . to line his own pockets.

"He's skimming!" Bala cries out. Lakshman nods. He plans to skim one tenth of the year's allotment. But how to hide that much money?

That's where Kalidas comes in. Mulana Ahmed will pass the skim to Kalidas. Kalidas will pass it to shady bankers in Agra. For his part, Kalidas gets a crore of hun. Lakshman waits a moment for the number to sink in.

"A hundred lakh of hun!" Bala says. "The wealth! The wealth!"

The caravan from Kalyan to Bijapur will travel by the Vyasa Pass. The captain plans to camp on the other side of the Great Ravine. It is there the transfer with Kalidas will be done.

"This is Kalidas's secret?" Jedhe says. "It's worth a dozen promises!" Trelochan frowns at him, but Shivaji's face is a mask of emptiness.

That is Ahmed's plan, Lakshman continues. Kalidas has different ideas. Why get a hundredth part, rich though it is? Why not take the whole allotment? A hundred men on either side of the ravine can cut off the caravan,

Lakshman says. There's no escape. The room is full of shadows now. Through the window comes the sounds of dogs, of children playing, the smell of chapatis cooking.

"What else does Kalidas want?" Tanaji asks suspiciously. "More than protection, I bet."

Lakshman shrugs. "He says that Shivaji should give him the gold that would have been his share."

"A crore of hun," whistles Jedhe. "We do all the work, face all the danger, and Shahu should just hand it to him?"

"He said it makes no difference. He told me to tell this to you, Shahu: 'If Shivaji gives or does not give, it is all one'—that's what Kalidas said. Still he says to tell you it was the agreed portion."

Shivaji looks up. "I will consider his request," is all he says.

"You'll need more than a hundred men," Tanaji says.

"No," says Iron. "Too many and you lose the surprise. Surprise is key."

"Do we know the day the caravan is to leave?" Bandal asks.

"Kalidas will tell us," Lakshman answers. "There won't be much warning. The captain of the caravan's no fool."

The men around the circle fall to talking. Plans are scratched out on the floor, maps drawn with fingertips. After they've argued for a while Shivaji motions for silence. "What do you say, Hanuman?"

"Three hundred men, lord."

"Make the arrangements."

There is a moment, just a moment, of awesome finality. "No good will come of this," Trelochan says quietly. "To steal that much gold . . . you think Bijapur won't react?"

"It's true," Tanaji says, frowning. "A moment ago Bijapur's attack was the only thing we could discuss. Afzul Khan the new commander? Do you think he'll just sit in Bijapur while we walk off with the whole allotment?

"His attack might come at any time, Shahu," Tanaji says quietly, continuing. "How will you manage that? You have no cannon, the army is . . . well, untried, to put it nicely."

Before Shivaji can answer, however, Bandal speaks: "What difference does it make? We're no worse off now than we were before. The only difference is, maybe we can get a load of fucking money."

"Tanaji is right," Shivaji says, "and so is Bandal. Lakshman, please go to Kalidas, and wait for word of the caravan. Hanuman, please plan the attack. The rest of us will set up a defense against Afzul Khan. There is no doubt he will attack." Shivaji stands. "Enough. I'm hungry. Let's go eat."

ೞ౧ೞ౧

Sambhuji waits outside. Shivaji's long arms reach for the boy and draw him in, half-pulling him from his feet. He squeezes him tight, until the little boy giggles and gasps for mercy, then lets him go, mussing his hair. "Let's go to supper, Sam."

"Are we going to war, father?" Sambhuji's eyes gleam.

"Maybe."

They look up and see Sai Bai coming toward them. "We'll see, Sam."

"There's a big war coming soon!" Sambhuji tells her. "Father might take me along!" He runs ahead to find more friends to tell.

Sai Bai's face is troubled. "Is it war then?"

Shivaji shrugs. "Maybe."

She looks at him for a moment as though her heart would burst with all the cares it carries. Instead she reaches for his hand, and presses it, and then turns and walks toward the palace. "I have a surprise, I think, husband." She leads Shivaji to the dining area.

"It's too early for dinner, isn't it?" Shivaji asks.

"You'll want some privacy for this, I think," Sai Bai says softly.

Seated on a cushion is Jyoti. Her face looks different though—the eyes are softer, rounder, lined around the lids with kohl; her lips darker, lead-reddened; the hands dyed with an intricate web of red-brown henna. She looks at him with a mixture of joy and terror.

"Aren't you glad to see Jyoti, husband? I told her you would be. She has come to ask a favor, husband." Jyoti blushes and turns away.

Shivaji waits. Finally Jyoti turns his way, keeping her eyes low. "I'm an orphan, you know."

"I think I've heard that, Jyoti," Shivaji replies.

"I'm not that old, you know."

"No, you are not old," Shivaji agrees.

"I've saved a few rupees, too."

Shivaji looks puzzled. "That's good. That's frugal. Very good." Sai Bai pats him on the hand, patience, patience.

"Also, I'm a good cook." This time Shivaji says nothing and merely waits. Jyoti looks up. "Do you get lonesome sometimes, sir?"

Shivaji seems surprised by the question. "Not often."

"No," Jyoti says. "No. Because you have a wife."

Now Shivaji starts to understand. "Jyoti, I am in a giving mood. Ask a favor."

Jyoti throws herself forward, pressing her head to the floor. "I bow to you, sir. You know what I want. Can you ask for me, sir? I have no one else to represent me. Can you arrange it? Please?"

"Who?" Shivaji says.

"Hanuman."

Shivaji sits up straight. "That could be difficult."

"But you could ask?"

"I'll ask . . . I'm only saying, maybe it's not so easy. Maybe . . ."

Sai Bai catches his eye. "Maybe it won't be as hard as you think, husband."

"Oh?" Shivaji sits up, crossing his arms, his eyes darting from face to face. "A love marriage? Is that it? Have you spoken to Hanuman already?" Jyoti turns to him and gives a tiny nod, terrified. Shivaji grunts. "This is not a good idea. Such marriages are doomed, I think. They always end in heartache."

Jyoti's face begins to crumble and Sai Bai reaches quickly for her husband's hand. "But we love each other, husband, do we not?"

"Our love grew, the way it should . . . *after* we were married." Shivaji looks uncomfortable. "I'm only saying what is well known, dearest. How can they be happy together?"

Again a look passes between Sai Bai and Jyoti, that woman's look that men find so unnerving. Shivaji shakes his head, resigned. "Very well, Jyoti. I'll speak to the family. May you find every happiness."

Jyoti tries to restrain herself—she shouldn't look too happy until the wedding is arranged. "I have a little money, not much . . ."

"Save your money. I'll take care of it."

"It will be a wedding gift from us," Sai Bai says.

"I'll ask tonight," Shivaji tells her. Jyoti bows, pressing her forehead to the floor as he steps out the door. Sai Bai watches him, and wonders what the future holds.

CHAPTER 20

Outside the walls of Golconda, where the Mogul armies wait in siege, Mir Jumla shifts uncomfortably in the ovenlike heat of Aurangzeb's war tent. He hates it here, for Aurangzeb's tent is most inhospitable. Would it hurt to have carpets? Cushions? Tables? Even the poorest of officers affords these things!

Aurangzeb has no furniture. He leans against his simple saddle, his legs stretched out on a rough blanket. In his hand he holds a small book, elegantly written, decorated in gold. Books he will spend money on. He flips a page and tilts his head with a nod, as though a passage catches his fancy.

He's a prince; he may soon be emperor if all goes well, thinks Jumla. Why must he live this way? Perhaps he thinks it will impress me? Very well! I'm impressed! Now may I have a cushion?

Aurangzeb looks up. "Of all poets, Hafiz is finest, don't you agree?"

Jumla ignores the question, waiting for Aurangzeb to close the book and get on with it. But Aurangzeb stares at Jumla with quiet eyes until Jumla realizes he's actually expected to answer. "Whoever you prefer, lord," he says, hoping that he doesn't sound too impatient.

Aurangzeb sighs and closes his book. "What did you wish to discuss, general?"

He looks into Aurangzeb's empty eyes and feels afraid. Even God fears a naked man—Who had said that? thinks Jumla "It's the digging, lord. The trenches you ordered. My men resent it."

"Tedious, but there is no alternative. The cannon can only do so much. We must breach the walls. That means explosives. That means trenches. But you know this."

"In Persia we had slaves to do this work."

"A single Mogul soldier is worth a dozen slaves."

"But it's so damned hot, lord," Jumla says, suddenly vehement. "Too hot to dig. My men are killing themselves." Another cannon volley rocks the air.

"If you want someone to control the weather, general, you must ask my brother Dara. I understand he's studied that and many other mystic arts. For my own part, I appreciate a soldier's honest sweat." He lifts his hands, looking at Jumla. "They're my men too, general."

"I worry for their health, lord. If Golconda should try to break the siege, I don't think my men will be fit to fight."

"Very well," Aurangzeb says. "Let them dig by night."

Jumla manages to hide his anger. When he looks up, Alu, that slender young eunuch, has floated into the tent. He carries two tight scrolls; these he places at Aurangzeb's side. The eunuch glances at Jumla, his dark eyelids highlighting his wide eyes. Alu leans forward gracefully and whispers into Aurangzeb's ear. Then, with another glance at Jumla, Alu glides outside. A sweet perfume, roses and sandalwood, lingers in the tent's warm air.

Jumla turns back to see that Aurangzeb has been watching. Jumla manages a feeble smile, while the prince's eyes bore into him. "He's quite a help to me, you know," Aurangzeb says quietly.

"Yes, lord," Jumla answers, trying not show his suspicions. Aurangzeb stares at him. Jumla feels a ball of sweat slide slowly down his back.

"If that's all, general?" Again the cannon boom, and the thud of the volley thuds against their chests. "How much longer until the trenches reach the city wall?" Aurangzeb asks, as if in afterthought.

"Maybe three weeks, lord."

Aurangzeb doesn't even say goodbye. Jumla eventually realizes he's been dismissed.

Aurangzeb opens the dispatch from Bijapur. Shaista Khan has written:

I've heard from Hing. Your brother Dara has delayed his move against your father.

From a letter that he sent me, however, it's clear that Dara is actively baiting the trap. He asked me to sound out the sultana's reaction to the planned coup. This request is typical of his womanish approach.

I have not the heart to do this. But I can't delay much more without arousing his suspicion.

Hesitate no more! I beg you in the Prophet's name to act quickly.

These Bijapuris are like hens without their heads. Without the forts of Maharashtra to protect them, they would be easy to defeat.

Word has come that Shahji's son, Shivaji of Poona, is starting to recapture his father's territory. He's taken a couple of Malve forts—without a shot, if you can believe it. The Bijapuris never saw it coming.

Afzul Khan is pressing hard to attack Shivaji. The Bijapuri hens are holding back. Fools. It would be easy to stop Shivaji now. Best to do it before the boy gets a foothold. This delay may work to our advantage, however.

I have made friends with Shivaji's emissary, a pleasant bumpkin who trusts me completely. You are more subtle in such matters than I, lord. I'll wait for your instructions. Should we help Shivaji? Or help Bijapur against him? Perhaps we gain advantage by letting matters take their course.

I trust the siege goes well.

By the way, a troupe of acrobats came to entertain the sultana's boy. One them was huge, a wrestler who might have been the twin of that giant bodyguard of yours. Does he have a brother? It occurred to me that you might enjoy a matching pair, but he left the palace before I could speak to him.

Shaista Khan ends the letter with the usual formal pleasantries. Aurangzeb closes his eyes. He might be sleeping he is so still. The cannon boom again but he shows no sign of having heard. He reads the scroll once more. Then he sets the end of the scroll into the tip of the lamp's flame.

Once he's stirred the ashes, he turns to the other dispatch. He takes a deep breath, then he rolls it out to read. It comes from Agra, from his sister Roshanara. And on the scroll there is but one word:

Soon.

Shivaji knocks on Tanaji's door. "There's no one home," Nirmala tells Shivaji when she answers. "I don't know where they are."

"But I have come to talk with you, auntie." Reluctantly, Nirmala swings aside the narrow door. She had sworn she would never let him come here, after what happened to her poor Lakshman. "You are well, auntie?"

Nirmala harrumphs—How well can a mother be who's seen her child mutilated? She nods for Shivaji to sit.

"Do you think Hanuman is lonesome, sometimes, auntie?"

Nirmala looks at Shivaji, eyeing him carefully, suspicious of his soft voice and smooth smile. "How am I to know? You keep him too busy . . . too busy for his own mother."

"That will not do, auntie," Shivaji replies. "I will tell him that he must not neglect his mother. Family is important, auntie."

"That is very true, Shahu." What's his game? she wonders. "But surely you did not come here to discuss Hanuman's family."

"Ah, but that is precisely why I have come, auntie."

Instantly she knows why he has come. Feeling suddenly rather wobbly, she sits nearby him. "You can't be serious. Who's the girl?"

Shivaji tells her. It takes Nirmala a while to figure out who he's talking about. When she does, she shrieks with horror. "That one! That one! A nautch girl's servant! You can't be serious!"

"She's not what you think, maybe, auntie. Jyoti's an orphan, but her parents were of good quality. She was raised by brahmins all her life. She is a servant now, but how should it be otherwise? All her life she was kept by the temple. The woman that she serves is not a nautch girl, not anymore; she is the guru of the devadasis at Welhe. In many ways Jyoti is quite special."

Nirmala lifts her head imperiously. "She has nothing to recommend her. No family, no accomplishments. You are infatuated with that nautch girl, and hope to gain her approval by recommending her servant."

Shivaji shakes his head. "I need no one's favor, auntie. I'm here at my pleasure, and because Sai Bai asked me."

"Sai Bai?" says Nirmala, widening her eyes. "I thought Sai Bai had better judgment. Hanuman will never agree. Haven't I tried to get him a wife? How many have I recommended, eh? And always he turns me down!"

"Maybe you haven't recommended the right woman, auntie."

Nirmala puffs her cheeks. "And I suppose some orphan servant of a whore is the sort of woman Hanuman would marry!"

"Maybe it is, auntie." Again that serene, infuriating smile.

Nirmala examines Shivaji's face. "She . . . They're not . . ." Shivaji lowers his eyes, but his silence tells her everything. "A love marriage," sighs Nirmala, half in awe, half in sorrow.

"It's not so bad, auntie," Shivaji says quietly. "Hanuman is no child. Marriage first, then love—usually that's true."

"You think I am an old fool? Your point, I suppose, is that sometimes love may come before marriage? This is, I think, a favorite plot of the songs that young men sing nowadays. Love before marriage! I'll have no part in it! It can only end in sadness."

"But I think Hanuman has found some happiness already, auntie. Isn't that what you want for him?"

Nirmala eyes Shivaji coldly. "Have you spoken to him about this?"

"No!" Shivaji exclaims. "Jyoti appealed to me to act in a brother's role. I would never speak to Hanuman before I spoke to you!"

"Well," she says, her lips tightening as though she's facing a terrible task, "I'll discuss it with him. I won't recommend it, though! I'll just mention it. We'll see what he says."

"Of course, auntie. You must do what you think is right." But his eyes are bright, because he knows the matter is accomplished. But at the door he turns to Nirmala, his face troubled. "What happened to Lakshman was . . . terrible. He was brave, so brave, and to be hurt that way . . . I don't know what to say, auntie."

When she looks at him, Nirmala realizes that his heart is overwhelmed with grief. Shivaji has been like another son to her; she cares almost as much about him as she cares about her own two sons, and her eyes cloud with tears. She sees now that he has shared her pain in secret. "Life is hard, sometimes, Shahu. How can anyone avoid its pain? We must all suffer. . . . But for a mother it is hard, you know? To see that face destroyed. Do you blame me for being angry at you, Shahu?"

"No, auntie. But, auntie, blame me, not Tanaji. I bear the burden, not him. He only did what I ordered."

"There's more than enough blame for both of you I think." She looks away. "Now go. I've heard your apology. Give me some time. About the other, I'll speak with Hanuman. Now go."

❦❦❦❦

In the courtyard, Shivaji sees Balaji hurrying toward him. "A letter's come from Bijapur. From Shaista Khan. He says General Shahji is still in charge. Afzul Khan is supposed to prepare the plan, but Shahji approves it." Bala's thick lips pull into a wide smile. "That's good news, lord."

Shivaji shakes his head. "Shahji will feel compelled to approve Afzul Khan's plans. If he doesn't, he'll look like a coward or a traitor."

"But even so, it means delay, lord. Both men will want to maneuver, each will seek to find a way to be superior. It will take days, maybe weeks, before they agree on a plan, longer still to implement it. In the meantime . . .

Kalyan." Bala's face grows almost rapturous, as though he can feel the Bijapuri gold spilling across his fingers.

"What if the gold is a lie, Bala? What do we do then?"

"That can't be, lord! Lakshman would not lie to us."

"Maybe not, but Kalidas would." He gets a foot in a stirrup and swings up over his horse's saddle. "I'm moving to a tent in the encampment. Stay here and keep an eye on the compound."

Just then a guardsman rides through the compound gates and rides quickly to Shivaji. "Sir, the sentries saw some activity in that copse near the main gate. It's a merchant caravan from Surat, lord. One of them is a *farang*. The *farang* claims to know you, sir. He sent this token." The guardsman holds up a small silver medallion that spins at the end of black string. Bala laughs, recognizing it. "Onil!"

ꙮꙮꙮ

Balaji rides with Shivaji through Poona toward the main gates. The city swarms with activity—so many have come to Poona in the past few days: soldiers, and their families, and vendors, and merchants—and all seem to be hurrying through Poona's main thoroughfare.

Outside the city walls, Shivaji and Bala canter about a mile to the copse of trees. O'Neil waves to them. He's dressed once more in *farang* clothing; his red hair glints in the sunlight. As they ride up, Onil gives them a low *farang* bow, waving his arms gracefully toward the earth.

"Onil, you have returned!" Shivaji says as he dismounts.

O'Neil lifts his hands Indian style. "Yes, lord, I returned. Come see what I have brought you." He walks toward the trees, where the captain and the caravan escort scramble to their feet. The oxcart drivers try to look important as O'Neil goes to the first cart and pulls aside the tarpaulin. Four bronze cannon lie in the cart. Each of them is about five feet long, with muzzle bores about wide enough for a fist-sized cannonball. Shivaji looks at them and for a moment disappointment crosses his face. "You have others, Onil?"

"Yes, lord," O'Neil answers. He walks Shivaji to the other two carts, four cannon in each. Shivaji looks at them in silence. Impatience and frustration seem to pour from him.

"But it's a start, lord," Bala whispers to Shivaji.

"A start," Shivaji repeats tonelessly. He walks from cart to cart. Shivaji looks closely at each gun, his hand trailing gently over the smooth bronze—over places where it's green with corrosion and places where it's shined smooth with use. "Wheels?" Shivaji asks.

"You must make wheels, lord. These have no wheels, lord." O'Neil's pale face wrinkles into a frown, and he starts talking to Bala in Persian.

"These are ship's cannon, lord," Balaji translates. "They sit on the deck in a small wooden dolly that would be unsuitable in the field."

"Ship's cannon, eh, Onil?"

"Yes, lord," O'Neil replies. "Dutch cannon, lord."

"Ammunition?"

Now it's O'Neil's chance to look uncertain. Bala says a word in Persian, and then tries another, and at last O'Neil's eyes light up. "Yes, lord. Here." He tugs further on the tarpaulin and reveals a dozen wooden kegs, heavily padded in wool batting. "Chinese powder, lord." He walks to another cart; here are four or five strange contraptions, like hinged buckets made of iron. When Shivaji shows no sign of recognition, O'Neil begins to talk again in Persian.

Soon Bala nods. "Molds, lord, for the cannonballs."

Shivaji opens one, then closes it with a dull *bang*. "We'll need iron, Bala."

"We can get it, lord. We can make these things, lord, wheels and cannonballs, very quickly, lord."

Shivaji nods. "Not much for a forest of teak, Onil."

"No teak, lord. Gift. My give." Shivaji looks quizzically at O'Neil. "Teak very good, lord. Lots of want. But no cannons on . . . on . . ." He stumbles and mutters some words to Bala.

"They wouldn't give him cannons only for his promise, lord," Balaji says for him.

"No for promise," O'Neil says, nodding seriously. "For bring teak, then cannon. For promise teak, nothing only."

"So where did these cannon come from, Onil?"

O'Neil seems embarrassed. "From buying, lord. From gold. From buying."

"Whose gold, Onil?"

"My gold, lord. These cannon come from Dutch ship, all wet ship lord. In water, lord, under, you understand?"

"Sunk," Bala suggests, and then says a word in Persian.

"Yes, sunk, lord," O'Neil says, nodding. "I buy, lord. I have some small gold, so I buy for you. Because you are good friend to Onil, lord. Save my life. Also I think you are to be king."

Shivaji looks carefully at O'Neil. O'Neil stares back uncomfortably. "I need many cannon, Onil. Not twelve, many. Five hundred, maybe. A thousand, maybe."

"I know, lord," Onil answers sadly. "I have only small gold, lord."

Bala asks O'Neil something in Persian. After O'Neil's long, slow answer, Bala turns to Shivaji. "He gave them everything and went into debt for the rest." Shivaji looks at O'Neil with a look that seems to mix gratitude and pity. Bala leans close to Shivaji and whispers, "He doesn't have enough to pay the caravan captain, lord."

Shivaji nods. Then he walks over and takes O'Neil by the shoulders. "The gods have blessed me, Onil."

"Gods don't give you enough guns, though," O'Neil says miserably.

"They've given me something better, Onil. They have given me friends."

ᏫᎾᏫᎾ

"I'm telling you, sir, it can't be done!" Rao, who used to be Shahji's captain of the artillery shouts even when he means to whisper, so deafened is he from cannon fire.

"Why can't it be done, Rao?" Shivaji yells into Rao's ear.

"I'm not deaf you know!" Rao shouts back. He hobbles around the cannon, which have been laid out in a shed near on the edge of the encampment, near the place where the blacksmiths have set up shop.

"Look here!" Rao shouts. "Here are five molds. Which molds go to which cannon, eh?" Rao nods toward O'Neil derisively. "Don't ask him. That *farang* has no answer." He opens the wooden, boxlike mold. "This mold is for a six-inch ball. None of these cannon have a bore over five inches. So this one is no good." He nods toward the others. "The others are too close to tell until we cast a few. Some may fit . . . who knows."

"Why should that take a week to figure out, Rao?" Tanaji bellows.

"Where's the other equipment, eh? The ramrods, the muzzle brushes, the swabs, the fusers, eh? Wheels, hammers, aiming blocks—you think you just point these things and they shoot?"

"We can build these things, Rao!" Bala shouts.

"Yes, you can build them. How long will it take though, eh? You'll need all of it before we can sound the cannon. Likely they were honeycombed to begin with, or those *farangs* would never have sold them. Likely they'll all blow up first time we try."

"But even this can't take a week, Rao," Tanaji insists.

"They must be tested for aim." Rao hobbles around the cannons. "Crews must be trained. How long do we have?"

Tanaji looks at Hanuman. "We move for the pass in two days."

Rao makes him shout a half-dozen times before he shakes his head and limps slowly toward Shivaji. "All right," he says as quietly as he can. "Two days. It's impossible, but I will do it out of respect for General Shahji. Your father saved my life once." Rao looks at Tanaji. "I want fifty men. We'll train night and day. My command is law. Agreed?"

Shivaji nods toward Hanuman. "Agreed!" Hanuman shouts. He shouts it twice before Rao pretends to hear.

ଔଽଔଽ

Two nights later, Sai Bai watches from the shadows of Shivaji's tent as the war council convenes one final time. The army will break camp tomorrow morning. She wishes she could speak to Shivaji's war council, but that is not her fate. She tries not to reveal her fear while the men bluster and preen. How she hates this foolishness.

Outside, the encampment is deathly quiet. All day long soldiers have been stowing their gear, getting ready for the morning; by now everything is packed away in saddlebags, and the tents are empty except for the soldiers trying anxiously to sleep.

The war council sits around campfire. Their faces, tight and grim, are lit by the flames. All of them wear weapons now; some have helmets wrapped beneath their turbans. They boast and laugh, but from the shadows, Sai Bai sees through that. Her eyes wander over the flame-lit faces: Iron and Tanaji, huddled next to each other; Hanuman nearby looking nervous; Bandal and Jedhe in their opulent armor; and sitting at Shivaji's right in a place of honor, O'Neil, who brought those awful cannon.

Lakshman rode away earlier. She saw him leave. His eye fell upon her, and when it did, Sai Bai grasped her tiny amulet against his evil eye. Since Lakshman has returned from Welhe, she wears it all the time. Maybe he isn't really capable of cursing her, but now she's carrying a child, better safe than sorry.

Lakshman is gone, she thinks, but where are Trelochan and Bala? Why aren't they here as well? Without them, the mood in the tent is unrelenting in its harshness. They're like a pack of dogs chasing a bitch, she thinks as she looks at them. And the bitch is war.

Only Shivaji seems thoughtful, his dark eyes darting from face to face in the dancing firelight.

Onil leans close to Shivaji. "Your sword. It is new, lord, yes? New?"

"Yes, Onil," Shivaji answers. "My sword is new." The sword rings as he pulls it from its scabbard, and its bright edge flashes.

O'Neil takes the blade.

"It's a very good sword," O'Neil says. He struggles to find the words to tell them about it. "It's German. German is a kind of *farang*. Very good sword is German. Very costly. Like for kings."

"Oh, for kings, is it?" says Iron, winking at Shivaji. "Now we know, eh, Shahu? You've got the sword—the rest should be easy, eh?"

"Is from Solingen, lord," O'Neil continues. "Best city for steel. Very nice. Make much hurting." O'Neil studies it more closely. The blade has the elaborate tracery of vines typical of Solingen blades, but this blade has two elements O'Neil hasn't seen before—wild looking dogs among the leaves, and in background, tiny six-pointed stars. Something about the design strikes a chord with Onil, but no matter how he tries, the thought remains obscured.

O'Neil hands it back, smiling. Shivaji grins. "Of course a *farang* would like a *farang* sword." He takes it and sets it at his side and looks around the circle. "Do we all understand the plan? Do we all agree?" he asks.

Hanuman answers for them all: "I think we're ready, lord. Tomorrow we break camp. I will take three hundred men and six cannon to the Vyasa Pass. We'll hide there and wait for the caravan from Kalyan. Lakshman will send word from Kalidas when it is expected. We'll ambush the caravan when it comes through the pass."

"Will you go with Hanuman to the pass, Shahu?" Iron asks.

Shivaji nods. At least he'll be safe, thinks Sai Bai. Safer, she corrects herself. For she fears most the dangers that Iron and Tanaji will face.

"Jedhe and Bandal will wait here for their men to arrive from the north," Hanuman continues.

"How many men will come?" Shivaji asks, turning to Bandal.

"Maybe six hundred, lord. That's as many as we can mount on such short notice."

"I thought you two had thousands," Tanaji mutters.

"We'll make do," Hanuman says. "Tomorrow morning, Iron and Tanaji will lead the two thousand men camped here to Welhe. And with you go the five remaining cannon that Onil has brought."

"Only five?" says Tanaji in surprise.

"One exploded this afternoon, father," Hanuman says. "Three men were wounded. Not badly."

"It's to be expected," Shivaji says quickly, but the faces around the table grow grim, and O'Neil seems in pain.

"Our men will bring another dozen cannon from Kari," Jedhe puts in.

"Let's hope they hurry," Tanaji mutters.

Hanuman continues: "Iron and Tanaji will disperse men along the Bijapur road. The bulk of the force will stay near Torna, to be joined by the men from Kari."

From the shadows, Sai Bai looks at the faces around the circle, all trying to look so brave. They are so foolish. How can they have any hope if Bijapur comes against them? Oh, they think the money will make all the difference. Will it, she wonders? Will armies materialize from nowhere? Will forts suddenly switch allegiance? Will money change anything at all? My unborn baby will be orphaned, she thinks. What good is money then?

As if he has read her mind, Shivaji begins to speak. "Who thinks that we will win against Bijapur?" The men glance at one another, and one by one they raise their hands. Shivaji places his sword with its point toward Iron and its ram's head hilt near his crossed legs.

"When I was a youth, I took a vow to drive the Muslims from this land. Others joined me, as you know." Shivaji nods toward Hanuman. "For good or ill, it is that vow that drives me. Not gods, not goodness, not money. Nothing drives me but my own determination." Shivaji's voice sinks to a whisper. "I think a warrior's word is all he truly has to give. I will be true to my word."

"That's right," Iron grunts.

The lamplight casts a flickering gleam in Shivaji's coal-dark eyes. "Tonight I name this sword. I call my sword Bhavani, and I consecrate it with a vow." He takes the sword by its bright sharp blade. "Before you all I vow to win the freedom of my people. And I vow this as well—never to fail you, my friends." Shivaji's voice grows hoarse. "In war, I shall stand beside you. In peace, I shall keep you close by. While you breathe you shall lack for nothing, and your children, if you die, will be my children."

From the flickering shadows another hand grasps the blade. "I too take this vow," says Bandal in a husky voice.

"And I," says Hanuman, placing his hand between the others.

Iron stretches out his hand, his jaw clenched. Then Jedhe reaches forward, and last of all, biting his lip, Tanaji. They sit like that for a while, hands touching as they hold the blade.

From the shadows, Sai Bai watches, and in the dim and flickering light, she has a frightening vision. She sees their faces dead and dying, the skulls stripped of flesh.

Instantly she looks away. Oh goddess, she begs, help me.

CCCC

Sai Bai holds Shivaji close all night. They lie awake but neither speaks.

When Shivaji rises at the rooster's crow, she wonders if she should tell him of her horrible vision. Before she can decide, he has dressed and quietly gone outside. Did he think that she was asleep? She gets up, swallowing back her morning nausea, dressing quickly as she can. The room seems to spin.

Outside the first rays of the sun paint the clouds with red streaks as dark as blood. Men mount their grumbling ponies. Many have tied saffron pennants to their lances.

Sai Bai finds herself one of hundreds of women who watch in frightened silence as the long line begins to form. She walks swiftly to the front of the line, where Shivaji waits on his Bedouin, talking with Iron and O'Neil. She'd like to run, but propriety and her nausea hold her back. Hanuman's horse trots past. She calls to him, but her voice blends into the river of voices crying out farewells.

She sees her husband nodding, hears Hanuman give the order to proceed, hears the bellowing of sergeants down the line of horsemen as the order is repeated. The army starts to move.

He'll be gone before she gets to say a word! She dashes for the city gates. The sentries let her pass of course, and mount the narrow stairs to the battlement. "Shahu, Shahu!" she cries out. Shivaji turns—maybe he's heard her!—but he turns back without making a sign. What about me? she thinks as he rides into the dawn. What about your vow to me?

"You see, your father is gone," says a voice beside her, dry as stones. Sai Bai looks around to discover Jijabai nearby, and standing next to her, Sambhuji. "Bite back your tears and be a man," Jijabai tells him, but she lets the boy bury his face in her sari, and pats him as he sobs.

Sai Bai is crying, too. She's too woozy even to comfort her son. A hand presses her shoulder, and Sai Bai raises her wet face to see Jyoti standing near her. "Did he say goodbye to you?" Jyoti sniffs. Sai Bai shakes her head. "Neither did Hanuman," Jyoti says. "None of them did. Two thousand men, and not one of them said goodbye."

CHAPTER 21

Kalidas offered Lakshman food. He offered him a woman. But Lakshman had come to Kalidas's hideout for only one reason.

Kalidas wants to hear Shivaji's response to his offer. Lakshman tells him, in a rush, just so, no more, for his thoughts are elsewhere.

Kalidas understands, of course: Had he not once felt the same desire? So Kalidas led Lakshman to Kali in her cloud of flies.

It's not like last time, thank the gods. She doesn't move, her eyes don't roll. She's just a statue. But this time, she laughs. Lakshman hears her clearly. He realizes that Kali's gaping mouth and hanging tongue are locked in a delighted endless laugh. She is the queen of laughter.

Even the decaying heads of her necklace are laughing. Each smiles as the blackening lips expose bright teeth. The liquifying eyeballs pour down the moldering cheeks like merry tears. What can they do but laugh? he thinks. They have come home. All our heads will someday hang around her black neck, strung through the ears, licked by her dangling tongue.

At last Kalidas returns, kneels before the *murti* and kisses her black, red-nailed feet. The flies buzz around him when he stands. "Come," says Kalidas. He helps Lakshman to his feet. "We've gotten word."

Lakshman's horse stands saddled in the clearing. "A gift to you, brother," Kalidas says, nodding to the new silver-studded saddle and matching bridle. "Are you all right, brother? Did she give you a good dose?"

Kalidas's smile is gentle and familiar, and around him his henchmen wear the same encouraging look. They are welcoming him into their brotherhood. He has come home.

As he helps Lakshman up onto his saddle, Kalidas tells him that Mulana Ahmed sent word: the gold caravan will leave tomorrow. "Tell Shivaji about the ridge behind the pass," Kalidas says smiling. "That's where I would wait."

"You look very happy, Kalidas," Lakshman says, liking him.

"Why not? Has she not given me everything? Even the protection of your lord, I have. Soon I will have more gold than I could spend in the rest of my life. Why should I not be happy?" Kalidas strokes one of the bright silver bosses on the saddle. "Don't forget to bring my money," he says, not looking up at Lakshman.

"I won't," Lakshman replies hurriedly. For it seems to him suddenly that Kalidas's voice is like a threat.

"I trust you, brother. I want to trust your master as well." Kalidas lifts his hands to his head. "Follow her commands, brother. She will give you anything. Just do what she asks."

"But how will she tell me what she wants?"

"Always she is talking, talking, talking. No one wants to hear, for they fear her words. Don't be afraid of what she tells you. However strange it seems, obey! Only listen, listen, listen." Then Kalidas laughs and slaps the horse's rump, and Lakshman canters away.

☙☙☙☙

Lakshman arrives at the Vyasa Pass just as the sun reaches the western horizon. Conditions at the encampment are spartan. No tents, no fires—the horses are kept saddled; bedrolls lie on the bare ground.

Lakshman gives Shivaji Kalidas's message: there's less than a day before the caravan clears the pass. Then he adds Kalidas's suggestion to ambush the caravan in the rise on the other side of the pass.

"I don't like it," Shivaji says after a moment.

Lakshman's good eye twists to Shivaji. "What don't you like, Shahu?"

"The place a caravan would most expect an ambush would be as they emerge from the pass. Just the place that Kalidas told us to go. They'll be ready for a fight. In a fair fight, our three hundred men can never beat their thousand."

Lakshman smiles. "Tell me you have an unfair plan."

❦❦❦❦

Shivaji's plan is so difficult that Hanuman begins deploying men immediately. The preparations are huge. Lakshman sees now why Shivaji chose
Hanuman to be his chief lieutenant. Hanuman has always been an enthusiastic fool, and that's exactly what Shivaji's plan requires.

What motivates Hanuman is hard for Lakshman to imagine. What motivates the three hundred men is obvious. Shivaji promised them a share in
the spoils. He even promised to count out their shares within their sight.
Of course, for this, even Lakshman pitches in. He thinks Shivaji's plan will
fail, but he wants his hand out in case it should succeed.

They work that night and all next day. The sun has begun to slip down
the western sky before everything is ready.

❦❦❦❦

Near the entrance to the pass, Lakshman scrambles to the top of a hill,
where Shivaji and Hanuman huddle together. Below them the gold caravan
stretches over the twisting mountain road. "Look," Shivaji says to Lakshman. "You guessed right."

Earlier, they'd argued over how the captain would arrange his caravan,
its wagons and its guards. Now they see that the forces are arranged much as
Lakshman had foretold. "You should always listen to me." Lakshman grins.

At the head of the line are rank after rank of lancers, riding four
abreast. Behind them come perhaps fifty horse-drawn carts, each surrounded by six horsemen. Then a hundred or more horsemen carrying
bows and arrows. Lakshman's eye gleams. "Just the way we want them,
Shahu. Made to order."

"The captain will have joined the real caravan: the one coming through
our pass. They're walking right into our hands."

❦❦❦❦

As the captain's section of the caravan enters the pass, the sun casts dark
shadows across the stony road. The sun is going down. The vanguard of Bijapuri lancers crowds together where the road narrows. The captain shouts
for everyone to move quickly.

The wagons struggle over the ragged stone of the mountain road, wheels
groaning and creaking. They're slower moving than the lancers, and soon a
large gap has formed. And behind the wagons, the archers clump together,

jostling against each other, since it's hard for them to move as slowly as the wagons.

The wagons have just reached the midpoint of the pass when chaos explodes all around them.

A loud *bang* echoes from the canyon walls on either side of the road. Suddenly a half-dozen horses and their riders fall into a crumpled heap. Those standing nearby find themselves splattered by blood, by chunks of meat and bone. Horses rear and run madly, screaming, their wounds still smoking. Another bang. More horsemen fly into the air as their horses disintegrate beneath them.

Smoke billows through the narrow passage. The smell of gunpowder and burnt flesh swirls around the chaos. The horses begin to dance, eager to run, pitching their riders. Fallen men scramble to avoid the hooves of their terrified mounts.

The cannon blast away again, leaving a score of horses and their riders dead, and dozens bleeding and wild.

"They're firing chains!" shouts someone over the screams of wounded. The remaining archers, who expected only to be firing arrows at a rear attack, now wheel their horses around and drive for the rear in panic.

More cannon fire. Screaming horses fall in a heap, pinning their broken riders. Unable to turn, the wagon horses run forward in a frenzy as another cannon blasts. The horses of the third wagon try to climb over the wagon ahead of them. They all spill over, and the upended wagons land in a heap against the jagged rocks.

All this has taken only seconds. Before the lancers can turn their mounts, an avalanche of boulders pours down. The phalanx collapses beneath the stones. Shouts and screams, crash and clatter, these echo in a jumble from the bluffs. Another cannon booms. Smoke billows out in brown, caustic clouds.

Then from the bluffs where the rocks crashed down, come high-pitched war cries: *Har, har, mahadev! Har, har, mahadev!* A hundred men, two hundred, some on ponies, come sliding down.

Soon the wagons are surrounded. The lancers are cut off from the wagons. The wagon guards try to form a line, but in vain. On their nimble ponies, Shivaji's soldiers dart toward them and dash away, attacking with lance and sword, and deadly arrows. Each time they leave a few more dead behind, then they circle and attack again.

Hanuman begins to shout orders. All the wagon guards have fallen;

most are dead. Riderless horses trample the bodies of the living and the dead alike. "Archers, archers!" Hanuman bellows. "Form a line!"

Less than three minutes have passed. The Marathi archers fire a rain of arrows. Lakshman, his lance bloody, is the first to reach a wagon. He heaves aside the canvas cover and exposes a dozen sacks. Dropping his lance, he slashes of the top of one with his serpent dagger and peers inside.

"Sand!" he screams, in a voice so loud that the others stop and look at him. He lifts the sack and pours its contents out in a brown cascade. He tries another and another. "Nothing but sand!" He runs down toward the rear of the convoy. Shivaji is trying to organize a rear guard against the fleeing Bijapuri archers. Lakshman reaches Shivaji and grabs him by the shoulder. "There's nothing here but goddamned sand! We attacked the wrong convoy!"

Shivaji looks at Lakshman for a moment, then tries to turn away, but Lakshman will not let him. He spins him around again, swinging his dagger toward Shivaji's face. Shivaji is fast enough to block the blow: with the hilt of his gauntlet sword Shivaji cracks Lakshman against the ear.

When Lakshman lifts his head, his ear is ringing so badly he can see the pain. He staggers to his feet and stares at Shivaji, trying to decide if he should drive his dagger in the bastard's back. But he does not. He growls and lurches back down the road.

In his pain, Lakshman sees the situation with icy clarity. All around is chaos and disaster. To the east, Shivaji is screaming at bowmen who are pelting the retreating Bijapuris with showers of arrows. But they're quickly running short of arrows. When they run out, Lakshman thinks, the Bijapuris will regroup. They outnumber us, and we'll all die.

Hanuman's men are firing arrows at any of the Bijapuri lancers foolish enough to attack. The lancers die by ones and twos, but there are hundreds of them. It's only a matter of moments before the lancers regroup and try an all-out assault, Lakshman thinks.

A cannon shot echoes through the pass. Lakshman turns to see that Shivaji has aimed a couple of cannon at the fleeing archers. A cluster of shot whistles mere inches over his head, over the wagons and riders, over the heads of Hanuman and his Marathi men. Then Lakshman hears the screams of the Bijapuris on the other side.

As the echo of the cannon's roar fades, an awful silence rings in Lakshman's ears. "Why are your handth empty?" he hears a voice whisper, a woman's voice.

Lakshman spins around, trying to find the source of the whisper. "Do you not thee that hammer?" the voice lisps again. Near his feet he spies a Bijapuri battle hammer and picks it up, threading his hand through the heavy leather thong.

"Thtrike him," says the voice. Lakshman sees a few feet away a Bijapuri gasping in agony, trapped beneath his broken, dying horse. "Thtrike him!" the lisping voice insists, and now of course, he knows whose voice he hears, and why it lisps. He sees the wide-eyed terror of the Bijapuri as the iron hammer falls. His head implodes with a wet *thwack*.

Lakshman looks down at the hammer lodged in the Bijapuri's skull, the Bijapuri's twisted, broken face, the blood and brain splattered on his pants. "What have I done?" he asks himself. He tugs the hammer free and staggers forward, self-loathing growing in his chest. In an agony of anger, he swings the hammer around his head once more, and smacks it viciously into the side of an overturned wagon.

The hammer splinters the wood with a loud crack. As Lakshman wrenches it free, he sees a glint of brightness. His eye widens, and he begins to batter the wood, again and again. Chips and splinters fly in all directions as the boards fragment under his blows. And then it spills out, looking almost a liquid; a river of golden coins flowing from the hammer hole, forming a puddle around Lakshman's feet.

❦❦❦❦

It takes Lakshman a moment to realize what's happened, a moment, but no more. Then he falls to his knees and begins to shovel coins into his pockets, laughing, rubbing them on his face like cool water. "Hey, Shahu!" he yells. "I found it! They hid it in the wagon sides!"

His shouts can barely be heard over the clamor of the battle. But soon Marathis all around him are leaping off their horses, tearing at the wagon sides with lances and swords, battering them with maces and bare hands. A pond of gold spills from the wagon. The Marathis scoop up the coins. Emptying the sacks of sand, they fill them with treasure.

CHAPTER 22

Word reached Bijapur in the middle of the night: A lone horseman, exhausted, covered with ash and mud after riding from the Vyasa Pass, carried the tale.

The story swept through the city like a fire. By dawn the nobles had gathered at the palace.

Gongs and trumpets blare; the dais door opens. The sultana appears, like a green tent gliding over the marble dais to the silver throne. Behind her comes the bony old eunuch Whisper, guiding the heir, still yawning, to a place beside his mother.

"He's coming," Wali Khan announces, lifting his silver-headed staff.

The throng of nobles grows quiet. The rear door of the Diwan-i-Am bangs open, its echo booming from the marble dome above.

Afzul Khan strides in, shoving General Shahji before him. His hands are bound, and he staggers drunkenly as Afzul Khan thrusts Shahji forward with his huge, hamlike hands. The nobles open a path, wincing as they see the bruises on Shahji's face. Shahji stumbles in gracelessly; lurching into a cluster of sneering nobles, and falling to his knees.

"I have brought the traitor as I promised, madam," Afzul Khan growls, and the room explodes in cries for vengeance. Wali Khan raps his silver-headed staff against the dais steps. The roar's echo lingers.

Shahji, facedown on the cold marble floor, hears but cannot see Wali Khan descending from the dais. "Surely this treatment is unnecessary, General Khan," he says hoarsely.

Grabbing Shahji's collar, Afzul Khan lifts him effortlessly from the floor. "How should a villain be treated, O Wise Vizier?" Afzul Khan snarls. He lets go, and Shahji's face smacks the floor.

"He is the queen's commander," Wali Khan says feebly, and again is greeted by furious shouts.

"That was a mistake, O Grand Vizier," says Afzul Khan, "but one which can be remedied."

"Let him speak," says the sultana's muffled voice. But Afzul Khan doesn't move.

Then Whisper, thin as a dry, old reed, comes to his mistress's side. There's something unnerving in his look. Afzul Khan slowly lifts his foot from Shahji's head. As he steps away, his heel clips Shahji's ribs, as if by mistake. Shahji's body lifts up, and then flops to the floor with a *thud*.

"Well?" the sultana says after long, uncomfortable wait.

Shahji lifts his head. "I have done no wrong. I have in all things done my duty."

The nobles groan in protest, bravely shaking their fists. Wali Khan bangs his staff for silence. "There is the matter of your son, commander . . . ," the vizier says.

"I know him not," Shahji growls. The nobles cry out. Some pretend to tear their exquisite, fragile garments.

"You know him, liar," Afzul Khan bellows. "He is your puppet, that is clear. You have played us false, traitor!"

"Madam, I beg you . . . ," Shahji whispers.

Surely she cannot hear him in the midst of all those voices, but she lifts her hand, hidden under the tent of her robes. "The queen will speak! The queen will speak!" rasps Whisper. Only when Afzul Khan raises his huge arms does the crowd grow quiet.

"We know your son, commander," says the queen. "First he stole our forts. But now he takes our very blood, commander! He has stolen the year's allotment! We are ruined!" Her words mingle with the shouts of the assembled nobles until Afzul Khan again signs for silence.

"This is Shivaji's evil, not mine, madam. I begged you to attack him."

"That was all talk, fool! You should have acted!" bellows Afzul Khan. He appeals to the queen. "Are we to think that foolish child has acted alone? Achieved success by luck alone? No one is that lucky! It is obvious who assisted him!" Afzul Khan kicks Shahji so savagely his body flips over like a sack of sand.

"This is not true," gasps Shahji. Blood stains his teeth.

Afzul Khan is set to strike again, when the sultana cries out "Stop! What good does it do to kick him, general?"

Then Afzul Khan lifts his chin ever so slightly toward the dais, ever so slightly nods. The boy playing at his mother's feet sees his uncle's nod. Instantly he stands. "Silence, silence!" Afzul Khan calls out. "The heir would speak!"

"The heir is but a boy!" Wali Khan protests.

"We've heard enough from the son of this traitor," Afzul Khan sneers. "Let us hear what the son of our sultan may say."

Though the sultana reaches out to stop him, her little boy moves to the silver rail.

"Let him be sealed, uncle," the boy's thin voice pipes.

"What did he say?" bellows Afzul Khan dramatically, holding out his arms to the other nobles.

"I said, let him be sealed!" shouts the boy.

"Let him be sealed!" Afzul Khan howls. "Let him be sealed!" Soon all the nobles take up the cry. The boy sultan slips beneath the silver rail to stand near Afzul Khan, his upturned face shining.

"What has he done to deserve this? Who will be next, Afzul Khan?" the vizier calls out. But the mob of nobles is already on the move.

"No!" Shahji cries as Afzul Khan hauls him to his feet. "No!" he screams again as Afzul Khan drags him from the audience hall.

The boy sultan, laughing and pointing, chases along behind. The noblemen follow after them like yapping dogs.

The alcove has walls of dark brick and a moldy smell, for there are only shadows here. Manacles black and heavy hang from bolts embedded in the walls. Afzul Khan fits these over Shahji's wrists.

"You shall be sealed, traitor," Afzul Khan intones. "We shall send letters to Shivaji. If he wants to save you, let him come here. Let him bring our gold. Or I shall go and take it from him. With these hands, I swear it!" He turns back to Shahji with a sneer. "Your son shall decide, general. I shall be happy either way."

"Will he be sealed, now, uncle?" the boy sultan asks, his small hand reaching into Afzul Khan's huge fist.

Afzul Khan looks down fondly. "Yes, sealed, but slowly, little one. One brick an hour. You will watch him die. Find the mason," he snarls to a nearby guard. "Make sure the bricks are large."

ଔଔଔଔ

"Have you seen Shivaji?" Hanuman asks, walking to Bala's room. Trelochan shakes his head.

Everyone wants to see Shivaji. But in the three days since he has returned to Poona, bringing with him in triumph the Kalyan allotment, Shivaji has scarcely showed his face. "Maybe he's with Sai Bai," Trelochan suggests. "Do you think he's all right, Hanuman? He seemed very distraught at the funerals, don't you think?"

"I don't know why," Hanuman replies. "We only lost eleven men. Eleven men against a thousand. The Bijapuris had almost two hundred dead." He frowns and scuffs the ground as he walks. "Why hasn't he sent for me? I'm supposed to be his damned lieutenant!"

They reach Bala's room. To their surprise, Bala is not alone. Seated beside him is a small, strangely dressed man. His skin is extremely dark, his eyes fiery. The fabric of his clothing is richly colored, decorated with hundreds of tiny white dots, and embroidered with silver thread and beadwork. Near the man's bare feet lies a long black dog. "What's Bala doing with a tribal?" Hanuman whispers to Trelochan.

"Come and meet this person," Bala says pleasantly.

The tribal lifts his hands in greeting, and Hanuman notices the network of white scars and black tattoos that circle his wrists. "Tell them what you were telling me," Bala says to the small man.

"I am Warli tribe man. Name Lion." Though heavily accented, the man's language is clear enough. "Bring story to you headman. Tell story. Strong place ours. We give." Puzzling this through, Hanuman glances at Bala, but Bala seems not to notice. Lion goes on, "Strong place, you understand? Pratapghad. We give you headman."

"Excuse me, sir," Hanuman says. "Are you saying you have captured Pratapghad? Taken the fort?"

"'Fort' means strong place, yes?" Lion answers carefully. "Yes, take strong place. Give head man. Give Shivaji. Give son of Shahji."

Trelochan whistles. "I've been to that fort. There's a big Bhavani temple there, on a hill inside the walls, very old. The tribals revere it—they think the Bhavani *murti* is their tree goddess. The fort itself is quite grand."

Hanuman leans close to Bala and whispers. "Tribals taking Pratapghad? Can it be believed?"

"I've never known a Warli to lie," Bala answers.

"But how?" Hanuman asks Lion. "How did you do it? What about the Bijapuris?"

"Warli sneak. Bijapur all dead men now. Bijapur bad men. Break tree. Tree goddess sad. Cry to Warli. Warli fix. Warli sneak. Bijapur bad men dead." Lion says all this quite calmly, patting his dog's long back.

Hanuman slides next to Trelochan and whispers. "Can this be true? I thought the Warli were peaceful."

"They're great archers, don't forget. And they're not peaceful when it comes their gods. They worship trees."

"Yes, trees. Trees good. Bijapur break tree. Bad. Now Shivaji take strong place. Not break trees. Yes? Not."

"This can't be happening," Hanuman says. "How can this be? Tribals come out of nowhere to give Shahu forts?"

"This is her work," Bala says reverently, nodding toward his *murti* of Bhavani. "Nothing is beyond her power."

"But Bala," Hanuman exclaims. "Forts, money, armies! These things have just appeared!"

Bala rises and bows to Lion. "My dear Lion, you must be exhausted after your journey. Let me get food for you. And for your dog." He goes to his door and calls out. Soon a servant girl escorts Lion from the room.

"Does Shivaji know about this?" Hanuman asks.

Bala shrugs. "All this news and no one can find him."

"More news than this, Bala?" Trelochan asks.

Bala nods. "The towns of Indapur and Baramati have written. They need our help—they've set up roadblocks and have stopped the flow of supplies to the forts there."

"A siege?" Trelochan gasps. "The fools. The Bijapuris will drive down from the forts and destroy them!"

"They ask us to send troops," Bala explains.

"We don't have troops to send," Hanuman says blankly.

"Don't we?" Bala asks, honestly surprised. "Have you paid attention to the encampment? Two or three thousand men have arrived in the past three days! I've had to set up special teams to find supplies. They all arrive hungry, of course. And more are on the way! Lonavala is sending men; Pimpalgoan is; Peth is. Other towns too. Jedhe and Bandal's men are arriving as we speak, and they say more are on their way. Lots more!" Bala's face, always smiling, now seems to glow as he speaks. "Do you think that the goddess is powerless? This is her work!"

Hanuman doesn't want Bala to see his disbelief, and he turns away. Trelochan catches his eye. "If you don't believe in the goddess, you can believe in money. Money changes everything."

"Yes." Hanuman nods. "The gold."

"Her gold," Bala says softly.

"Have you finished counting it?" Trelochan asks.

"Nearly," Bala replies.

"And how much is there?" Trelochan prompts.

Bala smiles. "Lots."

"Damn it," exclaims Hanuman. "Where the hell is Shahu?"

❀❀❀❀

At an old temple on a hill overlooking Poona, as the air grows cool and the evening breezes blow, Shivaji weeps. Though he knows Bhavani is everywhere, he comes to this small dark temple, as though it contains the door to her heart.

Wiping his eyes with his palm, Shivaji stares across the river at the lights of Poona. The river sparkles like a cloth strewn with tiny mirrors. At length he picks his way down the hill, his path lit only by the stars.

At the riverbank, Shivaji walks slowly past eleven heaps of ashes. In some the embers still glow orange. "You hardly knew them," Hanuman had said as the flames of the funeral pyres leapt into the air.

"I knew them well enough," Shivaji replied.

Now only ash remains, and soon the wind will blow the ash away. Shivaji steps into the river. The water comes up nearly to his armpits, so he holds his gauntlet sword above his head. Once on the other side, Shivaji walks along the outside of the city walls. A shadow catches his eye, and Shivaji turns, reaching for his sword.

Amidst a pile of rags lies the wizened, naked body of Ram Das. "What are you doing here?" Ram Das croaks.

Shivaji sheaths his sword. "I should be asking this of you!"

"But then I would know for certain that you are fool," Ram Das answers. "Do you have any food?"

Shivaji shrugs. "Sorry, father."

"Never mind." Ram Das peers into Shivaji's shadowed face. "Hold out your hands." Slowly, uncertainly, Shivaji lifts his hands. In the moonlight he sees blood pouring from his palms. "Those are your scars are bleeding. Remember how you got those scars, lord?"

There's a long pause. "When I took my oath."

"Did you think they'd never bleed again?" With a clawlike finger, Ram Das traces the bleeding scars on Shivaji's palms. "You think you're the first person to bleed, lord? You've died a million times already. Now give some other men a chance to die!" Shivaji says nothing. Ram Das strokes his shoulder. "But give them something to die for. Look what you've done since we first met! Think it's all your own doing?"

"I don't know what to say, father."

"Say whatever you want. I don't give a shit. Your answer makes no difference. It's all decided anyway." Tiptoeing to reach, Ram Das kisses Shivaji on the forehead. "Close your eyes, lord," Ram Das says solemnly. Shivaji stands there with eyes closed, expecting who knows what. After a minute, he opens one eye and peers around. The old man is gone; his rags have disappeared as well. Shivaji lifts his bleeding hands in the moonlight.

ଓଡ଼ଓଡ଼

By the time he reaches his home, Shivaji's hands have stopped bleeding. It will be dawn soon—too late to sleep. So he goes to Sai Bai's room and slumps against a cushion near her bed. He hasn't spent the night with his wife in many days—making war instead. And as the night passes, he grows concerned. He can feel it: something is wrong with Sai Bai.

The door of Sai Bai's room opens just a crack, letting in a shaft of the dawn sunlight. "I thought you might be here," Jijabai whispers.

Shivaji frowns and nods to Sai Bai, who sleeps restlessly beside him. "I think she's sick."

"Maybe," Jijabai says. Then she realizes that with even a single word, she has revealed too much.

"You know this? What's wrong with her?"

"We all must die, Shahu," Jijabai says. "I blame your father. She was never a suitable wife. Shahji should have sent her back." Her voice trails off and she looks at Sai Bai's face. "I once was pretty, Shahu," she says quietly.

Shivaji stares at her. At length, Jijabai scowls. "Stop mooning about. You must finish what you have begun. She is nothing!"

"Hold your tongue! What if she hears you?"

"You think I don't say this to her face? I am no hypocrite." She sighs. "Never mind now. Bijapur has responded to your attacks. They're holding Shahji for ransom."

Shivaji comes bolt upright. "In Bijapur?"

"You're surprised by this?" says Jijabai, lifting her eyebrows. "Now I am concerned. Go. The others want to talk with you—they're quite disturbed."

Shivaji begins to fix his turban. "And you are not?"

"I hope you let him die."

ଓଓଡ଼ଓ

The circle of men sit in an open space, a hundred yards from anyone. Bandal sweeps a spear around the grass before he sits, as if worried someone hides there. "Are these precautions really needed, cousin?" Trelochan asks.

"You think we're not at war?" Bandal snaps back. "You think that we're surrounded only by our friends? Afzul Khan likes spies, brahmin. There may be spies in this very circle."

"There's no harm in being careful." Shivaji says. Trelochan looks around the circle dubiously. There's Jedhe, Bala, Hanuman, Lakshman, and finally Shivaji. Their eyes are fixed on the parchment just arrived from Bijapur.

"Well? What does it say?" Lakshman asks, looking bored.

Bala speaks: "It's from Shaista Khan. He writes that General Shahji has been arrested. They're sealing him, even as we speak. One brick an hour until he's sealed behind a wall."

Bala continues: "They want the gold, the Kalyan gold. Unless they get it, Shahji will be sealed completely within a week." Bala looks around the circle. "Official word from Bijapur should come soon. The arrest was two days ago. Five days remain until General Shahji's sealed."

When Bala stops speaking, to the surprise of all, Lakshman stands. "I'm going, Shahu. All this foolish talk has become a nuisance. I will fight no more." He lifts his hands to his forehead in with an exaggerated bow.

"Where are you going, cousin?" Jedhe asks, looking stunned.

Lakshman bows again. "I'm off to Bijapur, cousin. They can use a man with my talents."

"What talents are those?" Jedhe asks, his face cold.

"I have no morals," Lakshman answers.

"I shall be sad to see you go, cousin," Shivaji says. "No matter what you do, I will always honor you as the son of my uncle, and as my friend."

"You see how it's done?" Lakshman looks at the others, pointing to Shivaji. "One thing more: Bala, when I send you a letter, here's how you'll know it's from me. The code word will be 'vengeance.'"

"Will you be sending letters, Lakshman?" Bala asks, looking confused.

"Why the hell do you think I'm going to Bijapur? You think you can beat Bijapur by force of arms? You don't stand a chance. I'm going to be your spy, you fools. Don't any of you understand?"

Now they do. Now the men in the circle stand and wish him luck, and bow him off, but Lakshman simply shakes his head and strides across the field as though walking from a pit of garbage.

"Do you think you can trust him, lord?" Bandal asks.

"You're talking about my brother!" Hanuman cries.

Bandal looks down for a moment. "I know who I'm talking about. Haven't you noticed how he's changed?"

"You can't let him go, lord," Jedhe says, finishing Bandal's thought. "He says he wants to be a spy. Whose spy? What if he tells Bijapur about our plans?"

"We have no plans," Hanuman says, disgusted.

"Let him go," says Shivaji. "For better or worse, let him go."

After a silence, Bala whispers, "What shall we do about this letter?"

"Ignore it."

"Let your father die, lord?" Trelochan gasps. "It isn't right that he should suffer for our actions."

"Shahji's situation is not our fault!" Hanuman declares. "He himself chose this course. He forsook his family for Bijapur. If Bijapur plays false, what's that to us? Does Bijapur think one man is worth all that gold?"

"How shall we have victory if we fail to honor our fathers?" Trelochan responds, but Jedhe stirs uncomfortably.

Shivaji stares at the ground. "I won't return the gold."

"Then they'll attack us," Bandal says.

"They'll attack us anyway," Hanuman responds.

"Then let's use the gold against them," Jedhe whispers. "Send gold to every town and village that sits beneath a Bijapuri fort. Tell the headman to block the roads. Some towns are doing this already. Encourage it."

"Yes, yes!" Jedhe says. "People are waiting for a reason to move against the jackals. Give them a reason! The gold will give them the courage!"

Bandal agrees: "Pratapghad fell to a bribe. When they hear about your wealth, other forts will fall."

"This is meaningless," Hanuman cries. "You're forgetting that we have no army. Afzul Khan will be here soon. He'll mow us down like grass."

"Maybe, cousin," Bandal answers. "But they'll come with a big army, and that will take time."

"In the meantime, we organize," Jedhe says eagerly.

"When we receive the demand from Bijapur," Bala says, reflecting, "we must promise to return the gold."

"They'll never believe it," Shivaji says.

"Write to Aurangzeb!" Jedhe suggests. "He's in Golconda. Offer to ally yourself to the Moguls. You're a force now, lord. He'll have to pay attention."

"Why should Wagnak give us any help?" Shivaji asks, using Aurangzeb's old nickname. "He defeated my father. Why should he rescue him now?"

"Because now we have the money and Bijapur doesn't," Jedhe answers. "Hell, it's worth a try! Look how quickly things can change. Delay, delay! Every day becomes our friend!"

Shivaji sits for a moment in silence, then nods. "Very well. Bala, send letters to Shaista Khan and Aurangzeb. Make promises. Beg."

"Yes, lord," Bala answers. "Shall I write to Bijapur too, and promise you'll return the gold?"

Shivaji thinks about this. "No. I intend to use the gold as you suggested, cousin. We'll offer bribes to the fort commanders. But we won't be able to hide this from Bijapur. Word will get around. Hell, we want word to get around. If I lie in their faces, it will infuriate Bijapur. Let the news trickle in. Jedhe, you and I will go to Welhe with the new arrivals, and prepare against Bijapur's attack. Bandal, will take a couple of hundred men and fortify Pratapghad." Shivaji turns to Hanuman. "Hanu, stay here and coordinate our efforts. I expect there will be new arrivals coming. Who knows, maybe another fort will fall without our help!" Shivaji smiles.

"This is a bad plan, lord," Trelochan says. "You're needed here. Maybe you haven't realized, but you are sparking an uprising. You must stay here and be the king!"

"I say I am no king!" Shivaji says. For once his face looks truly angry.

"As you wish, lord. Even so, you must not leave Poona. Stay here, lord; send others." Shivaji looks around the circle, and the others nod agreement. "Please, lord," says Jedhe. "Do us this favor. We'd all rather face Afzul Khan than stay here with Jijabai."

৩৩৩৩

Hanuman almost doesn't say goodbye to his mother. Ever since Lakshman came back injured, she acts so worried. His thoughts turn then to Jyoti. Shahu told him that he tried to make the arrangements, but that Nirmala had not been pleased. "She made me promise not to give Jyoti any money," Shahu told him.

"Can't you do something? She'd never let me marry a woman with no dowry," Hanuman replied. But Shahu refused to disobey Nirmala's wishes.

Hanuman sees Nirmala stirring rice and dal over the fire in the back kitchen. The warm smell of wood smoke mixes with the heavy scent of spices. He sees that her waist has grown thicker, and her shoulders smaller, that the braid along her back is longer now, and streaked with gray. When did she get old? he wonders. But her eyes are just as bright as ever.

"Are you just going to stand there?" Nirmala says.

Embarrassed to be caught staring, Hanuman says "I came to say goodbye. I'm off to join father at Welhe."

"Well, if you're going, go," she answers, turning back to her cooking. The pot of food is far too large for a woman who will be eating all alone.

"I'll be back," he says. She just goes on stirring. "We'll all be back."

"She's not good enough for you, Hanuji," Nirmala says softly. "Why didn't you tell me you were lonely? Now I know you're interested, I'll find someone suitable. You had only to say something."

"Never mind, mother."

She turns, and her face is full of hope and sadness, as though her heart is splitting open. "I forbid you to see her anymore," Nirmala tells him. "I didn't raise my son marry some nautch girl's maid."

"Her heart is full of love."

"You may say as much of any beggar. Your father has raised this family out of poverty. You're important now. You need a suitable wife. Don't you want your mother to be happy, Hanu?" she asks.

"Don't you want me to be happy too, mother?"

She turns away, and begins to stir the pot once more. "Maybe things will be better when you return." She puts down her wooden spoon, and spreads her arms to him. Finally she pulls back, clutching his arms. "Want what I want, son," she whispers. "Is that so hard? Want what I want."

He presses his folded hands to his forehead, and walks silently away. "She's too poor!" he hears her calling after him. "Do you hear me? Too poor for you!" He feels a lump of sorrow burning in his throat, and when he passes through the door, he starts to run.

CHAPTER 23

"If we had your Rajputs," Aurangzeb says to Jai Singh, "we should have won by now."

Outside the walls of Golconda, the Mogul siege goes on. As the prince speaks, a cannon volley rocks the night air, and the sides of Mir Jumla's extravagant war tent puff as though blown by a gust of wind. Mir Jumla chuckles, hoping to show that he enjoys Aurangzeb's words. "You see, general, even the cannons agree with Prince Aurangzeb! And I agree with him . . . though what is he saying, really, eh? He's saying I'm an incompetent old fool, eh?"

The evening is ending up exactly as Jai Singh had dreaded: dinner with Mir Jumla. His tent is as grandiose as the food had been. The center pole supports a massive ink-blue canopy embroidered with silver stars. Silk tapestries hang on every side. They recline on brocade pillows stuffed with down, breathing air perfumed by vases of fresh tuberoses. It's difficult to believe that Jumla's tent is in the middle of a battlefield; it seems more suited for a royal palace.

Naturally, Jai Singh thinks, our host has kept the guest list short—just Aurangzeb and Jai Singh, for Jumla would never think of inviting anyone less important than himself. So here they sit, pretending to be amused, in an opulence that would rival any residence in Agra. A score of half-used serving dishes rest on the thick carpet; in Jai Singh's honor, most were prepared without meat. Aurangzeb, Jai Singh notes enviously, has taken only rice and dal, the simplest of foods.

Can Aurangzeb truly be the man he appears to be? Is he truly a man without pride, without ambition? Jai Singh wonders, comparing Aurangzeb to the heir apparent, Dara. What a contrast. How unfortunate the accident of their births. If only Aurangzeb had been firstborn . . .

When he had arrived, Alu, that young eunuch who acts as Aurangzeb's *khaswajara,* sought him out at once, and led him to the prince. Aurangzeb had embraced him like a brother.

And then Jumla had appeared. Jai Singh studies the Persian general. Has Jumla been gaining weight? Gaining weight in the middle of a siege!

"What about it, general?" Jumla asks, setting down his wine cup and licking his long mustache. "Will you send us some Rajputs so we can end this siege and go home? Better yet, won't you lead them yourself, so I can go home?" He winks at Aurangzeb.

"You flatter me, general," Jai Singh laughs politely. "Your army is powerful and dedicated. What are the Rajputs now but soldiers for hire?"

Aurangzeb snorts. "Your people, general, are the greatest warriors that ever fought. I mean this," says the prince, waving away Jai Singh's protest.

"Yet your ancestors defeated us, highness," Jai Singh answers.

"Only by treachery, general. The greatest army may be defeated by a single coward. When a coward leads, the army surely fails. And if a coward should gain a throne . . ." Aurangzeb leaves the though unspoken.

Jai Singh turns away from Aurangzeb's penetrating glance, wondering if the prince has read his thoughts about Dara. He sits in silence, hoping that they'll drop the subject. At that moment another cannon booms, rattling the silver-covered tent poles and jangling the chains of the hanging oil lamps. "Do you fire the cannon all night, general?" he asks Jumla.

"Only until midnight, general," Jumla replies, holding out his cup for a refill. "Our men must sleep, you know. Last thing, we send a volley of flaming rockets, and then off to bed. But the Golcondans must stay up all night fighting fires. It won't be long until they surrender."

"I don't doubt it," Jai Singh nods. "As you know, Shah Jahan sent me to review your progress . . ."

"You mean Dara sent you," Aurangzeb says quietly. Jai Singh lifts an eyebrow but says nothing.

"And how do you find things, general?" Jumla asks.

"You have concentrated your attack on the south approach to the city, and placed great strength on the west and east sides as well."

"The south gate seemed to us the hardest for the Golcondans to defend," Jumla agrees. "It is there that we have thrown the main weight of the attack."

"Your front to the north, however, is weak, general—weak to the point of breaking," Jai Singh says.

"In just a few hours visit, you saw that?"

"Has the enemy noticed? That's the real question."

"They don't appear to have seen it yet. Your opinion of this weakness, general?" Aurangzeb asks quietly.

"Excellent, your highness." The Rajput's eyes are bright. "It is wise— brilliant!" Jai Singh continues—"To contrive a weakness for your enemy to spot. It gives your enemy a foolish hope; hope that guides them to their ruin. If you smoke the cobra in his hole, he'll coil and wait for days. But give the old snake an exit and he'll run for it. Stand there with your bag and you shall have him. This show of weakness is a masterstroke."

"It was Aurangzeb's doing," says Jumla, smiling.

"The inspiration was your siege at Lodi, general," says Aurangzeb giving a nod to Jai Singh. "But Jumla is too kind, I may have made a suggestion here or there, but the planning all was his."

"In any case, gentlemen, I see that the endgame approaches. Is the bag ready when the cobra runs?"

Jumla nods. "We have hidden cannon here, here and here," he says, drawing an imaginary diagram on the floor. When the servants come in bearing a salver full of cakes floating in rose-petal syrup, they must set them down elsewhere so as not to disturb the diagram.

"Let's discuss this later, gentlemen," Jumla says. He nods to a servant, who brings a hookah forward, lighting it with a burning coal before he hands it to his master. "You won't join me, either of you?" Jumla asks, sucking on the mouthpiece, setting the pipe bubbling. The smell of spiced tobacco mixes with the perfume of the rose syrup.

"So, general, what's the news at court?" Jumla asks expansively.

Jai Singh begins to tell of entertaining scandals: cuckolded husbands, enterprising eunuchs, devious wives. But soon, the night grows darker and Jai Singh's tales grow darker, too. The cannon volleys stop, and outside the tent the chatter of the camp grows quiet. "You know that Dara has sent out letters, of course," Jai Singh says, looking disturbed.

"What letters?" Jumla asks.

"To all the generals. Demanding that they confirm their loyalty to the throne."

Jumla glances at Aurangzeb. "I never got such a letter."

Jai Singh looks at him steadily. "Neither did I. I thought I was the only one. Everyone else seemed to have received one."

"Did you ask Dara about it?" Aurangzeb says softly.

"No." Now Jai Singh, like Aurangzeb, stares at the carpet, eyes forward, head still.

"Surely Dara felt that your loyalty is beyond question," Aurangzeb whispers.

"What about mine?" Jumla asks. "Am I not loyal?" A small trail of hookah smoke drifts from his mouth.

"Since you didn't get a letter, general, Dara must have thought so. No one can doubt your loyalty to my father."

Jai Singh looks up, troubled. "You know that the letter had nothing to do with your father, highness." Jai Singh studies Aurangzeb's face. Is he any better than his brother? Are any of his family to be trusted? "You know about what happened to my family in Amber?"

"Some difficulty with your bodyguard, I heard," Jumla answers. "Is there more than that?"

Jai Singh strokes his beard with his small, neat fingers. "The guard's captain died—was killed, they tell me—while trying to assassinate my wife and son."

"Betrayal is reprehensible," Aurangzeb says.

"Now my wife is guarded by a Mogul bodyguard," Jai Singh continues. "The captain of the guard is Dara's man."

"Ahcha," Jumla nods, understanding Jai Singh's worried tone.

"General," says Aurangzeb softly. "I hear the question that you must not ask, and that I must not answer." Aurangzeb leans forward. "He thinks he has you, general. Because of your wife, he thinks he has you."

"Because of my wife, he does."

"You can always get another wife, general," Jumla laughs. But Jai Singh does not.

❧❧❧❧

At that moment, Alu enters, and turns to Aurangzeb. "I'm sorry to disturb you, highness, but a dispatch has come." He opens a rough leather tube and draws out a letter.

"Who sent it, Alu?" asks Aurangzeb.

"It comes from Poona, lord."

"Where the hell is Poona?" Jumla asks.

"It's in the Malve, general," Jai Singh answers, trying to be polite. "A small city in Bijapur territory."

Aurangzeb reads the letter, then reads it again before speaking. "It's from some Marathi chieftain calling himself Shivaji," Aurangzeb tells the others, without looking up. "He claims he's taken a number of Bijapuri forts." He looks up at Jai Singh. "Is this possible? He says that he has captured the bulk of the Bijapuri allotment from the Kankonen."

"That would be a fortune, highness," Jai Singh says. "I suppose it's possible, but . . ."

"Read it yourself, general," Aurangzeb hands the parchment to Jai Singh. Jumla slides near, peering at the dispatch in the dim light.

"The fellow's Persian is quite presentable," Jumla says.

"I don't know what that proves," Jai Singh snorts. "Any fool may speak Persian." Jumla glares at him as he continues to read. "What's this? He wants you to save his father!"

Aurangzeb smiles. "I thought that would interest you." He looks at Jai Singh. "Shahji . . . Do you remember him? He used to be quite a nuisance during the Ahmednagar wars. And now the son appeals to me. The wheel turns, general." He turns to Alu. "How did this arrive?"

"Some courier. A bumpkin. Strangely dressed, highness, on a stolen horse that bears a Bijapuri brand."

Jumla snorts. "It's a Bijapuri trick."

Alu turns to him. "Believe me, the rider's not from Bijapur. He looks like a lost dog."

" 'Bumpkin' . . . Where have I heard that word recently?" Aurangzeb shakes his head and turns back to the letter. "So what are we to make of this Shivaji fellow? If we save his father, he'll become a Mogul ally." The prince looks amused. "How ironic. Asking old General Wagnak to rescue Shahji, his fiercest enemy."

"We all know Shahji, of course," Jai Singh replies. "I seem to remember he had a son. Shahji was made commander of Bijapur's armies. How did he come to be arrested?"

"Obvious, isn't it?" grunts Jumla. "The kid takes the gold; Bijapur takes the father."

"The Kankonen allotment . . . what would that be worth?" Aurangzeb wonders.

"A fortune, highness," Alu says in his soft, husky voice. He looks at Jai Singh strangely. Like a nautch girl sizing me up, thinks Jai Singh with surprise. Then his big smoky eyes turn back to Aurangzeb. "Bijapur's gotten rich by taxing the sea trade."

"Where is Poona, exactly?" Jumla asks Jai Singh.

"Just to the east of the ghats," Jai Singh answers curtly. "The entire area is peppered with forts. Shahji had quite a run against us."

"And this new fellow, Shivaji?" Aurangzeb's eyes light up. "I remember. Fetch that dispatch of Shaista Khan's."

"Yes, highness," says Alu, who glides silently from the tent.

"You're not really taking this seriously?" asks Jumla.

"You think the Peacock Throne needs no more allies, general?"

Alu returns with a parchment. Aurangzeb glances through it quickly. "This dispatch came from Shaista Khan, who is acting as my father's emissary to Bijapur. He mentions that Shivaji has taken a couple of Bijapur's forts. That was only two or three weeks ago. Shahji's son has been busy."

"He's trying to pick up where his father left off," Jumla suggests. Aurangzeb falls silent.

"You should send a letter to Bijapur, highness," Alu says. "Have Shaista Khan deliver it. He can be quite persuasive."

"Shaista Khan is not in Bijapur," Jai Singh says. "He was called to Agra for an urgent consultation." Jai Singh says this as one announces a death. "Called back by Dara, highness."

Alu glances at Jai Singh and lifts an eyebrow. Jai Singh turns away, embarrassed. Such a glance might mean anything!

At last the prince lifts his head. "How many men are actively employed in this siege, general? How many would be available for a second line of attack, should the need arise?"

Jumla seems rattled by the question. "Well, there's fifty thousand, total. But at this point—digging trenches, waiting—I suppose only eight or ten thousand are active."

"Could five thousand men be spared, general?" interrupts Aurangzeb.

"Of course they could be spared, highness, if that is your wish," Jai Singh puts in. Jumla glares at him. Let him glare; I outrank him, thinks Jai Singh.

"If you think it might be done, general," Aurangzeb says with quiet deference, though of course he could order anything he wished. "Jumla, please give orders that a company of five thousand be set upon the western road by noon."

Jumla's eyes bulge for a moment, but he recovers himself and inclines his head respectfully. "As you wish, highness. But you can't mean for them to attack Bijapur . . ."

"Of course not, general. But they'll put some steel behind our words.

Alu," he says. The eunuch looks up, alert. "Draft a letter to the sultana telling her it is our wish that General Shahji be set free. Make it clear that he is the father of an honored ally, Shivaji, and we would regard any injury to him as an injury to our own person."

"Yes, highness. To be signed how?"

"As Viceroy of the Deccan. In fact, don't request it, order it, by the authority of the Peacock Throne. Let them mull that over."

"They'll never free him, highness," Jai Singh says.

"That's all one to me, general," Aurangzeb replies. "It's the son I want, not the father." He turns again to Alu. "Send copies to Shivaji . . . have that 'bumpkin' bring them."

"Yes, highness," Alu answers, rising. Jai Singh again finds the eunuch glancing at him.

"Do we have any sources in the Malve, general, who can assess the credibility of this chieftain?" Aurangzeb asks.

Jai Singh thinks this over. "Traders, perhaps, or *farangs*. Let me see what I can find."

Aurangzeb stands. "Things are coming quickly to a head, I think. As Jai Singh says, we approach the endgame. I trust that both of you are ready."

Jai Singh bows again as Aurangzeb slips out, wondering how ready he needs to be. He thanks Jumla, bows to him, and walks back toward his tent. His sentries jump to their feet as he approaches. "There's someone waiting for you, sir," one of them says.

In the firelight, Jai Singh sees a graceful shadow standing by the entrance to his war tent. It is Alu, his dusky eyes glowing by the light of the flames. "I hope you don't mind that I've come, uncle," he says in a murmuring whisper.

With any other eunuch, Jai Singh would be abrupt, but this one is the subject of many stories. Everyone in Agra talks about him, and the tales are strange. "Forgive me, Alu. I'm tired and morning comes soon."

Alu smiles. "Whatever did you think I meant, uncle?" Jai Singh wonders if he got the wrong idea. "It's only that I never got the chance to tell you of my admiration for you, uncle. You have always been a favorite of mine."

"Really?" Jai Singh answers, trying to appear pleased.

Alu steps closer, as close to Jai Singh as a woman might stand, though still polite, with his long hands folded together beneath the sleeves of his dark silk jama. "Among the *mukhunni* you are much respected uncle. You have always dealt fairly with the brothers."

"Thank you," Jai Singh answers. His head comes scarcely up to Alu's shoulder, and he can feel the eunuch's breath, warm and sweet.

Alu slowly moves one hand from under his robe and places it tentatively on Jai Singh's chest, the long fingers resting gently on his shoulder, the palm on his breast. "You will find us helpful, uncle, should the need arise. Pliant. You need only make a sign . . . the subtlest sign, and you shall have us."

Jai Singh's lips don't seem to work. Alu's hand moves, rustling the stiff silk of Jai Singh's robe. "Dark times approach, I fear. And in the darkness, one wants a friend, yes?" Jai Singh nods, not sure where things are leading.

"But you told me you are tired, uncle." Again, silently, Jai Singh nods, and Alu smiles knowingly. "Some other time when you feel more rested we must speak again. Longer. Much longer." He slides into the shadows, his fingers trailing across Jai Singh's chest as he departs.

ೋಲ೦ೋ

A few weeks ago Maya had been a nautch girl, her life filled with softness and scents, with silk and serenity. Now she is the guru to a dozen devadasis in training, and every moment of her day is busy. The change came so quickly that she sometimes wonders if she would one day wake and find that it had all been but a dream.

Her head covered with the end of her sari, she slips across the torch-lit courtyard to the steps of the Bhavani temple. The night air feels crisp, and above her the canopy of stars explodes in splendor. The courtyard is silent, and the temple carvings, touched by silver moonlight, seem about to breathe.

She almost bumps against him, he sits so quietly at the top of the temple steps. When he raises his bearded face, she sees thin gleams of light reflecting on his cheeks. It is Tanaji, looking older than she remembers.

"What's wrong, father?" Maya asks.

"You should not call me 'father.'" His eyes, damp and dark, look at her for just a moment. "What have I done to deserve such an honor, eh?"

Maya sits beside him. The stone floor of the temple feels cold through her thin cotton sari; Tanaji slides over slightly to give her room. "Look at me. How many men have I killed, eh? How many men mutilated by my hand? You'd think I'd feel some regret. It never crosses my mind. Yet when I think of how I've failed my boys, how I've failed you, I blubber like a baby. I've been a fool."

"Tell me what's troubling you, father?"

"That you should call me that, for one thing. Have I ever been a father to you? When things were hard for you in Poona? I could have protected you from Jijabai! I could have taken your part!"

"You did your best."

"No. I failed you. Just as I failed Lakshman. And Hanuman. And Shahu, too."

Everything she thinks to say seems empty. She should argue . . . she should comfort. Instead she merely sits beside him.

"Maybe Dadaji had the right idea. When his time came, he shaved his head and became a sadhu. At least now he spends his time in penance, winning the favor of the gods instead of disappointing those he loves."

"But he was old, father, and his time had come. You have much to do. You must not chastise yourself. It is the gods that choose our ends. How shall we avoid the twists and turns of karma?"

Tanaji thinks about this for a while, then shakes his head. "I fear Lakshman is ruined. When I look at him, I cringe."

"Many men bear battle scars, father."

"It's not his face that's scarred, but his soul. He's so full of anger."

"It must have been hard for Lakshman, father."

"But see what I have done . . . Just made things worse! And now I abandon Shahu when he most needs my help! I was his lieutenant. Now out of cowardice and anger, I resigned when he most needs me. How he must despise me!"

"I'm sure he doesn't! And you wouldn't have done this unless you thought he'd be better off with some other lieutenant."

"I thought only of myself. I never guessed that he would turn to Hanuman in my place. Now I've placed my other son in danger. There's no way to fix it. I've made a mess. Each step I take brings misery."

She hears the choked sound of Tanaji weeping, and without thinking puts her arm across his shoulder. His back is broad and strong, but wracked with sobs. So they sit for a while, as they evening breeze stirs around them.

"You've done much good. How you cared for Shahu and your twin sons! Surely you must place those good deeds in the balance of your thought. Do they not outweigh these small missteps?"

He lifts his head to look at her. She feels, for a moment, that she should wipe away his tears, but she thinks this would just embarrass him.

"Why do you act as though your life is at an end? Do you think your store of good deeds is empty? Even a dry well may fill again, father!"

"You're right," he says after a long time. But then his face changes as another thought flits across his mind. "Your servant girl . . ."

"Jyoti?" Maya says, smiling.

"Nirmala won't let her marry Hanuman. Says she's too poor. How can he be happy with a poor wife?"

"Maybe she can get money someplace. Maybe Shivaji . . ."

"Nirmala ordered Shahu not to help her. She said it would be as though Hanuman were marrying Shivaji."

"Foolishness. That's no reason at all." Maya stands, and Tanaji gets up, afraid he's disturbed her after her kind words. "I must go, father," Maya bows. "I have not much time. Those girls take all my thought. You are a good man."

He stands and bows to her. She calls him "father," with a voice so soft and warm, it seems the sun has risen. I might yet do some good, he thinks. I might. I might.

ᏋᎤᏋᏋ

What a dreadful place is India.

Hot and dusty or wet and musty. Never comfortable. Never easy. Nothing the way it ought be: the food a horror, more spice than meat; the cities a disaster, filled with crushing mobs, all of them trying to rob you directly or indirectly; the roads no more than trails; the rich extravagantly wealthy; the poor near starving. The officials he has met are either pompous, self-aggrandizing buffoons, or servile, sniveling toadies—but all of them ready to do anything for baksheesh. The *farangs* are no better—the very worst of Europe has found its way to Hindustan.

Who can understand the ways of fate? How odd that he should stumble into this lot, he thinks. These Marathis, Shivaji's people, have a core of honesty and courage that sets them apart. Few of the *farangs* he's spoken with even know of them, and those that do dismiss them, either lumping them in with the Bijapuris or calling them tribals and shaking their heads. "Stick to the Muslims," most tell him. "That's where the money is."

True, O'Neil had come to India to get rich. He won't go home unless he has enough money to build a noble life. But he doesn't much like the *farangs* here; the Portuguese shun him ever since the death of Da Gama; the Dutch shun him because he is a Catholic; and what few English there are, shun him because he's Irish. The Indian Muslims ignore him altogether.

Only among these Marathis has he found a sense of comradeship or honor, or most important, a place to laugh.

For their part, the Marathis seem to enjoy him. Sometimes he feels like a trained monkey. When he walks down the market in his high leather boots, a gawking crowd forms. Children sneak in to watch him bathe, even adults huddle nearby, staring with wide eyes at his pale, freckled chest and its mat of copper hair.

ꙮꙮꙮ

So O'Neil now finds himself in Welhe, making *granadas*. It's strange that these simple items are considered to be some sort of *farang* magic, thinks O'Neil. The Hindis, who have embraced the cannon and the matchlock so completely, have some sort of terror of *granadas*. They're simple enough to make: hollow balls of bronze, packed with Chinese powder and bits of steel and a paper fuse.

But O'Neil has no bronze, so he's using balls of fired clay, which he has heard will work if the walls are thick enough, and steel is scarce, so he packs the Chinese powder with sharp gravel. He's tried a few, lighting the fuse and watching it burn down before heaving it as far as he can, praying that the damn thing won't blow up in his hand.

They will do.

O'Neil sits cross-legged beneath a mango tree far from the encampment, about a hundred unglazed balls sitting empty near his knees. He looks up to see Hanuman walking cautiously toward him. O'Neil laughs. If he's crazy enough to come there, he's welcome.

"How is it going?" Hanuman asks, taking a place across from O'Neil.

"Sure, good," O'Neil answers.

Hanuman watches fascinated as O'Neil scoops powder mixture into a clay ball, cuts a length of fuse, and packs the ball with a wad of cotton. As he starts to melt wax on the opening, using a butter lamp, O'Neil shakes his head and chuckles. "We maybe die together, Hanuman." Hanuman tries to laugh. When the *granada* is complete, O'Neil tosses it casually to Hanuman, who catches it in his lap, eyes full of terror.

"Not banging, Hanuman," O'Neil tells him. "Must make fire for banging, or strong hit."

"How long until you are done, Onil?"

"Maybe sundown," O'Neil answers.

"Need any help?"

"I think men maybe very scared of *granadas*, Hanuman. Maybe too scared for helping?"

"Maybe," Hanuman laughs nervously.

"Bijapuris come soon, Hanuman?" O'Neil asks, as he starts another.

"Maybe."

"Can make many *granadas*, Hanuman. Who will throw?"

Hanuman shakes his head. "You can teach us how to throw, *farang*?"

"Sure," O'Neil answers. "Some men maybe die. You understand?"

Hanuman nods, his face tight, and it seems to O'Neil that he's working up the nerve to ask a hard question. At last Hanuman proves him right. "You have a wife, Onil?"

"Wife dead. Why? Maybe you have a sister?"

Hanuman looks shocked. O'Neil tries to restrain his amusement. From what he knows of these people, he can imagine how shocking the idea of O'Neil and Hanuman's sister must be.

"No sister, no sister!" Hanuman says, laughing as he realizes that O'Neil is teasing him. Hanuman looks O'Neil over, as though considering how much to reveal. He's going to tell me a secret, O'Neil realizes. I'm a damned *farang*, and it makes no difference what you tell a damned *farang*. I'm lower than a barber, and men will tell their barbers anything.

Soon Hanuman says: "I have a woman I like, but I cannot marry her. My mother does not like her, I think. Maybe you know her, Onil. She is Jyoti, the servant of that nautch girl, Maya."

O'Neil tosses a newly finished bomb to Hanuman. "I know that one. Why servant girl, Hanuman? Why not nautch girl? She is pretty, eh?"

Hanuman seems amused. "She's a nautch girl, Onil. Not suitable, you understand? Also, her family. She is a something, you understand?"

O'Neil isn't sure what sort of something the nautch girl would be that would make her even more unsuitable. An orphan, maybe? He seems to remember that Maya is an orphan. Then a thought occurs to him; he remembers the sword that nautch girl gave to Shivaji, the Solingen blade with the six-pointed stars engraved on the steel. "That nautch girl, that Maya. Her father is a *farang*?"

"I think maybe yes. But I think her father is dead now."

"Ahcha," O'Neil answers. What does that make her? he wonders. Makes her an outcaste, I suppose, not a fit companion for a Hindu. And then an image occurs to him unbidden: Maya walking back from her bath, her hair flowing unbraided in the breeze, her skin shining in the sunlight.

And a thought strikes him—one both practical and pleasant. He thinks about voicing it aloud, but on second thought, he holds his tongue. He's managed fine without a woman so far. But as he tries to work, his mind seems intent on conjuring up images he has until now kept at bay, and the woman he imagines is one fair and slender, with burning, gold-flecked eyes.

CHAPTER 24

ᙁᙍᙍᙍᙍ

Outside it is bright afternoon, but in this part of the Bijapur palace, it might be midnight. Some of the people waiting in the line cough from the smoke of the torches. Just ahead, someone has overturned a narrow wooden box, because the opening grows smaller and higher every hour, and many of those in line are now too short to see.

Of course, those who get the best view also get the worst smells. For manacled as he is, the prisoner has few options. His pants are stained with urine and excrement. Once an hour, the hourglass sands run out. A weary old mason ambles forward with a wet lump of mortar, a well-worn trowel, and a single brick. The corridor echoes the scraping of the mortar and the ringing of trowel as he taps the brick in place.

When they see the mighty Hindu general kneeling in his own excrement, what do they think? That ruin may come to anyone? That in the end, even the greatest warrior must soil himself like a baby?

A one-eyed man lingers while the others peer into the shadows and move on. When others stay too long, the guards scowl and poke them away, but this man has been free with his baksheesh and they leave him alone.

At one point the corridor echoes with the *bang* of an opening door, and the *clack* of thick heels on stone. A huge, heavy-set noble stomps down the hall, a little boy scurrying ahead of him. Bright rings glitter on his heavy fingers. He scoops up the boy and lifts him so he can look. The boy giggles. After a moment the man sets him down, and glances inside himself, taking a moment to spit into the cell before he leads the boy away. The guards bow until they hear the palace door slam shut.

The next time the hourglass is turned, the guards push everyone aside; they even hold the mason back. At their nod, the one-eyed man steps onto the overturned box and tosses a brass flask into the cell; it clatters across the stone floor and rests against the prisoner's knees. This moment has cost him twenty rupees.

Shahji looks up at the one-eyed man. For a moment he seems to recognize the face. But no, the general thinks, for he knows no one with a face scarred so, with one eye ruined so. He considers mouthing some word of a thanks. But how will he reach that flask, just inches from his knee, and even if he could, how would he open it, and even if he opened it, how would he drink? Thirsty as he is, the gesture seems to him most cruel.

Shahji prays to all the gods that he might die, but from his lips what comes is only a long and incoherent moan.

ⓔⓓⓔⓓ

The sultana still sits upon the throne, still hidden beneath a mountain of green velvet, but the faces of the nobles turn her way no longer. Instead they cluster around the towering form of Afzul Khan as he holds forth, standing with his back to the queen. "This is what comes of pandering to infidels!" Afzul Khan cries, his neck swollen with rage. "We must only crush them! We must grind their idols into dust!"

He is only starting to warm to his subject, however, when the major domo calls out: "His excellency Ali Rashid, ambassador and messenger of Prince Aurangzeb, Viceroy of the Deccan!"

A young man dressed in black robes shot with silver walks confidently forward. Ambassador Rashid moves to the dais, and makes a sweeping bow.

"Your highness," he says in a clear voice that carries easily through the hall, "I bring you greetings." He holds out a roll of parchment heavy with ribbons and seals. "Madam, sadly the urgent nature of my mission prohibits the exchange of pleasantries. I beg you read this letter straightaway." He holds out the parchment until Wali Khan, with that special care that men of size are apt to use, picks his way down to receive it.

Soon all is quiet except the ticking of the Persian clock. Wali Khan breaks the seals and unrolls the parchment. Slowly, his fat lips moving, he reads it silently. Then he shuts his eyes and stands as still as stone.

"Read it," comes the sultana's muffled voice.

Wali Khan's face voice is tight. " 'To our much loved servant, the sultana of Bijapur, greetings.' "

"Servant!" bellows Afzul Khan. "He says that? Servant?"

"Let him read, general," says the queen.

"That is not right!" Afzul Khan protests, turning his angry eyes to the messenger.

The ambassador lifts his head proudly. "I am the embassy of the Great Mogul and my person is inviolate," he says softly. The messenger is weaponless, but his soldiers place their hands upon their sword hilts. Afzul Khan glares at him, nostrils flaring.

Wali Khan continues. " 'It has come to our notice that Bijapur has imprisoned Shahji, the father of our ally, Lord Shivaji of Poona.' "

An angry murmur stirs through the crowd of nobles. They look to Afzul Khan, but the general stands mute. He appears baffled: eyes wide, mouth working, speechless. He may be brave and full of bluster—but he has no skills, the nobles now realize, to respond to the subtle thrusts of a Mogul ambassador.

Desperately nobles shift their gaze to the dais. Surely the sultana can answer. Or Wali Kahn, or Whisper. Even Afzul Khan turns around to look.

"Fetch him," comes the sultana's muffled voice.

The nobles explode into anguished cries, but Wali Khan looks to his guards and lifts his chin. Without a word, the guards begin to move. "No!" shouts Afzul Khan, glaring at Wali Khan. His eyeballs seem about to burst from their sockets. "No!" he says again, this time quietly. "No, I will do it."

He turns and stomps from the hall. The nobles watch him go. The wiser ones, sensing the unexpected shift in the mantle of command, bow appreciatively toward the silver throne.

"Lord Ambassador, how kind of you to bring us this letter," pipes Whisper, his voice barely perceptible. "We might have thought to receive it from the hands of our dear friend, Shaista Khan. Is he not well?"

"Prince Dara requested General Shaista's presence. Viceroy Aurangzeb, concerned for General Shahji's safety, sent me. I am an unworthy substitute, I fear. My main advantage was proximity." The ambassador waves his hand, the vague, unconcerned gesture of a man born to nobility. "I was so anxious to come, I fear I even outpaced the small honor guard the viceroy sent with me. No matter, they shall be here presently."

"We shall be glad to welcome them, Lord Ambassador," Whisper says. "The guesthouse of Shaista Khan—"

"They are too many for that guesthouse, I would think."

"How many are there, Lord Ambassador?" Whisper asks.

"Some five thousand, with horse and elephant, Lord *Khaswajara*," the ambassador says. "Imperial guards detailed by the viceroy. I am most honored to be favored by their company."

Whisper's eyes grow wide, but he recovers himself. "It is no less honor than you deserve, I'm sure." The ambassador inclines his head, his point driven home.

"Bijapur welcomes you, lord. We are pleased to hear that Shaista Khan is well," comes the sultana's voice, softened by her many veils. She lifts a covered hand, and Wali Khan and Whisper step close to her. "What shall I do?" whispers the muffled voice.

Wali Khan looks fiercely toward the face that he has never seen. "You must free him, madam."

"It will be seen as weakness, madam," Whisper answers. "Afzul Khan will seize upon the act to depose you."

"He would not dare!" the queen gasps.

"He'll declare himself regent to the heir. Any hope you have of power will be lost," Whisper insists.

"What if you do not free him, madam?" Wali Khan whispers. "What of Aurangzeb's imperial guard? They are enough to rescue Shahji, maybe even enough to capture you, madam. If we fall upon them, Aurangzeb will send armies to invade us. It will be war, madam."

"War must come, madam," Whisper replies. "We've known that for years."

"But who will lead your armies, madam?" Wali Khan protests. "Shahji? I think not. Afzul Khan? Give him the army and he will depose you! You must release Shahji, madam—you have no choice!"

"If I release Shahji, then I hand over the regency. There must be some way to contain Afzul Khan," the sultana says, sounding desperate. "You are my advisers! How shall I do this?"

Whisper shakes his head. "I know not, madam."

"Give me time to think, madam," Wali Khan says.

"There is no time," she answers. "You men! You act as though you have forgotten our most important problem!"

"What is that, madam?" Whisper says.

"The gold!" she answers. "The Kankonen gold! How shall anyone rule without a treasury?"

ℰ☉ℰ☉

As Afzul Khan strides along the dark corridor, he at last begins to think. Who knew that Shahji had allies in Agra? He's played a double game the whole time, Afzul Khan realizes. Well, now we know. He's always been a traitor. I alone understood the threat! I alone acted!

Maybe I should kill her, he thinks. It would be easy enough. She's only stolen her power from that boy of hers. And who better to help the boy to grow into manhood?

The guards have heard him coming and pushed the crowds away. Afzul Khan glares at everyone. The wall is nearly finished now—the remaining opening would be filled by only one or two more bricks. For a moment he stands beside it, head bowed, nostrils flaring. Then he strikes.

Inside the alcove that has become his tomb, Shahji kneels and prays for death. Soon, he prays with all his heart. Soon.

He hears the crash and clatter. Despite his weariness, his eyes turn once more toward the wall. A half dozen bricks go flying through the air, crashing to the floor around him. Shahji ducks his head.

Then the great bulk of Afzul Khan looms over him. Kill me, prays Shahji. He waits for the heavy foot to kick. Instead Afzul Khan unlocks his chains.

Shahji pitches to the floor. Afzul Khan grabs him by the collar and tosses him through the broken opening. Shahji rolls over and sees the cowering faces of a line of people in the torchlight, and the dreadful face of the one-eyed man who threw the water flask.

But the moment ends quickly. Shoved and dragged and thrown and carried, Shahji lurches toward the throne room. At last he falls at the dais steps, on the very spot he landed—when? A day ago? A week? A month?

"As you requested, madam," Afzul Khan growls out, gasping for breath. "Here is the traitor."

"Your wish, Lord Ambassador?" the queen asks.

"I pray that you put him in my care, madam," the ambassador answers.

The sultana nods to her *khaswajara*. "You may take him to Shaista Khan's residence," Whisper says.

"There he may stay, but no other place," says the veiled queen.

The ambassador bows. "As you say, madam."

Soon Shahji is hoisted to his feet by the two Mogul guards. Though he has no idea how he comes to be free, he doesn't care. Somehow Shahji manages to walk from the hall like a man.

"You got what you came for, Lord Ambassador," the queen says. Her voice is strong behind her many veils. "You have the father." She pauses. "The son, however, is a different story."

The ambassador straightens. "I have no instructions about the son, madam." He looks at the mountain of velvet, but there is no face to read.

"Then sir, leave with our blessing." With these words, the ambassador takes his leave.

For a moment silence blankets the room, and then the sultana speaks.

"Shivaji," she says. The word becomes a hiss that echoes through the room. "Who will rid me of that mountain rat?"

At last a noble speaks. "I will," answers Afzul Khan.

Tension grows as the days pass. In the bazaar, a crowd of angry Bijapuris stone a Hindu merchant to death; no one is quite sure why, but everyone, at least the Muslims, seems certain he deserved it. The few Hindu shopkeepers in the great city board up their stalls.

Lakshman buys the white knitted cap of a *haji* and begins to sit amidst the *qwali* singers at the tomb of Ibrahim Roza, the Sufi saint buried in the shadow of the massive dome of the Gol Gumbaz.

The *qwalis* echo through the courtyard. The lead singer is a blind man with white, wandering eyes. His voice like a trumpet rings pure and strong over the drone of the tamboura and the *thud* of the tabla. The singers join the chorus as the blind man ends the verse. As Lakshman becomes familiar with the songs, he joins in. After a while, one of the singers slides over, making a space for Lakshman.

From time to time Lakshman enters the tomb, placing his head under the grave cloth of the saint. The third time he does this, he kisses the stone over the saint's feet like a devout Muslim. When he rises, he accepts the gift of flower petals scattered on the tomb, eating them one by one with closed eyes as a true believer might. The tomb attendants embrace him as a brother. They smell funny, Lakshman thinks.

Sometimes Lakshman sits apart, moving his lips, babbling any nonsense that comes into his head. Before long pilgrims approach him, cautiously kneeling to drop coins at his feet as though he too might be a saint. He reaches to touch their bent shoulders and says something, anything, and they look at him in gratitude, their eyes sometimes damp with tears. One day, the imam giving the lesson uses Lakshman as an example of true devotion.

Lakshman tries to look wild and strange. With his scarred face, with his broken eye that now weeps almost constantly, he succeeds. He sleeps in an alcove near the tomb, and wakes to find warm food placed near his feet.

When he gets bored, which is often, he goes to the bazaar. As he wanders through the marketplace, Lakshman hears the rumors: the Mogul guard camped just miles from the city gates; Shahji slowly coming back to health at the hand of the young ambassador; Afzul Khan readying a massive force to recover the stolen Bijapuri gold.

Holding out a cup, mumbling nonsense to the passersby, Lakshman walks among the market stalls. Some people recognize him from the tomb. But most prefer to ignore beggars than to see them, so it's easy for him to stand nearby unheeded as men discuss the latest news.

One day a strange procession pushes down the streets of the marketplace: cruel-looking soldiers accompanying a line of ten covered palanquins, each alike with black lacquer and silver decorations. The air fills with the shouts of the soldiers, the protests of the people they shove aside, the indignant barking of pariah dogs and the lowing of the street cows, with the cries of the shopkeepers and rough-edged street singers' songs.

Lakshman follows. At last the bearers lower the palkis outside a fabric store. From each box a woman emerges, some middle-aged, some young, and each one veiled. Lakshman wanders closer, hearing "the wives of Afzul Khan." At the shop door, the owner and his men bow as they pass inside.

Lakshman pushes close. The last in line, a slender graceful woman, lifts her head, and Lakshman glimpses behind her veil the outline of her face. From beneath her robes she drops into his cup a golden hun.

As the days pass, Lakshman thinks that he should write to Shivaji. He decides to wait until he has firm news of Afzul Khan. It does not occur to him to tell Shivaji of the rescue of his father.

Meanwhile in the marketplace, the men talk of little except the stolen gold. It's slowly dawning on everyone just how serious their situation is: without the gold, cash is growing short, credit strained.

Guards and soldiers have not been paid. Some have begun to walk through the bazaar in packs, taking what they will. The nobles insist on buying things on credit. Supplies grow short. Prices rise.

One day there is a riot over bread. The guardsmen simply watch as the mob runs down the street, looting any store that isn't locked.

The next day Lakshman hears a commotion at the mosque: a crowd of young men, all wearing white, chanting for Shivaji's death. It gives him an unexpected satisfaction to join in. He screams so loud that he's pushed to the head of the crowd. Death to Shivaji! Kill the thief! Death to Hindus! He shouts until his throat hurts. Others cluster near him, shaking their fists. He can hardly keep from laughing. But when the crowd marches out, Lakshman stays behind, relishing the silence of the quiet tomb.

Later he hears that the mob burned down a Hindu temple, leaving a brahmin trapped in the flames to die.

At prayers next morning, he lifts his head from the mosque floor to see a rich procession moving toward the tomb; Afzul Khan and all his captains bearing deep baskets of roses. One by one they enter the tomb and dump the flowers, shaking out the roses on the tomb of Ibrahim Roza.

Afzul Khan barely manages to squeeze through the door. When he emerges he kisses the threshold, the doorjamb; he spreads the dust of the floor upon his heart. Tears stream down his heavy face. At last he lifts his head and shouts in a voice that rocks the quiet: "I shall crush the infidel beneath my heel!" He shouts this two more times. Then his captains join him, calling "*Jai, jai* Afzul Khan! *Jai, jai* Afzul Khan!"

The fakir who sleeps in the next alcove slides over to Lakshman, saying, "His army is assembled. Tomorrow they set out for Poona. What men will do for gold!" The fakir shakes his head.

Lakshman merely sighs. I really should send word to Shivaji, he thinks.

It so happens that as Lakshman walks through the marketplace later that morning he sees again the line of ten black palkis. He feels a sudden urging, and follows them. The procession stops at Gold Street, and again the bearers help the wives of Afzul Khan to their feet. The last one, the small one, notices Lakshman again, and hesitates but then moves toward him.

This time, however, Lakshman speaks to her. "I must tell you something! I've had a vision!"

"What vision, fakir?" says the whisper from behind the golden veils.

"I saw your husband at the mosque. I saw Afzul Khan," he croaks. "He prayed to the saint for victory, but when he rose . . . he had no head! Just a bloody stump between his shoulders where his head should be!"

"Oh, Allah!" she cries, clutching her veiled cheeks.

"If he does this terrible thing, he shall die. Do you hear? He shall die!"

"Angels of grace!" she whispers.

Lakshman strides off into the crowd.

ༀༀༀ

The next morning, things are not peaceful in Afzul Khan's harem.

In anticipation of his departure to battle, Afzul Khan had taken a strong *vajikarana,* and all night long his lingam had been swollen and his balls boiling.

But he had no pleasure.

His wives, horrified by the tale of the one-eyed fakir and his vision, had wailed and wept in their beds. Just when he'd calmed one wife enough to mount her, he'd hear another start to cry. Thrust as he might, she'd be too upset to give him any pleasure.

From room to room, from bed to bed he'd gone, his lingam ready to explode. Finally he'd stormed off to his room and slammed the door. Then at last he found relief.

He brought all his wives in the garden. Dewdrops cling to every rose; birds sing. The women stand in dressing gowns, eyes red with weeping.

Afzul Khan stomps into the garden, dressed for battle. Weapons hang from his belt, spurs protrude from his black boots, and his broad curved sword slaps against his leg. The older wives gulp and lift their tear-stained faces, while the younger ones weep aloud.

Afzul Khan comes to his first wife. He stands by her—feet wide apart, jaw clenched, neck bulging. "I am not satisfied!" he shouts. He waits. She struggles not to sob. The birds stop singing, and only the babble of a nearby fountain breaks the silence.

"I am not satisfied, wife!" he screams, bending down so his face looks into hers. His wife lifts her damp eyes, but she knows better than to answer. "I am not satisfied!"

He moves down the line from woman to woman, his face a mask of rage. "I am not satisfied!" he yells at each, until the fifth wife bursts into sobs.

"But husband," she cries. "We don't want you to die!"

At this, Afzul Khan wheels around. The fifth wife's eyes reach scarcely to his breastplate. "You think that I will die?" he whispers.

The fifth wife can say nothing. She falls to her knees. Soon all his wives are wailing. Afzul Khan strides down the line, turning each wife's face with a gauntlet-covered hand and staring fiercely into her eyes.

When he reaches the tenth wife, the wife who spoke to Lakshman, she looks at him as though her heart would break, a look so searching and so deep that Afzul Khan drops his hand. "Husband," she whispers, her voice raw, "I could not bear to see you dead." She lifts her hand, but he pulls away so quickly that the heavy sword slaps against his leg.

"Is this so?" he asks softly. "You could not bear to see me dead?" She nods. He moves back to the ninth wife, and the eighth. "Is this so? Is this so?" They nod, silently. Down the line he walks, asking; down the line they nod, one by one, too anguished even to speak. "Even you?" he asks, when he reaches his first wife. "Even you?"

"Husband, you know I could not bear this!" she cries.

Afzul Khan bows his head. "So be it," he says softly. Then he turns. His broad sword flashes from its scabbard in a whirl.

One by one he mows them down, slashing through neck after neck, killing the next before the last has slumped to the ground.

By the time he's reached the middle of the line, the ones that still breathe have begun to scream. On the ground behind him, heads fall with mouths still gasping, dark blood pumps from hearts still beating. Green grass, white robes, black hair, red blood. The sword rips through their necks like stalks of wheat.

By the time he's reached his tenth wife, she starts to back away, begging. Afzul Khan points his sword to her, and blood drips from the blade. "Come back, you!" he calls, his voice hoarse. "Come back and die!"

Without thinking she begins to run, running and turning, running backward, and her little feet get tangled in her robes. She falls and creeps upon the ground. "No!"

Wearily, Afzul Khan shuts his eyes. Then as calm as a man about to strike a snake, he walks over and thrusts the broad blade of his long sword into her belly, thrusts it through so hard it cuts the bones, thrusts it till it penetrates the soil beneath her back. Blood bubbles from her mouth, and when he pulls away his sword, blood fountains from the wound.

With the folds of her white skirt, while her mouth still moves and her wide eyes stare, he wipes the gore from his blade. Then he sheathes his sword, and without a look behind him, walks to the garden door. "Bury them in a row," he tells his *khaswajara*. "Except the last. Bury her where she fell. She at least showed some courage."

Afzul Khan strides from the garden, ready now for battle.

CHAPTER 25

❧❧❧❧

Bala knocks on Sai Bai's door, and when there is no answer, he pushes the door open and steps in. The shutters are closed, and the room in shadows. Shivaji sits by Sai Bai's low bed, holding her hand. Her face, once round, now is gaunt, her eyes enormous, dark-rimmed. Beautiful eyes, thinks Bala, but then he realizes that they are wide with pain.

A servant girl tucks a crisp white sheet tight around her mistress; nearby in a wooden bowl, sits a dark wad of bandage oozing blood. The servant takes up the bowl and as she passes Bala, a smell rises from the bowl, sick and sweet. Bala knows that smell; anyone who has seen death knows it. It will linger in his nostrils for a long, long while.

Shivaji looks up, his face full of anguish. "What is it?"

"Word from Lakshman, lord."

Shivaji glances at Sai Bai. "Go," she says. "I'll be all right." She even tries to smile. Shivaji rises, pressing on her hand all the while. It takes a while for him to let her go. Her wide eyes never leave him.

When Shivaji shuts the door, Bala asks, "Still bleeding?"

"Much less than yesterday, I think."

"Good," Bala says. But they know this might be a sign of a body giving up. For a moment he considers placing a hand on Shivaji's arm, but he does not. It would not be seemly to touch Lord Shivaji so.

The bright sun bathes the busy courtyard, and Shivaji blinks as though unaccustomed to the light. Bala notices how worn his face appears. Bala hands a wrinkled paper to Shivaji. "This came a few minutes ago, lord, brought by an Afghan trader. A one-eyed fakir paid him a gold hun to bring it. He gave Lakshman's code word, 'vengeance.' "

Shivaji unfolds the note.

Shahji freed. Afzul Khan setting out for Poona. 100 elephants. 500 cannon. 2000 horses. 15000 men.

"Is this all?" Shivaji cries. He says each word aloud once more. "All that time in Bijapur, and this is all?"

"Fifteen thousand men, lord," Bala says, as shakes his bald head. "How many men have we in Welhe?"

"Two thousand, maybe three. Perhaps another thousand in Poona. A couple of hundred more in Pratapghad or on their way. Maybe a thousand ponies."

The thought occurs to Bala that there are many signs of coming death: a blood-filled cloth in a wooden bowl, for instance; or a thousand ponies and four thousand untrained men. They sit in silence for a moment. Around them the bustle of living carries on: men carrying baskets on their heads, women singing as they wash clothing at the well, birds flitting to the ground to peck at unseen seeds, a bony cow poking through a pile of garbage. "What shall I do, Bala?"

This is not what Bala wants to hear. He wants the plan laid out for him, he wants to act upon it. He does not want uncertainty. "If you need guidance, ask the goddess."

At that moment, a young sentry, running hard and out of breath, dashes through the courtyard calling to Shivaji. "A dozen Mogul soldiers at the city gates, lord, asking for you!" the sentry sputters. "We didn't know if we should let them in."

Shivaji glances at Bala. "Escort them here."

Soon, a pair of sentries on ponies come through the compound gates, followed by two rows of soldiers riding on proud Bedouins, pennants fluttering from the tips of long lances.

The captain of the Moguls rides forward. "We seek Lord Shivaji of Poona," he says, enunciating each word.

"I am he," Shivaji answers.

Hanging from the captain's belt is an elaborate silver tube, which he hands to Shivaji. "I bring this message from my master, Lord Ali Rashid, who sends you greetings and begs that you read it at your ease. He bids me to await your answer, if you have one."

"Tell your master that we are in his debt, captain," Bala answers before Shivaji gets a chance. He calls to the sentries. "Take these guests to our dharmsala and give them every comfort."

"You are kind, lord," the captain says, bowing again to Shivaji.

Shivaji opens the silver message tube and breaks the seals. He unfurls the bright parchment and tosses it to Balaji. "Persian," he says.

Balaji looks the paper over. "It's from Aurangzeb's ambassador to Bijapur. He says that they have rescued your father. Shahji is being given every honor a man of his greatness deserves."

"That's good," Shivaji says. "That's very good."

"Maybe," says Bala. "He says that he has brought five thousand imperial cavalry to Bijapur. They're encamped at the gates of Bijapur, ready to attack if he should give the word." Shivaji raises his eyebrows. "He says that Afzul Khan is on his way to attack you."

"That we knew already."

"He suggests that a Mogul foray into Bijapur would force Afzul Khan's return. You have only to request this action." Bala looks at Shivaji, his face serious. "He apologizes but with the siege of Golconda, a small contingent is all that could be spared on your behalf."

"Five thousand imperial guards?" Though Shivaji shakes his head, all he can do is laugh. "A small contingent? This fixes everything!"

"Wait, lord. The note goes on to say that your presence is requested— no, it says 'required'—in Agra. There you shall confirm your fealty to the Peacock Throne." Shivaji's face hardens. "They will send a hundred men to escort you, and to protect the tribute that you naturally will wish to offer to the *padshah*." Bala looks up at Shivaji and rolls the parchment. "The rest is an insult, lord. Such bad manners are unforgivable."

"What does it say?"

Balaji seems hard pressed to say the words aloud. "He suggests—that's the word he uses, 'suggests'—that you would wish to bring no less than nine crore hun to lay in tribute at the *padshah*'s feet."

For a moment, Shivaji stares at him in silence. Then he starts to laugh, and laughs some more, and soon Balaji is laughing, too. "Well," Shivaji says finally, lifting the silver tube, "it's an elegant bill, I'll say that much. Whoever thought I'd be rich enough to get a bill for nine crore hun?" He looks at Bala bitterly. "Think Shahji's life is worth nine crore hun, Bala?"

"At least then your troubles will be over, lord. Give them what they want and live in their protection."

"No, Bala. Our troubles would only be beginning."

☙☙☙☙

"He should have come himself," Iron grumbles to Jedhe once they return to his house in Welhe. "I keep thinking Hanuman will be different than his father. Honor doesn't run in their blood, Jedhe."

They'd just returned from a war council, where they heard the message sent by Lakshman, and Shivaji's terse note: "Prepare a defense."

"Why didn't you speak out, uncle?" Jedhe says.

"I tried! Weren't you listening? Every time, he shut me up. Told me to talk to him later! Me! Iron! He tells me this! We're outmanned and outgunned—and there sits Hanuman brimming with confidence. Truth wasn't welcome there, Jedhe."

"It's true, uncle. We're sunk."

Iron laughs. "Take the advice of an old man, nephew. Never trust anyone completely. Never. Not even your old uncle Iron."

"You don't trust Shivaji, uncle?"

"In the end, what difference does it make? Unless we watch our backs, we'll all be dead. What do you think of Tanaji's plan?"

"You mean Hanuman's plan, uncle?"

Iron sniffs. "I've seen this plan before; always the same thing. You think I don't recognize Tanaji's tactics?"

"But I think the two of them are hardly talking now, since the trouble over Hanuman's marriage."

"Then the son is just a copy of the father. Too bad. Lakshman at least thought for himself. Too bad we got the other twin as captain. As for the plan, I can't see any part of it that doesn't end in death."

They talk about the plan: a series of quick feints by small squads of bowmen mounted on ponies. Hanuman expects Afzul Khan to follow the squads into the Torna valley, where the combined Marathi forces will perform a double-flanking attack, rushing down from the hills, supported by the Torna cannon. "I never heard such nonsense," scoffs Iron. "As if Afzul Khan would follow those squads into a fortified valley. Maybe he'll also aim his cannon at himself and shoot his own head off."

"What do you think he'll do, uncle?"

"What would I do if I had fifteen thousand men?" Iron laughs. "I'd break off a phalanx of cavalry. Chase down the bowmen and crush them.

Make it ugly. Make an example. The main force goes straight to Poona."
Iron looks at Jedhe seriously. "That's the goal, nephew—Poona! Why
would Afzul Khan be distracted? He doesn't want battle. He wants gold!
He wants Shivaji! Both are in Poona."

Jedhe considers this. "So what do we do?"

"I'll keep my word. I'll fight next to Hanuman. At least until it's clear
all hope is gone. Then I'll decide. There's nothing to prevent us from cutting a deal with Bijapur if it's clear Shivaji's doomed."

"Then why wait? Isn't the outcome already clear now, uncle?"

"To us perhaps. Not to my men. It's sad that men will have to die. But
if I do things my way, some will live." Jedhe merely looks at the floor.
"You're young," Iron says gently, "and you don't like an old man's plan. I
understand. Don't you think I'd rather die gloriously?"

"If you don't like your own plan, uncle, why do it?"

"Dying gloriously is still dying. The point is staying alive."

"Maybe it's not so bad to die, uncle."

"That's the spirit! Go and die!" Iron puts a calloused hand on his
nephew's shoulder. "Listen to the way an old man thinks: if you lose and
live, Jedhe, you can always fight again. If you die, you're done."

Jedhe, for a change, has nothing witty to reply. "This isn't how I thought
that it would be, uncle."

"When you're young, you want a hero's life. When you're old, any life
will do. Hanuman's playing at being a hero. You want to die for his dreams?"

◈◈◈◈

Meanwhile, across the courtyard from Iron's house, Hanuman says to
Tanaji, "How do you think it went, father?"

Tanaji tugs at his mustache, and grimaces. "About as well as you could
expect. No one likes to think about facing a big army, least of all one led by
Afzul Khan."

Hanuman considers this. "What should I do?"

"You can't do anything. In battle the plans will fall apart, and then, in
all the smoke and noise, someone will take the lead. You, maybe, or Iron, or
me. Jedhe, maybe. And everyone will follow in a glorious attack. Or a
rout." Tanaji sighs.

"Why doesn't Shivaji come?" Hanuman says bitterly. "Shivaji should
lead us. I no longer think he's needed in Poona. Anybody who is going to
join us has already made the move."

Tanaji thinks this over. "Write him. Ask him to come."

Hanuman turns to a little writing desk in the corner of the room when a servant enters. "A visitor for you," he says. "A woman."

As the woman steps shyly through the door, Hanuman jumps to his feet. "Jyoti!"

In the dim light her dark face seem to glow. She bows deeply to Tanaji, eyes lowered, then to Hanuman, but looking straight at him. Then she turns back to Tanaji. "I know you asked me to have no more to do with your son, sir, but something has come up. Something wonderful and strange." Hanuman's first thought is that Jyoti is pregnant. That would explain the way her face glows, but not her happiness.

Tanaji glowers at her. "You have heard my judgment. You have no dowry; my son and you have no future."

"All that has changed, sir," Jyoti says.

"Changed how?" Tanaji asks gruffly.

"Two nights ago, when I lifted the covers of my bed I found a gift. A gift that I can only guess the gods sought fit to give me. A purse. A yellow purse, a purse of soft leather, tied with a golden cord. The cord was cut in two. Inside were coins—heavy golden coins I have never seen before: not hun, not rupees. I showed it to the *shastri.* He said the money was *farang* gold."

"*Farang?*" gasps Hanuman.

"Yes. Suddenly I am a rich woman." She giggles nervously. "When the *shastri* saw how much, he nearly piddled. He told me I should give the gold to the temple. Then the gods would give me blessings; otherwise the gold would bring evil. I refused."

"The rich give nothing away," Tanaji says. "That's how they stay rich."

"Then I am rich. Rich enough, maybe, to be worthy of your son."

"But where did the purse come from, Jyoti?" Hanuman says "How did it come to be in your bed? Had someone been to the temple that day?"

"No. Only the regular villagers been there that day, other than your father," she says, turning to Tanaji. Tanaji braces himself with a big frown. "Did you see anyone around that night, someone who might have had a bag of *farang* gold?"

Tanaji harrumphs. "There was no one there but me."

Jyoti seems confident now, strong. "You can't deny, sir, that I've answered your objection now."

Tanaji shakes his head. "You're right. I'll talk to Nirmala."

"My prayers are answered, father," Hanuman says.

"Is the letter to Shivaji finished?" Tanaji snaps, turning so no one can see his face.

"Nearly," Hanuman sits back at the small desk, writing hurriedly, and Jyoti watches him, beaming. She doesn't notice Tanaji wiping at his eyes.

When Hanuman is finished, Tanaji takes the letter. "I'll be back tomorrow," he says. But Hanuman isn't looking at him, nor is Jyoti. "I'm leaving now," Tanaji says, louder.

The moment he is gone, they fall into each other's arms.

An hour later, the servant calls through the door. "A messenger has come, sir. The Bijapuri army has been spotted."

ᏮᎧᏯᎧ

The sun shines hot and bright on the Bijapuri plain, on the heads of the thousands marching toward the mountains like a swarm of carrion beasts. Ahead the mountains loom like teeth thrust out of the earth, with black flanks dark beneath the shadows of huge clouds.

The howdah of Afzul Khan's great war elephant rocks like a boat in a turbulent sea. Through a fog of dust, Afzul Khan sees his cavalry spread across the plain, bright lances gleaming. Ahead of them ride the ten banner-bearers, carrying on silver-studded flagpoles the dark green flags of Bijapur, snapping in the breeze.

Behind him tramp war elephants heavy with armor, trunks upraised. In the rear, their faces streaked with dust-stained sweat, follows an ocean of soldiers. In the distance, oxcarts strain beneath the weight of weapons and supplies, and behind them, high-wheeled cannon tugged by man and ox alike. Trailing away behind, hidden by clouds of dust, the servants and cooks, the fletchers and smiths and whores straggle slowly, slowly onward.

The swath the army cuts across the plain is wide: crops and huts are crushed beneath its heavy step. The peasants grab what things they can and flee. From the dust clouds that hang around them like a war god's chariot, the music of destruction blares: the pounding of the battle drums; the blasting of war trumpets as tall as men.

The track of the army moves across the plateau like a stain.

Rocking in his howdah, the general of all, Afzul Khan, sweats in the noontime heat, propped on silk and velvet cushions. With each step sounds the *clunk* of the elephant's armor, iron bossed with leather, that covers its flanks.

The sun is so hot that the mahout, who half-kneels, half-sits on the beast's wide head, must ladle water on its war helmet; otherwise the elephant's brain would surely bake beneath the bronze. The water sizzles into steam.

A man rides up on an energetic Bedouin. Dust streaks fall in lines along its flanks, and strings of foam hang from its lips. The man spurs his mount to walk beside the elephant, and calls to Afzul Khan. "Nearly time for prayers, general."

Afzul Khan points to the mountains. "No more stops for prayers. When I pray next, I'll be in Poona. I'll use Shivaji's skin for my prayer rug. Not until then, captain, will I stop for prayer."

"But, general!" the captain protests, until he sees the face that lowers at him from the howdah. "As you say, general." He hesitates. "But sir . . . the men. I mean, we're going into battle soon, and the men . . ."

"Captain, which way are we facing?"

"West, sir."

"Which way's Mecca?"

"West, sir."

"So anyone may pray. Pray in your saddle. Pray on your feet. Trust me, Allah will understand." Afzul Khan stares at the mountains, and points to the pass. "We must be there tonight, captain. I want to eat my dinner in Welhe."

"But, sir, those mountains are fifteen miles away! And it's another eight miles through the pass to Welhe."

"You heard me, captain." And with that Afzul Khan heaves himself back amidst his velvet cushions.

❦❦❦❦

They don't make Welhe by the evening, though the captain sets the lash to many. It's just too far and too hot. They've barely reached the foothills as the sun goes down. The captain looks at the rugged, narrow road that winds into the heights, curses, and calls a halt. It takes a quarter hour before the word has spread, before the whole ragged force, stretched for miles across the Bijapuri plain, stops to collapse exhausted on the hot ground.

The captain screws up his courage and rides back to Afzul Khan. "I had to call a halt, general. There was no way to bring the army through that pass at night. Our men are exhausted. The road's a mess and probably protected." He shouts this in a rush, waiting for the heavy sword to fall and split his head in two.

"You did what you had to, captain," the general says at last.

"I know you said that we must . . ."

"But of course, we could never have made Welhe, could we? Clever of you to work that out. We're here, at least, by sundown. That's something."

Afzul Khan twists his face, and it occurs to the captain that he's trying to smile. "Come and meet me in an hour. I have something I wish to discuss with you."

The captain bows as a man condemned bows to his judge. "But first," says Afzul Khan, "spread the word among the men. No tents. We sleep beneath the stars tonight. Tomorrow we break camp at dawn."

An hour later the captain returns to find the general seated by a bright fire in a camp chair of wood and leather, talking with a small man he's never seen before. Not far away he sees servants fluttering around a dinner table; a table set—the captain notices—for one.

"Ah, captain," says Afzul Khan, standing at his approach. "I've been waiting. Come and look at this."

The captain joins him. When the small man lifts his head, the captain sees the deep brown scars where a cross has been branded into his face; one ragged scar from forehead to lips, the other where his eyebrows must have been. An Abyssinian, the captain thinks. He hates them, but the general is fond of them. Most of them are Christians, and all of them are soulless, their shifty eyes like jackals' hunting for an unsuspecting prey.

"This man, Simon, has been helping me," Afzul Khan explains. The captain inclines his head in greeting. The Abyssinian merely squints in reply. He holds an oiled leather thong, twisting it tightly around his fingers and untwisting it.

"Come and see, captain," says Afzul Khan. Despite his bulk, the general slides easily between some carts parked end to end to form a private area. The captain follows. Behind him comes the Abyssinian. He can smell the oil and onions on his breath.

Two torches driven into open ground between the wagons light up a messy heap of long bamboo poles, and nearby a small pile of oiled leather thongs. Propped up against a tool box rest a wooden mallet, a thin saw, and a two-handled drawknife.

"Simon's weaponry." Afzul Khan chuckles, nodding at the toolbox. As if in response, the dark man moves silently to the tools and begins to cut a bamboo pole.

The captain notices that the poles form some sort of assembly: an open framework bound with leather thongs. "Simon's handiwork," says Afzul Khan. "He's an expert, you know. A master of his craft."

"What is it?" the captain asks. Afzul Khan lifts his chin, encouraging the captain to pick up the assembly. When he lifts it from the ground, it expands: the poles drop down on leather hinges with a clack, forming a box.

A cage.

"Are you hunting, then, sir?" the captain ventures, though suddenly his blood runs cold.

"Trapping," Afzul Khan says, taking a step closer.

The captain tells himself to calm down. What are you afraid of? But then he smells oil and onions, and spins around to see the Abyssinian inches from his back, the thin leather thong twisting in his hands.

"I had my Christian build this cage for Shivaji. It's based on my ideas, but the execution is all his own, and I must say, it is superb." The Abyssinian nods his head. "In this cage I shall bring Shivaji to Bijapur. In this cage I shall parade him as a prize. In this cage I shall watch him as he dies."

The Abyssinian swiftly lashes the sides and corners together, the contraption takes form, like a pair of flat, oddly shaped boxes, both but a few inches high. Soon he stands back, puffing slightly from the effort.

"I don't understand," says the captain, walking around the assembly. "How is this a cage? How can it hold anything?"

"I agree, it's difficult to appreciate without a—well, a specimen to demonstrate." Afzul Khan looms over him. "Would you care to volunteer?" Before the captain has a chance to answer, before he has a chance to move or even think, Afzul Khan has reached his thick arm around his head, squeezing his skull until it would seem to burst. Then he throws him effortlessly down.

Then the trap is sprung.

The captain lies on his back. Something's in front of his eyes; he can't see what. The bamboo slats of the cage press against his limbs. He's in a sort of lattice cross, his torso and his limbs twisted painfully. The bamboo is loose in places, tight in others; his head for example, can move forward but not side to side. He pulls his head back far enough to see what's in front eyes.

Bamboo spikes. Sharpened.

Probably there are others hidden from his sight. It's not just a cage, the captain realizes. It's an instrument of torture.

"Well, what do you think, captain?" The heavy, jowled face of Afzul Khan comes into his sight as the general stoops beside him, grunting with the effort. "Now, this part here, around the head and eyes, that was my idea."

Perhaps he's only testing me, thinks the captain. "Ingenious, sir," he whimpers.

"Ingenious, yes. You have no idea," Afzul Khan laughs. "For one thing, you're upside down."

No, I'm not, the captain thinks. But in that instant, the general grabs the side of the contraption and flips it over.

It takes all the captain's strength to stop his head from hurtling to the spikes before his eyes. Now he sees the ground below him, and inches from his eyes, those spikes, sharp and terrible.

"Now you understand," the general chuckles.

"How do I get out?" the captain gasps. Or maybe he just screams.

"You don't, captain. I thought that was clear?" Afzul Khan turns to the Abyssinian. "Make a sign: 'He disobeyed.' Put him and the cage upon a cart and drive him around the camp. Let all know what happens to those who disobey. Then make another cage; this one for Shivaji. I approve of the design."

The captain, struggling to keep his head from falling forward, hears the crunching of the general's thick-soled shoes as he leaves. He can no longer contain himself. "Allah!" he screams. His eyes, just inches from the blinding spikes, are suddenly wet with weeping, and mucous and saliva pour from his nose and mouth. As if in answer to his wailing, he hears the footsteps of the general's return, and his growling voice. "Don't do this, captain. Don't weep like a woman. Show some courage. You weren't much good as a captain, after all. Just think of all the good you'll do as an example. Before you were but one captain among many. Now you are unique. You'll give each man incentive to obey."

"Don't let me die this way, general!" the captain wails.

Afzul Khan considers this. "Am I not known for being merciful?"

"Yes!" the captain sobs. "Afzul Khan the merciful!"

"Very well. Stay alive until we capture Shivaji, and I'll let you go. By then the men will have no more need of your example."

The captain gasps. "I will pray for our quick victory, general!"

"Allah attends to desperate prayer, captain."

Tanaji rides into the courtyard of the Rang Mahal, struck by the quiet hanging over Poona. Where have the children gone? he wonders. People walk through the courtyard silently. And no one sits outside—the verandahs are empty. It's as though a cloud hovers overhead.

The cloud, thinks Tanaji, of war approaching.

When he enters his doorway, Nirmala gives him a long, desperate embrace. It's been a long time since she has thrown herself against him so. He pats her, whispering softly to her.

Then he sits, and listens to her, while (of all things) she unwraps his turban and combs his thick black hair. "It came to me to do this, husband," is all she'll say. But he must admit, it feels good, her hands soothing him, the ivory comb whispering through his hair. They talk of many things, but of course it isn't long before they speak of Hanuman, and of Jyoti, and of Jyoti's sudden wealth.

"Shivaji!" she cries when she hears it. "This is his doing!"

"Maybe," her husband says. "But he was in Poona the whole time. And he promised you, didn't he? To you, at least, he has always kept his word."

"Hmmph. There's always a first time. Besides, who else could it be?"

"Who else had a bag of *farang* gold?" Tanaji asks, as if he has no idea. "She'll be a servant girl no more, I'd guess. She's rich enough now to buy a town."

☙☙☙☙

At the door of the palace, Jijabai greets Tanaji. She starts to speak to him when Sambhuji runs in and hugs him hard around his legs. Tanaji tousles his hair and Sam runs off.

Jijabai shakes her head. "He's been like that for days. Shivaji gives him nothing. He sits with that sick wife of his, as though he can make up for years of neglect. Shameful what he did to her—but what he's doing now is even worse. He should be with his army!"

"That's why I've come."

"Good. Talk some sense into him. It does us no good for him to wait there in the dark, watching her die."

"Is there no hope for her, then?"

"We must all die, Tana." She shows Tanaji to a small room, and goes to get her son. The narrow steps seem steeper these days, her legs shorter. By the time she reaches the top, she must press her hand against a wall to catch her breath.

When Jijabai enters, Sai Bai's eyes move to her, but nothing else. Shivaji sits up, startled. His hair hangs down around his shoulders. "Tanaji is downstairs," Jijabai hisses. "Make yourself presentable."

Shivaji slumps when she says this. He presses Sai Bai's hand. "I'll be back soon."

Jijabai closes the door as Shivaji leaves, and sits at the edge of Sai Bai's bed. "Well?" she says.

"I'm feeling much better, mother," Sai Bai answers, but her eyes are wide and dark and her face is thin.

"This lingering illness of yours is more than a nuisance. It's dangerous. He sits by your side when he should be commanding armies. Your indulgence may cause many to die." Jijabai stares angrily at Sai Bai. Slowly however, she grows softer. She touches a single finger to Sai Bai's hand. "A woman's lot is never easy. Much less a queen's."

"I'm not a queen, mother," Sai Bai whispers.

"You must act like one."

"But how, mother? You can't mean for me to die." Sai Bai's eyes now seem filled with fear.

"Not to die. But you must free my son to do his duty. You must let go his hand. You must be braver than he."

"But how can this be done?"

So Jijabai tells her.

ᘓᘍᘏᘐ

Servants bring in butter lamps, and their golden flames casting flickering shadows on the plaster walls. Soon Balaji and Trelochan join Tanaji in the darkening room. As they wait for Shivaji, the smells of evening drift through the high windows; the dusky smell of dung fires, the tang of oil on hot metal pans, the golden smell of chapatis being fried.

A servant comes to the door, and shows a cloaked figure into the room. "Bandal!" Bala exclaims, as the visitor takes off his cloak.

"I thought you were at Pratapghad," Tanaji says, rising to greet him.

"I just came from there. Where's Shivaji?"

Trelochan chuckles. "That's what we all wish to know."

"Now you have your wish," Shivaji says, stepping through the door.

Tanaji tells of the situation in Welhe. "All in all, not good," he says. "We're outnumbered five to one. Our men have had no training."

"But what about the Bijapuris, uncle?" Balaji puts in. "An army that size, gathered in a short time. They won't have had much training either."

Tanaji shakes his head. "Afzul Khan's armies live in fear; he stands behind them with a whip. Death at the hands of an enemy is better than living to face Afzul Khan's displeasure."

"We've heard all this before," says Bandal. "Whether they're trained or not, what difference does it make? They have five men for every one of ours. And he has elephants. And Abyssinians." Bandal turns earnestly to Shivaji.

"You send untrained men against Afzul Khan, led by an untried captain, and what do you think will happen? Disaster!"

Tanaji bristles. "You agreed to the plan. And it's not like Hanuman's alone. Iron is there."

Bandal snorts. "I don't trust him, cousin," he says to Shivaji. "I'm guessing that Iron will go his own way; he always has."

"We'll discuss Iron later," Shivaji says wearily. "We have another problem to solve." He nods to Bala.

So Bala tells Bandal of the letter from the Mogul ambassador, the offer of support and the demand for nine crore hun.

"What are we to do about this, Shahu?" Tanaji demands.

"Nothing," Shivaji says flatly.

"But they'll attack us!"

"We're already under attack. Afzul Khan isn't writing letters; he's here in force, today. The Moguls are far away."

"But the Moguls have Shahji. He's practically a hostage!" Trelochan says. "What about your father?"

Shivaji shakes his head. "Do the Moguls mean to use my father to control me, like the ring in a bullock's nose?"

"But, Shahu," Tanaji says quietly, "if you accepted their offer—if the Moguls would move against Bijapur . . ."

"That's nothing but smoke, uncle," Shivaji replies. "Five thousand men against Bijapur? Do you seriously believe that they'd attack?" Tanaji shrugs. "Anyway, how would that stop Afzul Khan?"

The circle is silent for a moment. "Well then," Tanaji says at last, "if that's how it is, we must gather all our strength. Shahu, you must lead the battle in Welhe."

Bandal shakes his head. "To go to Welhe is a fool's errand. We can't defeat Afzul Khan in open battle!" He leans close to Shivaji. "Why should we fight on a flat field? Our strength comes from our mountains! Those Bijapuris come from the plains. They ride Bedouins, not mountain ponies! How can they hope to win, if we choose the place of battle?"

"The battle plain is chosen, Bandal," Tanaji says firmly. "The plan is to face them in Welhe!"

But at the moment, the door opens, and Sai Bai enters. The argument is forgotten as the men look up in wonder. Yes, it is she, Sai Bai, in a bright blue sari, with golden earrings, with kohl around her eyes and vermilion along the part of her braided hair. She sweeps across the floor, a tray of toddy cups in her hands.

"I thought you might be thirsty, husband," Sai Bai says, lowering herself gracefully to him.

"But can this be?" Shivaji asks, eyes wide.

"I am feeling much better, husband," Sai Bai laughs, moving around the circle. "Yes, much better now." She stands, and maybe a look of pain steals across her face, but in an instant it is gone and her smile returns.

"My heart is glad to hear it," Shivaji answers.

When he starts to rise, Sai Bai shakes her head. "You have business, husband. Do what you must do. See, I am well now, by the goodness of the goddess!"

"It is a miracle," says Bala quietly. Sai Bai nods, her dark eyes beautiful and deep, and shuts the door behind her.

ಹಹಹಹ

Outside, Jijabai takes the tray from Sai Bai before it tumbles from her hand, and takes her arm before she falls. Sai Bai collapses against her. A servant girl moves to help, but Jijabai glares at her. "What are you looking at, eh? This doesn't concern you!"

Grunting and scolding, Jijabai helps Sai Bai up the stairs. She's surprisingly light. Behind them the bright blue sari's train sweeps across a trail of drops: dark red blood, freshly fallen on the wooden floor.

ಹಹಹಹ

The flames of the butter lamps flicker as the door closes, and then burn bright once more.

"I will join the battle," Shivaji announces.

"Excellent!" says Trelochan. "Sai Bai's recovery is a sign. Soon all will be well. Shivaji's sword will lead us!"

Bandal leans forward intently. "The battle's better joined at Pratapghad than in Welhe. We can put the Bijapuris where we want them. In Welhe, we have no advantage."

"If Welhe falls, then Poona must fall as well," Bala answers. "Afzul Khan will march straight for Poona. The treasure will be lost."

"I disagree. He wants vengeance more than treasure. He'll follow Shahu." Bandal looks earnestly at Shivaji. "Pratapghad's perfect, Shahu. The place is a fortress. I can't imagine how those tribals did it. The fort was empty when we got there; the gates still barred from the inside. Inside, nothing: no sign of life, no bodies. Nothing but ghosts."

"How did they do it?" Bala says.

"As I say, I have no idea. Pratapghad's impregnable. There's a long road leading to it, narrow, twisting. Deep forests on each side. A perfect place to stage an ambush."

"The time has come for battle, not for ambush," Trelochan insists. "Win in open battle. Don't win by deceit!"

Shivaji smiles. "Since when has lying ever failed me?"

"But what of the Moguls, lord?" asks Bala.

"Delay. Tell the captain I'm considering their request," Shivaji says. "Who knows what the morrow may bring?"

"With any luck, we'll all be dead by then," Tanaji says, trying to make a joke, but no one laughs.

Shivaji turns to Bandal, placing a hand on his shoulder. "Shall we go to Pratapghad?"

"Yes, lord," he answers. "I'll die at your side."

ⓒⓢⓒⓢ

Shivaji collects his gear, and straps on the sword Bhavani. He glances around the room, fixing it in his memory. He's about to visit Sai Bai, but Jijabai stops him at the door. "She's sleeping, Shahu."

"Good. She hasn't slept for days, not really."

"As you say, Shahu. This is good news. It is the sleep of healing."

"Her recovery is a miracle."

Jijabai walks him to the courtyard. By the light of torches, they see Tanaji and Bandal already mounted, with Shivaji's pony at the ready. Nirmala stands nearby, covering her mouth with the end of her sari.

"Tell her I said goodbye." Shivaji hoists himself onto the saddle.

Jijabai bows as they ride off. Men can be so foolish, she thinks.

CHAPTER 26

The stone walls of Adoli temple shake like the kettle of an elephant drum.

Through the columns, Maya sees the night sky flash, and then, a moment later, she hears the thundering blast. A great, deep-throated roar rips the air like the laughter of a rakshasa. The mountains flash, the smoky air glows, and eerie shadows swirl.

An hour ago her nose began to sting with the smell of gunpowder smoke. Now tears stream from her burning eyes. She leans against the stone wall of the inner temple. Inside that room sleeps Bhavani. Its doors are locked, and the brahmins have taken the key. Who will wake the goddess in the morning? she wonders.

I should have left, I should have left, I should have left! They told her to leave—the *shastri*'s wife begged her, Jyoti in tears, but she had broken free. At last they fled the temple for the hills, and left Maya behind.

Her fingers tighten on the handle of a sickle. She had suddenly felt the need of a weapon, and the sickle was the only sharp thing she could find. Her butter lamp is guttering: the flame sputters and all is dark. The air flashes again. For a moment she sees clearly, and then her world dissolves in blackness.

No, she tells herself. She thought—she must have been mistaken—she thought she saw a man standing in the doorway. She raises the sickle. A series of flashes sputters through the darkness. The shadow has moved.

A man.

Maybe the *shastri* has come back for her.

Then the sky flashes again, and she sees now only steps away a haji cap, a grizzled beard, the wild look of a fakir. She lifts the sickle over her head. In another burst of light, the fakir waves his hand. As he does, the sickle flies from her grasp. The clatter of it echoes from the walls.

The lights flare again, and Maya sees who it is. "Hanuman!"

"No," the man answers. And in the next roaring flash, she sees the ragged scars, the moisture seeping from the flat and empty eyelid. "Recognize your handiwork?" Lakshman asks, with a voice like acid.

Suddenly Maya is utterly alone; no gods, no friends, just her and this half demon. When the light flashes again: there he stands, one eye bright and evil, and in his hand, he now holds her sickle.

"How did he do that?" Lakshman asks in a harsh falsetto. "I'm so frightened! Oh dear! I'm alone with a magician!"

"What do you want?" she whispers.

"What do I want, indeed? For I can have anything. Anything at all."

She flinches as she feels his cold touch in the darkness. "Do it and get it over with. I've had so many. Another man, what difference will it make?"

She hears his ragged breathing in the darkness. "When I take you, you'll know. You'll never be the same." The cold hand moves to her neck. "You think that I'm the same as other men? No more. No more." The hand creeps down her shoulder, the fingers slide across her breasts. Through the thin fabric of the sari, Lakshman pinches Maya's nipple.

"I've come to take you out of here," he says, lifting his hand, just so, as if he'd never touched her. "Afzul Khan is coming. He's going to destroy this temple. Because it is Shivaji's goddess." The words hang in the air, like the echo of a gong. "You think your precious Shivaji would come to save you? You poor bitch. He's sitting on his ass in Poona. He doesn't care a shit. Bastard." He takes her upper arm, firmly, not rough as she expected. "We've got to get going. Afzul Khan is almost here."

"I won't leave the goddess. Someone needs to protect her!"

"It's your own safety you should think of, not hers. She's just a piece of rock. So what if Afzul Khan breaks her: imagine what he would do to you! Come. It's me or death." A flare streaks light on his dead-white scars. "Come on, I'll take you to him. That's what you want, isn't it?"

Beneath his grip she stumbles, driven blind into the darkness.

❂❂❂❂

"Stand fast! Stand fast!" Hanuman screams into the night, as his pony wheels and bucks beneath him.

Around him, the battle boils: dust and smoke, the crack of matchlocks and the boom of bombs, the screams of elephants and horses, and of men. Around his pony's feet, shrub grass smolders; burning trees spew sparks into the breeze like swarms of fiery insects.

"Stand fast!" Hanuman cries, his long sword waving. "Stand fast and form a line!" His voice can't be heard for the roar of O'Neil's *granadas*. Hanuman swings around to see Jedhe ride up. Blood streaks Jedhe's face. "They're running like rats!" he shouts to Hanuman.

"Where's Iron?" Hanuman shouts back.

"About a half mile behind us."

"Pull back!" Hanuman shouts, spurring his horse. "Tell everyone to pull back!" He drives his pony over the bodies of dying men. A bullet rips his pant leg. On he rides. "Fall back!" he cries. One by one the archers see him, eyes wide with terror. "Fall back!" he screams.

"Onil!" one shouts to Hanuman. "He's still up there!" The air flashes, and Hanuman sees a lone figure on a rise a hundred yards ahead. The man hurls something toward the Bijapuris and throws himself onto the ground.

The *granada's* roar blasts the air. Hanuman peers into the smoke. He glimpses the army of Afzul Khan, sees the silhouettes of elephants and horsemen. And a strange, unearthly sight: a man suspended in a bamboo cage. For a moment Hanuman thinks the man is floating over the lurching cart. Hanuman spurs his pony to O'Neil, and hauls him onto the saddle. The pony dashes madly into the darkness, racing from the noise and fire.

❧❧❧❧

Iron sits next to a tree, holding his head in his hands.

"What's happening?" Hanuman asks, as he jumps from his horse. O'Neil dismounts and goes to look for water.

Iron looks up, his white mustache stained with soot. "The men are running! I said no good would come from attacking at night!" Iron scowls. "The gods are set against us. We're finished!"

"Keep your voice down, uncle!" Hanuman whispers.

"What I'm saying everyone already knows," Iron says, but he lowers his voice. "Surrender. It's useless to go on."

Jedhe interrupts. "Forget surrender, Hanuman. Fall back. Collect the men. Make a plan!"

Iron glares at him. "Why should more men die?"

"You surrender then, old fool," Jedhe spits. He turns back to Hanuman. "We're no good here. Move fast! A retreat is better than a rout."

"All right," Hanuman replies. "We'll fall back to the Poona road. Leave the cannon if we must."

Without waiting another moment Jedhe races toward a cluster of men, shouting the order to fall back.

"What about Torna?" Iron grunts. "You mean to abandon it?"

"Torna can hold out a long time."

"Against ten thousand men? With no relief?" Iron's face creases. "You are more a coward than your father is!"

"Fine! Stay here and die. Or come with me and fight. I don't give a shit." With all the strength he can muster, Hanuman strides away.

"Wait!" Iron cries, catching up. "I know the men in Torna, nephew," he says, suddenly looking very old. "What you ask is hard for me." He lifts his hands to his face and his whole body seems to shake. Then he turns to Hanuman eyes cold as death. "By the gods, I'll triumph or I'll die."

❦❦❦❦

Afzul Khan clambers down the elephant ladder. His captains sit on a carpet spread on the bare ground. Not far away, the forest burns, spreading a ghostly light across the clearing. "Where is my best captain?" he shouts, and of course the others know exactly who he means. In a moment an ox-cart rolls into the clearing. Lashed to the cart is a swaying bamboo cage, and in the cage is Afzul Khan's captain. The sign HE DISOBEYED bounces against his chest. His legs are stained yellow and brown.

The men around the circle cannot help but stare. They fear the prisoner will look at them, but he focuses only on the twin blades of bamboo mere inches from his eyes, his face nearly mad with concentration.

"How goes it, captain? Still alive?" Afzul Khan laughs. He reaches out and shakes the cage; the leather lashings squeak as the bamboo flexes, and the captain's face grows pale.

"I'm having six more made, just in case," says Afzul Khan, his eyes moving from face to face. It doesn't take the men too long to count seven faces in the circle, and one of those is Afzul Khan's. "Let's have reports."

An Abyssinian is first to speak. "We met very little resistance, general," he says. "They are very bad fighters."

"Casualties?" grunts Afzul Khan.

"On their side, hard to tell. They pull the bodies from the field."

"What about us?"

Silence as the captains glance nervously at one another. At last one of them speaks; the oldest, small and wiry, with a grizzled beard. "Not so good." Afzul Khan's eyes narrow as he turns to face him. "We lost six, seven hundred men, maybe, mostly wounded but a lot of them dead."

"Wounded is worse than dead," Afzul Khan says, with a voice smooth as oil. "How many Marathis fell? How many bodies on the field?"

Again the grizzled captain glances around the circle. He might as well already be dead. "Maybe fifty."

The captain in his cage takes just that moment to moan. Everyone looks up, and then looks away. Except, of course, for Afzul Khan. "So, tell me, captain," he says, leaning in, so great folds of flesh well up over his chin, "how we lost fifteen times as many men as those mountain rats."

"*Granadas,* general. *Farang* bombs. Most times they only hurt the men who throw them. That's why we don't use them. But this *farang,* he was a crazy man. He stood maybe twenty yards from our line, lighting them and throwing them and never thinking twice. Blew up a hell of lot of men, and a hell of a lot of horses."

When the captain stops speaking, Afzul Khan stares at his grizzled face very quietly, for a very long time, as though sizing him up, then leans back. "Fine. We can afford to lose a few men. They cannot. Things are good."

"Yes, general," the captain says, and the others nod and mumble along.

"Well, what's your advice, my captains? Shall we rest here for a while? Or should we pursue them while their trail is hot?" Afzul Khan's eyes flit from face to face. "Well?" No one speaks.

A young captain gulps. "We should do, general, whatever you say."

There's silence for a moment. Around the circle everyone hesitates; no one even breathes. "You see?" Afzul Khan says. "When is a fool not a fool? When he obeys me. And you, captain, are no fool."

"Thank you, general," the young man gasps.

"We'll rest here for the day." He places a heavy hand on the young captain's shoulder. "You will be my new aide," he says. "Prepare the men to leave at dawn. We move up the Poona road, capture the city, and Shivaji. And of course, the gold." Afzul Khan eyes the captain. "Cheer up. Not all my aides end up in cages. You might return a hero."

"Thank you, sir," the young man manages to say.

"You," Afzul Khan says to the Abyssinian. "Get fifty volunteers. I have a special project they'll enjoy."

"What sort of project is it, general?" asks the Abyssinian.

"Light work," says Afzul Khan, his face glowing. "Tell them each to bring a hammer. And torches. And we'll need a cannon too, I think." He gives the cage another violent rattle and stalks back to his tent.

❦❦

Bandal, Tanaji, and Shivaji have stopped to rest. With their ponies stumbling so often in the dark, they give up and wait for dawn. No one says much: they each feel the bitter hopelessness of their situation

Shivaji, lying on his blanket stares into the sky, to the cold light of the stars. Soon he is asleep.

He wakes with a start. He's seated before a doorway. Its shape reminds him of the gateway of a fort.

The wooden doors swing open, and a figure glides toward him. At first he thinks it's Maya. Her dress is stiff, colored the deep green of old ivy leaves, but her skin is pale gold like the youngest grass, and she has many arms.

I know you, he thinks.

There is no sound when it happens; no crash, no cry. Just her hand breaking off at the wrist and flying through the air. The stump that's left is dry and white.

Her eyes implore him as the rest of her arm explodes in a shower of shards.

Great dents sink silently into her body. Her dress begins to shatter.

A great white gash appears where her nose once was. Then half her face flies off.

Help me, she mouths.

Her head explodes into a powder, leaving a broken neck, white as snow.

Shivaji wakes with a scream. "What is it?" shouts Bandal, sword in hand. Tanaji scrambles for his mace.

"We must hurry," Shivaji answers. "Afzul Khan. He's destroying Adoli temple."

❦❦

A makeshift camp has sprung up near the turnoff of the Poona Road. A few sentries stand up wearily as they hear the sound of their approaching ponies. "Hanuman!" one of them shouts. "We thought you must be dead!"

"Not dead, just slow!" Hanuman urges his pony forward. In the clearing are a cluster of soldiers. Some look up as he passes; some wave their fists; some shout his name; some boo. "Who's in charge?" Hanuman asks.

"Him, maybe," the soldier answers, pointing. "I don't a give a shit." In the center of a crowd, Hanuman sees Jedhe, arguing with some men. The words are unclear, but not the tone; the voices loud and full of blame.

"Here comes Hanuman!" Jedhe shouts.

Soon a dozen men surround him. "What's going on?" asks Hanuman.

"Mutiny," Jedhe whispers calmly, but the worry shows in his face.

Just then Iron strides into the circle. "You'd think they'd never seen a battle," he growls.

"Most of them haven't," Hanuman answers. "Not until tonight."

"You're going to have to act fast," Iron tells him. "A lot of them are leaving."

"One battle! One battle and they quit!" Jedhe spits. "Cowards."

"It isn't cowardice to run from certain death," Iron says. He turns to Hanuman, face taut. "These men are ready to kill you."

"Why?" Hanuman looks baffled.

Iron slaps him on the back. "Part of the pleasure of command. Win, and they'll follow you through fire. Lose, lose even once, and they turn on you like jackals. You've started off losing. Nothing's worse than that."

Hanuman looks at the faces of the soldiers in the camp lit by fire glow. They're drawn and serious, and some are wild with anger. He turns, and turns, and sees not one friendly face, until he's made the whole circuit and looks back at Iron. "What should I do now, uncle? They're starting to wander off! I must get them back!"

"How? How do you mean to do it?" Iron asks, staring at him levelly.

"I don't know, uncle. I need to think."

"You don't have time." Iron frowns. "Fortunately, I came prepared. I can get an hour for you, maybe. Expect no more! And watch out for tiger claws." With that he strides into the hostile crowd.

Jedhe shrugs. "He's right about the tiger claws, cousin. A lot of these men are angry. I wouldn't stand too close."

From somewhere Iron has scrounged a black cauldron. Soon the smell of frying mustard seed and coriander floats through the air. As Iron cooks, he sings: a song about a soldier with a woman in every town—Lakshmi in Adoli whose ass was roly-poly, Parvati in Welhe, whose slit was kind of smelly—on and on. Soon a circle forms. Iron stirs the pot, and waves his ladle in the air to keep the beat.

As Iron sings, Hanuman moves to the edge of the crowd, where exhausted men sit at a distance. "Wait a little while," he says, reaching out to touch an arm or shoulder. "Get some food." He nods toward the fire, toward the steam from the boiling dal, toward the laughter. Some of the men ignore him; others shrug at one another and amble over to join the others.

In the dawn light, Hanuman sees just how exhausted the men look. Their heads droop forward as they eat.

Jedhe catches up with him. "Iron says it's up to you. You've got to say something. You've got to inspire them. Otherwise they'll just go."

Iron is finishing the song about the man whose lingam was so long it needed a shoe when Hanuman steps to his side. The men who had been laughing grow suddenly silent. Then from the rear comes a long boo, and another, and soon the air is filled with booing.

A voice shouts out, "Let's hear what the bastard has to say!" Soon there's shouts of "Quiet down!" The crowd readies itself to listen.

"Men," he starts off, "our lands are under attack!"

"Your lands," says a heckler. "My land's just fine!" The boos begin again.

"Look here," shouts Iron, rising to his feet. "Do you call yourselves men? You're acting like goats! This man's an officer, isn't he? So give him some room!" With that he lumbers back to his seat.

Hanuman tries again. "Should we just lie down like dogs while that jackal Afzul Khan insults us? Should we run away? What about our honor?"

From the back the heckler calls again: "Ain't no honor when you're fucking dead, captain!"

Jedhe leaps up. "Who said that? Step forward and show yourself." But now the men close ranks, hiding the heckler, and boos and shouts of anger start again to fill the air.

"He's right!" comes a clear voice, calling loudly.

They all turn to see Shivaji on his pony, followed by Tanaji and Bandal. The crowd opens a pathway for him.

"What good is honor anyway? Who should die for honor?" Shivaji looks around the circle. "Can you eat honor? Can you spend honor?"

"You can't fuck honor either!" shouts the heckler, and everybody laughs.

"No," Shivaji says. "So why die for honor?" His face grows hard. "Why die for anything?" He pulls out his sword; its bright blade whistles through the morning air. "Why do I even have this sword? Is nothing worth dying for?" Shivaji glares at the men, one by one, as if challenging them.

"Your own life?" comes the heckler's voice, now uncertain.

Shivaji shrugs.

"What about your family?" shouts another man. Shivaji shrugs again. "What about to defend your home, lord?" shouts a voice from the back.

Shivaji looks up. "Would you die to defend your home?"

"Yes, lord," the man replies.

"Good for you!" Shivaji waves to the man. "Step forward, fellow."

The man shuffles forward, a tubby barefoot fellow with a disheveled turban and a greasy beard. An old bare sword bangs against his thick legs. He stands before Shivaji as though expecting to be struck.

"But would you let me fight with you?" Shivaji asks. "Would you let me die with you—to defend your home?"

"Sure!" the man answers, looking stunned.

"Swear that you will let me join you!" Shivaji says, his eyes on fire. "Swear it, that we may be brothers!"

"Well, sure you can join me!" He looks around at his comrades, enjoying the stupid joke. "Of course I swear it!"

"Then let it be so, brother," Shivaji answers, looking pleased. "Give my brother here a decent sword." Instantly, Jedhe unsheathes his own sword, and hands the jeweled hilt to the startled farmer.

"Anyone else?" Shivaji calls out. The faces turned up toward him are full of consternation. "Who else will let me join him? Who else will let me stand beside him, until death takes me? Who will have me for a brother?"

"I will, lord!" a voice calls out. "And me!" "And me!" soon the crowd is clamoring, calling out "Lord!" and "Shivaji!" and "Brother!"

"Then I will join you all!" he cries. "My sword ever ready at your side! My life to stand beside you! I will be your brother if you'll have me!" The crowd erupts with cheers. Soon they all are yelling, and the chant begins: "*Har, har, mahadev! Har, har, mahadev!*" Soon the men are shuffling in a silly dance, waving their weapons in the air: *Har, har, mahadev!*

Suddenly Shivaji's voice cuts through the air. "But hold!" The chanting stops. "Would you do the same for me? Will you stand beside me against a murderer? Against a jackal who would kill me and all my family? Against a brute who means to crush our gods beneath his heel?" He wheels his pony, sword aloft, looking at them all. "Will you help me, brothers?"

"Yes!"

And now the bedlam cheering starts, the swords and lances flash in the morning sun. Shivaji raises the sword Bhavani high above his head. And if he says more, no one knows, for the morning skies now ring with cheers: "*Har, har, mahadev! Har, har, mahadev!*"

෧ාඔ෧

Outside the doorway of the upstairs room in the Rang Mahal in Poona, Trelochan stands with Bala. The incense in the air cannot hide the smell of dying. The door cracks open, spilling light into the corridor, and Sambhuji steps out, his face pale. Bala spreads his arms. The boy runs to him and buries his face against his chest. "Why did I have to kiss her, uncle? She was fast asleep! She'll never know I kissed her."

"She'll know," Bala tells him, holding him tight. Then through the door walks Jijabai, calm and stately. She looks at them and shrugs.

"What's wrong with her? What's wrong with mother?" Sambhuji cries.

"She's gone away, Sam," Trelochan says softly.

"Don't coddle him," says Jijabai. "Your mother is dead."

"It's your fault!" the boy cries. "You killed her."

"No, child. She just died," Jijabai replies. "Now you must be a man and face it." But he wails and runs away. Bala looks to Jijabai, offering to catch him but she shakes her head.

"She never stirred," she says, annoyed. "Not even to say goodbye to her own child."

"The gods grant her peace," Bala whispers.

Jijabai snorts. "She'll have more peace than we will, Balaji."

"I will tell Shivaji, madam," says Trelochan.

"No, I'll go," Bala insists.

"Fools," says Jijabai. "I need you here. We'll send a courier. Anyway, what difference does it make?" She walks slowly through the shadowed corridor and down the narrow staircase, suddenly looking very old indeed.

ೞ⦿ೞ⦿

"We must move quickly," Shivaji says to Hanuman as they ride together on the road to Pratapghad. "I want to reach Pratapghad by nightfall."

Hanuman's eyes grow wide. "Can this happen, lord?"

"I rely on you to make it happen, Hanu," Shivaji replies. Hanuman bows.

"That's a hard order, lord," says Bandal to Shivaji.

"But not impossible, I think," Shivaji says. Hanuman wheels his pony and begins to shout orders.

Shivaji trots until he rides next to Jedhe. "I was glad for your help back there. You made all the difference."

Jedhe shrugs but his face lights up. "You would have done it without me, lord. And now you have three thousand extra brothers."

Shivaji smiles, then grows serious. "I need to ask someone to do a task that's very dangerous."

"Ask me, lord."

Shivaji checks that no one can overhear them. "What's wrong with my plan, Jedhe?"

"Nothing, lord." Shivaji waits. "All right," Jedhe says impulsively. "The flaw's obvious. We're off to Pratapghad. What's to stop Afzul Khan from going straight to Poona, taking the gold and murdering your family?"

"Exactly. What can I do, Jedhe?"

"You must send someone to Afzul Khan. Lie to him. Say you've taken your family and the treasure to Pratapghad for safekeeping."

"Who should I send, Jedhe? Anyone who would ride into the camp of Afzul Khan would be a fool indeed."

"Maybe a fool could be found, lord." Jedhe shakes his head. "What do you want me to say to Afzul Khan?"

They talk quietly for some time. Finally Jedhe bows and turns his horse, and trots back through the marching men. Though Hanuman calls to him, he does not answer, but trots on, head high, face set. Hanuman peers after him for a moment, and then spurs until he comes to Shivaji. "What's happening with Jedhe?" he asks.

Shivaji tells him, and the color drains from Hanuman's face. "Why the hell did you send him, lord? Why not Iron? Why not me?"

"What's wrong with Jedhe?" Shivaji asks.

"Father says that he's a traitor." Hanuman looks back. "Do you want me to stop him?"

Shivaji peers behind him. "What's done is done," he replies. "We'll play the cards we're dealt. Maybe it will turn out right."

☙☙☙☙

"What's needed, captain, is greater speed," says Afzul Khan, leaning over the railing of his howdah to glare at the anxious face of his young captain.

"Of course, general," the captain says, looking frantic, "but the pace is exhausting, sir. I fear the men . . ."

"You fear the men altogether too much, captain. Show some spine. Draw blood, and they'll get the idea."

"Yes, general. But will they be in any condition to fight?"

Afzul Khan sneers. "That's my concern. Yours is speed. Put an empty cage at the end of the line . . . reserved for the last man to arrive."

The captain gulps. "As you wish, general. I'm sure we'll make better time, sir."

"See that we do. The Abyssinians like using their whips, captain. Don't be afraid to ask their help."

ⓔⓞⓔⓞ

The sun has risen high into the sky when Maya wakes. She sits up, and straightens her sari. In her sleep it became disheveled; her braid has come undone.

"Good. You're awake," says Lakshman. "You can see Pratapghad from here. We can be there in an hour." He lifts his chin to the west, to a great sloping mountain ringed around its crest with stones, like a black crown. "We must be on our way. There's a stream over there, if you want to use it."

Maya nods, and walks stiffly to a nearby stream. Her legs ache, and the insides of her thighs are chafed. She drinks and splashes her face with water, reties her sari, braids her hair. Her muscles ache. I'm not used to riding, she thinks. She looks up to see Lakshman on his pony. "Changed your mind about sitting up front?" Maya shakes her head. Lakshman helps her up behind his saddle, his bright eye never blinking.

"You moan in your sleep," Lakshman says after they've ridden for a while. "You make lots of noise. You kept calling out: 'Shivaji, Shivaji!'"

Suddenly her head clears, and with startling clarity she remembers her dream. Shivaji had come to her in the forest, tall and strong. He had lain beside her, held her in his arms. She was willing; he was ready. She'd never had a dream so real. Even now she recalls the power as he thrust inside her, the violence of it, the heat. Wrapping her legs around his waist, pounding his buttocks with her heels, calling out his name, gripping him as she felt the spasms shudder through her, melting as he exploded deep inside her.

She finds herself trembling at the memory. It had all seemed so real. So very, very real.

Lakshman chuckles. "How you enjoyed it. How you groaned. How you begged for more." As if he sees into her thoughts, he lisps, "It all seemed so real!" Lakshman's lip curls and he whispers in Maya's ear: "Did I not say you'd know? Did I not say you'd never be the same?"

And although the sun is high now, Maya trembles.

CHAPTER 27

"But can this be, general? Do the walls of Golconda still stand?"

General Jumla scowls at the smug prick sitting on the other side of Aurangzeb's humble war tent. He readies, to launch a stinging response but catches Aurangzeb's look. "Ali Rashid," he says, grinding his molars, "since I have left the Bijapuri court to you, perhaps you will be good enough to leave the conduct of this war to me."

"Nothing in war is certain," says Aurangzeb's quiet voice. "The diggers ran into an unexpected layer of rock." Ali Rashid nods as if to suggest that if *he* had been in charge, there'd have been no rock at all. "Suppose you tell us how things went in Bijapur," Aurangzeb says.

"Extremely well, Lord Viceroy," Ali Rashid replies. "I demanded that the Marathi commander be released. Of course the sultana complied." Aurangzeb gives the slightest nod. Ali Rashid hesitates: he expected a compliment, at least a smile. "I took the poor man to Shaista Khan's residence."

Jumla lifts his head at this, and shoots a glance at Aurangzeb, but the prince only stares at his carpet. "Shaista Khan is still in Agra? With Prince Dara? When's he expected back?" Jumla asks.

"He's away indefinitely, general. I think it may be best to bring this Commander Shahji here, or to take him to Agra. I'm not sure of his safety when Afzul Khan returns."

Aurnagzeb's head snaps up. "Returns?"

"He took a small force to Poona, I believe."

"How small?" says Jumla.

"Fifteen thousand," Ali Rashid says, surprised that this information is causing concern.

"We've got Shahji. Afzul Khan's gone. Who's in charge of their eastern armies?"

"I don't know, lord," Ali Rashid says. "It should be easy to find out." Aurangzeb glares at him. "Of course, I sent a note to Shivaji as you suggested, telling him Shahji had been freed, offering him help. Also to say he should present himself in Agra with the nine crore hun as tribute."

Aurangzeb blinks. "You put both the offer of help and the demand for tribute in the same letter?"

Ali Rashid shifts uncomfortably. "At the time, it seemed . . ."

"What was Shivaji's reaction?" Jumla asks softly. His lifted eyebrows bulge over his thin nose.

"A very prompt response, general. Shivaji said he had matters in hand. But he agreed to go to Agra. He's probably on his way there now."

"Probably?"

"He said that he was making preparations, and would leave as soon as he was able. I understood—"

"Fool!" shouts Jumla. "You understood very little, it appears!"

"Keep a civil tone, sir," Ali Rashid says haughtily. "I trust I've managed this affair appropriately."

"You haven't managed it at all!" Jumla snaps.

"And then you sent your men to Poona?" Aurangzeb asks.

"There was no need, lord," Ali Rashid replies, his face confused. "My men are marching back from Bijapur, even as we speak. With the war moving so slowly here, I assumed . . ."

"I told you not to send him!" Jumla cries. "I told you he'd botch it up!"

Ali Rashid's face grows pale. "How dare you, sir! My father—"

"Your father is an imbecile," grunts Jumla, "and you, sir, are a fool."

"Lord," Ali Rashid pleads to Aurangzeb.

"Jumla's right," Aurangzeb answers, staring serenely at the carpet. "You've killed Shivaji and you've lost the gold. More important, you've lost the trade routes. Shivaji might have been our ally. I thought you might have gained some sense from your mother. Sadly, you're your father's son."

Ali Rashid looks as if he has been struck. "I'll send the army, lord! I'll make things right!"

"It's too late," Jumla snarls. "Afzul Khan will have captured the gold and killed Shivaji by this time."

"Maybe Shivaji has defeated him!"

Jumla sneers. "If Shivaji defeats a Bijapuri army under Afzul Khan, he'll have no trouble defeating you!"

"A Mogul soldier is worth a dozen Bijapuris!" Ali Rashid shouts. "How dare you insult our soldiers!"

Aurangzeb stands and turns away. "He's not insulting our soldiers, Ali Rashid. He's insulting you. Take a rug."

Ali Rashid stares; he has no idea what Aurangzeb might mean. Then Aurangzeb unfurls a small carpet to face west, toward Mecca. He takes from his pocket a small brown disk, clay fired from the soil of Mecca. He places his forehead on the disk, and begins to say his prayers. Jumla, glaring at Ali Rashid, hurls a prayer rug at him, then rolls out one himself.

Then a slender eunuch stoops through the entry of the tent. "Highness! A dispatch from Agra! Highness, it's important," he insists.

He taps the prince's shoulder but Aurangzeb does not stir. Only when he has finished praying does he turn to Alu. "Never disturb my prayers."

"This is important, highness," Alu says, giving him a silver tube.

Aurangzeb frowns and takes the tube.

"It's from Murad," Jumla whispers to Ali Rashid, now so caught up in the moment that he has forgotten his anger.

"Murad? Aurangzeb's brother?" But Jumla doesn't answer; his eyes are locked on Aurangzeb's face for any sign as to the scroll's contents.

At last Aurangzeb sighs, and his shoulders slump. "Not important enough to interrupt prayers," he says finally, with a face of sorrow. "But I forgive you this time." Aurangzeb closes his eyes. "My father's dead."

"*Allah akbar!*" Ali Rashid whispers. "God is great, lord. How did the *padshah* die?"

"My brother, in his grief, has neglected to tell me." He looks down once again, studying the parchment intently.

"So the time has come at last, my old friend," says Jumla gently.

"Yes," Aurangzeb replies. "Dara has mobilized his armies around Agra. Murad has begun the march from Surat."

"For a funeral?" asks Ali Rashid. He seems confused to be discussing tactics at this time of tragedy.

"For a battle," answers Jumla wearily.

"This is the moment I have dreaded, general," says Aurangzeb. "Somehow I thought the day would never come. A foolish hope. Vain to think that death might somehow pass us by."

"I'm so sorry about your father, lord," says Ali Rashid.

"Don't be," Aurangzeb replies, his face now empty of any emotion. "When my mother died, he lost all perspective. He lived in vanity and debauchery. He fancied he'd make a paradise on earth; all the while he sank deeper into hell. I fear he's in the fire even now, cursing the Prophet with each burning breath."

"Never you mind, Ali Rashid," Jumla says, voice dripping venom. "You've still got Dara. Your father is Dara's favorite."

"Well, Dara will be a good emperor, won't he? You act like there's something wrong with him."

Jumla nods toward Aurangzeb. "Remember where you are, fool. What do you think is going to happen to *him*?" At the young man's puzzled look, Jumla explodes: "He'll be killed, and his children and his wives! A new emperor kills his rivals!"

"But everyone knows that Aurangzeb has no designs on the Peacock Throne."

Aurangzeb looks up. "Pray, tell my dear brother that when you see him. But I don't think that he'll believe you."

Ali Rashid seems stunned. "Lord, please excuse my—"

Aurangzeb waves his hand. "What Allah wills. I am but a poor fakir, Ali Rashid. What difference to me life or death? Still, out of kindness, think well of me when I am gone." He sighs. "I suppose you wish to go to Agra? At times like these, a son's thoughts bend to his beloved father, no? Go. Travel fast. Dara will set his armies on me soon. You won't want to be here when he does."

Ali Rashid looks alarmed. "Your kindness, lord, will never be forgotten, not by me or by my heirs."

"You see his quality?" Aurangzeb smiles to Jumla. "What an idle promise that would be, coming from me."

"You have sons, lord," Ali Rashid protests.

"Not for long, I fear."

Ali Rashid stands. "Then I swear here, by the Prophet, that my children will pray for you, and my children's children, for seven generations!"

"I am much comforted. Now do go quickly."

When he's gone, Jumla groans. "What a pompous jackanapes!"

"He's an improvement on the father."

"Pray Allah that I never see either man again."

"Be careful what you wish for, Jumla," Aurangzeb says.

Alu stoops through the door flap and glides gently forward. "Highness, what are your commands?"

"Murad brings his army to Rathanbore. We will raise the siege at once and with all haste rendezvous with him there. I myself will leave immediately with a hundred guards. Leave the tents behind. Rathanbore fort is well stocked." He turns to Jumla. "Now listen: forget the cannon, forget the elephants. What we'll need the most is men."

"You can't mean to leave everything here, lord," Jumla protests.

"Things have changed, Jumla. A moment ago the Marathi, what's his name—Shivaji—was all I cared about. Now he has lost all importance."

Jumla frowns. "I'm not leaving five hundred cannon for the Golcondans. They'll end up being used against us."

"You're correct of course, general. Detail four thousand men to bring them north. Alu, I'll set you in charge of the transport of the cannon."

"I'd prefer to go with you, highness, in the vanguard."

Aurangzeb gives him a grateful smile. "Thank you. But Jumla's right, we need to bring the cannon, and I too am right; we can't afford to wait. You know how to get results. You have effective means of persuasion, I understand." Alu's face pales for a moment. How much do you know about me? he wonders. Alu inclines his head and looks up with his softest smile.

Less than an hour later, the Mogul armies have pulled back from the Golconda walls. From the hilltop Jumla can see the dust cloud of Aurangzeb galloping north to Rathanbore.

❦❦❦❦

Afzul Khan lifts his hand, and a eunuch quickly brings a great goblet that he drains in a gulp. Only then does Afzul Khan turn his face toward Jedhe. "Well?" he rumbles.

"I bring greetings from my lord Shivaji, general," Jedhe says at last, lifting his hands to his forehead.

"You bring greetings from a dead man. But you know that. Your name?"

"Jedhe, general. I am one of Lord Shivaji's captains and *deshmukh* of Kari."

"I thought that belonged to Tukoji," a captain with a grizzled beard speaks up.

"Tukoji is my father. He . . . retired," says Jedhe, feeling uncomfortable.

"Enough," says Afzul Khan. "State your purpose and be gone."

Jedhe licks his lips. "My master seeks a parley, general."

"Why has he not come himself? No matter. He can talk to me in Poona, if he lives."

"He's not in Poona, general. He's moved to Pratapghad, with his family." Jedhe pauses: "And the gold."

As his comrades begin to shout in protest, Afzul Khan lifts his hand for silence. "This can't be true, lord," a captain stammers. "We've had watchmen at the city gates. It would take a caravan to move that gold! Our watchmen have seen nothing!"

"Bijapuri watchmen, captain?" Jedhe lifts an eyebrow.

"I told you to use Abyssinians!" shouts Afzul Khan. "Who knows what the hell those men were up to!"

"General, I swear!" But Afzul glares at him, and the captain holds his tongue.

"Lord Shivaji wishes a parley, general," Jedhe continues. "He does not wish harm to you or to your men."

"He doesn't want to die, you mean," Afzul Khan growls in reply.

"Lord Shivaji hopes that you and he can reach some settlement."

"What's wrong with death? That settles all. Your man is a coward!"

Jedhe glances around the fire and speaks guardedly, leaning closer. "You're right, general."

Now Afzul Khan sits up straight. "Go on."

Jedhe feels the sweat begin form small beads beneath his turban. "Shivaji is just what you say. A coward."

"Like his father," growls the general.

Jedhe nods. "I lied about Tukoji. My father wanted to to bring Shivaji to Bijapur. I arrested him, and pledged my forces to Shivaji." He looks up helplessly. "I was a fool."

"Not just a fool. Also a traitor!"

"Let me make amends!"

Afzul Khan leans back. "I'm listening, traitor."

"Shivaji is holed up at Pratapghad. He has at most three thousand men, farmers mostly. You've seen them fight."

"I've seen them run, you mean."

"Exactly! Not a warrior in the bunch! Cowards all!"

"Even a coward will kill if pressed, lord," the grizzled captain says, staring hard at Jedhe.

"Not these men, general. Not these farmers! When they see Bijapur's might, they will surrender!"

"Why haven't they surrendered already, then?" the captain asks.

"They think Shivaji will protect them. They think he's on some mission from his goddess. They are fools."

"There, captain," Afzul Khan says. "That's why I drive my men with fear. A leader may inspire his army for a little while, but in the end, a coward will lay down his arms unless forced to fight."

"I see you are a man of wisdom, general," Jedhe answers. "Kill Shivaji and you end this foolish rebellion in one stroke!" Again Afzul Khan drains his cup; again the eunuch fills it. "Shivaji hopes to make a deal, lord," Jedhe says. The young captain's eyes flash when Jedhe calls Afzul Khan "lord," not "general." Jedhe presses on. "Pratapghad is a difficult place."

"That much at least is true," the grizzled captain says. Afzul Khan nods for Jedhe to continue.

"Shivaji quakes at the mention of your name. Everyone knows your power and fears it. Shivaji most of all! He was raised by his mother, lord. He thinks like a woman."

"At least his father was a fighter." Afzul Khan leans back, drinking slowly from his cup.

"This man should not be trusted," the grizzled captain protests. "With his own mouth he admits his treachery."

"Silence," Afzul Khan replies. Again he drinks, his eyes focused on Jedhe. "What do you say, traitor?"

"You call me traitor, lord. That name is often given to men of initiative. I won't deny that I have ambition. I've been told that you are generous, lord." Afzul Khan nods. "I tell you, lord—go to Pratapghad. Meet with Shivaji. If you plan things right, you'll have Shivaji in your palm."

"What of our lord's honor, eh? Are you suggesting he should take Shivaji by deceit?" The grizzled captain spits.

"Is it dishonorable to use a lie to strike a liar?" Jedhe answers.

Afzul Khan licks his lips. "Send word that we accept Shivaji's parley."

"I will ride to Shivaji and tell him, lord," says Jedhe, bowing.

"I don't think so." Afzul stirs in his cushions, his face suddenly alert, full of malice. "I need someone I can trust, not a traitor." He nods to his Abyssinian sentries. "You want to go back to Shivaji? Very well. I'll send you. In chains. I should kill you myself, and send your hands to Shivaji. But much better if he hears your treason from your own lips."

The general rises and turns to the young captain. "Send my Simon to Pratapghad to set up the parley. Send this traitor with him."

Afzul Khan steps from the fire and goes to the cage, where he looks at the tearstained face of his former captain. "Did I misjudge you, captain? Was I too harsh?" He stares at the captain's quivering limbs, at his face now wild with lack of sleep, lost in some endless waking nightmare, staring at sharp spikes just inches from his eyes. "Don't sleep captain; you'll just hurt yourself. Here—let me help!" Then Afzul shakes the cage fiercely and stomps off, while the captain's whimpers fill the night.

ᏣᎤᏩᎤ

As soon as they saw the Marathi force approaching in the distance, Tanaji and Bandal began the long trip down the Pratapghad fort road. The narrow, rocky path clings to the edge of the mountain, rough and broken, so their ponies take steps haltingly.

The vegetation grows thick and verdant. Huge trees bend beneath the weight of vines. Vine and branch combine to form a living, woven wall. It is not only the mountain's steepness that protects the fortress high above them, but this extraordinary forest.

Together Tanaji and Bandal have prepared as best they could, gathering into the fort all the food that they can scrounge from the villages below. And as a consequence, the people of the outlying towns have made their way up to the fort, to huddle in the doubtful safety of those stone walls. Bandal at first was wary of letting in so many, but where else, asked Tanaji, were they supposed to go? Better to let them join us, he said; at least we all might die together.

It will not be the Bijapuris that defeat us, thinks Bandal, but hunger. Even so, he opens the gates. He wonders if they'll end up eating rats. He'd heard it often came to that during a siege. That, and worse.

Fortunately the walls of Pratapghad are tall and wide, and the space inside is large; and the cannon are numerous, and the shot and Chinese powder plentiful. They could hold out a long time inside those walls.

But who, Bandal wonders, would break the siege, if it came to that? Maybe Shivaji has a plan.

By the time they've reached the mountain's foot and had a little lunch, the sun has passed its zenith. They rest at the side of the road. A mile or two down the road, they know, the Marathi vanguard approaches, but the trees are so thick that there is nothing to see. At last, they see two horsemen trotting toward them: Shivaji and Hanuman. "What news from Poona?" Shivaji asks straight away.

"None, lord," Bandal answers. "Did you expect some?"

"Maybe," Shivaji shakes his head. Then he explains how he sent Jedhe to Afzul Khan. "I wonder if that bastard has taken the bait."

Tanaji shakes his head. "I tell you, Shahu, he'll never accept your parley. He'll think it's a trap."

"That's exactly why he will accept it, Tana," Shivaji says.

"Either way he comes here," Hanuman says. "He'll either come here first, or he'll go to Poona first and then come here. Either way he comes here, because this is where Shahu is. Am I right?"

"The difference," Bandal tells him quietly, "is whether he first kills Lord Shivaji's family. And your family too, cousin. He'll leave no one alive. He is a demon, Afzul Khan."

Hanuman seems taken aback. "The fort is prepared, Shahu," Tanaji says. "We're as ready as we're going to be."

"If he comes here directly," says Shivaji, "he'll be here by tomorrow night." It occurs to Hanuman that Shivaji never says "they'll be here" or "if they come"—always it's: "he'll be here" or "if he comes." The realization begins to gnaw at him, and he finds a fear growing inside him.

"We can hole up in that fort for a long time, Shahu," Tanaji says, nodding toward the mountain.

"No. We're not going inside the fort. We'll fight him here."

The others share glances. This is something no one expected.

"There is no here, Shahu," Tanaji says. "This is a road, not a goddamned battlefield!" Hanuman has never heard his father take this tone with Shivaji. "What's the point of coming all this way if you don't mean to use the fort?"

"We must use the fort," Bandal says, coaxing him. "They have fifteen thousand men. We have three. What other defense do we have, lord?"

"We won't have a defense," Shivaji says quietly. "That's just a slow death. We'll attack before they ever get there."

"But he would never make it up this road, Shahu!" Tanaji sputters.

"I do not mean for them to reach this road. I mean to build another." Shivaji points to the fort. "I mean to make a road from there, straight up to the ridge below the outer wall." The others look where he's pointing. If not for the forest, a straight road might be built. If not for the wall of trees and vines. The notion is absurd.

"A hundred men might do it, lord, if you gave them a month."

"How long then for three thousand men?" Shivaji replies.

Hanuman begins to work this out, but before he can answer, Bandal says "This is madness, lord! Let us make a last stand in the fort. Why not die with honor?"

"I don't mean to die, Bandal. I mean to win. If you have doubts, then leave."

Bandal's eyebrows shoot up. "I've never heard such words from you before, lord."

"We have no time for doubts. The enemy is at our back."

Shivaji then unfolds for them his final, desperate plan.

"Your plan has a lot of ifs, Shahu," Tanaji remarks.

"Have you a better plan, uncle?"

"If it's what you want, lord," says Bandal, "I'll stay here with Hanuman, and help him."

About a half mile from the summit, beneath the black stone walls that bristle with cannon, the road spreads out upon a promontory. A small stone building, about the size of a doll's house, is there. Shivaji jumps from his horse and steps toward the tiny temple. A fresh garland of tuberoses hangs around a lead-red rock inside.

"It is a self-born Ganesha," Tanaji tells him. "The villagers revere it." Shivaji peers inside. The round rock bears a surprising resemblance to the god; a curving bulge sweeps across it like a trunk; cracks resemble ears. Eyes are painted on it, and it is ringed around with cut flowers.

"This is a good sign, uncle," Shivaji says. "It is here that we will have the parley."

Tanaji snorts. "If he agrees to parley."

"He'll agree."

"Maybe. It won't be easy to defend you here in any case, particularly if things go wrong."

"If things go wrong, what difference will it make?"

Tanaji shakes his head. "You think you've got this all figured out. The gods will have their surprises. Always there's a scorpion hiding in the flowers."

"What choice do we have?" As their horses walk on, they see more rice drawings, swastikas, and mangoes traced on the ground, and dozens of tiny clay lamps.

"Dewali already," Tanaji says. "The village women are putting out lamps."

"Not much of a festival this year, I'm afraid."

"People always find a reason to celebrate, even when all seems dark. That's what Dewali's about, right? Set out light against the darkness?"

As they pass below the massive basalt walls, watchmen on the battlements call down and wave. By the time the two men ride through the small

horse door of the fort gates, word has spread of their arrival. A hundred villagers watch as they enter. The children shout, old men wave their walking
sticks. But the disappointment on the faces is clear: They had wanted a su-
perman, but what they see is just a man, only a man. So much more will be
needed—if Afzul Khan should come.

Tanaji rides with Shivaji round the wall's perimeter; Bandal's men
have set the cannons gleaming, piled shot and kegs of Chinese powder on
the shoulders of their bezels. Near each redoubt a fire smolders for the
fuses, over it a caldron of water boils against a seige. They see armories of
matchlocks, lances, arrows, swords.

When Shivaji and Tanaji complete their circuit, it is nearly night. In the
main courtyard, Bandal's men have formed two uncertain lines. Shivaji dismounts and walks between them. Most have the sun-worn faces and grizzled stubble of men who only shave when they go to town, but they stand
tall, with exaggerated stiffness, pulling back their shoulders and puffing out
their chests. Many are barefoot, and their clothes, though clean, are ragged.
Most have bare swords hanging from their belts, others carry only long
knives used for cutting underbrush.

When he reaches the end of the line, Shivaji turns and calls out, "How
many here have been in battle?" A scattering of men raise their hands.
"How many here have killed?"

"You mean, killed a man?" a voice calls from the rear.

"Yes. How many?"

A few more raise their hands than last time.

"Before we're through, we'll all be lifting our hands," Shivaji tells
them. "The time has come to take back what is ours!"

"Shivaji *ki jai*!" a voice shouts, and soon a hundred men shout "Shivaji
ki jai!"

"Have we no flag to fly?" Shivaji calls. From his pony, Tanaji shakes
his head. "Who will give me a flag?" Shivaji asks the men. They glance at
each other, wondering what to make of the question.

Shivaji strides back along the line of men. Their turbans come in a
rainbow. At last he stops in front of a tall man wearing a saffron turban.
"Will you give me your turban, soldier?"

Instantly the tall man unwinds his turban hands it to Shivaji, bowing
his head. He's shiny bald.

"Take this to the main gate. Have the watchmen hang it from the flagpole." The soldier nods and races for the gate. "We fly a saffron flag! Just as
a *sanyasi* puts on saffron clothes, our flag is saffron, for we dedicate this

battle to the gods! *Har, har, mahadev!*" And the men pick up the cry: "*Har, har, mahadev! Har, har, mahadev!*"

Tanaji steps over to Shivaji, pumping his arm in the air as he joins the cry. "Bandal has made a place for you, Shahu," he says into Shivaji's ear. Tanaji leads him to a house of brick and stone; the residence of the fort commander.

Near the door is a dark man with the cap of a haji. He lifts his hands to his head and greets Shivaji, but it takes Shivaji a moment before he recognizes the broken face. "Lakshman," he says, as if trying to appear pleased.

"As you see, Shahu."

"You did well in Bijapur, cousin," Shivaji says, placing his hands on Lakshman's narrow shoulders. He seems to have grown thin since Shivaji saw him last. And his face looks devious now, like an old snake.

"I did what I had to do, cousin, no more."

"What do you think of your son, eh, Tana? He went his own way, but he has served us well, eh?" Shivaji slaps Lakshman on the back. "Tomorrow, when the army assembles, I'll give you a robe of honor."

"I want no gifts. I have my own resources now. In fact, I've brought you a gift."

He lifts his chin, and Shivaji turns to look. Across the courtyard Shivaji sees her, her yellow sari lit by the glow of the setting sun, her face brilliant in the sunset's luster. "There, I give her to you, cousin," Lakshman says though Shivaji eyes him coldly. "You can't pretend that you don't want her! Maybe you can fool others, but I know your heart."

Shivaji stares at him. "You know nothing," he says at last.

Lakshman's eye now changes, bright, mocking, amused. "I know she wants you. She dreams of you, Shahu. She moans your name when she sleeps." For a moment it seems to Tanaji that Shivaji might strike at Lakshman, so much anger fills his stare. But he turns on his heel and strides away.

"What sort of man have you become, Lakshman?" Tanaji glares at his son. "What were you thinking?"

Lakshman lifts his face, his smile an empty sneer. "You think because I've lost an eye that now I'm blind? You've got Hanuman; you've got Shivaji. You don't need another son, not anymore. I'm just a nuisance now."

"You're still my son," Tanaji protests, but Lakshman shakes his head.

"Not just your son, your better son. That's right, father; someday you'll see this; someday you'll understand." He nods toward Shivaji's closed door. "Always you cared for Shahu more than me."

"That's not true! What has happened to you, Lakshman? I hardly know you!"

Lakshman glares at him, and bends down to pick up his pack. "In the end, father, all the lies must stop. You'll see it, in the end. He's evil. He's as greedy as his father, and he's getting worse. You think you are his friend, but you are only his tool. In the end, he'll betray you, just as Shahji did. Then you'll know who loved you best. Good luck in the battle." Without another word, Lakshman begins to walk away.

"Where are you going? The enemy is almost on us!"

"There's the enemy," Lakshman answers as he walks off, nodding toward Shivaji's door.

◔◑◕◑

She has tossed for hours on the bedmat. When she finally gives up trying to sleep, Maya goes to the temple.

He looked at her and looked away. She tries her best to think of other things. Where are her girls tonight? Hiding in some cave? Are they safe? Has Afzul Khan discovered them? Always though her mind returns to just one thought: He looked at her and looked away.

He's nothing! Why do you even care? How many men have you forgotten? Forget one more, just one more! Still that image burns. His face so angry. What has she done to deserve such treatment? At last she rises from her bed, ties her sari, and slips into the courtyard.

In front of her, spreading through the courtyard, are the snoring, sleeping bodies of several hundred soldiers. So many still here, she thinks, even though most have gone to the foot of the mountain to cut a new road to the fort.

She tries to find a path through the sleeping bodies. Sometimes her bare foot bumps against an arm or leg, but no one wakes. As though some other power wills it, she finds that her footsteps bring her right past Shivaji's house.

A few yards from his door, she stops. Is he alone? Asleep? The high window in the wall flickers, as if a lamp burns inside.

She looks away. The temple, not this door, she whispers to herself.

Across the moonlit courtyard a few lights still burn in the stone lampposts of the temple. As she enters the shadowed, dark pavilion, her memory flashes back to her dancing temple in Adoli. I'm sure it's destroyed now, she thinks sadly. The sudden appearance of Lakshman there still troubles her. I should not have left, she thinks, not with him. I should not have come here, she thinks.

Then she notices: the temple doors are not locked, as they should be. How can this be? she wonders. She hesitates. From within the *murti*'s room, a lamplight wavers. She tiptoes forward. Her eyes have opened in the darkness. She sees the bright eyes of the goddess staring at her. The air here chills her and she starts to tremble.

Something is moving in there, just beyond the door. A spy, she thinks. Mice. A dog. One of the brahmins. She sees the shadow now, someone in the corner, some dark form. A Bijapuri. Lakshman. Shivaji. She inches forward. "Come in," she hears—just a whisper, but it echoes.

"Who is it?" Maya whispers back. Screwing up her courage, she steps up to the goddess's threshold, and stoops until her head touches the worn wood. Any moment she expects to feel a knife thrust into her neck, but when she lifts her head, the shadow has not moved. "Who is it?" she hisses again.

"She couldn't sleep, so I came to keep her company," the whisper answers. The words strike Maya strangely; it occurs to her that the voice might be speaking of the goddess, or of Maya herself. The voice whispers again, "Come in. You took so long. I thought you'd never get here."

"Mother!" Maya cries out. "Mother, is it really you?"

"Yes, child," answers Gungama, her old eyes beaming. "Did I not say that we would meet again?"

They hug each other, and then they laugh, and they hug each other again and then they cry. The goddess near them stares into the distance while the small stone room rings with sobs and laughter and whispers.

It isn't long before she's told Gungama about the attack on the Adoli temple, how she sent the girls away. Then she tells of Lakshman's strange arrival, and of how they fled from the Bijapuris. She even tells of that vivid dream she'd had.

"Is that so," is all Gungama says.

"What's wrong with me, ma?" asks Maya. "Why is he always in my thoughts? I don't even like him!"

"He is not one to like or dislike. His role is only to disturb everyting, as he has disturbed you."

"You said once that our fates were intertwined."

Gungama strokes her cheek with her soft palm, her eyes tender. "How that is to be, I cannot see. I only know that you are here for him, just as I once was. You're stuck with him!" Then she looks at her anxiously, as if telling her some hard secret. "But now you start to sense his purpose. And your own purpose, which is tied with his. How it all works out I can't imagine. Somehow all will be well." Gungama peers into Maya's gold-flecked eyes. "He's come to stand the earth upon its head, child. And he starts with you."

☙◦◦◦❧

Bandal has found some words to drive his men: "If you want to live, then cut." It gets the point across succinctly. He tried explaining, and cajoling, and pleading and threatening, but now he merely points to the west, to the dust cloud hovering in the air that surges ever closer.

"If you want to live, then cut." The men slash furiously through the vines and trees. They push great heaps of brush beside the new-made road. The sun has passed its zenith, but the air is cool. And to everyone's amazement, the road is nearly finished: a clear, wide track that leads directly to a promontory a few hundred yards from the fort's first gate. It looks as if some god has taken a razor to the forest and shaved a swath down to the bare soil.

In truth, Bandal feels a little perturbed. In the morning, Iron gave him orders. Hanuman too, was telling him what to do. At noon Shivaji came riding down the new road, Tanaji behind him, picking his way through the half-cleared places, and the men had cheered.

Shivaji then shouted out his plan. Afzul Khan will march his men along this new road, Shivaji told him. The Marathis will hide in the forest on either side, and attack. The Bijapuris on the road will die like dogs.

The men cheered. That smile of Shivaji's, so confident and certain, made them feel that anything is possible.

☙◦◦◦❧

It is Bandal who sees them first, the riders from Bijapur.

A half-dozen horsemen burst into the wide clearing at the foot of the mountain, riding quickly. Even from this distance, it's easy to see that they ride expensive Bedouins and fly dark green pennants from their lances.

Bandal finds a jug of water, splashes his face and hands, and slaps the dust from his clothes. "Keep working," he growls as the men stop to look. "We must finish the road by sundown." He reaches the foot of the mountain road just as the riders get there.

Bandal blinks when he sees them; dark men with crosses branded across their faces. Except for one: blindfolded, gagged, hands tied behind his back—his cousin Jedhe.

"Where is headman?" barks the lead rider.

"I am Bandal. I'm in charge. Why have you bound my cousin?"

The rider laughs. "I am Simon, messenger of Afzul Khan. I come to see Shivaji."

"Release that man and I'll take you to him."

"You are quite rude," the rider answers. "I bring this man to Shivaji, not to you. Take me now to Shivaji." Suddenly the other riders lower their lances, though Bandal saw no sign from the lead rider.

"Let him go." Around him he hears his men stop their work, can feel them approaching though he does not turn.

"Don't ask for death, fellow. Take me now to Shivaji."

Bandal looks things over, does the math in his mind. For a moment, looking at Jedhe, he considers fighting. His muscles cry out for violence. But instead, he calls out "Bring me my pony."

"Let's go," Bandal growls when he has mounted. The riders lift their lances.

"Keep working!" Bandal calls to the men. He spurs his pony, and the riders follow him up the new-built road.

"You know this traitor, fellow?" the lead rider calls to him. "My master says he is traitor. I say this right? Means 'stinking liar'?" Bandal grits his teeth. "You do not answer me, fellow? Is that not rude?" Again Bandal says nothing. The rider says something in a language that he does not understand, and the other riders laugh.

By the time the riders reach the main gate, Shivaji stands before it, with Iron, Hanuman, and Tanaji at his side.

The Bijapuris form a crescent, with the captain at the center, next to Bandal. Bandal dismounts and walks back to Jedhe. He sees that his hands are not tied but wrapped in chains, his wrists raw and bleeding. "Don't, fellow!" the lead rider calls. "He is not for you."

"What is your business?" asks Shivaji.

"You are Shivaji? I am the messenger of Afzul Khan. He sends me to make arrangements. I say this right?"

"Go on."

"Afzul Khan is not far. You see?" The captain nods toward the west, where the dust cloud of the army now seems only a few miles off.

"Why is my man treated so?"

The captain chortles. "Is traitor. I say this right? Means 'stinking liar.' He try to sell you to Afzul Khan. Say you are coward. You are coward, Shivaji?"

"Shivaji is our lord," Hanuman calls out. "He is no coward."

"This rude fellow talk for you, Shivaji?" The captain sneers.

"Let him go," Shivaji answers.

"Sure." The rider holding Jedhe's horse shoves Jedhe so hard he falls from his saddle. Bandal manages to break his fall, and sets to work, pulling off his blindfold and gag.

"Take him inside," Shivaji says to Bandal, as he helps Jedhe to his feet.

The captain throws a key at Shivaji's feet. "In my land we kill such a man."

Shivaji doesn't move. Bandal leads Jedhe into the fort as again the captain snorts. "Say your business and be gone," Shivaji orders.

"You don't be rude. You send messenger, Afzul Khan sends messenger."

"I would not send back a messenger in chains."

The captain frowns. "But I am not traitor. I come to arrange this parley. I say this right?" Shivaji nods. "I find place for parley. Then comes Afzul Khan. Tomorrow. Noon, maybe. For parley. I find place."

"We will parley in the fort. A place has been prepared"

The captain laughs out loud. "I think not inside that fort. I think not inside is good idea."

"Then where?"

The captain looks around him, considering. He clearly has something in mind. "You make nice road. Is for Afzul Khan very nice. All army can come up this road very fast. Why you do this?" The captain studies Shivaji, sizing him up. Shivaji stares back until the captain starts to squirm. "Something here is not right," he says. He turns and whispers with the man beside him. Then he looks back at Shivaji. "Back there. At place road ends."

"There?" Shivaji asks, looking shocked. "That's no place for a parley."

"Yes, fellow. That place only."

Shivaji's eyes narrow, and now it is he who stares at the captain. "All right. I'll make the arrangements."

"No!" the captain answers. "I make arrangements. Also I make rules. I only, or no parley. I do this."

Shivaji nods. "I'm listening."

"No men. No archers." He points to the battlements. "Walls only. You understand?"

"I understand."

"Parley in tent."

"We'll put up a tent, if you want."

"No!" the captain answers, glowering. "Afzul Khan tent only!"

Tanaji steps beside Shivaji. "Don't do this, Shahu. It's some kind of trap."

"How can a tent be a trap?" Shivaji nods at the captain. "Agreed."

"Good. In tent Afzul Khan only, Shivaji only."

"No!" Tanaji bursts out. "This is bad, Shahu." He turns to the captain. "Bodyguards. One guard to each man."

"Agreed," the captain says. "But no weapons in tent."

"Agreed," Shivaji answers, though Tanaji again protests.

The captain leans back and says, "Good. Done. Parley at noon tomorrow."

"Wait!" Tanaji strides forward. "No soldiers near the tent! It would be a death trap!"

"Ten soldiers," the captain offers. "Ten soldiers, Shivaji; ten soldiers Afzul Khan. Ten soldiers each man only."

"Enough," Shivaji says. "Our arrangements are done."

"Yes, done," the captain looks at the faces of the watchmen on the battlements. "You have bad men for soldiers, I think." The captain says one unknown word out loud, and the Bijapuri riders laugh.

Shivaji stands solemnly. "Go while you still breathe." Iron and Hanuman move to his side.

The captain considers Shivaji, measuring him. "Tomorrow. Noon." He nods to his men, and they ride off slowly down the new-made road.

ᕯᕲᕯᕲ

At that moment, Jedhe stumbles out of the fort. Behind him, Bandal waves his bare sword at a crowd of angry Marathis, shouting and throwing stones. They begin to form a circle around Jedhe. A stone clips his ear and he staggers to his knees.

Shivaji runs to stand in front of Jedhe. "What are you doing?"

"He's a traitor, lord! He deserves to die!" someone shouts and the others cheer.

"Quiet!" Shivaji orders. He bends over Jedhe and pulls him to his feet. Blood trickles down Jedhe's face. "I will deal with this, not you. Go back inside the fort."

Hanuman rushes out from the fort, and behind him, Iron and Tanaji. They stand in front of Jedhe, hands on their sword hilts.

With their arrival, one by one, the men obey. Last to go is a tubby, barefoot farmer, his face twisted in anger. "Take back your goddamned weapon," he says, throwing a jewel-hilted sword at Jedhe's feet. "I won't carry a traitor's sword."

"Are you all right?" Shivaji asks. Jedhe nods. "Bring him to my room," he tells Bandal.

"Are you going to try him, lord?" asks Bandal.

"No."

"But he's a traitor!"

Shivaji glares at him, then turns to the others. "You believe that? You'd take the word of that—that mercenary?"

Bandal shakes his head. "I don't know what to believe, lord."

"If he betrayed you, he must die, Shahu," Iron says softly.

"You can't let a traitor live, Shahu," Tanaji agrees.

"Stop it," Shivaji cries. "Are you a traitor, Jedhe?"

Jedhe lifts his head wearily, glancing at the faces that watch him. "I did only what you told me, lord," Jedhe answers. "I wouldn't betray you." He looks at the others, pleading. "I did only what Shivaji asked."

Shivaji smiles. "I believe him. You must believe him, too."

"But we don't know what really happened, Shahu!" Hanuman cries.

"So we must take his word. How will we succeed if we do not even trust each other?" He looks from face to face. "The only way to convince Afzul Khan to come alone was to make him think that he might take me by treachery. So I asked Jedhe to play the traitor."

"Why didn't you tell us about this plan?" Tanaji spits out.

"Your father also did shit like this," Iron tells him, his face ugly. He shakes his head. "It's bad business. You make us weak, Shahu. Afzul Khan will think our ranks are full of traitors."

"We'll sort this out later," Tanaji says. "That army will be here soon. If we're dead what difference will it make?"

Shivaji nods. "Afzul Khan will bring his army up that new road. That's my plan, at least." The others say nothing, but Shivaji's words seem to hang in the air, suddenly hollow. "We must hide the men in the forest along the road's edge before he gets here."

"Sleep in the forest?" Hanuman says. As he says this, the plan sounds more and more doubtful.

"Yes. We'll set our cannon along the road. Also any cannon we can move from the far side of the fort. You've heard this plan before," Shivaji insists. "You all agreed!"

"No one is disagreeing, Shahu," Tanaji says, his eyes cold.

"How is Onil progressing, Hanu?" Shivaji asks.

"He's got about a hundred *granadas* ready, Shahu," Hanuman answers.

"And the bombs for the road?"

"He says he isn't certain that they'll work, Shahu."

"They'll work," Shivaji answers, confident as ever. The other men look skeptical. "We'll plant the bombs along the road as soon as they're ready."

"What about the parley?"

"We'll launch the attack as soon as Afzul Khan goes in the tent. Bandal, you will be my bodyguard."

Bandal looks up, surprised.

"How much of your plan did Jedhe know, Shahu?" asks Hanuman. "How much has he betrayed?"

"I betrayed nothing," Jedhe whispers.

"So you say," Tanaji replies.

"You want to make a different plan?" Shivaji says. "You want a different leader?" No one answers. "Then do as I say." Shivaji leads Jedhe toward the fort.

As they stand there, looking after Shivaji and Jedhe entering the fort, Bandal nods toward the road. A courier on a Marathi pony hurries forward. "Here comes more bad news," Bandal says.

"How do you know that, cousin?" Hanuman asks.

"Because it's all bad news, cousin." He shakes his head, disgusted. "I'll see to finishing the road."

"What about this courier?"

"That's Shivaji's look-to, whatever it is. Let him handle it. I've had enough for one day."

 birth

In the darkness behind him, the walls of the fort twinkle with a thousand tiny Dewali lamps,. Around the blazing fire in the central courtyard, soldiers and villagers are singing, a long, energetic chant. But here on the walls of the high place, Shivaji sits alone, staring across the moonlit mountains. He sees his new road through the forest, like a white scar on dark skin beneath the crescent moon.

At his side, his sword, Bhavani, lies unsheathed, its ram's-head hilt glistening. The basalt stone is rough where he sits. The singing voices seem a hundred miles away.

He sees beyond the hillside the campfires of the Bijapuris blinking through the forest. Eastward, the horizon has begun to glow, the first hint of dawn, of death approaching.

He turns his head toward the north, and stares hard into the darkness, as if he might see a wisp of smoke from Sai Bai's funeral pyre.

Shivaji stands. Slowly he unfolds his turban, and unties his hair, which falls across his shoulders, blown by the breeze. The turban slips from his uncaring fingers—caught by the wind, it floats and spills like a ghost in the shadows. Finally it whispers out of sight into the darkness where the fort walls meet the mountain, falling into emptiness.

Shivaji steps forward, until his toes have reached the wall's edge and touch the empty air.

"How does this help, darling?" comes a soft voice behind him.

Shivaji looks around to see the wrinkled face of Gungama. For a moment he ignores her, and begins to lean over the edge of the wall. Instead he turns to her, and carefully, for the wall is narrow, he manages to kneel. "Give me your blessing, ma."

"Not for this, darling. I don't have that many blessings left. I've got to be careful how I use them."

With a light touch on his chin, Gungama lifts his head. "Have you been crying? Your wife was done with that body, darling." Gungama combs his long hair from his face as though he were a child. "She needed it no more. She played her part; and she's off to play another." Shivaji drops his eyes. "Your part is not yet over. Why do you wish to die?"

"Maybe dying now would be the best," he stammers. "My men no longer trust me. Why should they?"

"So what happens if you jump? Then, poof, your men will triumph?"

"No. Then my men will die. But at least I won't be to blame."

"You don't know that, darling. Maybe you end up floating in the sky up there, a hungry ghost, watching their blood flow like a river down that nice new road."

"Our only freedom is to choose the moment of our death."

Gungama shakes her head. "To me you say this foolishness? I am too old for it, child. What matters is how we choose to live, not when we choose to die. Consider your wife. Was she not faithful, all her life? Faithful even in her death? Did she not rise and feign recovery so that you would come here free from worry?"

Shivaji starts. "How do you know that?"

"Jump, and you prove her life was worthless. And your life, and mine as well. Jump and I will jump with you, darling, for with your death, all hope will flee the world." She points to the horizon. "The man who waits out there—he is no man. He is a demon incarnate, come to earth to destroy you. He must die, and you, my sweet, must kill him."

Shivaji looks over the battlements with a face filled with grief, or longing. "If it's what you want, mother."

"No!" Her voice fills the air like a shriek, harsh and terrifying. "You must do what you want. I'm old and dying. She's dead. You have life. You choose."

"What do you want of me?" Shivaji yells. "These hints, these knowing looks . . . They mean nothing to me! Either you're crazy, or a fool, or both. But I will not be persuaded by you! If I live, or if I die, it's none of your affair. Leave me!"

She stares up at him, a tiny doll. At last she speaks: "Throw me down if you think I'm lying."

He grabs her up and lifts her from the stones. As easily as one might lift a bird he holds her in midair. The look upon her face is one of ecstasy. Her legs sway in the emptiness. "Ah, ah!" she cries. "I'm dancing! Dancing!"

Shivaji whirls away from the edge, and thrusts her to ground. Then he strides off into the darkness.

After a moment, Gungama gets up, and presses her hair with her old palms, and creeps carefully down. At the bottom of the wall, she finds Maya hurrying toward her. "What happened, mother?"

"Who can tell, child? Anyway, he's alive; that's something. Go to him, child. Tonight of all nights he needs comfort. You, of all women, know how best to comfort him."

Maya looks up in surprise. "He'll just turn me away, mother."

"Not tonight. Go to him child. Go now."

In what seems like an instant Maya finds herself before Shivaji's door. She knocks, and tries the latch.

It's open.

CHAPTER 28

It had been like a cloudburst; first the tension—unbearable, fierce, heavy—then the sudden, shuddering release. As Gungama had predicted, this time Shivaji had not sent her away. But there'd been no joy in it, that first time, no pleasure, no desire, only the cloudburst, only the release.

Later, though, it was different, oh my yes. Later it had been slower, gentler, finer: eager hands stroking warm flesh, lips brushing lips, tongues darting, teeth nipping. There were moans, and gasps, and pleasure building; she had locked herself around him, felt his strong arms and hard thighs, felt his heart gallop against her breasts, felt the spasms crashing through her like waves as he burst inside her, calling out her name.

After that, she had used the skills a nautch girl knows: the whispering caresses of fingertips and eyelashes; her soft breath and moist lips teasing him, swirling him back to hardness; her tongue coiling around him until he groaned and begged for mercy. Only then did she lower her hips upon him, twisting and squeezing while her hands smoothed the tightening muscles of his belly, while her hair fell over him, while her fingers teased his nipples, until he strained against her, clutching her tight. Then the agony and rapture filled her so she could stand no more, and she fell upon him, mouth pressed against his neck to keep herself from crying out.

It had been nothing like her dream, not at all: rougher and more gentle, stronger and softer than her dream. So different from her dream. How many times? She wonders now, as she dozes, her skin still tingling, the smell of him still lingering in her hair. I lost count, she thinks, smiling. However many, it was too few.

She rolls over, and reaches out her hand, but he is gone. That jolts her awake. She sits up, alert.

At that moment there's a knock at the door. Another knock and the door begins to move. She finds her sari and clutches it about her. Tanaji looks in, glances at her. "Where is he?" he growls. She turns away. His eyes dart around the room. "Shit," he says, and pulls the door shut, hard.

ᏣᏫᏣᏫ

"He wasn't there," Tanaji tells Hanuman.

"Damn." His son shakes his head. "I just sent men to walk the walls."

"You don't think he jumped?" says Tanaji, aghast.

"I don't know what to think. Last night when he found out about Sai Bai . . ." Hanuman leaves the sentence unfinished.

Tanaji decides against telling him about Maya in Shivaji's room. "We don't have any more time. Disperse the men into the forest now, before the Bijapuris get here. Are the cannon in place? And the bombs?"

"Yes, that's all done. But, father, what about the signal?"

Tanaji frowns. "Same as we agreed: when Shivaji comes out of the parley tent, attack."

Hanuman looks desperate. "What if he doesn't show up for the parley?"

"For that matter, who's to say that Shahu will be the one to come out of the tent and not that demon Afzul Khan? If Shahu's gone, we're all dead anyway. For now, we'll follow the plan, and pray."

"Shit," Hanuman says, and he hurries away.

Tanaji has an inspiration. He runs to check the Bhavani temple. Empty. Then he checks the stables, even peers down the well. Nothing. Tanaji even goes to the powder hut, but no one is there but O'Neil, making still more *granadas*. "Seen Shivaji?" Tanaji asks.

"Not until yesterday," O'Neil answers, not looking up.

"How many *granadas* are you making, Onil?"

"Make three hundred yesterday. Now fifty more. Enough?" O'Neil studies Tanaji's face. "Something wrong?"

"Nothing. If you see Shivaji, say that I am looking for him." Tanaji strides off. Near the main gate, he catches up with Jedhe. "Seen him?"

"No. No luck?"

Tanaji snorts. "I think he's left us."

"No!" Jedhe gasps. "What are we doing, uncle? Without Shivaji, what's the use?"

"Hell, I don't know." He glances at the sun, reckoning the time. "No! He'll come back—he must come back!" Tanaji sighs. "This is a bad day, Jedhe." Tanaji walks away, and Jedhe feels more afraid even than at the camp of Afzul Khan.

ဗဩဗဩ

The Bijapuri war elephants, with armor glistening in the morning sunlight, plod to the front of the line. In the clearing around them stand several thousand men, spears and helmets gleaming. Into their midst lumbers the huge war elephant of Afzul Khan.

Afzul Khan, dressed in robes of green, lifts his legs over the railing of the howdah, and slides to the ground. Without missing a step he strides to the head of the line. The cart that carries the captain in his bamboo cage trundles a few yards behind.

The captains bow as he approaches. "Report," Afzul Khan commands.

"You can see where the parley tent is being raised," the young captain says, lifting his hand to the promontory at the top of Pratapghad. "All will be ready by noon."

"What about this road, captain?" Afzul Khan asks, with a hard, steady look, as if testing him.

"It's new, lord. Looks like they built it for our convenience."

" 'For our convenience,' " Afzul Khan repeats. "And what do you think?" he says, turning to the older captain.

"I think it's a trap."

"But you think everything's a trap, captain!" Afzul Khan laughs. The other captains join him.

"I say it's a trap because it is one, general."

Afzul Khan eyes blaze. "Of course it's a trap. You think I don't know a trap?"

"Then what are we doing, lord?" the young captain asks. The others stand impassive, eyes glued on Afzul Khan.

"You're the captain. You're the one who marched us into this trap. So, captain, what's your plan?"

The young captain gulps. "I place my trust in you, general. Whatever you may order will be best for all."

Afzul Khan throws a heavy arm across his shoulders. "You hear how he answers? This is why I've chosen him to be leader!"

The old captain spits. "Let's get out of here, general. We're like tigers driven toward the ring. It's madness."

"Why? If you were Shivaji, what would be your plan?"

Simon jumps in. "If he is Shivaji, he is now shitting his pants." Afzul Khan laughs, and the others laugh, too.

"If I were Shivaji, I'd have you right where I want you," the old captain answers. "I'd get you in that tent and hold you."

"How?" smiles Afzul Khan. "How would you hold me?"

"I'd think of a way. Then I'd launch a flying attack down this new road. Horsemen at full speed. Cannon from the fort for cover. Archers there and there." The older captain points to some nearby rises.

"Do you see any archers, captain?" Afzul Khan asks. "No. Why? Too obvious. Besides he has not got enough men." The other captains chuckle. "Still, I agree with some of what you say. He will try to hold me at the tent, and then he'll throw everything he can at us. That's what this road is for. He thinks he's got us where he wants us."

"So then you'll move us back to cover, lord?" the captain asks.

"Do I look like a coward?" Afzul Khan replies. His eyes are empty, and his tone flat.

"It isn't cowardice to protect your men."

Afzul Khan walks slowly around the circle of captains, looking carefully at each. "Simon, what do you say?"

"Shivaji is a fool. He is not a good leader. His men are very rude. We should have not a worry with him, lord."

Afzul Khan nods. "That's right. We have an army here, not a bunch of farmers waving pitchforks. Shivaji is a coward and the son of a coward. I will bring that mountain rat home in a cage." He turns to Simon. "Your men have their instructions?"

"They make tent just as you say, lord," Simon answers, bowing.

"No, captain, he may try, but Shivaji shall not hold me. Rather I shall do the catching." He smiles at the old captain. "But what about this road? How to keep them from flying down upon us, waving their pitchforks?"

The young captain's face brightens. "We could block the road, lord!"

"Ahcha!" says Afzul Khan, now grinning like a jackal about to feed. "We could block the road! How could this be done?"

"Move the army up the road," the captain answers "Elephants at the head, then infantry. Archers at the rear."

"And what's wrong with that plan, eh?" Afzul Khan asks, lowering his face over the captain like a vulture.

"Those cannon…But they'll overshoot the road," the young captain beams proudly. "Look—they'll never manage the angle!"

"Yes," Afzul Khan agrees. "The mountain rat has miscalculated. His cannon overshoot the road! Would he aim cannon at his own troops?"

"But what if Shivaji holds you, somehow, in that parley tent?" the old captain asks.

Afzul Khan's face grows cold. "You've outgrown your usefulness. I think you might be growing cowardly."

The captain sets his jaw and stares back. "Then, with all respect, general, I resign from your service."

"No one quits me, captain." Afzul Khan smiles his terrifying smile. "I was going to make you my bodyguard for this parley, but you stink of fear. Instead, I'll place you at the front of the attack. Let's see if you still have any balls." The captain stands mute. "Arrange the troops. Push to the very top of the road. Place yourself at the front of the charge."

"Yes, lord," the captain says stiffly.

"No one is to move except upon my order. Upon my order only, captain, do you hear? Unless you hear the word from me, you do not move. Not one inch, except when I give the order!"

"Your command is clear, lord."

"Let me be bodyguard, general," Simon offers. "I will not fail you like some coward."

"I'll take the boy," Afzul Khan replies, nodding toward the young captain. "He's faithful. Besides, I have a special order for you, Simon. If this fellow moves before I say, if he even blinks, put him in a cage."

ꙩꙩꙩꙩ

Tanaji has given up looking for Shivaji. He watches the Abyssinians set up the parley tent. It is a rich affair, tall and wide, silver tent poles, carpets on the floor, sides of woolen cloth, ropes wrapped with silk.

Below him, the army of Bijapur has begun to move up the newly built road. It's wide enough for three elephants to walk side by side. Tanaji watches as they trudge up its length, groaning as the mahouts kick their ears. Behind them comes an army, a real army, with gleaming lances and shining shields. He thinks of his son's troops, ill-equipped, untested—men who stepped off the farm a few days ago. Now they're hiding in the trees and underbrush along the road. What do they think when they see that army? How can they face an enemy like this?

Where the hell is Shivaji?

In his anxiety, Tanaji begins to pace beside the parley tent. The Abyssinians pay no attention to him. They bring carpets now, and a strange, folding camp table. Seems too big for that tent, thinks Tanaji. He shakes his head. Why am I watching these fools? I should be making preparations. I should be sharpening my mace. I should be praying.

Praying . . . Suddenly he remembers the tiny Ganesha shrine, a few yards from where the tent is being raised. Before he knows it, he stands before its open door. He kneels so he can peer inside, and it seems to him he sees a shape stretched around the red-painted stone. He's here. The great leader! Sleeping! Clutching the *murti* the way a child might clutch a doll!

Crawling into the tiny shrine, Tanaji reaches in and jostles Shivaji roughly by the shoulder. "Come out, damn it."

"Hello, uncle," Shivaji says as he crawls through the tiny doorway. His long hair falls over his bare shoulders; he's not even wearing a shirt. Tanaji glares at him. They walk past the tent, but the Abyssinians don't recognize him—they scarcely look up. Tanaji glares up at the surprised sentries standing on the wall, and lifts a finger to his lips.

Once inside the gate, Tanaji wheels on Shivaji. "What were you doing?" he shouts.

"It doesn't matter. Nothing matters."

"Quiet!" He pulls close to Shivaji. "Goddamn it, it matters!" Shivaji shrugs, and starts to walk off. "Where do you think you're going?" Tanaji shouts. "You've got to get ready!"

"I'll be at the temple," Shivaji answers blandly, not even looking back. Tanaji watches as Shivaji ambles off, and then runs to Shivaji's room. It's empty; Maya's gone. He rummages through Shivaji's bag; finds clean clothes, a turban, a jeweled *katar*. Shivaji's *farang* sword hangs from a hook on the wall; Tanaji grabs that, too.

As he runs for the temple, Bandal and Jedhe hurry toward him. "What do we do?" Bandal calls. "Afzul Khan will be here any minute!"

"He's back," Tanaji answers. "He's gone to the Bhavani temple." Bandal's eyes grow wide. "He's not even dressed!"

"What the hell's going on, uncle?"

Tanaji shakes his head. "Can you find a mail shirt?" Jedhe nods. "Bring one to the temple. Hurry!"

"Don't forget the honor guard, uncle!" Jedhe says. "The ten men. Shivaji never chose them! We need them now!"

Tanaji mutters curses. "Here, take this stuff to the temple. Shivaji's there. Get him dressed. Get the mail shirt; make sure he wears it. Do whatever you must to get him ready I think Shivaji's gone crazy."

"You want him to meet Afzul Khan if he's crazy?"

"I don't know, all right? One step a time. First we get him ready, then we figure out a plan!" He thrusts the clothes and sword into Jedhe's hands. "I'll fetch men for the honor guard."

"What are we doing, uncle?" Jedhe calls after him.

☙☙☙☙

At the temple Jedhe sees Shivaji seated before the image of the goddess. A strange old woman kneels beside him, whispering in his ear. They do not see Jedhe as he enters.

"It is that time," Jedhe hears the woman say. "The wick of righteousness burns low; once more the gods take birth as men. Once more do demons wear the skins of men to halt the flame of truth. Your time has come, my darling. You must now take on the yoke you have been born to."

Shivaji doesn't move. "Who is that approaching?" the old woman asks. Then she smiles. "Oh, it's you." Jedhe blinks; he's never seen her before. "Shivaji's ready for you, darling," the woman says. "Dress him here."

Jedhe stops short, realizing what the woman has said. "Here?"

"Here before the goddess, yes," she says.

"In front of you?"

"Am I not his mother?" She laughs when she sees Jedhe's reaction. "Never mind, I'm leaving." She kisses Shivaji's forehead, and hurries off.

At that moment, Bandal hurries up, a dark bundle in his hands. Taking Shivaji's shoulder, Bandal shakes him. "Come on, Shahu. Let's go. It's time. He's coming. You've got to dress."

"Do it here," Jedhe insists. Bandal starts to argue, and sighs. Then he shakes out his bundle, revealing a shirt of fine steel rings, and a narrow, tight-fitting helmet.

"First the mail," Bandal slips the metal shirt over Shivaji's head. "Now the helmet." The helmet fits tight, like a cap.

Jedhe slips a white cotton shirt over the mail. Then he takes the long turban cloth and wraps it over the helmet. Shivaji's eyes never leave the goddess.

"Isn't he ready yet?" calls Tanaji, hurrying toward them.

"Almost done," Jedhe says. He wraps the sash belt around Shivaji, and then begins to fasten the jeweled *katar* dagger.

"No," Shivaji says, breaking his silence. "I'll take no weapon. I have sworn it," Shivaji repeats, eyes focused on the goddess.

"Damn it, pay attention!" Tanaji yells. "You're meeting a killer! You'll take weapons, damn it, or you'll die."

"What good are weapons against a demon, uncle?" Shivaji asks, turning for the first time to look at them.

"Don't be a fool. He's flesh and blood same as you."

Bandal steps forward. "Take these, at least, Shahu," he says, holding out his *wagnak*.

"Yes, yes!" Tanaji says. "Tiger claws. Take them Shahu! At least then you'll be able to defend yourself."

Shivaji ignores him. Bandal bows his head. "Please take these, lord," he says, again holding out the tiger claws. "As your bodyguard, I insist. Even if you're searched, they're easy to conceal."

"I gave my word. And the goddess has told me to go unarmed."

"The goddess is crazy," Tanaji snarls.

Shivaji laughs. "I'm crazy, too." He bows to the *murti*. "Come on. Let's see what fate the gods hold for us."

As they walk across the courtyard, they see O'Neil carrying a cloth sack carefully in front of him. "You are going, lord?" O'Neil says. "I hope is good. No dying, now!" he adds, smiling.

"Be ready for my signal, Onil," Shivaji answers.

"Go with God," O'Neil replies in English, and hurries on.

Near the gate they find the ten guards Tanaji selected. Shivaji points to two. "You two are excused. Get with the others and await my signal."

"They're good men, Shahu," Tanaji protests. "I'll vouch for them."

"I want you and Jedhe in the guard," Shivaji answers. "Tanaji, you'll hold my *katar*. Jedhe, you'll hold my sword, Bhavani." Not waiting for answer, he turns and begins to stride ahead.

"Lord, I beg you once more, take the *wagnak*!" Bandal whispers urgently. But Shivaji shrugs him off and he strides across the courtyard. Bandal struggles to keep up. As they march through the gate, soldiers cheer. Shivaji lifts his hand casually, exuding confidence.

"First no one can find him, now he's everybody's hero," grumbles Tanaji.

ᑯᑯᑯ

"What's that, uncle?" Jedhe asks, pointing to a metallic glint that shines through the trees.

"Those are howdahs of the war elephants," Tanaji replies, hurrying behind Shivaji on his way to the parley. "You'll see soon enough."

The Bijapuri army has pushed to the very top of the new road, and now stands packed into a tight line aimed at the parley tent. At its head, war elephants stand three abreast, howdahs gleaming. The sounds of the great army echo from the fort walls.

As they approach the parley tent, Tanaji smells the elephants: a rich, rancid odor of shit and sweat. With it, the smell of hot wax, for the soldiers have lit the fuses of their matchlocks.

Tanaji catches Jedhe's eye and nods with his chin toward the birds circling in long spirals over the road. Vultures. Jedhe's eyes drift to the trees. "Look only at the road!" Tanaji snarls.

"I just wanted to see where the men are hiding—"

"I know what you wanted! Do you want the Bijapuris looking there?"

ᑯᑯᑯ

At the parley tent, Tanaji snaps out orders, arranging the men. From their howdahs, the Bijapuris offer mocking comments. "Ignore them!" Tanaji snarls. Stretching down the hillside are dozens of elephants and hundreds of horses, and in the wide clearing below Jedhe sees an ocean of men surging forward. How can we ever hope to defeat them? he wonders.

Suddenly a commotion erupts on the new road; the throbbing blare of war trumpets, the clatter of cymbals and booming of drums. The Bijapuris cheer. The elephants squeeze to the edge of the road, as twelve riders come forward.

One by one the horsemen emerge between the elephants and peel off in a row, facing the Marathi guard. All are Abyssinians. Though he's seen their scarred, branded faces before, even Jedhe's heart quails at the sight.

Last of all comes Afzul Khan, dressed in green silk robes and a white turban fastened by an emerald pin fashioned like a peacock feather. His horse sags beneath his bulk.

Oh gods! It *was* him! Tanaji thinks. It was Afzul Khan we saw in Khirki! Afzul Khan that Shahu made a cuckold! The night we rescued Maya—the night it all started. It's been fated from the beginning!

Behind Afzul Khan rides his bodyguard, the young captain. But the Bijapuri procession is not yet finished: up the hill comes the oxcart carrying the prisoner captain in his bamboo cage. He's babbling; drool hangs from his lips, and his head flops with each bump, yet somehow he manages to avoid the sharp spikes only inches from his eyes.

Afzul Khan dismounts and strides to the captain with the grizzled beard. "Remember!" Afzul Khan shouts so everyone can hear. "No one is to move without my order!" He points to the cage and shouts again, "Remember the penalty for disobedience!" Then Afzul Khan takes a step closer to the old captain. "Are my orders clear, captain?"

"General, look," the older captain answers defiantly. "There stands that traitor—standing in Shivaji's honor guard! This is a trap, not a parley! Why else would Shivaji give a traitor a place among his guard?"

"Because he is arrogant, or stupid, or both," Afzul Khan replies. "For the last time, captain: Obey my orders or face my wrath!" The captain's eyes glare with such fierceness that a line of fire seems to burn from them.

Afzul Khan turns to Shivaji. He frowns, as if seeing Shivaji had awakened some distant memory. But he lets it go. "All right," he says. "Let's talk."

"Not here. Inside, as we said," Shivaji replies. Shivaji's head barely reaches Afzul Khan's shoulders.

"You see the forces I array against you?" Afzul Khan replies. "You see the might of Bijapur ready to assail you? Where are your armies, little mouse? Cowering behind those walls?" Afzul Khan laughs. "Huddled around the treasure you have stolen? How long can they survive? How long will those gates keep out my elephants, eh?"

Shivaji's eyes grow hard. "If you think yourself invincible, why parley? You asked for this. Let us go inside and talk."

Afzul Khan squints at Shivaji, sizing him up. The sapphires and diamonds of his turban jewel glitter in the sunlight, the gold embroidery of his green silk robes gleams. In his white shirt, Shivaji looks as plain as any farmer. "All right. We'll talk. You and me, alone."

"No!" Tanaji comes forward. "Each with a bodyguard, as we agreed. And with no weapons, as we agreed."

Afzul Khan's black eyes gleam as he turns his heavy face toward Tanaji. "Does this puppet speak for you?"

"He only reminds us. I know you keep your word."

"Yes, unlike your coward father, I keep my word."

"Then let your man be searched," Tanaji snaps. Afzul Khan scowls, but nods to the young captain, who steps forward. Face taut and pale, he lifts his arms. Bandal pats his sides and legs, then probes his turban.

"Now the general," says Tanaji. Afzul Khan's face grows dark, but after a pause, he too lifts his arms.

Bandal scarcely needs to lower his head to pass beneath the general's arms. When he pats the silken robes, he must make two passes, so wide is the general's form. Bandal steps back. "Your turban, general."

Afzul Khan looms over him. "Be careful of my jewels." He slowly bends at the waist, until Bandal can just reach the thick white silk of his turban. Bandal works quickly. Then he steps back, and Afzul Khan settles his turban and its gleaming jeweled pin with a vain, almost feminine gesture. "Now you," he says to Bandal.

Bandal lifts his arms. The Bijapuri captain pats his sides and legs, and then his turban. He doesn't notice the two dark rings on the fingers of Bandal's hand. "Now you, sir," the captain says to Shivaji.

Shivaji lifts his arms. The captain feels the mail beneath the cotton shirt and hesitates. "Don't take all day," Afzul Khan mutters. The captain looks at Shivaji uncertainly, then probes his turban as well. Again he hesitates. "Well?" says Afzul Khan. "A weapon?"

"No," the captain says, uncertainly. "No weapon . . ."

"Then step inside," the general growls. "What are you waiting for?" The captain shrugs. "Now you," Afzul Khan says, nodding to Bandal. Bandal glances at Shivaji and steps through the entrance flap.

"You go first, mouse," Afzul Khan says to Shivaji. "It's my tent." Shivaji at last walks into the tent, and Afzul Khan, stooping carefully, follows.

ಅಅಅ

Over the battlements of Pratapghad peek a thousand hidden eyes. The villagers have crept up the tower steps to watch. They huddle in clusters, peering around the basalt stones, through the bow slits, at the confrontation near the tent.

Maya hunches near a shepherd and his family. In vain she searched for Gungama. Shivaji looks to her like a king from the old tales; Afzul Khan like a rakshasa. "Daddy, where have all the soldiers gone?" the shepherd's daughter asks. "No one's here. Who will protect us?"

"Hush," says the shepherd. "Shivaji will protect us." But Maya sees his fingers check for his knife. "And if he fails, I will protect us." Maya realizes that he will kill the girl if he must.

And who, Maya thinks, will protect me?

◑◐◑◐

"I see him! Shivaji's there!" Hanuman whispers.

"Where?" whispers Iron, crawling up beside him. "Are you sure?"

Hanuman points through a small clearing in the underbrush. "Look, there by the tent."

"I can't see a thing with all these damned elephants," Iron mutters.

Hanuman looks again. "And now I can't see anything either." He turns to Iron. "It had to be him."

Iron tugs his mustache. "If it was Shivaji, it means our attack is on."

"What if he doesn't come out, uncle? What if Afzul Khan comes out?"

Iron scowls. "Shit, I don't know. Worry about that later. They'll only be in that tent for a short while. Spread the word: time to get ready."

Hanuman suddenly gives Iron a hard embrace. "When the signal comes, there won't be much time. I've enjoyed your company, uncle."

"Stop talking like a woman!" Iron replies, pushing him away.

◑◐◑◐

Afzul Khan drops the entrance flap behind him. Shivaji takes a seat at the far end of the tent. Behind him stands Bandal, the tiger claws hidden between his fingers. It dawns on him that this could be the last place he ever sees. He glances at Shivaji, but from behind there's no way to tell whether Shivaji looks confident or frightened. I'll just do my best, he thinks, and hope the gods will help.

The tent is tall enough for Afzul Khan to stand comfortably. He prowls the edge of the tent, first one way, then the other, like a bull elephant choosing a place to rest. He stops beside the low camp table that is covered with green cloth.

What the hell is it with that table? Bandal wonders. Something about it seems wrong. It seems so out of place.

When he first entered and saw it, Bandal had lifted the cloth, expecting maybe an assassin to be hiding there. But it was just a table, some strange design of bamboo slats, probably fashioned to be light and portable. Easy to see that there was no one hiding there. While the young captain watched, Bandal had replaced the cloth. But even now Bandal's eyes are drawn to it. Something about it gnaws at him. Something about it is all wrong.

Afzul Khan nods to the young captain, who hurries forward, placing a cushion close to the central tent pole. Afzul Khan then sits on the cushion. His knees jut up into the air, as though his huge thighs are unable to relax, and his hulking shoulders hunch forward.

Afzul Khan's voice is soft. "Ever been to Khirki, mouse? Ever sleep with some fool's wife there, and then run away? Ever done that, mouse?" Shivaji stares back, silent. "Well, you wanted this parley," Afzul Khan says. "Speak."

A moment passes. Bandal looks at Afzul Khan's glittering turban pin, suddenly troubled that he didn't look at it more closely. But then Shivaji's cool voice says, "I'm here to offer you a deal, general. Leave my territory. Now."

It takes a moment for Afzul Khan to collect himself. "What kind of deal is that, little mouse?"

"Leave and live. That's a good deal."

Afzul Khan begins to chuckle, then he laughs, a low, growling laugh. "I thought you were a coward, mouse. Now I see you are a fool. Maybe we're both fools, who can say?" The general lumbers to his feet. "Come and embrace me, and we will talk as brothers." He spreads his arms.

Don't do it! Bandal thinks, as Shivaji stands.

No! Bandal calls out, only his voice isn't working. Shivaji steps forward, lifting his arms.

Afzul Khan folds his arms around Shivaji. He clutches him to his chest. His huge arms squeeze so tightly Shivaji's heels leave the ground. Shivaji groans as Afzul Khan wraps him tighter. The general's face grows taut with the effort of squeezing Shivaji, his thick neck begins to swell, and he leans backward, pulling Shivaji from his feet.

The general nods to the captain. With a sudden gesture, the captain whips the cloth from the table, and suddenly Bandal recognizes it. A cage! Lying on its side—a cage like the one that holds that babbling prisoner outside! But before Bandal can move, the young captain has knelt to the side of the cage and flipped its top open. Afzul Khan drags Shivaji toward it, step by step, as Shivaji struggles furiously, his muffled voice groaning.

Do something! Bandal thinks. He lurches forward, reaching out for Afzul Khan. As if in a dream, he notices the blades of the tiger claws protruding between his fingers. With a yell, he drives them into Afzul Khan's shoulder.

His next image is of Afzul Khan's hideous, twisted face turning toward him. He hears Afzul Khan's voice roaring like a bull, sees an anvil fist whip toward his face, sees Shivaji pulling free.

Then Bandal's sight explodes in a starburst of pain as he's hurled backward. He falls against the tent poles near the entry, and heavy cloth collapses on him. He pulls himself free of the tangled cloth only to see the young captain's foot swinging for his head. He turns aside, but the captain's shoe catches him by the ear and sends him spinning.

Bandal scrambles to his feet. His vision is a swirling blur of light and pain. He catches a glimpse of Afzul Khan and Shivaji circling each other, and sees some sort of weapon in Afzul Khan's hand.

Then a blow strikes the back of his neck. He collapses. A savage kick catches him in the ribs, flopping him onto his back. The captain drops to drive his knees into Bandal's chest.

Only then does the captain discover them, the black steel blades glinting between Bandal's fingers. The razor points slice his shirt and glide along the glistening skin of his chest. Then they catch the flesh and dig deeper, so sharp his wounds gleam white before they start to bleed. Then they rip into the captain's throat and shred his neck. His head flops forward and he falls.

Bandal feels the warm blood pumping from the captain's wound, feels the captain's body shuddering. But he hears behind him grunts and blows and remembers Shivaji and Afzul Khan. Somehow he manages to shove the captain's body from his chest, somehow manages to stagger to his feet.

Despite his dizzy vision, Bandal sees Afzul Khan attacking Shivaji. The general's arm bleeds from Bandal's stab, but not enough to stop him. In his hand is a bright knife, its handle the jeweled turban pin. It was a hidden weapon after all, Bandal thinks stupidly. He stumbles forward. But Afzul Khan sees him. He swings the jeweled knife in a wide arc, slashing Bandal across the throat.

Bandal tries to scream, but he cannot. He reaches for his neck, and his fingers slip into the wet gash, as if he has a new mouth. He gasps and quivers as he struggles for air, for there's an emptiness where his throat should be. Blood bubbles over his tongue and pours over his lips; blood gushes down his arms. He's staring up at the top of the tent now, but he doesn't know when he fell. As he dies he hears the gagging as he drowns in his blood.

◉◉◉◉

"Now who will help you, mouse?" Afzul Khan laughs.

Shivaji watches as his cousin shudders into his death, then backs away.

Afzul Khan's face is flushed with triumph. "My knife or my cage, mouse. You decide," he growls. With unexpected speed, he lunges, knife held high, point toward Shivaji's heart. The force of the blow knocks Shivaji down, but the blade is turned by his tunic of mail. Shivaji springs to his feet.

Afzul Khan's small eyes gleam. "You won't fool me that way again."

Shivaji steps backward, his eyes fixed on Afzul Khan's bloated face. Again Afzul Khan lunges, this time the knife's blade aimed for Shivaji's unprotected face.

Shivaji ducks, and the blade drives through his turban, piercing the helmet above his ear, but breaking before it can kill him. Afzul Khan stares at the jeweled hilt of the broken knife. Then with a laugh he tosses it aside. "Now we are equals, mouse. Now it is just you and me."

Moving backward, Shivaji bumps into one of the tent poles. He tugs it, as if to use it as a weapon. But when he pulls it from its place, part of the tent comes crashing down, burying him and Afzul Khan in darkness.

Afzul Khan curses and thrashes in the cloth. Shivaji crawls backward, and bumps against Bandal's wet, warm body. A few feet away, Afzul Khan emerges from the fallen tent, his face a mask of rage.

The knife cut Shivaji's scalp, and now blood streams from beneath his helmet, into his eyes. Blindly he feels along Bandal's body. He feels the hand and finds the fingers, feels the fingers and finds the *wagnak*. He tugs at the steel rings, cutting his own hands as he peels the weapon from Bandal's death grip.

There's a sudden moment when the rings slip free and Bandal's hand falls, leaving the *wagnak* in Shivaji's grasp. As Afzul Khan staggers toward him, Shivaji slips the tiger claws onto his own hand. He squeezes his fingers and Afzul Khan sees the black blades.

"A coward's weapon," he says. "A toy. You think that will stop me?" Afzul Khan steps closer, spreading his arms. "Come then, mouse. Come and scratch me with your tiny claws." With that Shivaji rushes forward, fist clenched tight. Afzul Khan does not flinch or move away. He wraps Shivaji in his massive arms and squeezes tight.

Pinned down so, Shivaji can slide the blades across Afzul Khan's torso—but only a little, for his arm is pinioned in a crushing embrace. Afzul Khan begins to pound Shivaji's body even as he holds him, battering him with fists like stones. Shivaji groans with every thudding blow. All his concentration bends to freeing his arm, just a little, just a little.

Somehow, amidst the blows, Shivaji gains a little space. He can lift his arm! In a flash he drives his blades with all his strength into Afzul Khan's side. Again and again he plunges the blades, but Afzul Khan is so padded with fat that the *wagnak* seems only to scratch his skin. The general never stops his blows. He squeezes Shivaji hard still. Shivaji gasps for air.

Unknowingly, though, Afzul Khan is squeezing Shivaji's blade hand, actually pressing the *wagnak* deeper into his own side.

Shivaji hears Afzul Khan groan. He feels something give. Suddenly the blades sink deep. The general's arms loosen. Shivaji thrusts his arm into Afzul Khan's wound. He smells the blood and shit. Afzul Khan screams. He strikes out wildly, trying to get away from the claws that rip his insides.

Shivaji thrusts upward, again! Again! A rain of blows falls on him, but he does not stop. With his hand twisting in Afzul Khan's gut, Shivaji leans into the massive chest, and pushes with all his might.

Afzul Khan staggers, but he will not fall. Instead with a roar he clenches his fists together, and smashes them against Shivaji's back. The blow is staggering: Shivaji crumples to his knees. As he falls, his arm, wet with black blood, pulls out from Afzul Khan's side.

Shivaji looks up to see Afzul Khan's face, contorted in triumph and pain. "You cannot kill me!" Afzul Khan shouts, and with those words hammers his foot into Shivaji's ribs. The blow hurls Shivaji within inches of the bamboo cage. "It is I who will kill you!" Afzul Khan staggers toward him. Blood gushes from his side, but he comes on, unheeding of his wounds. He pulls back his foot for one more kick. Twisting, Shivaji stabs, catching Afzul Khan from below, ripping the tiger claws up his thighs, his balls, slicing his lingam. Afzul Khan screams and plunges forward.

Into the cage.

At the last moment, he manages to turn his head.

One spike breaks; the other pierces his ear, emerging bright red through the white folds of Afzul Khan's turban.

☙✺❧

Outside the tent, the guards wait. They began by watching each other with grim faces, but as the tent collapses, as the muffled shouts and groans emerge, their eyes grow tight with tension. What should they do?

When the first tent post fell, Tanaji rushed forward, but one of the Abyssinians spurred his horse to block his way. The two stood, eyes locked, listening to the grunts and unintelligible words.

Now the whole tent collapses, and worry slips across the Abyssinian's face.

"We're going in!" Tanaji yells to the Marathis. He lifts his mace like a club, with two hands, and the Marathis bare their swords. Jedhe waves Shivaji's *farang* sword, still sheathed, above his head. The Abyssinians quickly form a line to stop them, but they look at each other with troubled faces.

"We should all go in!" Tanaji shouts to the Abyssinian. "Something's wrong in there! Let's go in together!"

The Abyssinian captain, glancing to the part of the tent that now twists and squirms like a living thing, considers for a moment. "No," he says.

Then the tent stops moving.

From within, no more muffled voices. Silence.

Tanaji looks at the Abyssinian and sees a face as troubled as his own.

Then the tent begins to move once more, as someone pokes and thrashes toward the entrance flap. Tanaji steps forward, wanting to help, but again the Abyssinian bars his way.

And then a man emerges: feet bare and soaked with blood, legs blood-stained, shirt slashed, turban gone.

Shivaji lifts his bleeding head to see the sky. His helmet, cracked and mangled, tumbles from his head, and his blood-soaked hair falls in thick wet ropes across his shoulders. He lifts the bloody *wagnak* so that all may see.

"Bring me my sword!" Shivaji cries.

❦❦❦❦

The grizzled Bijapuri captain stands in his stirrups and shouts, "No one move! Not one inch!" The Abyssinian guard scowls at the captain and lifts his lance. "Stop! Keep still! Not one inch, I say!" the captain screams.

Shivaji now moves quickly to Jedhe, who stares at him with horror. "Do I look that bad?" Shivaji asks. The white teeth gleaming from that red-streaked face look like a demon's. "Courage, cousin," Shivaji says. "Give me my sword."

"It is yours, lord," Jedhe cries and hands over the ram-hilt blade.

As Shivaji takes it, he sees that he still wears the bloodstained tiger claws. He tears them off and hurls them to the ground. Then he grasps the sword and tears off its sheath. The *farang* blade, polished mirror-bright, sparkles in the sunlight. Shivaji holds the sword high, walking toward the road.

"Stand your ground! Move not one inch!" the captain screams.

Shivaji steps to the captain, his demon smile gleaming. Then Shivaji lifts the sword above his head and cries out in a loud voice: "For the goddess! For Bhavani! *Har, har, Mahadev!*"

"We will not move until we hear the general's order!" shouts the captain.

"*Har, har, mahadev!*" Shivaji cries, and from the crackling, leafy woods along the roadside, shouts are heard.

"Stand your ground!"

"*Har, har, mahadev! Har, har, mahadev!*" Shivaji shouts, waving the sword above his head with each word. The voices in the woods begin to raise the call as well, "*Har, har, mahadev! Har, har, mahadev! Har, har, mahadev!*"

"Not one inch!" the captain yells, his eyes wide. And then the blasts begin.

෨෧෨෧

Hidden in the foliage of the woods, Hanuman squints through the underbrush, trying to see the parley tent at the top of the hill. "What do you see, captain?" one of his soldiers whispers.

There's a stirring on the hilltop; the elephants are stamping more emphatically. Hanuman thinks he can make out his father, lifting his mace.

All around him a deathly quiet has fallen. I wish I knew what the hell is going on, he thinks. What is happening up there? He strains to see the parley tent.

And then a figure, bloody and obscure, emerging from the tent. "Shahu!" he whispers involuntarily.

"Is it him?" the soldier whispers from behind. Hanuman holds up his hand for silence.

Not until Shivaji lifts his sword above his head is Hanuman convinced. And when Shivaji gives the signal cry, *Har, har, mahadev!* Hanuman turns and yells as well: "The signal! The signal! *Har, har, mahadev!* Attack! Attack!"

The forest bursts forth with sudden violence. Out of the leaves and vines, men emerge, and bright blades.

"The fuses!" Hanuman screams. "Throw the *granadas!*" Can anyone hear him?

All around comes a chant that sounds like roaring: *Har, har, mahadev! Har, har, mahadev!* Buried beneath the road, the first of O'Neil's hidden bombs explodes. The blast thuds like a book dropped beneath a dome. The blast of other bombs follows. "Get down! Get down!" screams Hanuman.

Another blast, and another, the blasts now heavier and stronger. Beneath the Bijapuris' feet the road becomes the mouth of hell. Fire leaps down the road; black smoke belches into the sky.

The forest brush begins to rattle as a rain falls; not a rain of water, but of bodies broken: arms, and feet, and sharply broken skulls; hooves and tusks and shattered weapons pelting through the leaves. Men cower against the damp earth, which shudders beneath them as though it were a great drum beaten hard.

Sound erupts around them, battering their ears though they have squeezed their hands against their heads. Smoke rolls through the forest like an angry river.

O'Neil's bombs, hidden beneath the road from the bottom of the hill to the top, explode in a rolling cloud of thundering death, spewing smoke and fire, sending death screaming through the blackened air.

On the hill road there is no warning, only death, death before the bomb's roar hits the ear. The soldiers watch in frozen terror, unable to move, unable to pray even, as the ground beneath them roils into fire.

At last the ground stops rumbling and Hanuman lifts his head. "Attack! Attack!" he cries. His ringing ears cannot hear his own voice. He dashes down the hillside, sword in hand, pushing the Marathis forward. "Attack! Attack!"

Amidst the broken bodies on the road, men still live. But not for long. The Marathis dash through the fire, swords and sickles waving, slashing anything that moves.

Blood pours down the smoking road in rivulets.

◎◎◎◎

The bomb blasts stop a hundred yards from the hilltop, leaving all the elephants alive. But though they have been trained to war, they are not ready for the fury of those bombs. Maddened by the flame and smoke and thunder all around, they rear up and the soldiers fall from their howdahs.

The great beasts collide into each other, goring and being gored by armored tusks, skidding on the gore of the men they squash beneath their heavy feet. Bellowing, eyes rimmed with white, the elephants drive mindlessly into the forest. Their howdahs and their armor tumble off, dragging behind them as they run. Sometimes they drag men still tangled in the traces.

❀❀❀❀

Jedhe siezes his *katar* and runs to the captain in the bamboo cage, miraculously unharmed. Jedhe slices through the thongs that secure the cage door. The captain, trembling and moaning, is too far gone even to notice. Jedhe releases the captain's feet, and catches his body in his arms—the smell is horrible—and lifts him so his eyes no longer face the pointed stakes. Then Jedhe cuts the bindings on the captain's wrists, and he collapses.

When this is done, Shivaji lowers his sword and looks to the Bijapuri captain, still standing in his stirrups. "That man is now free," Shivaji says. "And so are you. Take what men still live and leave my lands." Blood trickles from the wound beneath his helmet.

"What about the general?" the captain answers.

"He's dead," Shivaji says.

"He should be buried," the captain says.

"I myself will do it. Leave or die."

The captain looks behind, down the road now burning, where Marathis slash and hack at anything still moving. In the clearing far below, several thousand soldiers mill in disarray. "I could still take you," the captain says.

"Try," Shivaji answers, and he lifts the point of his shining sword toward the captain's heart.

The captain looks at him. "I never moved, did I? Not one goddamned inch." The captain turns to the Abyssinians. "Come on, you, bastards," he calls. "I'm the general now."

The captain turns once more to Shivaji. "Shall I take him?" he says, nodding to the prisoner Jedhe has released.

"He's mine now."

"So's the goddamned treasure. And the goddamned forts. And any other goddamned thing you want, son." The captain starts to pick his way down the bleeding, broken road, the other riders following.

Tanaji comes forward, grabbing Shivaji's arm. "You've won, Shahu!"

"Have I?" Shivaji whispers. Then he collapses to the ground.

EPILOGUE

Maya's feet slap the black stone floor of the temple, punctuating the complex rhythm that Gungama taps behind her on a drum. How long has she been dancing? She has reached the wild ecstatic moment near the end. Maya has merged into the goddess.

No more can Maya tell if she is dancer, dance, or goddess. She can no longer tell the jingle of her ankle bells from their echo. The small drum sometimes seems to guide her feet; her movements sometimes seem to wring the rhythm from the drum. This is why she dances, this one moment that expands beyond eternity. As she whirls, perspiration flies from her limbs like stars.

Then the drumming stops, and the stone walls ring with silence. Maya lifts her hands to bowed head. It takes many seconds before she feels the pounding of her heartbeat, the pulsing ache of her limbs, the heaving of her breath.

Gungama comes beside her. "You did well," she says. "Be careful of the wideness of your left eyelid during the Kharunabhava. You must emphasize the goddess's compassion, child; one can't do this with eyelid held so wide."

"Yes, ma," Maya answers when she can catch a breath. Gungama throws a shawl across her shoulders, for Maya's silks are wet from dancing, and the morning air is cold.

Maya hesitates for a moment outside the *griha* doorway as they leave. There she sees Shivaji, bare-chested, wearing only a lungi, prostrate on the floor, head buried under his arms. A brahmin stands nearby, holding a bowl of fragile rice cakes. "The *sraddah* gift," Gungama whispers. "It is the eleventh day since Sai Bai's passing." Maya turns her eyes to the goddess, remembering Sai Bai. Today Sai Bai's will soul occupy a new body.

May my sister's next life be happier, Maya prays.

Outside the temple, dawn lights the street. The Poona market stirs to life. Gungama and Maya walk together, arm in arm: one woman bent from exhaustion, the other bent from age.

Shoppers have begun to stroll the market stalls. Poona is aflood with visitors come to see Shivaji, the hero of the Malve. The city has been filling since the day they came from Pratapghad. And since that day, a week ago, thousands more had come: every bed filled, every inn packed. Outside the walls another city has sprung up, a vast metropolis of tents.

Each day Shivaji sat cross-legged on a dais in his courtyard, greeting his unexpected guests. High caste and low, even untouchables, received a look, a touch, a piece of candy or of gold.

In the midst of all this hubbub, Hanuman's wedding to Jyoti began four days ago. In the mad excitement of the victory at Pratapghad, Hanuman had invited all his soldiers. Of course they accepted, bringing with them wives and children, grandparents and servants, all joining the crowds already at the city. It soon became impossible to tell who was invited and who was not, and at last Shivaji let everyone take part.

Workmen adjust the wedding *pandal* that covers half the courtyard, tightening the canopy of bright cloth by shinnying up the long support poles. A plaster *murti* of Ganesha, nearly six feet tall and pink as a baby, rests on a bed of rose petals. Some servants sweep, others hang fresh garlands. From the kitchens of the brahmin chefs, the smells of fires and cooking fill the air.

The women reach the palace guesthouse, where a servant girl tells them that Jyoti is still asleep. Her eyes sparkle. "I guess she won't get much sleep tonight. Lucky girl." The girl turns back to Maya. "And what of you, mistress?"

"We still mean to leave tonight, after her wedding. See that our bags are packed."

When Maya has changed clothes, she and Gungama eat chapatis. Jijabai enters without a knock. "Am I to understand that you are leaving?" she asks, with a cold formality that might almost pass for politeness.

"That was always our intent," Maya replies.

"I have come to ask you to change your mind. Do not go to Adoli. Stay here, and be my son's wife."

Astonished Maya looks up, first to Gungama, then to Jijabai, whose hands are folded in supplication. She takes a long time to answer. "Does Shivaji know that you are here?"

"What difference does that make?"

Gungama whispers to Maya. "There's your answer, child."

Maya lifts the end of her sari over her head. "I decline your offer." She turns back to her breakfast.

Jijabai has managed to contain herself, but no more. "How dare you, little whore! I come here begging, and you treat me so!"

"And now you know why I decline," Maya answers.

Gungama speaks without looking up. "It is her destiny to wed a king. Is your son a king?"

Jijabai glowers at the old woman. "She is a pauper and a whore."

"Show her," Gungama tells Maya.

Maya slips like a shadow into another room and comes back with a wooden box. She opens it and takes out the jeweled headdress. The diamonds and pearls glitter like water in her hands. "You see I am no pauper," Maya says. "Ask your son if I'm a whore." Jijabai whirls on her heel and stomps out the doorway.

☙☙☙☙

Last to arrive at a hastily called meeting in the main palace are Tanaji and Trelochan. Bala, Lakshman, and Shivaji wait for them.

"I have news," Jedhe tells them. "Iron and I rode behind the Bijapuris as they retreated. We took five hundred men, just to keep an eye on things. As we neared Bijapur, we heard that the Moguls had lifted the siege of Golconda." Jedhe glances around the circle, letting the news sink in.

"So we took the men east. On the road, moving slow, were a couple of thousand foot soldiers. Led by a eunuch." Jedhe looks around, enjoying the expressions of surprise. "But that's not all. They were escorting five hundred cannon."

"Five hundred cannon and two thousand men?" Tanaji blinks in astonishment.

Jedhe nods. "Iron set our force up on a hillside. We attacked their flanks. Imagine being led by a eunuch! The better soldiers had been part of the earlier divisions, and these were the the dregs. They ran off. They left more than four hundred cannon behind."

"That's twice what we took from the Bijapuris," Bala says. "We have nearly a thousand cannon now."

CRCRCR

It's the final day of the wedding.

Jyoti enters from the guesthouse, splendid as a princess, her face hidden beneath a long veil of golden silk, led by Shivaji, since she has no father. Maya follows behind her former maid, their roles now reversed.

Then Shivaji escorts Hanuman, decked out like a prince, to a seat of honor in the shadow of Ganesha. He places honey in Hanuman's mouth to sweeten his welcome. His parents sit nearby. Nirmala sobs into the end of her sari while Tanaji pretends not to notice.

Shivaji leads Jyoti to Hanuman's side, and with a sweeping gesture, places her hand in his. Trelochan and another brahmin bind their hands together.

Together, Hanuman and Jyoti walk a slow circle around a fire and a vessel of Ganges water. Three times they walk, and each time offer roasted *bakri* to the gods. "I am the melody, you are the words," Jyoti says.

"I am the earth, you are the sky," Hanuman replies. "Let us live a hundred autumns."

Then Trelochan brings them to a place a few yards from the fire, and places seven heaps of rice in a line before them. Side by side, they step from heap to heap, with each step repeating a prayer. "For food," Hanuman says. "For strength." Another step. "For wealth." Another. "For happiness."

Nearby, Maya's gaze drifts to Shivaji, his face radiant with joy and edged with sorrow. Never has Maya felt more longing. She is about to turn away when he bends toward her. As their friends walk the final three steps, his eyes lock with hers.

Jyoti and Hanuman throw ghee into the fire, the crowd in the courtyard presses close. This is the part they've been waiting for. Every hand is filled with kumkum-stained rice; the younger boys have bags of the stuff.

Shivaji and Maya hold a silk sheet between Hanuman and Jyoti while Trelochan intones a verse. When he finishes, the crowd pelts the two with a shower of colored rice. Seven times he does this, seven times the rice rain falls. Maya and Shivaji are too busy laughing to stare into each other's eyes. Then Trelochan says the word, and Maya and Shivaji drop the silk curtain. Rice falls on Hanuman and Jyoti so fiercely they must cover their faces. When things calm down, they garland one another with roses, and sprinkle rice on each other's heads. Kiss! Kiss! Kiss! the crowd chants, until Jyoti pecks Hanuman's cheek and everyone applauds.

⊘⊚⊘⊚

Fifty miles from Rathanbore, Aurangzeb makes camp. He and his guard have built fires, but keep their horses saddled, for they will leave before the dawn.

As Aurangzeb puts down a wooden bowl of rice and dal, two soldiers hurry up; one a sentry of Aurangzeb's company, the other a mud-stained courier.

"The Princess Roshanara sent me, highness," the courier tells him. He takes out a simple leather tube. "She said to say she had very little time, highness." Aurangzeb opens it.

The parchment inside, of course, bears no seal. It is small and completely covered with the princess's manic script. Aurangzeb peers at the writing by the flickering firelight.

Brother:
  Father did not die from the poison, but he is too sick to rise. The court is in an uproar, and begs for Dara to take the throne. I am a prisoner in my own room. I beseech you, hurry!

Aurangzeb reads the words again: "*Father did not die!*"

"Is there an answer, highness?" the courier asks.

Aurangzeb considers. His brows knit. For a long time he is silent. "Tell her that I come as quickly as I can."

"Is that all, highness?"

"One thing more. Ask her this." Aurangzeb seems to struggle to say the words. "Where is he? Where on earth is Jai Singh?"

Aurangzeb tears the parchment to shreds and thrusts them in the fire. The courier backs away, frightened by Aurangzeb's twisted face.

⊘⊚⊘⊚

At the wedding feast, Sambhuji leads Maya up the back stairway of the Rang Mahal. A long receiving line waits outside Shivaji's door, but Bala hurries Maya inside. "Please don't take too long," he whispers. "There are so many waiting."

Shivaji, still in his wedding clothes, leans against a satin cushion. He's removed his turban, and his dark hair falls against his shirt. The sun strikes him like a crown.

"You look like a king," she breathes.

He turns away, embarrassed. "I understand my mother visited you. I apologize for her rudeness. If I had known what she was planning . . ." He looks at her, and his eyes are dark as night. "If I had known . . ."

Lost in his eyes, her mind searches for an answer. "Never mind her words," she whispers.

He stares at her and she at him. "I understand you wished to see me," he says at last.

It takes Maya a moment to gather her thoughts; suddenly seeing him, suddenly close, she had forgotten her purpose. Finally she says, "I came to say goodbye. Gungama and I are going back to Adoli. We shall rebuild the dancing school and temple that Afzul Khan destroyed."

Shivaji's eyes seem to burn, that look of wild impatience that she first saw the day they came to Poona, but his voice is gentle. "Can I help?"

"I would ask a favor. It will take money to rebuild, a lot of it." He nods and Maya goes on. "You know that wedding headdress that I have? Let me sell it to you."

"Save that for your wedding day. I will underwrite your project myself. Tell Bala; he'll give you whatever you need."

Maya bows, then falls to the floor and places her forehead at his feet. "Oh, why can you not be a king?" she whispers, then looks up. "Forgive me. I should not have spoken."

"I heard nothing," he replies, "so there is nothing to forgive." She sees that his eyes are full of longing, too.

Maya rises, smoothes her sari into place, and bows to leave. "Do you know," she says at the door, "this was only our third time alone together." She stands by the door, looking at him, memorizing his face. She turns, certain they will never see each other again.

"Our fourth time," Shivaji answers, before the door *clicks* shut.

☙☙☙☙

After she fetches their belongings and says her goodbyes, Maya, changes into a simple cotton sari, and joins Gungama in the *shastri*'s oxcart that will take them to Adoli.

As they pass the courtyard gates, the din of the wedding feast fades behind them. A lonesome sentry watches them depart. The city streets are so deserted there's little to hear but the creaking of the cart wheels. Outside the city walls, the tent city is deserted. Everyone's at the wedding.

Through the overhanging branches of the mango trees that line the road they can see the Poona hills shining bright in the afternoon sun. By the time they reach the river, the sun has dipped behind the trees. "I hope the ferryman has not gone to the wedding," the *shastri* tells them. But it isn't the ferryman who comes out of the hut; it's Tanaji, looking very pleased with himself. "This is a very large load." He winks at Maya. "I must call my helper!"

That's when Shivaji steps through the doorway. "You didn't think I'd let you go without a last goodbye," he says to Maya.

Tanaji and Shivaji lead the bullock cart onto the raft and tie the bullock's nose ring to a rail. Then they haul on the rope, towing the ferry across the broad river. The diamond waters dance in the setting sun.

At the other shore, Shivaji leads the cart from the ferry, and his hand grips the rail just inches from Maya's. Then they all must say goodbye. With a bow, Shivaji places a purse in the *shastri*'s hands. "To begin your work," he says, looking at Maya.

"It is I who should bow to you!" the *shastri* cries.

Gungama insists on giving Shivaji another kiss. "Remember," she tells him. "Your work has just begun."

The oxen tug the cart toward the Adoli hills.

"We're not far," the *shastri* calls. "Come see the goddess in her new home."

"Trust me," Shivaji calls back. "I hope to see the goddess very often."

☙☙☙☙

After the cart has passed the turn, Shivaji points with his chin to the small shrine of Bhavani atop the Poona hillside. "Let's go to that temple, uncle." Wearily, Tanaji agrees.

It's a steep climb and Tanaji is winded when they get there. Shivaji's face glows in the setting sun. Tanaji finds a lump in his throat. Like that day by the river, he thinks, when the birds flew by. He wishes he were a poet.

At their feet the hills turn golden, and the river glows as if lit from beneath. The trees wave gently, and their leaves rustle in the breeze like clapping hands. On the walls of Poona the watchfires have been lit, and from the Rang Mahal comes the sound of dancing. "Look around you, uncle," Shivaji says. "What do you see?"

Tanaji's head sweeps the horizon. The fields of the plateau spread like a great blanket; in the far distance, forests of teak; and on the jagged peaks of far-off mountains, the squared-off shapes of forts. "Land," Tanaji says at last.

"Whose land, uncle?"

Tanaji suddenly remembers when Maya had asked him this same question, months ago. Then the answer had been complicated, but it was no longer. "Your land, lord," he answers. "Yours."

Shivaji smiles. "No, uncle. Ours."

ଘଡ଼ଡ଼

On the floor of an abandoned mosque near Khirki, a wandering troupe of acrobats beds down for the evening. In the far corner, a giant stretches on a bedmat, and wraps his enormous arms around the plump figure in a sari who lies beside him. "I never thought I'd come to love this life," whispers the soft, high voice. "Always moving, never enough to eat. But with your strong arms around me, it's not so bad."

The voice pauses. "Can you hear me, or are you sleeping already?" The giant grunts. "We've been together for one year today. Do you remember? One year ago you released me: you freed me from my golden cage into the forest of freedom."

The giant presses closer, purring like a big kitten. His companion whispers: "I don't suppose I'll ever know how you managed that trick in the river, but I bless you for it. It was worth dying to be born again with you. Oh, Karm, I owe you everything."

With that, Basant (for of course it is he) kisses the giant's hand and snuggles closer to his warmth. Through a high window, the crescent moon beams down and bathes them in silver.